A Turn of Light

The Finest in DAW Science Fiction and Fantasy
by JULIE E. CZERNEDA:

NIGHT'S EDGE:
A TURN OF LIGHT (#1)
A PLAY OF SHADOW (#2)*

***

THE CLAN CHRONICLES:

Stratification:
REAP THE WILD WIND (#1)
RIDERS OF THE STORM (#2)
RIFT IN THE SKY (#3)

The Trade Pact Universe:
A THOUSAND WORDS FOR STRANGER (#1)
TIES OF POWER (#2)
TO TRADE THE STARS (#3)

***

SPECIES IMPERATIVE:
SURVIVAL (#1)
MIGRATION (#2)
REGENERATION (#3)

***

WEB SHIFTERS:
BEHOLDER'S EYE (#1)
CHANGING VISION (#2)
HIDDEN IN SIGHT (#3)

***

IN THE COMPANY OF OTHERS

*Coming soon from DAW Books

A TURN OF LIGHT

Marrowdell

JULIE E. CZERNEDA

DAW BOOKS, INC.
DONALD A. WOLLHEIM, FOUNDER
375 Hudson Street, New York, NY 10014
ELIZABETH R. WOLLHEIM
SHEILA E. GILBERT
PUBLISHERS
www.dawbooks.com

Jacket art by Matt Stawicki.

Maps by Julie E. Czerneda.

Photographs by Roger Czerneda.

DAW Books Collector's No. 1616.

Book designed by Jackson Typesetting Co.

First Printing, March 2013
1 2 3 4 5 6 7 8 9

DAW TRADEMARK REGISTERED
U.S. PAT. AND TM. OFF. AND FOREIGN COUNTRIES
—MARCA REGISTRADA
HECHO EN U.S.A.

PRINTED IN THE U.S.A.

For Jennifer Lynn Czerneda,
whose smile lights my life.
(We did it, Princess!)

Rhoth and Surrounding Domains

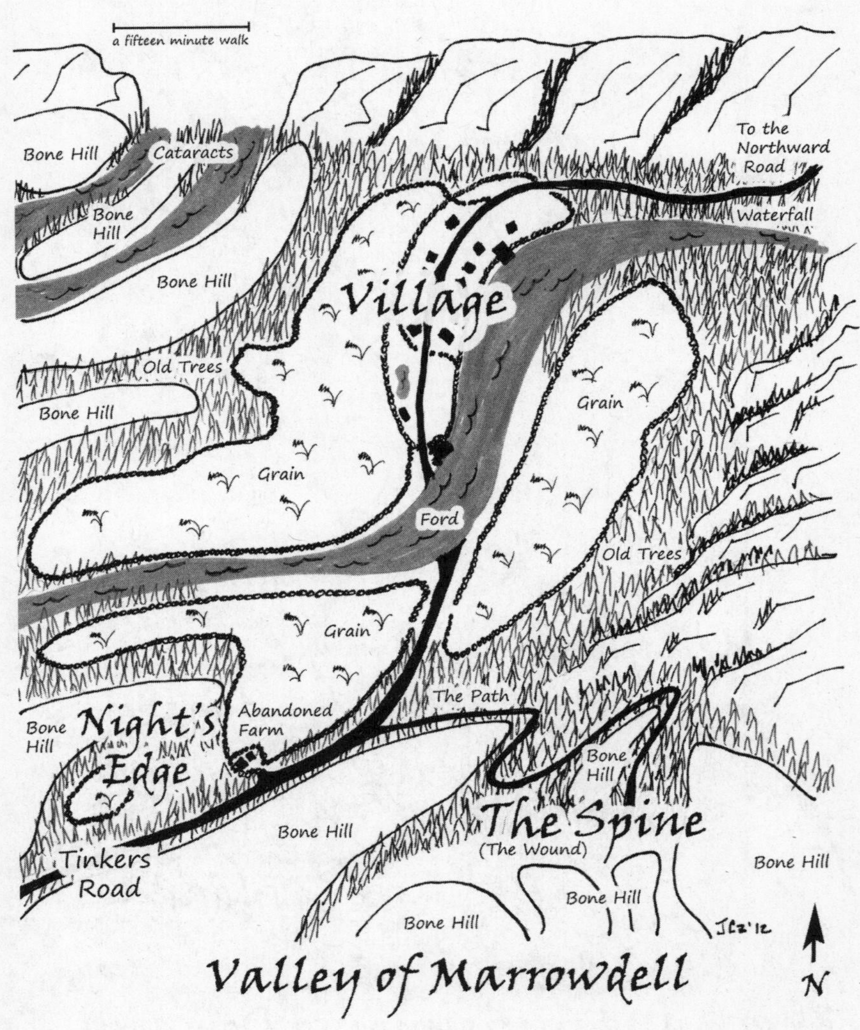
a fifteen minute walk
Bone Hill
Cataracts
Bone Hill
Bone Hill
To the Northward Road
Waterfall
Village
Old Trees
Bone Hill
Grain
Grain
Ford
Old Trees
Grain
The Path
Abandoned Farm
Bone Hill
Night's Edge
Bone Hill
Bone Hill
The Spine
(The Wound)
Bone Hill
Tinkers Road
Bone Hill
Bone Hill
Valley of Marrowdell
N

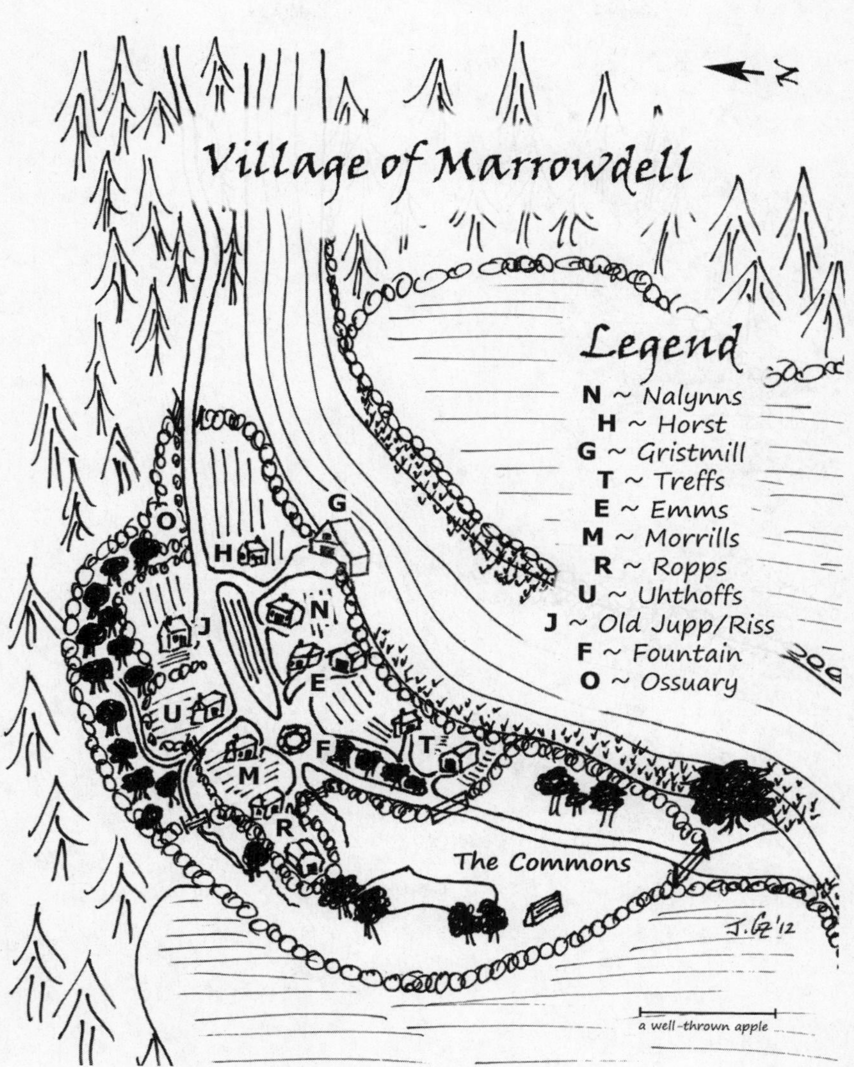
Village of Marrowdell
N
Legend
N ~ Nalynns
H ~ Horst
G ~ Gristmill
T ~ Treffs
E ~ Emms
M ~ Morrills
R ~ Ropps
U ~ Uhthoffs
J ~ Old Jupp/Riss
F ~ Fountain
O ~ Ossuary
G
O
H
N
J
E
U
T
F
M
R
The Commons
J. Cz '12
a well-thrown apple

ONE

JENN NALYNN DUG her toes deeper into the sweet meadow grass and scowled at the river sparkling in the distance. For good measure, she scowled at the golden fields spread between the crags that cradled Marrowdell in sunkissed arms, then at the blue arch of sky that dared be dotted by clouds whiter than the daisies nodding shoulder-high around her. Even the small village nestled by the river had taken on a glow, its crude wooden structures burnished rich bronze. Home. She scowled at it too, so fiercely her eyebrows almost met.

A cage was a cage.

Eighteen days from now, not counting today, she'd turn nineteen. Adult at last, with all that meant. Freedom. Choice. Adventure! She'd urged the summer to end, excepting the daisies, eager to start her travels. Wasn't it cooperating? Just yesterday, Old Jupp had complained fall was in a hurry. His joints could tell. Everyone agreed the weather couldn't make its mind up this year, so best be ready for an early change. Sure enough, today purple asters with eyes of gold bloomed like a royal cloak all around her.

All for naught.

Because her dear, doting father wanted her married before she left home.

Jenn sighed and dropped her gaze to the flowers spilling over her lap. Someone thought she needed cheering up. "Thanks," she mumbled, though the last thing she wanted right now was to make daisy crowns. Her fingers fretted at a stem; it snapped instead of split.

She plucked petals instead. "Go." *Pluck.* "Stay." *Pluck.* "Go." *Pluck.* "Stay." *Pluck.* Petals began to fly like snow and an approaching butterfly thought better of coming close. "Go. Stay. What do you think?"

Given the little meadow where the girl sat was home to nothing larger than butterflies, single-minded bees, and the occasional indiscreet mouse, it would seem unlikely she expected an answer. But this wasn't any meadow; this was hers. Too close to the old trees. Too close to the Bone Hills. Too close to sunset's first, deepest shadows. Night's Edge, the settlers called it and no one else came here.

Which made it hers. For as long as she could remember, Jenn had come to Night's Edge as often as chores and her father allowed. From harvest till planting, she'd run across the fallow fields, past the empty farm, to where her meadow waited within its shelter of dark pines. Now, at summer's end, with ripe grain bending the stalks, she walked the longer way within the cool shade of the Tinkers Road, or rode, if she could borrow Wainn Uhthoff's pony. How didn't matter, so long as she could be here.

Where she was never alone.

Sure enough, a voice softer than the petals in her hand warmed her ear. "Go home? Stay home? Both. Sunset's close, Dearest Heart. It's time you left."

Jenn's round cheeks flushed and her eyes flashed rebellion. "It's too soon. I don't want to go home. Not yet." She flung the petals into the air.

The air shimmered. *Snap, snap.* The petals disappeared. "You must leave before the sun touches the Bone Hills. I shouldn't need to remind you."

The note of aggrieved, if tolerant, patience was a perfect match for her aunt's, today's reason Jenn had fled to the meadow. Something about hems. Or had it been husbands? Her aunt's speeches on proper deportment and dignity blurred to a sameness on rainy days, let alone when the sun peeked in the windows and birds sang. She hadn't paid proper attention, Jenn thought contritely. Instead, she'd squirmed until her aunt threw up her hands in atypical frustration and shooed her away.

Had the point been to hem a husband or husband a hem?

Was one behemmed or behusbanded?

Jenn laughed. The sparkling sound brought up the nose of a curious digger, crowned with a moist dab of soil. Nearer the forest, a rabbit paused, ears flat back to listen for the swoop of an early-hunting owl, and found the strength to jump into the safety of a thorn bush.

While on the Northward Road, a weary stranger lifted his head and caught the scent of sunwarmed pine.

"You shouldn't mock what keeps you safe."

She'd laughed at her own silliness, not in disrespect; well, not exactly. Jenn dumped the remaining flowers from her lap and drew up her knees. Her skirt, the one with the hem she wasn't supposed to drag in damp grass, presumably in case of husbands, she tucked snugly around her ankles to discourage curious ants. "I've rules enough at home, Wisp," she complained. "I don't need more from you. Night's the same here as anywhere else." Except for being forbidden to her, like the rest of the world. "I'd like to stay—"

"No. No. No!" The shimmering spot beside her on the hill began to whirl, the long rays of late afternoon sun picking out confused motes of dust caught by its frenzy, yellow pollen spiraling up in streaks of gold. "You can't. You mustn't!" The little whirlwind swept up the ruined flowers and spun them into chains. "Go or it will be dark!"

Dark? Her lips twitched. "I'd never finish my outside chores if I worried about the dark. Besides, there's a lovely full moon tonight. Really, you make no sense at all, Wisp."

Neither did husbands. Jenn's small round chin jutted in defiance. Her father knew full well she was free to leave Marrowdell. He'd—to be fair, he hadn't said she could go at nineteen, but he hadn't said she couldn't, had he? What he had said, far too often this summer and again at breakfast, was that fall was the season favored by the Ancestors for weddings, and how happy he'd be when she and her older sister took husbands.

What possible use would a husband be? There wasn't a filled set of pants in the village interested in anything outside the valley.

Making them fools. There was so very much outside. Marrowdell might be in the back pocket of beyond, but Master Uhthoff was as good a teacher as any in Rhoth and they had books. Books that spoke of innumerable wonders. Oceans and plains. Creatures with legs like trees and mines that dove to the heart of the earth. Jenn's curiosity stole the rest from her sleep, her peace when awake.

Outside must be what she longed for so desperately. This summer, as the light of each day faded, she felt emptier than the day before, as if she slowly starved from the lack of . . . what? She didn't know, only that it wasn't here. She'd know it, when she found it. It had to be among the wonders she dreamed about.

It had to be.

Which led back to husbands, her father, and her visiting aunt. Her aunt's stories of life in Avyo, the great capital of Rhoth, made her longing worse. Chandeliers and peaches. Parties and dances!

Her aunt, who carried her campaign to salvage the manners of her widowed brother's so-neglected daughters to the supper table, regardless of its impact on anyone's digestion.

Meaning shoes.

"I won't mind being late for supper," Jenn announced with great sincerity, digging her bare happy toes deeper into the sod. "Let me stay just a little longer. Please?"

The pollen stilled, a column of dust leaning toward earth. A flower-scented whisper caressed her cheek. "If you answer not to law, Dearest Heart, answer friendship. Go home now. For me. Because I ask it. I wish you safe."

"That's not fair—"

"Neither is abandoning your father and sister to fend for themselves. Hurry to save them. Dearest Heart. Good Heart."

Good-hearted Jenn. That's what everyone said of her—usually before asking a favor. The bane of her life, she decided, vowing to work on being strong-minded.

Tomorrow.

Jenn gently brushed the line of ants from her skirt, lifting the hem by handfuls to check for stains. "I hope you know—" She paused, lips parted.

There, in the shadow of her skirt.

The tip of a claw.

Not like a hawk's or chicken's. Not like any of the bear's claws hung above Uncle Horst's fireplace.

This was a blade of ancient bone, as long as her longest finger. The underside of its elegant, deadly curve was serrated, as if the needle-like tip was insufficient threat.

One glimpse, then it lifted into the light and was gone.

"—what I'll have to put up with," Jenn finished as she stood.

Over the years, there'd been other shadows, other glimpses. A tuft of wiry hair, curled like the end of a beard. Paired tendrils of what might have been steam—or breath. A patch of textured cloth or skin that had reminded her of woven chain, but tighter, smoother, as fine as the best linen. Now a claw.

Wisp didn't want to be seen, that much she understood. If she reacted to a glimpse, he'd shred grass and sulk.

She couldn't imagine a shape that fit the glimpses, let alone how Wisp kept the rest of himself from sight. Nothing in Marrowdell—and nothing in any book she'd read—held such a being.

He might let her see the whole of him one day. She sighed inwardly. Might. One day. The world kept its best secrets from her and demanded she wait and wait and wait.

It wasn't fair.

"I'll go home before sunset," Jenn said, resigned for now. "If I didn't, Aunt Sybb would fuss."

"Dear Heart." A contrite breeze tickled the fringe of pale hair on her forehead. "Your aunt means well."

She did. Their father's sister was neither hardy nor young, but every year she undertook a pilgrimage to Marrowdell for the summer, bringing dry goods and cloth for dresses, impractical shoes for her nieces and a pair of her husband's barely worn boots for her brother, books and biscuits and delicious hard candy. Best of all, she brought stories of life in the great cities, for Sybb Mahavar's impeccably Rhothan marriage had saved her from the politics that sent so many of Mellynne heritage to the north woods.

She and her coach would head south again after Jenn's birthday. Her coach of black and gilt, that smelled inside of leather and lavender. When they were little, Jenn and Peggs had played in it, closing the doors and pretending they traveled along Avyo's magnificent cobbled streets, waving at imaginary passersby out the windows.

"That's it!" Jenn pushed her hair back. "You're brilliant, Wisp!"

"I am." The breeze flipped her bangs forward again, then paused as if confused. "Why am I?"

"I don't know why I didn't think of it before. Aunt Sybb has lots of room. They have a huge house—bigger than all the homes of Marrowdell put together. All I have to do—all we have to do—" she couldn't leave her sister to take over all the chores, "—is climb in her coach and hide—"

The breeze went from tickle to grit-heavy shove. "What's wrong with you?" Jenn caught her balance, coughing, eyes wide. She hadn't meant it. She'd been daydreaming out loud.

"Go home." A breath in her ear. "Stay home." Another.

Then, so feather soft she might have imagined it, save for the uneasy stir of fine hair along her neck, "Never leave."

"I won't spend the rest of my life here, not for my father and not for you!" Jenn tossed back her head, braid thumping her shoulder, and stomped away through the meadow, skirt gathered in her hands and uncaring where she stepped. Though, somehow, her feet missed both asters and ants.

She wouldn't come back tomorrow, she fumed. Or the next day. Or the next. Let the opinionated wind play with mice and bees. Serve him right.

She hadn't been serious. Now she was.

No matter what anyone planned for her, she'd find a way to leave Marrowdell and see the world.

She would.

~ Oh, that went well. ~ From above.

Sarcasm from his peers wasn't safe to ignore. The being Jenn Nalynn knew as Wisp shrugged his shoulders, which were in no sense like hers, and made his slow way to the shelter of the old trees and what lay beyond. ~ She'll be back. ~

~ And if not? ~ A different speaker, from below. They cared not for the pretty meadow, nor did they waste effort to bend its fragrant air into words. ~ What then? ~ From behind. They circled him, mocked his care-filled steps with their grace and speed and power, buffeted him with wind. They didn't dare touch him. Power, he still had.

From above. ~ Will you fail? ~

They'd crossed hoping for trouble; his penance, their amusement. Once word spread of the girl's outburst, would there be bodies pressed against bodies for their next meeting? Had they nothing better to do?

He'd supply a pestilence to keep them occupied, a whimsical something with pus and a fearsome itch, but those whose opinions did matter would know. Know, and likely visit it on him threefold.

Instead, Wisp shrugged what weren't shoulders once more. ~ She'll be back. ~

He would miss her, however long frustration kept her from the meadow this time. She'd grown dear to him, goodness and bright expectation being rare in his life. Something he hoped no one discovered, or that life would swiftly become a greater misery.

Of course, should Jenn Nalynn, turn-born and forever cursed, try to leave the valley, his would be the first teeth in her throat.

He would regret that most of all.

TWO

THE POUND OF Jenn's callused feet on the packed earth was almost as loud as the pound of her heart. Wisp and his stupid law and silly tricks . . . he was worse than her father. Much worse! At least Radd Nalynn truly needed her. She helped him in the gristmill, as much as she could, and did her share, almost always, in the gardens and around the house. Little wonder his cheerful face would cloud whenever she or Peggs talked of life beyond Marrowdell. How could he manage without them?

If Aunt Sybb could stay year-round to keep house for him, everything would be different, but she had a home of her own, a better one, in Avyo. As for her father taking another wife? Jenn shook her head. Even if he'd been willing and let it be known, Marrowdell was home to just two unmarried women of the right age. Riss Nahamm had her hands full with her great-uncle's household and Wen Treff talked to toads.

Jenn paused at the river to hitch her skirt well above her knees. Though this time of year most of the ford was ankle-deep, the low sun caught every dancing ripple, dazzling the eye and making it impossible to discern shallow from hole. Best be safe than soggy.

The cool water soothed skin prickled by grass and ants, and eased the burn of the roadway from her soles. By the time she reached the rushes, dancing with black damselflies who flashed vivid blue as they tilted their curious heads at her, the river had washed away her temper as well. Wisp was Wisp, Jenn chided herself. As well expect sense from Wainn's old pony, who would oh-so-cleverly find his way through any latch to eat himself sick on fallen apples. Both needed to be loved and properly managed. Her next visit to Night's Edge, she'd take Wisp some of the thistledown she'd collected for a new pillow. He liked to fling the fluff-tailed seeds high and wide, so they caught the wind and headed for the upper meadows. Why, he never explained.

Glimpsing a white pebble under the water, she gathered her skirt and stooped to collect it, adding the small damp treasure to the others in her pocket. White was best and hard to find, at least others said so; Jenn felt quite pleased with herself as she walked out of the river and up the slight slope. The dry sand was warm underfoot until she reached the shade of the massive oak that marked this end of the village proper. The tree had a wide curved branch it would lower, if asked politely, for a child who wanted to watch for travelers on the Tinkers Road.

Or a vantage point to throw acorns.

Squirrels excelled at that. With their help, the shade of the oak would be brown with fallen acorns; to judge by those already on the ground, they'd started. It'd soon be time to open the gate to let the big sows amble through. Satin never minded a child lying on her warm broad back. Or acorn throwing, especially close to her clever snout. Filigree, though covered in pretty black spots, had no patience when feasting and, if bothered, she'd grunt a terse command to the hanging branch, which would shake loose both child and acorns.

For now, the tree was empty of children and the gate closed. Jenn climbed its cedar rails and jumped down the other side. The road led through the commons, as her aunt called the pasture where the villagers kept livestock in summer. High hedges surrounded it, full of twittering birds and the deep drone of bees. Davi Treff's great draft horses stood slack-hipped and nose-to-tail with Aunt Sybb's fine matched bays in the shade of the trees by the pond. The sows and Himself, their lordly, if lazy, boar, lay in the pond's shallows and wagged their long ears at flies. Good'n'Nuf, the Ropps' pampered bull, must be hiding behind the shed again. The cows crowded the middle gate, anxious to be milked. Seeing them, Jenn picked up her pace. Must be closer to suppertime than she'd thought.

This year's weanlings, a tight little herd of brown and white, pranced toward her through the thick grass, huge eyes brimming with curiosity, then suddenly lost all interest and turned their attention to a game of head butt.

Last year's calves and the riding horses, all but Uncle Horst's and Dusom's, grazed the ravines beyond Marrowdell under the watchful eyes of the Emms' twins, Allin and Tadd. Bandits didn't set foot in the valley but menaced anyone on the Northward Road. Every so often a horse or calf would manage to get itself stuck or slip into a chancy mountain stream, not that many, she'd heard, were as dangerous as the deadly cataracts that roared between the tips of the Bone Hills. Come fall, the animals would be brought back through the village and let into the fields after the harvest, there to fatten with the rest of the livestock till frost.

Maybe this fall, Allin Emms would realize she had no intention of marrying him, ever, and Tadd would break his abashed silence to speak his heart to Peggs.

Then again, Jenn grumbled to herself, some things never changed.

Come winter, everything else did. Here, snow didn't conveniently melt, as in the cities to the south. Marrowdell shrank to narrow icy paths between homes, barns, privies, and larders, those structures roofed in white. When the weather permitted, Davi would take his team from the village to the more-trafficked Northward Road and back, the horses' huge feet and wide chests doing what they could to keep a passage open. After storms, every adult who could lift a shovel or rake helped dig out the road. It was that, or risk being cut off from the outside until spring. Isolated, an entire village could die unnoticed, by starvation, fire, illness, to be smothered by snow.

With the sun warming her shoulders, the road dry and warm beneath her feet, Jenn found it hard to imagine winter. Fall, yes. By her birthday the grain fields would be harvested, their bounty stored as feed and flour. Larders were already filling with that from gardens and orchards: sacks of dried beans; jars of jellies, chutneys, and pickles; precious pots of honey; and onion braids. Wheels of pale cheese and crocks of brined butter rested in the cool dark of the springhouse while sausages and hams—last year's piglets—hung in fragrant smoke. Soon they'd press apples for cider and dig the root crops. The children would collect rushes and down from nests by the river. The older ones would gather kindling; charcoal bins were already full, fuel for the cold months, and barrels of ash stood waiting. They'd be traded this fall for a share of lye in Endshere; no one in the village had the knack.

Jenn climbed the far gate, more mindful of her skirt within the village proper. Cynd Treff looked up from berry picking and smiled, her big hat tilted so the sun caught her freckles. From the clanging, her husband Davi was busy at his forge. Off to milk the cows, Hettie Ropp and her stepmother, Covie, waved a cheerful greeting. Cheffy and his sister Alyssa went ahead, arms wrapped around empty milk jugs almost as tall as they were, laughing as they tried to bump into one another. Birds chirped in the apple trees, laden with fruit, that filled the heart of the village; Zehr Emms whistled as he worked on his house. Supper smells filled the air. Everyone was busy. Everyone content.

Jenn scowled. Didn't they know?

The world was bigger than this.

Dark and twisted trees, skirted in moss, lined the road. Their tips leaned together, hiding the sky. The road twisted as well, hiding its future and past. A fine place for an ambush, Bannan Larmensu thought, and didn't care. There'd been a time he'd have been on alert, his every sense tuned to the limb out of place, the rock ready to fall, the deadly lurkers in the brush.

No longer. Rhoth's prince had lured the merchants of Eldad to his bed at last, with Vorkoun and the eastern marches the dowry. What generations of raids and thievery couldn't defeat, a stroke of a pen laid waste. Once-proud Vorkoun now belonged to Ansnor, and he was on this road.

"Lovely place, sir." Tir Half-face used a thumb to pry up the pitted metal that gave him his name. He spat at a lichen-crusted boulder. "Just lovely." He settled the crude mask over the ruin left when a sword took his nose and most of his chin.

"It's a road, not a place." Bannan used the whip to flick a bloodfly from the ox's wide back, not that the creature appeared to notice, then leaned back, boot braced on the plank that separated the front of the settler wagon from the end of the ox. He regarded his companion with fond exasperation. Easier to leave behind an arm than shed the man who'd guarded his back since he'd come new and foolish to the border, and been his truest friend since.

A short wiry beard, brown with traces of gray, sprouted below the mask; above, bright blue eyes returned his regard. What tanned skin showed was scarred and puckered, his ears were ringed in metal, and, on his bald head, Tir wore the straw hat he'd bought in Endshere. To blend in, he'd professed, tossing his helm into the wagon to rattle loose. Blending, Bannan noticed, hadn't extended to removing the throwing axes from his belt.

He'd removed his weapons. Removed them. Dropped them. Walked away from them without a second glance or regret. As he'd done with his life. The settler's garb was too new for comfort, but the leather and woven flax would fit better after sweat and rain. And work.

He needed work.

"When will we arrive—at a place, sir?"

Good question; a shame he hadn't an answer. "I'm in no hurry," Bannan replied, then added with a straight face, "By the map, the Northward goes beyond Upper Rhoth. We could take it to the barrens."

"We couldn't, sir, and that's the truth. Ancestors Frozen and Forgotten." Tir took a deep breath and spoke as though reasoning with the feebleminded. "No one survives winter in that wasteland. A winter, might I say, sir, coming closer by the day."

"I promise we'll stop before it snows."

"'Snows?!'" A moment's aghast pause, during which Bannan enjoyed the unopinionated sounds of creaking wood and the breathing of the ox, but a sly look warned him Tir wasn't done. Sure enough. "Could be, sir, we should have stopped already. They say the best land was that before Endshere. Behind us. They say there haven't been settlers this far north since those Naalish squatters were kicked out of Avyo."

Bannan grunted something noncommittal. Debate the twisted politics of the Fair Lease law with Tir? He'd rather clean up after the ox. Before their time, anyway. What had it been . . . fifteen? Twenty years? Those settler land grants, to his advantage now, had been the prince's sop to the newly poor.

Being poor was another topic not to broach with Tir, or he'd not hear the end of it all day.

"They say, sir," Tir needed no prompting to continue, "that the locals call this the Doubtful Road. Seems no one who takes it past Endshere can trust their future."

"'They say. They say.' Heart's Blood. When did you take stock in gossip? There are valleys. Settlements." Bannan shifted listlessly. "The place doesn't matter." A dirty brown shadow strutted up to the wagon and blew a noisy response to this. Without a change to his plodding walk, the ox tipped his horned head nervously at the sound. The two animals weren't friends; the ox, being wiser than he'd looked, had to be hobbled at night to keep him close. "Scourge agrees with me." Bannan stretched to slap the horse's dusty shoulder. "Don't you, boy?"

Tir's forehead wrinkled. "Bloody beast."

Thus addressed, Scourge flung up his huge head and rolled his eyes till the red showed. At least he didn't show teeth. This time. "Peace, Tir. I couldn't leave him behind; he'd eat my nephews. What would my sister say then?"

Stiffly. "I would never presume to speak for the baroness."

"'Baroness,' is it?" Bannan chuckled. "Lila'd box your ears for that, after all the times we got drunk together." In the worst part of the city, too: the slum beneath the high bridge where no one would expect a Larmensu, let alone both heirs. His mood soured. They'd left Vorkoun as if for another patrol, pretending nothing had changed, that the farewells weren't forever. Lila had hugged him more fiercely than usual, that was all. "You could have stayed in her household. You didn't have—"

"And risk the baron's jealousy, sir?" Tir protested. He laid a hand over his heart. "I'll have you know Lila wrote of her undying love, sir. Heartbroken, she was, seeing me leave. Sent me with you to protect her marriage vows. Such a brave woman, she is."

Bannan half smiled and shook his head.

The brows came down to scowl over the mask. "Not in so many words."

Bannan waited.

"Heart's Blood!" Tir threw up his hands. "All right. Sir. Being every bit as mad as you are, sir, your dear sister wrote if I let you turn around she'd take off my ears herself. I'm allowed to hit you on the head, but no unnecessary maiming. Ancestors Witness—" with vast admiration, "—I believe she means it."

The truth at last. "I'm sure she does," Bannan replied mildly. "Right, Scourge?"

The big horse snorted his disdain, then sidestepped into the shadows where he preferred to travel, moving his bulk between the trees and over twigs without sound. He could do it with a rider, too, and carry that rider into battle. Not any rider. Not Scourge. Bannan's was the only hand he tolerated; he didn't doubt his mount would, in truth, try to eat the sons of his sister's unsoldierly husband, given provocation.

The foul-tempered warhorse wasn't the only threat to Lila's household Bannan took away with him on this road, nor the worst.

"The exchange was yesterday, wasn't it?" The treaty that moved the border moved people as well. Ansnor would free any Rhothan prisoners; Vorkoun her Ansnan ones.

"The start of it, yes." Tir gave him a somber look. "It'll take a few weeks. No one wants blood on the streets." The treaty said deeds on either side were forgiven, political prisoners and soldiers alike honorably discharged, to be left in peace.

Bannan thought it more likely his fat new ox would sprout wings. Of royal purple.

"How long before they compare notes?" He'd lost track of how many "they" were. The faces blurred; easier to remember the astonished anger, then fear. Every one who'd seemed innocent until he looked at them as they spoke, until he'd declared each a liar or spy. His gift, to see others for what they were, to know the truth when he heard it from their lips.

Truthseer.

They didn't know his name. No one used a real name in the marches, not in a conflict with such deep roots on either side. Bannan had taken "Captain Ash" from the officer he'd replaced.

Those brought before him knew his face; by campfire, by torchlight, more rarely by the light of day. The Rhothan captain who was never wrong. The well-bearded Rhothan captain. Bannan fingered the novelty of a smooth chin and jaw, hoping road dust disguised the contrast between pale and well-tanned skin. All those years, the beard had hidden his relative youth; with luck, its absence would hide him now.

"They'll figure out what I must be," Bannan went on grimly.

"It'll be talk, sir," Tir objected. "Nothing more. Who'd believe?"

"Scourge does." No coincidence that the creature chose as rider the Larmensu who saw him for what he was. "You do."

"You can't think I'd—"

"Peace, Tir." Bannan sighed. This man, as all those in his company, would die for him without hesitation; he'd seen it in their faces. Had chosen them for that true loyalty.

How different from Vorkoun's high society where he'd been so desperately unhappy as a child, hearing the lies, seeing through masks of flesh. As soon as he could pass for a man, he'd taken service at the border, where he faced an honest hate and finally found use for his gift.

He was what he was. The heritage of his line, to be a truthseer. Now his curse. A fair trade, if those he loved were safe.

"Lila gave me orders, too," Bannan said, lightening his tone. He pulled out the precious letter that had been waiting in Endshere and made a show of reading it. "'Little brother. Find a wife and raise some brats of your own. Surely there are women in the north.'"

"Wife? Here?" Tir shook his head vehemently, almost losing the straw hat. "Your sister can't be serious. Sir. They'd be—farm maids."

"What—you don't think one would have me?"

Tir caught his mood and gave a low whistle. "Have you? You'll have to fight them off, sir. And their mothers."

"A battle worth the effort. I'll share, by the way," Bannan grinned. "You'll need a wife, too."

"I've had three," Tir boasted. "Don't be charmed by a pretty ankle. The trick's to taste her cooking first—"

"So now you're giving me advice."

"Wife hunting is serious business . . ."

"Says the man who can't keep one."

"I've kept them all," Tir said smugly. "Just not in the same city."

They both laughed.

The wingless ox plodded forward, half asleep, each step putting distance between future and past.

Jenn lengthened her stride but didn't run. Children ran, not dignified almost-nineteen adults who expected to be taken seriously; this according to her aunt, the most dignified person in Marrowdell. Also, running made her look late, and she wasn't today, not quite.

As she passed the village fountain, Jenn dutifully, if absently and in haste, dipped a finger of thanks into its cool water. The practice was one her father's generation insisted upon; like the rest born here, she saw nothing remarkable in the deep basin of gleaming blue tile, always full of sweet water that never froze or fouled. The basin was rimmed by huge blocks of weathered gray stone, so cunningly fitted that only the tiniest strands of emerald-green moss could grow between. The ground surrounding the blocks was paved in riverstone cobbles that stayed free of snow or ice.

Though she found precious little good about her brother's family's exile, Aunt Sybb declared Marrowdell's fountain to have water finer than any in Avyo, and each summer brought bottles to fill and take home.

Night was night and water was the same everywhere, Jenn assured herself. She passed the Emms' house and glanced toward the mill. No sign of her father heading home yet. She walked faster. She wouldn't be so much as tardy if she got home first.

Shoes. She mustn't forget to put on shoes for supper. She'd do whatever it took to convince her aunt she was a person who should live in the great city.

Which Marrowdell was not. The village consisted of the commons, the fountain, the mill, and eight homes linked by its meandering road and footpaths. Its buildings were simple structures, made from stacked, ax-hewn logs with any chinks between filled with red clay from the riverbank. Their slanted roofs were protected by shakes of cedar wood, themselves coated in moss, bright green after a rain. Repairs left bare patches, especially in summer. Doors, never locked, hung open on their wooden hinges in this pleasant mild weather. Precious hand-sized panes of glass, carefully framed in wood, were set into wide windows, with shutters ready to protect them from wind or weather. Some had curtains, some did not.

Each home had its privy set conveniently between garden and woodpile, so return trips weren't empty-handed, as well as a larder dug deep into the cool earth, with sturdy doors that did lock. A spring-famished bear might break through, but not quietly. More likely thieves had clever paws and snuck about on moonless nights. Three homes had barns towering behind them, with room to store feed and provide warm quarters for all the village livestock come the cold.

Cities were grander, Jenn thought as she walked. Warmer, too. For one thing, Aunt Sybb said city people didn't go outside to the larder or privy, trips that, come winter, were made only when desperate, followed by thawing numbed flesh by the stove.

Cities had oil lamps and furnaces and water indoors. They had crowded, busy roads, with pavements to keep shoes free of mud. The largest, like Avyo, had trolleys that ran along metal rails, though Aunt Sybb pronounced those noisy and abrupt. Every building was a lofty edifice of marble and brick and glass, with new ones built all the time.

Nothing new was built in Marrowdell. When the settlers arrived, twenty-three years ago come fall, the homes and barns had been here, empty and waiting. The fountain had been here too, though it hadn't filled until Zehr Emms touched its stones, the water having waited to be needed. The rust-red road and hedges had been here, gates open, and the fields of grain. The gardens had been ready to plant with vegetables. Though they'd found berry bushes, the apple orchard arrived with the settlers, Kydd Uhthoff having filled his portion of the family wagon with saplings from their home in Avyo.

From then on, all had stayed the same. The house picked by the Nalynns stood by the tall gristmill and overlooked where the river's slow meander quickened into the first rapids and the bank became steep. The Emms took one nearer the fountain; old Jupp and the Uhthoffs lived across the garden and road, next to the orchard. The Treffs, Morrills, and Ropps lived near the common pasture.

The mill was Marrowdell's largest structure, half again the height of a barn. Traced by dust, golden sunbeams slipped between its weathered outer boards into its open heart. Whole logs, stripped of their bark, rose through the floors to the roof high overhead, their girth wider than the arms of three children could hold. At each level, support beams met them like dancers who gripped one another against the strain.

The floors were of thick planking, gray and polished by use. The main floor, reached through sliding doors wide enough for a wagon, housed the great wheel that hung over the river. In summer, the wheel was still, its pulleys and wooden gears loose and patient, the hopper tipped up. The millstones lay beside their open case, being dressed for the coming harvest. Jenn could draw their elegant pattern in her sleep, having spent the last few years as miller's apprentice. This season, she'd been trusted to deepen the grooves on her own, her father doing the final sharpening. The hard stone was reluctant, which also described Aunt Sybb's feelings about one of her nieces wielding a chisel. But no one else in the village had the talent.

Below, in the basement, was the stone-lined raceway, dry for now. Once its gate lifted in invitation, the river would run through to turn the great wheel. Gears would engage, leather belts take the strain, and everything would move. Jenn loved it all, from the millstones and their dancing shoe, to the conveyor that caught the millings and took them up to the loft to be cooled, screened, and bagged. She'd run errands up and down the wide open stairs that went up alongside the hopper, stairs in winter the villagers decorated with pine boughs and ribbon for the Midwinter Beholding, when the loft would be transformed with light and music.

Otherwise, until harvest, the mill was an empty, peaceful place, redolent of grain, dust, and the river, a useful spot to house Aunt Sybb's fancy Avyo coach, carefully tarped against the damp in a back corner of the main floor.

On the far side of the mill, closest of all to the outside world, stood the solitary building Uncle Horst called home. He wasn't really her uncle. He'd come to Marrowdell without family, so the Nalynns added him to theirs. Horst wasn't really his name, but once a very small Jenn pronounced it that way, he'd kept it as his. Uncle Horst helped Radd in the mill, when he wasn't hunting, and at all times he watched the road, though for what Jenn couldn't imagine. He avoided the tinkers' tents, other than to have his knives sharpened or boots resoled, and, though he escorted her from Endshere and back each year, likewise avoided Radd's sister. Which might have had something to do with relinquishing his place at the Nalynn table during her visits, except that Uncle Horst wasn't like that. He wouldn't begrudge family their rightful place. He respected Aunt Sybb, that was all, and was shy.

The Nalynn home wasn't full of noisy small children and bags of dripping cheese, like the Ropps'. It wasn't austere like the Uhthoffs', with Master Dusom's shelves of books, or full of industry like the Treffs'. It might not contain the fine cabinetry of the Emms' or the musty secrets of old Wagler Jupp—and lacked bear teeth—but it was,

Jenn nodded to herself, as she always did walking up her sloping path, the best home of all.

Stripped of other wealth, Melusine Nalynn had nonetheless brought treasures to start her new life: a baby daughter in her arms and a cutting from her favorite rose. Both had grown strong and beautiful. Peggs, with her black flowing hair, glad smile, and doe-soft brown eyes, had no equal in Marrowdell—an opinion that whenever expressed drew a flustered blush to her fine white cheeks and a quick denial to her lips. Which made it no less true.

The rose climbed the river side of their home, covering its logs with a blaze of red blossom all summer, reaching around to frame the girls' bedroom window and nod over the roof, filling the breeze with heady fragrance. Bees and butterflies loved it. Each summer, bluebirds nested within its thorns. Each spring, Radd pretended he didn't check the bare woody stems every morning until the first buds appeared. The tender plant shouldn't have been able to survive the winter, let alone thrive.

But this was Marrowdell.

Jenn couldn't make herself scowl at her mother's rose. She'd ask it for a cutting herself, when she left. And return, often, to visit.

Feeling better, she went around back. Aunt Sybb didn't approve of bare feet in the parlor, which was what the front half of their house became during her visits, even though it was also Radd's bedroom, the dining room, and where the entire family sewed or read or talked during winter, when not at the mill. Separated by a curtain, the kitchen, with its fireplace, oven, and cookstove, filled the back half. A ladder beside the fireplace led to the loft and the warm cozy room Jenn shared with Peggs; a little too warm, admittedly, some midsummer nights, but perfect in winter.

Jenn stuck her head through the open kitchen door, too sunblind to more than guess at her sister's shape, and whispered urgently. "Did she notice I was gone?" Their aunt also didn't approve of "traipsing off," her term for the myriad earnest excuses, some of them real, Jenn produced for having been outside in nice weather instead of inside. Inside being lectured. "Am I late for supper?"

"Not to eat it," came the tart reply.

Jenn winced. She'd promised to help with the preparations, hadn't she. Time flew in the meadow. "Sorry, Peggs."

A basket was thrust at her. "Run this to Uncle, Good Heart, and all's forgiven."

Jenn slipped her arm through the handle and lifted one edge of the covering cloth. The aroma wafting upward with the steam made her mouth water. It wasn't as if Peggs needed help anyway. Until the dishes. "I won't be long."

"While you're there, Jenn Nalynn," her sister suggested dryly, "thank Uncle for filling the cistern."

"Oh." Her chore, most definitely, to lug buckets from the fountain to fill the clever holding tank Zehr had built behind their kitchen. "I will."

Determined not to be at fault again, at least not today, Jenn crossed the road to the mill and took the short path to Uncle Horst's, exchanging an absent smile and greeting with Riss as the two passed one another, Riss with her darning basket over one arm and a pair of plump, skinned squirrels in hand, doubtless courtesy of Uncle Horst's arrows.

Jenn didn't slow to admire his small garden, though the pumpkins were nicely plump, with orange creeping over their round sides, and she could almost taste the pies and breads and soups. They'd lost last year's. The twins had let the yearlings lead the way into the village and, with the single-minded cleverness of cattle, they'd headed for the nearest garden, trampling what they didn't eat. She'd had words with Allin over that disaster.

He'd still proposed at her birthday. As if she'd forgive him for the pumpkins. Besides, all he wanted was to be the next miller, which he wouldn't, since everyone knew Tadd was the twin who could hear when a gear was failing, let alone—

"Thought I heard a visitor." Uncle Horst, who their father swore could hear a feather fall, appeared in his doorway, smiling. He was older than their father, the corners of his eyes and mouth creased in small soft lines, his gray hair starting to thin. His body was thin, too, which only went to prove Aunt Sybb's assertion that you mustn't judge someone by their looks since Horst could outwork any man in Marrowdell and only Davi the smith could lift a heavier weight. He'd been a soldier in Avyo; beyond that bald statement, he wouldn't speak of the past, not even when a younger Jenn had coaxed, being curious how he'd lost the tips of two fingers on his left hand and what old wound made him limp in the damp chill of fall and become, as Peggs put it, cranky as a bear himself.

"Greetings, Uncle. I brought supper."

"Most kind." He took the basket from her and sniffed, closing his eyes in rapture for a moment. "You're such a fine cook."

Jenn chuckled. "Peggs' the fine cook," she corrected as always, then grimaced. "I'm sorry I forgot the cistern, Uncle. Thank you for taking care of it."

"It was needful." He raised an eyebrow. "Tomorrow's laundry day."

So it was. Meaning he expected an explanation for her negligence. In many ways, Jenn thought glumly, her "uncle" was stricter than her father. "Aunt Sybb was talking about hems," she began. "Hems and husbands. And the sun was shining so very brightly," that was important to mention, since Uncle Horst preferred the outdoors, too. "And I thought asters might start to bloom on such a bright sunny day and they have and—"

"And you, my dear, must respect both your aunt and your responsibilities."

Quashed, Jenn ducked her head and said in a small voice. "Yes, Uncle. I am very sorry."

"Actions. You must take more care to think of their consequence, Jenn Nalynn." Uncle Horst did his best to look stern but the lines beside his mouth creased into little dimples, the way Jenn knew meant he wasn't really angry and was having a hard time not smiling. She gazed up at him through her lashes and waited. As if sensing he'd lost his advantage, he went on, "I'm an old man. I won't always be here to do your chores while you play in the meadow."

Of course he would.

"Let me do your laundry," Jenn offered. He wouldn't ask for himself. Not for supper. Not for anything. "It'd be no trouble." Well, it might be. His clothing ran more to well-aged leather than homespun, and as a hunter he was particular about the scents that touched his things.

"No need, thank you." The smile she'd been waiting for. "Now go. Behave yourself. You can tell me tomorrow about the asters."

Jenn stretched up to kiss his stubbled cheek. "I promise."

Being the best sister imaginable, Peggs had left Jenn's shiny black shoes, as well as a damp rag, by the kitchen door. Jenn sat on the barrel by the washtub and quickly wiped her feet, rubbing them dry on the inside of her skirt before working on the shoes. She was supposed to wear stockings with them, but her only pair had made a fine lining for her mittens last winter.

She stood gingerly, getting her balance. That was the worst of shoes. They tipped the world in a most uncertain manner. She drew herself up straight, shoulders back, and, upon consideration, used the rag on her hands as well. With less result. She should have washed them in the river. Maybe the green nails wouldn't show.

Jenn folded her hands together and walked decorously through the door.

Peggs smiled. "Welcome home." She plucked a stem of grass from Jenn's hair, then licked her thumb and applied it lightly to the tip of Jenn's nose. "Pollen." She resumed arranging bowls and spoons on a tray. The bowls were white porcelain, decorated with long-feathered birds in blue; the spoons were lovingly-polished silver, with handles shaped like horses jumping. The bowls were chipped, the spoons weren't the same size, and the tray was a slab of wood Jenn had painted when she was little. Normally, she didn't notice. Today, with leaving and cities and plans filling her thoughts, Jenn wondered what elegant matched settings graced homes in Avyo.

"Any pebbles?"

She blinked, back in the kitchen. "Some pinks. And a nice white one." She tipped them from her pocket into the pottery jar waiting by the fireplace, then wiped her hands again. "What can I do to help?"

Peggs held out the tray. "Hold steady while I fill these." She'd made a stew, brimming with late summer vegetables and topped each bowlful with a dollop of cream. A fresh loaf of bread waited beside the pot of butter and a berry pie sat in the bake oven, steam and purple juice bubbling through slits in the crisp golden pastry. Basic fare, Aunt Sybb called it. Her mouth watering, Jenn wondered what could be better.

Another reason to see the world, as if she needed one.

Peggs' sketchpad leaned against the windowsill, illuminated by sunlight. Charcoal sticks of varied lengths poked up from the broken-handled baby cup she used for brushes, when in a painting mood. She'd been working on wildflowers again. "I forgot to bring asters from the meadow," Jenn said apologetically. "They're out now."

"And was your meadow in a good mood today?"

No one else knew of Wisp. Whether Peggs believed or played along out of kindness wasn't important. She listened. "No," Jenn admitted. "We argued. But it was his fault," she emphasized. "He said I'm never to leave home. Never!" The tray tipped, bowls sliding, and she quickly firmed her grip.

Her sister pursed her lips thoughtfully. "Do you know why?"

"There isn't a 'why.'" Jenn couldn't help the sullen note to her voice. "No one will let me do what I want with my life."

"And what might that be today?" their father inquired, stepping through the kitchen door with a broad grin. He'd scrubbed until his already ruddy cheeks shone like little apples, his sister having told him very clearly how a man mustn't bring the soil and dust of his work into his home. As Radd Nalynn was the miller, and usually coated from head to toe either in chaff and flour, or powdered rock from dressing his stones, coming home clean took special effort. That he did it with such goodwill said everything necessary about his love for his sister.

His daughters kissed him lightly in greeting, one on each damp, overscrubbed cheek. Jenn showed him the tray. "What I want is to put supper on the table."

Their father looked at the bowls, then at the door to the parlor. His eyes crinkled at the corners. "It's glorious outside. Birds singing. Sun shining. We could eat on a blanket by the river."

Peggs handed him the loaf and butter, then collected the pottery cups and ewer of water. "No, we couldn't."

"I suppose not." Like a man girding himself for battle, Radd Nalynn led the way into his own home.

A more unlikely battlefield couldn't be imagined. The Nalynn parlor was a welcoming place: bright, warm, and comfortable. This time of year, the potbellied heat stove was filled with cut flowers and the heavy throws were neatly folded in a chest against any damp, ready for winter's comfort, while pretty quilts covered the bed in the corner. On the floor, baskets of bright rags waited to be made into rugs and bundles of straw waited to become baskets.

And, though formidable in her way, Sybb Mahavar was hardly a foe. She was the female version of her younger brother, though diligent application of powder forestalled any unseemly apple spots on her cheeks. The two had the same thick dark hair, salted white at the temples, and the same strong lines at jaw and chin. Both had soft creases at the corners of eye and mouth that suggested old grief until they smiled, which was more often than not.

Radd wasn't a heavy man, but decades in the mill had laid muscle through his chest and arms until his body resembled a smallish barrel. Sybb was frail beneath her layers of linen and wool, her wrists and neck skin over bone. Neither was tall. Peggs was a head taller and Jenn, since last year, could look her aunt in the eye.

Something she carefully avoided doing as she carried the tray to the family table.

To encounter an unexpected problem.

For the first time ever, the long wooden table that filled the other half of the room was covered by a cloth; one of the sheets from the chest, by the look. Worse, there were flowers in what, this morning, had been a large jar of pickles in the kitchen.

As for the flowers . . .

Radd stopped in his tracks, loaf and butter pot forgotten in his hands. "We don't pick her roses," he said in a strangled voice. "You know that, Sybbie."

"Which is why I was surprised to see them here," his sister replied calmly.

Everyone turned to Peggs, who shook her head. "I wouldn't touch them."

The roses nodded from the jar, each dewy fresh. Loose petals patterned the white cloth beneath, forming a perfect spiral outward.

"I wasn't home," Jenn reminded them. The display was Wisp's work; she was sure of it. Another apology.

But . . . he didn't come to the village.

Not that she'd noticed before.

If it was Wisp . . . a breeze was one thing. How had he managed the pickle jar?

And, a new worry, where were the pickles?

"I'll look after this." Peggs put down her tray to take hold of the jar, not without a meaningful glance at Jenn, and carried it to the window right of the front door. It fit, just, on the deep sill.

"Supper smells marvelous, dear. Radd?" Aunt Sybb rose gracefully from her place on what she called their settee—a wide bench against one wall, layered with blankets and backed with cushions—and stood by her chair at the table.

Radd's eyes hadn't left the roses.

His sister gave a delicate cough.

"Your pardon, Sybbie." He hurriedly put down the bread and butter in order to pull back her chair. It was more a lift of the chair to get it over the edge of the thick braided rug that filled the center of the wood floor, the chair itself made of rounds of birch with their bark peeled off, tied together. It was their best, free of creaks and with new soft cushions tied to seat and back.

The cushions, along with many other useful items, had been made by the Treff from dresses Aunt Sybb had brought last summer, seams carefully picked apart and every scrap of fabric saved. Their aunt had given the cushions a most thoughtful look on her arrival, but made no comment. Jenn wondered if she'd noticed the small pearl buttons were now on most of the men's shirts.

It was likely. The reversal of fortunes that left her brother penniless and exiled wasn't something discussed, nor was the ultimate use of her gifts. Wisp was right; her aunt didn't lack kindness.

Or resolve. When Jenn finally looked directly at her aunt's face, the lift of one shapely eyebrow made it clear their earlier discussion of the day—be it hems or husbands—wasn't over. She gave an accepting nod. Being dignified and adult probably included listening to all of a lecture, not just the part she couldn't avoid.

Radd helped his sister sit and took his place. As he cut thick slices of bread, steam rising from inside, Peggs placed a full cup at each setting, doing her best to avoid the rose petals on the cloth.

Having put down her own tray, with some relief, Jenn put a bowl of stew in front of her aunt, from the left, with a spoon. She served her father, then put out her supper and Peggs'.

The sisters sat, hands neatly folded. No need for a lantern or candles yet; the late afternoon sun shone through from the kitchen and played its beams over the table, picking out the deep red of the petals, embossing the simple cloth. Their aunt's keen eyes studied them, then lifted to regard Jenn's nose.

Jenn froze in place.

Aunt Sybb's brows began to draw together.

Slurp!

Her glance flashed to her brother, who halted his spoon halfway from his lips to return the most innocent look possible. "I expect poor manners from these deprived children, Radd Nalynn, not from you."

Jenn focused on her bowl, doing her best not to smile. There was nothing—beyond rust, according to their aunt—wrong with their father's table manners. After all, he'd grown up in Avyo, and once owned six of the city's great mills, as well as a tannery.

"Of course. My apologies, Sybbie." He put the spoonful of stew back in his bowl. "Please say the Beholding for us."

"I'd be honored." Aunt Sybb brought up her hands, beringed

forefingers and thumbs touching, the rest of her fingers spread wide, then brought them down to frame her heart, or rather the delicate clockworks pinned to her fine lace shawl. "Hearts of our Ancestors, we are Beholden for the food on this table, no matter how plain, for it will give us the strength to improve ourselves in your eyes. We are Beholden for the opportunity to share this meal, for as you know it's impossible to keep certain young people from running wild outdoors when they should sit still to listen and learn from their elders—"

Jenn sank in her chair.

"—We would be even more Beholden for the opportunity to find certain young women husbands to help them in their future lives before we're spirits ourselves."

Her sister gave a faint "meep" of protest; her father shook his head. "Sybbie . . ."

"Please let me finish. Hearts of our Ancestors, above all we are Beholden for this time we've spent together, as family. It's never—" her voice wavered. "It's never long enough." Radd's eyes softened and he touched her sleeve. She blinked fiercely as she said, "However far we are apart, Keep Us Close."

"'Keep Us Close,'" Jenn echoed with the others, exchanging a worried glance with Peggs. They all shed a few tears the night before Aunt Sybb left for the winter, but that was weeks away. It had to be. "Aunt Sybb," she began, "you aren't—you can't be leaving yet. You'll miss—" to say her birthday, her very special, coming-of-age birthday, would be selfish. "You'll miss the tinkers," she finished lamely. Their arrival and the harvest marked the high point of the year, as far as Marrowdell was concerned.

"I—" Aunt Sybb looked to her brother and Jenn's heart sank. They'd talked about this, her father and aunt, and the decision was made. It was on their faces.

"What matters is your birthday, Jenn," he said firmly, "We'll have our own party before your aunt leaves. Now. Let's enjoy this excellent supper."

He didn't want a fuss, that meant. She struggled to be calm and reasonable, but this was the worst news and her voice cracked shamefully. "How soon?"

"Jenn—"

"It's all right, Radd. Dear Hearts, I leave the day after tomorrow. Horst will bide with me in Endshere while my escort travels from Weken."

In such haste? "But why?"

"Because it's started." Peggs, usually the quiet one, leaned forward with a troubled frown. "You've stopped sleeping, haven't you, Aunt?"

"Peace, child." Their aunt's hand fumbled at her cup. "Eat your suppers."

Jenn looked more closely, seeing what she'd missed. Powder muted, but couldn't hide the dark circles beneath their aunt's eyes. "Is it true?"

"The Hearts move us at their whim."

"It's this place," she countered, furious at everything. "You know it is. Why won't it let you stay?"

An astonished silence fell over the table. The roses on the windowsill turned in their jar to face her. Peggs, who noticed, made a point of trying her stew.

Jenn flushed and bent her head. The sun on the cloth moved from petal to petal. The ones it deserted grew dark and dull, like stains.

No one talked about Marrowdell. About how the valley rejected some and chose others. About the dreams that drove the unwanted away.

"Jenn. Look at me."

Reluctantly, she lifted her eyes to meet her father's.

"Don't make this harder for your aunt than it already is. Our home's here. Hers is in Avyo, with your Uncle Hane."

Her aunt nodded, eyes too bright. "I miss the city, child. Don't worry. I'll be back next year."

"Let me come with you." The words fell out of her mouth before she'd thought them.

If the silence before was astonished, this was worse. They gaped at her, Peggs included, as if she'd lost her mind. Jenn pressed on. "For the winter. I'd be no trouble."

The roses withered as one, brown petals dropping to the floor.

Jenn refused to look at the now-gaunt stems. Why should it matter to Wisp or Marrowdell where she was? Others came and went. Just this spring, Anten Ropp had taken his stepsons all the way to Endshere to trade their extra bull.

Flowers hadn't died with drama over that.

"Uncle Horst helps more than me in the mill. I'd be home by spring plant—"

"Enough!" A roar. "No more of this—this nonsense, Jenn." Their father thrust away his bowl of stew, slopping its contents on the cloth. "Marrowdell is your home. High time you both grew up and took husbands!" He stood before either daughter could protest, turned, and stormed out of the house.

The three left exchanged shocked looks. Jenn couldn't remember her peaceful father leaving the table during a meal—let alone like this.

Aunt Sybb coughed delicately, dispelling the stunned silence. "He wants what's best for you."

And it didn't matter what she wanted? Jenn's flash of rebellion faded under her aunt's too-knowing gaze. "I'll apologize." She gathered her courage. "But I did mean it, Aunt Sybb. I want to go with you. I'd listen to lectures every day."

Distress etched lines across their aunt's face. "I wish you could, child, to the depths of my heart. I wish it were possible for you both to attend university, the theaters—"

"Why not?" Jenn sat straighter in sudden hope. "My name's not on a bind. Hettie said her father wants to send Cheffy and Alyssa to the university when they're old enough. I could go—"

"Jenn, don't," her sister whispered urgently.

Too late. The petals on the table shriveled in their pattern, starting with those near Aunt Sybb's hand. She might have missed the rest of their misbehavior, but this she did see and was transfixed; her face lost all color beneath its powder.

"Aunt?"

She started, then covered her eyes with a trembling hand. "You must stay. I can't. Not here. Not in this place . . ." her voice choked.

Peggs nudged Jenn and mouthed, "Behave!" Out loud, "Let me make you some tea, Aunt." As she rose to go to the kitchen, her fingers closed on Jenn's shoulder, pressed gently. Look after her, that said.

Much as she longed to shout at Wisp to behave, if indeed the petals and roses were his fault, Jenn quieted. Aunt Sybb never grew used to what she called Marrowdell's "eccentricities." Only yesterday, she'd taken refuge in the kitchen from the house toad, as if there was anything harmful in the creature with its soulful brown eyes, so like those of the puppies she described. Most of the time, the toad acted as a doorstop, ably keeping mice from the house. Unfortunately, it had decided to yawn and show its needle teeth when Aunt Sybb was sitting on the porch.

Whenever she visited, it was her nieces' duty to ensure nothing upset her. Which wasn't easy, Jenn thought with some frustration, when they didn't know what would.

Was the outside world so different?

She'd find out, Jenn vowed again.

Her stew cooled in its bowl. She didn't dare taste it, no matter how hungry, not with her father and sister fled the table, and her aunt sitting there, quivering, trying to be blind.

All she could think to do was sweep the offending petals from the cloth into her hand. They were crisp and dry, dead as if this was late fall and well past the frost.

No thistledown for Wisp.

Peggs arrived with tea, her lips pressed together in an unfamiliar line of disapproval. She'd cut thin slices of warm pie, topping it with strips of pale cheese, already melted. Normally, Jenn approved of going straight to the sweet course, but having missed lunch, she'd wanted her stew. She swallowed any objection. Supper had been disrupted by her selfishness, making Peggs' efforts in the kitchen for naught.

Everyone was upset, when she was the one being put upon. Jenn didn't see the fairness in that at all, but it was as it was. How did a simple request to visit Avyo for the winter mean she wasn't mature? They could have refused and that would have been that. What she'd said to Wisp had been in fun. How could she hide in Aunt Sybb's coach? Besides, their aunt would turn right around and bring her home.

The aunt who must pack and leave, through no fault of her own. Their father worried for good reason; his sister's will was stronger than her body, and sleepless nights quickly took their toll.

The aunt who was still trembling.

Jenn sighed, deep and long. Only one sure way to take Aunt Sybb's attention from the dying rose petals. She swallowed and plunged. "I won't marry Allin Emms. He's more interested in the mill than me. Besides, he's like a brother. An annoying one."

Aunt Sybb, who'd roused to grip her cup of tea with both hands, giving Peggs a murmured thanks, looked over in pleased surprise. "No one said you should, my dear."

"I won't marry Tadd either. He's moony over Peggs."

"Jenn Nalynn!" Peggs sank in her seat, having put the abandoned bowls of stew on the tray.

"Well, he is."

Her sister took refuge in her tea, cheeks pink.

As Jenn hoped, her new willingness to discuss marriage revitalized their aunt. "The Morrills come from excellent family."

Now she was well and truly stuck with it. Jenn felt her own cheeks flush.

Riedd Morrill had been a baron in Avyo, with a seat in Rhoth's House of Keys. That power and influence hadn't outweighed the heritage of a Mellynne bloodline, forcing him and his household into exile with the rest. It hadn't mattered to the horse who caved in his skull either, leaving his family to find a new life. Which they'd done, with varied success. Covie Morrill had raised her sons, then married widowed Anten Ropp and cheerfully begun raising his three children. Riedd's cousin, Riss Nahamm, took on the care of their great-uncle, Wagler Jupp, who refused to bend his ways one iota from his former life.

The grown sons, Devins and Roche, remained in the Morrill

home. Both had their mother's thick brown hair and green eyes, though Devins, being tall and lean, was said to take after their father while Roche was compact and sturdy.

"Devins likes you," Peggs offered, a mischievous gleam in her eye. "Remember how he'd pull your hair when Master Uhthoff was reading to us?"

"Devins talks about udders all day," Jenn retorted. "You can have him."

"I don't want him."

Aunt Sybb's regard shifted to Peggs. "Whom do you want, my dear?"

The pink in her sister's cheeks drained away. "There's no—I don't—"

Taking pity, Jenn stepped in. "I won't marry Roche Morrill either." She had no intention of elaborating.

Roche, when he could avoid helping his brother and stepfather in the dairy, hunted with Uncle Horst. When he wasn't hunting, he was spying. He'd followed her once, as far as the empty farm. It hadn't been a good feeling, like playing hide and seek in the hedges. She'd turned back, passing where he lurked in the shadows without a sideways glance.

The fierce wind that bent the trees behind her had done no more than fling leaves and dirt at Roche, but she'd smiled at his shout of fear.

He hadn't followed her since.

Like Wisp, Aunt Sybb was not to be denied. "Peggs, dear. You can tell us. Who has caught your eye?"

Peggs jumped up. "I should put Poppa's supper back in the pot before it's cold. Please excuse me." She grabbed the tray of bowls and almost ran to the kitchen.

Leaving Jenn alone with her aunt.

"I don't know," she said hurriedly. Who hadn't been moony over Peggs? Not that her sister offered any encouragement.

Her aunt touched the tip of her napkin to the corners of her mouth. "I wouldn't ask you to betray a confidence, child. However, unless more settlers with eligible sons arrive or you somehow conjure a prince from that vile toad of yours, if you want a husband you'll have to pick one from here sooner or later."

"What did you say?"

A faint frown. "Pardon me, Aunt."

"'Pardon me, Aunt,'" Jenn repeated quickly, blood pounding in her ears. "What did you say?"

"I said you shouldn't waste time hoping for more settlers to arrive. It's been over six years since the last, and they stayed but a night." Aunt Sybb gave a delicate, unfeigned shudder. "I can't blame them."

"No," Jenn corrected. "Not that. About the toad."

Rarely was Sybb Mahavar rendered speechless. She took a too-hasty swallow of tea, color rising to her face. "It was nothing. A bit of nonsense from an old story. My point is that you and your sister have four healthy men of the right age, right here. Allin and Tadd. Roche and Devins. Any one—"

"You forgot Wainn Uhthoff."

"I did not." Jenn watched her search for words. "Wainn is a kind and gentle person," Aunt Sybb said at last, "but an unsuitable husband. He is—disadvantaged."

The Uhthoffs, arriving too late to join the others at Endshere, had taken the Northward Road alone and been chased by bandits. In their desperate flight, their wagon had overturned, crushing Wainn's mother and sister, injuring young Wainn. He'd grown up with wide brown eyes ever puzzled by what they saw and a mind slow to understand. He helped his Uncle Kydd with his bees and stayed with the cows during calving.

"I'd rather Wainn than the rest," Jenn assured her aunt. But she was thinking about toads.

While on the windowsill, had she looked, she'd have seen a jar full of pickles.

And not a rose petal in sight.

Progress, of a sort.

Efflet had borne Wisp over the kaliia fields, to the hedge that bordered the village. Unseen, of course. They, like dragons, concealed themselves with light. Unheard would have been better still, but efflet couldn't help but talk among themselves. Fortunately, the villagers thought their raspy little whispers came from crickets.

He'd arrived ahead of the girl, as he'd planned. Heard her shocking request. Done his utmost to express an opinion. The aunt had listened, he thought.

Now, to get home.

Unfortunately, while he'd been occupied with pickles and roses, the efflet had abandoned him. Some sound in the field must have caught their attention. A grasshopper. A bird. A foolish mouse. Though efflet were the most peaceful of creatures otherwise, whatever small life threatened the growing kaliia would be torn to shreds and fed to the soil. Larger threats? Oh, those were torn to shreds and left as reminders of the value of well-tended hedges.

Wisp hurried as best he could along the strip of dirt the villagers called the Tinkers Road. It was nothing like a road, or was much more than one. At its end was the turn-borns' crossing. Its length? Were he on his side of the edge, he'd be wading though a shallow river of the purest mimrol, its thick silver warm and far more comfortable than that chill, damp, and muddy stream he'd had to cross to leave the village. Water. Bah!

There'd been a time he could have used the air itself, or taken the solid paths of earth.

The time might come again. Or not. He'd been as he was long enough to no longer care. What mattered was his duty, what remained of it. He no longer led his kind, but he would protect them with his last breath.

From what he could. Just ahead, the Tinkers Road was forced sharply west by the massive Bone Hill the villagers called the Spine. The narrow path to the upper meadow met the road where it bent, a path hidden until one was right beside it.

Wisp cringed and twisted to keep that dreadful opening in sight until safely past. Because nothing bled through by the light of Marrowdell's day didn't make it safe. It was never safe.

Not for those aware.

The villagers, in their blissful ignorance, could walk there unharmed if they chose; not so on his side of the edge, never so. There, the Wound showed its true nature. Ugly, stained. A trap with no escape.

But a place, nonetheless, easy to avoid. Wisp continued on, consumed by greater concerns. He had allies near the girl. The father held his daughters close, for love's sake. The aunt, who might have belonged in Marrowdell if not for heartstrings pulling her elsewhere, protected her brother and his family against the outside. The old soldier watched the road, for guilt's sake and a promise. Each helped in their way. Could they prevail against the girl's growing will? Not alone. That was the crux of it.

Why now? Or was now, why? This year's harvest would take place during a Great Turn, a moment of extraordinary potency and risk. He doubted coincidence. Wisp's next step clawed deep furrows in the packed dirt. Whatever the world, there were those drawn to power; most fools, some dangerous, a few of utter peril.

A chill, as though water ran down his spine. Turn-born. He didn't need the lingering daisies in their meadow to know the girl was coming into her heritage.

His bones felt it.

This Great Turn, for the first time in memory, there was a key on the Marrowdell side of the edge. An innocent, unknowing key.

In the shape of Jenn Nalynn.

THREE

JENN STOOD BEFORE the Treff porch and smoothed her skirt. The open door was framed by shoulder-high vases filled with dried flowers. The overhanging canvas—which tended to accumulate snow and collapse in winter, but there was no arguing with Treffs, as the saying went—provided welcome shade to the benches beneath, though these benches weren't for sitting. The one on the left was home to a row of pale gray crocks waiting their turn in the kiln; Jenn paused to study them carefully, but found no hint of the lovely colors and patterns sure to be revealed, once fired. Hettie said, having heard it from her Auntie Cynd, that her grandmother's latest glazes used rare pigments all the way from Thornloe. Davi had collected a mysteriously heavy package from Aunt Sybb's coach when she'd arrived. Not that Lorra would say.

Tiny bells chimed softly. They hung from the birdhouse at one end of the porch, to ring when its occupants came and went. The right-hand bench stood up against the wall to allow room for a quilt to hang in the light breeze. Frann wouldn't put such special work in the sun.

Jenn rubbed dust from her shoe.

She'd reason to be nervous. Aunt Sybb was a lady of refined manners, whose idea of expressing disapproval involved a certain sternness in the stirring of her tea, and whose heart was as soft as her brother's. Lorra Treff was also of refined manners, but visiting her domain was more like plunging into a bear's den. Where a short-tempered and hungry bear could be waiting. Or rather, two.

Lorra Treff, as she'd remind anyone who might have forgotten, had done more than rule a prominent family in Avyo. She'd been the head of its famed potter's guild and, as such, fully capable of expressing her disapproval in terms as sure to shock her illustrious riverside neighbors as they were to wilt the most stubborn dockside apprentice. In the company of peers—or family—she relied on verbal flaying and dismemberment to end any argument in her favor. Or at least silence her opponent.

Stripped of title and wealth, Lorra had chosen, like most, to go north with the shards of her household. A daughter, Wen. A son, Davi, and his wife. The wife's brother—Anten Ropp—and his family.

Though she doted on Davi and was glad of the rest, exile became bearable, to hear Lorra tell it, when she'd discovered her arch rival, Frann Nall, at the settlers' camp in Weken. Frann's prosperous holdings had included Avyo's riverfront warehouses, used by, among others, Lorra and her guild. Their battles had been legendary. Guild representatives cried foul in the Lower House time and again over what they called outrageous fees and preference for foreign artisans; the barons of the House of Keys, beneficiaries of the fees and fond, truth be told, of the luxury of owning foreign-made art, heard such recommendations from the commons and dutifully ignored them.

When Lorra and Frann met at a social gathering, those nearby would place wagers on the length of time before sparks flew. Without doubt, none would have bet the two could survive in the same village, let alone thrive in the same house.

But the two recognized in each other a kindred spirit and left their feuds with the wealth that spawned them. They arrived in Marrowdell with an eye for new opportunities. Lorra, seeing the quality of the clay lining the riverbanks, immediately instructed her beloved son to assemble her potter's wheel, then build a sequence of larger and larger kilns. Frann claimed organization of the village stores, keeping records for the mill as well as overseeing trade. Lately she'd taken up weaving, trading for wool from Endshere to add to flax. Useful, lovely things came from the Treff household.

Not that it was ever peaceful.

Jenn stepped up on the porch, careful of the pottery, and eased inside the door.

The Treff home was twice the size of the Nalynns'. Davi and Cynd slept on one side of the loft, Wen the other. Lorra and Frann each had their own rooms on the main floor. The large airy central room, where Jenn stood, served as kitchen and workroom. It extended from front to back, well lit by windows at both ends and by light streaming through the open doors on either side, and held an argument unlikely to end while its proponents lived.

Tidy shelves filled the left wall from floor to ceiling, with clever pegs to hold bobbins and spindles of thread. Baskets of leather and fabric scraps shared space with bottles of homemade buttons. The irreplaceable scissors and forms and needles, Frann's most precious millinery supplies, were, Jenn knew, safely tucked into the long boxes on the topmost shelf. In front stood a loom, threads hanging from the rafters above, beside a small desk and chair.

The wall to Jenn's left formed the opposing side. Great messy clumps of clay sat in bowls on the floor. Or on the floor. Bits and pieces of a pottery wheel leaned against the wall. The wall itself?

Bare but for a single painting, showing a tall young man beside a table. Jenn leaned from side to side, entranced as always by how the eyes in the portrait seemed to follow her. Creamy lace erupted from the young man's collar and cuffs, gold brocade shimmered down the front of his coat, and he looked, in Jenn's opinion, thoroughly uncomfortable. The table in the painting held a bowl of exotic peaches. The bowl was a Treff family heirloom; the elegant young man, hard as it was to imagine, had grown into Davi, the village smith.

The room was divided by more than each woman's passion. A wavering line of chalk, fresh by the look of it, led along the floor from front door to kitchen. Streaks of clay and bits of thread crossed it here and there, sorties into enemy territory. Jenn wasn't surprised. The shouting that went on when both women were at work could be heard all the way to the mill, if the wind was right.

For now, to Jenn's relief, serenity reigned. Davi must be out in his smithy, attached to the barn beside the house. Cynd, his wife, would be in her garden. As befitted her former station in Avyo society, she was accomplished in embroidery and other fine handwork, skills she turned to good use during winter when she, Wen, and Frann sewed most of the village clothing. Though uninterested in plants before, she'd quickly realized gardening would keep her out of the house in summer, when Lorra and Frann were most at odds. To no one's surprise, the Treff gardens produced the best gourds and potatoes. Cynd's childless state hadn't endeared her to her husband's mother in Avyo; her abilities in Marrowdell did. They'd grown closer.

Which could not be said of mother and daughter. Wen Treff lived in the same home. She sewed and cooked with Cynd. She listened to the flute Frann would play come winter evenings and drew designs for her mother's pottery, but Marrowdell had claimed her more than any other.

Wen talked to toads.

Not only toads. She chatted with birds and squirrels. Jenn had once caught her lecturing a butterfly, her face animated and glad, mouthing some soundless language of her own.

Come a person too close, and Wen fell still. By her actions, she understood what was being said, but no matter how others railed or coaxed or reasoned, she uttered not a word in return.

The silence of her daughter might have explained something of Lorra Treff's fiery temper. Or Lorra's temper explained the silence. No one was quite sure.

"I swear, Lorra Treff, you'll poison us by the time you're through. What are you thinking? Get this mess out of here!"

The heated complaint came from the kitchen. Jenn took a step back. This might not be the best time for a visit.

"I'll work where I want in my own house!" Hotter and louder. "And how many times have I asked you, Frann Nall, not to leave your wretched great loom in the middle of the floor so no one can move without you shrieking? Cynd! Stop fussing with those loaves and help me carry this—"

"Don't you dare take that mess near my loom!"

Not the best time at all. Jenn turned and fled out the door.

"Hello, Jenn."

She started and almost knocked over one of the doorside vases, steadying it with a hurried grab, then smiled with relief. "Hello, Wainn."

Wainn Uhthoff stopped short of the porch, his hat crumpled in both hands, a shy smile on his handsome face. "You're wearing shoes."

"I am." She lifted a foot for his inspection. "Were you visiting Davi?"

He blushed bright crimson.

Ordinarily, Jenn wouldn't have noticed. After all the talk of husbands and who was suitable at supper, she blushed herself, unsure why.

They might have stood there like fools a while longer, but Davi chose that moment to step out of his barn for a piece of harness hung out to dry. Spotting them, he waved a greeting, aimed a big thumb toward the river, then went back inside.

"What does he mean?" she puzzled.

She hadn't thought it possible for Wainn to blush hotter, but he did. "That's where she is."

Shouts still rattled the dishes inside the Treff house. "She" could be only one person. "Wen? Good. I was looking for her."

"That's where she is." As if she hadn't heard, all the while twisting his hat. "May I visit with you?"

Visit Wen. Suddenly, Jenn felt ridiculous. What was she thinking? She'd left Peggs with her aunt and the dishes. The two of them probably thought she'd rushed after her father to apologize, which she should have done and assuredly would do as soon as possible, as well as the dishes, but she'd known Lorra Treff most definitely would not welcome a visitor after dark and . . .

Jenn couldn't wait. The sun was abandoning another day, leaving her behind. Wen was the only person in Marrowdell who might know if toads could be made into princes. Yes, she didn't speak, but surely she could give an informative nod or two?

When Jenn didn't answer, Wainn gazed longingly toward the river, then back at her. "I'm not allowed to visit alone."

Her lips formed a soundless "Oh."

He waited patiently, another of the ways he wasn't like the other young men of Marrowdell. Wainn could stand so still, you forgot he was there. If it wasn't for his father being Master Uhthoff, their teacher, he might have truly been forgotten. But Dusom Uhthoff and his brother had made sure Wainn was included, in classes, in activities, in the chores they all shared.

Though until this moment, despite what she'd said to her aunt, Jenn hadn't thought that could include being a husband one day. As for Wen Treff? She was . . . she was old, wasn't she? True, Wainn was twenty-eight, but no one thought of him as grown. And Wen? She had to be at least thirty.

Not to mention the toads.

The reason she'd come in the first place.

Jenn gave a resolute shrug. If she helped Wainn, she hadn't totally wasted her time. She took off her shoes and tucked them safely inside her shirtwaist. "Come with me," she offered.

The sun touched the first of the Bone Hills, drawing long shadows from the village buildings, torching the fields to red gold. A swathe of light paved the road toward the valley's mouth and everything she wanted, an invitation she wasn't allowed to accept. Turning from it, Jenn led Wainn through the Treff farmyard to the riverbank. There, she took the path through the bushes to the shore.

The river sparkled and burbled to itself. Behind the Treffs' it was shallow and rich with reeds, home to waterfowl and frogs. No one hunted here, other than down from old nests or to collect the occasional egg from a large clutch. In return, the birds would sound the alarm when a log floated downstream and lodged in the shallows, a treasure the villagers would quickly pull to shore.

The water was a deep blue, almost black. Beetles whirled in the still patches, playing tag with their tails. Tiny midges careened back and forth in straight lines from shoreline to midriver, faster than the eye could see, preoccupied by their own affairs. A heron stalked past as Jenn and Wainn came down the bank, its great yellow eyes alert for careless pollywogs. Other than the clang of Davi's hammer and the river, the loudest sound came from crickets in the grass. The air smelled of water and growth and decay. With a hint of summerberry.

Wen Treff stood bent in the shallows, skirt hitched to her thighs, her mass of brown curls dusted with cobwebs and pollen. Her gaze was fixed on something in the water.

"That's where she is," Wainn said breathlessly.

His voice drew Wen's attention. Her eyes were gray, almost colorless. Her eyebrows met in a distracted frown that cleared when she saw Wainn. "This is where I am," she agreed.

Wen spoke?

Heart thumping in her chest, Jenn glanced over her shoulder at the Treff house, tensed to rush back and tell the family the news.

Then, she hesitated.

Wen's speech or lack of it wasn't her business. Didn't she run to her secret friend in the meadow at every chance? Maybe Wen did the same, in her own way.

Meanwhile, Wainn had waded into the water, stopping when it reached his knees. "Hello, Wen," he said happily. "We're not alone. Jenn Nalynn let me come with her to visit."

The pale gaze switched to Jenn. A brow lifted. "Why would she do that?"

"I've a question," Jenn said carefully. She moved forward until her toes sank into dark bubbly mud. "About toads and princes."

Wen, it turned out, possessed the same quality of stillness Wainn could display. For an endless moment, she regarded Jenn. The river eddied around her knees and a curl fell loose over one eye. A fish gulped air near Wainn, as if making a comment. A dragonfly landed on Jenn's wrist, regarding her with emerald eyes. Just as Jenn began to believe she'd imagined Wen could speak, she did. "I know toads. The only prince I've heard of is the one who sent us here. Mother calls him the Fat Old Fool. She writes him a long letter once a year and gives it to Davi, who is supposed to ask your aunt to deliver it. He burns it in his forge instead."

"My father calls him Prince Ordo Arselical," Wainn offered. "He rules all of Rhoth." He lifted his foot from the water and splashed it down again. "Except here."

Wen's smile transformed her face from plain to extraordinary. "Except here," she agreed.

From what Jenn had been taught, Marrowdell was indeed part of Rhoth and so subject to its prince, because the prince had decided it should be. Rather than leave the quiet north to the hunters, trappers, and foresters who made it home, he'd declared to his barons that an unsettled northern border was an invitation to invasion, Rhoth being in a constant state of disagreement with its prickly eastern neighbor, Ansnor, and never sure of the intentions of the vast civilization of Eldad to the south. As to the west, well, there lay peaceful Mellynne, who'd put up with the prince's great-grandfather's border raids no longer than it took to overrun the Rhothan capital and place its own people in positions of influence, before leaving with a treaty of binding friendship.

A treaty that hadn't spared those of Naalish descent when Prince Ordo needed families to settle the north for him and, not coincidentally, wealth to buy the support of both the House of Keys and Lower House in Avyo. He'd declared all the original property leases at an end, offering those left penniless the choice of Mellynne, a domain as foreign to them as to any Rhothan, or to take his gift of land to the north and start anew.

A handful of settlements were his legacy, Marrowdell among them. No other domain contested the border. No one of Rhoth appeared to care about those sent into the wilds and left to fend for themselves.

Not that Jenn thought of the world in such terms. Her breath caught imagining what it would be like to travel to scholarly Mellynne, with its fountains and art, or to cross the inland sea to Eldad's great cities, said to spread across the horizon—even mysterious, dangerous Ansnor had its charm. Anywhere, she decided, coming back to her problem, but here.

"I've heard there's a way to change a toad into—" Jenn paused. She didn't need or want a prince, she needed a way to leave Marrowdell. "To change a toad into the perfect husband. For me."

"I would be a perfect husband," Wainn asserted, looking at Wen.

Wen actually blushed.

She was doing an excellent job helping other people's futures, Jenn fumed to herself, just not her own. "Wen. I need a toad," she insisted.

"Toads prefer other toads," Wen told her, pushing the curl from her forehead. She appeared amused. "Why would one want to marry you?"

"I don't want to marry a toad." Jenn collected herself. "I want to know how to change a toad into a man. A man to be a husband." Now her cheeks burned.

"Have you tried this?"

"How could I? I don't know how."

"Then toads should be grateful. For if anyone could do such a thing, it would be you, Jenn of Night's Edge."

For a woman who hadn't spoken for most of her life, Wen Treff had no trouble robbing Jenn of speech.

"I can't tell you how to accomplish this," Wen continued. "Nor would I betray the small ones. But I do know a change in shape does not bring a change in nature. If you want someone to give you his heart, I suggest you follow your own." Wen bestowed her glorious smile on Wainn once more, then bent to the water again, her face behind a fall of cobwebbed curls, to talk to fish.

"Well, isn't this convenient."

The ox thought so, having pulled the wagon halfway off the road before agreeing to stop.

"I'd say someone wanted to help new settlers, sir," Tir agreed, coming back to the wagon. He'd been walking alongside the animal to stretch his legs and escape the dust.

"The ideal spot, too." Bannan glanced upward. What sky showed between treetops was the deep blue of a late summer twilight, a warning they'd soon have to break out lamps to see the way ahead. And here they find the first roadside clearing since Endshere wide enough for one or more wagons, complete with a patch of grass beside a burbling mountain stream? Pretty.

Unfair. Having left the border guard, he'd hoped to look at a pleasing landscape and not see where lurkers could hide or how easily any escape could be cut off. For that matter, he'd like, for once, to look at an earnest face, like any in Endshere, and not see the lie.

Tir leaned on the wagon as Bannan jumped down. "Do they think we're fools, sir?"

"The good people of Endshere did warn of bandits." And been willing to provide escort—for a steep price. An escort likely to be the bandits themselves, in his opinion, but he'd been polite in his refusal. No sense leaving ill will behind.

Or revealing himself.

Doubtless word had gone ahead. The wagon and its contents had worth here; there was always the chance a once-wealthy settler had hidden something valuable, not that he had.

"A fire," Bannan decided. "And a good supper." He took an appreciative sniff. The afternoon's warm pine lingered, mixed with road dust, fresh ox droppings, and the grass underfoot. Nothing of the city, nothing of before. "We may," he added cheerily, "need to open the brandy."

"Here? Sir?"

"Relax, Tir." Bannan pursed his lips and gave a soundless whistle. Scourge jerked his head from whatever had him rooting in the bushes. "Watch," he told the horse.

There was something anticipatory in the baleful stare this produced.

"No bandits tonight," he announced. Scourge rarely had to attack. Few on foot waited to learn what crashed toward them in the dark, and no strange horse would approach if they had his scent. The wily veterans of his company had valued that assurance, especially during their endless patrols into the broken wilderness across the

Lilem River, land Ansnor had claimed and defended as fiercely as Rhoth. The soldiers would curse the horse with affectionate pride by day, and sleep better by night.

When anyone slept, he reminded himself. They hadn't been at war; they'd never been at peace. Patrol was—had been—a weary sameness of hunting one another through the dark. They'd aimed to survive it, not win. He supposed the Eldad treaty accomplished that much.

"He has his use," Tir admitted, watching Scourge shove his head back into the shrubs, hunting whatever feckless rodent had his attention. "But on a farm? You can't tell me, sir, he'll let you hitch him to a plough."

"There might be bears." Bannan grinned. "Or wolves. Rabbits—right, Scourge? You like rabbits."

An ear flicked in his direction.

"Oh, and that's going to be easy to explain." At Bannan's look, Tir added, "Sir. You do realize it's not normal for a horse to eat rabbits."

"In Rhoth," Bannan reminded him. "Scourge is Ansnan."

"If you say so, sir."

"I do. And so must you, from now on. After all, he could be." Since no one had ever seen an Ansnan mounted, and they used tall horned cattle to pull their wagons, who was to know what their horses looked like? When it came to it, Bannan reasoned, Scourge easily passed for a horse—a powerful, oversized, and ugly one, to be honest—from a respectful distance. Any closer, and there was something odd about the lower jaw, a predatory awareness to the eye, and no stallion had balls quite that shape. Mind you, that close and you'd best be a friend or quick on your feet.

In a public stable, Scourge would mouth hay, though he preferred the mice that nested in it, and delighted in sweet mash, provided Bannan or Tir slipped in meaty table scraps.

Whatever the great beast was, he was a legacy. Bannan's father had been his rider, as had his father's uncle. Scourge chose whom he would endure, as he had ever since stalking from the mist that morning into the Larmensu paddock.

Had the closeness of the Larmensu holding to the troubled border attracted him? Or simply a temporary overabundance of rabbits?

Regardless, as a mount, Scourge proved more than ready for what he loved most. Battle and blood.

If Bannan didn't produce a worthy heir to Scourge's saddle, he assumed the war steed would abandon him to seek his own. Eventually. He'd miss him. Cantankerous, irritable, dangerous. Tireless, courageous, and, above all, loyal.

Well, above all, bloodthirsty. Scourge's loyalty depended on his opinion of what his rider had in mind.

That he so willingly took this road?

"Rabbits," Bannan said firmly.

Jenn stormed all the way to the village fountain before she noticed her shadow. She stopped. Wainn stopped. He didn't speak. His eyes were wide and sad and unutterably patient.

"What do you want?"

"I'm not allowed to visit alone."

Did he expect her to walk back to the Treffs' with him and spend more time watching Wen mouth soundless words at perch? Before she could snap a reply, Wainn continued. "I wanted to thank you, Jenn Nalynn, but you walk very fast."

What was wrong with her? After dipping her finger in the water, Jenn shook her head and sat on the fountain's ring. She patted the stone in invitation. "I'm glad I could help, Wainn. Wen's talked to you before?"

He dipped a finger in the water too, catching the droplets on his outstretched tongue, then sat his lanky frame with care. He did everything the same way, she realized, as if unsure the world around him could be trusted to wait as it was. "I hear everything she says. I'm a good listener." A mottled gray toad hopped toward them over the cobbles and made itself comfortable against Wainn's bare feet. He bent to look at it. "You won't turn him into a man, will you?"

Jenn eyed the toad. It blinked its limpid brown eyes at her, then yawned toothily. "Not," she said dryly, "if it means a man who wants mice for supper."

Wainn chuckled. "You have a good heart."

Good or not, it felt empty. She offered the toad a toe to rub its chin against. "All I want is to see more of the world," she said gloomily. "Why is that wrong?"

"I thought you wanted to marry a toad," he said, looking confused.

Jenn burst out laughing. Birds chirped in answer and a late beam of sun found its way through the apple trees to sparkle on the fountain. "I can't believe I bothered Wen with such nonsense." She lost her smile. "I guess I was desperate. You can't visit Wen alone. I can't choose my life alone. I'm sure Poppa won't let me leave Marrowdell without a husband." She patted his hand; it still clutched his hat. "And you, dear fellow, are spoken for."

"'Spoken for?'"

She touched the concerned furrow between his brows. "Wen likes you."

"Yes." His puzzlement faded, replaced by a dazzling smile. "I'm a good listener."

"You are indeed. Let me know when you want to visit again. I'll come if I can." Jenn looked along the road to the mill, thinking of her father working when he should be home, eating his supper alone if he had any appetite left. Her fault. She'd best go and make amends. He could never stay angry at either of his daughters; it wasn't fair to leave him unhappy. Then she would spend time with her aunt, as much as she could. "I have to go. Good night."

Wainn stood and offered his hand to help her to her feet, a courtly gesture as natural as his muddy bare feet. Hers, Jenn thought ruefully, were no better. She might be wearing black stockings.

"My uncle has a book," Wainn informed her as he released her hand. "A book about changing one thing into another."

From nonsense to instruction?

She shouldn't encourage this, Jenn told herself, fighting a surge of hope. Not in herself or Wainn. "It's not possible."

"Wen said if anyone could do such a thing, it would be you."

The sunbeam disappeared. Silence made a wall around them until a bee buzzed past on her way to the hives. One of Kydd Uhthoff's bees. Not the lesser of the two brothers, Jenn reminded herself. Not in knowledge. In Avyo, Kydd had been in the midst of studies at the university when his family was exiled. What those studies had been, no one said, but his keen dark eyes had a way of looking through a problem—or person.

If anyone here could have a book to help her, it would be Kydd.

Wainn nodded as if he'd followed all this. "I can ask him for the book for you, if you like."

If anyone here would immediately want to know why she was borrowing that particular book, it would be Kydd. He was curious to a fault—and, like his brother, a close friend of Radd Nalynn. Jenn swallowed. "Leave that to me, Wainn. I'll visit your house tomorrow." If it was on one of the many shelves, she should be able to borrow it with no one the wiser. Dusom was always glad to share, especially if a former student took interest in reading. "What's the title?"

"It's not in the house. It's in a hive. All the Mellynne books are in the hives. The books from Ansnor are in the hives too. Uncle says they make good winter coats for our bees."

Books from Mellynne? Ansnor? Who would . . . Jenn closed her mouth and took Wainn's sleeve, tugging him with her. "Show me."

The main orchard nestled in the lee of the cliff behind Marrowdell, protected from wind, exposed all day to the sun. There were six more apple trees where the road split in the village center to go around the fountain. At this time of year, every branch bent under its load of ripening fruit, tempting the milk cows on their way to the shed and driving Wainn's old pony to feats of inventiveness at the latch. Or, as now, to lean his head over the gate to nicker plaintively about his lack of apples, hairy lips working as if to summon the fruit closer.

Beneath the trees, behind the Uhthoffs' home, were the hives. Whenever Uncle Horst found a wild colony, he'd tell Kydd, who'd would march off with his sack to invite the bees home. Jenn didn't think there was conversation involved, other than gentle hands and a knowledge of their nature. Once in Marrowdell, the bees seemed content to stay. Like most villagers, they avoided the Bone Hills and meadows beyond, but there was plenty of nectar to be had between the village gardens and the wildflowers lining the gullies.

Despite the lengthening shadows, they droned back and forth, head height, knowing better than any where to go.

Seven hives. "Which one?"

Wainn peered into the nearest. Bees bumped into him, crawled over his shoulders, then flew off on their routes. "Wen could ask them for you."

She could use Wisp, not Wen. Wisp enjoyed playing with bees. He'd whirl them dizzy then set them on a flower without a hair of their bodies left ruffled. Then again, bees didn't appear to find this game as entertaining as she did. Best not have Wisp involved.

Not yet.

Which was as far as she let that tendril of thought go. The book first. Learn what was needful.

A bee landed on her nose. Jenn went cross-eyed trying to read its face. "Would you help us find a book, please?" she asked.

"You have to use its words, not ours," Wainn told her. "Like Wen."

The bee left. Feeling foolish, Jenn crouched to look inside one of the hives. Something lined the outer walls, but she couldn't tell if she looked at honeycomb or leather binding. Bees walked softly over her hands and arms, wings never still, their hum its own kind of music.

Music that would change to a battle cry if she tried to take anything from their hive. Jenn had watched Kydd lift a panel of honeycomb, dripping and golden, using his free hand to guide the bees back inside. He cared for them, they trusted him.

Who'd think to look for books here? Even if they did, who could, without being stung? She wasn't sticking her hand in there.

As for why these books were hidden instead of on a shelf—only Kydd Uhthoff could explain that.

"What if he wants to read one?" Jenn mused aloud. "Isn't it too much trouble?"

"No trouble. He asks me. I know all the words."

She straightened to stare at Wainn. "You do?" She hadn't known he could read Rhothan, let alone any other language. He'd been with them during classes, yes, but she'd never seen him open a book.

He nodded. "I know all the words in all our books. Father calls me his library. He asks me for words too, if he doesn't want to reach to the top shelf."

"So you know what this book says about changing one thing into another."

"Oh, yes." A wide smile. "All the words."

Jenn smiled back. "Would you like a piece of Peggs' pie?"

The turn had come. It slid as night's leading edge across the trapped ones, brushed blue over their ivory flanks, pooled darkness where their edges bled beneath the forest. It faded greens and etched black under flowers, intensifying their colors until the meadow drowned in waves of yellow, white, and mauve. The wide golden fields, rooted in the dark, reaching for the light, took fire as the edge passed over them and showed their true nature.

The turn had come and shapes revealed themselves, small and anxious, wings ablur. Efflet. They fell silent and left their fields. Approached and settled carefully beyond reach, row upon row, pale eyes unblinking, claws knuckled at their breasts. Wisp ignored them. Unreliable creatures, efflet, but they sought his presence despite his tempers.

Company, of a sort.

The light of this world faded; the light of his lingered. In their fleeting balance, what belonged elsewhere could no longer hide. Wisp gazed bemused at his own claw, used it to snap the head from an aster. Such particular magic, light. Beyond the grasp of the wise, outside the reach of fools, though neither hesitated to try. For during a turn, the edge between worlds softened. Here. Elsewhere. Crossing between was easier, for those burdened or less able.

Disturbing what slept. That was easier too, in a turn, but nothing sane would try.

Ease and threat were fleeting. The turn swept across Marrowdell, unstoppable, uncaring. It passed him by, and his claw disappeared. The pale eyes of efflet winked out, row after row, while along the branches of the towering neyet flared a multitude of tiny stars, as what seemed leaves became hordes of busy ylings, the stars the light caught in their hair. The tiny beings had been trapped on this side of the edge, like other small ones, disdained by the mighty, overlooked by those who should have taken care and offered rescue. Resilient and industrious, they'd made new homes along the neyet's exposed roots. During each turn, their multitudes held hands and sang, or threw themselves with abandon into the air to dance, cloaks rustling.

Though some stood guard, barbed weapons at the ready. Nyphrit would eat them if they could.

The turn passed the neyet.

Leaves giggled in trees. Ylings weren't the most serious of folk.

Wisp watched the night's edge unfold shadows along the Tinkers Road. Soon it would douse the glistening water and cross, bringing the turn to the village. The few small ones who dwelt there were too wise to leave themselves exposed. The roses on the girl's home became only more beautiful, though, like the oak at the river's edge, they'd sent roots into his world and now held opinions.

When shadows met the road's last bend, when night followed the plunge of the river and slipped down the final scarred cliff of Marrowdell, their worlds would part company and this day's turn be done. The limit of the edge, of his duty, and the line the girl must never cross.

The villagers would light their fires and lamps, draw curtains, close doors. He'd asked the girl if inside their buildings they pretended night hadn't come. She'd laughed her beautiful laugh and said, not at all. Night was a time of rest and peace. Of sleep and dreams.

For those who could rest. The girl blamed Marrowdell for the whispers that disturbed her aunt and sent other would-be settlers away, but Wisp was aware of no malice or intent. Their dreams crept to the edge of their world. Here, they met the edge of his. That was all. Some could tolerate that glimpse; most, it seemed, could not.

This turn ended. Dew, that nuisance of late summer evenings, began to sparkle on the plants around him. Despite his thorough distaste for damp, Wisp remained. He would wait for the lights in the Nalynn home, wait till those lights disappeared again.

"Don't dream," he would say then. "Stay here and content, Dearest Heart."

For her sake, and theirs.

FOUR

LEAVING WAINN TO wait outside, cautioned to keep from any window, Jenn tiptoed into the empty kitchen. She was careful not to step through the late day sunbeams leaning through window and door, and kept behind the ladder and half-drawn curtain that separated the necessary clutter of the kitchen from the rest of the house. Her aunt and Peggs murmured peacefully in the parlor, something about tomorrow's supper. Grateful to avoid explaining either Wainn or her mud-stained feet, Jenn chose a stick of charcoal from Peggs' cup and put it in her pocket. The sketchpad securely under one arm, she went to the pie and quickly ran a knife through the pastry, separating a generous slice for Wainn and a slightly smaller one for herself so he wouldn't eat alone. She'd no more put the pieces on a plate, adding forks, when she heard her name and froze.

"Jenn should be home by now." Their aunt's voice was concerned. "I hope she hasn't gone off again."

"Not this late," Peggs reassured her. "I'm sure she's with Poppa at the mill."

She would be soon, Jenn told herself guiltily. She eased toward the back door, avoiding the plank that creaked . . .

"I'd be happier if she was slipping out to see a young man."

"Aunt Sybb! Jenn would never—"

. . . she stopped and nodded vigorously.

"A pity. Many a good marriage began with playful indiscretion. You should try it sometime."

Had Aunt Sybb been into the cider?

"Come now, Peggs," their aunt continued. "We're grown women. It's natural to have a fancy for someone. Natural and healthy. Surely you do."

Jenn tightened her arm over the sketchpad and made sure she had a good grip on the plate. Nothing could make her budge from this spot now.

But when Peggs finally answered, her voice was heavy. "Is it natural and healthy to want someone who doesn't know you exist?"

Who in Marrowdell didn't know her sister? Jenn frowned.

"Of course. As well as frustrating, maddening, and tiresome. Men can be such fools, adorable as they are. That's when—" a pause during which she imagined their aunt gently patting Peggs' hand, "—you turn to your family."

"Oh, no," Peggs protested. "No. I don't want—I don't need—"

"Oh, yes, you do. As does your father, not that he'll take my good advice and scoop up that fine and capable Nahamm woman before someone else realizes old Jupp won't live forever."

"Aunt Sybb!"

This was better than one of Roche's spooky storytellings in the Emms' hayloft. Jenn eyed the out-of-reach counter wistfully; the plate grew heavier by the moment.

"Don't fuss, child. It's unbecoming. There's nothing wrong with a discreet word in the right ear. That's the problem with this place. You've grown up too close together. No wonder it takes someone from outside to stir the pot, get people to notice who and what they should."

If not the cider, definitely something.

"Please, I'm sure you have the best intentions, Aunt Sybb, but this isn't—he isn't someone like that. Let it be, please. I'm—for Poppa's sake, I'm willing to marry anyone who'll help him in the mill. You know that. I'm sure Jenn feels the same way."

She most certainly did not. Jenn closed her mouth just in time.

"Wherever did you get that idea?" Aunt Sybb sounded horrified. "Your father doesn't want an apprentice. He—We want you happy, that's all."

"Happy?"

The word hurt, the way her sister said it.

"Yes, happy. It's not impossible, Peggs." Her aunt spoke so softly, Jenn had to strain to hear. "Trust me. It only seems that way because you're young."

"It's that way because I'm young! Don't you understand?"

Jenn shrank from the anguish in Peggs' voice. She didn't want to be here anymore. She didn't want to listen. But her feet wouldn't move.

"Ah." With calm certainty. "The talented beekeeper has your heart."

"How—? Don't say anything, Aunt Sybb. To anyone. I beg you."

Kydd Uhthoff? The plate almost slipped through Jenn's fingers. What was Peggs thinking? Yes, the younger brother was handsome, in a distant, scholarly way, and kind, she supposed, having noticed Peggs' talent and given her all those private drawing lessons, but he was—how old was he?

Old enough to be her father, Jenn thought, that's how old.

"No, dear, no. Trust me. This is a delicate matter. Not impossible, whatever you think. You're mature for your years. He's a man who missed much of his youth. I applaud your taste. I do. Dry your eyes and mind your posture. You're a Nalynn. We fight for what matters to us—"

"Is the pie ready, Jenn?"

Jenn jumped and everything flew into the air. Wedges of pie hit the floor, the plate smashed on the oven bricks, and the forks followed the plate, their tinkle and fall like rain after thunder.

She lunged for the sketchpad and managed to grab it, then looked up.

Wainn blinked down at her.

Aunt Sybb stood beside her sister and shook her head.

While Peggs had never looked so furious in her life.

"More tea, young Uhthoff?"

Their aunt was the gracious hostess. Peggs gave Jenn another "I'll get you" look before she passed Wainn his second piece of pie. The last piece. With a thick curl of cheese.

How was this her fault? Jenn supposed Peggs in a temper was better than Peggs unhappy, since her tempers lasted about as long as it took bread to toast on a stick. Though she conceded this might be an uncommonly fierce one. Her sister hadn't spoken to her, not yet; she'd watched, grim-faced and arms crossed, while Jenn cleaned the floor and her muddy feet.

"Now," her aunt said, having arranged everyone and everything to her satisfaction, "tell us about you and Jenn, young Wainn."

Jenn gulped a hot swallow of tea and tried not to choke. A promising dimple appeared in one of Peggs' cheeks.

Wainn methodically chewed his mouthful before answering, a period during which Jenn frantically tried to think of something to say to deflect Aunt Sybb's interest. Tried and failed. The man finished and smiled happily. "I'm not to visit Wen alone. Jenn has a good heart. She let me visit Wen with her today."

Not what her aunt or Peggs had expected. "Why would you visit Wen Treff?" her sister demanded.

"Why shouldn't I?" Jenn countered, recovering her voice. "She's a neighbor."

"She doesn't talk to neighbors. She talks to toads."

"Toads?" Aunt Sybb quickly raised her napkin to her lips. Her eyes sparkled. "Oh my."

"Wen talks to me too," Wainn said solemnly. "And Jenn."

"She does? She did?" Peggs' surprised smile lit the room. "That's marvelous news. The Treffs must be so happy—"

Wainn shook his head. "Wen doesn't talk to them. They don't listen."

"'Toads,'" their aunt repeated, napkin lowered but at the ready.

"Dear Heart, surely you didn't believe me, about changing a toad into a prince. It was a story."

"I don't want a prince," Jenn began. "I—" Her sister and aunt were looking at her with identical expressions of amused skepticism.

"Jenn wants to make a husband who will do what she wants," Wainn finished for her, all too helpful. "I can tell her how."

She buried her face in her hands.

"You can?" Peggs asked.

"I have the words from my uncle's book."

"K-Kydd's involved?!"

Jenn raised her head at this. "No. Yes, but he doesn't know he is." Another "get you later" look was forming. "Kydd has a book with something about the—the topic. Wainn remembers reading it."

"I can't read," he said calmly. "I know all the words. Would you like to see?" He rose from the table, bowed politely, and went into the kitchen.

Aunt Sybb looked decidedly unhappy. "So much for being rid of them," she murmured. "That poor boy." At her nieces' stares, she shook her head. "An old, sorry business, Dearest Hearts, and not my place to say more."

Wainn returned with Peggs' sketchbook before either Jenn or Peggs could say a word, smiling from ear to ear. "Would you like to see?"

The three women exchanged glances. Aunt Sybb lifted her shawl-wrapped shoulders and let them drop.

Wordlessly, Jenn passed Wainn the charcoal from her pocket.

He sat, placed the pad in front of him and put the charcoal carefully on top. One hand lifted and pantomimed taking an invisible book from an invisible shelf and putting it down on the table. With great care, he turned invisible pages.

Jenn, Peggs, and their aunt watched, mesmerized.

Wainn stopped. "Too far," he apologized, and flipped back a few "pages" before making a satisfied sound. "Here it is."

He bent over the drawing—a cluster of summerberry flowers—and printed several lines of dark lettering overtop. When finished, he held up the result, as if uncertain who should get it first. Peggs reached. Jenn was faster.

The letters were neatly done, but the words weren't Rhothan. "I can't read it," she complained, passing the sketchpad to her sister.

Peggs looked up, eyes wide with wonder. "I think this is Naalish, the language of Mellynne."

Wainn nodded happily. "Yes, it is."

"Let me see, please." Peggs passed the sketchpad to Aunt Sybb. The older woman tilted it to the sunlight coming through the kitchen, then frowned and beckoned.

Understanding, Jenn rose and brought the reading lamp. Lighting its candle, she aimed its mirror to shine on the pad. "Can you read it, Aunt Sybb?"

"I was more spiritual once," their aunt muttered. "Before the world turned on us regardless." Louder, "Naalish is used in the temples of our Ancestors. What are children taught these days?"

Jenn ignored the question. "What does it say?" As the older woman hesitated, she pleaded, "We have to know, Aunt Sybb." She had to know, was the truth.

"And will I have no peace till you do, child?" Jenn held her breath until the corner of Aunt Sybb's lips curved up. "Still, I see no harm in it. I'm curious too. Please bring me my writing case. I'll need to transcribe this word by word. It's been many years . . ."

Jenn launched herself at the hutch their aunt used for her things while visiting. It was the only furnishing their parents had brought from Avyo, gleaming with inlays of red and yellow wood, its cupboard doors latched with such cleverness that a simple touch opened any one, or locked it. Aunt Sybb's case was in the middle cupboard to the right side, the one that also held a pullout shelf to use as a desk. Jenn gently picked up the flat leather case by its handle and rushed back to the table.

"I wish you were this eager for sewing lessons," her aunt commented. "Let's see what Wainn has remembered for us. With more tea, please," she added.

"You make the best pie," Wainn said wistfully as Peggs stood.

She tousled his hair fondly. "I'll see if there're some shortbreads left."

Leaving Wainn to watch Aunt Sybb open her case and set out her ink pot, fountain pen, and a small sheet of the creamy linen paper she insisted was for invitations and not childish doodles, Jenn collected the empty cups and plates and followed her sister into the kitchen.

Peggs took hold of the handle of the big kettle on the stovetop, with a folded rag to protect her hands, and nodded to Jenn to add fresh tea to the pot.

"I shouldn't have listened to you and Aunt Sybb," Jenn said earnestly as Peggs poured the hot water. "I'm sorry."

Her sister's eyes met hers through the steam. "Don't be. I'm not. I shouldn't have kept it secret from you." She managed a smile. "You told me about your friend in the meadow. I should have trusted you with this long ago."

"How long—" Jenn stopped there.

"How long have I known?" Peggs refilled the kettle and returned it to heat. Their father would take a hot cup on the porch when he came home from the mill. "Since the art class in the orchard, last spring. Remember? The blossoms were like snow in the trees. Master Uhthoff asked Kydd to show us how to mix watercolors. I had trouble getting the pink I wanted and he—he knelt beside me to help. His eyes as he—" She turned pink herself. "That's—that's when I knew."

"I remember Cheffy Ropp poked his paintbrush into a hive." Jenn grinned. "Hettie tried to help and she was the one stung." The eldest Ropp daughter was calm and gentle, strong enough to be her father's best assistant in the dairy, her round face always wreathed in smiles. She'd come from Avyo with her family, like Peggs; they'd been best friends ever since. "What's Hettie think of this?"

"I can't tell her." Her sister clutched the tin of cookies. "I—I think she likes him too."

Jenn promised herself another look at Kydd Uhthoff, a long one. "So the extra drawing lessons . . . ?"

Peggs sighed. "Were just lessons," she admitted. "I love drawing," this hastily, in case Jenn might suspect an ulterior motive, "but I—he was—he was always so courteous and helpful and kind, I—I drew!" This last with such woeful emphasis, Jenn pictured her tongue-tied sister pretending day after day to be enraptured by paper and charcoal rather than by her teacher, a teacher unlikely to be immune to the charms of his pupil, for wasn't Peggs the loveliest and most accomplished woman in Marrowdell? Kydd Uhthoff's generous offer of lessons took on an entirely new light.

If so, Kydd Uhthoff had a great deal to learn about proper courting. Where was the romance in blackened fingertips and scribbling? She'd assumed the lessons had ended with the approach of fall and the harvest; maybe it had been mutual frustration. They needed help. Though tempted to tease, Jenn said as seriously as she could, "Maybe Aunt Sybb's right about having family—"

"No." Peggs put cookies on a plate, her fine fingers trembling. "Leave it be, Jenn. He doesn't know I exist, other than as an art student, or Radd Nalynn's eldest—the one who bakes."

"You do make the best pies." Which garnered the exasperated eye roll she'd hoped.

"Back to the parlor with you," Peggs ordered affectionately. "Before Wainn comes after his cookies."

The two carried their trays to the table. Aunt Sybb sat, rolling her pen between her palms so it clicked, just, against her rings. It was the sort of habit she thoroughly discouraged in her nieces. She looked up at Jenn with the oddest expression on her face, part wonder, part dread.

"You've finished." Jenn sat, the tray in front of her, tea forgotten. "What did it say?"

"It rhymes." Wainn was clearly pleased.

Peggs took charge of distributing the tea and cookies. "In Naalish, you mean."

"In Rhothan." Their aunt returned her pen to the case and closed the lid with a little pat. She lifted the piece of paper. "It rhymes because it was written in this language first. The book Kydd Uhthoff brought with him is of Rhothan wishings, most likely collected by one of the Mellynne scholars who settled in Avyo. What Wainn remembers is a translation; I simply put it back as it was."

The sisters looked at one another; it was Jenn who asked. "What are 'wishings'?"

"Ill-conceived pagan magic. I find it remarkably apt in this place." Aunt Sybb tapped a finger on her teacup. "When Master Dusom omitted the entire matter from your lessons, I agreed under protest. I've never condoned keeping historical truths, however sordid, from the young. But he had his reasons." By the fire in her eye, Jenn was surprised "his reasons" had been enough. "Now, however, it's time you knew."

"About magic?" Peggs sounded as Jenn felt, half excited, half appalled. Magic was in stories. Wasn't it?

"About history," their aunt corrected primly. "Rhoth and Mellynne have always shared a seemly and proper worship of our Ancestors, but before Mellynne exerted her civilizing influence, alas, many Rhothans held a belief they could entice a favor from the departed through the use of objects and the saying of special words."

"Like the Beholding," suggested Jenn.

"Not like that at all, child," Aunt Sybb frowned. "Wishings were recipes, written as riddles. Anyone, the old Rhothans believed, could use them to obtain what they wanted. Back then, raids into Ansnor were as much to obtain rare ingredients as they were to steal livestock or metal. Which didn't, let me tell you, endear the Rhothans to Ansnor's people. Though to be fair, Ansnor raided Rhoth in turn. Still do, come to think of it. Avyo has progressed, but to the east, sad to say, the old ways linger. Vorkoun's market is rumored to be rife with token merchants and those who claim to know their use."

Aunt Sybb tended to ramble at dusk, which it was, Jenn realized, not needing to look out the window. Her emptiness eased once the sun sank fully behind the Bone Hills, past the time Wisp wouldn't bear her near him.

So she wouldn't see him.

That could change, she thought fiercely. That would change. She didn't need to see whatever he was, not when she could wish him to be as she was. "What does this one say? This wishing. How is it done?"

"This wishing is a pretty bit of nonsense," Aunt Sybb said firmly. "Don't forget that, Jenn Nalynn."

She nodded.

Their aunt gave her a doubtful look, but continued. "It is, as you wanted, a wishing to change an animal into a man. Not any man, however. A lover, to take to your heart. You're far from the first young woman," she said lightly, "unwilling to trust fate." She didn't glance at the paper as she recited:

"Something of you
"Something of love
"Something of dreams
"In a silken glove."

"Turn into ash
"By moonlight's glow.
"Give to the chosen
"Love's shape he'll show."

"When you give him the ash," Aunt Sybb told her rapt audience, "you would say: *'Hearts of my Ancestors, grant my heart's need.'*"

"I told you it rhymes," Wainn said, shortbread paused before his mouth. "Except the last part."

"Why don't I send the rest of those home with you?" offered Peggs, drawing the youngest Uhthoff to his feet.

"To share with your brother." Jenn winked and her sister blushed.

Wainn followed Peggs to the kitchen peacefully, only to turn in the doorway, his face troubled. "You should ask. Before you change his shape. Ask him."

"Ask the toad?" Aunt Sybb smiled into her napkin.

Jenn didn't smile. She stared at Wainn, who remembered books he couldn't read and loved a woman who wouldn't speak. He had his own wisdom, a Marrowdell wisdom. She suddenly felt of all the advice she'd ever been given, this was the most important.

"I'll ask," she told him. "I promise."

Bannan crossed his arms behind his head and gazed at the ribbon of sky above. Blue still. A star showed. The Mistress, most likely. Her companion at this early hour, before moonrise, was the Rose, soft pink, low and toward the east. Too low to see from the narrow Northward Road, that snuck through crag and hill like a thief.

Night here, courtesy of the steep slopes to either side and their cloak of dark vegetation. He'd shared camp duties with Tir, along with an early supper. Once Scourge disappeared into the surrounding trees, the ox had lowered himself to the grass, contentedly chewing his cud. Tir had rolled himself in a blanket and now slept, a sure sign he planned to be awake later and on guard, no matter what Bannan said.

The small fire they'd made had shrunk to a few glowing embers. His bones ached from the wagon. Traveling this road was slow and monotonous. He supposed it taught patience. He felt in no hurry.

Or was he still numb?

The Ansnans worshiped the slow dance of the moon and drew faces from stars, faces they believed watched and remembered your deeds, good or ill. Based on that sum, judgment would be passed upon your death. You could try to cheat. Rhothans learned to expect the bloodiest raids on cloud-obscured nights. But from what Bannan knew of their religion, nothing went unnoticed.

The aloof star had witnessed all of his life, then. The privileged childhood, the closeness of family. The loss of parents eased by work, friends, his sister. Scourge. The training and lessons that let him pretend to be adult. The skill that let him lead others. Years on the restless border. Raids. Counter raids. Spies, betrayals, blood. How many times he'd lain in the dark like this, between wild trees and rock, listening beyond his own heartbeat for footsteps, sword to hand because a pistol flash would give him away . . .

Bannan deliberately rolled over and pulled his blanket up to his ear. He was a farmer now.

He'd claimed a settler's portion from Vorkoun's treasurer, a woman who knew him, his family. She'd been flustered but managed the right stamps and seals. The law was dusty, not changed: any citizen of Rhoth willing to move north for life, upon relinquishing his or her property to the crown, was entitled to supplies and land. In Weken, signed and witnessed by a rather surprised magistrate, the document had become binding. It also became the sleepy-eyed ox, a wagon, older than he but sound, and the wagon's contents. Contents he hoped would prove worth their weight. It was one thing, Bannan reminded himself ruefully, to live off the land while scouting enemy terrain, quite another to prepare to live peacefully in one place forever. The trader had given several of his purchases, and himself, an amused look. Worrisome, that.

Tir, who knew all about farms and life on them, could have helped. Oh no. He'd disappeared into a tavern, since it was Bannan's name on the document, Bannan who wanted to dig dirt for a living, and Bannan who had them heading away from civilized parts where they might have found work wearing fine for-show-only swords, with the worst hazards being parade duty and sore feet from standing outside the House of Keys through long debates, and had he mentioned the admiration of beautiful, civilized ladies for uniforms?

What, he'd asked, was wrong with that?

Everything, Bannan thought bitterly, shifting to avoid a root. Officers from the border guard were being scattered across Lower Rhoth, their companies disbanded, while the people of Vorkoun, people he'd protected most of his life, waited for their new overlords. Too many had histories better forgotten, for Vorkoun had been rife with smuggling and secrets. How else to survive, when your enemy was closer than any ally?

Now, they'd be at the mercy of Ansnor, who'd shown none before.

Yet his sister . . . all the family he had left . . . gladly remained in the thick of it. Lila's letter hadn't been about finding a wife. She'd written of what life could be without war. Of how Vorkoun—how all of Rhoth—could change. She planned for a future he couldn't imagine and urged him to do the same. To look ahead, not back. And, because no one understood him as she did, to find his own peace. "Keep Us Close," she'd finished, her handwriting sure and strong, as if will alone would be enough.

Ancestors Lost and Adrift, he missed her already.

Should have insisted on the brandy, Bannan decided wearily, opening his eyes to stare up at the sky. The star gazed back, indifferent.

"AIEE—argh!!!!!" The scream was accompanied by the SNAP-CRASH of something large taking the shortest path regardless of the undergrowth. More screaming, at a distance.

An approving grumble from the dark. "Bloody beast."

Some things hadn't changed.

Bannan smiled as he closed his eyes.

Once Wainn left, the three women gathered around the table and regarded the paper with the "wishing."

"Something of me," Jenn said at last.

"That's easy." Peggs tugged her braid, then lowered her voice ominously. "Or . . . your blood." She laughed. "Just nothing irreplaceable."

"Something of love." Aunt Sybb's eyes sparkled. "I enjoy a riddle. Perhaps one of your mother's roses?"

Jenn preferred not to think about the roses. "Dreams I can do. I'll be right back."

She went to the kitchen. The ladder to the loft pulled down easily and, as she climbed, there was sufficient light to make out the bed she and Peggs shared, the chests their father had built for their clothes, and the wonderful window seat. When they were young, they'd both been able to curl up and sleep on it. They still sat there and talked by moonlight.

The window seat was cushioned with a mattress. Mindful of the sloped ceiling, Jenn crouched and unbuttoned the end. She shoved her hand inside, eyes closed, and felt through the straw for . . . there. She pulled out the folded paper and hesitated.

Was she sure?

Jenn sat, the paper in her hand. It had been folded and unfolded until its creases were mostly gaps; handled until its outer surface was smooth and tanned, like leather. She opened it with care.

A map of the world. She'd found it years ago, between the pages of one of Master Uhthoff's books. It hadn't belonged there. It had belonged here, with her.

Jenn traced the Northward Road with a fingertip. So small. Insignificant. It crossed a gap in the paper, met Endshere, then Weken. It followed one river and met others, wider. Crossed a bridge and plunged into Lower Rhoth where it split, half reaching to Vorkoun to stop at Ansnor, which was silly. Surely Ansnor had roads too.

The other half, the exciting half, went to Avyo and burst in all directions. Roads and rivers took her finger to the famous trade cities of Essa, to the west, or Thornloe, to the south. From Essa, a great bridge arched into Mellynne, whose roads curved and flowed like writing. Thornloe, connected to Avyo by road and bridge and tunnel, was the sole Rhothan port, squeezed into the mouth of the canyon where the mighty Kotor River emptied into the vast freshwater lake Rhothans called the Sweet Sea and the Eldad called Syrpic Ans, the Mother's Elbow. All the names were here. Eldad itself lay on the far side of the sea, beyond the southern mountains, its straight roads crossed at neat and tidy angles like well-sewn seams.

The map ended there, inviting her finger to draw more on her skirt. Mysterious places. Unknown domains. New sounds and shapes and . . .

Jenn folded the map and pressed it to her heart, the promise her emptiness could be filled. Would be.

If the wishing called for dreams, this held all of hers.

When she climbed down to the kitchen, Jenn found her father pouring his evening tea. The weariness in his face eased at the sight of her. "There's no pie left," he noted wistfully. "Or cookies."

Her remorse rushed back. "Peggs gave them to the Uhthoffs. Would you like bread with some jelly?"

"Tea's fine. I didn't work tonight."

So he'd gone to the mill to avoid her. "Poppa. I'm sorry. I truly am." Jenn leaned forward and kissed his cheek. "I spoiled supper."

Radd gave a rueful smile. "It took the both of us. Hopefully your aunt will let me back in the house. The last thing she'd want is a dispute before—" his smile faded, "—before she leaves."

"Does she have to go so soon?" Jenn asked in a low voice.

"Your aunt's stayed longer than she should. The journey to Avyo isn't easy on her, Dearest Heart. Best we can do is help, don't you think? I brought her cases from the mill," more briskly, "and left them on the porch. You and Peggs can pack for your aunt tomorrow. So. Do I dare?" With a meaningful glance at the parlor.

"I think so. Aunt Sybb's much happier." At his lifted eyebrow, Jenn made herself say, "We've been talking. About husbands. Aunt Sybb's been giving us advice."

His eyes widened. "And you're listening?"

"Yes." She scrunched her nose. "I won't say it's easy."

"I imagine not." Her father raised his cup in invitation. "Care to escape?"

She couldn't very well say no, though the map burned a hole in her pocket. She nodded.

"Let's sneak around," he whispered conspiratorially and led the way outside.

The porch ran the full width of the Nalynn home. Most of it disappeared under snow each winter, but the rest of the year, its wide planks became an extension of the front room, used for whatever was best done outside by sunlight, from shucking beans to reading. On hot summer nights, there was no better place to sit and talk after chores. Or sleep. It took a foul wind and rain to keep Radd from his hammock. He slept either here or in the mill while his sister visited, leaving her his bed.

His favorite chair sat on the porch all summer. Zehr Emms, who'd made fine furniture in Avyo, had put a seat in a broken barrel, tacked on wide arms, and added curved rockers beneath. It had been a gift for the pregnant Melusine Nalynn and the babe to come.

Jenn had been rocked to sleep in it, but by Zehr's wife, Gallie. Gallie had been her wet nurse, about to wean her twins when Melusine, her dearest friend, died in childbirth. Gallie's big heart had easily accommodated not only another baby, but a grieving Radd Nalynn and his young daughter as well.

They saw too little of Gallie these days. She was busy tending Loee, the tiny baby a joyful surprise to both parents, as well as her much older brothers.

Her father settled into the rocker's cushions; Jenn sat on the nearby bench. The forlorn stack of her aunt's luggage waited against the wall; the house toad, for whatever reason, was in the midst of slowly climbing to the top, moving each clawed foot with implacable precision. She'd have to make sure it was gone in the morning, before Aunt Sybb spotted it.

Porch lights were beginning to glow here and there in the village, though the last rays of the sun flooded the valley.

The treeless ivory of the Bone Hills was almost white, tinged blue in the distance. From here, she could see every one. She idly counted the five to the west, lower than the surrounding crags. They were called the Fingers and ran alongside one another, herding the river into the valley then splitting it, so part ran through Marrowdell while the rest writhed north in impassable cataracts. Their work done, the Fingers buried their tips in the fields. To the south rose the Spine, its massive slope and crown heaves of barren rounded stone, girdled by meadow and rugged forest. A path led up it. A path no one took.

Nestled between the base of the Spine and the first curved Finger, alongside the Tinkers Road, lay the empty farm, Jenn's meadow, and Wisp.

Elbows on her knees, she leaned her chin into her hands and pondered what to say to him. No need to mention marriage right away, she decided with relief. She'd ease in to the subject of his taking a man's shape, how they'd be better friends, the many other advantages, such as Peggs' pie. If the wishing could be trusted, the marriage part would take care of itself anyway. They'd be in love, wouldn't they?

Meanwhile, her father rocked back and forth, sipping his tea; a comfort and company.

Until he planted his boots on the porch and leaned forward, cup between his hands. "I visited your mother."

Meaning he hadn't gone to the mill at all, but past it and Uncle Horst's, and through the gate to the secluded glade the villagers had made home for their dead. It wasn't a great ossuary, like the ones in Avyo, where, as Aunt Sybb explained, for a small tithe your bones could mingle with those of your Ancestors. Instead, there was a peaceful spot beneath the crags, shaded by old trees and carpeted in wildflowers. Those who'd moved on and were now Blessed were buried in the ground, as close to one another as could be done without disturbance. Little Ponicce Uhthoff, in her mother Larell's arms. Mimm Ropp, who'd drowned saving her son. Riedd Morrill.

And Melusine Nalynn.

There was a fine bench for visitors; Zehr and Davi had crafted it, complete with fanciful iron legs. It was taken into a barn before the snow each winter and its return, freshly painted, each spring was a festive event. Uncle Horst had bought carved blessing sigils for each of those buried, having them shipped all the way from Weken. These were raised on poles, set so the sun would shine through and cast their names and Heart's Blessing on the ground throughout summer.

Aunt Sybb thought it a much better place to rest than a proper ossuary. Jenn wanted to see one anyway.

Her father's going there . . . it was his habit when troubled or perplexed. A condition usually brought about by his beloved daughters, truth be told. Jenn gave a little shrug. "I ask your pardon, Poppa—"

"No need, Dearest Heart. I find it easier to think, near your mother." He seemed to find his tea of engrossing interest, then looked up at her. "I realized I've never asked you why you want to leave Marrowdell." Quietly. "Aren't you happy?"

"Of course I am." Her father's eyes were steady and kind. Hers fell. "Not always," she admitted. "Poppa, I love Marrowdell. I love our home and the mill. It's just . . ." How could she tell him that every time the sun set, she felt she'd lost another day? That what had been a normal restlessness this spring had blossomed into wild impatience over summer, until now she ached inside as if she starved? "I need something. Something more."

"What?"

"I don't know—only that it isn't here." She wrapped her arms around her knees. "Is that so wrong, Poppa?"

"No." Almost bleak. "No, it's not."

Her heart pounded. "Then you'll let me go with Aunt Sybb?"

"I can't." The unhappy words low and hard to hear. "Jenn, no. It's not possible. I'm sorry."

"It's all right." She sat back and sighed in resignation. "I know why."

This gained her a slight frown. "You do?"

"You want me to take a husband first." Jenn did her best not to sound put upon and misused. Dignity first, Aunt Sybb would say. "Very well. I'll pick one." Or make one, she dared add to herself.

Her father carefully set down his cup. "You believe that's what I want? What your aunt wants?"

"Isn't it?" Jenn asked warily.

The scent of roses filled the warm evening air, rich and impossible to ignore. Her father lifted his head and closed his eyes. His nostrils flared as he drew in a long, reverent breath, then he exhaled and gazed at her, his face strangely at peace. "It's time I told you about your mother and Marrowdell."

Implying something she didn't already know, which surely wasn't right. Her family didn't have secrets. The world stilled around her, as if astonished too. All but the house toad, busy settling its unwieldy bulk atop the luggage.

"When my mills, our home, everything was taken? Like the rest, I was given three choices. Stay, with nothing. Leave, and take exile in Mellynne or the north. Not that it was a choice," he reminded her. "We were Rhothan, born and raised, regardless of our great-grandparents. What welcome would we have in Mellynne? At least to the north, we were offered land, a chance to start again. Your mother being pure Rhothan . . ." her father began, then confounded her. "Understand me, Jenn. Your mother didn't have to leave."

About to say, "But she did," Jenn hesitated and changed her mind. What could he mean? Everyone knew the decree had stripped wealth; it hadn't split families. Not directly. "Aunt Sybb was able to stay." Why hadn't he?

"Hane's family accepted her as their own. Melusine's?" His lips twisted as if over something sour. "Our marriage wasn't to their liking, in any way. They cast me loose once the decree was law, glad for the excuse and to see me gone. Melusine and Peggs were, naturally, to stay with them."

They'd relatives in Avyo?

She couldn't wait to tell Peggs.

Then, all at once, the full import of what he'd said struck home. "They wanted Mother to leave you?" Jenn echoed in disbelief. "To take Peggs? How could anyone want that?"

"For the same reason I begged her to obey them," he said heavily. "Fear of what this life would be. Fear for her safety, and little Peggs'. None of us knew what to expect."

Jenn had heard the stories. Exiles had died, in the exodus north. Whole settlements had failed that first terrible winter. She understood why, in the Midwinter Beholding, all in Marrowdell gave thanks for the sturdy buildings they'd found waiting, for the water and grain. Who had lived here first, raised the buildings, cleared the land, no one knew. They must have been driven away by their dreams, as had some of those who'd arrived with the Nalynns. What they'd left behind saved those who came after.

Her father had been very brave to take that journey. And her mother. "She came anyway."

"Yes." At his radiant smile, Jenn drew a soft wondering breath. "Yes, she came. Melusine laughed at her family's fears. Kissed mine away. 'For love,' she said, and would hear no more arguments.

"The truth, Dearest Heart? Life was hard, but joyous. Exile, the cold, learning the mill—an undershot wheel, Ancestors Witness, and me used to turbines and ordering others to their work. I sent a stone flying through the wall the first harvest, did I tell you? Lucky I didn't kill someone, including myself. What did it matter?" Warm and sure, "I had Melusine at my side and Peggs in my arms.

"Your mother made this place our home. She loved it. So much, she gave you to us before she—before she had to go. When she passed you to me . . . 'For love,' she said then too." His voice thickened. "Her final words."

Eyes brimming with tears, Jenn rushed to kneel at his feet. She put a tender hand on his knee. "I'm so sorry, Poppa—"

"No. No, Jenn." He took her hand between his callused ones. "Nothing about her death was your fault, sweet child. You're what helped me survive it." He bent to press his lips to her forehead, then sat back. "I'm telling you this so you understand. So you believe me when I say I would never want you or Peggs to marry for convenience or to leave home. All I want—with all my heart—is for you to have a great love, a lasting one. Like mine with your mother."

His eyes searched her face. "Is it possible," her father continued with the air of a man crossing ice of unknown thickness, "this is what you want too? What you feel you must leave Marrowdell to find?"

Was it?

Jenn's brow furrowed.

She hadn't thought so before. No. Her hunger was much too personal to include anyone else, intimate in a way she could barely express to herself, let alone explain to her father.

Anyway, she already loved Wisp. Wasn't he her dearest, truest friend? The wishing, though. Sitting here, with Night's Edge lost to shadow, her belief faltered. "What if that love isn't here, Poppa?" she asked forlornly. "What do I do then?"

"Give Marrowdell time, Dearest Heart." He held her eyes with the earnestness in his. "Here you're loved. Here you're safe. And here's where you'll have a bright future—whether you see it yet or not," with mock sternness. His fingers squeezed hers lightly then let go. "Trust me to know what's best."

Jenn's heart beat against her chest like a bird trapped beneath a basket. Here wasn't enough. Not nearly enough.

"I can't stay, Poppa," the words forced from numb lips. "I can't spend my whole life in Marrowdell. I can't."

"You mustn't say that. Don't. Please, Jenn." Her defiance should have made him angry. To her consternation, her father's eyes sparkled with tears and the pleading hand he raised trembled, as if he aged before her. "You must promise me. Promise you won't ever try to leave."

To refuse was cruel.

But to stay?

To promise?

Impossible.

She scrambled to her feet and ran from him. Through the door, through the parlor, into the kitchen. Past her shocked aunt and sister. She tugged down the ladder.

Footsteps. "Jenn! Wait!"

She scrambled up to the loft.

There, Jenn threw herself facedown on her pillow and pressed her hands tight over her ears.

Peggs followed shortly after. The mattress shifted as she sat on the bed. Jenn ignored her for a moment, then freed one eye. Her sister had loosened her hair from its tidy knot and now drew a comb through the long black locks, her face pensive.

Jenn mumbled into the pillow, "It's too early for bed."

"I brought a fresh candle. We can read, if you like." A meaningful pause. "Aunt Sybb and Poppa want a private conversation."

She rolled over to stare at Peggs with both eyes. "About me."

"Who else?" Her sister regarded her, a dimple almost showing. "I wasn't the one running wild through the house."

Their aunt's phrase, beyond doubt. "He wants me to promise never to leave Marrowdell." Jenn sat, drawing up her knees. The breeze from the window felt good on her cheeks, hot from the pillow. The pillow, and growing despair. "He's not being fair."

"You're his baby. Don't make that face at me. You know I'm right." Her sister shook her head. "You can't expect Poppa would encourage you to go."

"It's worse. He won't let me leave. Ever."

"How could he stop you?" her sister said, ever the voice of reason. "No one can. Your name isn't on a bind; you're free to travel Rhoth or anywhere. Soon you'll be nineteen and responsible for yourself. Poppa can't make you stay, Jenn. He wouldn't," as if delivering her most telling point. "When has he said no to you for long?"

"This is different." Jenn climbed from the bed. She went to Peggs' clothes chest and put her hands on one end. "Help me."

"Jenn—"

She gave her sister a pleading look. Peggs sighed and rolled her eyes. "See what I mean?" she grumbled, but put down her comb to help Jenn lift the chest and move it away from the wall.

Jenn dropped to her hands and knees. The dust tickled and she squeezed her nose hurriedly to stop a sneeze. She inched her way to where a narrow gap between warped floor planks had—through diligent use of a kitchen knife years ago—become a finger-width hole in the parlor's ceiling. They'd made it to spy on their father's gatherings with his friends, which turned out to be long boring conversations not worth hearing at all. But now . . .

"Can you hear anything?"

Jenn put her finger to her lips. If she could hear voices from below, theirs could be heard too.

She gathered back her hair, but before she could press her ear to the hole, voices did came through, sudden, loud, and distressingly clear.

"—her father!"

"And I'm nothing?"

"The decision's mine and made. She stays." Footfalls, heavy, as if he couldn't settle. Aunt Sybb would take a seat; her opinion, oft expressed to her restless younger niece, consigned pacing to pigeons. Not that Jenn had yet seen a pigeon, but she did try not to pace like one.

"Be sensible, Radd. You've seen how she is. Marrowdell's too small—"

"Don't you think I know that?" Furious. "Don't you think I've longed to show her the world? To show them both?"

Jenn rocked back on her heels. Peggs came and sat on the chest, hair spilling over one shoulder.

"I haven't lost hope," their aunt returned with equal passion. "You mustn't. We'll get you back. We'll get you home."

"Sybbie, stop." Such regret filled his voice, Jenn fumbled for Peggs' hand and gripped it tight. "We've discussed this. There's no will in Avyo to repeal the law. The same prince rules. The same barons. Do you think those who've enjoyed our wealth and property all these years would vote to give it back? And how could any of us return without setting neighbor against neighbor? Family against—" A pause, then, "Melusine lies here. So gladly will I when my time comes. Marrowdell's my home, Sybbie. Accept it—"

"I will not! I've hope, I say. Hope that lets me smile and bow and entertain those who believe my beloved Hane married beneath himself. Hope that lets me endure such petty meanness as searches at the gate—"

Sharp and anxious. "What searches?"

"For you, Radd. For Peggs. As if I'd hide you in my simples," an acerbic bite to the words.

"The Semanaryas." The grim voice was a stranger's, not their father's.

"Who other? They know full well where I go each spring. A simple thing, for them, to have the gate guards watch for my return. We can't match their bribes, so I don't complain. The guards are civil."

"Sybbie—I didn't realize—"

Jenn reached for Peggs' hand, gripped it tight.

"It's none of your doing, Radd. Our girls concern us now." Earnest. "Peggs. The House suspended for the summer divided, as I predicted in my letters. Some would allow the return of those exiled as children, others argue to leave what's done, done."

"Pigs will sing opera first."

"Inelegant, dear brother, but I fear you're right. Few press the issue. Peggs isn't the worry. I do believe she could be happy here, if it came to that. I can't tell you why, not yet, but I do. Jenn—"

"Heart's Blood, woman! How many times must I say it? Jenn can't leave Marrowdell!"

"Kindly listen before you bellow." A pause, during which Jenn imagined their diminutive aunt fixing their father with a quelling stare. "I agree."

"You do? But—"

"I've eyes. This past year, Jenn's grown into the very image of Melusine. Ancestors Witness, if she were seen by anyone who knew her mother . . ." Aunt Sybb stopped, then went on. "Even as a child, Peggs favored the Nalynn side. Jenn could pass as theirs—"

"She's not!" Radd snapped.

"Here." The word left such an appalled silence, the girls didn't dare move. After what seemed far too long, Aunt Sybb continued. "The Semanaryas don't forgive. They don't forget. Nothing would please them more than to take Jenn from us. In Avyo, they have the means. Legal or otherwise. I tell you we'd never see her again. Never!"

Peggs let out a gasp. Jenn shook her head urgently.

"You can't let that happen, Radd. You can't." All at once, muffled sobs.

"Sybbie. Sybbie, stop. I won't. You know I won't." A nose being blown. A heartbreaking pause. Then wearily, as if he'd given up. "You're right. About everything, you're right. I'm so sorry. I don't want to rush the girls, but what else can I do? I worry they're getting older. I worry I'm getting older. What if there's an accident in the mill?" Something too soft to hear, then louder, with anguish, "I'm lost. Melusine . . ."

"Melusine, Ancestors Blessed and Blissful, would tell you to stay here, where you're safe, where you've good, trusted friends. Peggs will be fine, Radd. Jenn will come around, you'll see."

"All she wants is to see the world." Jenn heard the pain in his dear voice; worse, it was for her. "I have to say no. I'll always have to say no."

"Calm yourself, Brother. First things first. Once Jenn settles a household of her own—happily, of course—she should be protected from any legal trickery they could attempt. Next spring, I'll bring a young man with me. Hane has a promising nephew. We'll find her someone, Radd."

"If only she'd look at one of the poor lads here. Between Zehr and Anten, I get no peace. None!"

Allin's father. Roche's. Jenn felt her cheeks burn.

"She might yet. Patience."

"What would I do without you, Sybbie?"

"You'd manage. You're a fine father. Though," she scolded gently, "it would help if you'd keep their feet in shoes when I'm not here."

"Husbands would be easier. Come. Sit with me." A cupboard opened. The clink of glassware. "I saved a bit of last year's summer-berry." Their voices faded as they went out to the porch.

Jenn stared up at Peggs, her eyes swimming with tears. "What can I do?"

Her sister looked pale but determined. "The wishing."

Jenn nodded. "The wishing."

No one was going to take her from her family. No one was going to stop her seeing the world for herself.

Poppa and Aunt Sybb didn't need to find her someone.

She'd make one of her own.

The girl's world grew elusive once its sun fully set. To see in its dark took effort Wisp couldn't afford often, not when his place—such as it was—in his own world was chancy at best.

He didn't need to see, to find where he belonged. The crossing—the only one in Marrowdell to be both dry and safe and, most importantly, unclaimed—was mere steps beyond Night's Edge. He need only make his way to that weak point and let himself be where he should.

And he was.

Not that his world wasn't chancy itself. As Marrowdell was

different from other parts of her world, so was this portion of his. Here, the two overlapped like twisted ribbons, neither free of the other. It had happened by accident. What the girl called the Bone Hills had tried to reach from his world to hers, only to flinch and be trapped in both. Such things were possible during a Great Turn.

Proving even the mighty could be fools.

When worlds touched, devastation followed. In the girl's, mountains had folded and rivers changed their course. What memory remained of that original cataclysm was writ in rock; what magic, set loose, scattered among those who survived and their descendants.

In his?

Oh, in his, something had been born. The Verge. A landscape, scoured and bleak and beautiful, emptied of life but impatient with magic. It called to any who dared live in it. It changed those who did. Those who endured made the Verge their home, a home full of promise, yet always at risk. Who knew how long it would last? The trapped ones need only flinch again to tear the worlds apart.

Or, as it turned out, be summoned. Time passed, bringing another Great Turn and a fresh set of fools, this time from her world, eager to reach to his, unknowing what they'd disturb.

Awakened, the trapped ones flailed out in torment. The edge between Marrowdell and the Verge tore and blurred once more, spilling life from world to world. Some died. Some were lost.

Some sought opportunity.

The sei, for their own reasons, intervened before the chaos spread further. Marrowdell was scarred.

As was he, Wisp grumbled to himself.

Their worlds settled as before, one into the other. Roots restitched the edge. The villagers left the old forest alone because the dullest among them could tell those weren't trees towering over their heads. What they saw above their soil were the roots of the neyet. Neyet who grew thus were a little different from their counterparts beyond the Verge; they stopped moving while winter gripped Marrowdell and sang in its spring.

The kaliia, on the other hand, were rooted in the Verge and grew through to the girl's world, thanks to the longings of efflet. On her side, they were boring brown fields. On this side, during Marrowdell's day, the kaliia were rainbows in the sky; by night, curtains of green. Until the harvest. Then, his sky regained its pure mauve and night its stars.

Not that Wisp looked up at the moment. Nor did he look left or right. He was tired and let it show. Those who'd pestered him earlier flew nearby and they'd return to their game given any encouragement.

No flowers where he walked. No bees or mice. The meadow between the Bone Hills wasn't a meadow here at all. Beautiful, yes. Wisp's kind preferred buttresses of naked rock, the clean strength of stone. Best of all, the heights, where a late summer storm drew all to ride its wind and chase lightning through the black roiling depths of cloud. Their wings would clap as loud as thunder and rain hiss to steam on their skin.

Jenn Nalynn loved storms too. She'd stand in the meadow, arms outstretched, soaked to the skin, and laugh at the thunder. At first, he'd been ready to catch any lightning that came too close. Then he'd realized none would. Even young, she could expect to be safe and was.

Safer for him to leave all thought of the girl and Marrowdell behind. Safest to make his way home before others noticed he was back.

His home wasn't like hers, shared with family. It wasn't in the heights, with his kind. He could no longer climb there. He could no longer fly.

He was no longer welcome.

Those who'd assigned his latest penance had made a sanctuary of sorts for his rest. To reach it, he shuffled down this steep winding path, mindful of the crystal growths whose tears made the footing treacherous. They wept whenever broken, and broke whenever stepped upon. In their way, they tried to warn him if someone or something else had gone this way first, and might be lying in wait. The greater danger was that he'd slip and fall on the damp, but crystals were dutiful, simple creatures. Like the efflet who kept him company, there was no reasoning with them.

A telltale glisten. Wisp stepped around it and found another the same size in his way. More ahead. Paired feet told him what the interloper was, a terst; daring to intrude here told him who. One of the turn-born.

The path went on and on, twisting as it descended. The air thickened and warmed, curling over his skin. Tempting, to let that soothing warmth relax his vigilance, but a mistake. A turn-born's expectations made their mark on the Verge. Warmth, in this case, didn't mean a wish that he, Wisp, be more comfortable.

It meant temper.

The path ended in a tall shimmer of opalescent blue, his "door." It kept out his peers, his old friends, his former prey, the rain. It would open to a turn-born. Most things did. Wisp hunched what weren't shoulders in the position of respect and walked through.

Inside, the blue shimmer became rounded walls, ceiling, and floor. They were aware of him. If he walked toward a wall, it would retreat a pace or two, then rebound in his face. When he lay down, the shimmer would close around him. On good nights, he thought of it as a comforting womb. On bad ones, he fought to breathe and not snarl.

Most nights were neither good nor bad and Wisp could ignore the nature of his home, be grateful for the protection it offered.

Protection those he served could remove in an instant.

The girl's kind ruled themselves, a method suited to their straightforward, solitary world. From what he'd read, some did profess to serve ideals but, as they were quick to idealize each other, it amounted to the same thing. In his world, everything capable of obedience obeyed the sei, which was perfectly reasonable, since only the sei were capable of insisting on it.

Which they did rarely. Their interests spanned times and distances greater than anyone else bothered to imagine. For the most part, the inhabitants of the Verge did as their natures dictated. Those who wanted to hunt one another for food, did. Those who wanted to taunt, steal, or make the weaker their target, did. Those who allied with one another to mutual purpose, including to avoid being hunted or a target, did.

Those who took all this to the level of war risked disturbing the sei. Disturbed, the sei would restore peace however they saw fit, and enact due penance from both sides. Otherwise, they remained aloof and left the care of the Verge to the turn-born.

For the turn-born and the Verge were one.

To amuse himself, Wisp sometimes wondered what Jenn Nalynn would think of her counterparts, if she could see them as they appeared here. The turn-born possessed skin, but neither flesh nor bone beneath it. Instead, the body, neck, and head were filled with light, as if a sunbeam had been poured inside glass. Extremities—arms and hands, legs and feet—were filled with what bound them to the other world. Most chose earth, selecting the color that suited them. Wisp had met one whose limbs were filled with teeth. Other someones' teeth. Presumably collected at some effort from the earth.

The turn-born who sat waiting for him—one wall of the shimmer having bent into a throne—had shards of black stone filling arms and legs. Like all terst, his head was crowned in thick white hair. With no face below the hair, turn-born wore masks when wandering, shaped in the semblance of man or woman, for terst were like the girl's kind. This one's mask had strong features, a hooked nose, and dark eyebrows. Real, save that here, light poured from the holes where eyes and mouth should be.

~ Did the cursed one tried to leave? ~ Turn-born went to the point the way fangs sought a throat.

There were no secrets. Wisp settled himself on the floor, too weary for ceremony. ~ She did not. ~

~ Then why enter her village? ~

~ I go where I choose. ~

The air grew chill. A warning. Scales clenched along his belly. ~ I went as a precaution. ~ Wisp admitted. ~ I removed an opportunity. She will not leave. ~

~ Her existence is an unacceptable risk. ~

Her existence was his life's sole pleasure, but the turn-born wasn't wrong. Wisp shrugged, felt a familiar pain. ~ Your doing, not mine. ~

The turn-born rose to his feet, the shimmer of ceiling rising to accommodate his looming height. ~ Fault belongs to the mother and her race! ~

He really was too tired for this. ~ Is there anything else? ~

~ Someone's coming. ~

The turn-born meant to Marrowdell. As he'd feared. Too soon. Did they hope to entrench themselves in the valley ahead of the Great Turn? Not while he breathed . . . Wisp began the arduous process of standing again. ~ I'll go. ~

~ Get your rest. It will not be until the kaliia's sun is high. ~

Midday, then. The kaliia's sun shone on more than the crop, Wisp thought to himself. It shone on Jenn Nalynn as well.

The turn-born walked out of the shimmer, which shrank, blue and glistening, until Wisp lay within its embrace. This night, he welcomed the protection, craved the peace; he had to regain his strength.

Tomorrow, it would begin.

FIVE

A LATE NIGHT TRIP to the privy was hardly unusual. The sisters going together wasn't either, since that way one could bring a lantern while the other carried whatever book they planned to share, especially when they were younger and the books were those their aunt might not have approved, and there were two "seats" anyway for private gossip. What was unusual was the two going past the privy and through the gap in the hedgerow to clamber down the riverbank.

Jenn eased the dew-damp branches back into place then joined Peggs, already arranging a handful of spills on the narrow strip of packed sand they'd chosen. The fire, if they kept it small and clean, shouldn't be seen from any window. Not that there should be anyone else awake at this hour, except Gallie Emms and her baby, but they'd agreed the fewer who knew what they attempted, the better.

Peggs unwrapped the hot coal from the kitchen, and tipped it into the curled shavings. They lit with a cheerful crackle. She fed larger sticks, then announced all too soon, "There. Fire's ready. Are you?"

Jenn set her bundle on the cool sand and carefully spread it open. The map. Hair trimmings. A lock was more poetic, and they'd discussed it in whispers, huddled in bed, but her ends had needed the scissors and she was, after all, only going to burn it. The bundle itself was silk, as the wishing required. One of the city undergarments Aunt Sybb had given them, finally of use.

They'd brought Jenn's small painted letterbox. She and Peggs had agreed she couldn't carry wishing ashes in her skirt pocket. She didn't write letters anyway, not like her aunt. When she left Marrowdell, she would. Many letters. Letters home, naturally, but there'd be letters to new friends as well. Invitations. Responses. She'd need a new letterbox then. A large one. With her own paper and fancy pens.

First things first, as Aunt Sybb would say. "It won't work, Peggs," Jenn pointed out. "We don't have the 'something of love.'"

"Yes, we do." Peggs, who'd smiled mysteriously whenever Jenn mentioned that part of the wishing, reached into her pocket and held out her hand. "This."

A little block of wood rested on her palm. A child's block. Jenn didn't need to see the carvings on each side, their paint worn thin with play. A lady's mirror. A mask. A mushroom. A mitten. A milk pail. Last and most important, the letter M.

M for Melusine.

Their mother's. She'd brought the toy to Marrowdell, to be a link between her childhood and theirs.

"We'd put it under our pillows," Peggs smiled. "Remember? You were sure it stopped bad dreams. Here."

The fire snapped impatiently. Moonlight touched the river, smoothing its glide over rock, and etched silver into the crags above the far bank.

Jenn couldn't touch it. The block on her sister's outstretched hand was more than a toy. It was a talisman. They'd take turns, holding it. Peggs—sometimes, when she thought Jenn was asleep, would whisper to it. They had no portraits of their mother, other than the hints in their own flesh, no letters or writings. A few clothes, her roses, the home she'd made them, that was all.

And the little block.

"It's too much," she protested.

"Mother wouldn't say that. Not if it brought you happiness. Take it."

This wasn't a game, Jenn thought, and shivered though the night air was summer warm. "What about your happiness?"

"After we do this for you."

"Aunt Sybb said magic was nonsense. It won't work," she fretted," and we'll have burnt the block for nothing." And her map, a not inconsiderable loss.

Peggs took her hand and pressed the block into it, folding her fingers tight. "If we don't try," she said wisely, "we'll always wonder, won't we? Come, Dear Heart. You're sure you remember the words?"

"Yes." Just as well, since their aunt had put the piece of paper and sketchpad on the small table by her bed. It was impossible, the sisters knew from experience, to walk on the parlor floor without a creak sure to wake their father out on the porch, let alone their aunt.

"I think you should say them as you put everything together," Peggs decided. "Like you would a Beholding. Serious."

Serious was how she felt. Serious and solemn.

And more than a little scared.

"Peggs. What if it works?"

Her sister prodded the fire. "Second thoughts?"

"Hundreds." Jenn pulled her shawl close around her shoulders. "Wisp is my friend. My best friend."

"If he doesn't want to be part of this, he can say no." Peggs chuckled. "Then we try a toad." She lost her smile when she glanced at Jenn. "You're worried he'll say yes."

"Of course I am. What if, when we're both—" Jenn waved helplessly, "—people—what if we don't like each other?"

"Maybe you'll like each other a great deal more. Did you think of that?"

Wisp was sunshine and flowers. Mystery and mischief. Playmate and friend and protector. "I couldn't like him more," Jenn countered, sure of that, if nothing else.

"Like him in a different way. A nice way." Did Peggs blush or was her skin reddened by the flames? "When it isn't maddening," she added under her breath. Louder. "The fire's not going to last. Let's finish this. You can decide the rest in the morning."

Morning. When she'd have to sit across the table from their father and aunt, pretending she hadn't heard. The words. The despair. The broken sobs.

She'd run to the meadow anyway. Wisp was her surest comfort.

" 'Something of me,' " Jenn said, giving in, and lifted the clump of hair in her fingers. She put it back on the piece of silk. They'd carefully saved the lace and satin ties from the undergarment, giggling at its impracticality in Marrowdell. Well, Jenn had giggled; Peggs had looked oddly thoughtful. " 'Something of love.' " The block joined the hair. " 'Something of dreams.' " Last, her treasured map.

Without letting herself hesitate, she tied the corners of the silk together. " 'In a silken glove.' "

They'd brought the heavy skillet. Peggs took hold of its long handle, her hands protected by a rag, and Jenn laid the bundle on the flat round of metal. The skillet should contain any ashes and keep them clean. The moon was almost full.

It would work. She just knew it would. It had to.

The night itself seemed to hold its breath.

Now, or not at all. " 'Turn into ash, By moonlight's glow.' " Taking a long spill, Jenn put its tip in the fire, waited for the spiral shaving to catch, then touched its burning end to the bundle of silk. "How long do you—"

Whhoomphf! The bundle burst into yellow flame.

"—think it will take?" she finished numbly. The silk should have smoldered to start, the map inside being the better fuel. "I—"

The flame winked out, leaving a tidy cone of white ash on the skillet.

"I wonder what else was in that book," Peggs said, her eyes wide.

Careful not to breathe and risk blowing the ashes away, Jenn used the lid to scrape them into her letterbox. They sparkled in the moonlight and flowed more like sand than ash, leaving not a trace on the skillet. She put on the lid, made sure it was tight, then slipped the box into her deepest pocket.

"Put out the fire. We'd best get back and get some sleep."

"Sleep?!" Peggs exclaimed in a shaken voice. She shook her head, braids sliding over her shoulders. "How can you think of sleep after this?"

"To bed, then. Or do you want Aunt Sybb to think we've been—" what had she called it? "—'slipping out' to see young men?"

"Jenn Nalynn." Her sister couldn't keep a straight face. "Fine. But we keep a candle burning. I've goose bumps. Don't you?"

Jenn didn't. She'd expected something remarkable to happen, and it had. The wishing wasn't what would keep her awake tonight.

Imagining tomorrow would.

Bannan cracked an eyelid at the noisy rattle of pot and spoon. The sun had barely touched the tips of the highest trees; mist slid pale fingers under the branches around their camp. The road itself was flooded in shadow and unappealing.

He shut his eye.

Tir made more unnecessary racket. That, he could ignore.

The heavy lump abruptly landing on his chest was another matter. "Wh—at?" He sat upright, shoving away what proved to be a wool cloak.

Most of a cloak, filthy and damp.

Scourge gave a satisfied rumble and bobbed his great head.

"Could be worse, sir," Tir commented. He'd left his mask off and a broad grin whitened the scar tissue ringing chin and nose. "There's no hand attached this time."

Bannan tossed off the blanket and found his boots. "Maybe they'll leave the next wagon alone." Standing, he found his way to the fire blocked by a mass of smug flesh. His fingers found the velvet under Scourge's jaw and he smiled as the horse who'd terrorized would-be bandits half closed his eyes and rumbled with satisfaction.

"We could be sure, sir. Go back to Endshere and check who's missing some clothing. And skin."

Go back? Bannan ran his hand up the powerful sweep of Scourge's neck, fingers digging into the shock of black mane. Tir was right. They'd never left a quarry unchased before. Never a battle unfought.

The horse brought his head around to rest his chin on Bannan's shoulder. The man pressed his cheek against the soft warm muzzle and stared into a dark, noncommittal eye. "The road goes north," he said at last. "So do we."

Like any visitor on the road to Marrowdell, the rising sun found the village first. It set birds atwitter and burst through windows. The cows mooed at the dairy gate. Wainn Uhthoff's old pony stood with them, slyly hoping to be let through into the orchard.

"You'll get sick," Jenn scolded as she passed. The pony whickered his disdain for consequence and leaned against the gate.

Consequence was something she couldn't ignore.

She'd slept after all. Overwrought, huddled under their comforter, Peggs' reticence on matters of the heart had abandoned her completely. She'd extolled the virtues of Kydd Uhthoff to her defenseless sister in a low, happy murmur that went on and on and on. He had, it seemed, a remarkable number—starting with the dimple in his chin. The litany had been better than a lullaby; Jenn didn't remember much after Kydd's singing voice.

At dawn's first blush, she'd slipped from bed, leaving Peggs sound asleep, dressed quietly, then stole out the kitchen door. Not without a wistful look toward the cupboards, but leaving without being noticed was better than any breakfast.

Jenn stopped at the fountain to dip her finger, then took time for a drink. She stared at her reflection, dismayed by her appearance. Why hadn't she brought a comb? She quickly undid her braid and ran damp fingers through her hair. About to braid it again, she hesitated.

She looked different with it loose. Older. The ripples of pale gold fell past her shoulders to her waist, gleaming in the sunlight. Her eyes looked bigger.

Sweeping back her hair, she braided it as tightly as she could, restoring the Jenn Wisp knew. She wasn't about to show him another.

The village was astir as she climbed into the pasture and broke into a run. The bays snorted and tossed their heads. The calves thought this a splendid game and ran alongside, their sharp little toes flinging clots of dew-wet grass into the air. They protested when she climbed the gate and left them.

Tendrils of mist hung motionless over the fields and blanketed the river in white. As Jenn forded the river, the mist curled around her. She was careless of her skirt, so when she climbed out on the far side, the hem hung heavy around her ankles and dripped on her feet. She didn't bother to wring it out. It would dry as she ran.

Not that she had to keep running. To leave the village, yes. To avoid her father and her aunt and anyone else, yes. But now?

The last thing she wanted to do, she discovered, heart pounding, was hurry.

Jenn slowed to a walk, the roadway cool underfoot. The morning birds were strangely quiet, the air so still she could hear Master Dusom's bell summoning Cheffy and Alyssa to class. Those had been the days, when her worries consisted of geometry and Roche dipping her braid in ink.

When she reached the point where the Tinkers Road should bend to follow the Spine, the path to the upper meadow to her left, she found herself confronted by a wall of mist, thick and dark and silent.

Mist was normal for a late summer morning, especially here, where it could hide from the sun between the old trees. Wisp always blew it from her path.

Why hadn't he?

She pressed one hand over the little box in her pocket. He knew about the wishing and wanted nothing to do with it, or her. He didn't want her in the meadow . . .

"Nonsense," Jenn said aloud. Wisp slept. He'd told her so. She was too early for him this morning, that was all. "So I'll be there first, for once." She'd never seen him arrive. Not that she saw him, but would there be something different about the meadow before Wisp was in it?

Curiosity made it easier to walk forward.

Two steps into the mist, and only the packed dirt beneath her feet told her she walked on the road. That, and a perceptible darkness looming to either side. Old trees lined the Tinkers Road, the kind the villagers wouldn't touch with an ax. In the mist, they leaned toward her.

Jenn closed her eyes and kept walking. If there was a way she knew as well as her own home, it was the way to her meadow. She imagined the sun burning away the mist and drying her skirt, imagined the full-throated songs of small brown birds and the drone of the first morning's bees. There'd be rabbits in the meadow this early, she told herself. Rabbits with whiskers bejeweled with dewdrops.

She quite liked rabbits.

So she wasn't surprised to hear a chirp followed by a serenade, nor to feel warmth on her face. She opened her eyes to find the mist gone as if it had never been, and herself almost to the opening that led to the deserted farm. Her shortcut to Night's Edge.

And Wisp.

The triumphant laugh bubbling in her chest stayed there. She should practice what to say, Jenn decided solemnly as she went past the empty house and barn, following the line of trees. Where they met the hedgerow was an opening, widened over the years of her using it. She gently stroked aside the cobweb that curtained it before stepping through.

The path from here led beneath the old trees, alongside the field. The grain stalks were shoulder high, nodding their heavy ripe heads. The livestock relished the dried stalks over any other foodstuff, thriving on that diet through the long winter; the grain became flour for the villagers. The villagers called it flax, when it needed a name, but it wasn't the plant she'd seen drawn in books. Something else to discover outside Marrowdell.

With Wisp.

Her breath caught in her throat. To travel the wide world in the company of her dearest friend. To find her heart's need and be happy together. What could be better than that?

As if in agreement, birdsong filled the fragrant air. She'd reached the meadow. Rabbits regarded her peacefully, clover stems sticking past their furry lips as they chewed, the flowers at the tips wiggling up and down. Bees hovered by her ears and pushed their way inside still-sleepy daisies.

If they came from Kydd's hives, they'd spent the night inside books. Just as well they couldn't read.

They couldn't, could they?

Stems bent here and there, though the air didn't move. "Wisp?" she called.

In answer, a big-eyed mouse peered at her before climbing a stem that gave under its weight.

Without Wisp, Night's Edge was simply another meadow.

But this was not simply another morning. She'd arrived first. She had time. Relief trembled Jenn's hands as she pulled the little box from her pocket and held it in both hands. What to say . . .

"My Dear Wisp." Too formal. Like her aunt's invitations in Avyo.

She wrinkled her nose like a rabbit's and thought hard. "Wisp, I've a new game. It's called being a man." Bah. She was almost nineteen, not ten. A grown woman.

What would a woman say?

"Wisp." Jenn closed her eyes and whispered in a low, husky voice, "Be part of my life always. Come with me wherever I go." Because that was what she wanted most. To see the wide world together. To have her friend with her all the time, her family happy and safe. To find what was missing from her life and be content at last.

Everything would be perfect.

She heard leaves stir and opened her eyes. The asters and daisies nearest the old trees bowed toward her. Then the ones closer to her. And closer.

"Wisp!"

The familiar breeze tugged her braid and caressed her cheek. "Dearest Heart. You're back. I'm so glad."

The breeze slipped along her arms to her hands, folded over the box. "What's this? Did you bring me a surprise?"

She'd promised to ask. Jenn braced herself. "If you could, would you be with me, Wisp? Always?"

"Always. Always. Always." The breeze began to whirl playfully around her. "What's inside? Thistle?"

It wasn't quite a yes.

Or was it?

If it wasn't, she had no hope of leaving, no way to fill the emptiness consuming her, no future.

It had to be yes.

Jenn tore the lid from the box, cried, " 'Hearts of my Ancestors, grant my heart's need!' " and tossed the ash into the air.

What had glistened silver by moonlight was black by day. The ash caught in Wisp's whirl like thistledown, spiraling up and around. All at once, it came free and poured to the ground in front of her.

No. Not the ground.

The ash fell to outline a shape, strange and bent.

"What is this?!" wailed Wisp. The shape moved as if struggling. On every side, wind ripped the heads from flowers, tossed dirt into the air, but the black stayed where it was—and then, began to squeeze inward.

"What have you donnnnnee?!" A howl.

"Wisp!" Horrified, Jenn dropped the letterbox and leapt toward him. She'd sweep away the ash. She'd stop this." I'm sorry. I didn't mean—"

Flash! CLAP!

As Jenn flinched, the black collapsed on itself and was gone.

The echoes of thunder rolled into the Bone Hills and across the fields. Behind them, the air fell silent.

Until even the birds hushed.

"Wisp?"

Where he'd been was a smoking ruin of burnt stems and scorched earth. Flower petals drifted down like cinders.

Jenn took a step and stopped. "Wisp? Don't hide on me. Please. I said I was sorry."

Nothing.

"Wisp. Please? Come . . ." No use. He was gone. She knew it.

From her feet outward, fall spread through the meadow. Stems drooped, flowers dried without seed. The bees fled and the birds flew up and away.

Jenn fell to her knees and brought her fists to her mouth. Had she driven her best friend from her too?

Or done far worse?

Jenn Nalynn forded the river without noticing it. Climbed Marrowdell's gate and ran through the commons without seeing how the calves cowered from her or the sows snorted in alarm. No one called to her as she rushed through the village. People saw her face and fell silent.

She'd called Wisp's name till she was hoarse. The only breeze had smelled of ash and dust and hadn't answered.

It wasn't her meadow anymore. Not without Wisp. She couldn't do anything there. She couldn't be there.

She wasn't welcome.

So Jenn ran, her still-wet skirt slapping her shins, bare feet pounding the dirt, and tried to think. Maybe, just maybe, Wainn knew another part of the book, a part that would tell her how to undo the wishing.

Or another wishing, a better one. One that turned back time, changed decisions, mended shattered trust . . .

She'd do anything to save Wisp.

Steps from her rose-covered home, all the maybes and hopes failed her. Jenn stumbled onto the porch. The house toad leapt from Aunt Sybb's luggage, landing with an offended grunt, and squeezed itself under the rocking chair.

Jenn half-fell into the parlor, catching herself with a hand on the cold metal of the stove. She wasn't surprised to find her father there, instead of at the mill where he should have been, nor her aunt or sister, whose expressions went from hope to shock at the sight of her.

But why was Kydd Uhthoff at the table with them?

"Jenn." The tall slender man stood at once, giving that gracious half bow so natural to him and his family. "Please. Take your seat."

"Kydd brought back the plate," Peggs said too quickly, rising as well.

"The cookies were delicious," he stated warmly. "Our thanks again. You're sure my nephew was no bother."

"No bother. Wainn's always welcome."

"Peggs makes wonderful pie," Aunt Sybb volunteered.

"I'd be happy to—"

Their babble made no sense. Mute, Jenn looked to her father, who came to her without hesitation, taking her in his arms as though she was fragile. He spoke over her head, quick and firm. "Peggs. More tea. Kydd . . ."

"I'll take my leave, Radd. Ladies." At the door, the beekeeper turned. "Unless—" his voice took an unfamiliar edge, "—there's something wrong."

Wrong? Jenn looked at him, seeing concern in his face, and something else. Suspicion. Of what? He couldn't possibly know. She trembled. Of course he could. Wainn, ever the innocent, might have told his uncle everything that went with the pie and cookies. Kydd would know how she'd used his nephew, how she'd learned about his secret library in the hives, which Aunt Sybb thought he'd got rid of and clearly hadn't, which meant it wasn't proper to own and surely not meant to share, and about the wishing . . .

He couldn't know about Wisp.

He mustn't.

At the same time, his dark eyes searched hers and found some answer that turned them cold. For the first time in her life, Jenn realized Kydd Uhthoff was dangerous. "Who was it, Jenn?" he snapped. "Who upset you?" Then, making even less sense, "We heard thunder."

"No one." Had they feared she'd be caught in a storm? So this wasn't about Wisp or wishing. Her confused relief must have been plain, for Kydd relaxed. She might never have glimpsed another side to him, except for the oddest feeling she'd just protected someone. "I don't feel well," she added faintly, and buried her face against her father's vest.

He laid a comforting hand on the back of her head. "Good thing you came home, Sweetling. We'll take care of her, Kydd. Thank you." With weight to the courtesy, as if the two shared an understanding.

"Good day, then." When the footsteps on the porch ended, her father spoke quickly, "Sybbie—"

"Bring her here."

Jenn found herself on the settee with Aunt Sybb, despite her dirty feet and wet clothes. For some reason, the older woman felt it necessary to take her hands and rub them between hers. She didn't protest. Nothing seemed to matter.

Peggs knelt, holding out a steaming cup. Her eyes searched Jenn's, asked a question.

Jenn shook her head, very slightly.

"He said no?" Her sister frowned. "What—"

Tears welled in Jenn's eyes. "I—the wishing—he's gone!"

"Who said no?" Radd's forehead creased.

Peggs gasped, "You killed him?!"

And Aunt Sybb asked with great concern, "The toad?"

Great steaming mugs of tea. Warm flaky biscuits dripping with butter. Slices of pale cheese, fragrant apple, and sweet ham. Peggs could produce a feast from thin air.

All wasted. The others had eaten earlier; Jenn doubted she'd ever want to eat again. The tea went down well, though. She wrapped chilled hands around her mug and nodded gratefully as Peggs offered more.

Her sister sat. Her father and aunt, seated, waited. It wasn't patience, Jenn thought miserably, so much as determination. None of them would leave her be without an explanation. They'd regard her with kind anxious eyes until she spoke or fell asleep on the settee. She supposed they'd keep watch while she slept, so as not to miss her waking again.

There was no escaping the truth. Jenn stared into her tea. "I tried the wishing," she said finally. "The one from the book."

"We both did," Peggs said at once, at her defense as always.

Not this time. Jenn shook her head. "It was my decision. I used the ashes." She paused to firm her voice. "I spoke the words."

"What ashes? What words?" Their poor father looked from one to the other of his daughters, perplexed. She couldn't blame him. "Why?"

"Jenn tried to turn a toad into a husband." She cringed. Despite Aunt Sybb's matter-of-fact tone, it sounded pure nonsense. "I wish you wouldn't carry on so, child," her aunt pleaded. "There are more toads."

She buried her face in her hands.

"Sybbie," firmly. "Peggs. We're done with refreshments, thank you. Kindly clear the table."

"Radd—"

"A moment alone with my youngest. Please."

"Place could use less toads," Jenn heard her aunt mutter as she and Peggs collected the plates and trays, then walked into the kitchen.

The settee creaked as her father sat beside her. "Now, Dearest Heart. Look at me."

She lowered her hands and obeyed. His normally apple-red cheeks were pale, and his throat worked as he swallowed before saying, "Was it your little wind? The one from the meadow?"

Of all the things he might have said, nothing could have shocked her more. "You—you know about Wisp?"

"'Wisp?' I knew something there kept you safe. Not its name. Wisp." He almost smiled at her astonishment. "Heart of my Hearts, did you think I'd let you run off otherwise? What kind of father would I be?"

It hadn't occurred to her. Night's Edge was part of her life, like her favorite cup or comforter. "How—?"

"How did I know?" Her father hesitated, as if unsure where to start within a longer story, then gave a short nod. "When you were a baby, if you weren't well, or became unhappy, all I had to do was take you to the meadow. The little wind would tickle your cheeks and you'd stop crying. You'd smile that wonderful smile of yours. I thought at first—" he sighed and tipped his hand over, "—whatever it was, it wasn't there for me." A chuckle. "For one thing, when it rained, only I got wet. It—Wisp—was there to look after you."

"He isn't!" Jenn sobbed, the horrid words spilling out with her tears. "Not anymore! Poppa, I tried—I tried to make a husband. I tried to turn Wisp into a man. What I did hurt him. I could tell. Hurt him and—" she hiccupped, "—then he—he was gone!"

Her father pursed his lips thoughtfully. "Hmmm." He took his handkerchief and tenderly wiped her cheeks. "Don't be too sure of that."

Jenn blinked. "Why?"

"Marrowdell's little curiosities are stronger than they appear. And so, my little princess," he put his arm around her shoulders and kissed the top of her head, "are you."

The mist was slow to leave the road; the sun slow to find it. Bannan eyed the wagon's hard seat with distaste. Going around the back, he pulled out Scourge's gear and gave a short, quiet whistle between his teeth.

Tir settled the yoke on the drowsy ox and glanced his way. "Scouting ahead, sir? Very sensible. There could be half-naked bandits lurking in the woods. Or bears."

"I'll take my turn in the wagon," Bannan promised. "Where's that—" He stopped and grinned at the loud trot coming up the road they'd traveled yesterday. No horse was as noisy as Scourge when he meant to be noticed. Sure enough, a moment later, he came into view, neck flexed and legs prancing. Making an entrance.

"They were only bandits," Tir pointed out dryly, eyes bright above the mask. "Probably armed with farm tools."

Scourge broke into a thunderous run straight at him. The poor ox bawled and tried to pull sideways. Tir stood his ground. The horse plunged to a stop, mane and tail flaring, his hooves almost touching the small man's boots. "Farmer bandits," Tir repeated, chin up. "With rusty pitchforks."

A hoof slammed into the ground.

"If you two are done," Bannan commented. "I'd like to get started." Tir's shrug and Scourge's snort were equally expressive. He hid a smile.

Riding was better. Not only did Scourge demand a good part of his attention, being nothing loath to dump him on the road if ignored, but the saddle's higher vantage let him see over the trailing mist. Not, Bannan thought ruefully, that he knew what he was looking for.

Something new.

Something different.

The horse's eager strides left the ox, wagon, and Tir behind in short order. Bannan waved as they turned the next bend.

The road didn't merely take them north; it climbed, slowly but surely, through steep, broken hills. The evenings were already cooler, easier for sleeping. He wouldn't miss the cloying heat of Vorkoun's nights. Winters would be harsher here; they'd been told few traveled once the snows hit. Fine with him, Bannan thought, envisioning a snug little cabin, evenings by a fire, a book. He'd brought some, planned to ask Lila to send more once he had a place of his own.

Thunder rumbled in the distance.

Scourge snorted and pretended to shy, a tower of muscle waiting an excuse to explode. Bannan grinned, keeping his seat with ease. "Too slow for you?" All at once, he was impatient too. The future lay ahead. He took a handful of mane and dug in his heels.

The horse's leap would have snapped his head back, if he hadn't leaned forward the instant those legs tucked beneath Scourge's haunches. The leap turned to a surging run and the road became a blur. Trees lost their shape. Bannan pressed his cheek against the hot mighty neck and half closed his eyes, letting the motion consume him, as safe as he could be. Scourge might throw him in a fit of pique; he'd not let him fall.

So when, a short time later, he found himself flat on his back and gasping for air, Bannan was understandably shocked.

He glared up at Scourge. The horse was standing, legs braced, where he'd decided to stop and launch his rider.

"Idiot beast!" Bannan finally managed to sputter.

Scourge ignored him, head high, nostrils flared.

Not good.

Bannan forgot the parts of his body that would undoubtedly not want to ride in the wagon later and lifted his head for a wary look around.

Just ahead, their road was joined by another, narrower and heading more west than north. No threat there. His eyes searched the rest of their surroundings. Trees and moss. Rocks and road. The same as every other stretch they'd passed since Weken. Rough terrain, impossible to move through with any speed or numbers. "What is it?"

Scourge relaxed, shaking his head and neck until dust flew. Birds sang. A bee buzzed past, taking the western road.

Bannan rolled to his feet, feeling bruises but nothing worse. He'd landed on dirt, hadn't he, though gray-pink boulders jutted everywhere, guaranteed to crack a skull. "You're up to something," he accused.

The horse gave him an innocent look, the only evidence of wrongdoing the rein left hanging after Bannan's flight over his head.

Tir's act was more convincing. Tir of the light fingers, who had uncanny luck with nillystones if unwatched. Tir, left well behind by their now-foolish gallop. They'd best go meet him, Bannan decided, his mood soured, and started toward the horse.

Scourge took a deliberate step back, a familiar wicked glint in his eye.

Bannan stopped. "Don't you dare," he warned in a pleasant, don't alarm the horse, tone. The idiot beast would turn contrary here and now, when he'd been the fool and come away without water or food, armed with naught but the short eating knife at his belt.

When Tir caught up? Oh, he'd never hear the end of it.

That great head swung toward the western road. A restless hoof tapped rock.

Was that his game? "We're not," Bannan said firmly, "going that way."

Scourge growled a singsong protest.

"No."

The horse's head lowered until his nose neared the ground. The rein trailed temptingly in the dust.

He readied himself, hands loose at his sides. "Easy, boy."

Scourge snorted as if stung and bolted. Risking his feet, Bannan lunged for the rein as the huge body rushed by. He grabbed it and held.

Leather and buckles gave way with a snap, leaving him flat on his rump for the second time.

Bridleless, Scourge thundered down the little road, tossing his mane, tail up and proud.

In an instant, he was gone.

Bannan leaned back on his hands to consider how best to skin his four-footed betrayer when he returned. Perhaps it was time for that overdue gelding. "Should have brought a normal horse," he told his deserted surroundings. Tir wasn't alone in his doubt of Scourge's usefulness on a farm.

Not that he'd brought Scourge. The beast was his shadow, impossible to govern or leave behind.

Until now.

Bannan got to his feet, brushed off the worst of the dust, and retrieved the remnants of the bridle, wrapping the long rein over elbow and palm as he pondered his options. Wait, he supposed. Tir and the wagon would be here eventually. A long and thirsty eventually, given the ox's lethargic pace.

Then what? Leave Scourge?

"Serve you right," he muttered, with a pensive gaze down the road the horse had taken. Less used than the Northward, but with signs of proper maintenance. Dead limbs didn't lean over it. Low spots had been recently filled. Which meant . . .

"Someone at the other end." He couldn't see much more; the cleft through which the road ran bent sharply.

Whatever had drawn Scourge, the creature would return in his own good time or not at all. The world would be a smaller, more ordinary place without him. Bannan felt a lump rise in his throat and he shook his head. No. He wouldn't believe Scourge had abandoned him.

He was about to turn back to wait for Tir when the rising sun peeked over the crags behind and flooded the road with light.

Making it beautiful.

What had been dark, moody trees became open forest, with glades beneath. The packed dirt warmed to reddish brown. Birds twittered and a heavy throated heron passed overhead.

A heron. He sniffed and nodded. Water ahead. A great deal of it.

And wasn't he thirsty?

Bannan hung the bridle over a branch so Tir would know where he'd gone and draped the rein across his shoulders. He wasn't chasing after the fool horse. He'd walk a little distance past the bend, see if he could find a stream.

The air was pleasant, the sun warm on his shoulders. He hadn't gone far at all when his steps gained a four-footed echo.

Bannan smiled and didn't look around.

Which was a mistake.

~ What's happened to you? ~ From above.

Another, closer. ~ Does it hurt? ~ The question held a hopeful malice. Those of his kind who'd escaped penance took singular joy in his.

Wisp spat black ash and ignored them all. He hobbled down the path to his home, desperate to be alone, to understand. He would have gone faster if he didn't keep . . .

He fell again, hard on one side, and fought to catch his breath. Crystal wept beneath him. Above, air pulsed, driven by great wings. Curious, they swooped perilously low, trying to see him within the narrow cleft.

~ What are you? ~

How could he answer, when he didn't know himself?

Wisp forced himself to his feet and stumbled downward, falling twice more before he reached the blue shimmer that was the door to peace and safety. He lunged for it, only to strike a solid barrier.

The impact threw him backward. He huddled where he landed, rocking back and forth in sullen misery as he stared at what was now forbidden. Why?

What had she done?

~ You cannot stay here. ~ From above, with none of the mockery of the others. ~ You must return to her world. ~ The bone-shaking timbre of the voice left no doubt.

Sei.

Wisp looked up. The being had shaped itself into one of his kind, though none of his kind would be this gaudy emerald green. Its clawed feet clenched the rock wall above the blue shimmer, but the limbs connected to those feet shouldn't have bent at such angles. The wings folded reasonably, but the bearded face and maned neck were too large for the body. As for the fanged jaw—that was farce. Though sei tried, their manifestations were never perfect. Which was just as well. It was important to know what you faced.

~ What did she do? ~ Wisp demanded. Tried to demand. Nothing came out. Why could he hear, but not speak? Instead, he lifted a limb. One ended in a man's hand, the other in a proper set of claws. The rest of his body was the same, a horrible blend of what he'd been and this—this travesty.

The sei understood. ~ You fled before the transformation was complete. ~

This was somehow his fault? Wisp trembled in fury, clawed feet—foot—shredding crystal. War was forbidden, not battle. And his kind excelled in battle.

~ We see an opportunity for your penance. ~

Opportunity and penance together in the same sentence was not, in his experience, a good thing. The sei had considered his servitude with the turn-born to be an "opportunity" too.

Wisp sank to his haunches, easing the wing he had left out of the way. He'd been doing his latest penance when the girl attacked him. He felt a different sort of anger, thinking of Jenn Nalynn, deeper, like a wound's pain. Why had she done this to him? They'd been friends.

Hadn't they?

~ We see the expectation of this turn-born. You will be finished and sent into her world. ~

Wisp tried to protest, to plead, but nothing came out. It might have been one of the bad nights, when the blue of his sanctuary smothered his screams.

~ Your penance remains. Keep her from harm. ~

Like this? He could barely stand. How could he protect anything like this?

~ Your penance remains. Only you may know the truth. ~

Truth? The secret the sei had sealed in him was worse than the ruin of his body.

Like any turn-born, the girl was of both worlds. Her life, like the roots of the neyet, should have bound their worlds together. But, unlike other turn-born, her birth had taken place in the midst of crossing from one to the other, and part of her remained there still, between worlds, caught like the trapped ones themselves.

Should Jenn Nalynn step beyond the edge, should she leave Marrowdell and so the Verge as well, her small, hollow form would tug its frail thread to the breaking point and so begin the unraveling.

All would be undone. All. Their worlds would be torn asunder. Nothing in the Verge, nothing along the edge of her world, would survive.

The trapped would be freed at last. Or finally die. The sei were unclear on that point.

The risk posed by the girl's very existence they told to him and no one else. The turn-born were left to believe her curse the same as theirs, to exist solely where the worlds overlapped. Wishing her ignorant, but not wishing her harm, they set him to keep her within Marrowdell. They cared only that Jenn Nalynn not cross into the Verge to challenge them.

Doubtless, they slept soundly.

The sei stopped wars and punished the perpetrators to ensure their peace, no one else's. They didn't explain why they wanted the girl to live. Perhaps they believed she'd be a check on the more outrageous of the turn-born. Perhaps they played games.

Wisp feared, deep inside, that the sei wouldn't care if Jenn Nalynn tried to leave. Her world was of no interest to them. The Verge must be a source of disturbance and conflict. A blight that produced the turn-born. A nuisance.

It was home. Home to so many. To too many. He clung to hope as if drowning. Surely their loss would disturb the sei more.

~ Your penance remains, so long as she lives. Ensure our peace. ~ The ill-formed jaws of the sei snapped. ~ Then, your penance will be complete. ~

What did that mean? Would he be restored? Allowed to come home?

Or dead?

The sei launched itself upward in an impossible motion that made Wisp's body ache. Instead of opening wings, it abandoned its form to become flame. As he flinched from the dazzling brightness, every shadow bleached away and the very air he breathed became fire and ash . . .

. . . then, air again.

He sat where he'd been before, but wasn't as he'd been. Wisp gazed numbly at hands and arms, covered in glittering green ash. The perspective was strange. His body was shorter, his head—his head turned on a stiff, too-short neck. He couldn't see his own back. Not that he had wings any longer.

A turn-born came through what had been his door and stood before him. Female in form, her limbs filled with sand, she wore a face set in aloof judgment. ~ Take him across. ~

She didn't speak to him. Who—? As Wisp took a horrified guess, claws sank into his now-tender flesh and he was jerked into the air.

His kind!

One carried him. Others flew beneath, beside, snapping at his dangling feet, crying insults. None pitied him.

Why should they?

Wisp closed his man's eyelids and pitied himself.

SIX

"THE THREE OF you tried to make a husband." Radd Nalynn ran one hand through his shock of gray-peppered hair. "Make one. Aren't real men good enough?"

Aunt Sybb narrowed her eyes. "Don't you have a mill to tend?"

Cheeks burning, Jenn gave her aunt a grateful look.

Her father snorted. "I don't dare leave you alone. What else might happen?"

"We might," Aunt Sybb said acidly, "get something done. I've to pack. We've a birthday celebration to prepare. Let alone the laundry!" She made a shooing gesture with her hands. "Go. Give the girl some peace." More soberly, "Everything can wait, Radd. Patience."

"Patience, it is." He took his lunch bucket from the table and headed for the door. A step short, he stopped and turned. "This was my fault."

"No, Poppa," Jenn said quickly.

"Yes. I should never have started all this talk of love and marriage. I pushed you both into rash decisions."

Peggs looked up from the table. "I've made no—"

"Giving my cookies to the Uhthoffs?"

Her lips moved without sound coming out.

"Make extra for Kydd, next time." With the faintest hint of a smile around his eyes. "Just not better."

"Poppa!" Peggs' turn to be thoroughly flustered.

"As for you—" to Jenn. Radd softened his tone. "Go to your meadow. Look for him. You've such a good heart. He knows that." Bright spots of apple red appeared on his cheeks, his only acknowledgment of their surprised looks. Without waiting for an answer, he left.

Tears ran down Jenn's cheeks; she didn't wipe them away. Go back? She couldn't bear it. Not the way it was now. Not without Wisp.

"Bath first," Aunt Sybb ordered briskly. "Then laundry." She laid a tender hand along Jenn's cheek. "Work helps. You'll see."

In winter, they sponged themselves clean by the stone fireplace. The rest of the year, the big tub sat outside the kitchen door. In summer, the climbing rose screened it from the mill and a curtain between poles provided privacy from the Emms' garden—added once Radd noticed the Emms' twins weeded with exceptional diligence on his daughters' bath day. Otherwise, the tub was open to the river and distant fields, and kissed by sun.

Peggs wouldn't hear of Jenn helping to fill it. She'd boiled the water herself, while her sister wiped plates, and shaved a bar of fine city soap to make bubbles.

The same water being destined for laundry, Jenn didn't know what their father would say about his shirts smelling of lavender, but when Peggs pronounced the bath ready, she sank into the hot water with a grateful sigh.

"Let me wash your hair."

She nodded thankfully and tilted her head back on the wide rim. Peggs undid the braid, hands sure and gentle. "You've a bird's nest in here," she scolded. "And look. A dead bee."

Jenn wasn't surprised. She closed her eyes and ducked underwater when Peggs tapped her shoulder, staying down until her sister lightly pulled on her hair.

"I shouldn't have done it," she said when up again.

Peggs rubbed suds through Jenn's hair, digging gently but firmly into her scalp. "None of us knew what would happen."

Jenn poked bubbles with a morose toe. "Which means I shouldn't have done it."

Before she could start to cry again, Peggs tapped her shoulder. "Rinse."

When she came up, her sister began to comb out her hair, pulling small sections together. "What I know, Dearest Heart," she said as she worked, "is we're responsible for our own lives. That means taking chances and making mistakes." Peggs finished by coiling the remaining length. She pinned it behind Jenn's head. "There. Like a grand lady of Avyo. I'll wager you do look just like our mother."

Jenn sloshed around to face her sister, elbows on the tub rim. "You didn't tell them we were listening last night." Peggs made a show of drying her hands. "You did? Peggs!"

"I didn't have to. Poppa and Aunt Sybb were waiting when I came downstairs this morning. They said it was time I heard the whole story."

"What do you mean?"

Peggs glanced around as if to make sure they were alone, then crouched by the tub, her hands by Jenn's. "Remember what Poppa told you?" she said in a hushed, urgent voice. "How Mother's family wanted her to stay in Avyo—to leave him? There's more to it, Jenn. They tried to make her stay. Aunt Sybb said they tricked her and locked her in their home, but she escaped with me in the night to join Poppa. They fled Avyo—chased by the city guard right to the gates!"

Jenn gazed wide-eyed at her sister. They'd made up endless stories about their mother. None had included daring escapes or chases in the night. "What happened?"

"In Weken, every settler took oath and signed their bind, the promise to the prince never to return home. Ever. Our mother signed one too. They should have been safe." Peggs, who was a wonderful storyteller, paused for effect. "But they weren't. It wasn't over."

Jenn almost forgot to breathe.

Her sister lowered her voice more. "Mother's family had her bind undone by the prince himself. Poppa didn't say how. That meant if they could find her, they could bring her back. By force, if necessary."

"They tried?"

Peggs hesitated. She gave a short nod, her lips pressed together.

"Well?" Jenn prompted eagerly. "You can't stop there. What happened?"

"They sent someone—" Pulling over a bucket, Peggs overturned it and sat. She'd grown pale and her eyes were huge; she swallowed hard before continuing, "They sent someone they trusted, someone who'd never failed the family. He came in disguise during the harvest, maybe hoping a strange face wouldn't be noticed. But—Mother saw him first. She knew who he was. Th—" She stopped midword and shook her head. "I can't."

"You can't leave it there!" Jenn protested.

Peggs got to her feet. Jenn grabbed for her with a soapy hand but her sister stepped out of reach, eyes suspiciously bright. "I—I can't."

"Of course you can." Aunt Sybb stepped through the kitchen door, shoulders back, eyes fierce. "You're neither of you children, Peggs Nalynn. That's become clear even to your father. You both need to know which roads you mustn't take—ever—and why."

Gooseflesh rose on Jenn's arms, despite the warmth of the bathwater.

Peggs shook her head again. "I can't tell her."

"I can." Aunt Sybb stared out at the river and fields beyond. "Melusine was alone when she spotted the man sent to bring her back. Before he could see her, she fled the village." Her hand lifted, the lace of her black shawl falling from a delicate wrist more bone than flesh. Her finger stabbed toward Night's Edge and Jenn didn't understand.

"Why did she run?" she asked.

"To protect your father. To protect anyone else who might try to help. Her family'd sent a formidable man, Jenn, a professional soldier. Melusine knew no one in the village was his match. Her hope was to hide till he gave up and left—but she was in no shape to run or hide." Aunt Sybb looked down at Jenn. "She was about to have you."

This wasn't romance or adventure. This was Wisp and the meadow and ash. Jenn wanted to sink under the water, to cover her ears, to not know. To never know.

Relentless, their aunt continued in her soft, steady voice. "The weather failed. Day was turning to night. Your father was desperate. Everyone tried to find her. The soldier guessed Melusine had climbed into one of the tinkers' wagons and gone with them into the Bone Hills. He had a fast horse. He found her first."

"And killed her." The accusation was harsh to her own ears. Ravens flew overhead and cawed a hungry echo. The air chilled.

"No, Jenn. No." Aunt Sybb came to the tub and sank beside it, the hem of her costly city dress spread in lavender-scented mud. Her eyes searched Jenn's. "He tried to save her. He found her lying in that meadow—your meadow. She'd—she'd given birth alone. Too soon. Too hard. He stayed with her until your father came and helped as best he could, but it was too late to save you both." Her hand found Jenn's and pressed gently. "Dearest Heart, you must believe me. This man had meant no harm. He vowed to your mother he'd keep you safe." A too-careful pause. "And he has."

"He's still here?!" Jenn scrambled from the tub, bubbles flying.

Tight-lipped, Peggs handed her a sheet. Jenn wrapped herself in it, a dreadful certainty growing in her mind.

Who in Marrowdell had been a soldier? Who guarded the road like an obsession?

"Uncle Horst." Jenn met her sister's eyes, saw the despair and confusion that must be in her own. "It's him, isn't it? The one they sent." The man who shared their table. Worked with their father. Had become family. "It's his fault she died."

"That wasn't his intention," her aunt said firmly. "If Horst hadn't found Melusine, we'd have lost you too. Remember that."

They'd meet. She'd have to look at him. "What will I say?" How should she feel? She'd never known her mother; now she didn't know this man who'd been their closest neighbor and friend her whole life. The mother she and Peggs had wanted—had needed—so many times? He'd come to take her from them.

And that's what he'd done, no matter what Aunt Sybb said.

Peggs helped Aunt Sybb rise to her feet, steadying her until she nodded. "I asked the same question."

"And?"

The older woman's smile transformed lines of grief to dimples. "And, because life moves on, that's when your sister's young man knocked at the door."

Peggs blushed prettily.

Jenn didn't try to think of Kydd Uhthoff as young or as her sister's. Life moved on? If so, hers had left her behind. Aunt Sybb was leaving tomorrow. Uncle Horst—Horst was a terrifying stranger. Her beloved meadow was where her mother had died.

Where Wisp—

Her hands shook as she dressed.

"It'll be all right, Jenn. You'll see. There are other—" Aunt Sybb hesitated, then added brightly, "—other toads."

Peggs hastily changed the subject. "Good thing it's laundry day," she said. "Look at your poor hem, Aunt Sybb. We'll need to wash that before packing, and be sure it's dry."

Dirty clothes, by unspoken agreement, pushed both future and past aside. While their aunt changed, Peggs and Jenn put the least soiled whites into the tub, adding hot water and chips of stronger soap. When her sister hooked the washboard on the side, Jenn numbly took over without a word, taking steaming handfuls of wet cloth and rubbing them with all the strength in her arms.

With each downward press against the ribbed board, she repeated to herself, I can't stay here. I can't stay here.

It wasn't about seeing wonders anymore. It wasn't about filling the hollow in her heart.

She had to get away from Marrowdell. As far away as she could.

Everyone had known.

Had Wisp?

Was that why he'd first come to care for her? Pity for her tragic birth?

Questions she couldn't ask. Jenn rubbed harder. She'd betrayed Wisp and he was gone.

Peggs came out with an armload, her nose held high. "Poppa tried to hide his favorite—" She stopped to yell at the top of her lungs: "Cheffy Ropps, get out of our garden!"

Jenn raised her head in time to watch the young boy bounce past on Wainn's old pony. Once persuaded to canter, the opinionated beast would go wherever he wanted, not his rider: at the moment, right through their vegetables and straight for the mill.

The boy shouted something. Jenn went to stand beside Peggs. "What's he saying?"

"I can't—"

Suddenly clear, "—river! Man in the riv—" the next bounce garbled the words.

" 'Man in the river?' It's Wisp!" Jenn hugged Peggs. "It has to be!"

Her sister turned the hug into a pull. "Hurry!"

They ran around the house. Across the main road, Old Wagler Jupp stood on his porch, leaning on his canes. Riss Nahamm, long hair caught up in a twist of rag—she'd been cleaning—came out the door behind him with a blanket in her arms. When she saw the sisters, she called, "Did you hear? There's someone in the river!"

"What's the fuss?" Old Jupp complained.

Riss pointed.

Jenn and Peggs looked, too. All through the village, people emerged, some with rope, others with blankets, only to stop and stare toward the river. The river that should be ankle-deep.

And now looked as it did at snowmelt, full and snarling at its banks.

The ford was gone.

"Poppa!" Peggs gasped. "The millstones!" Once the stones were set and the loft full of grain, all their father need do was throw open the floodgate and the water would rise in answer.

"It can't be," Jenn protested. The stones were outside their case, the race closed and dry. Just as well. In this fearsome state, the river would tear the wheel from the mill.

How didn't matter. Not far past the mill, the river plunged from the valley through a narrow rock cut. No one could survive that drop. She tugged at Peggs' arm. "We have to get to the falls!"

The sisters ran together. As they took the path by the mill, Peggs veered away, shouting, "Go! You can find him. I'll bring Poppa. And rope!"

Jenn nodded. She tore past Horst's home, barely flinching, then through the open gate in the hedgerow. Leaving the village behind, she pumped her arms and drove her legs faster. The road followed the river but water flowed with dreadful speed. Her only chance—Wisp's only chance—was to reach the flat rocks above the waterfall first.

And do what then?

She concentrated on running.

The man on the gray-muzzled gelding had seen his share of days. That didn't, Bannan thought ruefully, empty hands away from his sides, make him less a threat. In fact, everything about the man who'd managed to ride up behind him proclaimed he was, from his sharp gaze to the well-kept weapons hanging from back and saddle. Callused fingertips kept tension on the bowstring, the notched and wicked arrow aimed uncomfortably low. This one knew how to incapacitate a foe while leaving him able to talk. Or scream.

"You look like a bandit to me," the man said evenly. "Where's your horse? Your wagon?"

"I rode ahead of the wagon. As I said, my horse threw me and ran this way."

"I've seen no horse."

Of course he hadn't. Bannan intended to have a word with Scourge. A very stern word. If he got the chance. "I mean no harm. Just let me go back to the Northward and I'll wait for my companion there."

"'Companion.'" An eyebrow lifted on the lean, patrician face, the kind of face he'd expect to find protecting a baronial household in Vorkoun or Avyo, not the crossing of nothing and nowhere. "You admit you're a scout." The bowstring pulled back.

"I admit I'm an idiot. I told you. I'm a settler." Without proof, he wouldn't believe the claim either. "My name's Bannan. If you'd come with me to the main road—"

"You are an idiot if you think I'll follow you into an ambush."

The truth. Bannan grinned. "What do you suggest?"

The taut string eased ever so slightly. "I suggest—easy!" This as the gelding widened its nostrils in alarm and shifted its weight.

Bannan didn't bother looking around. "Lower your bow," he advised. "Quickly." Scourge taking up the hunt was nothing to trifle with; this man and his horse wouldn't stand a chance.

The man giving him an incredulous look. "Why should I?"

"On my honor, I mean you no harm, sir. I can't speak for my hidden—" horse? "—companion. You're in danger. Believe it."

Something flickered across those intent eyes. The bow lowered, string loosening. The man let the arrow tumble to the ground, then held his hands away from his body.

A shadow between two pines elongated into a leg, then a head carried low, like a snake ready to strike. A long body followed. Hooves met the road with no sound at all. Lips pulled from teeth that belonged to no horse.

Scourge growled.

The gelding rolled his eyes and trembled, but didn't break. More proof, if Bannan needed it, that this was no ordinary settler. This man had trained in an elite soldiery.

"Looks like we found my horse," Bannan commented. He didn't dare move; by his wide-eyed stare, the former soldier didn't either. Scourge wove closer. "You wouldn't happen to know any border guard passwords, would you?" the truthseer continued with deliberate calm. "Doesn't matter how old."

The man didn't hesitate. "Ordo's Precious Arse."

Bannan chuckled. That would do.

With a disappointed huff, Scourge became a big ugly horse again. He made a show of lipping a leaf from the dirt. The poor gelding wasn't convinced. His rider patted his neck, then nodded at Scourge. "I didn't know you folk used the Northward. You should have said you were a tinker."

Something about Scourge was familiar to this man? "I'm not," Bannan said easily, his mind racing. "Just looking to farm. My horse was a runaway; wound up on the family pasture. Ugly as he was, no one else wanted him." A rude snort from the animal thus disparaged. "I've an ox too," he added. "The best in Endshere, according to the trader."

"Lanky fellow, one eye?" At Bannan's nod, the man unstrung his bow and almost smiled. "You're lucky to have made it this far. The name's Horst. Excuse the welcome. Bandits occasionally try the road to Marrowdell."

"We were warned in Endshere." Scourge arched his neck; Bannan ignored him. " 'Marrowdell.' A village?"

Horst tilted his head down the road. "Valley and village both."

Bannan waited politely for him to extol his home's virtues. New settlers must be rare; he and Tir had been enticed with all manner of unlikely claims between Weken and Endshere. Water like wine. Turnips the size of melons. Beds filled with eiderdown. And daughters. To hear some of the threadbare farmers brag in their cups, simply following them home would guarantee a life of bliss. They lied, possibly to themselves as well. Most likely, the guarantee was life as a laborer for someone else. He'd keep going till he found a place where he could farm for himself, thank you.

Marrowdell. Now he remembered the name. Tir had heard it in the Endshere tavern. Something about people who kept to themselves and had little to do with the outside world.

Both suited him.

Horst, however, didn't say another word. Instead, he sat his horse, patently waiting to watch Bannan leave.

Curious.

"Is there an inn—" Bannan stopped as Scourge lifted his head and stared toward the valley, ears pricked. The gelding followed suit.

An instant later, he heard the drum of hooves. A high-pitched hoarse shout followed. "Man—man in the river!"

"Heart's Blood," Horst cursed, wheeling his horse around and digging in his heels. The gelding burst into action, doubtless happy to be leaving Scourge.

Scourge, as always, had his own notions. He walked to Bannan and stood waiting. After a moment, his head bent around as if to ask what was taking his rider so long.

"We are not following them," Bannan said firmly as he stepped into the stirrup and swung his leg over. "Tir's waiting." The Northward was straight ahead. He dug in his heels.

With an amused rumble, Scourge wheeled to pursue the gelding.

"Idiot beast!"

Jenn took the footpath from the road as quickly as she dared, hands up to keep branches from whipping her face, trying not to slip on the mossy rocks. It wasn't used this time of year, fishing being best in spring. The waterfall thundered in her ears, vibrated through her feet.

She burst into the open and grabbed a sapling to stop herself from falling forward. Directly below was the trout pool, relatively calm and shallow. Massive flat rocks lay beneath its surface, fitted like a giant's puzzle. On the opposite side, fierce rapids slammed against jagged stone, eating away the wall. Roots hung exposed, bleached and dead. Trees clung to the upper edge; most leaned inward, doomed.

The plume of the falls filled the air to Jenn's left. She needed no reminder how close the deadly drop was.

Where was Wisp?

The safest way to the river was simply to sit on the moss and slide. Despite her hurry, Jenn used whatever she could reach with her hands to slow her descent.

At the bottom, thorn bushes and round slime-coated stones became the challenge. Cloth and skin caught and tore. She teetered her way through the shallows until she felt flat rock underfoot.

The current tugged at the bottom of her skirt. Quickly, Jenn tucked it up, securing the ends through the waist. She eased forward, step by careful step. The water should have been warm. It was numbingly cold and reeked of wet ash.

A massive log that should have floated to an easy stop against the riverbank behind the Treffs, heralded by ducks, careened through the rapids and splintered as it flipped end over end.

Barely midcalf and Jenn could feel the power of the unseasonable current, trying to knock her down and wash her over the falls with the log. She stopped, afraid to go deeper.

Where was Wisp?

She searched the tumble of water coming toward her. Half the river was in deep shadow; the rest glared with sunlight. Her foot slipped and she caught herself in time, heart pounding in her throat. Where was Wisp? Others asked her to find things all the time. Well, now she had to find him. She would!

A confusion of branches spun from the shadows against the opposite bank, caught by an eddy. There! A pale arm showed, then disappeared. Showed again, found a hold. A head. A bare back. The mass tipped with every movement, tipped and shed parts. Instead of lodging, it slipped inexorably closer to the rapids with each slow turn.

"Wisp!!!" She was on the wrong side. She couldn't reach him. A rope. Where was her father? Anyone?

"Help!!!" Jenn shouted. "Someone! Help!"

It was no use. The river drowned her voice, kept her powerless.

"Wisp!"

"Who's in the river, Cheffy?" Horst demanded, leaning from his saddle to grasp the pony's halter and pull him to a stop.

The pony looked grateful, Bannan thought, amused.

The freckle-faced boy on its back gasped for breath. "A . . . man. With . . . no clothes!" This with relish. He noticed Bannan and his eyes went wide. "Who . . . are you?"

An excited child. A naked swimmer.

Doubtless some prank or drunken escapade. Having committed sufficient of both, Bannan was disappointed. This road had pulled him, had promised something new.

A lie. This Marrowdell was no different.

"Someone who'll leave you to your business," he told the boy. They'd try another road, farther north. Another place.

Horst gave him a curt nod of dismissal, his attention on the boy. "Where did you see this man?"

Bannan kneed Scourge to turn him back to the Northward Road.

Scourge didn't budge.

"Not again," he said under his breath. He started to dismount, intending to use the rein as a halter, and almost landed on the road again as Scourge chose that moment to leap forward.

The gelding and pony shied out of the way. Bannan grabbed a fistful of mane and hauled himself upright in the saddle, waving mute apology.

The horse, meanwhile, galloped toward Marrowdell as if determined to prove his rider had no control whatsoever.

Which was, at that moment, true.

"Idiot beast!" he shouted. Scourge didn't slow his headlong rush. "Ancestors Mad and Besotted, I should have left you in Vorkoun's stables!" Which would have been a thorough disaster once Scourge ran out of mice, but the notion did entertain.

A sudden shift in balance. Warned, Bannan flattened himself over the horse's neck as Scourge plunged into the thick forest beside the road. As he clung with all his strength, somehow the mighty body beneath him found gaps between tree trunks. Whatever Scourge sought, he wasted no effort on stealth. His breath came in loud urgent bursts, like one of the cursed engines of the Eldad climbing a hill.

While they ran down one. Bannan had ridden treacherous terrain, but this? The slope was too steep even for Scourge, who began to bound from side to side like some fool oversized goat, finding footholds in midair, as far as Bannan could tell.

Worse, the air filled with a roar that could be only one thing. A waterfall. A big one. Right below where his insane horse was more falling than running.

If he'd been on any other mount, he'd have thrown himself clear and counted himself lucky not to break both legs.

On Scourge? "This the best you can do?!" he shouted, all at once as mad as the beast. "Go!"

An ear flicked back. Approval.

More leaps, a twist that came close to throwing him, then they were in the river, Scourge splashing his way toward a figure in its midst.

Not naked. Nor a man.

The woman shouted, but he couldn't hear over the waterfall. She realized at once and pointed desperately.

He rose in the saddle to look. Yes. There. A man clung to a mass of flotsam against the other bank. Unconscious? No, he moved.

Which meant a chance.

The woman was in no safe place either. Bannan kicked free a stirrup and extended his hand. She took it in one of hers, pulling herself up and astride with reassuring strength. Farm maid, despite hair pinned like a grandmother's. She settled behind him, arms around his waist.

This time when he squeezed his legs, Scourge stepped forward with a will. The riverbed here was as level as city pavement, the powerful current like silk. The rapids ahead? Those were deadly. Narrow, though. If they could get close . . .

Suddenly what had been silk rose and battered against them as the river tried to spit them out. Water covered Bannan's boots and boiled against Scourge's flanks, yet a short distance away the pool remained smooth and unruffled. The woman tightened her grip. Grimly, he urged the horse on, trusting Scourge to keep his feet. If he didn't, well, the poor fellow would have company over the falls.

Bannan felt the rumble through his hands and legs as Scourge growled. Guessing what was to come, if not why, he pressed his arm over the woman's and gripped the saddle with his free hand.

The horse reared on his hind legs, hung in midair an impossible moment, then pounded his front hooves down on the water in fury.

Instead of a splash, the water flowed aside, meekly returning to its smooth self.

"Take that!" Not that he had the least idea what had just happened. Regardless, Bannan grinned and slapped Scourge's still-curved neck.

They continued forward as far as they dared, Scourge stopping on his own at the limit of flat rock.

Bannan shook his boots free of the stirrups. Understanding, the woman let go of his waist. If he looked straight down he'd see nothing but untrustworthy water, so he didn't. He worked his way forward over the saddle. All he had was the rein, a woefully short ten feet, and the strength of his hands and arms.

Scourge swung his head around, jaws agape.

Once those jaws took hold of something, nothing could pry it loose. Usually, this involved a bloody trophy Bannan preferred his mount not brandish in front of his men, Scourge's true nature being difficult to explain at the best of times.

Now, he gladly offered one end of the rein, relieved when Scourge snapped his teeth over it.

Still hopeless, he warned himself. The rein wouldn't reach. The man wouldn't be able to grab it. The thin strap would slip through wet hands. The current would tear him away.

Arms tightened around his waist as he sat back. She wasn't giving up.

Nor would he.

It wasn't long before the clump of branches and man turned lazily into the rapids. Caught instantly by the fast current, the clump bounced and snapped. The entire mass broke apart!

Somehow, battered by water and stone, the man clung to a piece that stayed above water. The river pushed him away and Bannan tensed. The girl cried out, her hand outstretched. He couldn't make out the words but, as if the man in the river could, he began to kick and struggle toward them.

Closer . . . closer.

Now or not at all!

Bannan lunged forward, throwing his end of the rein as far as he could. Scourge stretched his neck and head, holding the other. The pitiful length of leather snapped out.

And a hand snatched it from the air.

Having sacrificed his grip on the branch, the man immediately sank beneath the river.

But the rein stayed taut.

Bannan leaned deep in the saddle; in answer, Scourge began to back away, step by step.

Somehow, the rein stayed taut.

What gave this man the strength to hang on? Fear could do that, Bannan told himself. Turn fingers to iron.

Or was it exceptional will?

The head came up, gasped for air. The current rolled him under again.

The instant the man reached the safety of the shallows, Bannan felt the woman drop from behind him. Scourge stopped. She steadied herself against his shoulder and neck as she splashed forward, following the rein to its end. Once there, she pulled the man's head and shoulders out of the water. When he sputtered and coughed, the woman looked up at Bannan and smiled.

As Bannan looked down, he saw two truths.

Her smile was the most joyful thing he'd ever seen.

And the man in her arms?

Was no more a man, than Scourge was a horse.

They'd used him as a plaything, flexed their might on the river's foul water, lingered in the girl's world for no higher purpose than amusement.

How they loathed him, his kind. Wisp shivered in the girl's arms, barely conscious. He'd earned their spite. This penance of the sei settled nothing, accomplished nothing. It left him alive to remind the rest. This is what defeat looks like. This is failure's cost.

See what happens.

They hadn't meant to kill him; they hadn't cared how fragile his body'd become. He'd have welcomed death, if it meant peace.

How weary he was of it all.

The girl's arms tightened around him, her body the only warmth he could feel.

Duty had kept his head above water. Duty had reached for the strap. Had held on.

Wisp opened his fingers and let the leather float away.

Everything went dark.

SEVEN

UNDER OTHER CIRCUMSTANCES, the dramatic appearance of a stranger, especially astride a huge horse ugly enough to pull a tinker's wagon, would have claimed all Jenn's attention. Now? She vaguely knew he'd dismounted to stand by her in the trout pool, that he wanted something, but she had to hold Wisp. He'd be swept away otherwise.

The stranger pointed to shore.

Of course. Jenn nodded and tried to move, but Wisp, though not much bigger, was limp and far too heavy. Thankfully, the stranger saw her difficulty. He lifted Wisp from her and heaved him over one shoulder. Jenn struggled to her feet, her clothes sodden with water, and tried to help. Instead, she slipped and would have fallen, but the stranger had her arm. He waited, supporting them both, until she was steady again.

Meanwhile the horse splashed close and stood with unusual patience. Jenn leaned on his flank; the best she could do was keep out of the way. The stranger eased Wisp up and over his horse's neck, then stepped into the stirrup and mounted behind. He reached for her.

She shook her head. The waterfall roared like a cheated bear; the river could come alive again and attack. Three would be too many, even for such a big, well-muscled animal. Instead, she grabbed the stirrup leather and held on, smiling reassurance at the stranger. The shore was in reach. After all this, they couldn't fail. Wisp would be safe.

He had to be.

The stranger frowned, but didn't delay to argue.

They were no longer alone; others waited on shore. The horse arched its neck, as if intending to protest their presence, but the stranger soothed the animal, kept him moving forward at a pace Jenn could match.

Life could be measured in such steps, counted by effort, summed by will. She didn't know why walking out of the river was so much harder, but Jenn didn't stop. She couldn't.

When her father rushed to her, when Peggs was there and more, when faces she knew and loved surrounded her and the stranger and his ugly horse . . .

. . . only then did she dare believe Wisp would be safe.

Bannan Larmensu, man of no home, would enter the village of Marrowdell a hero. Explaining this to Tir would take some doing, and doubtless involve an incredulous stare or two, but for the moment, he rode the happiness of the villagers. For the woman, it appeared, was a favorite.

The man lying limp over Scourge's withers, something the horse acknowledged with an unsettled twitch every so often? He was something else again.

They'd thrown a blanket over his naked, shivering flesh, but the villagers didn't know him. That was plain.

The woman did.

But did she know what he was? There was the rub. His family's talent, to see the truth of a thing, had never put him in this position before. To know a liar, yes. To know Scourge was special, of course. But now, when Bannan looked at the man lying limp in front of him, he saw beneath the blanket, the chilled skin, the gooseflesh. He saw . . .

What?

Shadows. Blurred images. Nothing stayed sharp, nothing stayed until he could understand it. But there was another shape beneath the man. A shape more real than the seeming under his hands. That, he knew beyond doubt.

As he knew he'd stay here, in Marrowdell, until he understood.

Going up the path to the road proved easier than the plunge down. Now that they weren't about to fall forward to their deaths, Scourge placed each hoof with such ponderous care it was a wonder the villagers behind them had patience to wait.

The man was limp. Unconscious, he believed. There were fresh wounds on the body: deep cuts and abrasions leaked blood, and bruises bloomed beneath the skin. The river journey hadn't been kind. Despite Scourge's care and Bannan's hold, there'd be more bruises from this rescue, but there was no gentler way to get him to safety.

Not that this man was used to gentle, Bannan thought grimly. The river damage was nothing, compared to the rest. The body in front of him had war carved in it.

Another mystery added to the shape. How had he survived such injuries? No healer of Rhoth or Ansnor could have put a body this broken back together.

Scourge gave the final heave up to the road, stepping into sunlight. As if he'd never thrown his rider, run off, or disobeyed, he moved forward a few smooth steps then came to a careful halt at Bannan's command. He was relieved, though in truth it wasn't the first time the war mount had carried wounded from battle. The fat pony and gelding, reins in the hands of the boy, lifted their heads but didn't try to bolt.

Bannan waited for the villagers to climb the path. First came a tall, dark-haired woman, followed by a man with his arm around the shoulders of the woman from the river. Concern and a shared shape to the mouth and eyes of all three said family. A sister, likely the father. Horst was on their heels, followed by a giant in a smith's apron.

Horst wasted no time. "Is he dead?"

"No!" The woman from the river pulled free.

"Your swimmer will be fine," Bannan assured her. "Unconscious. His wounds need tending."

"We'll take him to the mill," the father ordered. "Davi, your cart?"

The smith shrugged. "It'd take too long. You—" a nod at Bannan, "—can get him there before I could catch up my team."

Horst pressed his lips together. Bannan didn't need to be told his opinion. He wasn't welcome in Marrowdell and neither was his burden.

"Would you? Please?" The woman laid her hand on Scourge's neck, a familiarity the normally testy creature accepted without a flinch. Blood stained her blouse and skirt, none of it hers despite the torn sleeves and scratches on her arms. Her eyes were the rare blue that darkened with emotion; as she gazed up at him, their color was almost purple. Younger than he'd thought by her pinned hair and mature demeanor, with round, pretty cheeks and a strong but delicate chin.

Younger and with a mouth he wished would smile for him.

"A pleasure." For a wonder, his voice sounded normal. "Where's the mill?"

The question appeared to startle her. Had she never been asked directions before? "That's the way to the village," she told him, pointing down the road. "You'll see the mill." Her hand left Scourge's neck to hover over the motionless form of the man. As if she longed to touch him, but dared not.

"I'd better go," Bannan said. She nodded and backed away.

The rein had tumbled over the waterfall. No matter. Scourge was well used to answering to legs and weight. When, Bannan reminded himself, he felt like it. At the moment he did, moving ahead when asked, stepping with fluid grace along the dirt road.

Trees lined it. Larger than he'd expect this near a settlement, where wood would be in demand. Old. Now that he had time to pay attention, he frowned and craned his head, staring as they passed. Old and . . . odd.

The cliffs towering to either side of the narrow gap weren't quite right either. Unlike those he'd passed on the Northward Road, these were riven by deep fissures from top to base, all running east to west. Again, odd. If he didn't know better, Bannan thought uneasily, he'd swear the stone had been raked by giant claws.

Scourge walked on, as if nothing was out of the ordinary.

Until they passed beyond the trees, and the great steed snorted and stopped, tossing his head as if startled.

Bannan gently urged him forward, startled himself.

The valley spread before him, a feast for the eyes. Closest, a trim little village, its gardens and orchards fenced by tall hedges, its buildings surrounded by flowers the like of which he hadn't seen since Vorkoun. The river, here tame and lovely, ran alongside a tall mill. It meandered from the west, drawing a serpentine line through wide fields of lush, waving gold. To either side, the torn cliffs, like scarred arms defending a treasure.

"Marrowdell," he whispered. The ordinary, made extraordinary.

The road forded the river, then ran through magnificent hills of smooth ivory stone, forested at their base. More of the trees that weren't quite right. Not only that . . .

. . . for an instant, the landscape took on a different shape, the sky another, nameless hue. The road became silver and liquid and took him by the heart. He had to race along it, meet what lay in the distance . . .

"Come no closer!"

Bannan blinked, finding himself on the russet road again. He brought his gaze back to the village and the people gathered before its open gate. People who weren't smiling.

Ah, yes. They were hardly a sight to engender confidence. Blood from the injured man—who likely appeared a corpse—ran down Scourge and soaked his own shirt. He lifted empty hands for the second time this day. "We need a healer." Scourge, seeing his way blocked, began to rumble in threat. Idiot beast. Bannan dug a toe into his hide, then gave those waiting his best smile. "Horst sent us."

At the name, the small crowd parted at once and everyone urged him through, hands gesturing. He kept smiling and hoped they'd keep their distance from Scourge's hooves.

And let him travel their silver road sooner than later.

The stranger's horse took such giant strides Jenn fell behind at once, too worn to run alongside. She eyed the pony wistfully as it passed, but Cheffy was too excited to notice. He drummed his heels constantly, which didn't affect the pony's plodding pace one bit. He'd had his adventure and wanted his pasture.

Without the old pony and Cheffy's warning, Wisp would have died. It didn't bear thinking about. Apples and pie, Jenn vowed. As soon as she could.

Her father and sister caught up to her, along with big Davi Treff. "You're sure you aren't hurt?" The kindly smith looked ready to sweep her up in his big arms and carry her home.

"I'm sure. The blood—it's not mine." The stains on her clothes were from Wisp. She'd never seen anyone hurt like that; the worst had been when Tadd Emms had cracked his head on ice and he'd spent two days in bed nursing a lump like an egg. She wasn't hurt, but she wasn't right. Jenn stumbled and Peggs put an arm around her shoulders.

"Horst!" Radd called before she could protest. "A ride for Jenn, if you please."

At the summons, Horst swung his gelding around and came back to offer his hand. "Jenn?" Like Davi, he looked concerned. Concerned and kind and familiar.

Were those feelings real? Was he?

Horst wasn't the family friend she'd known all her life; he couldn't be, not until she'd heard the story of her mother's death from his lips, not until she understood him. Jenn threw a desperate glance at Peggs, who, though doubtless having the same thoughts, could only shrug.

"Thank you." She accepted Horst's hand and stirrup, but avoided a direct look into his face. Once she was settled, Horst urged the gelding to catch up to the stranger—something the horse protested with pinned back ears and a jolting trot. At least it wasn't far to the village.

The village with Wisp in it.

Wisp who was—for the first time, the reality of it sank home—who was now a man.

The stranger's horse stood outside the mill, given respectful distance by the others. Jenn rushed through the big open doors and took the stairs to the loft, Horst behind her. Her father kept a pallet bed in one corner, to use during the long nights of milling. Surely they'd take Wisp there.

Yes! His still form was lying on the pallet, Covie Ropps by his side. None better, Jenn told herself. Not when it came to stitching wounds or making poultices. Given the tendency of her children, grown and young, to scrape knees and bump heads, Covie'd had plenty of practice. Not to mention the cows.

Wisp wasn't a child or cow. Jenn didn't know what he was. But if Wisp as a man could be hurt, surely he could be healed.

Riss Nahamm held a basin and steaming kettle at the ready. With no open flame permitted in the mill, she'd have brought the water from her kitchen. Dusom Uhthoff and Zehr Emms waited at a short distance, their attention divided between the stranger on the bed and the one who stood in the sunlight by the open gantry door, his idle hand on one of the ropes used to hoist the heavy bags of grain, his gaze over the village and the valley.

Jenn hesitated as Horst went past her to the other villagers. Much as she longed to rush to Wisp's side, the older women didn't need her crowding them, nor would they understand her interest. Worse, what if he awoke, saw her, and . . . what would he say?

What should she?

All consequences she wished she'd thought about, before wishing at all.

Jenn let herself be drawn to the stranger instead, who surely deserved more than to be left waiting. His clothes were as blood-soaked as hers. And as wet, from the growing puddle around his boots.

Another advantage to bare feet.

"I haven't—" Jenn began when she reached him. He turned and she lost whatever else she'd planned to say.

He was younger than she'd thought. His face had fooled her, set and stern during their crisis, and weathered save for pale skin where he'd recently shaved a beard. In tinker fashion, his hair fell loose to his broad shoulders, unlike the men of the village who kept theirs neatly trimmed to the collar. Dark wavy hair, with pine needles stuck in it. Hers likely held the same.

Dark hair and darker eyes. No, his eyes were like apple butter, dark brown with a warm amber glow in their depths, a glow that grew more pronounced as he returned her scrutiny.

Despite the settler shirt, homespun pants, and leather jerkin, this was no farmer. She could attest to the strength of his lean body, his quickness, his courage. The farmers she knew were strong and could be quick, if need be. She didn't know if they were brave—she thought so.

But the man in front of her, he was different.

Roche Morrill had injured a fish hawk with an arrow; he'd claimed to be shooting at a goose, but she'd never believed it. His stepmother, Covie, had nursed it to health. The stranger reminded her of that hawk, wary by nature.

"—haven't thanked you," she finished.

"No need. You are most welcome." A wide smile transformed his face and sparkled in his eyes. For the first time she noticed the subtle lilt he gave some words when he spoke. Different from the voices she knew. So were tinkers', who rarely paused when they spoke and used a breathless "na" to indicate a question. That was confusing. This, she quite liked. "Though I believe it's our friend over there who owes us." A half bow. "My name is Bannan Larmensu. And yours, brave lady?"

She'd never been called a lady before. Or brave. Or, for that matter, encountered anyone who hadn't known her name since she was little. "I'm Jenn," she offered almost timidly. "Jenn Nalynn. This is my father's mill."

"Greetings, Jenn Nalynn. You don't get many visitors, do you?" Bannan observed, his smile fading. When she looked a question, he nodded to where Horst stood talking with the other men in urgent, low voices.

"In Marrowdell? No. The tinkers and our aunt from Avyo. Years ago, a couple from Endshere who knew Anten thought they'd settle here but only stayed a night. You're—" the most handsome stranger she'd ever met? Not something to admit, not when she planned to travel the wide world. Jenn temporized, "You're the first visitor who's rescued someone."

His gaze touched Wisp, then came back to her. "The others don't know him." He lowered his voice. "You do."

Jenn nodded. "He's my friend. My best friend."

"Are you why he almost drowned?"

"I—" Her protest died in her throat. "In a way," she admitted miserably.

"Ah." With a wealth of meaning to the sound. "A lover's quarrel."

Jenn scowled. "No. It's not—" like that? Or was it?

"It's not?" For some reason, this brought back Bannan's smile. "Don't worry. Whatever happened, you saved his life. Your friend will thank you."

She hoped so.

He glanced past her. "My turn for introductions." He nodded a greeting to the three approaching, his expression turning bland.

Horst. Jenn stiffened. She couldn't help it and knew Bannan noticed.

"Surely I'll get supper," he said lightly.

Supper?

He meant to stay the night. Which was good, wasn't it? Bannan Larmensu, being awake and interesting, would take attention from Wisp. She'd have time to think. To plan. Not to mention eat. She'd missed breakfast and lunch. "Of course you'll get supper," Jenn found herself saying. "Has someone looked after your—" she hesitated. She'd seen the teeth snap over the rein; what he rode didn't belong with their livestock.

"Horse," he supplied, as if daring her to say otherwise. "No need, thank you. I'll take care of him. Scourge is shy with strangers."

Shy? "As you wish," she murmured, tensing as the three villagers stopped in front of them. She realized he couldn't know their names either and introduced them as Aunt Sybb had taught her, gesturing to each in turn. "Bannan Larmensu, this is Dusom Uhthoff, Zehr Emms, and—"

"We've met," Horst interrupted harshly. He looked like a stranger himself, Jenn thought, the lines of his face hard and grim. "Quite the coincidence, your arriving in time to help this other stranger."

Bannan crossed his arms and leaned nonchalantly against a sun-touched beam. "Oh, you can thank my horse for that."

"Your horse?" Horst's eyebrow lifted.

Bannan nodded. "Dumped me at your road, then ran this way. I assume for good reason."

"Your horse," Dusom echoed. Jenn could tell he thought Bannan had landed on his head.

"A creature of rare perception. Just as well, or that fellow wouldn't be breathing."

"Or me." Jenn pushed forward. Perhaps an exaggeration, but she wasn't about to stand by and let them twist what had been the bravest, most selfless act she'd ever seen. "Bannan saved me too. You should be grateful he was here."

Zehr looked embarrassed. "We are, Jenn. We are. But Horst watches the road and . . ."

"And you should heed his concerns," Bannan finished for him, abruptly serious. He straightened and brought his right hand to his chest, touching forefinger to thumb to circle his heart. "Hearts of my Ancestors be witness, I swear I mean no harm to you or yours." He lowered his hand. "Permit me to bring my wagon and companion to Marrowdell. Let me prove I'm what I said, a settler in search of a peaceful home. If you aren't satisfied, we'll be gone in the morning."

"You didn't—" Zehr bit off the rest, giving Horst an annoyed stare.

Dusom looked intrigued. "A new settler? Your companion too?"

"Only me. Tir's convinced I'm mad to try farming." Zehr chuckled at this; Horst scowled. "But he's the kind of friend who couldn't see me travel alone."

"The good kind," Dusom nodded.

"Yes."

Jenn took an easier breath. She wasn't sure what to make of Horst's animosity, but the others were now more interested than concerned. Just then, Peggs, Aunt Sybb, and her father appeared at the top of the stairs; Peggs spotted her and waved. Relief flooded her from head to toe.

Until she saw the flood of people following behind.

The curious must have waited for the miller before coming inside to see for themselves. Gallie Emms, with tiny Loee on one hip. Anten with Cheffy, whose younger sister Alyssa stared at him with admiration. Hettie Ropp, who rushed to Peggs, her cheeks flushed with excitement. The Morrill brothers: Roche glowering at Bannan, Devins at Wisp. Kydd behind them, but not Wainn, who stayed away from crowds. And a crowd it became as the entire Treff household, less Wen, arrived at the top of the stairs with big Davi behind, last but not least.

Lorra and Fran had donned feathered black hats for the occasion. From the flash of chagrin on Aunt Sybb's face, the powerful ladies of Marrowdell had scored a significant social victory.

In short order, the spacious loft was full of people, people who fell silent, people looking at her.

Jenn didn't realize she'd reached for Bannan's hand until his fingers closed warm around hers. "Quite the welcome," he commented.

Aunt Sybb had paused with the rest, probably taken aback by their blood-soaked clothing, but recovered first. She walked briskly toward them. Radd and Peggs joined her, as did, for some reason,

Hettie and Kydd. The rest waited where they were. A dignified but firm nod moved Horst, Zehr, and Dusom from her aunt's path. She stopped in front of Jenn and Bannan and waited.

Hurriedly letting go of Bannan's hand, Jenn performed the introduction. "Bannan Larmensu, this is my aunt, Sybb Mahavar. Of Avyo," she added loudly, to make up for the hats.

Bannan gave a deeper bow than any Jenn had seen, one leg back, almost sweeping the floor with the fingertips of his right hand, his left over his heart. "Bannan Marerrym Larmensu, dear lady. A pleasure."

"Ah! A modern gentleman." Aunt Sybb actually dimpled. "Please excuse Marrowdell's manners," she told him. "I'm sure you wish to freshen after your adventure." To Jenn, "Bring your young man along, dear." To them both. "A wash and clean clothes. Then a meal. I won't take no for an answer." To Bannan, "We're so very happy to meet you at last. I confess, I had no idea you'd be so personable."

Bewildered, Jenn looked at Peggs who mouthed what looked like "toad."

Toad?

Jenn's confusion cleared. Aunt Sybb thought Bannan was Wisp.

Meanwhile, having no idea what was going on, Bannan took it in stride. He bowed again, not so deeply, with that wide smile. "You honor me, dear lady."

"Lucky man." Zehr grinned. "Peggs Nalynn is the best cook in Marrowdell. And our beauty."

Hettie giggled, Peggs turned a lovely pink, while at this vindication of her assurance of manners, or rather the lack thereof, in the village, Aunt Sybb gave a delicate sigh.

"But first." Bannan looked at Horst. "My companion?"

"There's another one?" Aunt Sybb's eyebrows rose.

No wonder, Jenn thought, losing track herself suddenly. Bannan hadn't meant Wisp. A third stranger was coming, making this a day Marrowdell's residents would remember and discuss far too long. No point going halfway, she told herself. "He's welcome too."

"Hold on—" Horst said roughly. "We can't allow—"

"Nalynn vouches for our guests," Radd interrupted in a no-nonsense voice, staring at Horst until the other man gave a short unhappy nod. "Then it's—"

A shriek rang out. Everyone turned as a masked man appeared at the top of the stairs, a blackened ax high in each fist. He gave another shrieking shout and launched himself up and onto the floor, crouching like a maddened bear about to attack.

Jenn gawked with the rest.

"I see my companion's arrived," Bannan said mildly, drawing his share of startled looks. "Tir," this with exasperation, "what are you doing?"

Unabashed, the man lowered his weapons and straightened. He put the ax handles through loops in his wide belt, then gave a short bow, hands wide and empty. "Apparently saving you from lovely farm maids, sir." Above the metal mask, his eyes shone bold and merry. He bowed again, this time at Hettie Ropp. "I advise surrender, faced with so fair a foe."

Hettie, for once speechless, pressed her hands to her throat and appeared short of breath. Peggs elbowed her in the side.

Aunt Sybb rose to the occasion. "I expect you both," she told Bannan, "at our table."

"Not so fast, Sybb." Frann Nall pressed forward. "We want to know what happened. Who's the man from the river?" She pointed dramatically to the corner with the pallet and the rest of the villagers shifted to give Aunt Sybb a clear view.

"More?" This time, her aunt looked thoroughly shaken. "Jenn?"

"I can explain—" Jenn stopped there. Not like this. Not in front of everyone, family, friends, and strangers. Her hand found itself wrapped in Bannan's again.

"That's Wyll, Aunt Sybb," Peggs announced. She had the audacity to wink at her sister. "You remember Wyll," she continued briskly. "He was coming to visit. Poor man was attacked by bandits. Did you encounter such terrible foes on your travels?" This with the full brunt of her earnest, gorgeous eyes on Tir. Jenn bit her lip to keep from smiling. Peggs could make any man blush with that look. And the number of times she'd talked them both out of trouble?

"Indeed, dear lady," Tir affirmed, a rosy tinge to his ears and bald head. "Some tried our camp last night. Dangerous, they are. Your friend's lucky to escape with his life."

"Not luck. Bannan pulled him from the river just in time," Jenn added. "And me."

"He did, did he?" For the first time, Bannan's companion looked directly at her. Whatever he'd planned to say stayed behind his mask. His eyes seemed to see right through her.

Jenn realized her hand was still in Bannan's and she pulled it free, blushing furiously.

"A wash, change of clothes, and something hot," Aunt Sybb pronounced, taking charge again. She wheeled with an elegant lift of her hand to collect everyone she expected to follow, and the rest of Marrowdell parted to let them through without a murmur.

Jenn looked longingly at Wisp, lying so still. Peggs leaned close, "Go," she whispered. "I've helped Covie before. I'll talk to her, find out how he's doing. Meet you at home."

Could there be a better sister? "Oh, Peggs . . ."

"Thank me by helping with lunch." Peggs gave her a quick, one-armed hug. "I want to know everything that happened."

From the questions filling the eyes of everyone she passed, Peggs wasn't the only one.

The reprieve would be short indeed.

Vouched for by Jenn's father or not, they'd yet to be trusted. Their wagon was tucked against Horst's homestead and their ox blissfully led to pasture at the farthest end of the village. All in good time, Bannan thought contentedly, and availed himself of soap and a bucket of cold water before changing into cleaner clothes. Done, he dropped his blood-soaked shirt into the suds to be scrubbed later and ran fingers through his still-damp hair. His cheeks felt rough and his boots needed more than a brush on the grass, but he was as impatient as any in Marrowdell to get answers. Besides, he smiled to himself. The Nalynns' formidable lady expected them at her table. Best be prompt.

He laid his hand on the side of the wagon. The sum of his possessions was inside, tightly wrapped and secured, a gamble on the future wider and higher than he'd ever made on the next turn of a nillystone. A future here? He studied his surroundings with heightened interest.

Horst's home was crudely built, of whole logs the size of which he hadn't seen in years. Despite being shaped by simple ax, the resulting walls were strong and snug, their cracks well caulked. The broad, deep-set windows had glass panes, small but of good quality. No curtains—someone like Horst would want to see out at all times. Doubtless he watched now.

Bannan resisted the impulse to salute.

The village gates were of split cedar, the fencing of tall sturdy hedge. Not a defensive barrier, but adequate to keep wandering livestock from the orchard and vegetables. By all accounts, apples didn't thrive this far north, but the grove to his right, nestled under the riven cliff, boasted fruit-laden trees every bit as healthy and lush as his cousin's in Vorkoun.

Like the apples, the gardens weren't what he expected here. Plots occupied most open space between the buildings, themselves filled with neat rows of exuberant plants. Perhaps the towering crags held warmth. Perhaps someone here was an exceptional gardener.

Perhaps the ground—like the road, the river, and the man—wasn't what it seemed. His pulse quickened at the prospect of so many puzzles.

Scourge, also not what he seemed, lurked somewhere beyond the gate; an old and familiar puzzle, suddenly reshaped. Why had he wanted to come here?

Unlike those in Weken or Endshere, Marrowdell's villagers hadn't offered stable or pasture. How did they know of Scourge? Could—unsettling thought—there be others of his kind here? If so, why had

Scourge seemed startled by the village, as if expecting something else?

Yes, he was going to enjoy this place.

Tir was waiting when Bannan came around the wagon, his forehead creased in a fierce scowl. He moved in the way, stepped close. "Not so fast. Sir."

"Not hungry?" Bannan inquired mildly.

"Ancestors Provoked and Tormented. Bandits with pitchforks." Tir poked Bannan's chest with a blunt forefinger. "Blood on your saddle." Poke. "A farm village. Where there would be pitchforks," the finger for this wagged emphatically, then poked. "Not a soul in sight. Why, sir? Because everyone's in the mill. The mill outside which yon beast is pacing, still saddled. The saddle with blood on it."

Laughing, Bannan deflected the next poke and rubbed the now-sore spot on his chest. "Granted. You had every reason to storm the defenseless mill. Now stop fretting," he grinned. "You didn't scare anyone." Though he'd add the unusual composure of the villagers to his burgeoning list of questions. "Be glad you arrived in time for lunch." No need to ask how Tir had known to take the road to Marrowdell. To a tracker of his skill, the only surprise was that he hadn't commented on Bannan's tumble.

"And how did you fall off, sir?"

So much for that mercy. "Scourge spooked. Don't ask me why."

"To rid himself of a fool," Tir retorted, not ready to budge. The scowl above the mask was real. He'd been truly worried.

Bannan clapped the other's leather-clad shoulder. "No luck yet." Or all the luck in the world, he added to himself. If he'd been an instant later, the not-man in the river would surely have drowned. Scourge had known, somehow. Had known and cared, which was more peculiar. "Now. Lunch?"

His point made, Tir relaxed and a twinkle appeared in his eye. "What's the hurry: lunch or lady?" he inquired as they began walking.

Bannan nodded a greeting to the young men by the mill door. The taller nodded back; the other glowered. Fair enough. "You appeared quite taken by one."

"Taken and caught aren't the same. Sir."

A cautionary "Sir."

Her hand had filled his like a tiny bird, full of life, with utter trust. Bannan cleared his throat. "A fair place, this Marrowdell."

"Seen worse." Between the mask and the shade cast by his farmer hat, it was impossible to read Tir's expression, but Bannan heard a smile in his voice.

They continued in silence, boots making little sound on the packed earth of the path. The village road could easily take a large wagon; it sent a short curved spur to the mill, then split around what looked to be a fountain at the village heart before continuing through the common pasture. The road wove past a total of eight homes, all like Horst's in shape and size, themselves joined by narrower footpaths separated by gardens or, in some cases, waist-high hedges. Three barns, of good size. The Nalynns lived next to the mill, up a small rise to the left, overlooking the river.

Where they lived . . . Bannan stopped in his tracks and clapped Tir on the shoulder again. "Fair? Tell me you've seen better."

The cheerful little house boasted a wide friendly porch, filled with seats and cushions, surrounded by tidy flowerbeds. A stack of elegant though well-used luggage stood waiting at one end, likely that of the lady from Avyo. Windows gleamed between carved shutters, framed by lacy white curtains. The door stood open, inviting visitors as well as sunlight. A colorful rug beckoned.

Above all, the roses. Huge red blooms, with a blush of orange at petal tip, leaves dark green and glossy, framed the house and nodded over the chimney.

Suddenly every bloom turned to stare back. As if measuring him, as if they protected some treasure. "Tir—" Bannan began uneasily.

A breeze passed and the roses nodded mindlessly in every direction, flowers again.

He closed his mouth.

"Haven't smelled better, that's for sure." Tir closed his eyes in bliss. "Told you. It's all about the cooking."

No, Bannan thought to himself. It was, for whatever reason, all about Jenn Nalynn.

Peggs was in her glory. The larder door had been unlocked and thrown open; she kept Jenn and Hettie, extra hands and feet, on the run for ingredients. Every pot, pan, and bowl in the Nalynn kitchen was in use. More arrived through the kitchen door, filled with offerings from curious neighbors who, duty done, lingered almost out of the way and almost out of earshot.

Aunt Sybb may have envisioned a cozy midday meal for the new arrivals, something gracious and peaceful, but Marrowdell had other ideas. Jenn had been in the loft, hastily scrubbed, barely dry, and fumbling with the ribbons of her second-best dress when the excited murmur of voices had drawn her to the window to see the first trestle table being set up behind the Nalynn house. With more being carried up the path.

Peggs brandished a large spoon. "Eggs!"

"I'll go." Jenn poked a tendril of damp hair back into the ornate braid; there'd been no time to redo it. She'd thrown an old apron over her dress and put away her shoes. With this many to deal with, what did it matter what she wore? She grabbed the empty basket, then knelt to collect a handful of pebbles from their jar.

Hettie squeezed by with a tray of cups, continuing her conversation without pause. "—only saying they make our own lads seem a bit, well, uninteresting."

"Novelty doesn't last," Peggs proclaimed, sounding as stuffy as Aunt Sybb. Which would have worked better if she hadn't been craning her neck at every chance to see if Kydd had arrived.

Her friend chuckled. "I'd gladly give it a whirl. That warrior, Tir? I'm sure he knows a few pleasuring tricks worth learning."

"'Tir?'" Jenn echoed in disbelief.

"What? You'd warm to the other one?" Hettie's sunny face clouded. "Not me. Oh, he's prettier, I'll warrant, but that Bannan's eyes go right through a body, Jenn Nalynn. You'd best hope they find no secrets."

"We've fine men in Marrowdell," Peggs asserted, a little too forcefully.

Hettie put down her tray, her smile returning. "And which one's put that gleam in your eye? Come now, I'll have the truth—"

"I'll get the eggs," Jenn said hastily and ducked out the door, avoiding her sister's pleading look. High time Peggs admitted her affection for the beekeeper. Hettie was right in one thing.

Secrets, she thought grimly, weren't good things to own.

Squinting in the bright sunshine, Jenn wove her way through the maze of people, tables, and blankets. The tables were thick slabs of rough wood supported by barrels at each end; the blankets were spread on the ground between for seating. Two chairs had pride of place at the end of one table. These were occupied by Frann Nall and Lorra Treff, their hats giving them a regal air despite the pink of their cheeks. Jenn had made sure Aunt Sybb's chair was waiting at the head of the other table, placed where the sun wouldn't shine in her eyes.

The tapping of last year's remaining cider casks encouraged a distinct party atmosphere in advance of the main guests. Cheffy, no worse for his adventure, chased his little sister through the forest of legs. Tiny Loee chortled and bounced in place, her chubby hands locked on a table edge. Beneath the same table, the house toad waited for something to drop, never averse to a treat.

It was going to be, Jenn decided, a very long afternoon.

Bannan Larmensu and Tir—the newness of the names made her tingle—were in the parlor, sharing what peace remained with Aunt Sybb, their father, Horst, and Dusom. Peace and the contents of a dusty bottle Old Jupp had brought with him when he'd wheezed through the door. Whatever it was, it had created quite a stir.

Wisp lay, injured and unconscious, in the mill. Oh, in no danger. Battered and bruised, was the sum of it. Peggs said Covie had grown strangely evasive after that. As if there was something else, something she wouldn't say.

While she hunted eggs.

If Jenn's greetings to her curious, cheerful neighbors were a little terse, she felt she should be forgiven. The most exciting day of her life would doubtless contain more cooking, followed by endless hours of dish washing. At least she'd been able to nibble when Peggs wasn't looking and, given the excitement, Aunt Sybb had postponed her departure by a day. Perhaps two.

Given the cause of the excitement, Horst had pronounced himself satisfied to remain in the village as long as she required, where he could keep an eye on the strangers.

"Jenn." Roche Morrill peeled out of his conversation with Davi and fell in step with her. "We need to talk."

No, they didn't. Convincing him being impossible, Jenn sighed to herself. "What about?" At the hedge, she squatted awkwardly to protect her dress, and reached, finding the burrow at her first try. Aunt Sybb loved a hard-boiled egg with her tea and professed Marrowdell's better than any in Avyo. Just as well, Jenn reminded herself, she hadn't noticed the lack of chickens.

Roche crouched beside her, annoyingly near, green eyes aglitter. Recently, he'd taken to wearing his hunter clothes all the time, the dark leather vest with its pockets and stains, dark leather pants. Knee-high boots, rubbed black with grease for waterproofing. She supposed he'd start carrying his bow next, for all that it was old and twice-repaired. Anything to be different. Anything to be difficult.

As now. "You know what," he said in an annoyingly reasonable tone. "That stranger."

"Which one?" Ah. Her fingers touched something smooth and warm. "There are three." She pulled out a brown egg.

"The one with the ugly mount. The one who grabbed your hand."

"Scourge isn't ugly." Jenn retrieved another egg and put it in her basket. She kept her voice down, trying to contain her temper. "And I grabbed his, not that it's any of your business, Roche Morrill."

"You should be more careful," Roche said, cold and quiet, stark amid the laughter and excitement around them. "It doesn't look right, you and a stranger. People are talking."

When she'd been a child and Roche picked a fight, something he'd always done despite being eleven years older, she'd push him into the nearest puddle or snowbank, hardly something Aunt Sybb would approve of now.

Being adult had such disadvantages.

"People always talk," Jenn told him with as much dignity as possible. She put her back to him and went after more eggs. She found four, which emptied the nest, and carefully replaced each with a pebble, adding one of the rare white ones for good measure. Something in the civil exchange kept the toads laying, which was certainly good for the villagers.

Roche hadn't left. She could feel his eyes on her.

As she started to rise to her feet, he clamped his hand around her wrist and pulled, almost making her drop the basket. "Listen—"

"No." Jenn tugged free and glared back. "You've nothing to say to me."

"There you are, Jenn." Kydd Uhthoff smiled pleasantly, appearing not to notice either Roche's tension or Jenn's embarrassment. "Your sister's looking for you."

"We're not done," Roche said, his eyes never leaving Jenn's.

The older man's voice became a knife. "Yes, you are."

For a heartbeat, for no reason, Jenn wasn't sure what was about to happen.

Roche turned with a jerk and stomped away, in his haste—or on purpose—bumping Wainn with his shoulder as he passed.

"I don't know what gets into him," Jenn muttered, grateful Wainn looked more startled than offended.

Kydd's troubled gaze followed Roche. "Neither does he." A shrug dismissed Roche and his tempers. The beekeeper smiled down at her. "You've had quite the morning."

He had, Jenn decided, a very nice smile. Not so old after all. She tentatively smiled back. "It's a blur," she admitted.

"This doesn't help." A nod to the busy crowd.

"It's all right. Peggs needs me. She's making the lunch." As if he didn't know.

"A feast, without doubt." Kydd gazed toward the kitchen. "I suppose she'll be in there all afternoon." He looked wistful.

Jenn took a guess. "My sister didn't send you after me, did she?"

A not-old smile, and now a shy admission, "I haven't been able to get near the kitchen." This with such transparent woe Jenn fought to keep from smiling in triumph. So. She'd been right. The interest went both ways, as did the inability to admit it to one another.

Hadn't Aunt Sybb suggested family assistance? Jenn thrust the egg basket at Kydd, who accepted it with a puzzled look. "Peggs needs these," she explained. "Desperately."

His eyes lit, answering every question. "You don't mind?"

In no sense, Jenn thought to herself, feeling her own glow. She made the little shooing motion their aunt used to such effect. "Go. I've another errand to run. Tell her I'll—" No point continuing. Kydd was gone, his long legs making short work of the distance, the humble basket clutched to his chest with both hands as he stepped around those sitting on blankets.

She smiled. No telling what would become of lunch now.

Before anyone else could accost her, Jenn nipped behind the privy. She hung her apron on the hedge, smoothed her dress, and patted her hair.

Then she looked toward the mill.

Finally.

He awoke and lay without moving, taking shallow breaths, and hoping in vain the pressure on his body came from the walls of his sanctuary and the memory of the river had been a dream.

Voices came and went. Soft, whispers. Voices like hers. He refused to understand the words. Sometimes he was touched and the violation made him want to tremble, but he would not. To react to them was to believe what he'd become.

And he would not.

There was pain. He'd felt pain for so long he didn't remember being free of it. Sometimes, he was touched and the pain tried to fade. He clung to it, afraid to forget himself. He would not.

Like the voices, darkness came and went. He lay along its edge, preferred it. Time passed, clocked by breaths he had to take.

"Wisp."

Air warmed by the word moved across his flesh and defined it beyond all denial. Ear. Cheek. Jaw. Eyelid. Something chill escaped the eyelid and ran down the cheek. Tear.

"Dear Wisp. I'm so sorry."

More words, more breath. Defining lips. Nose. Chin. Stirring hair. "I never meant to hurt you."

She was making him and he could not refuse.

He could not.

Wisp trembled and took a deeper breath, one that hurt ribs and back and stomach. He moved his free hand and found fingers, thumb, palm and wrist. Shifted, and found legs and feet.

"Wisp!" So full of joy it gave him blood and heart and skin, though still a whisper. "Wait. I can't call you that here. Wyll. That's your name. Wyll."

Neither was, but it didn't matter. He must answer to whatever she named him, no matter what he was.

Wyll opened his eyes and found Jenn Nalynn.

EIGHT

HIS EYES WERE SILVER.

Silver with bronze flecks.

A shock, those eyes, open, staring at her from what was otherwise a plain, ordinary face, pleasant enough. It might be any young man's, save for the eyes.

A blink, and the eyes were a plain, ordinary brown.

Like the glimpses she'd catch in the meadow. How quickly he'd hide himself again. More than anything else, this convinced Jenn who lay on the pallet. "Oh, Wi—Wyll. You're all right."

His mouth moved before words came out, then motion and sound caught one another. "What have you done?"

The question from the meadow.

She looked over her shoulder. Covie'd been grateful to have her take a turn watching her sleeping patient, especially once told of the party developing behind the Nalynns. She'd wanted to collect more supplies—and check on her children—but she'd be back soon. Riss sat by the window, a hoop of fine work on her lap; she'd greeted Jenn with a peaceful smile, then gone back to her needle and thread.

A needle and thread that weren't moving. She'd nodded off in the warm sun. Good.

Jenn rose from her knees and took the barrel seat Covie had used. She folded her hands together and sat very properly, her aunt's voice in her head. Dignity avoids disaster. Good posture conveys confidence.

He waited for her to settle, his head on the folded blanket they'd given him as a pillow. His face was bruised along the right side; the eye encircled in swollen purpled flesh. A beard, russet brown and neat, covered his chin. His brows and lashes were darker and thick, his hair lighter, its brown streaked with red. Hair that would hang to his shoulders, like Bannan's, but straighter.

He'd been air and sunshine. Whispers and tickles. This . . . he was too real. She didn't dare touch him, didn't know what to do.

All the while, he watched her, as unmoving as the millwheel.

Finally, faintly, Jenn found words. "I wished you could be—like me."

"A wish did this?"

She grimaced. "A wish with a little help." What had Aunt Sybb called it? "Pagan magic. There was a book . . ."

"I see." Now that his voice worked, it sounded ordinary. Pleasant. A bit like Dusom's, for that matter. "You wished this upon me without my permission. Was that fair?"

Her eyes dropped to her folded hands; her fingertips pressed until the skin beneath turned white. "I did ask." Hadn't she?

"Dearest Heart." The familiar endearment shouldn't sound the same, from this mouth. It shouldn't—should it?—have the same tolerant note of much-abused patience. "You remade me at your whim, not mine. Tell me, please, why I lie here. Like this."

Only the truth would do. "I wanted you to be part of my life. Not just in the meadow—to come with me wherever I went. To leave Marrowdell and see the rest of world with me." How much did he know about people? How much could he know? Her cheeks flamed, but she forced herself to finish. "I didn't want anyone else. I love you."

"How blind the mighty," he said, making no sense at all, then made a peculiar rasping sound. She looked up as the rasp became a low chuckle, the kind that invited anyone who heard it to smile. "And how this—" He lifted the hand that was above the blanket and gestured downward. "—must disappoint."

"I don't understand."

"You will." His eyes closed. "Go home. Stay home."

Jenn stood, but hesitated. "Will you be all right?"

"Is that also your wish?"

"Of course!"

"Then I will." As if they played in the meadow, and she'd asked a silly question on purpose. "Let me rest, Dearest Heart, and learn what you've made of me. Go."

And there was nothing else she could do.

Jenn didn't go far. She went down. Down to the main floor of the mill, then, knowing the last thing she wanted was to see anyone else, down the narrower stairs to the basement.

It was cool here, cool and quiet and alone. Light filtered through gaps in the riverside wall. Water gurgled on the other side and she followed the sound across the dirt floor to the wheel within its dry raceway. She eased around it, the stone lining chill underfoot, to where small pieces of wood jammed between the wall slats made a crude ladder. She climbed above the wheel to the ledge made by the beams supporting the second floor and roof, and walked around to her window.

Not that it was hers. She just liked it. Her father took down the shutters for the warm months and no one else came up here. Jenn sat on the thick windowsill, dangled her feet over the riverbank, and sighed.

"I say 'I love you,'" she explained to the bluebirds perched on the eave by her ear. "He's supposed to say it back."

All the stories said so.

Maybe Wisp was more honest. She loved Wisp; did she love Wyll? They were the same—but they weren't. A man lay on the pallet. A man she'd met today.

Uninterested in her loves, the birds dove away and down, swooping to the water and up again. "'Patience is rewarded more richly than haste,'" Jenn informed them haughtily. Aunt Sybb's sayings were quite reassuring.

She wished she'd paid closer attention. She wished, most of all, that Aunt Sybb wasn't about to leave. If ever she'd needed her wisdom, it was now. "What am I to do?"

Whatever Wyll looked like, he'd shared all the years of her life. He'd always been there, to play, to listen, to protect. He was as close as anyone in her family, wasn't he? He was family. Aunt Sybb always said family should look after one another. "I should be taking care of him," Jenn decided.

And she was, wasn't she? First, she'd helped save him from the river. Now . . . her chin firmed. Now she would help him be happy with what he was, and where he was. He needed rest, that was all. Rest and time. There was no rush to leave before the harvest, so long as they were away before the snows threatened the road.

Besides. She loved the harvest. The tinkers were old friends, especially Mistress Sand, whose pockets would bulge with toys she'd made over the winter for the village children and who always remembered her birthday, and Master Riverstone, whose piping made everyone want to dance. She thought of them as Mistress and Master, since the two were in charge of the others, but in truth, all the tinkers preferred plain names as they did plain clothes. They'd helped celebrate Covie's wedding to Anten Ropp, it being the custom to have as many as possible bear witness for the Ancestors, though they hadn't dressed up like the rest. It wasn't their way.

When Jenn had been very little, she'd believed the week's excitement—the heavy wagons of grain passing through the village, the cheerful tinkers, the busy mill, the evenings of feasting, song, and laughter—was a celebration for her, since the last and best day was most often her birthday, or close to it. The minor disappointment of learning in Master Dusom's class that the harvest happened when it did simply because the tinkers insisted the grain be gathered and milled by the fall equinox, which they called the Balance, and then being teased relentlessly on the subject by Roche Morrill until she'd rubbed snow in his ears, had been eased by knowing she'd been born on such an auspicious day. She'd kept track since then.

This year, her birthday would be the equinox again, seventeen days from now. It wouldn't be the same, of course, without Aunt Sybb. Or without the tinkers. The sunset on the day of Balance held special significance for them, not that they'd say what, and meant they would leave Marrowdell while the sun remained in the sky. The village would still dance that night, but without Master Riverstone and the tinkers' music, it wouldn't be as good a dance.

Still, Jenn felt a tingle of anticipation. This year would be the most special birthday of all. Usually she looked forward to the party and, of course, to presents, it being the custom for each household to give one. In Marrowdell, such gifts were most often something received the year before by someone in that family. There was a lovely purple scarf that she might get this year from the Ropps, since Hettie'd received it last year from the Treffs and knew how much she liked it.

This year, though, presents didn't matter. This was her being adult birthday. Jenn was sure it would be the best ever.

Because she'd have Wyll to share it. She hoped he liked to dance as much as she did.

So. After the harvest and her birthday. They'd need a wagon. From this vantage point, she could see Bannan's, tucked beside Horst's home. It wasn't as big as Aunt Sybb's coach, who preferred to ride inside, but big enough for two. A wagon like that would be perfect.

Thinking of Bannan, Jenn drew up one knee and leaned against the side of the window. Her lips curved in a smile. They'd have moved outside for lunch by now. He'd be surrounded by eager villagers, he and his companion. She imagined what he might say about her. How brave she'd been. How determined.

She toyed with the ribbons of her second-best dress. The skirt was sky blue, with little white birds embroidered along the hem; the bodice, also white, had a strip of delicate Avyo lace from one of their mother's dresses around the neckline. The ribbons were the best part. They were bright yellow, like sunshine.

Would he think it pretty?

Something moved in the distance, under the old trees beyond the hedge and gate. Bannan's great horse. Instead of grazing, he walked onto the road and stood in the sun.

Then looked up at her.

Whatever he was, Scourge wasn't a horse. Not like Horst's gelding or Davi's team. His head reminded her of the animals who pulled the tinkers' wagons, though he was taller at the shoulder and leaner. To be sure, Master Riverstone called their powerful beasts "horses," and it was only polite not to argue, but every child in Marrowdell was carefully taught the difference. Offered an apple, a tinker's horse would take little fingers instead.

"What are you?" she mused aloud.

A voice softer than feathers warmed her ear. "Forgotten."

She leaned forward, hands on either side of the window. "You can hear me? You can talk?"

Scourge flicked his tail and moved back under the trees.

She hadn't imagined the voice. It came as a breeze, like Wisp's, but wasn't the same. This voice had been deeper, with a strange roughness. Like something unused for a long time. Iron, left to rust.

He was Bannan's. Why talk to her?

She'd grown up knowing Night's Edge was her place, that Wisp wasn't something to share with other children like a new rope or puppet. She'd thought him her secret, that only Peggs understood. She'd thought, Jenn squirmed inwardly, she'd thought herself special.

Apparently not. Here was proof.

Had Bannan needed a mount and wished his invisible friend into one? She grinned. It would explain Scourge's grim disposition.

Nothing else moved, other than birds, the river, and a cloud shaped like a melon that floated from one crag to the other. Jenn didn't move either, too tired to do more than slowly swing one foot in the air. She rested her head against the window frame and made a list. Wisp was Wyll and safe. Peggs had Kydd in her kitchen. Aunt Sybb finally had someone to entertain in Marrowdell who appreciated fine manners. Maybe she'd feel up to staying a few extra days. Roche—well, he'd always been annoying. She'd been called a lady.

A satisfying sum, all told.

Or was it?

Jenn looked toward the solitary house between the mill and the road. Simple on the outside. Simpler inside. The string of yellowed bear's teeth draped over the mantle was the only ornament. There was a workbench covered in fletching tools under the window; bags of feathers hung from the rafter. A single fireplace sufficed, open on two sides. No bake oven or stove. When Uncle Horst wanted to eat something other than what he could toss in a pot, he went elsewhere and was welcome.

Nothing soft. No rugs or cushions. A bed, its straw mattress covered by an old woolen blanket. A chair, positioned to look at the door. A rack on one wall, where he kept the paired swords that so entranced children, the one long and curved, the other straight and the length of Jenn's arm from elbow to fingertip. His other belongings were in the chest at the foot of his bed, as if he lived ready to leave at an instant's notice. The sparse home of a confirmed bachelor.

But Uncle Horst—she mustn't think of him like that—Horst hadn't come to Marrowdell to make any home at all. He'd come to take Melusine back to Avyo and stayed, according to her aunt, because he'd made Melusine a promise. Because of guilt.

Or had he nowhere else to go, without his prize? She rubbed her bare forearms, suddenly chilled. Would he have been punished for failure?

Regardless of why he'd stayed, Horst was as much a part of Marrowdell as anyone here, his life woven through theirs. Suppers and winter evenings with the Nalynns. Clothing from the Treffs. Cheese and milk from the Ropps. He'd taught the Emms' twins to ride on his horse. Helped Riss with the heavy work around Old Jupp's place. Took the wettest, coldest nights for his turn tending the charcoal pits. In the ice-cold of midwinter, he'd head north on the road toward the barrens, to return with packhorses laden with hides and meat.

He'd made her a hat of soft white fur. Told them stories by the fire of the great herds of elk that wintered in the valleys, of the wolf packs that hunted them, of the people from the barrens, belonging to no domain or prince, who sang like birds and never stayed in one place. Nothing of Avyo. Only of now.

It was like Wisp and Wyll, Jenn thought with a pang. The Horst she knew and the one she didn't.

"Thought I'd find you here."

Shaking her head in disgust, she twisted on the sill to glare at Roche. "Because this is where I come to avoid you."

He stepped from the ladder to the ledge and leaned his back against the wall, thumbs hooked through his belt. "Because you like the road." He tipped his head to the view beyond her, a lock of hair dropping over one eye. "I understand that. It's the only way out of here. For either of us."

He blocked the only way down from her perch, short of pushing him off. She resisted a childish urge to stick out her tongue. "Why would you want to leave?" All Roche did, as far she could tell, was to hunt as often as possible to avoid his share of work at his stepfather's dairy. That, and bother her.

"Do you think I want to stay in this crotch of a village?" He spat at the wheel, missed, and shrugged. "You were born here, Jenn Nalynn. You don't know what it was like, being taken from your friends, from your home. No one asked children. Father dragged us with him and put our names on settler's binds, then left us here to rot."

His father had died, not left. To a bitter boy, Jenn thought, what was the difference? To a baron's son, how great had been their fall? "You've never said anything about this before."

"You've never—" He stopped and thumped the back of his head against the wall, as if she tried all patience. "Heart's Blood."

"I've never what?"

His eyes burned through her. "Had a way to leave. I saw you with the stranger. I could tell what he wanted. A smile like yours, it goes to the heart of a man. You've only to lift your skirt to own him." His breath came faster. "He'd take you with him. Who wouldn't? But it doesn't have to be like that—"

How dare he?! Shadows dimmed the sunbeams coming through the wall. A cold wind slapped Jenn's hair against her cheek and fluttered the ties on her dress, a cold wind that smelled of ash. She welcomed how it drained the heat from her face.

When it reached Roche, he paled and swallowed but didn't, or couldn't, stop. "Jenn, listen to me. By the bind, I can't go south of Weken, but there's an old farmer in Endshere wanting to take in a couple as help. I've talked to him. If we work hard, last him out, he might leave it to us. Or I could apprentice to a trade there. You could work in the inn."

His dreams, spilling out of control, snares to trap her. She didn't blame him. How could she? She hadn't asked Wisp, not properly, if he minded being in hers.

Wainn had been right.

The sun came out again, the wind died, and Jenn caught a whiff of roses. "Take me home, Roche." She held out her hand in graceful request. "I've deserted Peggs too long."

His fingers, callused and strong, clamped over hers. "Didn't you hear what I said?"

"I heard." She struggled for something to say that would be kind—and final. "Roche—"

"We can leave now," he urged, taking her other hand, pulling her to her feet. "The stranger's horse could carry us both. We'd be in Endshere and married before anyone's the wiser." His eyes traveled hungrily over her face. "Allin Emms will sulk for months."

Was that what she was? A prize in their squabbling? They'd loved to outdo one another as boys; she should have realized that hadn't ceased with beards and deeper voices. Feeling as though she tumbled down a hill, Jenn had to ask, "And your brother?"

"Fool can't speak his mind. He doesn't deserve you." Roche jerked her hard against him, shifted his grip to her shoulders. "He can't please you," the words thick in his mouth. "Not like I can."

What was he thinking? Or was he? This was hardly the way to entice her to leave Marrowdell with him—an offer she might have considered a few days ago. No, she realized, turning her face so his clumsy kiss slid wet along her jaw. She wouldn't have considered Roche had he come on bended knee with all the grace of his noble father.

When he groped at her ribbons, she took advantage to quickly slip past him on the narrow ledge to reach the ladder. Before the fool could grab for her again and knock them both to the stones below, likely breaking legs if not heads, she suggested breathlessly, "You catch the horse. I've things to pack."

As Jenn climbed the ladder to the raceway, then hurried to the stairs and up, she felt a twinge of conscience. Scourge wasn't to be toyed with, that she knew.

Hearing Roche panting close behind took the twinge away.

Bannan untied the thong around the oiled leather wallet and unrolled it. He pulled out his settler's bind with its officious rustle of seals and waited for the reaction of those around him in the Nalynns' overcrowded parlor. In Weken, it had been avarice or pity, depending on whether there was profit to be made from him, both concealed behind some lie.

Dusom and Radd leaned close to run their eyes over the document, but didn't offer to touch it. They exchanged grim looks as they straightened.

"You'd think something would have changed," Dusom commented.

Radd glanced at his sister. "Same prince." He looked straight at Bannan, the oddest combination of hope and relief on his face. "That you've taken the bind says all we need to know, Bannan Larmensu. You've committed yourself to a future in a new land. I won't say it will be easy, because it won't. I can say it's yours to make and you've found those willing to help, if you wish to stay in Marrowdell."

The truth and a hand, freely offered, from someone who had such a wallet. They all did, here, each and every one. He'd been looking for such a place, without knowing it, and something tight and dark eased inside as he retied the fastening. Bannan found himself unable to do more than nod gratefully as he took Radd's hand in a firm grip.

"Not so fast. You could have stolen that," Horst challenged

harshly. "Even if it is yours, everyone knows a royal easement can be had for the right price." He turned to Radd. "We can't trust him. I say he's another motive for coming here."

"One like yours?" Bannan guessed. Horst tensed; the others looked unaccountably shocked. Interesting. He tucked yet another puzzle away for later. "I'm sure you understand," he went on smoothly, "what it's like to be a retired soldier looking for a peaceful home." As he'd hoped, that produced relieved nods and a few smiles.

Except from Horst. "Don't think to look here," he warned. "We've no room—"

"Nonsense." The woman's hat threatened the rafters of the Nalynns' parlor as she worked her way in front of the others, nothing loath to use her elbows. She must have been listening from the kitchen; there was no other open space left.

From her chair, Sybb gave a gracious nod. "Bannan Larmensu, may I present Lorra—"

"Treff. Lorra Treff." The woman glared at Horst. "I say we've room to spare. There's the farm up the road."

The road. Silver and liquid and . . . Bannan's heart hammered in his chest.

Horst's eyebrows shot up. "You can't be serious, Lorra."

"I most certainly am. Cynd tried to start a garden, but there's no point without someone living there. The vermin steal any crop. As for the rest? A shameful waste, if you ask me. Why not give the place to this fine young soldier?"

Nods from most of those standing around, though a couple of faces were thoughtful.

"It's a ruin," Horst snapped.

"If there's property available, I'd like to see for myself." Bannan tried to contain his eagerness. "I'm not afraid of work."

Tir coughed behind his mask.

One of the thoughtful was Radd Nalynn. He nodded and Horst made a sharp gesture of dissent. The two locked gazes; Horst looked away first.

"I'll take you," Radd promised. "First thing tomorrow."

He wanted to go now. That urgent desire being totally inappropriate and likely to cost him any chance of living here in these people's good graces, Bannan forced himself to relax. The farm and road weren't going to disappear. "Thank you."

The elderly man who'd brought the very fine, very old brandy—Wagler Jupp—lowered his ear trumpet and thumped his cane on the floor, barely missing someone's foot. "Anyone against the allotment, speak up. No? Settled. The farm's yours if you can keep it, young man." Another thump. "Where's lunch?"

Sybb rose from her seat before Lorra could speak, taking command of the room. "If our guests are ready?"

Bannan smiled. "We defer to our most gracious hostess."

A dimple. "I'll make you wait no longer." A slight turn of her elegant wrist indicated the open door behind him. "We mustn't waste what remains of Marrowdell's lovely summer."

He offered his arm and was rewarded with a charming smile. "My eldest niece is an accomplished cook," Sybb confided as she nestled frail fingers in the crook of his elbow. "You'll enjoy your meal. Although I trust you're prepared to be the center of attention. Novelty's rare here."

Bannan covered her fingers with his own, feeling a warmth that wasn't the brandy. "A pearl such as your good self would be rare in any domain, dear lady." In Vorkoun's halls he'd never enjoyed playing the courtier; with her, he did, very much.

"Most kind." They went out on the porch.

He nodded at the luggage. "I trust you aren't leaving soon."

"I may linger." Her eyes twinkled. "Marrowdell's become much more interesting with your arrival." They stepped to the turf, the rest following like some processional. "These are good people," she assured him quietly. "A little crude, at times, but they have overcome great adversity and loss. But so have you." The faintest hint of a question, exquisitely polite. The kind of question not to ignore.

Was he fit to be near her beloved nieces?

They walked around the house, and Bannan saw what had to be the rest of the village assembled and waiting. He bent his head near

Sybb Mahavar's. "Ancestors Witness, no dishonor sent me on this path."

The fingers lightly pressed his arm. "Welcome to Marrowdell, Bannan Larmensu." A wave toward the throng. She smiled, eyes sparkling, at his look of mock dismay.

Then he was in their midst.

It was, of all things, a summer picnic. The last time he'd sat to eat on a bright blanket, children laughing, blue sky overhead, he'd been a child himself. Lunch being served took precedence over curiosity and, seeing the abundance on the plank tables, Bannan didn't hesitate to join in and fill his plate. A feast indeed.

He traded greetings, absorbed names, and kept watch for Jenn Nalynn. Those around him had been banished because of their heritage, but he was hard-pressed to find Naalish traits among these people. Perhaps the tighter curls of those with dark hair, or the slight sallow cast to otherwise well-weathered skin, but such could be found throughout Rhoth.

The largest family was the Ropps, responsible for the cheese, butter, and cream. Their eldest daughter, Hettie, had freckles and an infectious grin, not to mention strong arms from the cheese press. She walked around with a ewer of milk, somehow managing to be near Tir more often than not.

Who was doing his best to repair the villagers' first impression of him, Bannan noticed. When Sybb offered her chair to the elderly Jupp, Tir had hurried to fetch her another from the house, blushing at her murmured thanks. He tolerated the youngest Ropps, the boy Cheffy and his sister, though they sat almost in his lap and stared, eyes wide, as he deftly tipped his mask to eat or drink. Though he'd left his axes in the wagon—at Bannan's insistence—the big smith, Davi, had brought one of his own making to compare and the two fell into a deep discussion about strops and oils. The children wandered off to chase butterflies.

A succession of villagers came to exchange pleasantries with Bannan as the meal progressed. To each, he freely offered his version of events: Cheffy's alarm, the fortunate timing, how anyone would do the same. Of greater interest was the news that he'd taken the settler's bind and meant to farm. Though it went carefully unsaid, he gained the impression new blood was rare here indeed.

Little wonder, given Horst watched the road.

For his part, Bannan studied the connections among the villagers as diligently as he'd ever pored over a map of new terrain. Davi's wife, Cynd—who'd brought a ham—was sister to Anten Ropp, linking those families. Anten's wife Covie, tending the man from the river, had two sons by an earlier marriage. The oldest, Roche, was elsewhere. He was introduced to the other, Devins Morrill, the man who'd nodded a greeting to him in front of the mill. Devins proved painfully shy until conversation turned to his stepfather's dairy cows. Bannan found himself with an invitation to inspect the new calves. The abandoned farm had a stout barn. Grazing for a cow, should he wish to trade his ox. The road? Nothing unusual about it. It was called the Tinkers Road. No one took it past the empty farm. Why would they? It was the tinkers'.

More and more interesting.

Desserts and fruit took the place of meat and cheese. He snagged a second thick piece of fresh baked bread before those baskets were whisked away, a delight after months of camp fare. Jugs of chilled cider made the rounds, along with pots of tea.

He received other invitations. Supper with Zehr and Gallie Emms, who had fine sausages. A tour of the forge from Davi, of the kiln by his formidable mother quickly followed by Frann Nall's insistence he see her loom. Cynd Treff, the calm rock of that family, promising turnips for his larder. They'd extra.

Should he stay.

Bannan found it a recurring theme. Other would-be settlers had come, he learned, and left before, as Davi put it, mud could dry on their boots. The villagers were friendly and willing, even eager. They had, however, entirely reasonable doubt.

None more than Horst, who didn't eat or drink with the rest. Instead, he took up station against the corner of the house where he could see Bannan and Tir at all times. The others let him be. Confident, perhaps, that the solitary soldier would protect them. Or was it habit? He had the impression Horst stayed on the outskirts at the best of times.

Let him. Stuffed, Bannan got to his feet, empty plate in hand. He'd noticed others taking theirs to the kitchen door and went to do the same, hoping to find Jenn at last, but Hettie spotted him and took it. "There's another pie coming fresh from the oven. I'll bring you a slice," she promised and rushed away in a swirl of braids and bright skirt.

More? He'd have to let out his belt.

"Hello."

Bannan turned to the voice, turned and froze in place. Standing before him, at the edge of the crowd but not part of it, was a most extraordinary man. "Hello," he managed.

They were close in height and he guessed age, though there was a rare youthfulness to the other's face. The straight nose and high cheekbones echoed those of the village scholar, Dusom Uhthoff, but his eyes . . . They shone, as if everything before them was wonderful and new. No. He shone, because everything within him was exactly that. Bannan found himself reaching out.

The man smiled and met his hand in a warm grip. "You can see me," he said with great delight and laughed.

"I can indeed." Bannan laughed with him. He couldn't help it. "I'm Bannan. Who are you?"

"This is Wainn." The man who spoke stepped close and put a fond hand on Wainn's shoulder. "I'm his uncle. Kydd Uhthoff." Similar features, but in the older man, sharper, more inquisitive. Another, like Horst, who didn't take him at face value. Unlike Horst, Kydd smiled pleasantly. "Welcome to Marrowdell, Bannan Larmensu."

Wainn looked at his uncle. "He can see me."

"He can?" Kydd gazed at Bannan with greater interest. "And what do you see?"

He didn't hesitate. "Joy."

The uncle's other hand shot out to grip Bannan's shoulder, grip and hold. Something warmed his eyes and his voice fell to a whisper. "Then twice welcome, truthseer."

Whatever showed on Bannan's face made Kydd smile. He gave his nephew a tiny push. "Check on the hives for me, will you, Wainn? In the excitement, I can't recall if I left some of the combs pulled out."

"I'd like to leave," he admitted. "There are too many here." He smiled at Bannan. "Except for you."

Honored, Bannan inclined his head. His eyes followed Wainn then went back to Kydd's face. The interest was real. The curiosity brimming.

The potential loyalty, as true as he'd seen in any of his former company.

Bannan smiled back.

"He can see me."

So much for her attempt to sneak home unnoticed. Not that she was sneaking, exactly. Jenn hefted the full water buckets, proof she'd had a reason to be gone for a while, if not for as long as she had. That Horst had filled the cistern behind their home to the brim yesterday was of no matter. After the lunch expanded to include all Marrowdell, there'd be dishes. Dishes needed water. Water she was bringing—she blinked at Wainn, registering what he'd said. "Who can see you?"

"The truthseer."

Not helpful. Wainn reached for one of the buckets, which was. "Have they started to leave yet?" Jenn asked hopefully, looking ahead. Someone stood by the house, but from here she couldn't see the area with tables.

"There are more pies."

Meaning no. Jenn slowed as she walked beside Wainn, taking her time up the path. "I'm surprised there's any left."

"Peggs will make more." With the calm assurance that all would be right with his world so long as this were so.

Jenn reminded herself it was her sister's own fault.

The cheerful murmuring grew louder with each step; low voices and high, laughter and words. They blended into a dull roar, like a distant waterfall.

Had no one left?

Wainn stopped. "There are too many," he apologized, giving back the bucket.

"Everyone wants to meet the visitors." And hear what happened. Such goings on! They'd be comparing notes all winter, Jenn thought dourly. Bannan would have told his story by now, several times over. They'd have to wait for her side of it. "Sure you don't want to come with me and meet them?"

"I did. He can see me." This with a smile of delight.

"So you said." The buckets were heavy, but Jenn hesitated. "I can see you, too," she ventured.

Wainn gave her his father's look, the one Dusom reserved for a student who'd completely missed his point. "You see what you expect, Jenn Nalynn. He sees me."

Patience, she told herself. "Who?"

"The truthseer. Bannan. He's looking for you." Then, to top it off, "I'm glad he's going to stay."

Finding herself gaping like one of Wen's fish, Jenn closed her mouth. Before she could sort any of this out, the figure by the house noticed them and started toward her. She knew his walk.

Horst.

Her heart sank.

"I'll leave now," Wainn told her, eyes somber. "You need to ask your questions."

"Wait—" She found herself pleading with his back as he strode off to the orchard, leaving her with the buckets and Horst.

"Here, Jenn. Let me take those." The man stepped close with a smile, then stopped, losing it. Something changed in his eyes as he looked into hers. "What's wrong?" The words were quiet; the demand was not.

She wanted to say it. Wanted to tell him she knew. About him. About Melusine. Demand to know the rest . . .

She couldn't.

Instead, Jenn blurted the first thing she could think to say, "Roche's gone to steal Bannan's horse."

Whatever Horst had braced himself to hear, it wasn't this. "Why would he do a fool thing like that?"

"He thinks—he thinks I'm leaving with him." It wasn't hard to seem embarrassed when she so thoroughly was. "I had to say I would. It was the only way he'd let me . . ." The terrible look on his face stopped the rest in her throat.

"Go to your father." Horst whirled and walked away with stiff unnatural strides, faster and faster.

"Uncle!" Jenn dropped the buckets, splashing water on her skirt. She caught up to him. "Wait!"

"Leave this to me, girl."

Leave what to him? What was Horst planning to do? She wanted to take his sleeve, but dared not. "Let me find Bannan. He can handle Scourge."

"I'm not worried about his beast. Go home." A sideways glare that froze her blood. "Go!"

She had no choice. Jenn started back, glancing over her shoulder every few steps. She saw Horst go into his home. Saw him come out with quiver and bow in his hands. Not the bow he used for teaching or practice. His prized hunting bow. The one that brought down elk.

She saw him go through the gate.

The Horst she knew could never harm Roche. Not for this.

The Horst who'd chased her mother to her death . . . would he?

Jenn broke into a run, this time for help.

"I'd rather the rest not know." A test, of sorts, though Bannan had reached his own conclusions. This was someone he'd trust at his back. Someone he'd gladly call friend, given any chance at all. "Not yet anyway."

"Too late," Kydd chuckled. "Some already do. Others will see it, if not understand what it is about you. Marrowdell welcomes the perceptive."

The promised pies arrived, a distraction that brought a surge of villagers to the tables. Including Tir, after an assessing glance toward Bannan and Kydd.

"Your man's careful of you."

"Tir's convinced I couldn't survive without him. Many's the time he's been right—but don't tell him I said so."

"Ah, yes. I—" Kydd's eyes trailed the lovely dark-haired woman who'd brought the pies. She looked up as if she'd felt his regard. With a shy smile, she went back into the house.

"I take it that's Peggs Nalynn, the accomplished cook," Bannan observed, straight-faced. "Is she spoken for?"

"Yes!" At Bannan's grin, Kydd looked sheepish. "No. Not yet. But a man can hope."

Could he?

Bannan tucked the unfamiliar notion away. "The empty farm. Surely it's promised to someone here." The fields would be harvested by the village as a whole, but there was another, distinct generation milling around the pies. Kydd himself, should he catch Peggs' eye, might need a home of his own.

"It's too close to the Bone Hills for any of us," Kydd said matter-of-factly. "You might manage, though."

Intrigued, Bannan was about to press for an explanation when Horst straightened from his post. Not to get pie; to leave.

At a guess, he'd gone to check on the man from the river.

If those of Marrowdell were perceptive, as Kydd claimed, had any of them seen what he had—the other shape beneath the flesh? "I wonder when the interesting fellow in the mill will stir," Bannan said as idly as he could. "I'd like to hear his tale."

"You find him interesting." Kydd raised an eyebrow. "Should we worry?" Not an ordinary question. Not when asked of a truthseer. Like Sybb, his instincts were to protect.

"He's survived more than most." The rest—the rest was like the road. Bannan found he couldn't share it. Not yet. Maybe not ever. As if Marrowdell offered its secrets to him alone. To deflect Kydd's attention, he went on, "I daresay Jenn Nalynn knows more. He's her friend, after all."

"What?" The color drained from Kydd's face. "What did you say?"

Heart's Blood. No one knew? "I must have misheard," Bannan hedged, well aware of the peril of betraying a lady's secrets. His dear sister gave a wicked pinch. When she could catch him. "A mistake—"

"Those with your gift don't make mistakes." He might have stirred a hive of Kydd's bees. "Why would you think she knows this man? How could she? Jenn's never left Marrowdell!"

"And I've just arrived," Bannan pointed out.

"Of course. My apologies." The man composed himself at once, giving the hint of a bow. "Our Jenn has a good heart, you understand, but she's a free spirit. It's not possible to keep her where it's safe."

Considering where he met her, Bannan wasn't surprised. "Here's your chance to ask," he observed with pleasure as Jenn Nalynn, as if summoned by her name, came around the house.

Instead of joining the gathering, she flattened herself against the wall where no one else could see her. She was barefoot, her hair falling from its knot and the hem of her dress soaking wet. Their eyes met, roses bent to stare at him, and she waved a desperate summons.

Bannan moved at once, Kydd with him. Tir's head lifted and he signaled him to wait as he was. If both new arrivals left, the villagers were sure to be alarmed.

As they weren't, he noted, by roses that moved.

Jenn stepped from the wall to meet them. Her eyes, huge and purple in a too-pale face, locked on Bannan's. "You must come with me," she urged, hands clenched together. "It's your horse."

No, it wasn't. Or was something more. He went stone cold, thinking of Horst's abrupt departure, thinking of the stranger in the mill. "What's wrong?" He kept his voice down.

"What's he done?" Kydd demanded, all trace of the affable beekeeper gone.

So. He wasn't the only one to suspect a greater problem than a stray horse though, to be fair, Scourge was capable of being an immense problem on his own.

"Nothing, if we hurry! Please." She turned and ran off toward the gate, tanned legs flashing.

The men followed, Bannan for his part regretting his enthusiasm for lunch.

A chill breeze swirled around them, nudged them from behind, raced ahead. It tore the head from a rose and spread petals on the road. The road that shrank until they were at the village gate faster than they should have been.

Than they could have been.

Bannan grabbed Kydd's shoulder. "What just happened?"

The other's eyes were full of wonder. "I—I don't know."

The road from the village. He'd taken it this morning, hoping for something new. Something different. Joy bubbled in his chest.

Marrowdell was both.

The sun burnished the dirt to red gold, framed by towering trees that should have been maple or oak, but somehow weren't. Jenn stood with her hand on the gatepost, staring down the road. The nearest trees tilted their tops the same direction. Leaves shuddered loose but didn't reach the ground. They hung in the air, as if surprised by the wrong season, then drifted back to their branches.

A nut fell to the road and bounced. A squirrel chattered in triumph.

"We don't cut the old trees," Kydd informed him quietly.

Bannan nodded in mute appreciation.

Not finding what she sought, Jenn sighed and glanced back at them. The trees stood straight again, simply trees. "We're too late," she said. "They could be anywhere." She gestured at the ragged wall to the side of the road. The slashes Bannan had noted met the ground as narrow ravines. He could see up the nearest. It was floored with rubble, choked by thick dark vegetation, and rose at an angle that would vex a goat.

Scourge would love it. Especially if there were rabbits.

"Jenn." Kydd laid a tender hand on her arm. "Please. Tell us what's going on."

"Horst's gone after Roche," she said miserably. "With his—with his bow."

The same hand gripped tight and pulled her to face him, not gently. Bannan took an involuntary step, then stopped. He didn't know enough to interfere.

"What did Roche do?"

Had he not heard such terrible surmise in a voice before, too many times? There were few innocents left in the border marches; those on both sides had been guilty of slaking more than bloodlust. Feeling sick, he looked closely at Jenn.

"What did he do?!" Kydd roared.

"Not what you fear," he interjected, relieved. It was there, the truth, written in her face. Misery and worry, yes. Nothing worse. Nothing . . . shattered. The other man's eyes shot to his and he replied, "I'm sure," to their unspoken demand.

Misery, worry, and now indignation. Jenn tugged free. "If you'd let me speak," she protested, "I'd tell you."

"Please," Kydd said tightly.

"Roche wanted to take me from Marrowdell." She glanced at Bannan. "On your horse."

Which Scourge would love more than rabbits. He grinned, remembering the many harmless stable hands the four-footed menace had laid flat. A would-be horse thief? "I hope your friend bounces," he said without sympathy.

The beekeeper remained tense. "When you left me, Roche followed you, didn't he?"

"Yes. He found me in the mill. Accused me of—" her cheeks flamed. "He made me angry, so I said I'd leave Marrowdell with him. To get rid of him, not because I ever would!" She waited for Kydd to nod. "Roche went to get the horse and I came home. He can't catch Scourge. I thought," this with some asperity, "he'd spend the rest of the day tromping through the brush."

She trusted Scourge to ignore a harmless fool. She might be right at that, Bannan decided cheerfully. Though he'd lead the fool on a chase he'd never forget.

"But Horst found out." Kydd stared over Jenn's head at the empty road. "He's gone after him."

"The man's grim," Bannan observed, still amused. "He's hardly going to kill the lad for being smitten." His smile faded at the dread on Jenn's face. It was real.

Kydd looked equally shaken. "We'd better find him first."

Jenn wasn't sure which was worse, the way Kydd covertly studied her as they walked, as if Roche's botched kiss had left drool on her face, or how, unlike Bannan, he'd immediately believed Horst capable of murder.

No, she was sure.

Kydd knew what Horst was. He knew about Melusine and Horst's promise. Of course he did. He'd been there. Wainn and Devins, Peggs and Hettie, the twins—all had been children, Roche barely more. But Kydd? At sixteen, he'd have been included in the hunt for her missing mother, been told the truth, been part of the secret. How could she have thought otherwise?

Because, Jenn told herself, everyone had lied to her. Not in words, but their lack.

All at once, it didn't feel like summer anymore. The road was cold underfoot. Long, thin shadows pinned the old trees to the dirt. She'd always looked forward to fall, with its blaze of colors, and loved its nippy air. She'd watch for the tinkers' wagons from the oak's branch, shout when she saw them coming. The hum and clatter of the millwheel would be music on nights aglitter with frost and stars.

This wasn't the same. This change was small and mean and troublesome, like the first deluge of spring, when larders were almost empty and even Davi's draft horses mired in the half-frozen mud.

Bannan whistled between his teeth, short and soft. "For Scourge," he explained. "Better safe than not."

"Horst would never loose an arrow unless sure," Kydd said.

"They've history." Bannan didn't elaborate.

Another worry, then. When he was sure, Horst never missed. Jenn walked faster.

Horst and one other. Of those who'd gone to him to learn the bow, Roche had taken it most to heart. The "*whisss*-thunk" of arrow tip into wood had gone on for years, leaving scars on the windowless side of the Morrill home. He no longer missed the straw targets; this winter, he was to join Horst in his hunt.

She was still angry at Roche. She'd love to push him in the commons pond with Satin and Filigree and Himself—after hugging him with relief. Which might confuse him.

No hug.

As for Horst . . . Roche was the closest thing to a son he had. How could he turn on him like this? Why?

They reached the path to the trout pool with no sign of horse or men. Bannan whistled again, this time with a small frown.

They'd be missed shortly, if not already. Just as well Kydd had come along. She cringed to think anyone else might believe the same as Roche, that she'd—that she'd try to convince Bannan to take her with him.

Though he wasn't leaving, according to Wainn. Bannan claimed to be a settler. Be that as it may, she thought. Surely there were better choices than here.

"You must be sorry you took our road," Jenn said abruptly.

Bannan had been focused on the brush to either side. He blinked at her, then gave a slow smile. "It's been interesting. And not your fault," this with emphasis. "I blame Scourge."

He'd said that before, at the mill. She'd taken it as a joke, the way the others had. Maybe it wasn't. She'd heard Scourge speak.

Did Bannan?

"Why would he want to come this way?"

"I don't know." The warm amber deep in his eyes intensified as he remembered. A pause and shrug. "There's no accounting for the creature. First he dumps me on the road, completely uncalled for, and runs off. Then he comes prancing to my aid as if he'd never left.

I suppose I'll forgive him. After all," his smile widened, "he heard your call for help."

Had he not . . . "I owe him apples," she said lightly. "A great many apples."

"Please save them for your sister's pies. Having been a hero, he'll be insufferable for days as it is. What is it?"

Kydd had stopped. "I fear we've passed them." He shaded his eyes to frown at the forest.

Bannan knelt, one finger tracing something in the dirt, his eyes flicking here and there. "We'd need Tir to read this." He rose, dusting his hand on a pant leg. "Luckily, Scourge is nosy, especially about trouble. If he's not here, they aren't. They must be ahead."

Ahead was where the crags closed in and folded the road between them. Jenn could see where the road bent to hide itself within smaller twisted trees. The river, to their right, had already plunged deep into its gorge.

Ahead was where both road and river left Marrowdell.

It didn't matter if the road past the bend was the same; it didn't matter that she hadn't actually promised her father or Wyll not to leave. If she went that far, she'd have left Marrowdell too.

Jenn gave herself a mental shake. A few steps along a road. She wasn't leaving. Well, she would, and soon, but this wasn't when.

"Let's go as far as the Northward Road," Kydd proposed. "If we don't find them by then, we'll head back for horses."

The junction wasn't far, Jenn told herself. Everyone said the Northward Road was closer to the village than Night's Edge and she could walk to her meadow from home faster than Peggs could boil potatoes.

It wasn't far.

But her heart thudded in her chest.

For the first time since leaving Vorkoun and the guard, Bannan found himself retracing his steps. In his defense, they were Scourge's steps and he was doing it for good reason. For a reason anyway.

For a woman.

A remarkable woman. Which was a good reason, he argued, wishing he couldn't so easily picture Tir's reaction. Instead, he kept his eye on their surroundings. The woman in question walked beside him in tense silence, no doubt worried about what might be ahead.

Besotted idiots ruled by their pants or mothers, his sister had called the eager young men who'd flocked around when she was presented at Vorkoun's court. Several to their faces. Lila had a low opinion of them—and of him too, when the occasion called for it—but would never suggest they be dealt violence for their misplaced ardor. A dunk in a cold fountain, yes.

He didn't know the people or the place, Bannan reminded himself. From what he'd seen of Marrowdell, eligible maids could be in short supply.

There couldn't be another with Jenn Nalynn's radiant smile, anywhere.

Not something he should think. Not while they were trying to save the current besotted idiot. Maybe not ever.

What he should think about was risk. Nothing to be done about Horst except hope he was sane and wouldn't shoot at them. Kydd and Jenn seemed to feel safe; somehow Bannan didn't find that reassuring. He caught up to Kydd. "I don't suppose you brought more than a dull dinner knife."

"I've this." Kydd deftly freed a paintbrush from his shirt.

Had that been a sliver of brown hide between the trees to his left? Bannan relaxed. "With such deadly blades at hand," he suggested, "no wonder everyone took Tir's entrance so calmly."

Kydd tucked away his brush. "Laugh if you like, Bannan. We've no need to arm ourselves. You'll see. Horst patrols because that's his nature, not because it's needful. I suspect if any bandits arrived in Marrowdell, we'd feed them supper. The valley's a safe haven."

Definitely brown hide. Scourge. Having shown himself to Bannan, the horse faded into shadow again.

"No place is safe." Distracted, Bannan spoke more harshly than he intended.

Jenn glanced his way. "Why do you say that?"

"Our friend was a soldier," the beekeeper told her. He gave Bannan a measuring look. "Easterner, by your accent. Mellynne heritage by the first name, Lower Rhoth by the last. You came from the marches." A conclusion, not a guess. "You're a border guard. You and your companion."

"Were," Bannan corrected. "We're at peace now. Have you heard?"

"News does find us." A faint smile. "Dusty and worn by the time it does, mind you, but sufficient. The world doesn't care about Marrowdell; we happily return the favor. News like that, though, has wings. When Anten was in Endshere, it was all the talk at the inn. The price of the prince's new train."

"Vorkoun." Bannan couldn't keep the anger from the word. He didn't try. "I hope it was worth it."

"As do we," with unexpected grimness. "I do not diminish your loss or theirs," Kydd continued before the truthseer could take offense, "but Vorkoun—in plain speaking, Eldad and Rhoth's long-sought access to Ansnor's mines—was far from the first coin spent."

"What do you mean?"

"Come, truthseer. Surely even in Vorkoun you'd have heard the names." Something flickered in the beekeeper's eyes. "They're familiar to us. Or did you think it coincidence those most in favor of Ordo's truce, from either house, own what we once had?"

"The Fair Lease?" Bannan's eyebrows rose. "You're telling me the prince planned this from the moment he assumed the throne?"

"Or before. He plays the fool, our prince, but behind it all has moved pieces across the board like a master. The irony?" Almost lightly. "Ordo tossed us from Avyo and indebted himself to his chosen barons for nothing. He'd feared our influence. That we'd side with Mellynne and oppose closer relations with Eldad, but—" a shrug, "—we're Rhothan. Most, I'm sure, would have taken his side."

"You favor the truce?" Bannan was taken aback.

"Freedom from conflict, however it happens, is the great step forward," Kydd said simply. "For the generations to come, if not the one that suffers for it. If the rail binds the domains in peace, Avyo will be at the heart of something new, something larger than a prince's ambition. Of course, the opposite could happen and history repeat itself. Mellynne might have ignored what happened to her children, but she could well take exception to a growing Eldad influence in the Rhothan capital. We live in interesting times, my friend. Or rather, outside of them."

Hadn't the elder brother been introduced as the scholar? Bannan eyed the beekeeper. "What were you in Avyo?"

"A student of our past mistakes and triumphs," was the answer, with a short bow. "In short, I studied history, culture, and politics at Sersise University and would have done so as long as they let me. Which wasn't long, alas."

The words said regret. The regret was a lie. "You don't miss it."

"There's more to learn in Marrowdell," Kydd assured him, "than in all the universities of Rhoth or any other domain." He added in the same tone, "Including a horse that skulks like a fox."

Bannan shook his head. "Poor Scourge. He'll be mortified you spotted him. You've sharp eyes."

Kydd gave a modest shrug. "The painter in me."

Jenn was looking around. "I don't see—"

"Stop!" A figure leapt onto the road, hands out. SNAP-CRASH! came hard on the shout as Scourge launched from the brush on the opposite side to confront him.

A second figure followed the first. Horst, shouting, "Don't take another step!"

Scourge snarled and lowered his head, keeping the two at a distance. Jenn frowned and started to walk forward.

"Jenn. No!" Horst tried to dodge past Scourge, who snapped viciously at the air in warning. "Any further and you'll die!"

The truth! Without hesitation, Bannan stepped in front of Jenn and braced himself.

"What's come over you, Horst?" Kydd demanded, more shocked than angry. "Why are you threatening Jenn?"

"Threaten—" Horst looked stunned. "I'd never—It's not me,

it's—" Words forced themselves from his lips. "There's a curse. On our Jenn. On this road. If she goes any further she'll die."

"Nonsense," Jenn protested, walking around Bannan.

Before she could take another step, the truthseer swept her up in his arms. Despite her startled struggle, he carried her several paces back toward the village before setting her on her feet, then kept his arms around her. "Believe him. He's telling the truth." His heart hammered in his chest. "There's something deadly here. Deadly to you. Something we can't see. You must believe me."

He stared wide-eyed over her head at the road, which, being a road, did nothing but lay there. A dried leaf tumbled across it. The sun stroked it with light. Shadows moved with the breeze. Dirt and tracks and nothing of harm.

He stared and held Jenn Nalynn tight, afraid to let go.

Everyone had gone mad. That was the only explanation. Since Aunt Sybb insisted you should be kind and humor mad people, Jenn stood still in Bannan's arms, though she could barely breathe and her ear was crushed against his leather vest.

Was Horst so desperate to keep her from her mother's family that he'd lie? That he'd threaten her life?

Threaten her . . . Jenn's eyes narrowed . . . with his bow slung over Roche's shoulder? She pushed with both hands. Bannan freed her at once.

"Why are you carrying Horst's bow?" she demanded.

The two traded guilty looks.

"So you're on his side now?" she accused Roche. "Is that all it took?"

He turned red. "It's not like that. I'm here to save you!"

"I'm here to save you!" Jenn wished the words unsaid the instant they left her lips, for pleased surprise wiped the indignation from his face. "We—" she added hastily, gesturing to Kydd and Bannan, "—thought Horst might kill you for trying to take me away." Oh, that hadn't helped.

Sure enough, Roche smiled possessively. "You needn't worry—"

"You thought what?" Horst broke in, his face like ash.

Scourge paced back and forth, a living fence, head low and very not-horse teeth and gums exposed with each snarl that rippled his lips.

Loud, distracting snarls. Jenn scowled at the horse. "Stop that!"

He swung his head around to look at her; she could have sworn with a mischievous gleam in his big dark eyes.

"Heart's Blood. Enough!" Bannan snapped.

A hoof dug into the road and threw up a clod of dirt. Scourge shook his head and arched his neck.

Bannan lifted an eyebrow. "Please?"

With a final rumble, the creature acquiesced, moving over to the roadside and dropping his head to graze. Not, Jenn noticed, on grass. He appeared to be lipping up ants. With gusto.

Roche went to take a step; Horst's hand shot out to hold him in place. He nodded a warning at the now-peaceful Scourge.

Who flicked his tail.

"How could you think such a thing?" Horst demanded. "Kydd?!"

His appeal to the beekeeper produced a grim, "You're the one who warned us of Morrill's intentions."

"My intentions?" Roche blustered. "Ancestors Witness, Jenn and I were running off to be married—"

"We were not!" Jenn protested.

"No, you weren't." Bannan's voice was strange and cold. Kydd gave him a sharp look, then stared long and hard at Roche.

"I had to tell the boy about the curse," Horst said heavily. "I couldn't take the chance you'd try to leave with him, Jenn."

"See?" Roche retorted. "There really is a curse. A curse on Jenn and this road. We saved your life." This to her, as if it were all her fault and she should be grateful.

He believed it.

He believed a great many things that weren't true, including what she was capable of, including what she wanted from life.

"Liar."

Horst cupped his hands over his heart. "Ancestors Blessed and Beloved, I swear it's true, Jenn. I'd hoped you'd never have to know." He dropped his hands helplessly to his sides. "You can't go beyond Marrowdell's scars." He pointed at the crags looming to either side. "Not and survive."

What "scars?" The crags were perfectly normal—their steep slopes riven by deep gashes, gashes filled with trees and hardy shrubs and loose rock—no different from any around Marrowdell. That was their nature, as the fields were flat and Bone Hills bare and smooth. First Wisp tells her not to leave, then her father, and now Horst.

"I don't believe any of this."

She would not.

She took a step.

"Please, Jenn. Listen." Horst appeared caught between frustration and anguish. "For your mother's sake!"

Jenn stopped, the blood in her veins having turned to ice and everything being wrong. Everything.

"Why can't I leave?" she asked him, the way her younger self would have asked about the blue of the sky or the lack of a mother, believing there had to be an answer she'd understand.

"Tell her, Horst," Kydd urged. "Bannan's a truthseer. He'll know what's true."

"I know the truth." Wind caught at her hair, flapped her skirt against her legs. It tossed leaves and dust and smelled of lightning. Scourge's head snapped up and he growled. The men traded uneasy looks.

Jenn felt Bannan's hands close gently on her shoulders. He stood behind her, silent and strong, no part of this yet offering support. As much for him as to confront Horst, she made herself go on, to say it. "I know the truth," she repeated. "My mother died because of you. Her family sent you to force her back to Avyo and she ran from you and she died." Wind howled through the tops of the trees; the sun dimmed. "As she died, she made you promise to protect me from them. Is this how? By making up lies to keep me here?"

Rain wouldn't be far behind. Driving, hard rain.

Horst dared shake his head. "This has nothing to do with them. Ancestors Witness, Melusine—" he stopped and appeared to age before her eyes. "When we realized she'd—she'd run, I tried to find her. I was so afraid. We all were. The day was dying and it was cold, for so early in fall." He shuddered. "I remember the cold.

"Radd sent me after the tinkers, in case she'd left with them. He and the others looked in the village while I rode across the empty fields, aiming for the road. When I saw farm buildings, I checked there first, in case, and lost time trying to find a way through the hedge. Before I could, the light turned. I can't describe it." His face filled with awe. "For an instant, everything looked different, everything was strange. I was lost . . .

"I heard a woman cry out. I couldn't make out words, but I followed the sound. When the world became itself again, I was in the meadow, Melusine lying at my feet, barely alive, and there you were, eyes open and bright, not even crying. Your mother looked at me. Looked at me and said . . ."

Horst swallowed and bowed his head. "She said, 'I've little time. I've been promised, guardsman. My daughter will live despite you.'" The words came out flat and harsh, as if heard that way and forever remembered thus. "'My daughter will live despite you, but only here. If she steps beyond the scarred hills, she will die." He paused.

Numb inside, Jenn couldn't take her eyes from him. No one else spoke.

He went on then, quietly, "She said to me, 'The House of Semanaryas sent you to this result and to them the guilt. By my Ancestors' Hearts, at my own heart's end, I claim your life's service. Stay with her. Keep her here and safe. Do this, and be forgiven.'

"I stayed. How could I not? I stayed and you—you grew around my heart." Tears glistened on his gaunt cheeks as Horst looked up at her, eyes pleading. "Please believe me. You must stay, Jenn. The promise made to your mother—Hearts of our Ancestors, Beholden are we—it saved your life then, I know it. It keeps you alive now. But only here."

Bannan's hands tightened on her shoulders. Jenn didn't need a truthseer to believe. She wished she did. But every dreadful word rang with truth.

She lived in a cage.

Lightning flashed, striking the road, the trees, everywhere but where they stood. Bars of blinding light.

Trapped, Jenn Nalynn tried to scream . . .

Thunder answered.

This body was useless, useless, useless! Wyll staggered and fell hard, face pressed to the wooden floor, and knew himself doomed.

The girl was at the brink!

A woman fussed over him, said things. When he pushed her aside, she ran off, calling for help. Whatever help she could summon would be as useless as he was.

The very brink!

He hadn't seen it coming, hadn't guessed, hadn't heard it in her voice. She'd prattled about seeing the world, but she always did. She'd never tried to leave.

Until now.

He should have known and stopped her. He was the guardian. His the duty.

If she left . . .

She had to be stopped, at any cost. ~ Here I am! ~ he cried, bile in his mouth, a mouth empty of fangs and useless too. ~ Here I am, helpless and weak!! ~ He'd lost pride so very long ago. ~ Be amused! Come mock me! I dare you!!! Come!!! ~

I beg you, he added, only to himself. Any of his kind. Several had been willing to torment him in the river—surely at least one hated him enough to do so again. One strong enough to dare approach the very limit of the edge.

One he could convince to act—

Footsteps along the floor. Someone touched him, turned his useless body over, breathed into his face. Wyll pulled useless lips back in a snarl.

"I'm he . . ."

~ . . . ERe ~

"What's wr . . ."

~ . . . ONg ~

Words came at him, echoing through both worlds, overlapped and confusing. Astonished, Wyll struggled to see the speaker.

Pale eyes. A wide mouth. Female. She had connection to his world . . .

More importantly, her body worked.

A toad rode her shoulder, half-tucked within her wild mass of hair, its eyes limpid brown and wise. Wyll spoke to it. ~ Little cousin. Who is this? ~

Pleased to be addressed, the toad yawned to display its fine rows of teeth. ~ Elder brother. In this moon cycle, I made thirteen eggs. I caught fifty-three crickets and a squirrel. No foul nyphrit lived to enter my family's home. I matter to Marrowdell. ~

A useless body; now a worthless ally . . . Wyll fought for calm. The little cousins were as quick to take offense as they were proud. ~ Important and accomplished cousin ~ he praised hastily. ~ I need this woman you've brought. Her help. Can she be trusted? ~

Somehow, the woman in question heard. "What c . . ."

~ AN ~

"I d . . ."

~ OO ~

Wyll winced. "Let the little cousin speak." To his relief, she nodded.

The toad's eyes sank into its head and popped out again. ~ Why would a dragon need help? ~

~ As you plainly see, I'm not myself. ~ Had he jaws, Wyll thought, he would close them on its smug little body and then see how co-operative a little cousin could be. ~ Tell me about her! Quickly! ~

Offended, the toad pulled back into its hiding place within her hair. ~ HELP ME! ~ Wyll shouted after it.

The woman knelt beside him. "My name is Wen. What can I do?"

The girl was too close . . . too close . . . "Stop Jenn Nalynn from leaving Marrowdell," he gasped and pushed this Wen with his better hand. "Tell the soldier—the one who guards the road! Hurry! Hurry!"

Instead of hurrying, she relaxed and gave a serene smile. "Do not worry. Jenn won't leave."

"She's almost past the edge now!" Wyll snapped. Pompous toads and inane women. Was his life to end in nonsense? "I beg you. Go. I—I can't do anything like this. You're the only chance. Find him. Tell him! He has to stop her before it's too late!"

"Calm yourself. She'll stop herself and come back. You'll see. Leaving isn't what she wants."

What were the sei willing to sacrifice simply to punish him? The immortals had no sense of proportion. Wyll felt tears leak down his face and struck out. He missed the woman; his fist splintered wood. He struck again. Again!

His fury and despair didn't trouble her. She looked away and half closed her eyes, sniffed the air. "There's a storm coming."

Had something of power heard his plea?

Or was this his true penance, to watch helplessly as worlds were consumed around him; to be powerless, while the decision of one brought ruin to all. To be like those who'd suffered when he and his kind last went to war.

Sei were nothing if not blunt in their justice. Blunt and cruel.

A gust through the glassless window. Dust rose, wood rattled. It stole the warmth from his skin. A second gust slammed shutters against the wall and toppled a broom. The room darkened until all he could see of the woman was her motionless silhouette.

This was no natural storm.

The daisies had given fair warning. Jenn Nalynn had come of age.

Lightning flashed, again and again and again. Despair. Rage.

Turn-born indeed, Wyll told himself, deafened by thunder. As if there'd been doubt.

As if there'd been any hope at all.

NINE

JENN LED THE way through the downpour, glad the torrential rain made it impossible to talk or listen, though less happy about the state of her second-best dress. Mud smeared the little white birds of her hem, her yellow ribbons hung bedraggled, and at some point the ornate braid had finally collapsed, leaving strands of hair over her shoulders.

Not pretty at all.

Easier to worry about a dress.

Easier to worry about anything but what she'd learned.

She was cursed?

Ignorance, Jenn despaired, was its own bliss. If she hadn't learned of wishings, and changed Wisp into Wyll with ashes and words, she could disbelieve.

But she had, so she couldn't. So she was. She truly would have died, had she taken one step too many. Jenn Nalynn. Young, healthy, and cursed.

What was Peggs going to say?

Their father had known. Now his distress over her plan to leave with Aunt Sybb made sense, as did his desperate plea for her to stay.

She sloshed through a puddle. Being cursed was bad enough. What about the rest? Her mother had spoken of a mysterious promise. By who—or what? Aunt Sybb had hinted, back when Jenn wasn't quite as well behaved as she could be, that each child, particularly naughty ones, might receive the personal attention of a Blessed Ancestor. A younger Jenn had thought that unlikely, since the Ancestors must have more interesting people to spy upon, people in cities or tall ships, but she'd not argued. Had their aunt been right all along? Did she have a—a watcher? Or more than one? If so, did they argue like the Treffs?

The corner of her mouth tried to smile.

But it was all she could do not to shudder at the closeness of her escape. Not escape, she reminded herself, with a rush of inner warmth. Rescue. Because of one man.

The rain went from downpour to drizzle.

Jenn lifted a streaming mass of hair aside to peer around at Horst.

His hair was flat against his scalp. Raindrops had caught on his eyebrows and stubbled cheeks. He wiped his face and met her eyes. His held a dreadful grief.

Quickly, she dropped the hair and looked ahead.

The drizzle lightened to a fine mist.

Jenn found herself stopping.

So be it.

She took a deep breath and turned.

Horst halted. They all did. Roche and Kydd, Bannan and Scourge; though Scourge's big hooves almost clipped Roche's heels. He snorted amusement as the man scrambled out of his way.

Horst. He waited patiently as she searched his worn, lined face for the uncle who liked honey in his tea but couldn't bring himself to that extravagance midwinter when supplies ran low. She'd sneak a dollop into his mug when he wasn't looking; he'd take a sip and act surprised. Not that he ever was, she supposed.

The uncle who did so much for the village, quietly, tirelessly, and even more for the Nalynns. Who swept the mill floors and worked through the harvest; who kept their bins full of charcoal and woodpile stacked. Did her chores when she forgot time in her meadow. And always . . . guarded the road.

Not out of shame, Jenn realized, her final doubt fading with the storm.

She could almost see the moment, feel as her mother had felt. Melusine must have looked at this honorable solder, seen him stricken by guilt, and known the only thing he could accept from her was a task. A penance. At the same time, she had to know the duty she claimed would lead him to love her daughters as she did. That she'd given Horst her family.

Her mother had saved him, Jenn suddenly understood, as surely as she'd saved her.

And what had she done? Jenn searched Uncle Horst's patient face and wanted to shrink. He must have been horrified to hear about Roche's scheme to take her away. He'd had to chase after the younger man. Not for some vengeance; she was ashamed she'd believed that.

"You gave Roche your bow to keep the secret from me, didn't you?" she concluded out loud. Not that it would have worked. Roche wasn't Horst; the only secrets he kept were his own. "When I followed you, you had to tell me to save my life."

"I saved—" Roche gave a startled, "—yip!" and shut up.

Bannan looked innocent.

Ignoring both, Jenn gazed wonderingly at Uncle Horst. "You've been saving my life, all my life. I never knew."

"We'd hoped, your father and I, foolishly perhaps," he admitted slowly, "that you never would." He gave a defeated shrug. "It was to be our gift, Jenn Nalynn. That you'd live free of shadow."

The mist cleared, replaced by tendrils of steam where sunbeams found their way through broken cloud and began to dry the sodden road.

"Heart's Blood! We're almost at the gate," Roche exclaimed.

Of course they were, Jenn thought. Had he no sense of distance? She offered her hand to Uncle Horst, her family and protector. Her smile came from somewhere deep inside, somewhere that held those she loved.

From her heart.

His mouth trembled. He took her hand between both of his, as if it were fragile or beyond price, then bowed to press his lips ever-so-gently to the back of it.

Once again, the sheer joy of Jenn Nalynn's smile took Bannan by surprise. Once again, it wasn't for him. If it had been, he thought with a pang, he'd be as overcome as the old soldier. And wouldn't kiss just her hand.

Bannan stopped himself right there.

He wasn't alone in reacting. Kydd smiled fondly and nodded to himself. Roche—

Roche ran his tongue over his lips and consumed her with his eyes. Unbidden, Bannan's fingers reached for the hilt of the sword he'd left behind.

Scourge shook his head and neck. Drops from his wet mane showered them all. As Roche let out an oath and Jenn laughed, the horse blew noisily and gave Bannan a look that said, as plain as if he'd spoken, that there were fools and there were dangerous fools and he'd best be sure which before he made one of himself.

"Dry clothes await," Kydd announced happily, waving at the village.

They were indeed almost to Marrowdell. Or had Marrowdell obligingly brought itself closer to them?

Not to them.

To her.

Jenn's smile might warm his heart, but Bannan's curiosity caught fire. Curses and promises made to a dying mother? Ordinary stuff compared to his wild surmise. Could it be true? Could he really have grasped when and why certain things occurred here?

The storm. Yes, yes, he told himself, it was the season for swift, deadly storms and here the hills hid their approach. He and Tir had been soaked more than once on the Northward Road. But this storm? This had seemed like despair.

Hers.

As for the road? He trusted his senses. There was no doubt it took less time to travel when they knew where they wanted to be.

Not they.

Jenn Nalynn.

Bannan wanted to laugh with the sheer impossible joy of it.

A thoroughly nonmagical figure tipped back his broad farm hat with a finger as he straightened from his slouch against the gatepost. Tir, no doubt waiting to berate him for whatever foolish risks he thought Bannan had taken this time. What would he say if he knew the greatest wore a pretty blue and white dress and splashed barefoot through the puddles, one small hand tucked in Horst's bent arm, the other in Kydd's, for all the world as if they returned from a pleasant outing?

If it were true . . . could it be true? Bannan's head whirled. Who else would know? He dismissed Horst and Roche at once. The two were too blinded by their own feelings for Jenn Nalynn to see her.

Wainn, Bannan nodded to himself, quite sure. He'd lay coin the uncle did as well.

If it were true . . . if the road and sky and who could guess what else answered this woman's whim?

He should be terrified.

He should grab his wagon and friend and haul their future back up the road as quickly as the sluggard ox could pull it. That's what Tir would do. Be sensible and run.

He didn't want to run. Bannan searched himself and found no fear at all, only excitement and that burning curiosity. Perhaps he wasn't afraid because neither road nor leaf showed any scorching; the ferocious lightning hadn't so much as singed a hair; not even that lying Roche's, more's the pity.

Or was it because she didn't know herself? Jenn's face was as open and honest as any he'd seen. The storm had shocked her too; she'd been afraid of the river. She was no more powerful than any other farm maid; she was, nonetheless, something far more.

Heart's Blood. He was half besotted already. With the place and the maid.

Not something to share with Tir, presently scowling more than usual. Bannan whistled distractedly under his breath as they neared, doing his best not to look inordinately cheerful.

"How's the wagon?" he asked, looking past to where it stood, canvas littered with debris but taut. Good thing. Depending on the state of the derelict farm Radd was to show him, he might be sleeping in it to start.

"Better than the ox," Tir replied, so grimly Bannan felt a chill and the others paused. "You. Horst. What hunts your fields that can drop a grown bull in his tracks?"

Roche frowned. "What was he doing in the grain? A calf on its first legs knows better. It's not harvested yet."

The truth. Another Marrowdell oddity. Bannan didn't need Tir's glower to tell him this one wasn't to be ignored. "What happened?"

"Seems he took fright in the storm, sir, and crashed through the hedgerow into yon field. Though that's not where we found him. He was left gutted and bled, as nice as you please, by the gate leading to the river. With no tracks to show how or who." Above the mask, Tir's eyes were chips of ice. "The villagers would like your permission to finish butchering the meat."

Horst and Kydd exchanged the slightest of glances. Tir picked up on it; so did Bannan. "You know."

"The crop's protected," Kydd admitted with obvious reluctance. Horst pressed his lips together, refusing to be part of any explanation. "From the first green sprout until harvest. Anything that trespasses—dies. Anything."

Bannan trusted his potential neighbors had planned to reveal that small yet crucial detail to him before he committed to life here. He glanced at Scourge, who raised his head and looked supremely uninterested. They'd have to be clear on where to chase rabbits—although if the fields didn't allow rabbits either, that might not be a problem. "Protected by what?" he asked, before Tir could.

"Whisperers." Roche lowered his voice conspiratorially. "That's what Dev and I call them. Can't see them. But if you lie on the ground, close to a row . . . at night . . . you can hear them moving about." Jenn's surprised look brought a defensive, "I'm not lying."

"I know," replied Bannan. Anywhere else, he'd scoff at invisible guardians. Here? Where the road through the valley every-so-often gleamed silver and flowed? "So if we don't trample the grain—and who would—" he said heartily, to reassure the air around them, "—we're safe."

He thought Tir's eyes would pop out of his head. To forestall the inevitable outburst—his companion not being prone to belief in anything he couldn't hit with an ax—Bannan moved his index finger in a tiny circle. In a pub, the sign meant "we're surrounded; stop insulting the locals." On patrol, deep in the marches where a false move cost lives, it meant "not here, we're being watched."

"Trample grain? Then where'd that lovely bread come from, I ask." Tir patted his stomach. "Fool ox."

Kydd looked relieved, Horst wasn't fooled, and Tir lied through his teeth.

Bannan gestured grandly to the wooden gate. "As you said, dry clothes await."

And a conversation he couldn't avoid, Bannan thought ruefully. Tir was not going to be happy. Not at all.

Uncle Horst lengthened his stride and left them to head for the mill. There could be storm damage, but Jenn guessed, with an oddly detached calm, that he hurried to prepare Radd Nalynn. Their secret was out. What would her father say?

She wasn't sure herself what she thought, not yet, not about anything. Well, she was sorry about the ox, though puzzled it hadn't known better. She was sorry to have sounded alarms over nothing, and sorriest of all for herself. No, she should be sorriest of all for poor Wisp, now Wyll.

Her nerves felt scraped raw; all she wanted was Peggs.

As for Roche Morrill . . . Jenn gritted her teeth and calmed herself with the image of him landing rump-first in the commons pond between Satin and Filigree. Preferably on his new bow.

Unaware, the cause of her irritation walked beside her, not too close but bestowing meaningful looks she refused to meet. She could almost hear the cogs turning in Roche's head. She'd come to save him; she'd said so. He'd take it as encouragement, no doubt. That she could deal with, though it might come to a dunking, but there was worse. He'd spoken his intention to marry her in front of Kydd, Uncle Horst, and Bannan. He didn't understand Kydd. He respected Uncle Horst. He detested Bannan. They hadn't taken him seriously; she certainly hadn't.

As her aunt would say, public humiliation teaches no one to sing.

Jenn wasn't too sure what that meant, but she was sure of Roche's temper once humiliated. Unlike his brother, who'd rant loudly a moment, then forget why he'd been angry, Roche would appear unaffected. But inside? He'd savor a slight, devise what he considered suitable retribution, and, when his victim least expected it, spring his trap.

To this day, she doubted Allin Emms knew who'd spread warmed pine resin around the privy hole that winter night. He'd come close to frostbite before being found and cut free. All because—according to Peggs who'd had it from Hettie who'd teased it out of Devins—all because Allin had claimed the last dance with her months before at the harvest, a dance Roche believed promised to him.

Which it hadn't been. He was an awful dancer, who held too tight and bounced too much.

Roche could spend the rest of his life with the sows, for all she cared. She did care about his spite. Roche wouldn't go after Kydd or Uncle Horst. He wouldn't dare. But the stranger would be fair game.

If Bannan planned to stay, he should be warned.

Which meant talking to him.

Jenn felt her cheeks grow warm.

Worse, it meant talking to him in private.

Ancestors Blessed.

She hadn't been able to so much as look at Bannan, not directly, not since . . .

Her shoulders tingled where he'd gripped them in support. If she closed her eyes, she could feel where his arms had wrapped around her, hear his heart . . . Her own pounded, remembering. How could his touch affect her like this?

What did it mean?

She had to talk to Peggs.

Kydd spoke. "Hello, Wen."

Jenn glanced up in surprise. Wen Treff stood in the middle of the lane to the mill, hands in her sleeves, patiently waiting. Her hair was in its usual mad cloud around her head, so she'd escaped the storm. For all she apparently cared; her feet were in one of the innumerable puddles.

Wen didn't look at Kydd or acknowledge his polite greeting. She ignored Roche, who muttered something under his breath about the witless and stalked off toward his home. Bannan and Tir hadn't come with them, Jenn realized with a start. She'd been that lost in her thoughts.

Wen's pale eyes locked on hers.

Did Wen have such thoughts about Wainn?

Not that she'd ever ask, Jenn decided, firmly reining in her imagination.

A fleeting smile crossed Wen's face, as if she'd heard anyway. "I told him you wouldn't leave."

Kydd's brow rose, but he prudently kept his peace and waited.

"Told—" Jenn looked beyond Wen to the mill. The violent storm would have been Wyll's first as a man. The mill wasn't a home. It leaked and shuddered and let in wind. She should have been here. Looked after him. "How is he?"

Wen tilted her head and considered her. A toad poked out from her hair, its wide clawed toes tight on her shoulder, and considered her too. "Broken."

" 'Broken?' "

Without waiting for an answer, Jenn bolted for the mill.

The floor was as damp as she'd feared. The sunbeams coming through the walls did little more than show the glisten of wet wood underfoot; the light sliced through air empty of dust, for now. There were voices below, deep and male. Uncle Horst had found her father in the basement, was likely helping, as he tried for the right words. After any storm, Radd made sure nothing had blown loose, that water hadn't pooled in gear casings, that nothing was broken.

Broken.

Forgetting Uncle Horst and the curse, forgetting Bannan and his touch, forgetting anything and everything else, Jenn hurried up the stairs, more afraid with every step. She usually liked the smell of the mill after a rain. It had a friendly tang to it, like a freshly-opened cask of beer. This? A too-full chamber pot. Sickness left on blankets. Neglect.

When the next step would put her head above the floor, she paused to calm herself. The rain made every smell stronger. Wyll was too hurt to climb down the stairs to a privy. Of course they'd brought him a 'pot for his comfort.

She stepped up, stared, and came the rest of the way with one hand on her throat.

Broken.

The pallet was empty, the blankets tossed and torn. The chamber pot had been thrown across the room, leaving a trail to explain the smell. The chair had been overturned. There were marks in the floor, deep and round, as if a sledgehammer had struck the wood.

"Covie?" Jenn looked around desperately. "Riss?"

"You came back." The voice, faint but steady, emanated from the shadows behind the stairwell.

Wyll. She sagged with relief. "Of course I came back. Why are you alone?" Jenn tried to make sense of what she could see. "What happened?"

"I believe I lost my temper, Dearest Heart. The others ran off."

Considering Covie's patience with the most difficult of cows, Wyll must have thrown quite the tantrum. "This isn't the meadow," Jenn scolded, "where you can rip plants apart. This is my father's mill. People will expect you to act—to act like them."

A thoughtful silence from the shadows.

She briskly rolled her damp hair into a knot at the back of her neck. "Come on. I'll help you back to bed, then clean this up." She'd need the mop from downstairs. Soap and some sand.

"I don't need the bed. You wanted me well, Dearest Heart. I am."

"Good. You can help clean." When he didn't move, Jenn walked around the stair opening toward him, her hand on the wooden rail that guarded its three sides. "What's wrong?" She could make out his shape now. He was standing—no, he must be leaning against an upright. "Are you sure you're all right?" She stepped closer; let her eyes adjust. "Wyll?"

"I am what you've made me, Dearest Heart." As she stepped into the shadow, he lurched part way free of it.

He wore nothing but Wen's lacy shawl around his shoulders. Shoulder. His right was whole and strong, the arm below it, the wrist and hand perfect.

The shawl couldn't stay on his left shoulder, for that was crushed inward, the arm and wrist and hand that dangled below shriveled and useless.

Had she done this?

Horrified, her eyes followed the sickening scar, as wide as both her hands and deeper than a fist, from the crushed shoulder, down his side, to a hip pried half from its socket. From the hip across a thigh missing half its flesh. From the thigh to a ruined knee. Like a joke, the calf and foot were without flaw, but thrust out at the wrong angle.

She hadn't seen it. How had she not? They'd been in the water, Jenn thought desperately. Bannan had taken him. Someone had covered him with a blanket. He'd been in bed. His eyes had been silver.

Had she done this?

His right side hadn't escaped, not entirely. Like poorly done seams, more scars stitched his ribs and marred the flatness of his belly. Without a word, he moved the end of the shawl so she could see he was intact, then let it fall again. Without a word, so she could see he could walk, he came to her.

It wasn't a walk; it was contortion. He used a powerful backward thrust of his good shoulder to twist his body and swing his bad leg forward. Once that foot was planted, his right came forward and he caught his balance. Pain flickered across his face.

She'd done this.

Jenn made herself reach out and touch him. First the right arm. Warm. Strong, though not heavily muscled. A graceful arm. A good arm.

The left. Fever-hot, bone-thin, wasted. She let her fingers trail along it to find his, but they were limp and flaccid and couldn't respond. She looked up, into his ordinary brown eyes, and hers filled with tears. "I did this. With the wishing. I did something wrong and this happened to you. It wasn't supposed to—I'm so sorry. I'm sorry. I'm—"

"Hush." Wyll's good hand lifted, fingers brushing her cheek as lightly as a breeze. "You came back," he said with a gentle smile. "Everything's all right now."

Jenn couldn't smile, but she managed a shaky laugh. "Spoken by the man wearing naught but a shawl. Don't you dare leave before I find you some clothes."

His eyes flashed silver—or did she imagine it through her tears? "Don't you dare leave." Not gentle. Not gentle at all.

Her other protector. Her best protector.

All these years, she'd made him listen to her prattle about seeing the world. Had it given him nightmares?

She'd glibly explained she'd done this to him so he could come with her, as if it was a gift, and left him broken.

"I won't," Jenn promised. "Uncle Horst told me. About the road and the curse and my mother." She settled the shawl closer to Wyll's neck, her hands trembling. The torn blankets, thrown chamber pot, the holes in the floor? He'd somehow known her danger and been desperate to save her, needing help those tending him wouldn't—

couldn't—understand. "And you," she concluded miserably. "I'm right, aren't I? You knew where I was. I scared you too. I'm s—"

Wyll placed a finger over her mouth. "Hush." The finger traced her lower lip, slowly, softly. His eyes followed it. "I always know where you are, Dearest Heart. I always know how you are. You came back and all is well."

Jenn couldn't move or speak. She didn't want to, though what she wanted wasn't the least bit clear at the moment. Other than to close her eyes and pay attention to nothing but his touch and how it made her tingle all the way to her toes and . . .

Footsteps. Wyll's finger abandoned its exploration.

"Jenn?"

Kydd. He must have followed her into the mill.

Of course he'd followed her into the mill. The wonder was everyone hadn't . . .

"What's going on?" With concern. Of course with concern. The room looked and smelled terrible and she was in the shadows with an almost naked—a lace shawl didn't count she was sure—naked stranger and . . .

"We're fine," Jenn said, raising her voice. "Wyll—needed a bit of help."

"Looks like a storm in here too." As Kydd came around the stairwell to where he could see them, his concern turned to icy disapproval. "Get away from him!"

Hettie Ropp, Jenn thought wildly, couldn't turn something into a scandal faster. She should be thankful it was Kydd, who never gossiped, though he'd had worrisome notions about Roche, she could tell, and now with Wyll . . . "Kydd—"

"At once!"

Her feet moved before she thought to argue, but Jenn didn't go far. "Wyll needs help."

"I need clothing," Wyll said.

Kydd's gaze dipped, then rose again. "That's obvious." He jerked the tie of his sodden shirt open, yanked it over his head, and threw it at Wyll. "Here. Cover yourself!"

Wyll let the wet garment strike his chest and fall to the floor. Was that a silver glint in his eyes?

Worse and worse. "Stop this!" Jenn protested. "Wyll's my friend."

"And what else? It's been mere hours." Kydd's eyes never left Wyll. "Where are your friend's bruises? His cuts?"

"I heal quickly," Wyll said calmly. "A family trait."

"Then why are you maimed?"

Jenn felt the blood drain from her face. How could he ask that?

Wyll lifted an eyebrow. "This?" His right hand lifted the withered left. He let it drop and it thudded against his hip like a dead fish. "I survived what you could not." He twisted his good shoulder and ducked his head. "I am Wyll, honored to be the friend of Jenn Nalynn."

Wise Wyll. Manners cooled tempers, her aunt said. Jenn held her breath as Kydd was compelled to return a short, if angry, bow. "Kydd Uhthoff."

"You are the bee friend. The truthseeker." The smallest of smiles, as if sharing a secret. "The almost wise and the lovelorn. Greetings, Kydd Uhthoff."

Kydd blinked. Curiosity lightened his face. "You have me at a disadvantage, Wyll. And know me better than most. How is that?"

Because Wisp had been her confidant and she'd told him everything? Ancestors Witness. Jenn couldn't count the number of secrets, silly or otherwise, her friend shouldn't share. Ever. "Surely we can leave such things till Wyll is properly dressed," she suggested.

"That won't be a problem," Kydd said. "Jenn, kindly ask my brother to let you choose from Wainn's clothes chest. Wyll's about the same size."

Curiosity, not trust. Not yet. Kydd didn't want to leave her here, with Wyll. Jenn cast about for a reason to stay. "You should go," she said brightly. "I have to clean before my father comes up here." Or anyone else, for that matter. The villagers would be preoccupied with storm damage, but all too soon, Covie or Riss would be back. After Wyll's fit of temper, it was unlikely they'd return alone.

"I'll help—" Naturally, Kydd turned to look at the mess as he spoke.

Wyll looked at her.

His eyes gleamed silver.

And things began to move.

"Heart's Blood!" Kydd stared, his mouth partly open, as breezes tossed the blankets back on the pallet and nudged them flat, rolled the chamber pot noisily to the bedside and upright, picked up the chair and set it in place, then, after hesitating over the smelly trail, whirled around the room to collect damp dust to cover the stain.

As a finale, rose petals flung themselves through the open window to land neatly atop the dust. Presumably to improve the odor.

Jenn shook her head in disbelief. What was Wyll thinking? This wasn't the meadow. "You can't do that here," she complained.

His eyes became brown and ordinary. "I helped."

"Don't help," she snapped.

Ordinary except for a wicked twinkle. "Shall I put everything back, Dearest Heart?"

Kydd's face worked, as if holding back a sneeze. He made a faint strangled noise, then broke out laughing.

"Don't," Jenn warned Wyll. "Don't do anything."

He stood statue still. Except for—Jenn did her utmost not to look there. Kydd, though shirtless, was decently clad; Wyll most definitely was not. Worse, she knew—she just knew—he was enjoying himself thoroughly at her expense. Like the Emms twins, who—until their mother caught them at it—would drop their pants, put their hands behind their heads, and wiggle their hardly impressive manhood at the Nalynn sisters while they hung the week's laundry. The number of times she and Peggs had resorted to throwing clots of mud? The result, she had to admit, had been pretty funny. Running with their pants around their knees was challenge enough, but Tadd had an absolute gift for choosing a direction that would collide with his twin.

"Only you, Jenn, could find such a friend," the beekeeper said, smiling. He retrieved his shirt from the floor and offered it to Wyll, who, having had his fun, held it modestly at his waist. "Marrowdell," Kydd concluded, with no doubt at all.

"A mere visitor till now," Wyll smiled. "Jenn wished me to stay, so I will."

Jenn winced. If he answered the truth to any question, what chance did she have of keeping anything private, let alone anything embarrassing?

On the bright side, Kydd wasn't alarmed by Wyll's little tricks. That boded well. Very well indeed. The others looked up to the Uhthoffs; they'd listen to Kydd's opinion about their new fellow. If only Wyll refrained from another display.

Which she couldn't expect. They were friends. She'd never controlled him. She wouldn't know how. Had never wanted to.

She'd wished him into this shape.

Jenn felt the weight of her soaked clothing, the chill damp against her legs, and shivered.

Wyll lost his smile. "Go home, Dearest Heart, and care for yourself," he said gently. "This man will see to my needs."

The beekeeper nodded. "It'd be an honor." From the glint in his eye, Kydd wanted nothing more than time alone with her Marrowdell friend.

She shouldn't worry, Jenn reasoned. If Kydd married Peggs, he'd be family and would have to keep secrets. Wouldn't he?

A warm breeze found her ear and whispered, "Go."

She nodded, her arms tight around herself, and left the two of them.

But it wasn't until Jenn stepped outside into bright sunshine that she remembered. What Kydd had interrupted.

Wyll's finger on her mouth.

Her heart pounded like a drum in her chest. She touched the tip of her tongue to her lip.

And tasted ash.

Bannan didn't have to be told stay back. With Horst about to bare past sins, the last thing welcomed by the villagers would be a stranger in attendance. So he let Jenn and the others continue on their way and followed Tir to the wagon. After changing into the last of his clean clothes—the boots would have to dry on his feet—he hung his wet things over a wheel.

Feet apart, hands behind his back, face composed, Tir waited.

He had a way, Bannan thought with mild annoyance, of waiting very properly, with the sort of attentive patience that made the person being waited for come to worry about something on his face or see flaws in whatever he'd done in his life. It was impossible to ignore a waiting Tir, though Bannan had tried in the past. The man was like an unscratchable itch.

Bannan crossed his arms and gave in. "What?"

"Sir?"

"Is this about my leaving the village without you, the 'whisperers,' or the farm?" That should cover the possibilities.

Tir surprised him. "It's about them, sir. Them and their plans for you." He pulled off his mask; the ruin of nose and chin added force to the accusation. "That nonsense about the field?" He spat. "The villagers killed the ox, plain and simple." A flash of puzzlement. "Or not simple. I won't say I figured how. But if you ask me, they did it to keep you here."

Bannan swallowed his instant objection. Tir couldn't see the silvered road. He wasn't distracted by it, either. How many times had his suspicions saved both their lives? "Putting aside for the moment I'd know if any of them lied to me, why bother?" He spread his hands to encompass the valley. "I told them I plan to stay. You were there."

"Not being a truthseer," Tir countered bluntly, "I didn't think you were serious. Maybe they didn't either." With exasperation. "Kill the ox and you don't have much choice, do you?"

Bannan half smiled. "What makes you think I want a choice?"

"Heart's Blood. You only met her this morning. Sir."

Bannan flushed. It was Jenn Nalynn. He couldn't deny it. But . . . "It's more than her. It's this place. I see—I can't tell you how—" He hesitated, then said helplessly, "Can't you feel the peace here? How special it is?"

Scourge, who'd been pretending to mouth flowers, found something that crunched.

Tir replaced his mask, taking longer than usual to settle it in place. When he finally spoke, his tone was quiet and thoughtful. "Maybe it says something, that you came to the guard too young. What were you—fifteen?"

"Fourteen. I lied." There'd always been a Larmensu in a Vorkoun uniform; he'd imagined or wanted no other life. Until now, Bannan thought. Until now. "Why?"

"Fourteen. Ten years in the marches." Tir gazed at the village, then gave him a somber look. "You don't know what peace is. Trust me on this, sir, this place—whatever you see here—it's not peace. Leave the wagon. We can walk out of here. Put a pack on the bloody beast if we—" Scourge shied sideways with a disgusted snort. "—take what we can carry," Tir amended. "I'm just say'n, sir. There are other places. Safer places. Ones without mysterious ox-killing whispers."

"Where's the fun in that?" Bannan said lightly, though it was all true and he knew himself perilously close to the kind of heart-driven foolishness that had, on several occasions in his youth, resulted in sister or friends or both hauling him back to reality by an ear, if necessary. "Besides. The food's good."

Tir heaved a great sigh. "The food's grand," he conceded, with all the enthusiasm he'd give a midnight watch in cold rain. "So we're staying, then."

"We?" A swell of gladness filled Bannan's throat. He hadn't asked Tir to take the road with him; he wouldn't have asked him to stay. He hadn't hoped. "You're sure?"

"With all this peace?" A sturdy finger poked him in the chest, hard. "Someone has to watch your back. Sir."

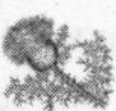

The girl left and Wyll no longer bothered to be social. He lurched his slow way to the window. He would see her from there, he thought, as she went home.

"Is there anything else you need, besides clothing?"

Surely not one of the questions burning in a beekeeper who hid books of what passed for knowledge in his hives. "What else should I need?" Wyll asked as he reached the window and braced himself.

As he'd expected, it was a trial to view Marrowdell through a man's eyes. Everything too close. Too low. The hills were askew and the colors? Gorge rose in his throat but he forced himself to look, to adapt.

He'd dealt with worse.

Kydd came to the window, glanced at what was doubtless comforting and familiar. "A place to stay. You'd be most welcome in our home."

This, he hadn't expected. Wyll looked away from the window. The man's demeanor was respectful, but unafraid. Was he foolish? "I will stay," he stated, "with Jenn Nalynn."

"You can't."

More foolish than was reasonable. How far would he go? "Why?"

"Because . . ." Kydd's cheeks took on a dusky hue. "Because Jenn lives with her family," with renewed confidence, "and they don't have room. Her aunt from Avyo is visiting."

"Aunt Sybb." The woman Jenn regarded so highly, the one whose opinion mattered to her most. A potent ally, should he need one. A formidable opponent, should he offend her. "I need shoes," Wyll declared, abruptly worried on that score.

"Shoes."

"I mustn't offend Aunt Sybb."

For some reason, this put Kydd back at ease. "Nor must I," he said with feeling. "A gracious lady. Very protective of her nieces." As if things had been settled in some way, he bowed. "I'll be back as quickly as I can, Wyll of Marrowdell. With clothes and footwear."

Wyll returned to gazing out the window, uncaring that the man waited for a response, oblivious to his eventual departure.

While distracted by Kydd's questions, he'd missed seeing Jenn leave the building. She was home now. Seeking the comfort of her aunt and sister. For she'd left in pain.

He should be glad. Pain taught lessons and the wishing was something she mustn't repeat. He should rejoice that her eyes had filled with tears, that she'd gazed at him with heartfelt misery, that her lip had quivered just so.

He'd touched the lip, curious. Been startled as the blue of her eyes deepened to rich purple. Twilight's color. The boundary of night's edge. Remarkable. Terrifying. As if a turn could catch breath and live.

He was, he assured himself, glad. If she believed his twisted body was her doing, it was a belief he'd let her keep. A constant reminder of guilt to prevent another, worse mistake.

Ask the sei.

Ask his kind.

Ask why he lived, still.

TEN

THE LATE SUMMER storm put an end to lunch and had sent the livestock scampering for shelter. While it lasted, it made a river of the road and a lake of the pond. There was no saving the last of the berries, but the melons, Cynd later averred, had appreciated a good drink. Between the glass that would need replacing, new panes having to come all the way from Weken; the missing shingles on Old Jupp's roof, which meant he'd have to stay with his niece Covie if he couldn't abide the hammering, though those children were hardly quieter; and the Emms' clean laundry, presently draped on the oak tree, the villagers cheerily agreed it could have been worse.

Bannan's ox was the only casualty, his regrettable passing an opportunity not to be missed, it being some time since the last outdoor roast and no new slaughter planned till early this winter. Davi proposed a new pit be dug once the puddles drained away.

Puddles were everywhere, glistening in the afternoon sun. The air was scrubbed to a sparkle and, though leaves littered the ground, those left on the trees shone as though polished. Rain-soaked clothes flapped in the remnant wind, no few being second-best dresses. Two black hats sat on the Treff porch, their sodden feathers leaning together.

The puddle in front of the Nalynn porch reflected the sky. Chin in both hands, elbows on her knees, Jenn sat on the step and watched the towering white clouds decay.

Peggs sat beside her. She watched the puddle-sized sky too.

Small, restless snores came from the parlor where, instead of packing, their exhausted aunt reluctantly took a much-needed nap. The dishes, deserted, sat in cooling suds. Peggs had taken one look at Jenn and made tea while her sister changed into dry clothes.

Their empty mugs beside them, the pair sat side by side to consider the day's events.

"I can't believe Poppa never told us," Peggs said, not for the first time. She lowered her voice. "How could he not tell his own sister?"

Both shook their heads at that.

"I'd tell you," Jenn promised.

"And I, you. We won't keep any secrets." Peggs paused. "Not ones that matter," she qualified. She tipped her head to the house. "Should we tell her now?"

"That would betray a confidence," Jenn pointed out. "Aunt Sybb wouldn't approve."

"She won't approve of any of it."

Both sighed.

Jenn drew a circle in the moist earth with her toe. "If we did tell her, she wouldn't need to worry about Mother's family anymore."

Instead of agreeing, Peggs sat up straight. "What if the Semanaryas send someone else? They still could." She gasped. "Jenn, what if they'd stolen you from your bed when you were little and dragged you from Marrowdell?"

"Then we wouldn't be having this conversation," Jenn said sensibly. "You've been reading too much. They don't know I exist. Besides, Wisp knew about the curse too. He told me to stay home. Remember the roses on the table?"

"Roses wouldn't have stopped you today."

Jenn knew how close it had been; her sister's dread wasn't helping. "Would you please stop worrying?" From here, she could see Night's Edge. The crags and river. The village and fields. The Bone Hills and forests. The span of her world.

Marrowdell.

And nothing more.

Kydd Uhthoff came in sight, walking toward the mill. He wore a fresh shirt and carried a thick bundle. A pair of boots hung from their laces over his shoulder. Things—as in Wyll—must have gone reasonably well after she'd left.

Spotting them on the porch, Kydd lifted his free hand in a friendly wave but didn't pause.

"Thank you!" Jenn called, waving back.

Peggs, who'd waved too, gave her a questioning look. "For what?"

"Clothes for Wyll. He's the same size as—"

"Wyll. Ancestors Foolish and Forgetful." Peggs caught her hands and turned Jenn to face her. "Dear Heart, there's something I must tell you. I'm glad Wyll's better, but before—before you visit him, there's something you should know," ever-so-gently, as if she were fragile. "I've heard he's—he's not quite right. Covie told Cynd at lunch, you see, and she told Lorra and Frann. Well, it didn't take long to reach the kitchen."

"It's all right. I know." She'd told Peggs about Roche and how she'd tricked him. About how stalwart Kydd had been in her defense. About their mother, Horst, and the curse.

Just, Jenn thought uncomfortably, not about Bannan.

Or Kydd and Wyll.

Or . . . Wyll.

Which was more than reasonable, since she could hardly bear to think about Wyll, let alone talk about him.

"You know?"

"Kydd and I stopped at the mill on the way home," Jenn admitted. Her lower lip began to tremble and Peggs' face swam as her eyes filled. "I've seen him."

"Oh." Her sister drew her close, a hand stroking Jenn's hair. Her apron smelled of cinnamon and apples. That was all it took.

"It's my fault!" Jenn wailed and burst into racking sobs.

Peggs waited patiently, hugging her until sobs became hiccups and Jenn sniffed noisily. At this, her sister eased her away gently and offered a linen handkerchief. Jenn took it dubiously; she hated using the fancy cloth, but their aunt insisted. "Better?"

She blew her nose. "A bit."

Peggs' dark expressive eyes held a wealth of compassion. "How bad—" she hesitated delicately.

Jenn sniffled. "The wishing went wrong. He's—broken." Wen's word. "His left side is crippled. There's a terrible scar," she traced it over her own body. "He can stand. Walk, in a fashion. But he's b—broken."

Peggs opened her mouth only to close it, a touch of color on her cheeks.

Jenn mumbled into the handkerchief. "Not there."

"He showed you?" Her sister digested that. "Well. Good," this firmly. "You wouldn't want—that—broken. Trust me."

"Peggs!" Jenn blurted, then giggled, surprising herself.

Her sister's lips twitched. "Shh," she cautioned, tipping her head at the open door. "Don't disturb our poor aunt." She turned serious. "Is Wyll angry with you? You meant no harm. I hope he understands."

"That's the only good part," Jenn sighed. "I won't say he forgives me, but he was more upset that I'd gone down the road. He'd thought I was leaving."

"Because he knows about the curse." Peggs looped a silky strand of black hair around her forefinger and held it across her closed lips, her habit when thinking. When younger and thinking very hard, the strand would end up in her mouth to be chewed thoughtfully; Aunt Sybb had worked diligently each summer to cure what she called a proclivity better suited to a cow than a young lady.

Jenn waited patiently.

The hair went free. "I wonder how much he knows."

"What do you mean?"

"Maybe Wyll knows how to make you not cursed. Is that how it's said, do you think?" Peggs' brows creased in deliberation. "Uncursed. Curseless?" A smile broke across her face and lit her eyes. "Oh, Jenn!

What if he's been waiting to remove this curse since you were born, but couldn't until—until—" That part failed her.

"Until I wished him into the shape of a man," Jenn pressed her hands to her bosom, "we fell madly in love," she pretended to swoon, "and were married before the sun could set on my birthday."

Peggs laughed. "Didn't we read that story?"

"Or one like it." Though in all such stories Jenn could recall, vile forces fought against the handsome protector and fair maid, leaving their future in doubt till the last page. She'd clutch a pillow while Peggs read the passages filled with danger and strife. If she'd had her way, it would be straight to the happy ending. With pie. "This isn't a story, Peggs."

Her sister gave her a quick hug. "Have a heart. Being romantic doesn't make it wrong."

"Or right. You," Jenn arched her eyebrows, "are under the influence."

"I shouldn't tease, little sister, if I were you." Peggs contentedly twirled another dark lock. "Your turn at love will come."

"If Wyll could uncurse me," Jenn reasoned, changing the topic, "he'd have said so. All he said was 'don't you dare leave.' "

Peggs looked deflated. "That's not promising. What else did he say?"

"It wasn't so much what he said . . ." Jenn ran her tongue along her lower lip. At the moment, it tasted of tea. "Peggs. Does it mean anything, feeling—odd—when a man touches you?"

" 'Touches you?' " Peggs' eyes widened. "Where? What did he do?"

"Nothing," Jenn hurried to say. "Nothing wrong. Wyll—" Where would sound safe? "Wyll put his hand on my cheek, when I was upset. I felt odd. Tingly."

Her sister ducked her head, a dimple showing past the curtain of hair. "Tingly's good."

"Peggs!"

"Not that Kydd—that we've—" Her surprising sister hesitated, then said, "He came to the kitchen with eggs and our fingers touched—on the basket." The basket's involvement making it clear the contact of fingers had been above reproach.

Jenn could picture the moment. She smiled. "Tingly."

"Wonderfully so," Peggs sighed with bliss. Then chuckled. "Of course, after that he hovered and was in the way and I knew I'd burn something if he kept watching me, so I had to shoo him out."

Poor Kydd. Jenn wiggled her toes thoughtfully.

"Why do I think there's more to this than a touch on the cheek?"

Because there was. Before she lost her courage, Jenn said the rest. "On the road. Bannan picked me up and held me in his arms—not that he had to, but he was worried about the curse and . . ."

"And you felt tingly with him too," Peggs finished with great satisfaction.

Jenn nodded.

The sisters silently pondered the significance of tingling as they watched Riss, across the road, hang damp rugs with little Alyssa's help. Once the two reentered Old Jupp's house, Peggs coughed. "Go on."

"What?"

"You know what. Was Bannan more tingly or less?"

"What kind of question is that?" Jenn rolled her eyes. "Tingly is . . . tingly."

Peggs chuckled. "I can't believe last night we worried you had no suitors. Today you've two. Three, if you count Roche."

"I don't count him," Jenn objected. "And I don't have suitors." Aunt Sybb's word. It went with courting, and invitations, and parties. With life in a great city like Avyo.

With freedom.

"Call them what you will." Her sister held out her right hand, palm up. "A dear and magical friend." Her left. "A handsome stranger who saves your life." She pretended to compare weights, as if choosing a turnip. "Who shall it be?"

Jenn stared into the puddle sky. The right number of clouds remained for a glorious sunset, a welcome for those new to Marrowdell.

"I shouldn't joke." Peggs lowered her hands. "Sorry."

"I made Wyll what he is."

"I know."

The sisters leaned shoulder to shoulder and watched the puddle shrink.

There was no need to say the rest.

There really wasn't. They both knew she would marry Wyll and care for him and they'd live in Marrowdell for the rest of their lives. She'd learn to be content. She could. She owed him that and more.

Jenn chewed her lower lip.

Except . . . there was that small detail she'd left out. It shouldn't make any difference. Still, for honesty's sake. Hadn't they pledged to keep no secrets from one another? Not any that mattered, and she was uncomfortably sure this one might, depending on how Wyll behaved in future. Something she couldn't guarantee, could she?

Peggs shook her head and half smiled. "Tell me the rest of it."

"The rest?" Jenn echoed faintly.

"I know that look. You might as well spill whatever it is." Her smile widened. "Wyll or Bannan?"

"Wyll," Jenn confessed. She folded her hands, which wanted to fidget, neatly on her lap. "Remember what Wen told me? How the shape of something might change but not the nature? She was right."

Peggs wrinkled her nose. "What do you mean?"

"Wyll—he can do Wisp's little tricks. Like the roses."

"What?!" Her sister launched to her feet. "He still has powers? He's—he's magic?"

"Yes, but—" Jenn began, neck twisting as she stared up in surprise.

"And Kydd's gone to him?! Alone??"

"Don't worry. He knows—"

"Jenn Nalynn! I—" The shout sputtered into incoherence. In frustration, Peggs waved her arms over her head and stomped her feet. "I—! You—! How could—!"

Awed, Jenn dared not utter another word.

"What's wrong?" Their aunt called from the window, barely awake and concerned. "Is someone hurt?"

"There'd best not be," warned Peggs, finding her voice. "You," she told Jenn, grabbing her wrist to pull her to her feet, "are coming with me."

"There's the boys' room, above the kitchen. Gallie wished me to tell you she's aired the beds." Zehr passed a rag over his sweat-damp face and considered the sky, burdened with the last of the storm clouds. "Late in the season for it, but it'll be a sticky night," he observed, then winked. "If I were you, I'd take hammocks on the porch."

"Our thanks to you both," Bannan said, remembering to use the villagers' short, old-fashioned bow. He couldn't help but admire how they'd kept the courtesies and speech of their former lives. Endshere's population shared the thick accent Tir still produced on occasion, a curdling of vowels that grew more pronounced the farther into Upper Rhoth one ventured, and no one else along the Northward Road bowed, being, as Tir called them, hill folk born and bred.

More and more hammers lent their music to the air, accompanied by at least one saw. Zehr had stopped by their wagon on his second trip bringing tools to Jupp's house, missing shingles thanks to the wind. "We're happy to earn our supper," offered Bannan. "Could we help with repairs?"

"I'll be using anything sharp," Tir broke in. "Unless it's a sword, he's apt to slice off a thumb."

Zehr chuckled. Bannan grinned, his hands out and open in mock surrender. "I'll learn."

"Start with fetch and carry," his helpful companion suggested. "It'll be safer."

Something villagers were doing everywhere, now that the storm had passed, including Kydd, who walked toward them with a thick bundle under his arm. He waved at the three, but turned off the road to the mill. Was Wyll awake? Bannan hoped so. He had questions. Innumerable ones. Starting with the shape beneath the wounded skin.

Zehr noticed too; his face lost his cheer. "Have either of you skill with injuries?"

"Wyll's taken a turn for the worse?"

"No, no. He's on the mend."

Good news, surely. "But there's a concern," Bannan guessed.

"He threw some kind of fit before the storm," the villager admitted uncomfortably. "Covie refuses to care for him and who can blame her?"

Tir came closer, eyes intent. "What did he do?"

"He pushed her to the floor, hard enough to bruise. I understand a man not being right in his head after an injury, but that's no excuse to hurt someone trying to help you. Wen took over, but she—Wen isn't—" The honest man floundered, but struggled on. "We're not sure she's capable, and Kydd—Kydd paints and keeps bees."

"I've experience in such matters." The vague wording would, Bannan hoped, imply all manner of battlefield stress and madness. "Tir, why don't you help our friend here with the roof? I'll see what assistance I can offer."

Relieved, Zehr didn't argue. "Most kind of you. Both of you."

Leaving Tir to rummage happily in the wagon for the tools purchased in Endshere, brand new and oiled in their leather wraps, Bannan strode to the mill, eager to solve the first of Marrowdell's puzzles: the man who was something else.

The air inside the mill was noticeably cooler and more pleasant; the night would indeed be "sticky" as Zehr had said. Bannan paused to listen. Someone worked below; pumping water, by the sound of it. Quiet voices above. There.

He climbed the stairs on his toes. What he hoped to surprise at the top, he couldn't have told himself.

At first, it seemed he'd surprised nothing more mysterious than a clothes' fitting. Kydd's bundle lay open on the floor, revealing an assortment of men's apparel. He stood holding a shirt against Wyll, who was definitely on the mend if he could dress.

Bannan hadn't made a sound. Before he could, Wyll turned his head to gaze at him with silver eyes.

No, they were brown. Why had he thought silver?

"Glad you're feeling better," Bannan said.

Kydd looked up and smiled a greeting. "Bannan Larmensu, this is Wyll. Of Marrowdell."

Of the valley, if not the village. Interesting. "I'm honored." Bannan stepped forward and swept a full bow, touching the floor with his fingertips. As he did, he saw that something the size and shape of a fist had crushed the wood in three places. Rose petals lay scattered nearby, with no flowers or vase in sight.

"Bannan." Wyll's voice was pleasant, with a trace of the villagers' Lower Rhoth accent. His seeming? Pitiful and twisted, the wreck of an otherwise comely man barely able to stand erect without help.

A lie. The wounds that had bled over Bannan's hands and shirt were gone. Pants hid the shattered hip and the stance was confident despite its bend. Where not disfigured or scarred, the flesh was strong and healthy.

And beneath the shape, if he stared long and hard, there was another. Stronger. Stranger.

No wonder Covie had fled.

"Tir won't let me near a saw or hammer," Bannan explained, deliberately casual as he walked toward the two. "I came to see if you could use a hand."

Kydd nodded. "Thanks. Pants were the easy part. The shirts will need tailoring, but the Treffs can take care of that," this to Wyll, who looked politely interested and wasn't, Bannan was sure. Going to the clothes on the floor, the beekeeper picked out a garment. "This should do for now." "This" being a well-worn, sleeveless leather jerkin, laced with leather strips along the sides as well as partway down the front. "Let me—"

"I can manage," Wyll said gently, taking it in his good hand.

Not one-handed, he couldn't, Bannan knew.

Then, what he knew changed.

Like supple snakes, the laces slipped from their holes and curled against the leather. Wyll pushed his head through the neck opening and shrugged the jerkin over his shoulders. Once the garment settled, the laces wove themselves back through and finished in tidy knots, save for a gap in the front; explained once Wyll took his withered left hand and tucked it securely inside.

"This is comfortable." He stroked the leather with his good hand. "Please thank your brother for me."

"Thank him yourself at supper," Kydd said, so calm Bannan gaped at him. Seeing his expression, the beekeeper smiled. "Astonishing, isn't it? What Wyll can do. I've never seen the like."

So this wasn't Marrowdell. This was Wyll. Magic, without chant or smelly potion. "What else can you do?" Bannan asked, pleased by how normal he sounded.

"Small conveniences." A faint, self-deprecating smile. "You needn't fear me."

Both were lies.

Bannan swallowed. Should he expose them? Dare he?

"Wyll is Jenn's friend," Kydd said, with a slightly anxious air.

Power to power. Of course there was attraction. It didn't mean the friendship was benign.

Just as well he was staying. Just as well.

Letting none of his concern show, Bannan offered his hand. "We have something in common."

Wyll met his grip after the barest hesitation. As their palms touched, Bannan again glimpsed silver in his eyes. And something else.

Grief. Deep and terrible.

His breath caught in his throat. His other hand rose to clasp Wyll's, not in compassion, but to hold himself steady. To somehow endure what he saw long enough, long enough . . . to . . . understand . . .

Wyll freed his hand with a tiny, irresistible flex of his wrist. "Excuse me," he said politely, "but I'm eager to leave this place."

Kydd rolled the clothes back into the bundle. "You'll accompany us?" He hadn't missed Bannan's moment of discomfort; he'd want an explanation.

"Delighted."

"Then we go." Wyll twisted himself forward, step by step, each awkward movement powerful; each with its cost in pain. Bannan could see it in his face.

At the top of the stairs, Wyll stopped. Bannan and Kydd caught up and glanced at one another. Fifteen wooden steps, wide but not deep, led straight down. Other than support beams every three, they were open to the main floor of the mill. There wasn't a handrail.

"Can you manage stairs?" Bannan asked, considering what they could do if not.

"How should I know?" With exasperated sincerity. "These are my first as a man."

The truth. But . . . "How—how can that be?"

Kydd's eyes shone. "Because Wyll's only been a man since this morning." He kept his voice low. "You were wished into this shape, weren't you? I was there, when Jenn came back from the meadow. I knew something profound had happened."

Jenn Nalynn had done this. Bannan felt no doubt, though the how was beyond him. But why? And why make him like this, misshapen and in pain? If she'd meant harm, which he refused to believe, she could have left Wyll in the river to drown.

"What were you before?" the beekeeper went on, his eagerness bubbling over.

Wyll narrowed his eyes. "Different."

He still was. That much Bannan knew. Like the road and the trees. Whatever altered Wyll's appearance went no deeper than eyes could see. Not that eyes could be trusted in Marrowdell.

"Let's keep all this to ourselves for now, shall we?" he suggested, remembering Zehr and what he'd said about Covie.

"I don't know who'd believe us if we told them," Kydd said fervently. "Marrowdell's eccentricities aren't like this. I mean no offense."

"None taken." Wyll looked at the stairs and murmured, more to himself than them. "I should fall and get it over with."

He could see the outline of . . . wings. He was sure there were wings. As his awareness flickered confusingly between man and other, filled with wonder, Bannan spoke without thinking. "Why don't you fly?"

Wyll turned, eyes molten silver. "You first."

A burst of wind, oven-hot with an abattoir's stench, slammed into Bannan and sent him sliding backward. His heels dragged and bounced along the floor. He craned his head around. He was being pushed to the open window!

He flung out his arms, tried to grab the frame. Instead, one hand found the pulley rope. With an effort that strained every muscle, he twisted to grasp the rope with his other hand as his feet and legs were swept from under him. Buffeted by wind, he hung halfway through the window.

The rope gave and he flew out!

The pulley brake caught with a snap and somehow he held, swinging over air. "Stop!" Kydd was shouting. "Stop! Bannan saved your life! He saved Jenn's!"

The wind pushed harder, flapping his body like a flag. He couldn't last . . . the fall wouldn't kill him, Bannan judged in an agony of fear. It would leave him maimed, like Wyll.

"Listen to me. He meant no harm! He's a truthseer! He can see you!"

The wind shifted, flipping Bannan back inside like a toy, dropping him on hands and knees. Arms shaking, he raised his head to glare at Wyll. "Ingrate."

Admirable restraint, that was. Lila'd be proud.

"What truth do you see?" Wyll demanded.

Not a question he felt safe answering; not a question safe to avoid. Bannan stood with Kydd's help, thanking him with a look and nod. Few would have stayed in the face of such extraordinary threat. He flexed his rope-scored hands as he eyed the not-man; his insides, being sensible, tried to tie themselves in knots. Weapons, strength, skill? Nothing against an opponent like this. "I asked if you could fly," he replied at last, "for when I look at you, I see wings."

"I'm a man. I have none."

"You're a man," Bannan conceded. "But I see a different shape beneath." Hopefully Wyll wouldn't ask for details. What he saw . . .

they were glimpses of a whole, a whole he couldn't comprehend, let alone express in words.

"What you see no longer exists," said Wyll calmly. "We should leave now." He resumed his careful study of the stairs. "One of you go first, please, so I see how it's done."

A real man would show some sign of having tried to kill you, Bannan thought, numb. Someone born in this shape would have the decency to feel remorse or at least be bitter about failure. He'd rather have anger than be forgotten.

Present company excepted.

"We could get the smith," Bannan said with an effort, unwilling to touch the not-man. "He carried you up."

Wyll shuddered. "I wasn't awake."

"Davi's butchering your ox." Kydd's voice wasn't normal either. "It strayed into the fields," to Wyll.

"Good news at last," Wyll declared. The smile was the first Bannan had seen on the not-man's face. "After dispatching an intruder of such size, the efflet's bloodlust will be aroused." At their blank looks, he added, "They'll stay close."

And that was good news? Allies, Bannan thought with dread, his pulse still a-race. Invisible beings capable of killing an ox, when Wyll himself was threat enough.

"What are efflet?" Kydd demanded. "Is Marrowdell in danger?"

"Of course not," Wyll appeared puzzled. "Efflet protect the kaliia, what you call grain. That's all. But they can be asked favors." His eyes turned silver. "If I can attract a few . . ."

Bannan held his breath, his fingers itching for a sword hilt, useless or not. Kydd looked in no better frame of mind, beads of sweat on his high forehead. When Wyll exclaimed, "Ah!" both men flinched and looked around, wild-eyed, but there was nothing to see.

But something had come. For an instant, Bannan glimpsed how the air around the not-man flickered, then thickened, as if he'd been wrapped in the finest gauze.

"Gently," Wyll admonished. He rose off his feet and floated in midair. Before Bannan or Kydd could react, he plunged down the stairwell shouting, "GENTLY!"

The men gave chase. "He said he couldn't fly," Kydd gasped as they thundered down the stairs.

Wyll hit the floor with a sodden thud.

"He can't," Bannan affirmed.

"Silly unreliable creatures," Wyll was muttering when they reached the bottom. He winced as he rose to his feet.

So. Not invulnerable.

Horst and Radd came from the basement, both splattered with mud, Radd clutching a shovel. "What happened?" he demanded. "We heard something fall." His eyes locked on Wyll and widened. "You're awake!" To Bannan's surprise, he bowed. "An honor."

"The honor is mine," Wyll said at once, managing his own bow in return. "You are Radd Nalynn, miller, father, and brother." He bowed next to Horst. "And the guardian, who today saved Jenn Nalynn."

Had Kydd told him? Bannan wondered, seeing the truth in Wyll's face, or had he somehow known what happened on the road? If so . . . a chill fingered his spine.

" 'Saved Jenn?' " Radd's face lost all color. "Horst? What does he mean?"

The old soldier closed his eyes briefly, then turned to face his friend. "It's what I came to tell you. Jenn was on the road—"

The miller dropped the shovel. His hand groped for the nearest column and closed, white-knuckled, on that support. "By the Ancestors . . . why?"

"It was my fault," Horst said quickly. "She wasn't trying to leave. She told me she'd argued with Roche. When I went after him, she followed. It shouldn't have happened. We brought her back with us."

With obvious effort, Radd composed himself, hand falling to his side. He picked up the shovel. "All's well, then," he said with forced cheer.

"No, it isn't." Kydd stepped forward, his mouth a thin line. "What's this about Jenn being cursed?"

"How do you—" The miller's eyes widened. He stared at Horst. "You told them. And Jenn? You told her?"

"I had no choice—"

"She was never to know!" The shout echoed from the rafters. He lowered his voice, but it was no less terrible. "I forgave you for Melusine. I forgave you and took you as my friend. You swore not to tell her!"

The old soldier flinched as Bannan doubted he'd ever done in battle. The two men had shared an unimaginable burden. He found he couldn't pity them; his compassion was for Jenn Nalynn.

The not-man's head tilted. "Since the girl's birth, I've watched this guardian's faithful duty. Did you so prefer her ignorance, Radd Nalynn, that you'd rather he'd failed to save her?"

Horst faced Wyll. His eyes slowly widened, as if seeing a spirit come to life. "Who are you?" he breathed.

All of a sudden, the air fell still. Bannan tensed.

A shadow broke the sunbeams at their feet. Though he didn't turn, though he couldn't know, Wyll's expression hardened and he snapped, "What are you doing here?"

Bannan whirled to see who stood in the mill door, head lowered to fit the opening, nostrils flared.

Scourge.

"Stop worrying," Jenn told her sister. Tried to tell her sister. It wasn't easy holding a conversation with someone walking as quickly as possible. Someone with longer legs. She gave a half-skip to catch up. "Wyll wouldn't hurt Kydd. He wouldn't hurt anyone." There might be a bee or two who disagreed, but Wisp hadn't squashed them. He could, Jenn supposed, but in all their time together he'd done nothing worse than pull up plants and throw them.

Anyone would do that.

"He'd better—Heart's Blood!" Peggs cried, breaking into a run.

"Did you just swear—" Jenn shut up. They'd come around the house and there was the mill.

The mill with a man hanging from the pulley, like a sack of grain.

Not hanging like a sack, Jenn saw numbly, running with her sister. Improbably straight out from two arms, legs and body flapping like a windblown flag.

Bannan?

"Hold on!" she shouted, which wasn't much help.

They weren't the only ones to see his peril. Bannan's great horse charged up the lane heading straight for the mill door.

As suddenly as he'd appeared in the air, Bannan was sucked back inside.

A prank, Jenn told herself with relief, remembering the bees. That was all. Wisp wouldn't have hurt Bannan.

Would Wyll?

Doubt. She'd never doubted her friend before.

If she had doubts, she'd never be able to convince Peggs, not now. Or anyone else.

"What do you want?" Wyll demanded.

Bannan frequently wondered the same about his strange horse; it had never occurred to him to ask. "Apples. Oats," he offered. "There's no food here. Go on, you."

Go, he thought, dry-mouthed with fear, this time for Scourge. Who knew? Scourge might listen.

Or not. A great hoof thumped against the wood floor. Again.

Horst and Kydd, having experienced Scourge, looked properly apprehensive. The miller sighed. "Kindly remove your horse, Bannan."

Lips writhed away from teeth as Scourge snarled his own answer.

"Idiot," Bannan told him, stepping forward with what he hoped looked the confident stride of a man familiar with his animal and not the truth, which was a man who had no idea what he faced but was responsible for it. "I'm fine."

Scourge moved too. He lunged through the doorway and took advantage of greater space to arch his neck and expand into the mass of intimidating muscle and bone he was.

Wyll, at whom all this noise and posturing was aimed, lurched to put himself clear of Kydd.

His eyes turned silver.

"Wait!" Bannan looked from Wyll to Scourge and back. "This is my horse," he said lamely.

To meet the silvered gaze was like staring into the sun. "Your horse. You ride him?" Amused.

Amused was safer. Talking was safer. "Depends how well disposed he feels," Bannan said lightly, with a meaningful glare at the creature in question, who ignored him, eyes locked on Wyll. Being ignored, Bannan faced the adversary who could talk, doing his best to ignore the blasts of hot breath on the back of his head. "You should remember him. Scourge saved your life in the river."

"Jenn Nalynn saved me."

Scourge rumbled in threat. Wyll braced himself. What would happen next hung on a breath, Bannan judged, holding his.

Which was when the next arrivals burst through the door.

It was instant bedlam. Crying, "Are you all right?" Peggs ran to Kydd and threw herself in his arms before he could utter a word. In public. Jenn would have liked to watch, but Uncle Horst ordered, "Get back!" for no reason while their father—Jenn's heart sank—added his own shout, "Get this animal out of my mill!"

The animal in question half reared and snorted. If he could produce flames from those flared reddened nostrils, Jenn thought with disgust, he would. Wyll was glaring back, his eyes that ominous color, while Bannan stood between the two, which was not at all a good idea.

How had things reached this state?

She'd also like to know how Wyll managed the stairs, which had been a worry of her own, but that wasn't as important as stopping him from doing something they'd all regret.

First. Jenn walked beside Scourge and leaned her shoulder into his flank to let him know he was in her space, as she would to Wainn's pony or one of the draft horses. They'd move; she expected he would.

And he did. Though with a surprised "Woomph!" as his hind-quarters shifted away. His great head snapped around to look at her.

"About time someone taught you manners," Wyll said.

Jenn walked past Scourge and Bannan, straight at Wyll, whose expression went from smug to uneasy as she approached. She didn't stop until they stood nose-to-nose, or would have, if he'd been shorter. "I promised my sister you'd behave," she said as calmly as she could, which wasn't calmly at all. "This is not behaving. I told her you were my best friend and I knew you would never," this with all the force of will she possessed, "ever harm anyone in Marrowdell. And you won't."

Unease changed to dismay; silver to astonished brown.

A breeze chased around the mill floor and flung dust at the mill-stones. It teased at hair and laces and skirts, ruffled a mane, then fled out the door.

In mute acquiescence, Wyll bent his head.

After a long moment, his eyes lifted to hers. She was startled to see they glistened with unshed tears. "You wished me a man, Dearest Heart," he whispered. "You've made me nothing more."

With a neigh like trumpets, Scourge pounced, pushing Jenn aside with a sweep of his neck to reach Wyll, knocking him to the floor with his huge head.

Jenn staggered. Bannan caught her. Kydd held Peggs, or she held him. Radd raised a shovel and Horst drew his knife.

Scourge, having planted a hoof on Wyll's chest, lowered his open mouth, dripping with saliva and filled with fangs, a finger's breadth from Wyll's face.

And roared.

~ Is this why you returned? ~ Wyll asked. ~ To see me fail? ~ The answer didn't matter. Nothing mattered. The first of the dire visitors he'd been warned against and the twice-cursed turn-born's expectation shackled him within this now-helpless, useless flesh.

Yesterday, daisies.

Today, his ruin. Leaving Marrowdell unguarded and the girl, exposed to harm.

The timing of her innocent rise to potency couldn't have been worse.

Why was he not surprised?

~ You give yourself too much credit. ~ The kruar snorted. ~ I heard the cackle of dragons tormenting their prey. ~ The hoof lifted from his chest to stamp beside his head, ringing through the floor with force enough to be heard in the Verge. ~ It pleased me to spoil their play. Had I known it was you, I would have left them in peace. ~

He'd have relished the irony, once. He'd had hope, once. ~ Your breath hasn't improved. ~ Wyll turned his face to avoid the drool and closed his eyes. ~ Be done. ~

Kruar preferred to ambush his kind, to kill up close. They'd use their wiles and tricks to lure their quarry to the ground and, once they had a dragon safely pinned, employ their tusks to tear an opening through the thin scales at the base of the jaw. Venomous fangs waited in a sheath below a kruar's tongue. One plunge of those fangs, a pulse of hot venom in that opening? Flame would ignite in the flesh, a flame that would burn till only scales remained.

A slow, hideous death. Dragon flesh tried in vain to heal itself, prolonging the agony. To be fair, kruar died no prettier in the talons of a dragon. Take now. If he'd his own instead of these useless feet, there'd be steaming kruar entrails on the floor.

~ I knew my mistake the instant your foul blood burned my skin. I knew it was you!!! ~ A singsong growl as the kruar happily worked himself to killing rage, then an unexpected pause. ~ Why are you here, like this? ~ the creature demanded. ~ Why are these women and men? Why are there buildings? Horses? And cows?! ~ the last with thorough disgust. ~ Why are there cows? ~

~ Why must I endure your rants as well as your breath? ~ Wyll countered wearily. ~ Why is anything as it is? The turn-born wanted them here, so they made this place— ~

~ Wanted them? Why? Do they not remember? ~

Stupid creature. Of course they remembered. Who did not?

Once before men had come to Marrowdell. They'd built mighty towers and studied the sky, awaiting the next Great Turn. And when it came, they'd cast their wishings, never guessing the consequence if they were answered.

While in the Verge, those who could guess had launched their little war, hoping the powerful would be distracted.

Utter folly seemed the privilege of both worlds.

~ They'll be here soon. Ask them yourself, if you dare. ~ Wyll kicked out with his good leg, connecting with one of the kruar's.

The kruar roared, as he'd hoped. It would be over soon.

"Scourge! Heart's Blood and Blithering Idiots! Stop!" The man's shout, but amazingly, the roar subsided. The growling ceased.

~ My truthseer pities you. ~

~ Be done. ~

~ Do not order me! ~ Another roar. ~ You command nothing and no one. If I choose, I will let you live. I would enjoy watching you suffer and be pitied. ~

Hope stirred, an unwelcome guest. It brought back duty. Demanded effort.

Wyll forced open his eyes to find the jaws no longer at his throat. ~ You were drawn here, ~ he told the creature. ~Your truthseer was drawn here. You will not be the last. ~

Another fearsome stamp. ~ I go where I choose! ~

More spit in his face. He remembered how much he hated this

particular kruar. Wyll moved his good hand listlessly. ~ Old fool. Have you been so busy playing the horse you forgot to track the years? ~

Silence.

Then, ~ Another Great Turn is nigh upon us. ~ The kruar's head rose. ~ Why else do you think I've returned? The sei will be distracted. My chance comes! ~

~ Chance for what? To slink into the Verge and hide from the sei? Your penance won't be forgotten, any more than mine. ~

~ I've suffered enough! ~ Another fearsome stamp.

~ When did that matter? ~ Wyll pushed himself to an awkward sit. The rest stood at a distance, wise for once. He refused to look at the girl. Not until he'd found a way to protect her from her own folly. ~ You know what she is. You can smell it. ~

~ Turn-born. ~ The great head swung to stare at Jenn Nalynn. ~ She pulled your teeth. You deserved it, toying with my truthseer. ~

Wyll refused to be deflected. ~ A turn-born of this world, not ours. ~

~ Impossible! ~

It would have been, had the mother's plight not met a foolish heart. How could he be glad, knowing what he knew? How could the girl's existence matter to him? How dare he let it?

~ Yet she exists, as even you can see. ~ The sei put value to her life; he shouldn't. Her existence threatened everything he once cared about, cared about still. Dead was safer, safest, best of all. Here and now. The kruar could do it.

He couldn't. ~ She is ignorant of that heritage and its risks. ~ Wyll continued. ~ The sei made me her keeper. ~

~ You?! ~ Fangs snapped in front of Wyll's face. Snapped, and stayed closed. Nostrils flared to take in his scent. Kruar rarely trusted outside their kind. He'd sorely perplexed this one.

~ The sei want her safe. ~ Wyll left the rest unsaid.

~ Then they should be disappointed in your service. It took the old soldier to stop her slipping beyond the edge. The old soldier and my truthseer. I was there. ~ A satisfied rumble. ~ You were not. You are of no use. You cannot protect her. ~

Had he ever felt pride? ~ But you can. ~

~ The sei will notice. ~

How long did it take a thought to travel that thick skull? ~ Making this an opportunity to serve your penance. ~ Use their words. ~ They may consider it favorably. ~

~ And allow my return! ~ A blast of hot, odorous breath. ~ I will take this opportunity. I declare common purpose! ~ The jaws snapped near Wyll's throat. ~ Until I decide to end your suffering. ~ Magnanimously.

~ Until then, a common purpose. ~ Wyll grabbed the kruar's neck and pulled himself to his feet.

"Nice horse," he said aloud.

ELEVEN

"'NICE HORSE?'" Jenn rushed to Wyll's side, not letting Scourge out of her sight. "He attacked you!"

"A misunderstanding, Dearest Heart."

She narrowed her eyes. "About what?" Neither answered.

They'd wanted to kill one another. She hadn't misunderstood that. Some private conversation had gone on between the two, Jenn was sure. Wyll's eyes had flickered silver. Scourge's remained black, but had widened or narrowed as if Wyll argued some point. A truce may have resulted, but tense quivers continued to shudder along Scourge's flanks and Wyll gave a tiny pained wince every so often. A truce, she thought, dry-mouthed, neither trusted.

Why?

"Jenn." Peggs beckoned urgently, her face pale. "Come away."

"What?" Jenn frowned in puzzlement, then her face cleared. "Scourge won't attack me." For assurance, she looked to Bannan, who'd gone to the animal.

Scourge, as suited the embodiment of "nice horse," laid his face against Bannan's chest with a ridiculously placid nicker. "Your guess is as good as mine," Bannan admitted as he patted Scourge's neck. "Idiot beast." With fond exasperation.

"Overly protective," Wyll offered generously. Scourge flicked his tail.

"Are you all right?" Jenn ran a worried eye over her friend. Dressed, he looked more normal, if she overlooked the drool drying on his jerkin. His face was drawn. Exhausted, at a guess. Who wouldn't be?

Wyll smiled gently. "I am well."

"Jenn!" Peggs' voice was shrill. "Come here this instant!"

Overwrought. Her sister was never overwrought. Or hysterical. Maybe it was her proximity to Kydd. "Everything's fine, Peggs."

"No, it's not!"

With a concerned look at his eldest, their father stepped in. "First things first," he said gruffly. "Bannan, this is not a stable. Kindly remove your horse."

Bannan took firm hold of Scourge's mane. "Of course. My apol—"

"Forget the horse! Poppa! Get Jenn away from him! Him!" Peggs cried, pointing wildly at Wyll. "He tried to kill Bannan. He has—he has powers! He's dangerous!"

"Peggs!" Jenn protested.

"I assure you, I'm quite harmless," Wyll said calmly.

Scourge blew loudly through loose lips. Bannan gazed at Wyll, his eyebrows raised.

"What's going on?" In rushed Dusom Uhthoff, with Zehr, Tir, and Riss at his heels, grim-faced and carrying whatever they'd been able to grab quickly. A pitchfork, hammers. Riss held a broom and looked ready to use it.

Wrong. All wrong. Jenn put herself beside Wyll, taking his good hand in hers to hold tight. "Bannan's fine. See?" she urged. "It was—it was a little bit of fun."

"Heart's Blood, girl!" Tir could growl as fiercely as Scourge. "Fun?"

She sent a beseeching look at Bannan, who hesitated, then gave a small nod. "No harm's been done," he said.

Jenn sighed gratefully.

"Not because harm wasn't meant," Kydd objected, shaking his head. He stood by Peggs, his arm around her waist as if he'd forgotten to take it away. "Jenn, your friend would have killed Bannan. I've seen his powers for myself. Without lifting a hand, he could kill any of us."

The villagers stirred.

"He wouldn't," Jenn insisted.

"I couldn't," Wyll put in, which wasn't helpful. Scourge snorted.

"He can't stay here," Kydd went on, avoiding her eyes. "Not in Marrowdell. He has to leave."

Send Wisp away?

Wind banged a shutter. The sky darkened. The storm should come back, Jenn thought, furious, opening her mouth to protest. Before she could, Wyll's fingers pressed hers ever-so-lightly and a familiar breeze whispered soft in her ear, "Peace, Dearest Heart. They aren't wrong. I let myself be angered and their fear is the result. Peace and patience, or you'll make matters worse."

To the rest, "I regret causing any distress, good people of Marrowdell. It won't happen again."

"How can we believe you?" Kydd pointed outside. "Look at this!"

"Now you're blaming Wyll for the weather?" Jenn exclaimed, outraged. Lightning flashed, a strike so close its thunder shook the mill. "Stop this! All of you! Leave him alone! You don't understand."

"Jenn, please—"

"Wyll came to Marrowdell to marry me."

Scourge's head shot up, making Bannan jerk back with an oath. Everyone else looked stunned.

Including Wyll, again not, Jenn glowered at him, helping. "We're in love," she snapped. Lightning flashed again, limning faces, turning those around her to strangers.

Why wasn't anyone saying anything? Why did they stare at her like that? Tears blurred her vision. Jenn blinked furiously and pressed her lips together, afraid to say another word, afraid she'd said too many. That was the trouble with words; once spoken, you couldn't take them back.

"Then congratulations are in order. The Ancestors Blessing on you both." Bannan put his circled fingers over his heart and bowed. When he raised his head, something in his eyes jolted her heart.

"Yes, they are," Jenn replied unsteadily. "Thank you." She tugged on Wyll's hand.

Prompted, he said, "Thank you."

Scourge snorted again.

Sunbeams flowed through the door; the storm must have been a passing remnant. Kydd exchanged a sober look with his brother.

Radd Nalynn bore that aggrieved expression his daughters knew very well indeed, the one that meant he had a great deal to say and wasn't going to say it until they were home and alone. "You." He looked up at Scourge, who looked back with a curled lip. "Out!"

The commotion had drawn Marrowdell together again. Outside the mill, silent villagers gave Scourge room to pass, then pulled close again. They looked over their shoulders. At the horse. At Tir. At him. Doubtful looks. Fear-filled.

Exactly what he didn't want. "Couldn't have gone worse," Bannan muttered once he and Tir were past the crowd. "Idiot." To Scourge.

To himself.

"What happened in there?" Still tense, Tir glanced from side to side as if they might be ambushed at any turn, instead of walking a lane of sparkling puddles and red mud, surrounded by pleasant gardens and hedges. A bee droned by, on its way to one of the hives under the apple trees.

"What happened was my fault." The words were sour in Bannan's mouth. "And if they throw Wyll from Marrowdell, it'll be because I lost all common sense."

Tir stared at him, scarred forehead crinkled. "Tell me you didn't fight over the maid."

That had been the worst of it. To hear Jenn proclaim her love, her intention—to see the truth in her face.

To begin to comprehend what he'd lost, before the chance of having it.

"We didn't fight," Bannan said numbly. "I gave him reason to strike at me."

They'd reached the wagon. He sat, arms limp, on the driver's step. Tir leaned on the wheel and pulled off his mask. He scratched his beard. "How good a reason?"

"You tell me, old friend." Bannan put his hands behind his head and studied the sun-drenched crags that loomed behind the orchard, his gaze caught in the deep scars that ran from summit to base. "This Marrowdell is a rare and wondrous place. So wondrous, it contains a farm maid whose best friend commands the very air. A friend who, only this morning, mind you, she wished into the shape of a man for love's sake. Misshapen, crippled, but a man nonetheless, who nearly drowned trying to reach her."

"I didn't know you'd hit your head, sir," Tir said kindly.

"I know how it sounds—"

Tir chuckled. "Like a child's story. A silly one at that." Bannan faced him and waited. "Heart's Blood." The other man's eyes slowly narrowed. "You're serious."

"Never more so. I look at him," Bannan said simply, "and see the man you see. I see what he was, as well. Not all. Not whole. Glimpses. He had wings."

" 'Wings.' " Tir shook his head. "You're seeing wings, now."

And so much more . . . something he'd rather not discuss. "They were there," the truthseer insisted. "Once."

To his relief, his friend merely shrugged. "That's a bad trade. As a man, he can barely walk."

"I know. I knew. But . . . when I met him, saw what he was capable of . . . I was dazzled. I lost sense of which parts I saw were this Wyll and which weren't. When he hesitated at the top of stairs, I—I suggested he fly." Bannan remembered the furious flash of silver. "He didn't take it well."

"I'd have hit you too," Tir agreed. "Though not hung you out a window. Sir."

"We are what we are." Was Wyll? He'd twice claimed to be no threat. The first time, he'd lied. The second? There was the rub. The second time, he'd told the truth. Something had happened. Had it been Jenn? "I don't believe he'll do it again."

"Belief is a fine thing, sir, and the Ancestors approve. But if you don't mind, I'll add this Wyll's not doing anything else unnatural to tonight's Beholdings."

Tir's Beholdings tended to lengthy grumbles about the food and weather or, lately, the condition of the Northward Road and his, Bannan's, mind. "I'd be grateful," Bannan half-grinned.

"What I'd be grateful for is a look inside yon bloody beast's head." Tir nodded at Scourge. "What was that nonsense in the mill? I've seen him do daft things, but nothing like that."

The beast in question tilted back an ear, then gracelessly lowered himself into a puddle like the brat he was to roll with grunts of delight, hooves flailing in the air. When he finally lunged to his feet, he was thoroughly coated in red mud and as thoroughly smug about it.

"You'll stay that way," Bannan warned him. The only thing Scourge loved more than a mud bath was the endless grooming to get him rideably clean again. He'd purr himself to sleep and, given any opportunity, be back in the mud the next day.

As for Tir's question, he'd been asking himself the same thing. Bannan gazed at Scourge. "For a being who can command the air," he suggested smoothly, "a horse can't be much of a challenge."

This garnered the full-on glare, complete with teeth and forelock toss, of Scourge at his most insulted. Point made, the horse strutted away, though mud-speckled haunches did little for his offended dignity. Bannan refrained from comment.

He waited until Scourge was safely beyond the hedgerow. "When Scourge charged into the mill—let's say to my rescue—"

"He has before."

"He has indeed." Bannan leaned forward. "What troubles me this time, Tir, is Scourge went straight for Wyll. He couldn't have seen what happened."

"They know each other, sir. That was plain enough." Tir's blue eyes held a chill. "Know and hate. I was sure there'd be blood."

He'd been sure too, just not whose. "None of it makes sense. If

Scourge came to Marrowdell to pursue an old foe, why help me save—what is it?"

Tir had come erect, tugging his mask into place, another mask sliding behind his eyes. "Company, sir."

Horst and Kydd, with Wyll between them. They didn't offer support; he didn't appear to need any, lurch-stepping his way around puddles, taking his time, his head held high. Like any of the maimed veterans Bannan had known, too young to be betrayed by their bodies, dealing with blindness or missing limbs with an ease borne of tiresome practice and the certainty of nothing better ahead.

He was caught by an incongruity that slipped away before he could name it.

"Think they'll send us all packing at once?" Tir tried not to sound eager.

And lose the silver road, the wondrous hills, the farm?

"We've nothing to pull the wagon," Bannan answered, for the first time glad the poor ox hung from a butcher's hook. "Scourge certainly won't."

"Bannan. Tir." Horst was polite and expressionless. His duty face, Bannan judged, the one he'd show no matter what he was called upon to do.

In contrast, Kydd was wan and tense, understandable in a man courting one sister and likely feeling the frowns of the other, Bannan thought sympathetically. "What can we do for you?" he asked.

"Wyll's to spend the night in my home," Horst said.

"There's a meeting this evening at the Emms," Kydd elaborated. "For villagers." The words drew a line. To his credit, he looked distressed.

A meeting doubtless to discuss the not-man's alarming abilities, during which they wouldn't want him unwatched. "We'd be glad to help Wyll settle," he offered. "Tir and I are sleeping by the wagon anyway." Thus keeping all the strangers in one place, as far from the other homes as possible. He'd have done the same.

Horst nodded gravely. Kydd tried too hard not to show relief. "Gallie's sending a supper."

Aloof to all this, Wyll studied Tir, a scrutiny the former border guard bore with growing discomfort. Finally he snapped, "What?"

"Why do you wear a mask?" the other replied.

"It covers this." Tir jerked the metal down.

"To what purpose?"

Tir scowled and scrunched his face into a grotesque shape. "So I don't scare children."

Wyll appeared puzzled. "The young respect the marks of battle."

While he enjoyed the rare spectacle of Tir speechless, Bannan took pity. "Why don't you save Gallie the trip and fetch our supper?" he suggested.

Tir gladly escaped, though he made sure to replace his mask and glare at Wyll first. Kydd hesitated, then took his leave as well. "Ancestors Baffled and Beloved." Bannan said in earnest. "I don't envy him tonight."

"The meeting concerns you as well. Kydd will speak in your favor," Horst said bluntly. "As will I."

The good regard of a man like this was not given lightly. Pleased, the truthseer gave a small bow. "My thanks."

"You acquitted yourself well." The old soldier rubbed one hand across his face then shook his head. "I wish I could say the same. This has not been a good day. My past—it's not something I'm proud of."

Bannan recognized the signs. The confession of a tightly held secret could burst a dam inside a man, spilling forth everything hidden. The relief was intoxicating, if temporary and, as Vorkoun's truthseer, he'd taken full and heartless advantage, time without number.

If there was more to Horst's past, despite his pity, Bannan knew he shouldn't be the one to hear it. Not until they were neighbors, or, better still, friends. "Scourge took the battle honors today," he said with deliberate lightness. "Best wait till you see my skills—or lack of—around a farm. Tir's taking wagers. I believe he's betting on the plough to win."

Horst gazed toward the gate and the road beyond. Lines deepened around his eyes and mouth, then he said in a voice already distant. "I won't be here. I leave with the Lady Mahavar."

He meant for good.

Bannan frowned. Having confessed, did Horst mete his own punishment? "You don't belong in Avyo," he protested, certain of that, though he scarcely knew the man. "Jenn understands what you've done for her and why. You belong here."

Horst gave him a sharp look. "Do I, truthseer? That welcome was based on duty. Duty I've fulfilled. Why shouldn't I go home?"

Wyll, who'd been gazing around as if seeing the village for the first time—as well he might be, through a man's eyes—looked at Horst. "You guard the road."

"From what?" the soldier demanded. "There's been naught but honest settlers off the Northward in all the years I've patrolled. Marrowdell's safe. The Nalynns too. Melusine's family knows she's dead, Radd and Peggs are beyond reach within their binds and this valley. Jenn?" His voice softened. "I promised to keep her safe. Well, now she knows of the curse and will mind herself. Duty done, I say. High time I went back to my life."

His life was here.

Horst lied with courage, yet revealed one truth. In the marches, he'd have leapt on that slip. Here? Let it pass, Bannan told himself. What business of it was his, why this man chose to leave?

Horst had earned a smile from Jenn Nalynn.

For her sake, then. "You say they know Melusine is dead," Bannan made himself say the words. "How did you prove it? Surely Radd buried her here."

"He stole her body and gave it to a bear." Horst whirled to stare at Wyll; the not-man merely smiled. "Not that he let the bear keep it."

"Then you took what was left to Avyo." It was more than clever; it was flawless. "The Semanaryas mourned a daughter killed by an animal, not childbirth. No wonder they haven't come for Jenn. They don't know she exists."

"Heart's Blood. You sound like you admire what I did," Horst said harshly, his throat working. "I defiled the resting place of a Blessed!"

More often than not, those killed in the marches rested where they fell, unless dragged away by wolf or bear. "You did what you had to do," Bannan countered. "Show me a bone in Avyo's ossuaries that hasn't been shoved here and there, or put in a box to suit some descendant's whim." He gentled his tone. "Horst, you saved Jenn. You fulfilled your duty to the Semanaryas and gave them back their daughter. I see no shame here."

"And when Radd Nalynn learns all that's buried in Marrowdell is a ring? That I lied when I demanded a token for Melusine's family as proof of her death? That he pours out his heart to an empty grave?"

By saving everyone else pain, the man took it all for himself. "Ancestors Lost and Misplaced. Does it matter where they are, if they hear us?" Bannan paused, then said simply, "Tell Jenn."

"I'm not the man they think I am." A muscle jumped along Horst's jaw. "I'll not stay to watch that man die."

"You underestimate her."

"I won't chance it. I can't. I ask you respect that, Bannan. Don't tell Jenn, or anyone else, my intentions. Let me play the uncle and leave in peace. It's better thus."

"It is not better." Wyll's eyes flickered silver. "You must not leave Marrowdell."

"Can you stop me?" Horst challenged. A fretful breeze swirled around his head, then rushed through the nearby garden to flip leaves in a temper, doing nothing worse than expose the warm gold of ripening pumpkins and startle a butterfly. "I see not," the soldier concluded with a grim smile.

The silver faded, not the temper. "Fool. You see and understand nothing. Go. Abandon her." Wyll lurched away, entering Horst's home without host or invitation. The surly breeze followed, shoving the braided doormat aside.

Bannan glanced at Horst. "I'll keep silent. I've a feeling he will too."

The soldier offered his hand. He gave his own, and received an unexpectedly warm grip. "Welcome to Marrowdell," Horst said in a low voice. "Most welcome, Bannan Larmensu."

Moved, he put his hand on the other's shoulder. "For my part in events, I'm sorry."

Horst went still; his set and weathered face like those of the carvings along Vorkoun's eastern wall: nameless warriors confined to their alcoves and the attention of pigeons.

"I was always to leave," he said at last. "Now I know when."

Aunt Sybb sat in her chair, her best black shawl adjusted just so, the polished toes of her shoes showing just enough from beneath her lavender skirt to remind those without shoes of the significance of their lack no matter how muddy it was outside and how unsuitable city shoes were for mud, and lifted one dainty finger. At this admonishment, the sisters fell silent and exchanged glum looks.

"So," Aunt Sybb said. "He wasn't a toad." This had become something of a sticking point. "Ever?"

Jenn held back a sigh. Her aunt, while insisting there was no such thing as a curse, had professed herself satisfied that the question of Jenn's leaving for Avyo had been, however oddly, settled. She'd dismissed Horst's terrible secret, attributing that airily to the reckless hearts of lonely men who took too much on themselves, this with a stern if sympathetic look at her brother. Toads, however, were another matter. "No, Aunt. Wyll was never a toad."

"Then what was he?"

"I—" Admitting she didn't know wasn't likely to go well. "My friend from Night's Edge. The meadow."

"Yes, dear, we're aware of that. But what was your friend before you made him into a man?"

Safer. Jenn stared at her hands, neatly folded in her lap. Better off. Happier. "He was a little breeze," she said after a moment. "He could always do things. Move the air. Talk to me. Nothing like—nothing like what happened to Bannan."

She hesitated and Peggs noticed. "But?"

"Wisp chased Roche home once. He didn't touch him," she added quickly.

Their father lifted his head. He'd been silent since walking in the door and taking a seat at the table; had listened as she and Peggs did their best to explain what had happened to their aunt. Well, thought Jenn, she'd tried to explain and Peggs had been difficult. Until Jenn brought up the beekeeper, which had made her sister almost impossible.

"He protects you, Jenn," Radd said heavily. "Without hesitation. Without regard to anyone else. Therein lies the problem. With his powers . . ." he let his voice trail away.

"I've told him not to harm anyone." She believed Wyll, but how to persuade the rest? "He hasn't been—it was only this morning, Poppa. You haven't talked to him yet."

"Quite right. You must speak to the young man, Radd." Aunt Sybb pursed her lips, then gave a nod. "As soon as possible, given such a public—" her eyes touched on Jenn, who blushed, "—announcement." Peggs' turn next. "And display. Both young men."

"Sybbie—"

"Aunt!"

Their bastion of right was unmoved by either outburst. "A formal visitation would be best," their aunt went on, as if instructing her household in Avyo. "A meal is too personal and we certainly can't have Peggs cooking. I shall ask young Hettie to wait on us. Surely her mother has a pair of shoes to fit the girl. A platter of cheese and fruits. Some sweet biscuits. There really must be cordials. Do you have any cider left? It was reasonably convivial."

Jenn wasn't sure whose eyes were widest. Their father's normally apple-red cheeks had gone the color of eggshells and Peggs seemed short of breath. "I saw two jugs in the larder," she said helpfully. The storm had ended lunch before they'd been brought out. There wouldn't be beer until the harvest.

"Excellent. I shall write invitations, of course." Aunt Sybb paused, then, delicately, "I assume your friend will have no difficulty?"

"Wyll can read." Jenn smiled. She'd take favorite books to enjoy on a sunny afternoon and Wisp would flip the pages. They'd sound out the words together when she was younger; once she could read for herself, he'd read along. Sometimes he'd keep reading by himself, while she made daisy chains. Every so often, he'd grow frustrated with the obtuseness of a character and lift the book into the air, threatening to shred it into pieces. He never did.

"Radd, dear. Whom do you suggest deliver them?"

"Enough! This is foolish, Sybbie. On a day like this—" his voice broke. "How can—"

The tiny woman in the birch chair sat straighter, if that were possible, her eyes fixed on her brother. "It is precisely on a day like this we must act as Nalynns. As family. Do I wish you'd confided in me from the start? Of course, for your sake, dear brother. But as our beloved grandmother would say, once a ship's passed the fourteenth bridge, there's no point chasing it." His lips quirked. "I trust there are no more secrets?" She waited until he gave a tiny shake of his head. "Well, then. You've daughters who've proclaimed their affections. Did you honestly expect them to wait for a more opportune time or one of our choosing?" Gently. "Radd, we urged them to follow their hearts. It's up to us to support them."

He gave her a doubtful look. "This is how? With invitations."

"The invitations," she said primly, "are but the beginning, if all goes well. We've a great deal to do."

She'd said "we." That had to mean . . . Jenn burst out, "You're going to stay!"

"Sybbie, you can't."

"Tsh, Radd." The smallest of dimples. "I managed a fine nap this afternoon. I believe the cider we had with lunch proved a most beneficial soporific, and shall take a cup before bed tonight." She offered her hands to her nieces. Peggs and Jenn exchanged delighted smiles as they each laid a hand in hers. Cool and soft, never callused, hands which nonetheless wielded strength. "I must—I shall remain as long as I can, Dearest Hearts," their aunt asserted, gazing fondly at them.

Her eyes suddenly widened. "Ancestors Blessed and Blissful! We might make the Golden Day!"

The rest of the Nalynns exchanged puzzled looks.

"As I thought. Marrowdell is on the outside of the world." Aunt Sybb tsked her disapproval. "The twentieth of Haveral? The autumnal equinox of this most favored year of our Blessed Ancestors? The best halls were booked ages ago. Every handfasted couple in Rhoth and Mellynne wants to be wed that day."

"On my birthday?" Jenn blurted. "Why?"

"The eclipse, of course." Aunt Sybb squeezed their hands. "Imagine, Dearest Hearts. To be wed on the most auspicious day in our lifetimes. Not that I," she added firmly, "adhere to the old ways, most of which came from Mellynne in the first place and look where that put us. But traditions have their reasons, that I truly believe, and what better reason than the Ancestors' wish for long life and good fortune?"

Jenn knew what an eclipse was, though she'd yet to see one herself; Master Dusom, who owned a little brass telescope that collapsed into itself and who knew the name of every cluster of stars, made sure Marrowdell's children had a solid grasp of the heavens. To have such a fabled event on her birthday? A few days ago, she'd have tingled with delight.

Now?

Now it was like the closing of a trap, with even the sky conspiring to order her life.

Radd coughed. "Let's not get ahead of ourselves. There are matters to be settled. Serious matters." The corner of his mouth twitched. "Still, there's no harm in planning ahead. I trust you'll provide me with a list, dear sister?" He laid his hand over Jenn's; reached across the table for Peggs. "You're both sure, now. Peggs?"

She blushed but managed a bold, "I'm sure, Poppa."

"Jenn." His hand pressed warm over hers. "Wait," as she opened her mouth and hesitated. "Don't answer. We'll go ahead as you wish. See how it comes out. How's that?"

She should be sure. Wanted to be.

Wasn't at all.

How did he know? Jenn wondered, and searched his kind face.

"Now," Aunt Sybb said, reclaiming her hands. "I think it's time we discussed dresses."

"That, I'll leave you to, dear ladies." Radd rose and went around the table to his sister, bending to kiss her cheek, his hand lingering on her shoulder. "Mind your aunt," he told his daughters with mock ferocity.

Seeing how Peggs' eyes shone, all Jenn could do was nod.

Despite better intentions, Jenn fell asleep somewhere between flounces and flowers, curled into the cushions of the settee. She roused for a little supper and tea, then did her utmost to pay attention as her sister and aunt discussed arcane subjects like households and draperies and many other things that had nothing to do with Wyll as far as she could tell and possibly were a little ahead of matters as they stood.

But Peggs glowed. Aunt Sybb was animated. Lists sprouted like spring flowers and roses nodded approvingly through the windows. So Jenn did her best not to yawn, though once the sun went down, the effort was painful.

Finally, her aunt noticed and shooed her off to bed.

Which would have been wonderful, Jenn thought with some irritation, save the moment her head met the pillow, she wasn't sleepy at all.

Nor was Peggs, who sat on the window seat, brushing out her hair. The long black locks shone in the candlelight. They should shine. There'd been a great deal of brushing. And humming. Endless humming. Which hadn't helped with sleeping. Jenn pulled the quilt up to her nose. "Must you hum?"

Her sister looked vaguely in her direction. "Was I? Sorry."

She hadn't stopped smiling, either. An introspective, full of secrets smile.

"What you are," Jenn grumbled enviously, "is giddy."

"I wouldn't say giddy." The brush paused as Peggs considered, her lower lip between her teeth. "I am, aren't I? Oh, my."

Jenn gave up on the bed and squeezed beside Peggs on the window seat. There was a meeting underway in the Emms' barn. A meeting at which they weren't welcome. A meeting she was sure should have ended by now, but their father hadn't returned. "What do you think's happening?"

"Maybe it's a good sign, that it's taking so long." Peggs undid what was left of Jenn's braid and applied her brush. After a couple of long strokes, she said, "About what I said in the mill . . ." a pause "I'm sorry. I was afraid for Kydd," she admitted. "More afraid than I've ever been in my life. I suppose that's the other side of love," lightly said, not lightly meant. "The fear of losing it."

"I told you Wyll wouldn't hurt Kydd." Her sister's panic still rankled. "You should have trusted me."

The brush tapped her lightly on the head. "You're used to him and what he can do. It's different for the rest of us."

True. She'd grown up with Wisp's little tantrums and tricks. Jenn squirmed inwardly. To be honest, she hadn't realized he could do real harm, if provoked. The dreadful confrontation in the mill played over and over each time she closed her eyes. What if it had gone too far? What if Scourge had killed Wyll? What if Wyll had killed Scourge?

What if they'd fought, and harmed someone else? Like Peggs or their father?

She couldn't forget Bannan either. What had Wyll been thinking, to hang Bannan from the grain pulley? "He won't do it again," Jenn insisted.

The brush dug in a little harder.

"He won't. Ouch!"

"It's not me who needs to be convinced." Peggs put down the brush and stood to plait Jenn's braid.

Jenn pulled up her knees and dropped her chin on top. "If they say he can't stay," she continued miserably, "what am I to do? I can't leave."

"Poppa will speak up for Wyll." Peggs finished and kissed the top of her head. "Time for bed." She blew out their candle and climbed under the quilts.

"Coming." The moon must be close to full, Jenn decided. Its light shimmered in the few remaining puddles and sparked the eyes of busy toads. It coaxed memories of color from the gardens and folded velvet shadows, blue and dark and soft, around the trees and mill.

She pushed the window wide open, to invite the cooler night air.

Roses framed the window. Pale moths, larger than her palm, fluttered around the largest. One tasted the tip of her nose with its thread of a tongue. "If we were married," Jenn told it, cross-eyed, "they'd have to let Wyll stay, wouldn't they?"

"Which is why Aunt Sybb made all those lists," Peggs said sleepily. "Come. Get some rest. Things are always clearer in the morning."

A flicker across the path; a shadow grew long, then shortened. Jenn leaned forward, curious, and the moth left her for a rose. Something moved.

Someone. The moonlight caught hands, trapped a face. Bannan Larmensu. With a pack over his shoulder and walking like a man late.

No, she thought, her heart in her throat. Like a man leaving.

Peggs rolled over and hummed to herself.

She should call out and stop him. She wanted to.

And couldn't.

Jenn turned from the window and climbed into bed.

By night, Marrowdell posted sentries. Massive toads lined the road to watch Bannan's passing. They shifted position to keep him in view and were unconcerned by mere feet, so he walked with care. Their eyes were perfect disks of moonlight, like so many silver coins tossed in his path.

For luck, Bannan told himself, ready to claim all he could find.

They weren't toads. Or rather they were something else as well.

Like the road, silvered by moonlight, also had an amber hue, and the sky, which was mostly dark and star-filled but also shot through with vivid colors for which he needed names. When he looked closely, the toads' loose folds of skin became coats of fine mail and their warts, rich gems. No idle gauds, he judged those, but medals of some kind. Accomplished toads. He hoped for their favorable opinion.

He hadn't stepped on one. That had to count.

Other than the moonlight, the village was dark, porch lanterns and candles as yet unlit. What light there was sifted through the timbers of Emms' barn and laid bright bars across the ground that flickered with the movements of those inside. Voices murmured. As he passed, Bannan didn't try to make out words. He'd learn their decision soon enough.

If up to him? He'd let Wyll stay. The not-man had as much right to the valley as any of the villagers, if it came to that. If it came to forcing him to leave, against Jenn Nalynn's wishes?

Bannan shook his head and bowed as he stepped around a particularly large toad. Best they didn't try.

The toad blinked, for an instant disappearing into the shadows.

Moonlight bathed the fountain at the village's heart. Bannan paused to touch his finger to its water, as he'd seen the villagers do, and was surprised to find it cold, which it shouldn't be after a summer's heat. He brought a palmful to his lips and let it slide over his tongue, ready to spit if it were foul.

Sweet as a mountain spring. Sweeter. Bannan swallowed reverently, then emptied his flask and refilled it. "I'd stay for this alone," he assured the toad squatting on the fountain's stone wall.

Flask at his hip, Bannan continued on his way. The gate to the commons was closed. Rather than fumble for a latch, he tossed over his pack and climbed the rails. Retrieving it, he slung it over his shoulder and set forth.

No more toads. The livestock had gathered for the night at a wide shed on the high side of the pasture. A pair of workhorses stood hipshot by one end, head to tail, deep in sleep. By the other, two more horses, their silhouettes suggesting an elegant length of limb. A great pig lifted its snout as he passed and wuffled the air; finding him harmless, it let its head drop back on its companion's side with a hollow thud. Within the shed, peaceful lumps dotted the thick bedding, likely the calves Devins had told him about.

He'd like one or two, Bannan decided, though what he'd left to trade after donating the ox to the village larder remained to be seen. He'd a bit of coin tucked in a box under the wagon, completely against the bind's strictures. As Tir'd eloquently put it, what barkeep or wench would serve without?

There being few such temptations on the Northward Road, much to Tir's disgust, the coin was still there. Enough for a calf?

At the next gate, Bannan stopped babbling to himself. He put both hands on the top rail and gripped. Good wood. Weathered and rough, but strong. If he looked at it, he'd see nothing beyond its purpose. To mark the end of the village.

And the start of everything else.

The road beyond sloped to the ford, marked by the great tree to his left, and the rich smell of reeds and water filled the air. The river was silvered by moonlight; the road on both sides silver and flowing to his deeper sight. To either side stretched wide fields, quiet and serene, and he spotted a dark clump of trees in the distance that must mark the farm. Beyond, the smooth hills, painted the palest blue.

Why did he hesitate?

He'd had to come. The last light of the sun had flowed across the valley and through the village like a curtain pulled across a stage, its fleet passage exposing another Marrowdell, a different shaped landscape, other life. As he'd stood by his wagon and stared in wonder and disbelief, the fields had blazed red, the hedges filled with bright eyes, and the very road beneath his feet changed to molten silver.

As soon seen as gone.

How could he ignore so tantalizing an invitation?

He'd rushed inside after Tir only to find his friend with Wyll, the pair hunched over a makeshift table with the set of nillystones and two heaps of nuts, the former guard intent on teaching the not-man the fine points of the game and, from the interested gleam in Wyll's eye, the concept of gambling a familiar one indeed. They hadn't so much as looked up when he'd mentioned stretching his legs, this being a such lovely night.

Bannan put one foot on the lowest rail and leaned his chin on crossed arms.

A stretch of his legs. That it was a slightly longer stretch, along the Tinkers Road to what could be Bannan's new home, and who knows, possibly an overnight stay because once he was there why leave? Trifling details, hardly worth the mention.

He'd apologize to Tir tomorrow.

Tonight? He had to see it first for himself, by himself. Where was the harm? He could hardly get lost. From Devins' description, the farmhouse and barn were the only structures on the far side of the river. The road was properly hedged on either side, Ancestors Blessed, he could walk it blindfolded and never trespass in the growing fields. From all accounts, he'd be perfectly safe.

So why was he still on this side of the gate?

"You're afraid it won't be true."

The woman stood on the other side. Bannan hadn't seen her approach; hadn't heard so much as a footfall. She stepped closer and moonlight struggled through the mass of hair that framed her face and tumbled over her shoulders, revealed naked arms, long-fingered hands, and tidy bare feet. She wore a white nightdress.

No, he thought, heart pounding in his ears. She wore Marrowdell. Silver lapped at her toes and other nameless light tangled with the moon's in her hair. The edges of her blurred between there and here until he wasn't sure where she belonged or if he dreamed.

Tir was not going to be pleased. Not at all. Bannan found himself standing straight, hands before his chest as if to ward a blow.

Her head tilted; he glimpsed a strong chin. "Now afraid of me?" With a note of amusement.

He lowered his hands. "I mean no trespass."

"Surely you do, Bannan of the border marches." She laughed and swept out her bare arm, stepping aside to grant him the road. "Be welcome."

Swallowing doubt, he shrugged off his pack, tossed it over, then climbed the rails. Once his feet were on the ground, he bowed graciously. "May I know your name, Lady of Marrowdell?" Though he thought she must be the smith's sister, Wen Treff.

"He sees you," crowed a new voice with great delight. "I said he would."

"You did."

"Wainn?" Relieved, Bannan sought any sign of the man in the shadows. "Where are you?"

"Up here!"

"Up" being in the tree. Bannan found his pack and went to stand underneath. It was shaped like a massive oak; by now, he wasn't surprised to see something else again, something curious that moved its twigs without a wind. Wainn straddled the lowermost bough, feet a-dangle. Rather than jump down, he waited while the branch lowered itself with a faint creak of wood on wood, like an old rocker, then leapt to his feet. "This is Wen," he confirmed joyfully, going to her side. He was shirtless, in loose string-tied pants. "We're going to swim."

Her moonlit smile, his sure arm about her waist, transformed them from magic and youth into something no less wonderful. Bannan grinned. "Please don't let me interrupt," he said with another, deeper bow.

And a twinge of envy.

"You want to see your home," Wainn nodded toward the distant trees. "It waits for you."

Bannan settled the pack on his shoulder. "Full of mice, no doubt," he said cheerfully.

"The mice are gone," Wen stated. "The truth remains."

He gave her a searching look. She gazed back, calm and silent; a pair of toad eyes appeared in her hair, doing the same.

Wainn chuckled. "You see."

"No mice," Bannan agreed, shaking his head in awe. He took off his boots and secured them to his back. "I hope you'll visit."

Wen answered, "I will not," and walked into the darkness.

Dismayed, he stared after her. Had he been too casual and given offense? These two had taken a journey toward that other place, the one he saw beneath this one, and would never be ordinary again. They were royalty, here. "I meant no disrespect," Bannan told Wainn.

"Wen would like to visit," Wainn explained cheerfully, "but before she stopped talking, she made promises to keep her mother happy. Her mother was afraid she'd forget the way home, so Wen promised to stay on this side of the river." He added, with charming honesty, "Her mother worried about men too, so Wen promised not to receive visitors alone. That's why we swim where there's fish. Wen keeps her word."

To the letter, if not the intent. Somehow Bannan kept a straight face. "Admirable."

"I can visit you," Wainn assured him. "I'll ask Peggs for a pie. She makes the very best. May I come tomorrow?"

"Yes." Bannan put his hand on Wainn's bare shoulder and grinned. "Yes. Any time," he said and meant it.

Satisfied, Wainn hurried after Wen, leading to an eruption of giggles from the dark, paired splashes, and more laughter. Promises kept. Bannan chuckled and stepped into the river himself.

Unlike the fountain, or this morning, this water was summer-warm, silk against his skin. The footing was secure, mostly firm sand with a few flat stones. He wouldn't have minded a quick dip, if it came to that, but the shallow ford was well maintained and even, and the river behaved as a river should. Within too few steps, he'd climbed out the other side.

His eyes found the village as he sat to dry his feet and put on his boots. The meeting must have ended; lights were being lit throughout Marrowdell, warm yellow beacons to welcome families home and keep them in comfort.

He rose and put the river behind him, facing the moonlit road.

"Jenn." The soft call came with a light rap of knuckle to wood.

Her father. The meeting must be over.

Careful not to disturb the motionless lump of her sister, Jenn slipped out of bed. She snatched a shawl and hurried down the ladder, trying not to jump to any conclusions.

Which was easier before she saw Radd's too-carefully composed face. "Oh, no," she gasped. "What did they decide? Must he leave?"

He put a finger to his lips. "Don't wake your—"

"I'm not asleep." The night curtain between kitchen and parlor drew aside. Aunt Sybb stood there, her hair tidy in its cap and the rest of her wreathed in ivory lace to her chin. She held a candlestick in her hand and its flickering light caught the worry in her tired eyes. "Come. Tell us both."

In the parlor, as Radd lit the table lamp, Aunt Sybb climbed back in bed to sit as straight as if the down pillows were iron rods. She invited Jenn to join her with a pat on the covers, then looked to her brother, who pulled up one of the dining chairs and turned it to sit astride. "I take it they plan to banish Wyll."

Jenn tensed.

"Not quite," Radd answered, giving her the faintest of smiles. She relaxed, ever-so-slightly. "Valid concerns were raised, without doubt. They've seen how important he is to you, Dearest Heart, but no one believes we're important to him."

What could she say to that?

"I explained Wyll's been a good but shy neighbor. That the two of you grew up together and you'd been meeting him at Night's Edge all these years with my permission. Don't worry," at something in her face, "I didn't tell them about the wishing. Ancestors Dire and Disgraced. Kydd's books." Her father shook his head grimly. "I should have known they wouldn't stay gone and forgotten. Not in Marrowdell. It'd be best, Dearest Heart, if the others don't think he's involved."

Another secret. "Why, Poppa?" Jenn asked for her sister's sake; she could guess. The books had been hidden for a reason.

"Remember what I told you," interposed Aunt Sybb. "In most of Rhoth, especially in Avyo, to profess belief in wishings and magic is unseemly. Such belief harks back to a time when people sought to take from the Blessed Ancestors, instead of giving them our Beholding. Kydd and Wainn are not at fault, and Marrowdell is assuredly a place of—" she pressed her lips together, then went on, "—of novelties. But there may be some who would be unsettled by such news."

"It's no time to bring up old trouble," Radd confirmed, unexpectedly mysterious. "As for your Wyll, many find him uncanny and worry what he might do. I did," sternly, before she voiced her protest, "promise you'd be responsible for him in future."

At her vigorous nod, he looked relieved.

"The poor child. You couldn't take longer to tell the tale, could you?" Aunt Sybb chided. "What was the decision?"

"Wyll's to have the abandoned farm."

Joy filled Jenn until she could hardly breathe. What could be better? The farm was as close to Night's Edge as could be. It needed work, but . . . her father wasn't smiling. "It's perfect," she sputtered, anxious and unsure why. "I mean, it's full of mice and cobwebs, and the well's dry, but I can help him set it to rights. Sew curtains. Fill the larder shelves." Domesticity flooded her with possibilities she'd never considered before. Not seriously. To avoid them, she went back to what mattered most. "It's right beside our meadow. It's—"

"Bannan Larmensu's," Aunt Sybb finished when Jenn paused for breath.

"He was offered the place first," Radd agreed heavily. "That was the sticking point for some, and I admit there were hard words said after the vote. To ask Bannan to give it up? You saw his face, Sybbie. I'm not looking forward to the task, let me tell you."

"A shame. A man of fine character and upbringing, if I'm any judge." The two paused and sighed together. Jenn looked from one to the other, wishing they'd stop agonizing and help her plan Wyll's farm. "Thank the Ancestors," Aunt Sybb said at last, "he hasn't seen or set foot on the property yet. That should soften the blow, don't you think?"

"Oh."

It was their turn to look at her. Jenn swallowed.

"What is it?"

She'd seen Bannan take the road, thought with regret he was leaving the village, been sure he'd be gone in the morning.

Scatterwit, she chided herself. Distraction was no excuse.

Bannan Larmensu had left the village, yes, but not Marrowdell.

He'd been heading for the Tinkers Road. There could be only one reason. He'd gone to the farm he believed was his.

"What if he's spent the night?" Jenn asked miserably.

She supposed it wasn't at all fair to hope for mice.

An easy walk took him to the first trees, the trees themselves the leading edge of a wilder forest. Kydd's caution about not felling such for wood tingled along Bannan's nerves. He could see the truth of it by moonlight.

They weren't trees. They were tall and tree-shaped and might pass by day, but not now, not when they awoke to whatever light played on them in the other world. They leaned toward him with interest, as if noticing his attention. Branches creaked, twigs snapped; echoes of other, unheard sounds. The occasional leaf startled him as it drifted by his face or brushed his body before rising again. Others—he could swear they moved along the branches.

Bannan stayed to the middle of the road and watched for roots. Not that he had any reason to think treading on a root would offend them, but he planned to be a very good neighbor. He'd take no chances.

No avoidable ones.

So when he reached the point in the road where trees to either side blocked out the moon, he deliberately slowed. The farm clearing should be to his right, past the first bend. By daylight, this was probably a delightful passage, shaded and level. Now, in the gloom, he wouldn't trust what he couldn't see.

Bannan tried looking beyond. The road had been silver and fluid earlier. To his relief, it retained a faint glow, sufficient to show the way. He walked a little faster.

The glow was stronger on the right, so he stayed to that side. No. Not stronger, he realized after a few steps. Some blight dulled it along the other side, something oozing from the wild forest.

More than once, following a skirmish, he'd seen where a blood-laden stream met another, how its darkness spread before being mercifully washed clear. This was the same. In that other Marrowdell, some darkness bled into the silver road.

Zehr Emms had been right. Thanks to the late-day storm, the night air was warm and sticky. Sweat soaked Bannan's skin, yet a shiver worked icy fingers up his spine. A bit late to regret his impetuous rush to the farm, wasn't it? He dared not stop here, but as he walked, his footsteps seemed to cover less distance. Or did the road grow longer?

Where, he thought ruefully, was Jenn Nalynn when he needed her?

Safely in Marrowdell, under a roof, within walls, surrounded by light and family. The life he would make, Bannan vowed, forcing his legs to move. He'd spent more nights on the ground than in his bed at the Larmensu estate, more years living among the guard, where luxury was a day's ease without rain or an Ansnan patrol nearby, tossing 'stones and trading stories. He'd dreamed of simple comforts, not the estate. Longed for family, not a throng of servants or strangers. Why the Northward Road? Why the settler's bind? He wanted a life of peace, where the work of his hands mattered to those he loved.

Would such lowly ambition dismay his loving sister? Who, though no stranger herself to rude camps or deadly campaigns, would live happily ever after in her baron's town mansion, taking summers at the lodge in the hills?

No. Lila'd be glad for him, should he put down roots here and grow into a hairy old farmer surrounded by noisy brats. Given any encouragement, she'd visit like Jenn's lady aunt from Avyo. Wouldn't that cause a stir in Marrowdell, the arrival of a Vorkoun baroness and her entourage? Though doubtless Lila would prefer to dress rough and sneak horses from the stable, considering herself sufficient guard for her husband's royal person and his sons.

A wonder Scourge hadn't picked his fiery sister.

The formless dread grew worse. He must be nearing the source of the stain.

Bannan clung to thoughts of Lila, of bright days and hope, doing his utmost not to look left. Harder by the footstep to avert his gaze. Instinct and training screamed at him to watch for ambush, to hold a nonexistent weapon, to be ready to fight.

Not this. This wasn't aware, not of him, not yet. To pay it attention, Bannan feared to his core, would draw what he couldn't survive.

The glow disappeared.

He halted, afraid to take another step. He'd packed candles. Dare he light one? The night pressed against his face, tried to stifle his breath, muffled his hearing. "Been in worse spots," he whispered, desperate for a voice.

A breeze chilled his ear. "I don't think so."

Bannan froze, sure the deep uncanny sound hadn't come from a mouth.

The breeze lifted hairs across the back of his neck, then found his other ear. "Though there was the time you let the Ansnans pin us in that swamp. Between the leeches and the stench—"

It couldn't be . . . "Scourge?"

A laugh in his ear.

Bannan stretched out his hand, sagging with relief when he touched hot, sweat-damp hide. He flattened his palm against it. "Keep Us Close," he exclaimed, low and fervent. "Wonderful idiot beast," with each word, he gave an affectionate slap. "Heart's Blood, but I'm glad to see you." Not that he could. See. But hear? "How can you talk?"

"I could always talk," Scourge said testily. "Just not so you could hear me."

"Now you can." They might be standing in the dark beside some dreadful unseen blight, but Bannan couldn't help grinning. "Ancestors Blessed. This is a marvel!"

"This is Marrowdell. The edge between worlds." Said with the finality of sufficient explanation. "Take hold and walk with me.

Unless," a surprisingly familiar dark humor, "you prefer to wait and see what might rise."

"No, thank you." Bannan ran his hand up to Scourge's back, then forward till his fingers tangled in that familiar coarse mane. He closed his eyes in utter trust.

Until the great animal turned and began to head in the wrong direction. Bannan's eyes shot open. "The farm's the other way," he protested.

"Who's the idiot beast?"

Rather than argue and lose, Bannan quieted and walked where Scourge led, unable to stop smiling. This would solve the old mysteries, he realized eagerly. What kind of creature was the not-horse? Why had he come to live with the Larmensu? Why allow himself to be ridden by men?

The unsettling question of why Scourge showed such relish for blood he might leave for daylight.

Before having a voice, Scourge had expressed an abundance of opinion. He'd believed the not-horse had his own particular wisdom, though there was one who might have a problem with a Scourge who literally spoke his mind. Bannan chuckled. "I can't wait to see Tir's face."

"You should have seen yours." The breeze in his ear conveyed great satisfaction.

Reassuring, that Scourge could somehow see in the strange darkness. Bannan readied another question, only to be told, "We're about to pass the opening. Not a sound."

The opening to what? If to the source of the stain affecting the road, Bannan was all too glad to be as inconspicuous as possible. He tightened his grip on Scourge's mane and stared ahead, hoping for moonlight, finding only the smothering dark. He listened to his own footsteps, heard the hammer of his heart in his chest, wished them both silent.

Scourge made no sound at all. If not for the fistful of coarse hair in his hand, the heat and living smell of the large body beside him, he'd have thought himself totally alone.

Something else tried for his attention. Bannan's head turned.

Turned, and couldn't turn away. Worse, now the something pulled at him! Bannan stumbled and caught himself against Scourge's side.

"Stay with me, truthseer," a faint breath warned. "Don't be drawn."

Good advice, he was sure. Advice he'd take to heart. What was this place? As Scourge led him, step by step, Bannan planned what he'd say to the kind villagers of Marrowdell about their road and their farm. If he lived the night.

Another step.

One more, and moonlight flooded the road.

Bannan gasped. He couldn't help looking over his shoulder.

Instead of the terrible darkness, the road stretched behind, brushed with soft light and tree shadow. It didn't simply bend, as he'd thought, but rather sent a fork steeply up the tree-cloaked hill. Another road, one unseen from the village.

One they hadn't mentioned. That had been the source.

Bannan didn't dare look deeper. Not so close, not at night. "What," he asked unsteadily, "was that?"

Scourge snorted and took a quick sidestep to pull free of his unresisting hand.

So now he played horse?

Accepting, for the moment, Bannan followed, lured by the swath of brighter light through a break in the trees ahead. It had to be the farm. His farm. His steps quickened as Scourge trotted ahead, tail flagged.

A lane welcomed him into as neat a yard as he'd ever seen. By moonlight, the buildings looked almost new. A generous barn with a loft. A trim little house with a porch. Over there, what might be a garden. A tree. Two more. By their shape, those could be apple, he thought. He hoped. Another tree, much taller, that should shade the home from summer's heat. If it was a tree. He'd respect it, and have the shade.

Bannan took it all in, breathing as hard as if he'd been running.

A shoulder-high hedge ringed the yard, separating it from the grain fields. Common fields, he'd been told; he'd have a share if he worked the harvest. Surely, the fields would be safe then.

Inside the yard, grass had grown hip-high and thick. It would have to be cut, or grazed. Both, if he could trade for a cow.

From this vantage, he saw the farm lay nestled between two of the long hills. The Bone Hills. A poor name for such lovely landmarks. Whatever the stone, the hills gleamed smooth and blue under the moon's touch, like the nameless peaks in Ansnor that stayed snow-capped year long. They could be seen from Vorkoun. He remembered how much he'd longed to climb one as a boy, to touch the snow and ice for himself, to see the world from such a height.

He supposed a Rhothan might make that climb, one day. Unless the railroad proved too thin a glue for peace.

Didn't matter here. Didn't matter to him. Bannan shook off the past as he headed for the house. Spotting Scourge by the hedge, head high and staring west, he changed direction.

The bright moonlight lost the battle to pull more than shape from the not-horse. His eyes reflected cold white disks when he dipped his head to acknowledge Bannan's presence, like the toads'.

Not a comparison Scourge would appreciate.

The creature wasn't staring over the hedge, he stared through a gateless gap in its growth. Bannan peered past him. A narrow, well-used path ran alongside the tall grain, disappearing in the shadows. "Where does it go?"

"To Night's Edge."

A name, he thought, delighted. And a curious one. "What's that?"

For a long moment, he didn't think Scourge would answer. Then, distant and faint, "The way home." With that, the not-horse turned away, his head low. "You should introduce yourself." Having thus startled Bannan, who could see no one else, Scourge ambled like a tired old workhorse toward the barn.

Bannan glanced back at the path. "So it was truly good-bye, my friend, when you left me on the Northward Road." If he hadn't followed? The truthseer shrugged. What was done was well done, as far as he was concerned. They were together, still. As for explanations, he knew better than to press Scourge now.

Besides, there was the matter of an introduction.

Going to the center of the empty farmyard, he gave a short self-conscious bow. "My name is Bannan Larmensu. I hope to live here."

No answer. Of course there was no answer. He was alone. Scourge had distracted him from further prying, that was all.

Meaning he'd lied.

Or had he?

Bannan found himself unsure of the truth for the first time in his life. It must, he decided, be how Scourge "talked," using the air itself. A fine state of affairs.

The answer not appearing before him, which would have been convenient, Bannan went to the little house, guessing that would be as good a start as any.

And there he met, if not someone, then something.

Squatting on the porch, blocking the door, was the largest toad he'd seen yet. And the fattest. Its pale belly expanded pillow-like beyond its legs, until he wondered if it truly sat or somehow balanced on a very full stomach.

To open the door, he'd have to move the toad. Bannan put down his pack, then bowed with all the grace he possessed, brushing fingertips across dew-damp ground. As he rose, he lifted his hands and circled his heart. "My name is Bannan Marerrym Larmensu, late of Vorkoun."

The toad's eyes sank into its head then popped out again, but it didn't budge.

"I've come with the consent of the villagers of Marrowdell. Like them, I have taken the settler's bind and wish to make my home here." He infused the words with all the formal pomposity he could. "I ask your permission to enter."

Moonlight glittered on an astonishing array of needle-like teeth as the toad yawned.

What else could it want to know? Bannan smiled to himself. "Wen sent me," he assured it, straight-faced.

With a satisfied grunt, the toad hopped to one side.

"My thanks, sentinel," the truthseer said sincerely. And to Wen, he thought.

Taking a candle from his pack, he lit it from his striker, then put his hand to the door latch. Though tempted to pause, he lifted it and pulled the door wide.

Tried to pull it wide. The door moved about a third of the way on creaking hinges then stuck fast. Bannan lifted the candle and slipped through the opening, mindful of his feet.

"Well, well." After all the strange, terrifying, and wondrous things he'd encountered today, nothing could have put him more at ease than the normal chaos of a long-abandoned cabin. He brushed a shelf clear for the candle, then took stock.

The place must have been den and playground for several generations of wildlife—including, from claw marks on one wall, at least one bear. Nothing scurried from his feet or light. Courtesy of friend toad, Bannan guessed.

And, somehow, Wen Treff.

He found a peg for his pack, took off his shirt, and set to work. Nothing fancy, this first night. He'd be satisfied with space for his bedroll. Bannan tied some straw from what remained of the bed to a poker for a makeshift broom, only to put that aside after his first sweep raised a choking cloud of dust. Instead, he used his boots to nudge debris out of the way until he'd cleared a small swathe in the middle of the room.

In the process, he discovered a stovepipe and stone hearth, but no stove. The left-hand wall boasted a fireplace with a stone bread oven to the side, but when he tried to look up the chimney, he found it blocked.

Too hot for a fire anyway.

He used his shoulder to force the rear door open as far as it would go, about a handsbreadth. A small breeze ventured in, cooling the sweat from his skin. There were windows. The two at the front of the house were shuttered fast. The one at the back looked to be the main thoroughfare for whatever had lived here, and would, he thought cheerfully, need a new frame. And glass panes. He should be able to order those.

The neglected room called to him like no place ever had. Reckless and driven, Bannan lit the rest of his candles. There was a table, missing a leg. He moved it to the fireplace and propped it against the bread oven to use for sorting. Not all was ruined. He uncovered treasures. Three forks. A rusty pot. A bucket with no handle.

Which led him to think about water and the well. "Daylight," he promised, carefully emptying an old nest from the bucket before setting it by his new pot.

The ladder to the loft was missing most of its rungs. He jumped and caught hold of the opening, then pulled himself up and through, hanging by his elbows.

A fine bedroom, Bannan thought with glee. He could stand easily under the peak. Windows at both ends let in moonlight and air. They'd been letting in birds as well, judging from the nests, and he hoped the toad had been thorough with the mice. Stars showed through gaps in the roof. A few shingles. Tir could help with that. Testing the floor boards he'd leave till morning.

At the thought of morning, Bannan yawned so fiercely his jaw cracked. He let himself drop back down. Tomorrow, he'd clean the place till it shone. Turn the damaged bed frame to kindling. Clear the chimney. Those first. He had tomorrow.

He had the rest of his life.

He pulled out his bedroll and laid it on the cleared portion of floor, then blew out the candles. Removing boots and belt, he lay down, folding his arms across his chest.

Moonlight slipped through the open doors. Softer now and lower. Peaceful, with its job done. A pale moth, large as his hand, followed a moonbeam through the ruined window to flutter here and there near the ceiling, before coming to hover close to his face. Moth? Each wingbeat sent a faint aroma of spice. Each leg bore a golden boot, and a tiny satchel locked with a jewel hung from its body. It flew off again, out the window, on whatever tasks a moth undertook here.

Here, Bannan thought. Marrowdell.

He smiled as he closed his eyes.

Home.

After opening the window, Jenn eased back into bed; Peggs rolled over but didn't wake.

Why hadn't she waited?

She pressed her warm cheek against the pillow, wide awake though so tired her bones hurt. The evening should be cool, not midsummer hot; what little air slipped through the window hardly helped.

Her churning thoughts didn't, either. This was all her fault. Wyll's poor body. The arguing among the villagers. Their father's worry. Peggs' fright. The rush to be married. If only she'd waited a day to do the wishing . . .

If only she'd met Bannan first . . .

Would she have wished at all?

A treacherous, unworthy warmth filled her. But wasn't Bannan noble? And brave. Strong. Handsome, too, no denying it. Those gorgeous eyes, with their apple butter glow, could melt a heart at ten paces. He smiled well and often, and laughed. She quite liked his laugh and the way he spoke. She quite liked everything about him, including how he made her feel.

If she'd waited . . . it wouldn't have changed a thing, Jenn told herself, and tried to believe it. Bannan might never have come to Marrowdell, had he not rushed to Wyll's rescue, and Wyll wouldn't have needed rescue—would he?—had she waited.

She'd consoled herself in duty to her friend. An easier duty, if Bannan left on his own. Now, it'd be her fault—hers and Wyll's—that he couldn't stay. How could he? There was no room for him in the village, no timbers suited to new buildings, nothing new in Marrowdell, ever.

A tear dampened her pillow. Jenn tried not to be selfish. She tried her very best. But as sleep claimed her, the image behind her eyes wasn't Bannan or Wyll or her meadow.

It was a map, edges shriveling as they caught fire, burning until it was ash and the world it promised was no more.

Wyll knew himself exhausted. After collecting his weapons, the old soldier had given him his bed: a caution he understood and a courtesy to keep him where they wanted. But to lie there, helpless, and expect to rest? "Another round." He pushed half his pile of nuts at Tir, who'd none left. The man cheated at every opportunity; he'd returned the favor.

"Not without a fist of ale," Tir yawned. "Losing's no pleasure dry, let me tell you. You like ale?"

"I know what it's for." What would the man think of the rush and numbness that came from not from drink but from roaring at the top of one's lungs? Of pouring out sound and fury until the weaker cowered beneath wings and rocks shook loose from the cliff tops? Now, that was intoxication. "I've read," Wyll said dryly, "a great many books."

"Ancestors Dull and Dubious." The man shook his head. "That's plain wrong. We need to introduce you to the real thing. Another night," he yawned as he swept the worn white and black 'stones into their sack. " 'Nuff's enough." The house toad, whose avid gaze hadn't left the playing pieces throughout their game, abandoned its place beyond the lamplight. Tir pulled in his feet with a jerk as it waddled past their table. "Heart's Blood! Was that here all the time?"

Wyll watched the toad go out the open door. "The little cousins have a fondness for pebbles." When the man scowled and shoved the sack deep inside his shirt, he added, because the little cousins had a right to their prickly pride and he wouldn't see them maligned, "They aren't thieves."

Tir looked unconvinced, but didn't argue. He yawned again. "It's me for my bedroll and you for bed."

The bed. Wyll glared at the unsettling object. "I've never used one."

"Never slept in a bed?"

At no point in the game had the man seemed hard of hearing. Cunning and interestingly devious, but not deaf. "Not like this."

"Ah." Tir scratched at his beard with two fingers and a thumb, eyes narrowed in thought. He'd left off his foolish mask. "There's no trick to it," he said at last. "Head on the pillow, if there's one. Blanket atop. 'Cept on a night warm as this. You'd cook. Be too hot," he clarified, as if Wyll wouldn't grasp the concept.

"Play again. I'll let you win."

"Sorry. I've had my excitement for the day." Tir scrunched his scarred forehead. "Anything you need before I go?"

Stupid man. What he needed was his sanctuary, its impenetrable walls tight around him. He couldn't defend himself, like this. Not against his own kind. Not against those here. Wyll's hand wanted to make a fist; he lowered it to his thigh and spoke as calmly as possible. "Do you trust these people? Should I?"

Tir's eyes traveled to the open door and the darkness beyond. "Bannan's likely found himself a soft spot," he muttered incomprehensibly. To Wyll, "Stay here."

And he left.

Without the man, it was worse. The room widened, its windows and doors gaping wounds, and Wyll imagined wingbeats. His kind. They didn't like to fly on hot moist nights. They liked him less. He stood to turn and turn, unsure where danger might strike first. Unsure what he could do, any more, if it did.

A loud thud made him turn again, so quickly he lurched off balance and had to clutch one of the bedposts to save himself.

Having dropped a roll of blankets in front of the door, Tir spread them with a kick of his foot. "That should do," he said gruffly. "Mind you blow out the candle. Bloodflies'll come to a light." He plopped himself down in his clothes and boots, an ax to each side in easy reach, and threw an arm over his face. "You'd best not snore. Or talk in your sleep."

"I don't know," Wyll admitted.

"It'd be my luck," Tir mumbled. "G'night."

Caution Wyll understood. This?

This was the girl, bringing him thistledown and silly secrets.

This was the truthseer, pulling him from the river. Kydd, bringing clothes.

Kindness. They gave it so freely.

They wouldn't, if they knew him.

Wyll blew out the light. Without a word, he lay on the bed like a man, his head on the pillow as he'd been told, and closed his eyes.

TWELVE

WAGLER JUPP'S HOME stood alone within the village. An unclipped hedge separated it from the Uhthoffs, the road and common gardens from Horst and the Nalynns. The world at large was held at bay as much by the temper of its occupant as the looming crags beyond.

As a rule, Jenn Nalynn gave Old Jupp as much space and as little conversation as she could, while remaining properly respectful. He was, after all, the most elderly resident of Marrowdell, having been by every account ancient before taking the settler's bind with his nephew Riedd Morrill. He'd refused the prince's so-called "Kindness," the small home and stipend granted those family members too old or infirm to settle a new land. Jenn had heard it said, by her own father, no less, late at night when he and his friends were in their cups, that Old Jupp had survived the journey and subsequent winters because bile pickled his flesh long ago.

In Avyo, Wagler Jupp had been important, the Secretary to the House of Keys, privy to goings-on both public and highly secret. He'd come to Marrowdell with a wagonload of locked chests filled, not with useful clothes or tools, but documents. Who they were to impress, or embarrass, so far from the capital, Jenn couldn't imagine. They'd grown musty and old along with Jupp, who must, she thought, take some comfort from their mere possession, for he kept the chests in his home. Not that she'd been inside more than the once, when at six she'd run through his door to hide during a game of seek.

Being summarily chased out by an irate Jupp, waving his canes and trumpet at her, had left Jenn with no desire to visit again. Ever.

So, of course, here they were, at the foot of the step to Old Jupp's narrow porch, because, according to Aunt Sybb and their father, there could be no one better suited to deliver their family's all-important invitations to Wyll and Kydd than the former secretary himself.

Jenn thought their choice had more to do with Old Jupp having napped through Wyll's ill-timed demonstration of his powers and being absent at last night's meeting, thus being more likely to agree, but if her elders preferred to invoke such convincing arguments as respectability and neutrality, who was she to argue?

"Do I look all right?" Peggs fussed again. To Jenn's chagrin, her once-serene sister who'd hummed herself to sleep was—by day and with family involved and matters taking a serious turn and whatever should she wear?—a bundle of nerves.

Obediently, Jenn cast a critical eye. Being anxious brought Peggs' huge eyes to life and planted roses on her cheeks. Her thick black hair coiled above her head, emphasizing her graceful neck; a confection so full of pins Jenn doubted they'd get them all out again. Her sister wore her second-best dress, its lace bodice tied with brilliant red ribbons, topped with one of Aunt Sybb's soft city shawls. She'd found stockings and her shoes gleamed with polish.

Good thing the mud had dried overnight.

In the basket on Peggs' arm was a twist of the sausages Old Jupp supposedly favored, fresh-baked biscuits, and a jar of berry preserves. There would have been a pie, but Wainn Uhthoff had shown up at breakfast with a wide smile and charming expectation. Peggs had given in, in Jenn's opinion, far too easily; at this rate, they'd run out of pie before her sister was officially betrothed.

Peggs almost bounced in place. "Well?"

"You look perfect. Very ladylike," Jenn pronounced. She wore her third-best dress, which was really her last-best and only choice; she'd no intention of wasting her very best on what was a delivery and it didn't fit all that well across her bosom anymore regardless. Her toes objected to the shoes, a concession to their aunt, and, as for how she felt today?

Impatient to have done, Jenn told herself. Impatient to start whatever new life she must. Like pulling a splinter; best suffered quickly.

Peggs gave her a suspicious look. " 'Ladylike?' "

"Mature. Elegant." Jenn tried not to roll her eyes. "What more can I say?"

"I wish you'd let me put up your hair."

Jenn lifted the creamy pair of envelopes, with their press-waxed seals. "Shall we?"

No one else closed their doors in summer. Jenn crossed the porch with Peggs, wincing at the noisy clack of their shoes on the wood, and rapped on the door as her aunt had instructed. Two firm knocks, then wait.

Anywhere else, she'd shout hello through the opening and wander in. Well, at the Treffs there was no shouting, because Lorra and Fran expected some modicum of manners and if a calm voice couldn't be heard above whatever was happening, it wasn't a good time to intrude anyway.

The door opened. "Fair morning, Peggs. Jenn." Riss Nahamm wiped her hands on her apron and smiled. "What a nice surprise."

Riss was, after Peggs, the loveliest woman in Marrowdell, with skin like porcelain and rich red hair, streaked with white above her ears. Jenn considered it likely she'd been the most beautiful woman in all Avyo before growing old. Being Riedd Morrill's cousin, thus of Mellynne descent, had brought her here with the rest. Being unmarried and of kind heart—and, in Jenn's opinion, courageous—she'd moved in with their great-uncle, to care for him in his declining years. Not a life to envy.

To prove the point, a loud and querulous, "Who's that at this unseemly hour?!" came from inside. "Send them packing!"

"Good morning," Peggs said hurriedly, thrusting the basket into Riss' arms.

Their aunt had been exacting in her instructions. Jenn steadied her sister with a look and showed the envelopes. "We're to ask a favor of Master Jupp, Riss. May we come in?"

Riss' green eyes shone. "Please." She lowered her voice as she gracefully stepped aside for them to enter, "You've picked a good time. He's quite cheery this morning."

Jenn braced herself and led the way, doing her best to smile.

She remembered the interior as dark, full of terrifying, half-seen shapes. Finding it anything but, Jenn realized with a twinge of conscience her younger self must have surprised the old man while he slept. No wonder he'd chased her out.

This was a bright, dignified space. Sunlight streamed through the windows, but couldn't compete with the lamp glowing on the table. It was unlike any Jenn had seen, of blue-black metal, ornamented with gold scrollwork, that rose from a heavy stone pedestal like a man with outstretched arms. The head and body formed a tall urn, doubtless for the sort of oil brought in from Weken, since each outstretched arm supported a beautiful clean flame enclosed in frosted glass. A dozen thick glass prisms, longer than a finger, dangled below.

The frosted glass bore designs that allowed the warm yellow light to pass. Jenn peered closer, fascinated, then stifled the urge to laugh. The designs were of dancing women. Naked, dancing women.

With parasols.

The giant lamp presided over sheets of paper, stacks of paper, bound bundles of paper, and quill pens. There were pens in cups, pens in pots. From the curls under the table, several had recently been sharpened. On the only open bit of tabletop lay a page half covered in the finest black lettering she'd ever seen. It put Aunt Sybb's elegant cursive to shame.

The walls were lined with chests, large and small. Two others formed the table's supports. An oiled tarp hung across the ceiling overhead, one end tipped so any leaks from an untrustworthy roof would flow to a bucket tucked to one side. There were other practicalities in the room Jenn judged Riss' work, a tidy little kitchen to one side of the fireplace, a curtained-off corner for Old Jupp's bed, and neatly darned socks hanging from the rafters. A ladder led to the loft, doubtless Riss' domain, but she had her place in the main room, too. An inviting pair of chairs sat side-by-side near the sunny window, accompanied by more small chests, themselves tables, each with its small lamp and a well-read book. Beside the leftmost were baskets filled with colorful skeins of thread, and a large embroidery hoop stood in reach, a piece of white cloth stretched taut and waiting. The seat cushions were tapestried with fanciful animals. Big-eyed toads on the one. Birds on the other.

The bedroom curtain, now that Jenn looked closely, was also a tapestry, a summer scene done in subtle greens and blues. There were tall buildings set in gardens and bridges of stone, like those she'd seen illustrated in books, arched over a wide peaceful river. Ships with colored sails plied the water.

"Avyo," Riss said with a small smile, noticing her attention. "What I recall of it, anyway. Uncle, you've visitors."

Wagler Jupp sat at the table, quill poised above the half-filled page as if determined to continue his train of thought the instant he was rid of them. His trumpet lay to one side and he didn't reach for it. He was scowling so fiercely his thick gray brows threatened to tangle together.

This was "quite cheery?"

Jenn kept her smile and, feeling silly, bobbed in place in what she hoped resembled the curtsy Aunt Sybb had taught them. Peggs followed suit, more graceful by far.

Riss shook her head. Instead of raising her voice, she went over to the old man, put one hand on his shoulder and leaned close to whisper in his ear. He looked suddenly interested and put down his pen. "You've letters for me?"

Jenn didn't hand over the envelopes. "We've a favor to ask, Master Jupp," she said.

"Give me my letters!" An age-spotted hand thrust out. "Hurry, girl."

Peggs dipped another desperate curtsy. "Our father asks if you would do us the honor of presenting these to—" she turned bright pink but continued, "—our suitors."

"What'd she say? What?" Riss gave him the trumpet and Jupp put it to his ear, aiming the end like a weapon at Peggs. "What'd you say? Be quick." His free hand thumped the table; the prisms swayed from side to side, sending rainbows around the room. "I've no time to waste."

"Uncle's writing his memoirs," Riss informed them. A dimple formed in one cheek, though she spoke seriously. "He's reached the controversy surrounding Prince Ordo's coronation—"

"'Controversy?' It was a travesty!" Old Jupp's eyes glittered. "Who could possibly mistake parrots for doves, I ask you? Doves are filthy, but parrots? They take aim! Do you know how many hats were ruined that day?"

"A pivotal moment in our history," Riss said soberly.

Her uncle stared at her. His breath caught with a wet rasp, his eyes bulged, and the trumpet began to shake wildly. Was it some kind of fit? Old people had them, Jenn had read. Which wouldn't please their aunt or father. From Peggs' ashen face, she feared the same or worse.

Old Jupp erupted in a bellowing laugh. "Pivotal! You should have seen their faces," he sputtered joyously. "All those pompous, pious, prince-licking hangers-on, with parrot dung dripping down their heads. Best day of my life, that was. One of the very best." He laughed some more, then smacked his hand on the page. "Right here, ladies. The sum of their antics and idiocies. Should get me skewered and boiled in oil." He grinned wickedly, showing very few teeth. "I plan to die first and spoil all their fun."

"Uncle," Riss chided, then chuckled fondly.

Life within the Jupp household, Jenn realized somewhat dizzily, was nothing like she'd imagined. "Please, Master Jupp." She held out the envelopes. "Would you deliver these for our family?"

Taking them, he turned them over in his hands to examine the seal. Their father had produced a thick ring they'd never seen before to press the imprint into the wax, so grim during the process, neither daughter had dared ask. "Important business, I see. Young Uhthoff I can find. Where will this newcomer, Wyll, be?"

"Horst's lent Wyll his home," Riss supplied. "I was at the mill when it was proposed," she added quickly.

"Of course you were," her uncle said blandly. "And where shall the worthy Horst lay his head the meanwhile, hmm?"

Riss lifted a shapely eyebrow and said, her tone matching his, "It's summer. I'm sure he'll manage."

Peggs looked from Old Jupp to his niece, frowning ever so slightly for no reason Jenn could see. This was all taking much too long, she fussed inwardly, and the longer it took, the worse it was going to be asking Bannan to leave.

Perhaps her concern wasn't as discreet as she'd thought, for Old Jupp rose to his feet. "The summer cloak. My hat. Quickly, Riss. And a proper satchel, if you please."

Riss looked astonished, but hurried to obey. In short order, she produced a faded green cloak from a chest and the tallest imaginable gray hat, free of bird droppings, from a box. The satchel took a moment's rummage under the bed while her uncle tapped his canes impatiently.

In cloak and hat, his silver trumpet tucked in his belt and the satchel carefully hung from a shoulder, Wagler Jupp was a different man. Jenn and Peggs bobbed another curtsy. He tipped his head slightly in regal acknowledgment, careful of the hat, then scowled and stabbed one cane at the door. "Out with you! I've important business to conduct."

Jenn and Peggs fled to the porch, stopped, and looked at each other.

Nodded once.

Then both took off, skirts held above their knees, running in opposite directions.

Bannan's eyes shot open. He gazed up at unfamiliar, cobwebbed rafters. Remembering, a laugh bubbled up, warm and triumphant. He rolled eagerly to his feet. "Day's wasting!"

Not quite day, perhaps, but dawn winked through every gap and opening in the little house. By the mess surrounding him, he hadn't made much progress at all, last night. But today?

Today was his.

This was his.

Bannan wanted to run outside and shout. Instead, he took a thoughtful sip from his half-empty flask. There was the sticking point. No point tidying the place further if there wasn't water to be had.

Proud at being sensible, he went into his pack for the short shovel and an ax, grabbed those and his confidence, and set out in search.

Moonlight was forgiving; sunlight showed the truth. The roof he'd judged mostly whole proved mostly holes, with few good shingles left. More to keep Tir busy, Bannan chuckled. The welcoming porch tilted along its length to disappear under the sod. Nothing that couldn't be fixed. It'd have to be dug out and new foundation stones added. Doubtless there'd be more to do. He'd wanted work, Bannan thought cheerfully as he explored behind the house.

Not everything needed repair. He was delighted to find the privy's roof intact. After hacking dew-wet grass and a prickly shrub from in front of the small building, he pulled open the door. "Of all things—" he exclaimed. Inside was clean and dry, with solid, sweet-smelling wood and nary a web, just like the Nalynns'—something he'd attributed to Radd's care for his home. If this was Marrowdell's contribution to its inhabitants, he was all in favor.

Wait till he showed Tir, who'd done his share of latrine digging.

Marrowdell's other welcoming gift? A perfect day. The air was fresh and dry, with a nip to keep it lively. The fields were free of mist, the sky a dome of blue. Bannan resumed his search for the well with a happy whistle, only to stub his boot toe on the door to the larder, half buried in leaves. The door, or what remained of it, had been torn from its hinges years ago. Likely the bear. He took a cautious look inside, ax at the ready. Leafy debris, more empty nests, the remnants of plank shelving. No bear.

A new door could wait. He'd nothing to store anyway. Bannan grinned. He would. Those were indeed apple trees and he hoped for berry bushes in what had proved to be the farmyard's garden patch, albeit weedy and overgrown. He'd no idea how to preserve fruit. Or weed. Or anything else.

He did know who to ask.

Later. Next, find the well.

Bannan took a few more steps, kicking at the grass.

"Fair morning!"

He looked up to find Wainn Uhthoff sitting on a large fallen branch, a pie balanced on his lap. "My first visitor," he smiled, pleased beyond words. "Fair morning to you!"

"I brought pie."

Fresh too, by the steam coming through slits in the golden pastry. Bannan's mouth watered. "Thank you. I hadn't thought about breakfast."

"Peggs makes the best pie." Wainn regarded him. "How did you sleep, Bannan Larmensu?" With emphasis, as if his comfort held some vital import.

In spite of the hard floor and musty room, all Bannan remembered was putting his head down and being at peace. Yesterday had been full to the brim; he probably could have slept standing up. He stretched with a grin. "Never better."

Wainn's eyes lit. "Wen was right. You belong!"

At his honest joy, a lump filled Bannan's throat. He didn't dare speak. Instead, he smiled and reached for the pie.

It was apple. Like the water in the village fountain, it was better than any apple pie he'd tasted before, the filling creamy and warm and fragrant, the pastry a confection that melted on the tongue. They ate it in thick wedges they somehow juggled to their mouths, a task made harder by the way Wainn would laugh at him, and he'd have to laugh back. Little brown birds, dark-eyed and bold, hopped around their feet, quick to pounce on crumbs.

A splendid breakfast, Bannan decided, licking the final sweet trace from his lips. "You're right," he told Wainn, passing him the flask. "Peggs makes the very best pies." The sun was fully up, drying the dew, warm on his shoulders. Too full to move right away, in his heart as well as stomach, Bannan leaned back against the branch and asked as idly as he could, "Did you see Jenn this morning too?"

When Wainn didn't answer, Bannan glanced at him. The usual smile was gone, replaced by a troubled look; the first he'd seen on the other's face. "What is it?"

"She should have waited," low and dismayed. "She should have asked Wyll first."

The truth. What did it mean? "What's wrong?" Heart's Blood, he'd never have left Tir with the not-man if he'd thought there was any risk. Bannan found himself on his knees, facing Wainn, hands ready to take hold and shake him. "Tell me!"

"Bannan," with profound concern. "Jenn didn't sleep well."

"'Didn't sleep . . . '" Bannan rocked back on his haunches. His sleep. Now Jenn's. He couldn't doubt Wainn, but why this? Perplexed, he ran one hand through his hair. "She was upset yesterday," he ventured. "Did your uncle tell you what happened?"

"Yes." Wainn brushed crumbs from his homespun pants. Eager birds rushed to his bare feet and he stood awkwardly, not to startle them. A flash of wise hazel eyes. "It hurts to need what you can't find. Jenn is unhappy."

Bannan's heart thudded in his chest as he remembered how the road had swept them with her, how wind and lightning had answered her despair. Wyll's twisted body. What did "unhappy" hold in store for the rest of them? He felt a chill despite the warm sun. "Will there be a storm?"

"Why would there be a storm?" Seeming as changeable as weather himself, Wainn smiled brightly as he tilted his head to study the clear sky. "This is a good day for laundry. That's one of my chores."

"I thought—" Had he been dazzled by Marrowdell, by Wyll, by her smile? "I thought Jenn had—that she could—" Finding no words for the impossible, Bannan shook his head. "There's something special about Jenn Nalynn, isn't there?"

"You are the truthseer," with touching confidence. "You see her."

"What I see . . ." What did he see? Eyes that held every color of the sky. A smile whose mere memory touched his heart. "Light," he said finally. "I see—I see light." Which made no sense at all.

But Wainn nodded. "You see Jenn."

"That doesn't explain what she can do!"

The young villager offered the empty plate to the birds. "She can't make pie." He rose, licked his thumb, and gave Bannan another too-wise glance. "Jenn Nalynn doesn't do. She is."

A riddle. Like Marrowdell itself. Bannan pressed the heels of his hands against his closed eyes. "I should be afraid," he muttered to the light-splattered darkness. "We all should."

"Father says fear makes people stupid."

Surprised into a laugh, Bannan dropped his hands. "It does indeed." He regarded Wainn fondly. "Then I promise I won't fear Jenn Nalynn. Though I hope the weather stays fair. I've work to do. Starting with locating my well."

A nod. "I'm thirsty."

Bannan tipped the empty flask. "Sorry."

Wainn smiled. "That's good. The well waits to be needed."

"You know where it is?" He hadn't looked for help; he was more than happy to receive it. "I've had no luck."

"Why do you need luck?" Wainn asked curiously. "You're a truthseer."

"I am at that." Bannan shook his head. Where had he left his good sense? "Thank you, my friend, for reminding me."

He turned and looked at the farmyard. Saw overgrown grass. Saw where he'd trampled it. Bannan looked deeper.

The path near the road flowed silver.

Lavender shot through the sky.

And there it was. A hint of cobalt in the grass, between house and garden. He'd walked over the spot more than once, Bannan thought wonderingly.

Trusting what he'd seen, he went to the hint and began to dig. It took the shovel, ax, and Wainn's help to pull out the weeds and chop through the thick sod. He was soaked with sweat and most definitely thirsty when the shovel clanged against stone.

Switching to his hands, Bannan quickly felt along the stone to where it met another and another. Once he had the well's proportions, he grabbed the shovel and dug on the other side. Faster and faster.

At last, he uncovered a ring of precisely set stones, like the one in the village but half the size. A pavement surrounded it, yet to be fully cleared. Within the ring? After removing the last handful of wind-shifted dirt and leaves, Bannan leaned forward eagerly.

Only to be disappointed. "There's nothing here." The well was no deeper than his arm, floored in ice-blue stone like polished marble, all of a piece. As dry to the touch now as it had been for years, by the dust his fingers streaked aside. "I can't stay here without water," he said miserably.

Wainn, who'd been watching a butterfly, chuckled. "It waits to be needed," he said once more. As if Bannan should know.

The truth.

Could it possibly be that simple?

This was Marrowdell.

Bannan ran his hand over the cool dry stone, then unstoppered the empty flask and lowered it into the empty well.

Water burbled and bubbled forth in answer, right through the stone.

He could scarcely believe his eyes. Water rose over the flask, filling it; it rose over his hand, chill and refreshing as a winter morning; it rose over his arm until it reached the lip of the surrounding stones. Then stopped.

Lazy rings crisscrossed its surface. The sky sat there, girdled in stone, his rapidly numbing arm thrust in its midst.

Bannan pulled out his arm, and the full flask. "It worked! Wainn—did you—?"

Wainn was gone. As was the pie plate. The toad, however, sat on the stones beside Bannan, considering him with huge brown eyes. He laughed and toasted it with the flask, taking a long, deep drink. The water coursed down the inside of his throat with each swallow, soothing, restoring, delicious.

Marrowdell's welcome.

Where was Tir when he needed him? Or Jenn? Anyone, other than the mute toad, to share this with? "Scourge!" Bannan bellowed. The not-horse had to be thirsty by now. "Scourge. Look! Water!"

When no dark ugly head appeared in the doorway of the barn, he went in search, flask in hand and no few backward glances to be sure the well was still there and still full. Why hadn't more people settled in Marrowdell, when it offered so much?

He refused to think about last night and the perilous nature of the road. Wainn hadn't mentioned it; somehow, he'd never found the moment, or the words, to ask. Every place had its cliff. You avoided its edge, that was all.

Bad winters, he assured himself, undaunted. Nothing wrong with being snug inside for a few months. He'd learn how to use his new tools. Make furniture. Beat Tir at 'stones. Read. How he'd longed for time—with lantern and roof—to read. He already knew which of his favorites he'd reread first.

The barn was empty of life, save for swallows dipping in and out and through. Bannan walked inside, appreciating its cool shade. A warm day to come. Hopefully, given the state of his roof, the first of several dry ones.

An empty, ordinary barn. A wide corridor ran end to end. There were three good-sized stalls to the left, with wooden hayracks and half doors, shuttered fast, that would open toward the sun. To the right, a low pen suited to piglets, a sturdy storeroom—the door locked in some fashion or stuck—an abundance of wooden pegs for harness, and the ladder to the loft. Admittedly, he was no farmer, not yet, but there had to be room here for all the stock he could handle, as well as their winter feed.

Empty. Bannan's brows knit together. The farmyard had gone wild. The house had sheltered a host of wildlife, as had the larder.

Why not the barn, with its open door? It hardly needed sweeping, as if not only mice, but dust avoided the place.

Something else about the earthen floor caught his eye. Bannan crouched to brush fingertips over long parallel tracks. Wagons. None of the impressions looked recent, but Tir could tell more.

Another puzzle. He, Bannan told himself with determination, would solve this one too. In the meanwhile? He pushed up his sleeves. He had a bucket and broom. Now he had water.

Time to clean house.

Not any house, he reminded himself with an inner thrill.

His home.

Spying, Jenn was sure, was neither mature nor polite. Their aunt would be horrified. A good thing neither she, nor Peggs, planned to get caught.

Easier for Peggs, who could always pretend to be on her way to visit Hettie and didn't have to deal with Uncle Horst's distaste for shrubbery or anything that might hide more than a squirrel. His was the only home without at least a berry bush or convenient barrel nearby.

But there was, Jenn discovered to her delight, Bannan's wagon. The back flap had been left open, doubtless to air after the night's damp. She wasted no time climbing inside and working her way forward to where she should be able to see in a window.

That is, she tried to work her way forward. The wagon was packed tighter than pickles in a jar, with not a speck of room wasted. Jenn squirmed over boxes and bags—apologizing under her breath when something went "snap-grissh" under her knee—and wiggled between hanging sacks.

A breeze followed her, chilled her cheek, and snarled. "Why are you here?"

Scourge.

Jenn twisted around to find his long horse face in the wagon with her. "Go away," she whispered, shooing him with her free hand. The other held back the hanging lamp threatening her head.

His nostrils flared. "Are you a thief?"

"No!" She hurriedly let go of the lamp, ducking to avoid its swing. "Go away."

"Are you hiding?"

"I'm doing nothing wrong." Well, she was, but poor manners should hardly matter to a creature as dangerous and unpredictable as Scourge. Who'd threatened Wyll, something she didn't forget. "This is between me and Wyll."

"Whom you plan to marry." A deep chuckle in her ear. "You could do better. Anything breathing would be an improvement. A toad—"

Jenn blushed furiously and flung the lantern at him.

Scourge dodged out of sight, then his head reappeared and shoved so deeply into the wagon something else in a bag went "snap-grissh." "You come out." The breeze became a howl in her ear. Those terrible jaws snapped near her shoes. "Out now!"

Voices, from outside. "I can't," Jenn pleaded. "They'll see me." That most of Scourge protruded from the wagon might look normal; given any chance at all, Wainn's pony would happily push his head and neck through an open kitchen window, not that Scourge was the sort, she was sure, to try for a loaf of bread cooling on a shelf. "I just want to hear Wyll's answer to Father's invitation," she confessed.

His head disappeared again. Jenn was afraid to move.

A breeze tugged her hair. "Toad."

The not-horse was insufferable. Hearing no more voices, Jenn eased her way to the back of the wagon. Maybe she could slip out—

"Why, hello."

Or not. "Hello, Tir."

With his mask in place, she couldn't tell if he was angry or surprised to find her in the wagon. Maybe she could blame Scourge—claim he'd chased her inside.

"Man can't find his head with his hands in the morning," Tir said confusingly. Worse, he winked. "So, what'd Bannan send you after?"

To her dismay, he gripped the back of the wagon, preparing to climb in, though there was hardly room for her alone.

Jenn hastily closed her hand on something and brought it up between them. "His—" She held a pair of pants. Could she blush any hotter? Worse, they weren't homespun, like those everyone wore—including Bannan. These were black leather, soft and supple. She imagined how they'd look and discovered—oh, yes—her cheeks could flame. "I'd better go."

Tir helped her down, his eyes searching her face. Once she was on her feet, he kept hold of her hand. "Heart's Blood," he muttered with a sudden fierce scowl. "How old are you, girl?"

"I'll be nineteen this harvest." Jenn clutched the pants, wishing she dared pull her hand free.

"Eighteen, then." He showed no inclination to let go. She was amazed to see a tinge of color rise up his neck and pinken his ears. "Eighteen and promised to himself, over there. What was Bannan thinking? Not that he was, I'll warrant. Not with his brains, at any rate."

Somewhere in there, Tir probably made sense. Just not to her. Jenn tugged gently at her hand. "I shouldn't keep him waiting." She lifted the pants.

"I'll take care of it." Tir gave back her fingers and took the pants. "You get home. Your Wyll's left to meet your father. He wasn't interested in waiting till this afternoon, invitation or no, and—" grimly, "—you've some explaining to do."

She ignored the last part. "He can't have gone already," she objected, dismayed. Afternoon was when everything would be ready, and Radd would have shaved—something Aunt Sybb would insist upon—and she and Peggs both would be home and settled upstairs—another insistence, but where they could listen. "He shouldn't—"

"You've changed your mind?" Tir sounded relieved. "Not that I've anything against Wyll as such. Man's seen his share of trouble and bears it better than most. But—" His voice trailed off as he looked at her. "You're going to marry him."

Jenn stared at him. "Of course. Why would I change my mind?"

"So last night meant nothing to you."

She blinked. "What about last night?"

"Are you telling me you weren't with Bannan?"

"Why would I go to the farm?"

"The farm." Tir shook his head and, of all things, began to chuckle. "The farm? This is about the farm. Ancestors Witness, I should have guessed. So that's where he spent the night."

He was the most confusing person. Jenn frowned. "Where did you think he was?"

"I don't tell you, young Jenn," Tir countered, tossing the pants back in the wagon, "and you don't have to tell me why you were in his wagon. Fair?"

She wasn't entirely sure of the bargain, but nodded.

"Good. Now go home and keep your friend out of trouble."

That, she intended to do.

Wagler Jupp was making his methodical way to the Uhthoffs by the time Jenn made it home. She couldn't see Peggs. Or Wyll. Taking off her shoes, she tiptoed onto the porch and stopped by the open window.

A breeze, warm and familiar, caressed her cheek. "Come inside, Dearest Heart. I've nothing to say you cannot hear."

Wyll might know all about Night's Edge; he had a great deal to learn about her family. Starting with her father and aunt and their rules about who should be part of conversations. Jenn stayed right where she was.

Rose petals dropped on her.

"Nuisance," she muttered, plucking them from her hair. She listened harder. No one was talking.

Why weren't they talking?

"Jenn?"

She looked up at her father, who stood in the doorway, not yet shaven. He arched an eyebrow. "You may as well come in."

After dumping his pack on the table, Bannan sorted the immediately useful from the rest. A strong thin rope. A bar of hard soap. Flint and steel. The half sausage and heel of bread, part of last night's supper from Gallie Emms, he put aside, full, thanks to Wainn's pie. Aside also went the rolled leather pouch containing his last few leaves of Vorkoun black tea, and the metal cup and bowl he'd used since entering the guard.

He started with the rope, stringing it from the porch to the not-oak tree east of the house. He tested the tautness with a finger before tossing his bedroll over it. Not that he'd be doing laundry any time soon, but the line was ready.

Next, Bannan tackled the windows and doors. The shutters on the front windows were secured by a wooden bar shimmed in place, easily hammered free. With the shutters removed, daylight and fresh air poured through the openings to fill the main room. He'd have to order the small glass panes, which meant measuring the opening. Later. Instead, Bannan took his ax to what remained of the front door's seized wooden hinges. He leaned the door against the wall, then did the same to the back door. More air, more light.

As for the hinges, the smith, Davi, should be able to make metal ones. Or he could order some from Endshere.

He'd have to watch his coin, Bannan reminded himself. Maybe he could trade labor for the hinges.

Inside, he freed a wide plank from the ruined bed and, starting at one corner of the main room, used it to push debris out the back door. What he couldn't push, he carried, tossing it all into a pile. The work was heavy and filthy, raising so much dust he tied a wet handkerchief over his face so he could breathe.

After the first pass removed the worst of it from the floor, Bannan tossed his makeshift shovel and broom up into the loft, pulling himself after. To his relief, its floor was solid, though strewn with droppings, old nests, and a neat pile of tiny bones that gave him pause. He swept everything out the open window at one end, then glanced outside.

From here, he could see over the hedge to the north and past the wide fields that flowed gracefully along the river. Beyond the fields, a wild forest nestled against the Bone Hills. Beyond those . . .

Beyond was a broad gap in the scarred north wall of the valley. The river split around the Bone Hills, he'd been told, with its greater flow leaving Marrowdell in an unnavigable cataract. And was that not mist, rising within the opening?

The morning sun teased a rainbow from the mist, drew shadows along the eastmost side of the gap, and burnished the west with light. About to turn away, Bannan glimpsed a shadow that didn't belong. "What . . ." He rocked back on his heels, one hand holding the window frame, the other his broom, and puzzled at what he saw until, abruptly, it made sense.

Stone. The sides of the great gap weren't cliffs; there'd been something there once, something built. Its stones were rounded now and broken, their edges blurred beneath shrubs, but the underlying structure was unmistakable once recognized. Sections of overhanging rock became the remnants of floor or roof. Openings stared back at him, hollow and dark, too square and level to be the work of water or ice or wind. "Ruins," Bannan said softly. "But of what?"

And why here?

Whatever it had been was immense. He must ask Kydd. Perhaps, after the harvest, there'd be time before the snow to climb into those openings and hunt for traces of the builders or inhabitants, to take the Tinkers Road and explore the unseen end of the valley, time to . . .

"Ah, Marrowdell," he chuckled as he rose to his feet, gripping his broom. "You're determined to keep me busy, aren't you?"

To everything, and every mystery, its season, Bannan assured himself, feeling the vast inner content of a man with a wealth of time.

He went downstairs and surveyed the waiting mess. Having only the old bucket and pot, he should wait for Tir and the wagon, for all the supplies he'd purchased in hope of this future.

But he couldn't.

Something drove him, as if he didn't just clean a room, but cleansed himself. The sweat stinging his eyes had nothing of death or the threat of it; the blisters rising on his palms came from no weapon. He grew exhilarated beyond all measure; the water from his own well might have been the finest ale.

His inexhaustible well. Bannan drew bucket after bucket, tossing water on the floor, going back for more. When his makeshift broom struggled to move what quickly became mud, he returned to his plank and scraped it to the door and out.

When the worst of it was gone, he rinsed his sweat-drenched and filthy shirt and hung it on the line. Time to tackle the fireplace.

Using his ax, he pulled what proved to be an old nest from the chimney. The twigs and down stayed in a reassuring clump and, when no movement of the damper brought more down, he squirmed beneath to look. Seeing daylight, he finished sweeping the opening clean, then started a small fire, holding his breath.

The tinder caught with a playful crackle. Bannan fed it splinters he'd saved from the bedstead until he had a tidy little fire. Rushing outside, he watched anxiously for the first faint curl of smoke and heat rising from the chimney. Once sure it was safe, he added more wood, hung the water-filled pot on the pothook, and swung it over the flames.

While the water heated, Bannan went out back and set fire to the pile of debris from the house.

He paused as long as it took to brew a cup of strong tea, taking it and the sausage on his slanted porch for his lunch. Birds sang to him. A bee droned by. Apples shone in the trees. His back and shoulders burned, his hands were raw, and had he ever been happier?

So before he ate the sausage, Bannan Larmensu framed his heart with his fingers. "Hearts of our Ancestors," he said solemnly, "I am Beholden for this food, for it will give me strength to improve myself in your eyes. I am Beholden for this work, for it has given purpose to my life. I am Beholden for the chance to keep Lila and her family safe by my absence. However far we are apart," he finished in a husky whisper, "Keep Us Close."

Wyll had been given a stool, rather than one of the chairs. Not discourtesy. His twisted hip would make a chair painful, Jenn realized. For this formal meeting, the stool faced not the table, but two other chairs, one her aunt's, one her father's, set at the edges of the braided rug.

When she'd walked in, her father had brought another chair, putting it to one end. Not with her family. Not with Wyll. She was allowed to be present, that chair said, but not to speak for either side.

So Jenn sat, her hands folded in her lap, her back straight, the toes of her shoes together, and remembered not to chew her lower lip.

Aunt Sybb gave her a look of approval before returning her attention to Wyll, who looked far more relaxed than her father.

While her father, Jenn thought with an inward squirm, looked more like Wagler Jupp. Or Uncle Horst. His normally jovial face was drawn in stern lines and, when he spoke, there was no mistaking who was in authority here.

"Before you arrived, Jenn," he didn't take his eyes from Wyll, "we made our introductions. Wyll was about to explain why he came with such urgency, rather than wait until this afternoon."

"As the invitation specified," Aunt Sybb stated. She didn't appear flustered or other than politely interested. Then again, Jenn thought with pride, she wouldn't.

Wyll ducked his head to one side. "I came to be with Jenn. Why should I stay anywhere else?"

Aunt Sybb coughed delicately into her 'kerchief; above the lace, her eyes twinkled. Radd put his hands on his thighs and took a deep breath.

Before he said anything she'd regret—or he would—Jenn jumped in. "Wyll. This isn't Night's Edge. There are different rules here. Rules you have to follow, like the rest of us. It was rude to ignore my aunt's invitation. They had no time to get ready for you and Poppa hasn't even shaved! You should," she declared with great finality, "apologize."

Wyll struggled to his feet and tipped in a bow. "I ask your pardon."

Jenn would have taken his effort more seriously if a breeze hadn't flipped the hair from her forehead at the same instant. She scowled at Wyll. He smiled back, taking his seat on the stool and stretching out his bad leg.

Whatever had made Aunt Sybb cough struck her father next. When Radd could speak, his face wasn't quite so stern. "We can, perhaps, dispense with some of the formalities." He glanced hopefully at his sister, who nodded. "Good. Wyll. We've asked you here to talk about—" he hesitated, then surged ahead, "—the future. Yours and Jenn's. I need to know your intentions, sir."

"I have no intentions," Wyll replied. "I have duty. My duty is to stay with Jenn Nalynn as long as she lives, to keep her from harm and here. Is that what you need to know?"

The room, though bright and airy, suddenly felt stifling. Jenn clenched her hands together and wished herself anywhere else, but she'd made him into this; there was no escape for either of them.

"I need to know," her father pressed, his voice gone harsh, "if you love my daughter."

Rose petals fluttered in through the open doors, swirled together in a cloud, then fell softly around Jenn's chair and in her lap, covering her hands, her hair. Their scent filled the room. Jenn's eyes shot to Wyll. There was something naked in his face, something vulnerable and sad. The next instant, it was gone. "I always have," he said.

Radd Nalynn's throat worked. His eyes filled with tears. Aunt Sybb, who'd uttered a soft cry at the petals, reached for his hand. Hers trembled. "That's all we needed," he said at last.

Wyll smiled.

Jenn stood, shedding petals like autumn leaves. "I'll make tea."

She made her way blindly into the kitchen. Found and filled the teapot. Gathered cups and cream and honey. Tried not to think. Tried not to feel.

"Jenn." Her aunt's soft touch stopped her hand as she reached for the tray. "What's wrong?"

Everything. "Nothing," Jenn said.

"I see." Aunt Sybb patted her hand. "We need biscuits." She pulled out the tin, opened it, frowned gently. "Which we'll have to bake, since Peggs keeps giving them away." She closed the tin and gazed at Jenn. "Dearest Heart," very gently, "too much has happened, too quickly. How can you know your own mind? That's why it's important to slow everything down. Give Wyll time. Give yourself time. You'll see."

"I've made my decision," Jenn said stiffly. "I'm marrying Wyll. I'm marrying him as soon as possible. On my birthday. The Golden Day. I'll be nineteen and adult and no one can say otherwise."

"There's no harm in baking first, is there?"

"I—" Unable to argue, she picked up the tray. "I suppose not."

"Considering the necessary preparations," her aunt continued relentlessly, "however minimal, we'll need every waking moment. Your wardrobes alone . . ."

She meant to stay. If will alone could do it, Jenn didn't doubt she would. "You aren't sleeping," she protested. "Not well enough. You can't—"

"Ancestors Bloody and Unbowed!" Aunt Sybb drew herself up, a fierce gleam in her eyes. "I'll drink myself to a stupor on your father's cider, if I must, and if that fails, I'll stay awake with toothpicks in my eyelids! Make no mistake, my dear niece. I will attend your sister's wedding and yours, dreams or no dreams!"

Setting down the tray, Jenn gathered her frail aunt in her arms. She closed her eyes tight, breathed lavender, and somehow didn't cry.

"We are Beholden for life's trials," Aunt Sybb said gently. "Facing them is what makes us women, not years or moon blood, and will give you strength, I promise. I'm proud of the woman you've become, Jenn Nalynn, and so should you be. Now," a smile in her voice, "the tea?"

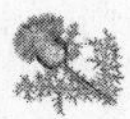

The rug and floor were strewn with rose petals. Wyll supposed, having served their purpose, he should remove them, but did not. For Radd Nalynn—miller, father, brother—couldn't take his eyes from them. Wyll supposed, having been accepted by the family, he could move from the torture of the stool, but did not. For Jenn Nalynn, twice cursed and turn-born, was making tea and would expect him here to drink it.

Having no idea what mattered to these people, he would take no more chances.

Radd's eyes lifted. "You look young," he said, his tone offering no clue if this was comment or accusation. "No older than I was, arriving in Marrowdell."

Was he? His kind lived longer than most; something he'd come to regret. Wyll shrugged his good shoulder. "This is how I am." Their kind lived such a pittance of years. Maybe he'd die sooner as a man; the sei's bent notion of mercy.

"But not as you were." Radd leaned forward, his words an urgent whisper. "You're older. You were in the meadow when Jenn was a babe." He'd gone pale. "Were you there—did you see how her mother—my wife—Melusine—did you hear—"

"Here's the—" Entering with a tray, Jenn stopped. She looked from one to the other.

Radd straightened. "Tea!" he greeted with a cheerfulness even Wyll could see was forced. "Most welcome. I don't suppose Peggs left us any sweets."

"We've made do," his sister said, keen eyes moving between them as well. "Toasted biscuit with honey."

Jenn's questioning gaze settled on Wyll, so he answered. "Your father asked if I saw your mother die."

The tray, with tea, biscuits, and honey, dropped from her hands. Wyll, finding himself hungry, made sure it and its contents landed gently, and upright, on the table.

They stared at him, not the tray.

Wyll shifted, hating the stool and their attention.

Jenn's lip trembled. "Did you?"

"No," he said. "I wasn't there."

Before Jenn, his penance had had another form, one without a kind child or meadow. He'd lived within the turn-borns' enclave, in a hole beneath their dwelling, permitted out when they had need for his service: to clean wastes or fetch water, to hurry away wailing terst parents or stand watch at the gate, whatever they couldn't make happen for themselves or chose not to. They weren't cruel, but they forgot him, more often than not, being unused to a servant. They'd leave for an endless time. When they returned, he'd stare up through the floor boards, listening to their interminable debates about this expectation or that, and wait to be remembered. To have any use at all.

Perhaps she saw the grim memory of it in his eyes, for hers grew soft. "There, then," to dismiss both question and answer. "You can't be comfortable like that, Wyll. Come stand by the table and I'll pour you some tea. Father? Aunt?"

Bemused, he let himself be treated as a man.

THIRTEEN

TO MOVE WYLL to his new home meant rolling the village cart from the Treff barn. The cart meant Davi rattling a grain bucket and bellowing "Come, Battle. Come, Brawl!" at the top of his substantial lungs to bring his team in from the commons. Either cart or bellow would catch the attention of everyone in Marrowdell, not that everyone hadn't already guessed what was up when Radd Nalynn went to the forge instead of his mill.

Davi's cart was a simple, honest vehicle, as he called it, with a pair of shoulder-high wooden wheels wrapped in iron that were replaced by runners once the snow was deep. There was a strong flat bed able to carry bales, which enticed children aboard for a ride, or logs, which did not. The cart had been out yesterday, to haul the remains of Bannan's dead ox from the commons gate.

Despite their names, Battle and Brawl were the gentlest of giants, with hooves like dinner plates and willing hearts. Harnessed and left in the pleasantly cool shade of the apple trees at the center of the village, the draft horses waited patiently on either side of the long cart tongue, eyes half-closed. In the commons, Wainn's old pony, after a plaintive nicker at being abandoned, laid himself flat on one side and went to sleep, yesterday's wild ride having been the most excitement he'd had in years.

Jenn fed the team apples, kissed their broad velvet noses, and tried not to fidget. After all, Aunt Sybb considered her a woman now, which assuredly meant she shouldn't fidget, at least where everyone could see. Everyone could, too, because her task was to wait with the cart while Frann finished fitting Wyll with one of Davi's old coats and Davi finished lunch.

Which was taking far too long.

She was sitting between Brawl's legs, making silly braids in his feathers, when Uncle Horst walked up, ax in hand. Jenn scrambled to her feet. "Fair morning, Uncle."

"Fair morning, Jenn. I've something for your friend." He laid the ax on the cart, fingers lingering on the handle. "It's served me well these years."

Jenn wasn't sure if Wyll could wield an ax or if he'd bother with one, but the gesture warmed her heart. "Thank you. I'll make sure he returns it as soon as he can."

Uncle Horst looked at her. He hadn't shaved this morning. His eyes were tired and full of secrets until he smiled. "As long as he needs it, tell him."

Before Jenn could say a word, he was gone, replaced by Lorra and Cynd Treff. Cynd had her arms around a basket of newly fired cups, while one hand grasped the handle of a chipped but serviceable pitcher. "Fair morning, Jenn," she said cheerily. "For Wyll."

This was more of a surprise than Uncle Horst's ax. Jenn dipped a quick curtsy. "Thank you. I know he'll appreciate them."

"I hope so." Lorra wore her black hat. She stepped around Battle, whose eyes followed the tall feather of her hat with the rapt intent of a well-mannered horse tempted beyond reason. She wore matching gloves, which she only did on significant occasions such as the Midwinter Beholding, and wagged one black-clad finger at Jenn's nose. "I don't know what Sybb's thinking," she stated. "This Wyll's no bargain, girl, farm or not. If you've any sense, you'll marry the other one."

Cross-eyed and speechless, Jenn could only blink.

"As for this curse business—" another wag, "—children should be kept close and safe. Especially here. I dare say Melusine meant well," Lorra added with unexpected gentleness.

Roche. So much for secrets. Serve him right if Horst took his beloved bow back.

"Cynd!" The gloved finger thrust imperiously at the cart.

Cynd, giving Jenn a sympathetic look, found a spot for the basket and pitcher. The two left before Jenn could recover, pausing to exchange brief greetings with Covie Ropp on her way up the lane from the dairy. She carried a small table, Cheffy a bucket of tools and hardware, while Alyssa balanced a wheel of cheese on her head. "For your friend," Covie announced unnecessarily. "Mind where you step," to her children as they clambered onto the cart and argued about where to put their offerings.

"Thank you." Jenn took the table and went to find a spot for it, Covie walking alongside.

"I heard Lorra's advice." The older woman leaned close. "You might listen. Your Wyll has a rare temper," in a low voice.

"He'd never hurt me." Of that, Jenn was sure.

"I'm glad to hear—Cheffy, don't push your sister!—Still," quiet again, "how well can we know one another or the paths we'll take? I can't tell you how glad we all are that my boy stopped you leaving with the stranger."

"My boy" being Roche. Easy to forget, with Cheffy and Alyssa bouncing around, that Covie was his mother too. Jenn swallowed what she wanted to say, beginning with how Roche had been the start of it all and certainly including how he'd been the one to almost lead her from Marrowdell, not Bannan. She looked up at Covie to meet a gaze as wise as it was kind.

"He's too like his father," confided Roche's mother. "Always restless, never satisfied. Avyo held opportunities for a man like that. Marrowdell?" She sighed and shook her head. "Roche won't stay here. Not even for you. I hope you understand."

More than she could say. "I do," Jenn said faintly. "I wish him well."

"You've a good heart, Jenn Nalynn." Covie smiled and raised her voice. "Alyssa, don't bounce so close to your grandmother's pottery. We'll be out of your way. There's more to come, I'm sure. But this is a start."

It was a wonderful start. Gallie Emms, with tiny Loee asleep in her sling, brought sausages and candles, promising a mattress once Zehr came down from Old Jupp's roof. As for Wagler Jupp, Riss came with one of her lovely tapestried cushions under an arm, a kitchen knife missing only part of its handle, and a spare cane, courtesy of her uncle who'd noticed Wyll's need.

Jenn touched each of the gifts on the cart, her heart swelling with pride. Marrowdell might not be a fine city like Avyo, but no city could have more generous people.

A bag dropped on the cartbed with a thud, startling Jenn and barely missing the pottery. "Charcoal," Roche claimed. "Tinder and flint."

"We don't want anything from you," she said icily, grabbing the bag and ready to hurl it back at him. "You told everyone about the curse!"

"Didn't." He shifted the bow further on his shoulder, green eyes sullen. "Just Devins."

Who would have told Hettie, who would have told Covie . . . which amounted to everyone, as Roche should have known, so Jenn scowled at him. "You said I was running off with Bannan." A chill little breeze overhead tossed leaves, and dropped an apple in Battle's reach. "Why?"

"You weren't running off with me, that's for sure." He folded his arms and regarded her coolly. "So who's the liar, Jenn Nalynn?"

Taken aback, she returned the bag to the cart with more care than he'd used. He'd salved his pride for a moment, no longer. The truth would come out once Uncle Horst or Kydd or Peggs heard his version, and not to Roche's benefit. He might, she thought, remembering what Covie'd said, leave Marrowdell sooner than later.

Despite their differences, she found herself sad to believe it. "Let's not fight," she said at last. The breeze died away. "Thank you for the gift."

"Doesn't mean I'm glad you've picked this Wyll," gruffly. "Or that I know why."

She almost smiled.

"Better than that Larmensu. We're well rid of him. A scoundrel, most likely. Or a bandit!"

Her sympathy vanished. "He is not!"

"He shaved his beard, you know. One he'd had for years. I noticed. I brought it up at the meeting. A man who does that," Roche nodded sagely, "is trying to hide his face."

Or start a new life. Jenn didn't bother to argue. "I'm sure you've chores to do, Roche Morrill. Don't let me keep you."

Roche flinched as though stung and stalked away with his shoulders hunched. She sighed to herself.

A toad hopped on the cart and blinked at her.

Jenn blinked back. Every home had its toad; until now, she hadn't realized toads picked their own. "Thank you," she said solemnly.

The toad settled, front legs bent, its long toes curled together around its plump creamy belly, and closed its eyes.

Birds sang, bees droned, and in every detail, the morning was perfect for anything. Anything but standing still. Jenn went back to trying not to fidget. Davi could eat a good-sized lunch, but how long could altering a coat take? She leaned against Brawl, who'd fallen asleep before the toad's arrival, and tried for patience.

Peggs arrived first, with a folded blanket and lunch bucket. She put both on the cart, wordlessly avoiding the toad, and leaned beside Jenn. "Aunt Sybb suggested we leave the rest till we know if Wyll's house has a roof."

"Never mind the house," Jenn said eagerly, "what about Kydd?" Peggs' turn at spying had been for naught. Of all things, Kydd Uhthoff had written a response to their father, put in a sealed envelope to be delivered by a delighted Wagler Jupp, who clearly felt this return to proper correspondence to be worth his unaccustomed exertion although he had, according to Riss, immediately gone to bed for a nap. "Surely Poppa's read it by now."

Her sister drew a ragged breath. "I've got to go. The bread's ready for the oven."

Jenn blocked her retreat. "Peggs?" Her sister's eyelids were red and puffy, as was her nose. "You've been crying. What's wrong? What was in the note?"

"It said—it said 'The Uhthoffs support the right of Bannan Larmensu to the outlying farm and decline to assist in his betrayal.' "

Explaining why no Uhthoff had brought a gift for Wyll, but not Peggs' tears.

"Father's invitation? What about that?"

" 'Until the matter is resolved in fairness to all . . . ' " Peggs' eyes filled. "Oh, Jenn. He won't come."

" 'Fairness?' " Jenn bristled. "How is that fair to you?" How dare Kydd Uhthoff refuse her sister? The leaves overhead fluttered.

"Hush." Peggs glanced around, as if worried she'd find him standing under one of his apple trees. Jenn hoped so; she'd give him a piece of her mind, she would. "Aunt Sybb called it politics and posturing. I'm to ignore him." Her sister sighed. "She couldn't say for how long."

"Don't bake," Jenn said firmly. "Wainn will have Kydd groveling at your feet in no time."

A sparkle in her sister's eyes. "Except for family."

"Of course." Jenn feigned horror. "You can't let us starve!"

"I've summerberry pies coming out of the oven," Peggs said thoughtfully. "I could cool them on the front windowsill."

Where the scent would waft throughout the village, especially toward the Uhthoffs'. Jenn nodded her approval. There was more than one way to deal with posturing. "I've changed my mind. You should bake. Make a few extra," she suggested with a wink. "Poppa loves summerberry pie."

"He does," her sister said with a smile that left no doubt which "he" was meant.

Soon after Peggs left on her mission, Wyll and Davi appeared on the Treff porch. Time to go. Jenn straightened and took a breath.

"What's all this?"

Jenn whirled to find Tir with one booted foot on the cart, his eyes shaded and inscrutable beneath a broad farmer's hat, stiff and new. Between the hat and his metal mask, he resembled a villain caught in the wrong story. "Gifts for Wyll," she answered. "He's moving to the farm."

"Does Bannan know?"

She hesitated.

He lifted the mask and spat eloquently. "I'll come along." It wasn't a request.

"Thank you," she said in a low voice. Surely Bannan would prefer to walk back to the village with a friend.

"Don't." Tir laid his hands on the handles of the axes in his belt. The heads were impractically thin, curved, and razor sharp. Jenn guessed, dry-mouthed, they weren't for wood. "I'll come to make sure there's no repeat of yesterday's madness."

"How reassuring," Wyll said as he approached, eyes a calm brown.

Frann had done wonders with needle and thread. The black coat crossing his shoulders might be worn in places, but it hung straight despite his crooked posture. Too warm for this day, but fall was doubtless in a hurry, now that she wasn't. "Look, Wyll." Jenn swept her hand to the cart. "See how kind everyone's been?"

"Relieved's my guess," Tir offered cheerfully and unasked. "Relieved to have you on the far side of yon river, that is."

Davi regarded Tir over Battle's back. "We're sorry to disappoint your friend, but we help our own first. Wyll is Jenn's betrothed and needs a roof over his head."

" 'On the far side of yon river,' " Wyll repeated, with a half smile. "From them."

Tir chuckled.

The big smith gave the two a searching look, then went back to checking harness. "We'll wait for Radd," he announced.

With a sigh, Jenn sat on the cart beside the toad and did her utmost not to fidget.

Bannan was in the loft when he heard the wagon. He tossed the wet rag he'd been using—the remnant of yesterday's shirt—into the bucket and lowered himself to the main floor, heart pounding. He added a handful of splinters to the fire, poked it to life, and swung over a pot of water. Tea for him. He'd surprise Tir with that obnoxious Essa brew he favored, having tucked the last canister in his pack before leaving Vorkoun, to be safely hidden in the wagon for this day.

That and more. Bannan looked around the now clean, empty room, struck for the first time by the significance of what he'd packed. The wagon's contents would help him survive. They'd make this a home. Of course, there'd be things he'd missed; such could be purchased or borrowed, he was sure. He chuckled. Doubtless he'd packed what he wouldn't need or want. The trader had shaken his head more than once. No matter. He had the necessities, coming up the road with his truest friend.

Bannan washed his face and neck, feeling stubble. No time to shave, though already it was a habit. He ran wet fingers through his hair instead, pulled on a shirt, and headed out the door.

Small blue birds chased crimson butterflies above the grass. The leaves on the trees fluttered silver and green. White flowers with golden hearts turned their faces to the sun. What a welcome! Bannan took a long deep breath and tried to settle his nerves, but joy welled up in him until he felt himself grinning like a fool. Tir would tease him, no doubt of that. A farm was work and nothing but, he'd grumble. All the while, understanding . . .

A breeze found his ear. "Beware."

Scourge. Grin fading, Bannan looked for the not-horse and spotted a shadow beneath the trees, darker than the rest. His heart began to pound. "Why? Who comes?"

"The dragon."

It should have been an occasion. That it wasn't, that they left the village in silence, with anyone who might have watched and waved seemingly busy with other concerns . . . Jenn hoped desperately that didn't make it a mistake.

Wyll was behaving, as Tir called it. Though a glint of feral silver had shone in his eyes when Radd bluntly told him he must ride in the cart, he'd let Davi lift him and found a way to sit, his crippled side supported on the Ropps' low table, braced with his good leg and arm between cheese and buckets. He faced forward, as if as eager to be done with the village as the village to be done with him.

Jenn sat with the toad, facing back. Tir was wrong. The villagers needed time to get to know Wyll, that was all. If Bannan hadn't gone off in such a hurry, this would be an occasion and Peggs wouldn't be miserable. The cart jolted across the ford and she stretched to dip her toes in the water. The gentle current swept clear the silt kicked up by Battle and Brawl and kissed her feet.

What else did the river touch, after escaping Marrowdell? The map had showed it winding south, between hills. Endshere and Weken. People and boots. Horse lips. Bridges. Boat bottoms. Fish nets and laundry.

Someone else's toes. Maybe someone nice or fun or full of stories. Someone different.

Someone she'd never meet.

The team stepped on shore; the cart tipped then leveled.

"So many thoughts," a tickle against her ear. "Are any of our meadow, Dearest Heart?"

Davi and Tir walked up front with the horses, her father with them. Jenn didn't turn to look at Wyll. "Night's Edge isn't the same," she said quietly. "It changed with you."

A damselfly pursued them, then darted back to the river and reeds.

The breeze toyed with her hair. "Did it? How did it? Did it really?" As if she played a game. "Are there more thistles?"

Wyll shouldn't be so glib, she thought, heartsick to remember the dead flowers and ash. "It died," she told him.

The breeze softened to a touch on her cheek. "Surely not, Dearest Heart."

"You'll see," she said, and refused to say more.

The big cart wheels shortened the road to a series of jolts and bumps. Before Jenn was ready, they were in the shade of the old trees. The villagers stayed out of their forest; there was no reason to enter. Nothing worth hunting lived there. Nothing grew beneath but clusters of red and yellow mushrooms, glossy and poisonous. The air itself was thin and reluctant to share. Having her meadow and Wisp, Jenn had spared the forest no attention at all.

Riding backward on the cart made the familiar . . . different. The old trees were graceful and tall, bowed at their tips as if too close to the sky or curious what went on below. And there . . .

The Tinkers Road bent to avoid the rise of the Spine, the cart followed, and Jenn found herself staring into the narrow, shadowed path that led up and away from the valley.

She'd always walked or run past it, to Night's Edge or going home. No one she knew had taken it, since it led deep into the old forest. Oh, Roche boasted he'd explored to the top, but with nothing to hunt, she doubted he'd gone past the first switch.

Jenn's eyes traced its winding course upward to where the forest smothered most of the creamy white of the Spine, but not all. The three tallest mounds were exposed to their base, surrounded by nothing taller than meadow. Meadow that flowed between and beyond Marrowdell.

Meadow every bit as lovely as Night's Edge. Lovelier. The longer she looked, the more flowers she saw, their colors richer and deeper as if better loved by the sun.

What else would she see, if she stood there? Was the Spine higher than the hills beyond?

Could she see to Endshere?

Farther?

Jenn leaned forward on her palms, swaying with the cart's movement. The narrow path, shadowed and dim, held such potent promise her breath caught in her throat and it was all she could do not to jump down and answer. Her father would surely call her back. She had adult responsibilities.

But, oh, how she longed to go.

"No. No. No!!!" The breeze tossed dust in her way, tossed leaves and petals, tossed grit and small stones until a whirlwind followed the cart and swept into her face.

She cried out, shielding her eyes.

"Don't look there! Don't notice! You must not!"

The cart lurched to a rocking halt. The whirlwind ended. Jenn dropped her arm and spat dirt from her mouth as she twisted to glare at Wyll. Her "Why?" died in her throat as she met eyes of molten silver.

"Speak no more of it."

There was an "or else." Jenn felt it, believed it. A shiver traced a path down her arms, trembling her fingertips. He'd never used such a tone with her before. She stared at this shape that was her oldest, dearest friend, who would be her husband, and refused to be afraid. "Yes, we will," she said firmly. "I want to—"

"Jenn!" Her father hurried around the back of the cart, Tir close behind, "What happened?"

Bedraggled hair hung over her shoulders, full of shredded leaves. She wiped grit from her face and shook off her skirt. "Bit of dust."

Both men looked at Wyll, who gazed back with eyes of innocent brown.

"I'll walk from here," Jenn added, hopping down.

It felt a momentous thing, to turn her back on the path. She could still see it, if she closed her eyes, climbing the steep slope, twisting up and up to the meadow above.

A contrite little breeze tried to pluck leaves from her hair. In no forgiving mood, Jenn slapped it away and went with her father and Tir, to walk the rest of the way beside the horses.

A dragon. No, Bannan corrected himself, the dragon. The word conjured memories of children's stories and naughty limericks. Dragons were ancient. Dragons were deadly. Above all, dragons were myth.

Weren't they?

In Marrowdell, he thought wryly, perhaps not.

In Marrowdell, perhaps they appeared as crippled men and traveled in wagons.

The slow, steady clop of hooves, the jingle of harness rings, said the wagon was close. Bannan sat on his slanted porch and rested his chin in his hands, eyes on the gap in the trees, to wait.

Depictions of dragons scarcely agreed. Immense or small? Scaled or feathered? Did they fly or crawl? Four fingers or five or none? The Dragon's Nose Pub in Vorkoun boasted a carved snout protruding above the door, complete with horns, wattle, and a snaggle-toothed grin.

The glimpses he'd had of Wyll were nothing so sure. Ancient, in some way. He nodded to himself. Deadly. Without doubt. He supposed the rest didn't matter, now that the dragon wore a man's shape.

Would he stay in it?

There was a question worth asking.

Big Davi appeared in the gap and waved a greeting. Radd and Tir were with him. Bannan stood eagerly as the big draft horses followed, heads bobbing in unison, tawny manes catching the sun.

But instead of his wagon, they pulled a simple cart, loaded with a few baskets and Wyll.

Because his wagon was designed for an ox, Bannan assured himself. Because they'd brought only what he needed first. Because . . .

What he feared wouldn't be true. Not till he heard it.

Swallowing what was too bitter for disappointment, Bannan went to greet them.

"Fair morning—" he stopped, startled when Jenn peeked at him from behind her father, eyes haunted in a filthy face. She looked as though she'd fallen from the cart and been dragged through shrubs. "If you wish to freshen up," he went on, trying not to stare, "there's hot water and soap inside."

The faintest shake of her head. Her eyes were more than haunted. They were purple with regret and he sank into their depths, losing all sense of what he'd asked.

"You've water?" Radd asked, sharp enough to shake him free.

Proudly, Bannan stepped to one side and held an open hand toward his well, full to the brim and surrounded by clean stone. There was no missing it, especially since he'd trampled the grass on this side.

Radd and Davi exchanged unhappy looks. They'd hoped he'd failed on his own, Bannan realized, heart sinking further. He glanced at Tir, who returned a resigned shrug and stuck his thumbs through his belt.

The signal for "battle ready."

If only battle could win this day.

The cart shook as Wyll rolled off, contorting his body into a stand with a pained grunt. He made his way, each lurch-step across the thick grass and uneven ground almost, but never quite, a disaster, until he reached Bannan. "Greetings, truthseer."

The villagers looked as miserable as he felt. "Tell me," Bannan said roughly. "Why have you come?"

The dragon smiled.

"To evict you. And exile me."

The homely washline upset Jenn most. She tried not to look at it. Less than a day, and Bannan had settled tighter than a broody toad in a burrow. It wasn't fair.

It wasn't fair that Wyll smiled, either. She'd have to speak to him about hurt feelings.

Bannan, today dressed like any villager in homespun pants and shirt, the unlaced throat showing skin still damp from washing and sleeves rolled up, wore what Aunt Sybb would call a "proper face." Nothing showed but calm, polite interest, as if they discussed nothing more dreadful than the care of hooves or how best to cool bread.

But this was dreadful, and not fair, and she—she wasn't going to stand here and let all their futures grow from such a poisoned start. "What Wyll means," Jenn stated in her best no-nonsense voice, "is that he hopes you have room for him. Here."

" 'Room?' " Bannan echoed, his proper face cracked by astonishment. "With me?"

Everyone looked astonished. An aster near her feet spun on its stem until its head popped off; she ignored it. She was right. This was better. "Yes. Until—" Jenn thought furiously, aware the others were staring at her as if she'd turned purple, "—until he builds a new home. Our home," she finished in triumph. "There." She pointed past the overgrown garden, over the hedge and grain, to Night's Edge.

The air stilled, thickened. Considering. Jenn set her jaw and waited.

A butterfly fluttered like laughter around Bannan's head.

Then two.

She saw the corner of his mouth twitch as the butterflies danced in his face. "I'd be honored," he said solemnly.

Two became a cloud. He disappeared behind wings of yellow, black, and brilliant violet, somehow keeping still as they patted his eyelids and perched on his ears.

Jenn gave Wyll a stern look; he returned an innocent one she didn't believe at all. The butterflies freed Bannan after one last swoop. He watched them leave and she didn't relax until he chuckled. "This will be interesting."

Her father smiled broadly. Tir frowned. Ever practical, Davi patted Brawl and said in his deep, calm voice, "Best we unload the cart and give my lads a drink. There's more to move, yours and Wyll's."

"Tha—" Bannan broke off. "Interesting, indeed," he finished with a grin.

Jenn turned with the rest to see the cart's contents stacked neatly on the grass, Uncle Horst's ax on top and the toad nowhere in sight. Wyll gave a modest bow. "The least I can do."

This earned him a too-thoughtful look from Tir, but Jenn didn't care. If Wyll was helping, he was happy with her solution too. She quite liked the idea of building her own home.

If not so much the idea of living in it.

Time for that when the time came, she told herself.

Davi led Battle and Brawl to Bannan's well. Leaving Tir and her father to take a count of missing shingles, Bannan came up to her. "Kindly done, Jenn Nalynn," in a low voice.

Jenn was glad he thought so. She looked at Wyll, who pretended interest in the roof discussion. "You'll let me know if he's any trouble," she told Bannan. "He's not used to houses. Not yet." A breeze flipped hair in her face.

"Neither am I." A wry smile. "Tir will have his hands full."

Returning his smile, she pushed back her hair and found leaves. Leaves and grit. They covered her clothes too. She sighed inwardly. He must, she thought ruefully, think she was never clean.

Be judged by your deeds, her aunt would say. "I'll help," Jenn promised. They'd need a kitchen, sooner than not. Especially with the repair work. "I'll bring breakfast tomorrow. I'll come as often as I can."

"To see Wyll."

Why did it sound like a question?

Because he waited for a reply, eyes warm and steady on hers.

Truthseer.

She couldn't say a word. She didn't dare. Wyll answered the truth to everything, which caused trouble enough, thank you. She wasn't about to be judged by Bannan. Not on this.

Not when she didn't know the truth herself.

At her continued silence, Bannan smiled. She tried frowning; his smile widened. "Visit whenever you like, Jenn Nalynn," he said, amusement making the unusual lilt to his words more pronounced.

Then he turned to invite Wyll inside, saying something about the main floor and how he'd already decided to sleep in the loft, but they'd need to see what Tir preferred, and did he snore?

Jenn didn't pay attention, busy frowning at the back of Bannan's head.

The porch was crooked. It wasn't broken. The windows were broken, but not crooked. All her life, she'd gone past this house, the barn, its little farmyard, without notice or care. Now their need overwhelmed her, as if their neglect was somehow her fault. It wasn't. The valley had a way of taking back what wasn't used or wanted and no one in Marrowdell had needed this place.

Until Bannan.

Jenn watched the cart leave for its next load. She turned, sending a longing glance over her shoulder at the gap in the hedge that led to her meadow, then straightened her shoulders and walked to the house. Stay here and help. Go home and do her chores. Everything was a tangle; anything she did had such consequence, it was a wonder she was willing to breathe. If she'd known this was what being adult was like, she wouldn't have wished so hard for her nineteenth birthday.

"Heart's Blood. Wyll! Stop!"

They couldn't be fighting already. Jenn hurried inside, fearing the worst. She halted in the doorway.

Inside was . . . spotless. The floor planks glowed as if freshly sanded, the fireplace might never have had a fire in it, and the rafters? Jenn could never keep ahead of the cobwebs at home, though she tried. These rafters might have been freshly built.

A shiny pot hung from its gleaming black hook.

In the midst of this unexpected magnificence, Bannan and Wyll stood, nose-to-nose. Neither acknowledged her. "Put it back as it was," the truthseer ordered grimly.

"Why?" A little breeze nudged a pack along the floor, leaning it just so against the wall by the fireplace. Wyll's smile was smug. "Think of it as my contribution."

For some reason, Bannan continued to glower. "Go build your own house. Leave mine alone."

"Fool."

"You heard me. Put it back!"

Jenn squinted as dirt, dust, and cobwebs whirled in through the open windows, draping themselves wherever they'd been and dulling the floor. "Heart's Blood!" Bannan swore again, jumping clear as pieces of wood flung themselves through the back door to assemble as half of a makeshift table leaning against the mantel. Soot swirled down the chimney to coat the fireplace and pot.

On its way out, the breeze dented the pot and toppled Bannan's pack, spilling its contents over the floor.

Jenn bit her lip, trying to keep a straight face.

"I swear it looked better than this," Bannan muttered, shaking his head. He pulled a sticky clump of web from his hair and tried to flick it from his fingers. Twice.

That did it. She burst into giggles.

The two stared at her. Bannan's lips quirked to the side. "I suppose I deserve that."

"You do," Jenn agreed.

The offended silver in Wyll's eyes faded. He stood in the bare dusty room like the house itself, broken and neglected. She'd done it again, hadn't she? Committed his life to what she thought best, without asking. Bannan's too. Jenn sighed. When would she learn?

Wyll's gaze rested on her. "Dearest Heart?"

"I'm sorry," she said quietly. "I should have asked you first—both of you." She gave a little shrug. "I didn't know what else to do. It wasn't fair."

"It was quick thinking," Bannan said with an approving nod that warmed her heart. "I, for one, am grateful."

"Because the arrangement benefits you, truthseer. I gain nothing from it."

Oh, Jenn knew that tone. Wyll hadn't forgiven Bannan for rejecting his "contribution." He was going to be, as her aunt would say, difficult. Something she recalled Wisp excelled at being, especially when she wanted him to play her way and he'd refused. "We gain a house in Night's Edge," she argued, eyeing Wyll. "You can do it, can't you? Build a house?"

"Like this?" Wyll glanced at the massive logs of the walls and moved his good hand in dismissal. "No. The neyet owe me no favors."

Bannan caught the odd word too. "'Neyet?'"

"What the villagers call the old trees. The neyet gave themselves once, to create the structures of Marrowdell. They would not be inclined to do so again."

What was he talking about?

Bannan spoke first. "Why?"

The question brought a smile to Wyll's face, a smile Jenn wasn't sure she liked. "They learned that to become wood, they must die."

Jenn didn't think Wyll had answered the "why" Bannan meant, but from his wary expression, the truthseer didn't plan to ask again, not right away.

"We'll use something else when the time comes," she said brightly, more concerned with the present than the opinions of trees. "Davi will be back soon with the next load. We should finish cleaning in here."

Wyll's eyes gleamed. "My way or yours, truthseer?"

"Both, if you please," Bannan conceded with a short bow. "Leave me the floor and fireplace for pride's sake; the rest I'll gladly leave to you." He looked up. "Oh, and there're some old nests—"

"Done." And it was, as fast as Wyll could say the word. He was like that, Jenn nodded to herself, when not making a point. Quicker than the eye could follow.

She rolled up her sleeves and tied her mess of hair back with the twist from her pocket, as if she could get dirtier moving dust. "I'll take care of the floor."

So now he lived with a dragon. Shaking his head in wonder, Bannan went for water, only to find Scourge by the well.

"I don't suppose you approve."

Scourge slobbered a mouthful of water and regarded him with placid eyes, every bit the horse. Without thinking, Bannan gave him a friendly pat. Coarse brown hairs stuck to his fingers, fair warning of the annoying clouds to come as the creature's coat readied for winter. "Touch early for the fall shed, isn't it?"

The breeze whispered in his ear. "Itchy."

"What would you do without me to groom you?"

"Itch."

The fall shed transformed Scourge from shadow to night, his dull brown hide turning almost black as the dark skin beneath showed through. He became almost handsome, or thought he was, tending to strut more than usual, but was prone to shiver at night until his heavy undercoat finished its regrowth. All of which involved hours of Bannan leaning on a brush while the not-horse burbled with pleasure. Hours he no longer had, if he was to get the farm ready for winter.

Bannan smiled. Scourge was notoriously averse to being handled by strangers, but he'd permitted Jenn's touch. She'd offered to help, hadn't she? A farm maid surely knew how to groom a horse. "I'll ask Jenn Nalynn," he decided aloud.

Well pleased, he dipped the buckets, old and new, into the well. She wasn't sure, so she wasn't Wyll's, not yet. All was fair. The more reasons he could find to have her here, keep her near, the more chance he had—

Low and grim in his ear, "What kind of fool have you become?"

He patted Scourge again. "The hopeful kind, old friend. The hopeful kind."

News of what Aunt Sybb called a "proper and civil settlement" arrived home long before Jenn, since she and, in the afternoon her father, stayed to help Bannan and Wyll while Tir and Davi plied back and forth with the cart. On his first such trip, Davi'd stopped to tell his mother the situation, she'd told Covie, and that was that.

On the cart's final trip, too tired to do more than glance wistfully at the mysterious path, Jenn leaned against Devins' bony shoulder and half-listened as he told her how Zehr had cleverly cobbled together a hitch to let Davi's team pull Bannan's wagon, their last trip for the day. He and Anten had lent their hammers to the most urgent repair, shingles for the roof, then helped pull the old porch free so the foundation stones could be reset.

Help that wouldn't have been offered yesterday, before Bannan proved himself. Finding the well hadn't been the only test. "So much for Roche," Devins declared with the satisfaction of a bet won. "I told you what he said about Bannan sleeping the night, didn't I? Said he'd believe a house toad could talk first."

Jenn gave a noncommittal shrug. The Morrill brothers—and the twins—gambled on anything and everything, their passion unaffected by stakes of acorns instead of coins. She grinned to herself. Except for the time Himself had gobbled Allin Emms' hidden stash, said plundering made possible by a carelessly latched gate. The blame had fallen on a protesting Roche, though truth was, Hettie, being annoyed by their latest game, had led the delighted boar to the hiding place.

"Roche tried to sleep there himself, just this spring."

Doubtless intending to annoy her the next morning, as she walked through the farmyard to Night's Edge. Jenn swayed with the motion of the cart and grumbled, "Has he nothing better to do?"

"Point is," Devins lowered his voice, as if his brother might be hiding nearby, "he showed up home after barely half the night, shaking so's he could hardly stand. He'd have lit every lamp we owned if I hadn't stopped him. Never said a word—I'm guessing he dreamed."

She shot him a sober look. "You shouldn't say that." Was this what lay behind Roche's restlessness? Why he'd wanted her to leave with him? "You don't know."

"What I know, Jenn Nalynn, is there's nothing else in Marrowdell that would make my brother turn tail."

Wisp had, which was hardly something she could tell Devins. Jenn changed the subject. "Will you work at the farm tomorrow?"

"I offered," he said, then sighed. "They don't need me."

An enthusiasm she suspected came from the pleasures of a change of routine and the curiosity all the villagers felt for the new arrivals in Marrowdell, though Devins had also been eager to see the farm where one or more of his beloved calves might come to live. Wiser heads had prevailed to delay such an arrival.

Scourge being here first.

Jenn wasn't interested in calves or anything but getting clean again. Leaves still rustled in her hair. The skirt would join next week's laundry, between the road dust and soapy water from washing

Bannan's floor. She'd done her best with the scrub brush Covie had sent along. To remove the lingering stains would take hours with a sanding stone and there'd been no real wear on the planks anyway, other than scratches near one corner she'd thought might have been the bear but her father, disappointingly, said were most likely carelessness when the bed frame had been put in place.

The bed Bannan had foolishly burned. Did the city bred not realize the effort obtaining a replacement would take? If they didn't want to share, they'd need beds for Wyll and Tir as well. Tir claimed to prefer a hammock, but a hammock wouldn't keep him warm in winter. Davi'd pointed out, in his thoughtful way, that the villagers had dismantled their wagons for lumber and Bannan had latched onto the idea, to the others' quiet approval.

He was determined to stay. That much was clear to anyone.

He'd welcomed her to visit. To visit him, not just Wyll. Her feelings on that weren't clear at all. Why did men have to complicate everything?

"Marry me."

Jenn twisted around so quickly she almost fell off the cart and had to grab hold of the edge. "Pardon?"

"Marry me." Every faded freckle across Devins' nose stood out, but he forged ahead, words spilling like milk. "I hadn't thought about it much, not really. But today, working together on the farm—well, it makes a man think, all this talk of homes and futures. It's time I had a family of my own. Shouldn't I? I'm a grown man."

Saying didn't make it so, Jenn thought, unconvinced. Nor did she believe a family was something one suddenly decided to acquire, like a new bull for the herd.

As for marriage? An impulsive proposal on the back of a bouncing cart was in no sense or shape romantic, even if she ignored the part where he didn't love her, nor she him.

To Devins' credit, if she said yes, he'd keep his word and be faithful.

Unlike his brother.

"I'm marrying Wyll," she said gently.

"Well, yes. So everyone says. But you don't have to," with urgent hope. "Once Roche leaves, I'll have the house. You could sew curtains and I promise I'll fix up the kitchen. Next fall, I could go to Endshere and trade some yearlings for a new stove, better than his—" the magnificent new appliance in Bannan's wagon having stirred lust in more than a few hearts, "—and I'd give it to you for your birthday. Jenn Nalynn, you should marry me!" When she simply stared, speechless, a flush replaced the pallor. "Or not."

What would Aunt Sybb say? "Be patient," Jenn told him. "I'm sure you'll find someone."

Devins slumped forward, arms on his thighs, and sighed. "The only someone left in Marrowdell," he said morosely, "is Peggs."

She couldn't argue with that.

The cart splashed through the ford and they stretched their toes to touch the water.

He sat up again, eyes alight. "Does she want a family?"

"Ask her yourself." Jenn leaned into his bony shoulder. "I can tell you her heart's unattached at the moment."

That, Kydd Uhthoff, for the tears in her sister's eyes.

Men.

Aunt Sybb stood waiting on the porch. She never waited on the porch. Exchanging alarmed looks, Jenn and her father hurried up the path. "What's wrong, Sybbie?" Radd asked anxiously.

Her mouth was slightly pinched, one eyebrow almost imperceptibly lifted, and creases drew together the corners of her usually sparkling eyes. Which held a glint that could be best described as implacable. This was the face her nieces, in private, called her "only for love" expression, since it presaged when one of them had tried her patience to the breaking point, not that a lady of their aunt's caliber ever broke, and a lecture was in the offing.

As able to read his sister as either of his daughters, Radd took one look and said quickly, "I'll go around the back to wash up." He fled.

Before Jenn could follow, her aunt crooked a finger to bring her closer. This was not in any way a good thing, since she needed to wash even more than her father, but she did her best not to fidget under Aunt Sybb's regard and schooled her face to polite attention. What had she done?

"Yes, Aunt?"

"There are pies," Aunt Sybb said grimly.

Of course there were pies. She'd smelled them from the road; her mouth had been watering all the way to the porch. "'Pies,'" Jenn echoed, hoping for a clue.

"Pies," the lady of Avyo repeated, in the same tone she'd used for "toad."

There were, Jenn conceded, an unusual number of pies cooling on the front windowsill, proof her sister had taken her advice to heart. But something in their aunt's demeanor suggested both worry and exasperation, for once not aimed at her younger niece. "Is Peggs all right?"

Aunt Sybb gave a faint, dignified sigh. The sigh that meant whatever wasn't all right had breached all bounds of reasonable behavior and dealing with it was beyond a mere lecture.

A sigh with which a younger Jenn had been unfortunately familiar. "Shall I take care of it, Aunt?" she offered, as she'd said all the times before. "The pies?"

"Please do."

Jenn went inside.

Peggs wasn't in the parlor. Pies were. Pies crammed the table, replaced the flowers on the heatstove, and covered the trunk. There were pies precariously perched on the arms of the settee and, while none had dared their parents' red and yellow lacquered hutch, pies sat on the chairs.

Swallowing her dismay, Jenn hurried through to the kitchen, where she found her sister surrounded.

Bowls of filling and pastry crowded each other, spoons sticking up like masts. Flour dust coated every surface, including the house toad who'd backed into the corner by the oven and puffed into an annoyed flour-covered ball. Steam filled the air. There were pies in the oven, pies waiting to be baked, and rounds of rolled pastry stacked like plates. In the midst of it all stood Peggs like some warrior queen, hair and dress plastered to her skin with sweat, apron long since abandoned, and fire in her eyes.

The battle for Kydd's heart—or at least his stomach—had been joined with a passion. Poor Devins.

"I've been—" Peggs admitted, "—baking."

Shaking her head, Jenn wiped a dab of flour from her sister's lovely nose. "We could smell pie all the way to the commons," she commented.

"But he hasn't come." Peggs hugged herself. "It's been all day—"

Their father appeared in the back door, toweling his face, and stopped in his tracks. "Ah. Pie for supper." He tilted his head, apple cheeks aglow, a twinkle in his eyes. "And pie for breakfast. A few suppers and breakfasts."

Peggs' mouth opened without sound, then closed with a snap. Jenn knew that look. Their father wouldn't have "pie for supper."

Though any cooking with the kitchen in this state would take Wyll's sort of magic. "Let me change and I'll help with the dishes," Jenn told Peggs.

Up in the loft, Jenn opened the clothes chest and rummaged for anything clean. Most of what fit her was hanging on the line or waiting for next wash day. Which might, she grimaced, need to come sooner. She borrowed one of Peggs' everyday shirtwaists and found an old skirt of her own. The hem had been let out as far as it would go two years ago, which made it perfect now for crossing the river or playing in the meadow. She'd put it away this summer after Aunt Sybb noticed more than her ankles showed—a fashion acceptable in Avyo, where ladies had the option of silk hosiery or tall boots with gilded buttons, but not with bare skin.

Bare skin. Jenn examined her arms, tanned below the elbows,

elbows red from scrubbing the farmhouse floor. Most people would have red knees, but she had a habit of pushing the brush too fast and far which, as anyone knew landed you on your elbows. Something that happened most if anyone was watching. They'd taken turns at that. Wyll one moment. Bannan the next. As if they didn't have chores of their own.

She sat on the bed, skirt in her hands, and wiggled her toes.

She'd watched them, too, through the window when she thought they wouldn't notice. Wyll's little breezes would unload each fresh cartload, Bannan would sort what was there and find a place for it. When her father returned, he'd helped Bannan scavenge planks for shelves from the ruined larder outside. A kitchen took shape around the fireplace. They'd shared the bucket lunch. Tomorrow Bannan's new stove would be set up, sure to be a wonder.

Tomorrow she'd bring breakfast, as soon as she could finish her chores here, then see what else she could do at the farm. The reward for a hard day's work was content by night. Father's saying, not Aunt Sybb's.

Content? She'd settle for falling into bed too tired to think. Except . . . she wanted to think about the path.

Wyll had been so angry. Why?

The path led up the Spine, that was all.

Jenn shook her head. "It's just a path." Yet her heart beat faster. From that height, what might she see? Might she see beyond Marrowdell?

Might her cage have a window?

Roses nodded at her. Melusine's roses, large and rich and red as blood. "You faced trials of your own, Mother," whispered Jenn, her fingers circled. "May your heart give strength to mine."

Tomorrow, before breakfast, she'd see for herself.

"Hearts of our Ancestors, we are Beholden for the food on our laps." Tir spoke loudly and with vigor, his hungry eyes fixed on the thick slice of ham waiting on his plate. "And we would be even more Beholden if this fine young pig's mother keeps popping them out."

Bannan hid a grin. Tir's exhortations to the Ancestors were always colorful.

"We are Beholden for new shingles on the roof, though a roof not needing shingles would have been better and saved all that time and climbing."

Colorful and rarely respectful. The dragon seemed fascinated.

"We are Beholden—" with such fervor the plate balanced on Tir's lap tipped dangerously, "—for the chance to work our fingers to the bone in this lovely dirt when we could have been living the life in a big city with women who don't make wishes that change one thing into a t'other, women who—" in time gripping his plate between both elbows, hands still piously over his heart, "—are warm and willing and wear those little black—"

Bannan coughed.

"—However far we are apart," Tir rattled off without pausing for breath, "Keep Us Close."

" 'Keep Us Close,' " Bannan murmured.

They'd taken their supper to the fallen branch where he and Wainn had shared pie, chairs or a bench not on the list of immediate tasks. The roof mattered most, closely followed by windows and doors. The stove, last in the wagon, so first out, sat in pieces in the midst of what would be the kitchen side of the downstairs room.

They sat in the warm sun and feasted on kindness. Leftover bread and onions from the lunch the men had brought to share from the village, the exceptional ham, and apples from his own tree. They hadn't uncovered the bag filled with Vorkoun wine before hunger claimed them, but water from his well more than sufficed.

His well. His tree. Bannan set his plate aside, discovering an appetite for more than food. "What do you know of Marrowdell's past?"

Wyll's knife paused. He was adept with one hand, or good with blades, or both. "More than I care to," he said, and stabbed a thick round of onion.

The truthseer rested his arms on his knees. "The ruins to the north," he began, undeterred. "What was there? What happened?"

Tir grunted. "Best ask what's wrong with this place," he advised around a mouthful of bread. "No one's lived here. Why's that?"

Wyll glanced at him. "You'll know," he replied, "or you won't."

Glowering, the former guard shoved a chunk of ham into his already full mouth and chewed, a spectacle few could watch without feeling queasy.

"The ruins?" the truthseer prodded. "I spotted them from the loft," this for Tir's benefit, not that he was one to take interest in an old forgotten structure unless the rubble made good cover. "It looked like there'd been towers once, on either side of the river."

"Men came and built." Wyll's eyes flickered silver and a breeze smoothed the bare soil in front of their feet like the sweep of a hand. Tir leaned forward with Bannan, absently keeping the food in his mouth with two fingers, as a line appeared.

Then another. Lines that drew themselves, or were drawn by sharp little winds. Circles met ovals. Straight lines converged, then splintered outward. A crumb-seeking bird fluttered from a line aimed for its toes.

The lines went deeper, sculpted, shaped.

Until they stared at a shadow of the past.

Thick spired masses, gilded with pollen, rose from the tops of facing cliffs, three on the left, two on the right. Beneath, rock had been hollowed away to leave wide openings staggered above one another, supported by graceful pillars. A petal-clad bridge of several levels, each with openings and arches, melded the two sides into a single structure, the whole held high atop the raging river on three improbably tall columns.

Nothing close to the ground, as if the builders chose to be part of the sky.

"Be a rare mess in winter," Tir concluded, and settled back to work on his ham.

Bannan stretched out his hand, but didn't dare touch what was a true work of art, both in the soil and what had been. "What was it? Who were they?"

A harsh breeze swept away petals and pollen, churning and scouring the ground. He gave an involuntary protest, staring up at Wyll.

The silver in the dragon's eyes faded to a somber brown. "The spark that set two worlds ablaze, truthseer. And they were fools."

"Psst."

Jenn looked up from the dishes. Her father had gone to the mill, after enlisting Cheffy to deliver pies around the village—excepting the Uhthoffs, of course. Her aunt and Peggs had taken to the porch, stitching by the last of the sunlight while Aunt Sybb instructed her errant niece on the perils of excessive pastry.

"Jenn."

Avoiding the remaining pies, she leaned through the open kitchen window to find Kydd Uhthoff crouched awkwardly beneath the sill.

He wore his winter Beholding coat, the heavy old velvet doubtless stiflingly hot, and looked to have shaved in a hurry, without a mirror to judge by the nicks on his jaw. Jenn scooped a cupful of hot sudsy water and held it at the ready. "What do you want?"

As if she couldn't guess.

"I heard what you did. For Bannan and Wyll." He started to rise. She warned him back with the brimming cup. "Jenn, please. Let me explain—"

Jenn scowled at him. "You made my sister cry."

"I did?" Kydd's eyes lit. "She did?" He hastily assumed a contrite expression. "I'm very sorry."

Jenn continued to scowl. "I'm not the one who needs an apology."

"I know. I'm sure. I—" Sweat beaded his high forehead. "I wrote one." He showed her an envelope. "Please take—"

"Jenn?" Peggs walked into the kitchen. "We thought we'd—what are you doing?"

The beekeeper sank in the shadows, pressing a finger across his lips. With a pleading look, he handed her the envelope.

Jenn dropped it in the dishwater. "Someone's here about a pie," she announced, and stepped away from the window.

Kydd rose to his feet. Being taller than the window opening, he had to stoop to peer inside, which wasn't at all dignified despite his fancy coat. She'd have felt sorry for him but for the way her sister's face lost its color.

"Pie?" Peggs repeated faintly. "Is that what you want?"

His well-thought eloquence afloat, the beekeeper gripped the windowsill like a man drowning and shook his head.

"Then what?" she asked.

"You," he gasped.

The faintest pink, like an opening rose, touched Peggs' cheeks. "Jenn, please take Aunt Sybb her cup."

"Are you sure?" Jenn asked suspiciously.

The two hadn't taken their eyes off one another. "Are you?" Kydd asked softly, leaning head and shoulders into the kitchen. His cuffs trailed in dishwater, but he didn't appear to care.

"Oh, yes," Peggs answered, stepping closer.

Jenn held her breath, her heart pounding. They were going to kiss. She knew it. Like in the stories . . .

Peggs put a hand behind her back to gently shoo her away.

Disappointed, Jenn grabbed the jug of cider and a cup, then left the two alone.

She'd get the details later.

Wyll watched night's edge stain the Bone Hills. His wish-changed eyes found the blue soothing. The rest of him did not. He'd kept the girl safely distant from the crossing during each turn, safe and away from what she might see. Now, she meant to live beside it.

Doubtless both turn-born and sei would blame him for that.

The kruar stood too close, an unpleasant wall of sweating hide. Any protest would please his obnoxious ally, so Wyll ignored him. The hordes of big-eyed flies that lifted with each slap of the kruar's long tail were harder to dismiss and that tail best not come near. His tolerance had limits, already strained by their conversation.

Tail slap. ~ You gave no oath. The villagers have no say in what you do. ~

~ I must stay. ~ Were there flies in the kruar's hairy ears? ~ Thus you must guard the road. Our common purpose— ~

The kruar snorted. ~ I'll guard it here. ~

Infuriating creature. ~ Our common purpose is to protect the girl. She sleeps in the village. ~

~ Where she is safe. She no longer tries to leave. ~

~ But the road— ~

~ I've heard what travels that road next will be cows. Go yourself. ~

Night's edge. Though he couldn't see it from the farmyard, Wyll imagined the turn washing over their meadow, finding flowers. It drew the efflet from the kaliia; they left their fields and approached him here, only to mill uncertainly, wary of the kruar.

He didn't blame them.

Without curiosity, Wyll watched the turn slip over his hand, then his body, finding no other shape. What the truthseer claimed to glimpse was mere memory, done and gone and lost. Unless the sei chose otherwise.

For his part, the kruar shifted uneasily as the turn scoured away the lie he wore, of hide and mane. Scars flared to life along his naked skin. His kind, grateful as Wyll's own, as gentle, had ripped away his armor, that vanity of the warrior sect. The light's passing followed his neck's curve and found the ragged stumps of its once-impressive crest.

Wyll averted his gaze.

The turn passed to the road and ylings threw themselves in the air to dance.

A heavy hoof struck the ground. The scent of dying grass caught Wyll's attention. The home he was to share, like the one last night, had been built of such unwitting corpses. The turn-born played with those weaker as wantonly as the sei, he thought dourly, and with less reason.

~ They wanted me forgotten, ~ the kruar crooned. ~ And almost I was. Years beyond count, I roamed without voice or purpose, unseen for what I was, until I began to forget myself. ~

Wyll glowered at his unwelcome companion. ~ Would I could forget you, too. ~

Would he could forget himself.

The kruar snorted with amusement, as if he'd heard the thought rather than the words. ~ Lucky for us both, I saw myself in a truthseer's eyes. Not this— ~ Skin shuddered from mane to tail, dislodging flies. ~ Not what the rest of his kind would see—but enough to remember what I am . . . ~

~ Yet Bannan doesn't see you as you are. ~ This being a sore point.

~ As he does you? ~ Another snort. ~ He sees what he needs to see. I'm of home and family. Once he finds the courage to leave those behind, he'll look deeper. Not before. ~

So out of pity, his old enemy avoided men's eyes, hiding here through the turn when his truthseer couldn't help but see him as he was. The fool was no more immune to fondness than he.

~ I can't go into the village, ~ Wyll insisted, returning to their argument. ~ You must watch the road. ~

~ No. I must protect my truthseer. ~

~ I mean him no harm, ~ Wyll said wearily.

~ You're no threat ~ the kruar pointed out with wicked joy. ~ She pulled your teeth. ~

~ Then explain yourself. ~

The kruar lowered his head until hot breath, unwelcome and foul, entered Wyll's nostrils. No joy now. ~ You know what touches the road between here and the village. ~

The path to the upper meadow. The Wound between worlds.

Yes, he knew. They all knew. The Verge was stitched in place and held solid, like the scars along his body and the kruar's. Everywhere but along the Wound. There, the puncture between had cut too deep to ever heal. The turn-born shunned that path for good reason. The Wound sought them, lured them.

Kept them.

He'd heard a turn-born speak of a labyrinth within, a maze in which their kind became lost. Maze, trap, or gaping mouth. Wyll didn't care which. Those fool enough to enter the Wound, from either world, were never seen again.

The girl had looked into that dread opening. Had looked and been drawn. He'd known the day would come when, like all turn-born, her passions grew beyond the fancies and frets of a child, and her expectations gained true force. But he'd hoped, the girl being of this world, confined to her sun's light, that the Wound would never catch her attention.

He'd stopped her in time. It had been in time. He had to believe that.

~ What of it? ~ Wyll demanded, rubbing the ache in his ruined side. He heard Bannan call to his friend. They'd pulled lanterns from the wagon, lit them to fend off the dark. Didn't they know the meaning of rest?

~ On his way here, last night, the truthseer saw the Wound. He was seen and he was called and only I saved him! ~ The neck arched with pride.

Bannan could see his true nature. It was possible he could see the oozing sore in the forest as well. The rest might be kruar nonsense, or might not. The turn-born were the ones who claimed only they could be lured, that others stumbled into their doom.

Turn-born, in Wyll's experience, were not always truthful.

Neither were kruar, with their magic of misdirection and guile, their preferred attack an ambush. ~ Nonsense, ~ Wyll said with calculated scorn. ~ You must be mistaken. ~

Foul breath, now the rude snap of jaws in his face. ~ Would I care to protect him otherwise? ~

~ It astonishes me you care at all. ~ Wyll pushed the kruar's snout aside.

Sullen silence. That had struck a blow. He smiled to himself.

~ If the truthseer is lost, ~ the kruar said with rare cleverness, ~ she will look for him. ~

Wyll wished for fangs. As well wish for a return to his youth and the chance to make any of a lifetime of choices again. He'd make the same mistakes, of course. Penance made him aware of his flaws; it couldn't remove them.

As for the truthseer, how was he to watch the man's movements? He could hardly keep up with him during the unpacking. What mattered was Jenn Nalynn. Wyll snarled. ~ Let him protect himself! ~

The kruar threw up his head and glared, a rumble starting deep in his chest. Before either could do or say anything Wyll was sure to regret, a rustle from the ground distracted them both.

Two pairs of limpid brown eyes peered up from the grass, followed by plump bodies as the toads worked themselves into the open. ~ Elder brother, ~ one said courteously as it settled on its toes. ~ Lord General. I have myself accounted for one hundred and four mice, fourteen squirrels, and a clot of nyphrit from this home. My companion provided thirteen eggs and caught fifty-three mice and a squirrel in this moon cycle. We matter— ~

The kruar lifted an impatient hoof.

~ —permit us to assist you, ~ it finished hastily.

A tail slapped. The toads gazed longingly after the disturbed flies, but didn't move. ~ Useless creatures, ~ the kruar dismissed them. ~ Leave your betters be. ~

More to annoy his ally than because he thought the toads of use, Wyll asked, ~ Assist in what way, most accomplished little cousins? ~

~ Watch the truthseer, ~ offered the second toad. ~ Alert you to danger, ~ said the first. ~ Be your eyes, ~ they said together.

Spies. Adept ones at that.

~ Why would you do this? ~ the kruar demanded, ever suspicious.

Wyll felt curiosity stir at the question. Why, indeed? Little cousins weren't so conceited that they risked themselves in the affairs of others. They kept close to their burrows, a safety left solely for the reckless pilgrimage to add their hard-earned pebbles to the white throne they built their queen. They believed she would join them, could they but demonstrate their worth.

Generations labored in vain. The reigning queen knew nothing of her lost subjects and had not the power to cross the edge to them even if she did, but he'd never been so cruel as to destroy their hope.

~ Bannan Larmensu belongs here, Lord General, ~ the bold first toad. ~ As do we. ~

The second, ~ As you do not. ~

Wyll prepared to lift the toads out of reach, but the kruar snorted its crude laugh. ~ We do not, ~ he agreed equably. ~ Brave little cousins, to speak so honestly. Have you more honest things to say? ~

Their eyes popped in and out, but they knew better than answer.

~ Enough, ~ Wyll pronounced. ~ Watch the truthseer. While my esteemed ally guards the road, you will tell me if Bannan strays where none should. ~ He shifted, wary of letting his side grow stiff. The twisted leg would fail him, if it could. The villagers had provided a cane. He had no use for it, unless on the kruar's thick skull. A cane could break or be taken, like any help that came from others.

Yet here he was, taking help from his ancient enemy and from those once beneath notice.

The girl's doing, Wyll grumbled to himself, feeling all three stare as he lurched away, done with them. She'd made him weak and needful.

She was worse than the sei.

The coming night would be interminable. The way Bannan and Tir worked, they'd collapse before playing a game with him. This close to the crossing at Night's Edge, his kind need only pay attention to reach him, should they want amusement.

Mist collected under the hedge, fingered the trees, mocked him as he made his way to the door. Damp, dark, horrid night. He hoped the men would work late, with lanterns blazing.

Regardless. He'd endure, as he endured all else.

Jenn Nalynn would return in the morning. She'd promised to bring breakfast.

The food didn't matter. Dawn didn't matter.

Having her near again, did.

The peace he found in her company was her trap; this flesh, her cage. Why had he set the kruar to guard the road? He should have begged the creature to rip out her throat and be done.

Before he had to learn if he still could.

What a sorry state he was in, Wyll thought as he lurched to this night's bed and fell atop it. He reached morosely for blankets; pulled one over his head.

Sorry indeed, to no longer trust himself.

FOURTEEN

WAINN LAID HIS arms across his pony's saggy back and considered Jenn with a thoughtful crease between his eyebrows, as if he knew full well why she wanted to ride this morning instead of walk. Which he couldn't, so she smiled and gave his pony another brisk pat. "He looks well rested."

The old pony turned its gray muzzle to regard her with one white-rimmed eye, then turned away, hairy lips working at air. A person who forgot apples, that said, was a person beneath notice.

Wainn shook his head. "I'm sorry, Jenn. When he likes, he will carry the children." He put his cheek against the bony spine, watching her with one eye of his own. "He doesn't want to carry you anymore. You're too heavy."

"But—" She hadn't been too heavy last spring; to be kind, the pony had been that much younger.

Jenn Nalynn curbed her frustration. She'd snuck downstairs before dawn to do her chores as quickly as she could. The day's greens were picked and ready, with a bit of weeding thrown in; she'd replenished the kindling and refilled the kettle before anyone stirred; and put on the porridge. She would have surprised Peggs by having the day's loaves in their pans, ready to rise, except just in time she noticed a few weeds mixed with the greens, the trouble with being in the garden before the sun, and had to sort those first. She did, however, manage to scamper out to the hedge and collect more eggs for breakfast, having boiled all they'd had to take to Wyll, since his toad would be unlikely to provide so soon and she'd promised, after all, to bring breakfast to the farm.

Once everyone stirred, Jenn had helped serve the table, whisking the plates out from under noses the instant she could, which may have been too quickly, since she'd had to return her father's mug because he'd wanted a second cuppa and her aunt pronounced herself dizzy. She'd been so very helpful, her sister had thrown up her hands with a laugh and pushed her gently out the door, after adding yesterday's baking to the eggs in her sack.

All for naught. Had she been able to borrow Wainn's old pony, Jenn would have had time to do her exploring before being expected at the farm. She sighed.

Wainn smiled. "Why don't you ride him?"

"Who—?"

He nodded toward the hedge.

Scourge, hipshot and eyes half shut, stood on the other side, dozing in the shade of the Ropps' barn. He wasn't easily seen; the giveaway was the line of offended cows glaring from their gate, the warhorse being between them and being milked. Had he wanted to annoy them?

"I couldn't," Jenn said slowly.

Could she?

He'd let her climb up with Bannan in the saddle. Those long legs would make short work of the road. Why, on a horse like that, she could make it to the upper meadow and be down again before Wainn's old pony could make it halfway up the Spine. She gave the pony an absentminded pat. "I should move him anyway," she murmured. "For the cows' sake."

"You should be careful, for ours," Wainn said soberly.

Before she could ask what he meant, he walked away with his old pony, one arm over its shoulders, their heads tipped together as if they conversed. She hoped about apples and not the folly of curiosity, because she couldn't stop, not if she would.

The cows, sensing an ally, crowded her heels as Jenn went to the milk gate, lowing with disappointment when she slipped through and carefully closed it behind her. "Hettie will be here soon," she assured them.

Scourge didn't budge as she approached. He might have been asleep.

But wasn't. A breeze tickled her ear. "Second choice, am I?"

Jenn hoped no one noticed her start. "You're very good at hiding," she said, coming close. Scourge wasn't merely larger than Wainn's old pony, he loomed. "May I ride you? Please," she added as his eyes snapped open, something red in their depths. She lifted the saddlebag. "I've breakfast for those at the farm. For your master."

The breeze turned chill. "I've no master."

He certainly had opinions. "Your rider, then," Jenn corrected impatiently. "Bannan. Will you take me to him?"

The great head lowered, flared nostrils snuffling at her neck and shoulder, lower still to nose the bag. "Where's my breakfast?"

"Not here." Jenn put the bag behind her.

"I like rabbits." Suggestively.

Her eyes widened. "You are not," she retorted, "eating my rabbits. Ever."

Scourge jerked up his head to glare down his long nose. She glared back. Finally, the breeze in her ear whispered, "How shall I know which are yours?"

Jenn paused. Tempted as she was to claim every one, she couldn't. After all, she liked foxes too. And hawks. Rabbits were like each year's piglets. Adorable, fun, and, unluckily for them, delicious. "Don't eat the rabbits of Night's Edge—of my meadow." She owed them protection; they were foolishly bold in her company. "And . . . please don't eat any rabbit while I'm watching," she added meekly.

He snorted; she took it for agreement and relaxed. "Will you let me ride?"

"Breakfast. Mine."

The cows lowed in growing desperation. Jenn's eyes wandered to the Ropps' barn and she grinned. "How do you feel about cheese?"

Scourge's lips were like Wainn's old pony's, without the gray whiskers. The anticipatory tongue that licked those lips—dark red, narrow, and forked—was not.

Jenn listened at the barn door. All quiet, except for the impatient cows. That was strange. Hettie should be shaking grain into the troughs with Devins and her mother, laughing about something as they prepared to milk. Cheffy and Alyssa had the chore of bringing the empty buckets, and those two couldn't be quiet if they tried. Jenn shrugged and pushed the door aside along its greased wood rail.

Inside, the barn was cool and dim, the air redolent of fresh straw and sour milk. Milking stalls lined one wall, windows open to the lovely morning. Bunches of drying thistle flowers hung from the rafters, waiting to be pounded fine and used to curdle milk. Ripe cheese would be in the spring house, that being pressed under stones in the Ropps' kitchen, but Jenn was after something else.

Across from the stables, on the wall warmed by the sun all day, hung yesterday's bags of curds, dripping whey into a lined trough. The trough tempted each spring's set of piglets to extraordinary feats to escape their pen to reach it and Hettie was forever chasing them out. Just as well, Jenn thought, Wainn's old pony wasn't a clever piglet, or there'd be no safe apples.

Jenn nodded politely to the Ropps' house toad, squatting in a sunny patch. It puffed itself into an indignant ball, patently disapproving of their presence. She couldn't help that.

She'd taken a few steps inside, Scourge eagerly following, when voices made them stop. Well, she stopped and the not-horse bumped into her, but gently.

"—who's the father?" The far door burst open, letting in a broad swath of light and Covie Ropp.

Hettie was close behind. "I can't tell you."

"Don't look at me!" This from Devins as he entered with them.

The three stood, blinking in the relative dimness of the barn, not yet aware they weren't alone. "She's my sister!"

"Stepsister. You wouldn't be the first to cast eyes where it's handy."

Hettie and Devins cried a dismayed "Mother!" at the same time.

During this charged exchange, Jenn tried to edge back out the way they'd entered, but Scourge wasn't moving. "Someone's been rutting where they shouldn't," the breeze in her ear dark and amused. "My guess is here. Stables bring it out in people. I blame the cows."

"It wasn't Devins," Hettie's voice cracked. "Or Roche. Can we leave it at that?"

They'd notice her at any moment. Jenn tried to look small.

"No!" More gently, "Dearest Heart, why weren't you using the moon potion I gave you?"

A moment's hush, then Hettie, in a small voice, "I didn't like the taste." Then, in a rush, "I only missed a few days here and there, Mother. I didn't know it would matter—"

"With you ripe as summerberries?" Covie sighed. "By your dear mother's heart, Hettie, I tried to protect you. It's not as though I don't understand. We're flesh, not stone—"

"I'll let in the cows," Devins offered hastily and set off.

Heading right for her.

Left without a choice, Jenn called a cheery "Good morning!" as if she'd just entered.

"Jenn?" Devins checked, staring at Scourge, who hung his head over Jenn's shoulder as if relishing the argument. A wave of shame passed over his face. "I—"

She understood. Hettie's revelation made his ambition to marry for curtains and a cook childish and shallow, which he wasn't, not really. "Hello, Devins." She gave a gracious nod.

The lowing grew frantic.

"My cows!" Devins gratefully escaped past them to the door.

"What can we do for you, Jenn?" Covie's eyes hadn't left Scourge.

"We—I came to see if you had curds to spare, please."

"Of course. Hettie?"

Hettie went to the nearest bag and lifted it from its hook. She gave it a twist over the trough, shook off the remaining drops, and handed it to Jenn. She didn't smile.

Hettie always smiled, the little gap between her front teeth somehow making her smile that much happier and warmer and more precious than anyone else's.

Jenn held the cool bag in both hands, her eyes locked on the other girl's. "I—"

The breeze interrupted. "Hungry."

She ignored Scourge. "I heard, Hettie. I'm sorry. I didn't mean to—I won't tell anyone."

"Do you know the father, Jenn?"

Her shocked look must have been convincing, for Covie said dryly, "I see you don't." She turned to her stepdaughter. "Word will get out, Hettie. If not from our lips, then as the baby grows. If you intend to let it," her tone formal; a healer offering that choice.

Jenn felt the blood run from her face. Women knew such things; women decided them. Maybe she was a woman, but she hadn't given the matter of babies and birthing any thought, till now. Oh, Peggs did. Whenever she minded little Loee, she'd cuddled her close and talk of having her own one day. Jenn would make a face. Loee was cute, like a piglet or baby rabbit, when she wasn't red-faced and crying. But to care for her all the time? Her sister would shake her head, with a look to say there were things Jenn couldn't understand yet, which almost always provoked a childish and highly satisfying pillow fight at bedtime.

This? She understood and wished she didn't. Being a woman was growing more complicated by the moment.

From Hettie's face, she was having similar thoughts. Her hands rested at her waist. "For my part, I do," she said slowly, "but I'd like to be sure of the father."

"You don't know?" Jenn blurted.

Scourge snorted.

Covie didn't appear surprised. "Who might it be?" she asked calmly.

Having experienced "tingly" from the touch of two different men herself, Jenn found herself confronted by the possibility of having—whatever sort of "having" one imagined—both. She hurriedly thrust the possibility as far from her thoughts as she could, having thought the thought of having being disturbing enough.

"I wasn't sure who I liked better, until, well—" A dimple appeared in one cheek.

She was blushing, Jenn knew. Worse, Scourge knew and was entertained. She felt the light brush of whiskers against her ear and restrained the urge to smack his nose.

"Who could it be, then?" Covie persisted.

Hettie arched an eyebrow. "One of the twins."

"The—?" Jenn closed her mouth, but not before Hettie frowned at her.

"I wasn't second choice, Jenn Nalynn, if that's what you're thinking," she stated, unwittingly echoing Scourge.

"I know." Jenn felt an odd pang in her heart. Every fall, Allin asked her to marry him for no better reason than the mill and to spite Roche. Every winter, Tadd pined over Peggs, for no better reason than her being the most beautiful woman in Marrowdell and who didn't? "I hope they deserved your—" she floundered.

Slowly, Hettie smiled her wonderful smile. "Attentions?"

Relieved, Jenn nodded and smiled back.

"With you and Peggs well settled, Jenn," Covie said matter-of-factly, "it's just as well both Emms are upcountry with the livestock." She chuckled. "That should give you, Dearest Heart, time to pick one."

Something soft and tender appeared in Hettie's eyes. "I already have, Mum, if he'll have me, too."

Jenn held her breath, waiting . . .

"Can we get some help here?"

"The cows are stuck," the breeze informed her.

Jenn turned in haste. Devins had opened the milk gate but, despite superior numbers, and horns, the Ropps' dairy herd jammed in the open door behind Scourge's hindquarters, eyes bulging. They weren't coming a step closer.

The breeze turned smug. "Stupid beasts."

"Take Bannan's horse out the back, please," Covie said, her normally calm voice tinged with some of the cows' desperation.

"Of course. Sorry." Blushing, Jenn took hold of Scourge's chin with her free hand and tugged. "Are you always this much trouble?" she muttered under her breath as he docilely walked beside her through the barn.

He feigned not to hear, his large eyes locked on the bag of curds she carried.

Behind them, Hettie and her mother hastened to settle their now-impatient herd, ending any chance of her hearing the name. Doubtless, Peggs would know first.

Jenn smiled to herself. She'd have her own secret soon, to share or keep as she chose.

The morning dawned fair again, the fields coated in the lightest of mists, already burned away where touched by sun. Bannan feasted his eyes as he worked, filled his nostrils with the scent of growing things and fresh-cut wood, felt the cool earth of the barn through the soles of his feet. Little birds flitted everywhere he looked; they'd been his serenade upon waking and kept him company now. Much more beauty, he warned his little farm, and he'd be unable to work for joy. An unlikely outcome, of course. He'd never been so full of life and the need to be doing something with it. He couldn't sit still if he tried.

Tir yawned. Again. He'd hung his mask by the fireplace with his axes, so his yawning was impossible to miss. Every yawn whitened the scars above and below his mouth, and exposed what few teeth he had left. Bannan couldn't help but take each as a mostly silent reproach. Yes, they'd had a decent amount of rest, but hadn't his friend worked with him last night until they'd stumbled with fatigue, then roused with him at dawn to help empty the wagon and remove its plank sides and canvas cover?

Wyll, who might have helped, lay curled on the bed they'd cobbled together for him last night. He'd taken to it as soon as it was ready, tucking his head beneath a blanket, and hadn't left that shelter yet.

Another yawn. "Did you not sleep at all?" Bannan demanded, feeling the guilt of the well-rested.

"With those eyes staring at me in the dark, sir, like to bore a hole in my head?" Tir spat eloquently. "Ancestors Witness, that toad was waiting for me to fall asleep. It'd make off with the nillystones, given a chance, and who knows what else. I tell you, sir, the things mean no good. No good at all."

Bannan hadn't seen a toad in the house last night, though lacking windows or working doors, he wouldn't have been surprised by such a guest. One was in the barn with them now, squatting in the shadows of the first empty stall. It was, truth be told, giving Tir—who hadn't noticed—its rapt attention.

He tried to appease his friend. "They eat mice."

"So do cats," Tir retorted, unimpressed. "What's wrong with a cat? What kind of village doesn't have cats? Or dogs? Mark my words, sir," he said darkly. "They've all been eaten—same as the mice. It's not natural."

No, it was Marrowdell and another puzzle, one Bannan doubted had anything to do with toads. He didn't attempt to argue. Tir grumbled most mornings until breakfast; he'd outright snarl after a late patrol. Meanwhile, there was another, more pressing mystery to solve.

Who was, or had been, using his barn?

He brushed his fingers lightly over one of the marks in the floor. "Wagons?"

Tir didn't let go that easily. "You can't," he pointed out, "pet a toad."

Thinking of the warrior-like demeanor of Marrowdell's toads by night, Bannan judged any such attempt unwise at best. "No one's asking you to," he said mildly. "Tir. Wagons. Am I right?"

His friend crouched to look, muttering something rude and unlikely about toads under his breath Bannan hoped the creature watching from the stall wouldn't understand.

Tir tilted his head, eyes following the tracks. He gave an interested grunt.

"What?"

"Too far apart for Rhothan." The other spat on the packed dirt and smeared the moisture with a thumb. Whatever he saw made him rock back on his heels. "Not Ansnan, not any that I've seen or heard of. Look here, sir."

Bannan knelt to peer at the drying spot, seeing lines, no wider than his smallest finger, as evenly spaced as tines on a fork. Together they formed an overlapping pattern, like so many fish scales. "What sort of wheel leaves such an impression?"

Tir shrugged his bafflement.

"There are sets of tracks," Bannan mused. "The same wagon, do you think?"

"Three wagons, sir." The former guard's hands described how the vehicles would have stood one behind the other, his voice slipping into the cadence of a report. "Good-sized—half again ours, at a guess. With loads, too. They've been here more than once, but I'd say months since the last. Maybe a year."

Bannan gave a slow nod. "Puzzle solved, then. The tinkers we've heard of, the ones who come to help with the harvest. They must have seen how the barn sat empty and put it to good use." He dusted his hand on one leg as he rose, perversely disappointed.

"If so, likely yon chests are theirs, too." Tir fingered his scruff of a beard thoughtfully. "What sort of tinker leaves belongings?"

"None we know," Bannan acknowledged, happily curious again. He joined Tir at the nearest chest.

Tir had found them in the storeroom, after solving the trick of its stubborn door latch with an ax. There were seven, more boxes than chests, square and knee-high. With no time yesterday for a closer inspection, they'd put them against the barn wall across from the stalls. It hadn't been easy work; it required both of them to lift one.

The boxes were of the same rough wood as the barn, though their planks were cunningly fitted and some effort had been made to round the outer edges. The lids were secured by metal locks, two per side, the black hardware pocked by rust and badly dented, as if each took a hammer to free its hinges as well as a key.

But that wasn't true. He looked deeper.

Bannan's lips parted in wonder as the sides of the boxes faded from rough wood to palm-sized pieces of stone, smooth and pale yellow, fused one to the other. The lids weren't wood—or stone. He thought the blue, shimmering material some sort of glass or crystal, but no crystal of his comprehension could melt what looked like thick fingers into the stone of the sides, nor could he imagine how anything could unlock such a grip. "If these belong to the tinkers," he breathed, "I can't wait to meet them."

"What do you see, sir, that I can't?"

Startled, Bannan looked up to find Tir's eyes boring into his. "I see the truth."

"And what truth is that?"

Roads that flowed and forests that bled and moths with tiny boots . . . where to start?

"I'm well used to your oddness, sir," Tir went on, determined. "You've been my captain and friend these many years. Closer than blood. I've seen to it no one learned of your gift who shouldn't. You know that."

"I—" Bannan closed his mouth and gave a grim nod. He wouldn't have lasted a month in the border guard, not in the beginning, without Tir's protection.

"Here, it's different. Since we arrived, you've been getting this look, like you're somewhere else. Like you're under some kind of wishing. Which," his friend said almost lightly, "I didn't believe more than my grandmother's tale of pearls in spoilt plums till we met him." A nod to the house where Wyll presumably still slept.

"Rest easy. I haven't changed—or been wished, or cursed. It's this place." Bannan took an unsteady breath. "Marrowdell. I see more here than I ever have. Things—maybe that don't exist anywhere else."

Tir looked decidedly unhappy. "Sir. Things that don't exist?"

Bannan carefully didn't smile. "They exist here. Take these chests. Wood and plain, aren't they?" He rapped on a lid. "Sounds like wood. Feels like it. But when I look deeper—the way I would to catch a lie in a man's face—I see a masterpiece of polished stone, surpassing any skill I know."

"Heart's Blood." The furrow across Tir's brow was deep enough to shadow his eyes. "Like the wings you saw when you looked at Wyll." He gave the squared timbers of the rafters a suspicious look. "What's the barn, then?"

"A barn." Bannan chuckled. "The house is a house. The trees—most of them," he amended, "—are trees. But the road is at times a silver river and your toads, believe it or not, are sentries. By their kit and demeanor, I'd judge them doughty fighters, not to be lightly crossed." He turned serious. "Two Marrowdells, Tir. The one everyone sees, and another whose truth I glimpse."

Tir swallowed. "How can that be?" he asked with great care.

"I wish I knew," Bannan admitted, unable to contain his delight. "Here, it just is."

"But only one's real."

The former border guard valiantly tried to make sense of the incredible, to put boundaries around it and keep them on the safe, familiar side; deep in his heart, Bannan knew it couldn't be done. "The water from the well's real enough," he countered. "I found it looking at that other Marrowdell, not this one. Then . . ." he couldn't help but smile, ". . . there's Scourge."

"The bloody beast?" Tir's eyes narrowed. "What about him? Don't tell me he looks other than ugly here, because that'd be stretching things, sir, well past my following."

"He looks the same." Of course he did. The sole constant in his entire life, Bannan thought nostalgically, had been the strange, dark not-horse. He'd measured his growth against Scourge's unchanging leg, his becoming a man by finally being accepted as Scourge's rider. The notion of a different Scourge . . . ? He shook his head. "Scourge is the same, but here, my friend?" Bannan tapped his ear. "He can speak."

Tir burst out laughing.

"As well as you or I," the truthseer insisted.

"From anyone else, sir," Tir said, mirth fading, "this'd be madness."

Was it? Bannan left his friend and walked the length of the barn, coming back to stand near the stall with the toad. He rested his shoulders and head against the upright beam, feeling its strength. What had Wyll said? That neyet had died to become this wood, to make the buildings of Marrowdell. Hadn't he'd glimpsed living neyet, leaning over the road as if curious about the smaller beings who used those buildings?

No, he thought. Not madness.

Wonder.

"I've spent my life enduring false smiles and promises," he said, as much to himself as Tir. "Spent my gift finding liars for a distant prince—and for what? So he could give away the city we protected and free those we caught. I swear to you, old friend, there were times I'd beg my Ancestors to blind me—to make me as other men. There were times I didn't think I could bear any more truth."

Tir's eyes turned bleak and his lip twisted above the hollow where he'd had a chin. "I asked mine for you, sir, some nights."

Moved, Bannan rested a fond hand on his friend's shoulder. "Not here," he promised, warm and sure. "Here, for the first time in my life, I rejoice to be a truthseer." A laugh bubbled from his chest. "Madness? If it's madness, Tir, to delight in beauty and mystery, to see wonders wherever I look, then I'll happily be mad."

"Be happy." Tir snapped a finger against his ear. "Just don't be careless," he advised gruffly as Bannan rubbed the sting. "Wonders are all well and good till they bite off your feet."

He looked past Bannan to transfix the watching toad with a glare of his own. "As for you. Call yourself a sentry?" in a parade ground snap, "Get to your post!"

Huge brown eyes blinked in astonishment, then the toad, with the immense dignity possible only to the warty and very round, hopped from the stall, hopped along the tracked floor and out the barn door, then, with one prodigious leap, disappeared into the uncut grass beyond.

Oh, the look on Tir's face!

Bannan grinned. "Ever made a recruit jump like that before?"

Jenn sat on the gate and stared at Scourge in disbelief. "You ate the bag."

"Hungry." His dark-red tongue fastidiously removed lingering flecks of curd from his slobbery lips.

The Ropps mightn't miss one, Jenn decided, though if he made a habit of this, they would. "Can we go now?"

He gave a shuddering sigh worthy of Wainn's old pony. "Very well."

She settled the plump saddlebags over his shoulders. Having been made for a pony, they looked ridiculous on his grand back. She probably would too, Jenn thought ruefully. "Come closer."

The breeze tickled her ear. "Jump."

She rose, balanced on the second highest rail, and hesitated. If he didn't move, and she didn't slip, she could do it.

If.

Jenn eyed Scourge with misgiving. He stood with seeming patience, but his tail slapped lazily back and forth. The creature enjoyed gossip. How much would he enjoy watching her fall flat on her face, at least here where the grass was soft?

Spotting Uncle Horst near the fountain, she beckoned urgently, relieved when he changed his path toward her. She sat on the rail and waited, as the breeze chuckled wickedly in her ear and a bee droned by.

"Fair morning, Uncle," she said as he neared. "Would you give me a leg up, please?"

"Fair morning, Jenn." Uncle Horst leaned the saddle he'd been carrying against the gate, hung the bridle and bags on it, then tilted his hat to consider Scourge. "Is something wrong with Wainn's pony?"

Jenn hopped from the gate to the ground and laid a confident hand on Scourge's massive flank. His skin quivered, as if warning off a fly. "Bannan lent him to me," she explained, dropping her hand to her side. "I'm bringing him breakfast. Not just his," this quickly, in case Uncle Horst read some meaning she most adamantly didn't intend he should. Or anyone else. "For Wyll and Tir as well."

"I see." Which could, Jenn despaired, mean anything at all. His eyebrows rose. "I'll help you with his tack. Where is it?"

At the farm, of course. Jenn thought furiously. Hardly anyone used a saddle. There were but a handful in all of Marrowdell anyway; Horst had one for his gelding, the twins for working livestock in the hills, and the rest, the fancy ones brought from Avyo, had been impractical here. They'd been traded for more useful things before she was born. As for a bridle or halter? She doubted Scourge would accept one if she had it.

She improvised. "He's had special training."

"I don't doubt it," Uncle Horst didn't frown, but his long face grew serious. "Still, he's no packhorse, nor a mount for someone used to ponies. If you want to ride, I'm happy to take you, Jenn Nalynn. Wait while I fetch Perrkin."

His gelding, who normally came trotting at the sight of Horst, could be seen peering from behind the shed at the end of the commons. He must share the cows' opinion of Scourge.

Two days ago—before so many truths intruded on her world—Jenn would have been offended at being treated like a child. Now, she found herself warmed by his honest concern and a little ashamed. "Thank you, Uncle," she began, fighting what was, after all, childish disappointment. She could explore the path up the Spine another day, any day. It wasn't as if she was leaving Marrowdell. Ever. "I—"

A leg straightened, another curled, and in a bow more graceful than any mere man's, Scourge lowered himself until his back was no higher than her shoulder.

"That's very special training," Uncle Horst commented.

"Isn't it?" Jenn said brightly. Hands on his neck, she vaulted astride, Scourge heaving up beneath her as she settled on his back.

Ancestors Named and Not, he was the size of a mountain. She hadn't noticed before, being too busy with Wyll and the river. Catching her breath, she patted the saddlebags. "Time to deliver breakfast."

Uncle Horst had to remove his hat to look up at her. His hair was thin on top, she noticed with sudden concern and the creases around his eyes and mouth were deeper this morning than she remembered. When had he grown so much older?

"Throw yourself off if he heads the wrong way," he advised her. Scourge bent his neck around to stare at him. Uncle Horst stared back. "Show up without her," he promised, "and it won't be the ox we'll roast at the harvest." He sounded so grim she almost believed him.

"We'll be fine, Uncle," Jenn replied, leaning forward to rub Scourge on the neck. A cloud of short brown hair was the result. Hair that stuck to her fingers. Hair she'd doubtless have over her skirt. "Ugh."

"Itchy," said the breeze rather apologetically.

"Say hello to our new farmers for me." Uncle Horst opened the gate. Without further comment or hesitation, Scourge walked through, moving as though he carried uncooked eggs. The livestock in the commons settled for watching from a wary distance as his long legs swept her along the road she knew.

To reach a road, Jenn thought eagerly, she'd never taken.

She lifted her eyes to the rise of forest and meadow and bone-white stone across the valley.

What would she see from its heights?

The sun kissed Jenn's toes, her knees, and most of her thighs as she rode, her skirt doing what skirts did in such situations. Since there was no one to see but the calves, who didn't care, a pair of equally uninterested waterfowl, and whatever other birds flew by, Jenn didn't care either. For a young lady her legs were, in Aunt Sybb's opinion, scandalously tanned already, but you couldn't help that, not if you forded a river daily and played in a meadow as often as you weeded the gardens.

Riding Scourge, she could almost see over the hedge. If she dared Allin Emms' trick, and rose to her feet on her mount's back, she could. Why bother? What there was to see, other than ripening grain, old trees, and Bannan's farm?

The way to Night's Edge.

Had Wyll gone there yet? Had he seen?

He hadn't believed her, that their meadow had changed with him, become blackened and withered and dead.

She wished she could forget.

"So quiet." The breeze, like Wyll's but not, slipped from one ear to the other. "No questions?" Slyly. "I know the truthseer in ways his own mother didn't."

Before Jenn could do more than blush, they reached the bend in the Tinkers Road. She looked for and found the opening in the trees. "That way!" she ordered, signaling the turn with her legs and hands as if she rode a real horse.

Being nothing of the kind, Scourge stopped in his tracks. The breeze against her cheek was wordless and winter cold.

"I just want to see what's up there. We won't be long." Greatly daring, she drummed her bare heels against his ribs. "Please?"

He shuddered, legs braced, ears flat. "Don't ask me!" A wail of despair. "I beg you!"

Leaves swirled around them as the trees leaned to listen. The air grew heavy and felt like storm, which wasn't, Jenn thought with frustration, going to help anything, including the laundry. Perplexed, she stared at the path. Too narrow for a wagon. Mounted, she'd have to duck under some of the branches. Used, but not often. She could tell because the undergrowth had been kept clear, but runoff carved deep furrows in its red earth. Otherwise, the path was utterly ordinary. Except . . .

Except how Wyll and now Scourge reacted to it.

Or, a new curiosity, to something up there.

Something they didn't want her to see?

Jenn settled on his back and dared a little pat. "We'd best go to the farm. They'll want breakfast."

"Yes. Yes." Scourge struck out at brisk, jolting walk, passing through the sunbeams that slanted through the forest.

As Scourge wasn't taking her where she wanted to go—she wouldn't ask him to anyway, after hearing the dread in what he used as a voice—Jenn took Uncle Horst's advice.

She swung her leg over and slipped off.

"Fool girl!" Scourge planted his hooves and tossed his head.

"I won't be long." Before he could block her way, Jenn ran to the opening of the path. He half-reared, making a strangled sort of noise, but didn't follow. She waved, feeling only slightly guilty. "Don't forget to take the men their breakfast," she told him cheerfully. Then she turned and started up the path.

Bannan paused in the barn door, eyes drawn to the hill that bordered the Tinkers Road and walled this side of the valley. Bare stone, the color and smoothness of cream, rose from behind the line of trees. The morning sun revealed not a single imperfection, as if to warn against any attempt to walk that slope. At the height, the stone erupted in separate masses, swollen and curved, each girdled by the green of meadow and forest. No two masses were alike and, from this vantage, the largest three stood close, almost touching, sentinels against the sky.

The path to that summit had tried to claim him, something he hadn't dared mention to anyone, yet, let alone Tir. If no one else could see how the Tinkers Road flowed silver, what would they think if he said something dark bled into it? That it had tried to lure him? That he'd almost been lost? Without a doubt, Tir would knock him on the head and drag him from Marrowdell. The villagers?

No. What he'd seen was real, he'd swear to it, but he wouldn't give them a dread that might be his alone. He needed to know more first. He'd hold Scourge to a full accounting, once the creature showed his long face. Bannan stretched and deliberately looked away from the hill to admire his mostly-new roof.

Tir had gone inside, to brew more of his drink in lieu of breakfast. Feeling somewhat hollow himself, Bannan glanced toward the opening to the road. No sign of Jenn. Perhaps she'd not be able to keep her promise. Perhaps, he thought with rather more disappointment than breakfast warranted, she wouldn't come today.

It wasn't as if they'd starve. They'd supplies from his wagon, plus what had come with Wyll yesterday. He'd learn to bake bread, once the oven was rebuilt. Biscuits in a fry pan, till then. Good campside food.

Like chewing on bark, compared to the loaves from the Nalynn kitchen.

It was early, Bannan reminded himself. Jenn would have chores of her own to do first. The garden being his next, he pushed through the tall grass to its supposed edge. There was a scythe among the shiny new tools in the wagon; they'd test its blade once the grass dried, later today. Well, he would. Bannan gave a rueful chuckle. He'd lost that bet on the 'stones the camp before Endshere. Tir wouldn't let him forget who was to sweat over the scythe first, and, with the luck he'd had on the road, the plough and churn. Though without the ox, or a field of his own, or a milk cow, for that matter, he was safe for a while.

The garden was a sea of lush foliage, doubtless all weeds. Still, Lorra Treff had said there'd been something planted this year. Bannan squinted, absently brushing grass seeds and spiderwebs from his arms, and grinned as he spotted promising color tucked here and there amid the greenery. Those had to be pumpkins. And long white pods that must be beans. Near at hand a veritable thicket of brambles held tempting clusters of dark blue berries. Despite his care, thorns snagged his skin and clothing when he reached for some; all the while little birds fluttered through with no trouble at all. His eyes followed one enviously.

He found himself looking toward the break in the hedge, where a twisted figure stood alone, intent on something beyond.

Wyll, awake after all.

Bannan disentangled himself from the maze of branches, happy not to bleed in the process, and tossed the berries into his mouth. They were . . . for a moment he closed his eyes in rapture as he chewed and swallowed, using his tongue to pry tiny seeds from between his teeth. The rich heady taste was familiar indeed. Peggs' pie. The garden held summerberries. His garden.

He licked the last trace of sweet from his fingers as he approached Wyll. The dragon wore yesterday's clothes, rumpled from sleep. His hair badly needed a comb Bannan doubted he knew how to use.

Without turning his head, Wyll spoke first. "Jenn Nalynn is crossing the river."

Bannan didn't question his knowledge. "And Tir's boiling the kettle," he said easily. "We'll have tea ready for breakfast." He stood beside the other, and looked out, seeing nothing more interesting than the narrow path between grain and trees. "I'm told that's Night's Edge." By Scourge, which he didn't think he should mention to Wyll, unsure of their truce.

Scourge had called it something else, too. The way home.

"Night's Edge is the girl's meadow," Wyll corrected. "Past the field." He lifted his good arm to point down the path. "It's been our meeting place since her birth. She wants me to build a house there."

"I heard."

"Where we are to live as husband and wife."

"If she doesn't change her mind," Bannan observed pleasantly. Maybe he was the fool Scourge thought, but he'd be an honest one. "People do, my friend. You should be prepared."

Wyll turned. "I can only build it," he replied. His brown eyes caught sparks from the sun—or from some silvering in their depths. "Perhaps you should be prepared as well, truthseer. Come. Let me show you where we'll live."

Bannan followed, more than happy to explore. Rows of grain rose shoulder-high beside them, heavy tops bent and whispering without a breeze. No birds troubled it. Nothing moved, not a fly or busy ant, between stalks so evenly planted as to amaze. The poor ox had died of his trespass; the man and dragon stayed clear.

Wyll didn't pause. Bannan marveled anew how each slow step and drag, each carelessly powerful thrust and twist, moved that ruined body with no other help.

Marveled, then abruptly understood. He'd been right to be reminded of the weary-eyed soldiers who hobbled Vorkoun's streets, their crutches held like lovers. The dragon moved too confidently for his injuries to be new. "You weren't maimed by Jenn Nalynn," Bannan accused. "What happened to you?"

"I led my kind in war," Wyll answered without turning or hesitation. "In gratitude, they broke my wings and let me fall."

"Because you lost." His mouth twisted as he thought of the marches and Ansnor, the years and blood spent for naught.

"Lost? No."

Taken aback, the man fell silent, as perhaps the dragon intended.

The morning sun pushed the shade of the old trees aside. It had already dried the lightly trampled grass underfoot. Wyll's steps left rough smears and gouges. Avoiding those, Bannan's bare feet found themselves in the tracks of someone smaller, someone who'd come this way often and alone.

The notion of stepping where Jenn had stepped washed away all thoughts of war. Bannan found himself inordinately pleased.

Lila. Oh, she'd laugh if she knew. Her little brother, who'd proclaimed himself—often and loudly—above such folly, to act like the worst moon-eyed, daft-headed . . . and not even care.

Wyll reached the end of the grain and stopped as if he'd struck a wall. His hand flailed for support and Bannan hurried to take it, wincing at the other's grip while he steadied him on his good leg. "What's wrong?"

"Night's Edge!"

Bannan lifted his eyes, and gasped.

The grain field curved away toward the river in a smooth line, leaving them standing in the open and exposed. Left, the line of old trees continued, hiding the Tinkers Road and framing the long lowermost slope of the Spine. Ahead, another rise of the naked stone flowed down to the valley floor at his right.

Heart's Blood. His little farm lay where the two came closest together, like a finger curled toward a thumb.

But it was what else lay between that had stopped Wyll and made the truthseer doubt his own eyes for the first time.

"There's no meadow here," he protested.

There—there at some distance stood more old trees, healthy and green. They made a narrow band of forest, wrapped around the nearer of the pale hills.

Here, at their feet? Everything was dead and withered, save for a patch in the center where a torch might have seared and blackened the surface. Winter, before any snow, without any cold. Even winter held promise, Bannan thought desperately, but there were no pods of seeds hanging from these flower stalks, no buds on the little shrubs.

Wyll pulled free of his hold, his twisted foot dragging through dead leaves. The smell of rot drifted up, thick and cloying.

Not winter. Bannan pressed his forearm over his nose. Something worse. "What did this?"

The dragon didn't answer until he stood where the ground had been scorched.

When he turned to Bannan, his eyes were brown and full of dread.

"Jenn Nalynn."

Bannan's heart hammered in his chest. The truth, but . . . "The wishing?"

"It happened here, but this—I fled before this."

" 'Fled?' "

Ignoring the question, Wyll frowned. "She told me Night's Edge had changed. Had died. But why destroy it? Was she so angry at me?"

"Angry women," Bannan pointed out with what he thought commendable calm, "throw things. Yell. Make life miserable for their brothers. They don't turn a meadow into—" What did he see here? "—despair."

A flicker of surprise crossed Wyll's face, then something softened in his eyes. "She couldn't have known," he said, with such profound relief Bannan wondered what the dragon had believed. "The result remains," more sternly. "Her feelings have grown stronger. Such matter to expectation, but never have I seen this. Those of Marrowdell were fortunate it wasn't worse."

Worse? "What do you mean?"

"How could the sei intend this?" Realizing the dragon spoke to himself, the truthseer held very still. "With no contrary expectations to dispute hers . . . if her strength grows . . ." Wyll remembered his audience. "Turn-born rarely agree," with a flash of silver, "for which all are grateful."

Bannan latched on to what he could understand. "Jenn wouldn't hurt anyone."

"She wouldn't want to," Wyll said heavily, which wasn't reassuring at all.

Not considering where they stood.

And what remained of Night's Edge.

Somewhere new. Somewhere different. Jenn hurried, her steps quick and light, tingling with the joy of it all. She wanted as much time as she could on the very top, this first visit. There'd be a wondrous view from there; she just knew it. And a meadow as lovely as Night's Edge. Lovelier, if that were possible. It could be. There would surely be rabbits, this time of year. As well Scourge hadn't wanted to come.

She didn't like to think how Night's Edge had looked after the wishing. She didn't want to go there, not until Wyll fixed it. He would; something else she knew. He'd make their special place the way it had been and should be, before he built his house there.

Though the Spine was steep, its path politely folded back on itself time and again, each sharp bend offering discovery to the traveler. The air was calm and cool, the rare breeze free of opinion. The trees leaned so close their branches touched overhead and what sunlight came through dappled the ground, inviting a game. With a grin, Jenn jumped from bright spot to bright spot.

When she'd had her fill of jumping, she walked through sunbeams and shadows, her bare feet making hardly a whisper.

She was, Jenn supposed, being ever-so-slightly irresponsible. Having Scourge deliver breakfast wasn't what she'd promised. Coming here instead of the farm wasn't what others thought she should or would do. Not at all.

She didn't care. "This once," Jenn told the interested trees, "I'm doing what I want."

Besides, she had a good reason. A responsible, adult reason. Wyll was here, as a man, because of her. She would take this path, wave down at him from the upper meadow, and once and for all, prove to him there was nothing to fear from his new home.

This was Marrowdell. Her world, now his.

A third bend, surely the last. Her heart beat faster as she rounded it, finding the way abruptly steeper, as if as impatient as she was, so that she must lean forward as she walked and was beside the tops of trees whose trunks she'd passed below. Bright little eyes watched her from sundrenched branches, her presence announced by squeaks and chirrups, and insolent flicks of tails. Finding her harmless, the squirrels rent leaves with their long thin claws, and tore the pieces with yellowed teeth.

She'd not known squirrels to grow this size, or be as foolishly bold. Then again, no one hunted here. "I won't tell Roche," she told them solemnly, though she was as fond of squirrel stew as anyone.

"Oh," she said a few steps later, her eyes wide.

Aunt Sybb had described the ossuaries of the Ancestors. How, after the famed arched bridges, they were the most beautiful buildings in Avyo, filled with light and air and music. She'd said you couldn't help but be glad when you stood inside, though they were solemn places, because they celebrated life and its remembrance.

As Jenn took the last, steepest part of the path, for the first time she understood that feeling, for ahead grew the largest old trees she'd ever seen, one on either side of where the path did indeed open to meadow and sunlight. Their trunks rose like the posts of some giant gate and she half expected to be stopped as she went between them, craning her head to see if their tops touched the sky.

But nothing stopped her. Jenn stepped from shadow to sunlight, from packed cool earth to sod, soft underfoot and warm. She held her hands out from her sides to let grasses and asters kiss her fingers as she walked forward, chuckling at the abundance of silk-headed thistles.

Wisp's doing.

Would Wyll play with thistledown? Somehow, she didn't think so.

The meadow was still. Nothing chirped or sang or rustled. No rabbits. Not a butterfly or bird. Or bee. She supposed they weren't used to visitors. Or was it too harsh this high in winter?

From this high, Marrowdell looked like one of Riss' tapestried cushions, all color and texture, the shapes she knew blurred at their edges. The river shrank to a creek and the village to a handful of blocks. If she'd hoped her world would look larger, she'd been mistaken.

Suppressing a sigh, Jenn dutifully waved in the direction of Wyll and the farm, though from here the hill's skirt of old trees blocked her view. She could walk over to where she could see and be seen—and would, she decided, when she wasn't expected elsewhere. She'd borrow Davi's cart and bring Wyll. Then he'd know how safe it was here.

First, to look the other way, over the hill. To see beyond and outside. She put her back to Marrowdell.

Like lace on a bodice, the meadow swept in a narrow band around the upper reach of the Spine and nestled between the creamy masses of stone. Four rose in front of her, crowning the hill like knuckles on a fist, no two the same or touching.

Jenn had never stood so close to one before. You didn't, that was all. She couldn't remember anyone giving a reason, other than it was easy to see from a distance that the Bone Hills were barren and boring.

And presently in her way.

The sides struck by the morning sun were bright white, almost blinding, the rest stark and black, the line between as crisp as if drawn with pen and ink. She couldn't tell if a gap led through to the other side, only that the shadows met.

The meadow slipped into the darkness, a carpet of green dotted with purple and pink, silent and still. A welcome. An offer.

A dare.

With a smile, Jenn left the light behind.

She mustn't! She couldn't! "No!" Wyll heard himself wail as Jenn Nalynn did the unthinkable. ~ NO!!!! ~

From above. ~ What have you done? ~ From below. ~ FOOL! ~

And commotion in this world. The other man, Tir, shouting about saddlebags and breakfast. The thunder of hooves as the kruar ran to him, as if he was anything but useless, too.

"What's happened?" A grip on his whole shoulder, a hard shake. Denied his first inclination, to fling Bannan away, Wyll tossed soot and rot into the air around them, blinding them both.

"Heart's Blood, Wyll," the truthseer cried. "Stop! What's wrong? Let me help!"

"You can't," Wyll snarled.

"I don't understand—Scourge!"

The kruar plunged to a stop, hooves deep in the rot of the meadow, neck and chest white with froth. ~ Why did she do that?! ~ he demanded, though he knew very well the turn-born were its prey. ~ Why didn't she listen? ~

Though he knew the trap the Wound could set.

"What's going on?" Tir, mercifully no longer shouting. "And—" in a newly horrified tone, "—what happened here?!"

Above, below. ~ Fool. Fool. Fool. Fool. ~ From either side.

Scourge rumbled and stomped his hooves, daring them to stay.

~ What's this? ~ Altogether, a chant that whirled around and around. ~ Fool with folly. Folly with fool! Fool with folly! ~ They had no regard for kruar, let alone this one. If he let the taunting continue, they'd be tempted to act and he'd lose his sole ally.

And possibly a few dragons.

Wyll gathered himself. ~ SILENCE! ~ he bellowed.

Rock cracked.

Bone bent.

He no longer ruled his kind, but hurt them?

It seemed that he could still do.

Abashed, they circled without sound.

~ Be gone. ~ This he said without sting; he knew they were afraid.

So was he.

FIFTEEN

BLEACHED STONE SWEPT upward to either side, walls so glassy smooth and flawless Jenn reached out, only to have some impulse curl her fingers away before they touched. Undaunted, she stepped forward. Shadow engulfed her like a plunge in ice water and she gasped, then made herself breathe normally.

As normally as someone brimming with excitement could.

She found herself walking through slices of darkness so intense she couldn't see her hand in front of her face. Once, the sun found her and she shaded her eyes before another step took her into the dark again.

It was all very strange.

Like the light, the path beneath her feet couldn't make up its mind. At times, she felt cool grass underfoot, at others, dried leaves gave way with a crunch. When her toes met something slick and damp, she was tempted to stop and bend down to feel what it might be, but she mustn't dawdle.

She'd explore more fully on her next visit.

The path between the stones turned. No wonder she hadn't been able to see through from the meadow side. Heart racing, Jenn walked faster.

Without warning, she stepped from the shadow's chill into the open. Shading her eyes with one hand, she eagerly gazed beyond Marrowdell for the first time.

The sun gazed back at her over the crest of a ridge, rugged and draped with dark trees, a ridge as high as where she stood, that stretched to either side as far as she could see.

Another rose beyond the first, taller, darker.

Another yet.

And nothing more.

The ridges were like the hedges around the village. Like the crags around the valley. Walls to contain her.

Walls to keep out the world.

Her eyes stung and Jenn blinked fiercely. Of course there were ridges and trees. What had she expected? Marrowdell was a valley within the northern range. Clearly, the range was greater than she'd thought. It meant the world was greater, too. She'd studied the map but failed to grasp the scale of matters.

She'd lost so much more than she'd imagined.

Mere steps in front, the meadow ended in a precipitous drop. She didn't bother to look over the edge.

Jenn turned. With the sun at her back, warm on her shoulders, she could see the path between the stones was wider on this side than the other. The shadow she'd walked through was gone and the ground, simply meadow.

There was nothing special here.

She'd been a fool.

Doing her best not to feel sorry for herself, which wasn't easy but as Aunt Sybb would say, "Self-pity makes a pitiful self" and she'd no wish to be that, Jenn retraced her steps. When she reached where the path between the stones narrowed then bent, her shadow hurried across the pale stone to follow. It didn't like being here either, she thought, eyeing it sadly.

Then stared.

For caught within her shadow was something darker, more blue than black, that curved away.

Something shiny, as if wet.

Jenn eased closer. It vanished.

Like her glimpses of Wisp in the meadow.

"Keep your secret," she told the bone-white stone. "I don't care."

She did, though. Wisp had never made her uneasy. The notion that the Bone Hills themselves had another, hidden shape wasn't right or good or safe. She wouldn't think about it, Jenn decided, walking more quickly. She would forget what she saw.

Marrowdell filled her eyes and heart as she freed herself from the stones' clinging shade. The Spine's meadow no longer charmed her, its asters dull and about to wither, its thistles mean and thorned. How had she thought it compared to Night's Edge?

Even the air here chilled. She rubbed her arms as she headed for the path down, cold inside and out. Cold and empty.

So empty . . .

A cramp struck her middle.

Another. With a cry, Jenn bent over and pressed her hands against her stomach. Why did she hurt like this?

She staggered forward, startling a moth, which proved something lived here, then felt a sharp pain. "Ouch!" She hopped on one foot, rubbing her now-sore heel. What had she stepped on?

A pebble, small and white, winked at her from the sod. "Something for my trouble," Jenn declared with forced good cheer. She'd collect it for Wyll and Bannan, who likely were unaware of the requirements of toads.

Her fingers closed over the little stone. It really was a lovely pebble. The nicest she'd ever found.

Her mouth watered. She lifted the pebble to her lips.

Jenn froze. What was she thinking? It didn't matter if she was hungry, which she wasn't since she'd had a perfectly nice, if hasty, breakfast. No one, including otherwise adorable babies who didn't know better and needed to be watched or who knew what would go in their mouths, should eat stones. Or dirt. Or anything not proper food. Ancestors Witness, she didn't need Aunt Sybb to teach her that!

Rejected, the pebble turned heavy, as heavy as a full bucket of water. Heavier! Desperate to keep it, she used both hands to hold on, but the pebble grew heavier and heavier until its weight pulled her off balance and with a cry . . .

She let go.

The pebble fell. It fell and sank from sight, as if the sod and solid earth beneath were water.

"I didn't want you anyway," Jenn scolded the pebble, though she had, more than anything she could remember.

What she wanted now, more than anything, was not to be here, standing on the Spine, so close to its pale stones she could feel the cold breath of their shadows on her neck. She wanted, Jenn decided quite firmly, to be at the farm having a cuppa and something properly breakfast with Wyll and Bannan and Tir. She wanted that now.

She left the Bone Hill, taking long, determined strides, and found the walk down the twisted path took far less time than the walk up, though the sun refused to play and the squirrels sulked and hid their faces. She ignored everything but putting one foot in front of the other, with care, since her heel stung from the pebble and she couldn't help but limp a little.

Served her right, Jenn thought glumly. She'd been a fool and foolish.

Near its end, the path became annoying, its unpredictable ruts larger and deeper. The trees leaned together to darken the shadows. She knew she should slow down, or risk a twisted ankle or worse, but something wasn't right, not right at all, and Jenn hurried as best she could to be anywhere else.

Which is when everything became as dark as night, forcing her to stop.

Bannan dodged left and low, but Scourge wheeled with a snort to hem him in the farmyard. "Heart's Blood!" he shouted, voice cracking with fury. "Let me by!" He tried again and almost made it, but at the last instant a fat toad appeared in his path. His lunge to avoid stepping on it gave Scourge time to whirl around, nostrils flared. Thwarted, Bannan glared up at his so-called companion. "You . . . let Tir . . . go," he panted, hands on his thighs. "Why not . . . me?!"

"Because Tir's blind," Wyll insisted wearily. "You are not." He'd been almost as quick as Bannan to return from the meadow, but only as far as the house. He leaned against it now, as if only the wood kept him upright, and his face was drawn and pale. Then, suddenly, his head lifted.

Something changed.

They all stopped moving, the only sounds Bannan's panting and the bellow-like heaves of Scourge's breath.

The air, he thought, and shivered in a chill better suited to early winter. The light dimmed and shadows crept around their feet, though there were no clouds.

"Jenn!" he shouted.

Jenn squinted, sure she'd seen a light. Yes, there it was. A bright happy yellow light round as a pumpkin that bobbed and swayed and didn't do much to reveal the road but shone on its bearer's welcome face.

"Wainn!"

The youngest Uhthoff carried an oil lamp at the end of a long pole, the sort of thing they used when a summer night was too glorious to spend indoors, and he wore his hat, which promised there was sunshine somewhere, if not here. "Hello," he said calmly. "Wen said you were lost."

About to protest, Jenn closed her mouth and nodded. "I think I was," she admitted. Not now, with his cheerful light and presence. "The road's that way, isn't it?"

"It's not up to me."

She blinked, disconcerted. "You came that way."

"Did I?"

This was as annoying as the path. Without sunlight, the air was chill and smelled of damp. She rubbed gooseflesh on her bare arms and considered Wainn with a small frown. "How did you find me?"

"I looked. You were here." He paused, lifting the pole. The light skittered across ridged bark and malformed rock, glistened over a half-eaten mushroom big as a cow's head, and sparked tiny fires in eyes that winked away. "Where is here?" he asked curiously.

Jenn sighed. She'd have to find the path for them both. "We're almost at the Tinkers Road." Wainn turned as she came up to him, the light swinging low so she had to duck. "It's—" she hesitated, her sure sense of the direction fading.

The pool of bright yellow around their feet shrank inward, not as if the light failed, but as if the darkness pushed closer. Jenn reached for Wainn's hand and wrapped her fingers around it, afraid to lose him. "I'm—I thought I—"

"Wen said you must know what you want."

What did she want?

A terrible longing came over Jenn for the little white pebble the Spine had offered. Her traitorous mouth filled with moisture. She turned her head and spat, rather than swallow. "I want—I want to go home."

Her heel throbbed vindictively.

"You are home," Wainn said unhelpfully.

Well, yes, she was in Marrowdell, but Marrowdell wasn't behaving. Not as it should. What did she want, then, if not home?

It was not the best time to remember Kydd's tender, if clumsy, avowal of love or Peggs' delighted response. Or the attentions paid to Hettie by the twins. For that matter, she'd better not think of Bannan's strong arms around her or Wyll's dear friendship.

Jenn thrust such decidedly confusing thoughts aside. She'd found her way down from the Spine and its pebble by wanting something simpler than love or happiness. "A cup of tea," she stated firmly, sure there was none to be had here. Wherever here was. Tea belonged where she wanted them to be. "Hot and strong."

The darkness slid back, retreating rut by ridge by rock, lifting through trees and leaves till Jenn and Wainn squinted at one another under the bright morning sun and a bee paused in surprise. "There's the way," he announced happily, and tugged his fingers free of hers. He lowered his pole, drawing the lamp close to snuff its small flame.

They were steps from the Tinkers Road. How could that be? Jenn thought with an inner shudder.

Wainn appeared unconcerned. "Bannan will have tea," he offered with the same pleased confidence he used for Peggs' pies. He headed off, and Jenn hurried to stay with him.

Once on the road, familiar and safe, her heart settled in her chest. She was even able to wave a greeting when she saw Tir coming toward them.

Despite his thunderous scowl. "Where've you been, girl?" he exclaimed, loud and rude.

Jenn flushed.

"She was lost," Wainn answered.

This—or something about Wainn—silenced what Tir might have said next. Instead, he peered at Jenn, his scowl slowly easing to a tired man's concern. "You're found, then," he said gruffly. "Come along.

"There's tea."

Tir escorted them to the farm without another word, expressing his disapproval in impatient steps and deep breaths, as though he struggled to keep what he'd like to say behind his mask. Jenn was tempted to ask what irked him, but she didn't know the man well enough. After all, sometimes Allin Emms woke so surly his mother sent him to the porch to finish his breakfast, even in winter.

Most likely, Wyll had caused a fuss last night. She hoped not, but he was capable of it. Or Scourge could have dumped her bags—and the men's breakfast. Like Wyll, the not-horse had a temper.

Whatever it was, she'd put it right.

As if she'd said it aloud, Wainn, on her other side, tilted his head to watch sunbeams and smiled peacefully.

They reached the farm in short order. Jenn looked longingly toward her path and Night's Edge, but the little house was where she was supposed to go. Having had her small adventure, she firmly intended to behave.

As for her adventure, the less said about that the better. Nothing would be gained from stirring trouble in life's pot. The best thing about Aunt Sybb's sayings, Jenn decided cheerfully, was how easy it was to choose ones that made her feel better.

Little wonder, then, that she cried out in surprise as a breeze, fever hot, swirled around her legs, then rushed upward to give her hair a painful pull. "I told you never to go there!"

Wyll leaned on a corner of the house, not content to wait until she was close enough to have a proper conversation.

Eyes smarting, Jenn shouted, "I'll go where I want!"

"And cause no end of grief doing it," Tir snapped, nearer and doubtless believing she'd spoken to him. "You do know they went near mad with worry, don't you? First the road, now this."

Jenn stopped in her tracks to stare at him as Wainn, with a blithe, "I'll find tea," continued toward the house.

"I was fine," she protested.

"Heart's Blood! So it was a game, was it? To see who'd rush to your rescue?" She shrank from the disdain in his voice. "Suppose you're sorry it was me." Tir turned and spat. "Fool girl."

He strode off toward the garden leaving her standing, openmouthed, in the midst of the yard. The torn and trampled yard. What had happened here?

A shadow detached from the row of trees. Scourge. As he approached, he flung his head high, nostrils flared till she could see red inside. Lather had dried on his chest and legs, but the breeze nipping her ear was frost cold. "Is he right? Were you trying to lure my truthseer into the Wound?"

"I don't know what you mean—"

"Jenn!" Bannan, who'd been sitting on the side of his well, rose and came toward her.

Finally. Someone glad to see her. Jenn's smile died. Why was he covered in leaves and dirt? And why the haggard look on his face? "I took a walk," she said in a faint voice. "That's all."

A whirl of hot fetid wind. "And what will be the consequences?" Oh, Wyll was in a mood.

"Are you all right?" from Bannan.

Suddenly, she wasn't sure. They were so upset, all of them. Not at her—she knew better. As if they'd been mortally afraid, for her. Why?

Because she hadn't been safe, Jenn thought unsteadily, remembering the white pebble and dark path. Not safe at all.

A fretful wind stirred grass and twisted leaves.

"Jenn."

She started, eyes wide.

Bannan gentled his tone. "What did you see?"

She shivered and rubbed her arms. There had to be another storm coming, the way the air took chill like this despite the sun. "Nothing. Nothing I wanted to." She couldn't hide her disappointment from him any more than she could hide the truth. "I thought I could see beyond Marrowdell from there, but all I saw were more hills. Hills, the stones, and a meadow. It wasn't nice, like ours." Like ours should be, she thought with despair. "It's not a good place," she whispered and wind howled through the treetops.

"Dearest Heart." The breeze wrapped around her and tried to warm her, but could not. "Peace. You're safe now. Trust me, when next I warn you."

Bannan's warm, apple butter eyes held hers. "It's all right, Jenn," he said soothingly, as if she was truly frightened, which she wasn't, just confused. She didn't dare be frightened. "You're here now. Thank you for sending breakfast. Are you hungry?"

Jenn shivered again. "No—no, I'm not. I—I would like a cup of tea, please."

"Nothing easier," he promised, and took her hand to lead her to a seat on the fallen branch.

There was tea, strong and hot. No milk for it, or honey, but the metal cup Bannan provided gave an interestingly unfamiliar taste.

The cup had a hinged handle that would fold to save space in a pack; Jenn thought it a very clever and soldierly item. Under other circumstances, she would have been curious. Had it seen battles? Was it old or simply battered? Did it come with a spoon?

Instead, she stifled her questions and sat drinking tea on the branch. With no porch, nor yet chairs or bench to put on one, they'd used the branch in turns yesterday as a handy place to rest; it was pleasant here, now that the chill wind had died down, and shaded by the large old tree. Though from here, with a lift of her eyes, she'd be looking at the long slope of the Spine; Jenn kept her gaze on her tea in its interesting cup.

Everyone else's gaze was on her, as if she was about to sprout horns or feathers or babble poetry in Naalish. She tried not to fidget.

Not so Scourge. "Will you please stop?" she begged again. He huffed at her and pawed the turf again with a hoof, sending dirt and bits of vegetation flying everywhere behind him. Wyll's eyes hadn't lost their silver fire, but at least he wasn't digging messy holes. Bannan, on the other hand, had a worrisome lack of expression on his face whenever Jenn stole a look at him. "I'm sorry I didn't come straight here."

"I'm sorry you trusted the bloody beast with our breakfast," Tir grumbled. He'd retrieved the saddlebags from the summerberry brambles and bore abundant scratches for his effort.

Though he shouldn't blame her for those. He could have asked Wyll.

Wyll leaned where the branch's jagged end turned up toward the tree from whence it came. Ripped away by a winter storm, perhaps. The snows affected the old trees, too, and brought limbs crashing down. Or lightning might have done it, though Jenn hadn't noticed any scorching. Wyll leaned because his body didn't favor sitting or standing straight. He leaned because of what she'd done.

And now he was angry with her too. Angry and disappointed.

She hadn't promised not to take the path; she'd said they'd talk about it later and done what she wanted. Having lost similar arguments with her father and aunt—most spectacularly when she hadn't promised her father not to skate until the ice was as thick as he'd wanted and wound up almost drowned beneath the ice—she knew better than to try.

A tiny sigh escaped her lips.

Wainn, who might have taken her side, stood quietly at a good distance from Scourge, his face shaded by the wide brim of his hat and a Treff-made cup in his hand.

Bannan stood as well, and Tir, the two lined up against her. She might have been at home—and a child—being scolded by her father and aunt. Jenn quenched a stir of rebellion; she'd put herself in danger, however strange, and might not have found her way home without Wainn.

Repressing a shudder, she lifted her eyes to look toward Night's Edge. "Have you fixed our meadow yet?" she asked hopefully.

"I cannot."

Wyll said it with such finality Jenn's heart thudded in her chest. She'd apologized, hadn't she? She'd come back safely—wasn't that the point? He couldn't mean to punish her—not like this. Her father'd only made her wait until after the Midwinter Beholding to skate with the rest.

"Of course you can," she replied lightly, though her lips wanted to tremble. "You must. Night's Edge is our special place—our home! You can't possibly leave it like—like that. Come. We'll go now and you can fix it."

The silver fled his eyes. His face went sickly white. "Dearest Heart—"

With a rude snort, Scourge pawed loose another spray of dirt and ruined leaves. Wyll's eyes flickered, and a quick little breeze snatched the debris and whirled it into a thin dense column, a column that bent to slap the not-horse smartly on the rump. He shied with an aggrieved whistle, hooves barely missing Bannan's feet.

"Wyll can't fix it." Wainn had a knack for being forgotten. Having startled them into noticing him again, he lifted his cup toward Night's Edge. "This was your fault, Jenn Nalynn, not his."

Her fault Wyll wasn't whole. That's what he meant.

"Something went wrong with the wishing," Jenn admitted with all the dignity she possessed. "Everything went wrong," she added miserably and couldn't help but sniffle.

Bannan went to a knee before her. "Not everything," he protested gallantly and pressed a handkerchief into her free hand. It was creamy linen, monogrammed with the prettiest "L" she'd ever seen, complete with trailing ivy and a little rosebud. She clutched what had to be a treasured keepsake and held back her tears for fear of soiling it.

"Not everything," the truthseer repeated, this time in a determined tone. He glanced over his shoulder at Wyll. "Tell her the truth," he ordered, with a snap that straightened Tir's shoulders, "or I will."

"T-Tell me what?"

"Tell you, Dearest Heart," whispered the little breeze in her ear, contrite and soft, "that you are not to blame. Your wishing shaped me as man; it did not make me thus."

"I don't understand," Jenn said slowly, looking at Wyll.

"Dearest Heart. Good Heart." He tugged his useless arm from its resting place inside his jerkin and let it fall against his twisted side, then spoke for all to hear. "This, you didn't do."

"But you said I did. You knew I believed it. All this time, I believed I'd—" The air grew heavy and tasted of lightning on her tongue. Jenn surged to her feet, Bannan rising to back out of her way. "How could you!"

"How could you?" Wainn said. He was at her side. When had he moved? He took the cup from her hand as if worried she'd spill her tea. "This is Marrowdell's guardian," the youngest Uhthoff went on in his careful, unhurried voice. "The penitent and punished." Tears glistened in his earnest eyes. "He didn't deserve to be wished into a husband, Jenn Nalynn. You should have asked first."

Wyll stared at Wainn. "What can you know of me? How?"

"I'm a good listener," Wainn explained, which Jenn knew to be true, though she hadn't realized he might listen to more than Wen.

"You dream of guilt and grief. You live by duty and honor. You love without hope." A sudden, small smile. "Yet you play."

Jenn pressed her clenched hands, and Bannan's handkerchief, over her mouth. She didn't know what would come out first and she daren't—she mustn't—make things worse. Yes, she was angry at Wyll for letting her believe she'd maimed him, but she was furious—or was she hurt?—because she hadn't known and had never known and they'd been friends, special friends, for all her life and she should have.

Thinking it through, she wasn't angry at all, but very very sorry. Tears smarted in her eyes. Had he lived like this all his life? Or . . . She lowered her hands slowly. "Wyll. What hap—?"

The breeze roared in her ear. "ITCHY!!!" Scourge twisted his big head around and began to chew loudly at the skin on his back. "ITCHY!"

Sticky brown hair began to drift through the air. Tir cursed, Wainn sneezed, and Bannan shrugged. "The fall shed. Sorry."

Jenn looked at Bannan. Had he heard Scourge? Could he?

It didn't seem so, when next he said, "We're going to use wood from the wagon to rebuild the porch. I say we grab a quick breakfast—"

"ITCHY!!!!" With a furious stamp, more chewing and more drifting hair. Jenn winced.

"Stop that!" Bannan looked annoyed. "Go on. The kit's in the barn," he told the not-horse, who gave a desperate neigh and trotted in that direction, only to stop and glance back with a pleading look that would have impressed Wainn's old pony.

Jenn didn't have an appetite anyway. "I'll look after him," she said, careful not to look at Wyll, and went after Scourge.

Anything to be away, where she could breathe. Away from them all, or most. Most especially from Wyll. For a heartbeat, Jenn gazed longingly at the Tinkers Road and thought of running home to Peggs.

Aunt Sybb wouldn't approve. Might have beens and if onlys don't mend socks, she'd say. A woman faces life's trials.

Jenn straightened her shoulders and headed for the barn instead.

If Marrowdell reflected Jenn Nalynn's most powerful feelings, Bannan Larmensu was relieved by the pleasant blue of the sky. With her safe arrival at the farm, warmth had returned to the air. He might have imagined those chill moments when the world seemed on the brink of . . . something.

He hadn't. She'd not told the truth, not all of it, about what had happened to her on the Spine. Something she'd remembered frightened her, and Marrowdell had shivered once more in answer. Ancestors Blessed and Beloved, that he'd been able to distract her with tea, or they'd have needed coats.

Wainn might have had some answers, to that and more, but after his astonishing insights concerning the dragon, he'd put down his cup and hers, and left without another word. Tir had collected those cups with a glower that warned away any conversation and stomped into the house, presumably to make breakfast, most likely his own.

As for Wyll . . .

Young Uhthoff had named him the penitent and punished. Wyll having admitted being cruelly maimed by his own, Bannan's urge to pity died stillborn. What did he know of dragons and their justice? Wyll might be guilty. As for him being transformed by Jenn's wish? That, from what he could see, was more an impediment to his hopes than penalty to the dragon, who appeared to manage quite well. Maybe better than a man turned dragon, if such were possible.

Duty. Honor. Bannan knew what those meant to him. What were they to Wyll?

The grief he'd seen for himself, felt still. That terrible grief. What had Wyll lost, besides wings?

The truthseer took a deep breath and shook his head. The dragon had stared after Jenn Nalynn like a man lost in the dark would look to a solitary distant light. That he was her guardian, Bannan could believe. That there was more than duty to his faithfulness?

He wasn't blind.

But was that duty to Jenn's benefit? There was a thought to draw gooseflesh from skin despite the warmth.

He'd ask—he'd dare that much—but Wyll had gone too, lurching through the farmyard to the path to Night's Edge, disappearing beyond the tall grass. Though he'd claimed he couldn't repair the damage, maybe he went to try. She'd asked, after all.

And now the focus of so much turmoil was in his barn, grooming his—Bannan shrugged and smiled to himself. Grooming Scourge, who'd never been his, and whose interruption had been suspiciously compassionate.

Making his choice, for better or worse, Bannan followed Jenn Nalynn.

"I wish you'd stop complaining," Jenn complained.

"I'll stop," the breeze informed her, a red glint in the beast's night-dark eye, "when you leave me to suffer in peace!"

The eye was well over her head, as was most of where Scourge itched, which didn't help. Nor did the fact that the lightest touch of the big fancy brush she'd found in the bag hanging from a hook—Bannan's kit—made his skin shiver madly, releasing choking clouds of stiff little brown hairs. She was coated in them already and she'd only just started. Jenn raised the brush, more than ready to toss it away.

A shadow crossed her feet. Bannan appeared in the stall door and smiled. "Need some help?"

"Oh, no. We're fine." To prove it, Jenn drew the brush as gently as she could along Scourge's side.

"ARGH!!! TICKLES!" the breeze scolded unhappily. Skin shuddered until Scourge's entire body shook, sending up another cloud. Hair twinkled in the beams of midmorning sunlight slanting through the barn, and drifted out the open stall window to the farmyard.

Jenn sneezed and spat, wiping at her mouth, then snuck a look at Bannan.

He wasn't laughing. That was good. Although there was a suspicious twinkle in his eyes. Jenn narrowed hers. "What am I doing wrong?"

The breeze flipped hair into her face. "Everything."

She frowned at Scourge. "I didn't ask you."

The truthseer stepped inside the stall. "You can hear him," he declared with wonder, eyes wide.

"When he wants me to," Jenn admitted. "He talks to you, too?" She had her answer in his involuntary glance at Scourge, who'd backed his hindquarters into the far corner of the wide stall to stand and huff as in terror of being touched with the brush again. "It's rude," she scolded the creature, "not to include everyone present in a conversation." Though Master Dusom hadn't breezes in mind when he'd chastised her and Roche for passing notes in his class, using his stern tone was most satisfying.

"ITCHY!" Forceful and aggrieved.

She and Bannan both winced, then he grinned. "Oh, yes. I hear Scourge. Here."

"Here?" she repeated. "Couldn't you where you came from?"

Scourge stamped one foot. "I couldn't speak there," admitted the breeze.

At the implication life outside Marrowdell might be lacking, Jenn tilted her head and frowned. "Why not?"

Bannan looked interested. "I've wondered the same."

"I didn't belong," the breeze said testily. "Beyond the edge is only you and yours. I smothered."

" 'Edge?' "

But the breeze became sullen, and Scourge flattened his ears.

"Let me have that." Bannan took the offending brush, then rummaged in his kit for a toothed band of metal, secured to a wooden handle. "The scraper's best once he's this bad." Scourge made a rude noise, but stepped up with an eager shake of his head. Bannan handed her the tool, showing her how to hold it, then laid his hand on the top of Scourge's neck. "Start here, at the poll, and work down with his coat. Press as hard as you can. Trust me, his hide's tough as ox's."

A smug, "Tougher."

Jenn nodded. No wonder Scourge had complained. Though she hadn't known better. Wainn's pony had grown so tender-skinned with age they had to rub him down with soft rags or he'd protest, and she didn't help with the village horses, having chores of her own in the mill.

Determined to do better, she rose on her toes and stretched, but with her arm fully extended, the scraper barely reached halfway.

"Tiny, aren't you?" Bannan chuckled. Before she knew what he was about, he put his hands on her waist and hoisted her to the windowsill. "Try from here."

For some reason, Jenn's breath caught in her throat. Hoping he hadn't noticed, she concentrated on finding her balance. Scourge gave her a doubtful look, but moved in reach. Copying Bannan, she put one hand flat against the beast's warm neck and drew the scraper down with the other, pressing with all her strength. Wads of hair collected and fell. The hair that didn't float up in her face. Jenn smiled, her lips firmly closed, and kept working.

After a few strokes, Scourge made a sound like a pot about to boil over. She stopped, alarmed, but Bannan merely gave him a pat. "He's just happy. Aren't you, idiot beast?"

"Itchy." But the breeze in her ear was mild. "Better."

Pleased, Jenn continued scraping. Bannan went to his kit and brought out a glove of woven rope, pulling that over his left hand. He applied the palm to Scourge's flanks in sure short strokes, whistling almost soundlessly under his breath as he worked. He was careful where bone rose near the skin, his hands strong yet tender.

Having noticed this about Bannan's hands, which was distracting and not what she should have noticed, Jenn began to feel warmer than she should.

"Where you're from," she said hurriedly. "Is it very different?"

"Vorkoun?" Bannan, thankfully, moved to the other side of Scourge. "She's an old crone, wrapped in shabby walls and prone to damp. There're ruins beneath her streets—none of which run straight, mind—and most families burn charcoal and oil, or haul dried manure from the countryside. There's a stench for you on a lovely fall morning. Though the Lilem's no sweeter, under her bridges."

"No wonder you wanted to leave." Jenn wrinkled her nose. "My aunt says Avyo is the most beautiful city in the world."

He'd bent out of sight. "Avyo can afford it." The words were bitter.

Maybe she hadn't traveled, but Jenn wouldn't have him think her unschooled. "Because Avyo's the capital and heart of Rhoth."

Bannan's frowning face appeared above Scourge's back. "Because our walls and blood protected her. Something those of Avyo, no offense to your lady aunt, chose to ignore when they bartered my city away!"

His anger wasn't at her. It wasn't childish, like one of Roche's sulks, or pointless, like Old Jupp's plan to embarrass other old people with stories about hats and parrots. This was a hard truth, an adult one, about the larger world and Jenn's heart pounded with pride. Bannan spoke to her as an equal. As someone who would care about important things.

So she thought carefully before responding. "You kept the people of Vorkoun safe as long as you could, the way Uncle Horst protected me. Now I know about the curse and won't take the road. Isn't it their turn, to look after themselves?"

Bannan's frown faded and he shook his head with a rueful chuckle. "You sound like my sister. Lila'd said, 'soldiers don't fix streets, peace does.' I didn't like hearing it. We argued up to the day I left."

He'd left his sister?

Jenn looked away and scraped hair from Scourge, who'd waited with surprising patience. Scrape. Scrape. How could Bannan choose a settler's bind if it meant leaving his family? What kind of person would do that?

"Jenn?" Bannan started around Scourge.

The only answer was someone who'd had to leave. Had Roche been right after all? Was Bannan some kind of criminal?

The scraper touched the line of cropped mane and Scourge

plunged aside as if stung. Caught off balance, Jenn tumbled from the windowsill to land, sitting, on the stall floor. The hard stable floor.

"Are you all right?" Bannan stripped off the glove and tossed it aside to offer his hand.

"Yes." Jenn scowled at Scourge. "What did I do?"

The great beast stepped forward, hooves a finger's breadth from her bare toes, and lowered his head until his soft warm nose touched her ankle. "Itchy?"

"You could have warned her," Bannan said testily. To her, "He's touchy around his mane. I'm sorry. I should have told you."

Jenn laid her palm along Scourge's cheek and firmly pushed his big head out of her way. As she rose to her feet, the wads of loose hair she'd so proudly scraped clung to her skirt. "I need to change." Bannan had yet to see her stay clean or tidy, she thought glumly. She brushed herself, managing to spread hair where it hadn't been. "I should go."

"Wait. Please." He took the scraper, but didn't move out of her way. "If it's something he said—" with a frown at Scourge.

"No."

The frown became a worried lift of his brows. "That I said?"

"I'd like to leave." Which was impossible when he wasn't moving. Jenn couldn't go around him without moving Scourge, who wasn't moving either. To ignore them both and climb out through the window, however tempting, would not only be childish but, from past experience, show more bare leg than she should, no matter how she tried.

"I truly meant no insult to your aunt," Bannan ventured earnestly. "You do understand—"

"How can I?" she blurted. "How could you leave your sister? You say you care about Vorkoun and her people, but you left them too." Once started, Jenn couldn't stop. "You shaved your beard!" Which made no sense. "Roche thinks you're a bandit!" she said fiercely. "So do I!"

His lips twitched. "No, you don't. I can tell, you know."

That wasn't fair at all. Jenn bristled. "If you're such a fine and wonderful man, Bannan Larmensu, why are you here?"

"Ah."

A rather pleased "Ah."

An "Ah" whose warmth made Jenn reconsider flight out the stall window.

Before she could, she found herself unable to move as Bannan cupped her cheek in one broad callused hand and captured her eyes with his.

"I see the truth, Jenn Nalynn," he reminded her gently. "Therein lay my use to Vorkoun. I found the liars. Exposed the spies. Sent them to justice and none of them loved me for that service, though they knew not my real name." He leaned close, his voice soft, its foreign lilt more pronounced. "The treaty will release them all and I cannot have them learn who I was. Not for Lila's sake. Not for her sons. I would die before risking them." She felt the heat of his body, though they didn't touch, as his head bent to hers. "Do you understand me now?" A whisper.

Jenn nodded that yes, she understood. She tried to say she thought him noble and valiant to sacrifice for his family, but the words were lost in her throat as Bannan's hand abandoned her cheek for her neck. His fingers slid into her hair, in a way that didn't feel at all like having Peggs braid it, and he dropped the scraper with an urgent clatter that startled them both in order to involve his other hand and its fingers in the same task.

How peculiar.

Jenn could have sworn she'd felt every feeling there was to feel, from joy to boredom to fury. Just this morning she'd been afraid and angry, pitied Wyll, and been sorry for herself. Not to forget being excited and hopeful and crushed by disappointment. This—this feeling that she had no feet and stood somewhere that wasn't here and time itself had paused?

This was new.

Bannan's breath feathered across her lips, inviting a kiss, waiting.

To accept, she need only close the tiny space between. A lift of her toes would do it. A tilt of her chin. She had only to want the kiss.

Which she did, didn't she? Warmth raced along her bones. She wanted to kiss Bannan and be kissed the way she wanted her meadow and Peggs' cooking, the way she craved candlelight and their father's easy smile, and anticipated the look on Aunt Sybb's face each spring when she stepped from her wagon and saw them waiting.

But not as much as she wanted the pebble.

Remembered, that hunger burned away all others, leaving cold, empty ash. "I need—" Jenn whispered desperately, her feet back on the cool earth of the stable floor, but nothing else right or real, "I need what isn't here."

Bannan's fingers fell from her hair to her shoulders. He drew a ragged breath, then another, and Jenn searched his troubled face, wondering what truth he saw in hers.

"So it's the dragon," he said at last.

And she didn't understand.

He could drown in the endless purple of her eyes, drown and be glad beyond any dream.

The breeze found his ear. "Fool," it warned, this time with pity.

"What dragon?" Jenn asked unsteadily. Her face was pale, though spots of rose red graced the high bones of each cheek and her lips—

Bannan refused to look at her lips. Bad enough his hands were loath to leave her. His fingers tingled still from the silk of her hair and, oh, how his body burned. Heart's Blood, when had such a simple touch affected him so? Never, was the truth.

Never again, it might be, too. He collected himself by turning away from her, gathering up the scraper and glove, taking another, slower breath.

There'd been such terrible longing in her face.

Just not for him.

"Your dragon," he told her as he turned back, schooling his tone to a cool and courteous interest—the discipline of the marches, that was, where revealing weakness gave weapon to the enemy. Tir would be impressed. "Wyll."

"Wyll's not—" Jenn's eyes widened. "Wisp?" Her surprise was genuine. "Why would you think that?"

"You do know what a dragon is."

"I know they aren't real," she said dismissively. "They're in stories."

"Like wishings?" She flinched and he wanted the words unsaid, but it was too late.

"He's not a dragon now." She held out her hand for the scraper and resumed grooming Scourge's shoulder, leaving Bannan no choice but to don the prickly rope glove and join her. As hair flew, he stole sidelong looks, seeing nothing more informative than the curve of a cheek whose softness he remembered all too well.

How was it fair, losing her to a creature of magic?

When Jenn Nalynn spoke again, her voice was thoughtful and low. "Wisp is what I called him, before. He didn't want to be seen. He wouldn't show himself, though sometimes I'd catch a glimpse in a shadow." She hesitated. "I think that's why he wouldn't let me stay till sunset."

"When he couldn't hide." At her questioning glance, Bannan admitted, "I know, Jenn. About Marrowdell and sunset."

Her nose wrinkled. "What about them?"

Her puzzlement was real; what did it mean? "I saw for myself, the night I came to the farm. I saw a different Marrowdell." Last night, he'd planned to show Tir, to see if sunset made a difference to his perceptions; being busy with lamps and unloading the wagon, they'd missed the fleeting moment.

Her small bare foot stamped the earth. "There's only this."

His heart sank. "To my eyes there's more," Bannan insisted. Was it only to his? "Come," he urged, suddenly desperate. "I'll show you."

She followed him willingly enough to the row of trunks against the barn wall. "What do you see?" he said, laying a hand on one.

Jenn gazed at it, then glanced at him. "A trunk. Yours?"

"No. I mean, what's it made of? Maybe if you look from here." He took her elbow and pulled her to the side where shadows dappled the wood. "Here. See? Like your glimpses of Wisp."

"I see it's made of wood." A tiny crease formed between her brows. "Isn't it?"

What were the rules here, that made dragons different from trunks? "It's stone," Bannan heard himself say, too eagerly. "Finely polished. Perfectly fitted." Ancestors Witness, he was making things worse. How could she believe him, against the evidence of her own eyes?

Jenn squeezed her eyelids tightly closed, her face scrunched with effort, then opened them again with a flash of intense blue. "Still wood." She sighed. "I wish I could see what you do, Bannan. It must be wonderful."

The truth. He found himself speechless.

As she regarded him, a dimple appeared, but all she said was, "Who would own a stone trunk?"

Jenn's belief rushed to his head like wine; he wanted to shout and grab her in his arms. Instead, he told her, "These were in the storeroom. There are tracks, from wagons, on the floor. Almost a year old."

"Mistress Sand," she replied promptly. "Master Riverstone."

Bannan blinked. "Who are—"

"Itchy!" The impatient breeze found his other ear. "ITCHY!"

"We're coming," Jenn promised, shaking her head. "Was he this demanding before he could talk?"

"Always," Bannan said with feeling.

"Always," the breeze echoed.

There was nothing to do but go back to grooming the not-horse, who settled under their ministrations with a smug flick of his tail.

The truthseer was glad of the respite. Sand and Riverstone? What sort of names were those? Made up ones, like Captain Ash, was his guess. Names used by people unwilling to reveal their own. He applied the glove to Scourge's hind leg with care—the mane wasn't the only touchy spot—and reminded himself this was Marrowdell, not the marches, and quaint local names shouldn't come as a surprise. Besides, she was Wyll's to protect, not his.

So now he lied to himself?

"The people you mentioned," Bannan ventured, keeping his tone easy. "Who are they?"

"Tinkers." The word sounded happy; these must be friends and he, wrong. "If the trunks are theirs, I don't understand why they'd leave them here. We've room in the mill; they know we'd be glad to help." Her tiny frown returned.

"I'll put them back in the storeroom," he said quickly.

Jenn gave him another sidelong look, this with a small smile. "I shouldn't bother. It's your barn. And they'll be here soon, anyway. For the harvest," she explained, then nodded. "I'll ask Mistress Sand about the trunks and why they look like wood, except to you."

Scourge turned his head to stare.

If he'd needed proof of her sheltered life . . . "Please don't." For a wonder, he sounded calm.

"Why?"

Bannan leaned a shoulder against Scourge, a creature doubtless aware of secrets and their cost, and said dryly, "My dear lady, not everyone believes what I say I see."

"You're a truthseer."

"Not everyone believes in the truth either." He was sorry to upset her, but he'd be sorrier still if Jenn's tinker friends were the type to fear those of uncanny ability, a lesson he'd learned long before becoming "Captain Ash.""Please let me judge for myself whom to tell, or not. Trust I've some experience in the matter."

Jenn shook her head, but not, he was relieved, in denial. "Once you've met Mistress Sand, you'll change your mind. She's a friend. And very wise. You'll like her."

Unshakable as Tir's, her loyalty. Was it another of her potent feelings? Bannan retreated behind courtesy. "I look forward to making her acquaintance," he said stiffly. Was he like Wyll, unable to say no to anything Jenn Nalynn wanted of him? Did she have that power? "I reserve the right to keep what I see to myself."

"Of course. That's your decision," she assured him, then gave him a shy look. "Though I'd be glad—very glad and grateful—if you'd tell me more of what you see that I can't."

His defenses crumbled. What should he say? What could he? "I see the dragon Wyll once was, and the silver of the road. I see—" you, Bannan thought, and stopped before revealing how she looked to his deeper sight, how radiance filled her slender form as though she were light itself beneath her skin. "Yesterday, as the sun's last rays passed over the valley," he said instead, "I saw the land itself as something new, something strange and beautiful at the same time. The light turned into—colors—I've no names for the colors," he admitted with frustrated joy.

"I wish I had your eyes." Jenn closed hers and leaned her forehead against Scourge. "This Marrowdell is all I have," she said with wrenching hopelessness. "All I'll ever have. I know what's here and it's—it's not what I need."

Wyll being here, Bannan told himself, heart thudding in his chest, Wyll being here. The dragon wasn't who or what Jenn Nalynn wanted either.

Her hand moved fitfully over brown hide. Scourge laid back an ear, but didn't object. "I was going to see the world, Bannan Larmensu of Vorkoun." She turned her face to watch her finger as she drew a shape in the hair with its tip. "I had a map. Of Essa and Thornloe. Of the Sweet Sea and Eldad." She reached further and drew more. "Mellynne."

No farm maid, Jenn Nalynn, content with her life. For the first time he realized the cruelty of her curse. He must be patient to win such a troubled heart, that Bannan saw clearly, and regretted his earlier impulse. Patient and understanding. Perhaps something more. "Lila's husband went to Mellynne, once," he offered. "All the way to Channen."

"The capital?" Jenn looked up, interest gleaming in her eyes. "What was it like?"

"He—" didn't say, wasn't the truth. The truth was, Bannan hadn't asked. They'd had little in common, other than Lila's fierce love. He'd been a soldier; Emon Westietas heir to a barony and destined, upon his father's upcoming retirement, to represent Vorkoun in Avyo's House of Keys. While Bannan patrolled the marches, Westietas had studied, appeared at public functions by the baron's side, and taught his pet crows clever tricks. He'd ridden not horses, but three-wheeled mechanicals; the rage among the idle rich and the bane of sheep on quiet country lanes. To hear Lila tell it, she'd been impressed by Emon's addled attempt to set a speed record by coasting down a local mountain, though he'd broken an arm and leg.

Bannan knew better. She'd found love and peace with the otherwise dreadfully earnest Westietas, who adored her and their sons, Semyn and Werfol, and spent what time his duties in the House left him at home. He was ashamed, now, to remember on his leaves doing his utmost to entice his sister away, rather than share her with his nephews or brother-in-law.

"Channen?" Jenn prodded.

"Yes." He thought quickly of the Westietas' home. "Channen nourishes the greatest artisans of Mellynne. Emon brought back astonishing works. A fountain of flame." The favorite of his nephews. "A painting that sings like a bird if you whistle at it." Lila'd moved that into a rarely used room. Bannan smiled to himself.

What else? Though she endured jewelry only when necessary, his sister was never without the Mellynne necklace Emon had given her. She'd bring the unusual pendant to her ear when she thought no one watched and smile at what it whispered.

That wouldn't impress Jenn Nalynn.

But he guessed what might. "Best of all," Bannan concluded, "a globe—a map—made from semiprecious stones collected from each domain." He watched her closely. "You can touch the world."

Her lips formed a perfect "O" of delight.

Bannan, torn between kissing those lips and Ancestors take the consequences, or riding to Vorkoun to fetch the globe even if he had to bribe guards, sneak through the gardens, and steal it—however likely that was to find him jailed or worse—grinned like a fool. Wait.

He could send Tir to do it. Better still, he'd write Lila and beg for the globe, or one like it. He'd send the letter with Horst, when he left with the Lady Mahavar—

Jenn's mouth snapped shut and her eyes clouded. "I should go." She made another futile attempt to brush hair from her shirtwaist then gave up. "I'll leave you to finish."

" 'Finish?' "

"Itchy," the breeze hinted.

"Of course." Bannan sketched a little bow and added with no shame at all, "I'm sure Tir's desperate for your help by now—to unpack the kitchen."

"Oh." She'd thought to go home, he could tell. Being good-hearted, now she wouldn't.

Good-hearted, but not so unaware as he'd hoped. Jenn raised an eyebrow. "I'll have Wyll clean my clothes, then."

He refused to be jealous. "If he can," Bannan challenged cheerfully, "I'll ask him the same favor."

A dimple, surely that was a dimple.

Then she was gone.

Scourge snorted.

Bannan listened to her quick little footsteps as she left the barn, then shook his head as he applied the scraper to Scourge's hide. "You don't have to say it."

"Then I won't." The breeze was sly. "A little higher. Back a bit. Not there. There!"

He pretended offense. "However did I manage all these years without your advice?"

"Barely. Now you'll do better."

Better he did, enough that Scourge soon fell silent, other than his deep burbling purr. His ears slowly drooped and his lower lips swung loose, until he looked more like a horse—a very content one—than usual. Bannan took his time with the scraper and glove, cooling his own blood in the pleasant monotony of grooming. A while since he'd done a thorough job, he thought with some guilt.

He took the finishing brush and swept it over Scourge with long, firm strokes, bringing up a shine. Then, because it had been a while, he exchanged the large brush for the silly little one at the bottom of his kit. It had been Lila's favorite as a child, festooned with white daisies. He'd borrowed it to use on Scourge. She'd let him keep it, after a brief but memorable skirmish that covered them both in mud—she'd won—and saw them stand at dripping attention in the kitchen to await parental justice—though she'd coaxed Cook into giving them fresh tarts while they waited, so it had been, overall, a most worthwhile afternoon.

Ancestors Witness, he missed her.

Bannan went to Scourge's head and held the soft little brush near one nostril until it twitched with interest. He smiled and began to gently brush the long muzzle. The flat cheeks were next, then the velvet around the half-closed eyes, Scourge cooperatively lowering his head. The finale, the spot sure to send the not-horse into a stupor, was underneath, between the cheeks. He reached.

Then hesitated. What was that odd shadow?

Bannan squeezed his eyes shut. "You're the same," he said desperately. "You have to be."

"I am what I am." The breeze slipped along his jaw to whisper in his other ear. "It's you who've changed, Bannan Larmensu. Boy to man. Man to truthseer. Soldier to what now? Lovelorn farmer, without a sword. I hardly recognize you." Sharper. "See me."

Slowly, Bannan opened his eyes. He took a deep breath and truly looked at Scourge, as he'd looked at the dragon, as he'd looked at toads and chests and Marrowdell's fickle road. "Heart's Blood!"

He ran a trembling hand over what should be flawless, gleaming black. Should be, but for what he finally saw beneath.

Scars, white and old, coursed like bolts of lightning over Scourge's muscular body. There wasn't a spot free of them that would fit Bannan's palm. The deepest etched the broad chest and up over both shoulders, as if he'd worn a harness of fire. By his lips were more. And where his mane arched high along his neck?

A series of sharp, flat edges marked the curve, like so many broken swords.

Tears stung the truthseer's eyes. "You idiot beast," he whispered.

"You see at last," the breeze said, amused.

"I—I don't know what I see."

"An old kruar, marked by one battle too many." The stamp of his great hoof was like a call to arms, but his soft nose found Bannan's hand. "Your gift—and your father's—let you see past what your world made me. For that—for the chance to stay myself—I gladly served your family. And now," his head lifted, "I am almost home."

Almost. "Isn't Marrowdell your home?"

"You know it isn't."

He did.

He finally understood.

There wasn't another way to see Marrowdell. There was another Marrowdell to be seen. One of dragons and—"Kruar." The word left a tingle on Bannan's tongue. "I want to know more."

"You know more than most," Scourge told him, but with an amused snort. "Ask the turn-born your questions, Truthseer. They may or may not answer. They may or may not lie. That is their nature."

"What are they?" Bannan asked. "How do I find them?"

"Don't worry." The breeze chilled his ear. "They'll find you, soon."

There were no rabbits or birds, nor anything for either to eat or live in or hide beneath should they return. Arms hugging her middle, Jenn Nalynn stood in Night's Edge, abandoned and alone, and worried.

Where was Wyll?

What had happened to their meadow?

Most troubling of all, why had he left it like this?

Was he still angry with her for being disobedient? If so, she had a right to be angry back.

"You're not my father—or my aunt!" she shouted into the rising wind. It turned sharp and cold around her, like winter's early scout, and spilled her words across the empty meadow, their anger lost in forlorn, unanswered echoes.

The way Wisp's name had faded, when she'd called for him after the wishing, when she feared he was gone, not just for a moment, but forever.

Right there. That had been the place, where the ground was scorched and black and dead.

But Wisp wasn't gone, she told herself, relief flooding through her as it had when she'd first held him in the river. He was alive and part of her life now. The wishing had worked after all. How could she be angry? She smiled and felt warm again.

Now, to find Wyll.

A bee droned by. Jenn looked up in hope, but it passed without pause, intent on the forest beyond. The forest hadn't been touched by whatever had ruined Night's Edge. The forest—it was from the forest Wisp had come, that final morning. Maybe every morning. Was he there now? She took a step toward it, then stopped.

The forest spread along the base of the Bone Hills, connecting one to the other, broken only by the cataracts and here, where the Tinkers Road entered Marrowdell. It flooded through the narrow pass between the downward plunge of the Spine and the rise of the first of the Five Fingers. After what she'd glimpsed on the Spine, she didn't want to go closer. She couldn't.

What if she saw—

Jenn found herself taking a step back, then another. Each step hurt her sore heel; each stirred new rot from the anguished ground. She kept her eyes on the nearest Bone Hill, wary—she wasn't sure of what.

Bannan shouldn't go there either, not with his ability to see the unseen. What was beneath the ivory stone shouldn't be seen at all, by anyone.

Her heel touched something neither soft nor rot.

"BruuUP!"

Jenn jumped. "Oh. It's you," she said with relief. "Sorry." She bent to gather up the offended toad, holding it gently under its thick arms. Its cool and heavy body hung loose, toes dangling to her knees, but it made no further protest. "What are you doing here?" she asked, not that she expected an answer.

Still, it had followed her.

She raised the toad until they were nose to nostril. It smelled a little of rot; so did she. Mostly, it smelled of sun-warmed grass, the way Night's Edge should smell in the warmth of the sun, and Jenn sniffled. "You're looking for Wyll too, aren't you? I don't think he can fix this," she said sorrowfully, more to her reflections in those limpid brown eyes than the toad, but it was company and listened. "He loved our meadow. He must be very unhappy."

A wise blink.

"Well, then." Jenn regarded the toad and thought. The toad regarded her; if it thought too, she couldn't tell.

If Wyll couldn't fix the meadow, she would. Plants grew where you put them, didn't they? It would take time.

She wasn't, Jenn reminded herself ruefully, going anywhere.

She gave a decisive nod. "I'll do it," she informed the toad. "By the river are wildflowers. And grasses. I'll collect seeds and replant the meadow. I want you," she added, happy to have a plan, "to find Wyll. Please tell him I'm very sorry and not upset with him at all." He hadn't deserved her temper or what she'd done; Wainn had been right about that. "I'll make it up to him." She squinted at the toad. She wasn't Wen, or sure if a toad could take a message, but if Wyll had been a dragon, surely anything might be possible. She'd believe it, that was all. "Can you remember? It's very important to me."

In answer, the toad gradually bent one knee then spread its long toes in midair, as if ready to move.

Jenn planted an impulsive kiss on its warty snout and set it on the ground. "Thank you."

The toad, after a meticulous settling of all its limbs, hopped slowly toward the forest. Where, to be honest, it had likely been heading before she'd almost stepped on it.

If she watched, she'd doubt, which wouldn't help matters or how she felt.

With a sigh, Jenn turned and walked back to the farm, following her little path between the whispering grain and the tall dark trees. Not that it was hers now, though with Night's Edge in such a state, Bannan surely wouldn't visit it.

She slipped through the gap in the hedge. The sky was blue, flowers nodded, and the farmhouse sat in the midst, loved instead of abandoned. Bannan's doing. Her heart, being willful and uncooperative, pounded in her chest.

"What do I do?" Jenn muttered under her breath. "Kiss a toad." A bee regarded her from an aster, but expressed no opinion.

The barn windows opened on this, the south and sunny side. When she'd left, she'd glanced back and been relieved to see Bannan busy grooming Scourge, as if nothing had happened.

Because nothing had.

She should have kissed him. He had a much nicer mouth—and teeth—than Roche, who she wouldn't kiss, thank you. Ever. Come to think of it, Bannan's mouth was nicer than anyone's she knew. And what was a kiss anyway? People kissed all the time.

If she'd kissed Bannan, she'd be done wondering how it would feel. Which would be good and settle her heart.

Unless his kiss felt like the kisses she'd only dreamed about, the ones in storybooks . . .

The ones that changed everything.

"Better the toad," she told the bee, who, upon sober consideration, turned its chubby body and dove into the flower.

The bee was right. There was work to be done. She'd help Tir unpack, then head to the river and begin collecting seeds for Night's Edge.

But as Jenn walked toward the farmhouse, a blue and yellow butterfly landed on a flower near her toes. She stepped to the side, only to find another in her path. By the time Jenn Nalynn walked around all the butterflies seemingly determined to get in her way, she found herself at the stable window.

Uncle Horst always said the easiest squirrel to catch was a curious one.

Still, being here, she couldn't not look, could she?

Staying cautiously to one side, at first all Jenn could see was the white rim of Scourge's eye as the ever-alert beast acknowledged her presence. She heard the expert swish of currycomb and brush; little wonder Scourge's deep purr rumbled through her bones and he paid no further attention to her. Hair sparkled in the sun and she held her breath lest she sneeze.

For Bannan hadn't noticed her.

His own hair had escaped from behind an ear to shadow his jaw. With a small toss of his head, he sent it back over his shoulder, then shifted to reach higher. Sunlight found his face.

It wasn't the face she knew. Unguarded, no longer attentive or charming or filled with emotion, somber lines settled around his mouth, making it almost grim. Bones were nearer the surface and his cheeks were hollowed with care.

The face beneath the beard, she realized abruptly. The face Bannan had worn through his years on the border, the one he feared to have recognized.

The one he hadn't yet left behind.

Uncle Horst showed a face like that, some winter nights by the fire. Radd would notice and signal his daughters to put aside the evening tea. He'd bring out a bottle and the two men would sit together, wordless and thought-filled. On those nights, she and Peggs would quietly take a candle and their books to the loft.

Bannan wasn't to look like that, Jenn decided, fierce and protective. It wasn't right that he should, being so young and full of life. And magical, in how he saw the world and shared it with her.

Just then, as though he'd heard her, Bannan put aside comb and brush to run a satisfied hand over the glossy hide in front of him. A fond smile pushed aside lines and hollows, restoring the face she knew.

Knew and hadn't kissed.

Jenn ducked below the window's sill and, finding no more butterflies in her way, hurried to the farmhouse.

Breakfast had improved Tir Half-face's disposition. Unfortunately, as far as Jenn was concerned, it improved it too much. Unmasked, his grin did little more than lift the bearded remnant of his chin and sink his cheeks, but there was no mistaking the gleam in his blue eyes. "Left Sir to finish on his ownsome, I take it. Guess he wasn't sweet enough for you."

Jenn closed her open mouth, unable to summon the sort of quick scathing retort she'd give Roche or the twins when teased. "I've chores at home," she said stiffly. "Do you want help or not?"

With a chuckle, Tir waved to the stack of boxes and bags against the wall. "Please."

If anything could take her mind off—off everything, Jenn decided, it was the intriguing contents of those boxes and bags. Aunt Sybb's wagon arrived well stocked with pleasant surprises each year, but this was different. What might Bannan have brought?

Pleasantly curious, she picked the nearest bag and sat on the floor to untie its top. The sturdy bag itself had value here, as did the bit of rope. Inside the bag, she found socks. Or rather, bottles stuffed into socks, she presumed to protect them during travel. Lamp or cooking oils? Jenn chose one and pried open the mouth of the sock to peer at its contents.

The label was plain, and disappointing. "It's just wine." If all the bottles were the same, Bannan had added bulk and weight to his wagon for no worthwhile purpose. Master Dusom and Zehr made wine each summerberry harvest, there'd soon be cider pressed, and, with the harvest, the tinkers' beer. Though once emptied, Bannan's bottles would be of use, she supposed.

"'Wine?'" Tir stopped unwrapping the parts of the new stove. "Ancestors Blessed and Bountiful!" He snatched the bottle from her unresisting grip and, stripping off its sock, hugged it to his chest. "Here's what I need."

Jenn blinked. "Now?"

Tir shot her an enigmatic look. "A tipple before bed," he said grudgingly. "Or however many it takes," a grimmer afterthought. He slipped the bottle into his bedroll, then went back to the stove.

Jenn gazed after him as she picked the sock from the floor and folded it. Tir Half-face and Aunt Sybb couldn't be more different, but something about him, his tired face, even the bottle, brought her aunt to mind. "You think the wine will help you sleep," she surmised, unhappy.

His back was to her, but she saw him tense.

"You hope it will stop the dreams."

He turned with a sharp arrested movement that made her flinch, his eyes like ice. "How could you— What do you know of my dreams?"

She'd been right. She hadn't wanted to be. "It's what Marrowdell does," Jenn told him. "To some people." The best people. People who wanted to stay, and should, but couldn't, making everyone else sad.

"What do you mean, 'some people?' "

"Most—we don't dream, not like you do. People who dream—they have to leave," she said, knowing he wanted the truth and not a kindly meant lie. Tir was Bannan's, the way Aunt Sybb was hers and Peggs' and Poppa's. It wasn't fair, that he dreamed too. It wasn't fair at all.

"I'm under attack?" He looked ready to grab his axes.

As well defend against winter as Marrowdell. "No," Jenn assured him. "There—it's just—not everyone fits. Not for long. Especially," as she thought about Roche, "here." She patted the wooden floor. "This is too close to the Bone Hills. That's why the farm was deserted. They say the dreams are worse here." They being her father and Master Dusom, talking late one night. Jenn didn't add how glad she'd been, then, to be sure Night's Edge would stay her and Wisp's private place. She'd been a child, then, with a child's selfish view of the world.

"They say that, do they?" After a wary look out the windows and doors, Tir crouched in front of her, balanced lightly on his toes. Twin furrows creased his scarred forehead. "Well, I don't plan on leaving, Jenn Nalynn. So where do they say they're easiest?" he demanded, low-voiced. He gave her a searching look and a muscle clenched beneath his beard. "I've my share of nightmares; what soldier doesn't? These dreams—I tell you the truth, girl. I dare not close my eyes. Me. And I'm no coward."

Neither was Aunt Sybb.

"The dreams are easier away from the Bone Hills. But—" he had to know, "—Aunt Sybb dreams, too." Regret thickened her voice and Jenn felt something stir inside, something determined. Dreams should be about good things. "She tries to stay, for us, but once they—once she can't sleep anymore, Poppa worries she'll make herself weak. I know she'll be back next spring, but—"

"So it's not always—"

To see such a man shudder sent a chill down Jenn's spine. "No," she assured him quickly. "Spring and summer, Aunt Sybb sleeps well—right through to fall, until this year." It wasn't right. Aunt Sybb should sleep like little Loee; better, since the baby still roused in the night.

For a heartbeat, she let herself believe it could happen, that Tir and Aunt Sybb could stay as long as they wanted and be well and have only good dreams.

If only belief was enough.

"I'll ask Poppa." With a sigh, Jenn offered the little she could. "There's room in the mill. You could sleep there."

Tir's eyes flashed. "Who's to look after him?" with a meaningful jerk of his thumb, as if the truthseer was a child.

"It's not as if you'd be leaving the valley," she said sensibly. "The mill's not far. You could be here every day. Besides, he has Scourge."

He looked outraged. "The bloody beast!"

"He's not a beast." She wasn't sure what he was, exactly, but Scourge wasn't someone to be mocked.

"Don't tell me you hear him, too?" Tir shook his head in wonder. "Sir said the beast could talk to him, but I hardly believed it."

"It's true."

He growled something she couldn't make out. "I suppose you see what he sees too."

"No." Jenn shook her head. "Bannan has a gift."

"A curse of his own's more like." At her questioning look, Tir hesitated, then said soberly, " 'It dims the brightest spirit, to stare into the dark.' " He touched fingers to heart in salute. "His sister said that once. Stuck with me."

The sister Bannan had left behind. She'd understood the price Bannan had paid, to keep Vorkoun safe; seen the look etched into his face. He should have stayed with Lila, Jenn decided. Sisters were important. Family was important. "What's she like?" she asked wistfully, imagining a gracious lady, like Aunt Sybb, but younger and more interesting. Not that Aunt Sybb wasn't interesting but . . .

"The bar—?" He glanced at her and changed what he was about to say. "Older by naught but a year, but you wouldn't know it. Lila's the wise one. More'n me or him, that's for sure." This last thoughtfully.

"Is she—" Jenn stopped, faced with his upraised, callused, and not very clean palm. She watched, fascinated, as Tir rose to stalk noiselessly around the pile of unpacked boxes and bags. What he suspected she couldn't guess.

He pounced.

When he stood, a too-familiar sack hung from his hand. A sack whose contents began to squirm, emitting angry little squeaks and growls.

She knew that sound. Jenn winced.

"Who," Tir said grimly, giving the sack a furious shake, "gave us vermin?"

She'd last seen it full of charcoal. No, Roche had said it was charcoal; she hadn't looked and, knowing his spiteful temper, she should have. "They didn't get out," she said weakly. The only things in Marrowdell that flustered Aunt Sybb more than toads were its mice, not that any toad would let a mouse indoors but that wasn't, Jenn had discovered, a comfort. According to Aunt Sybb and storybooks, mice should be tiny, furred, and have cute noses, not be the size of big Davi's palm, dark gray and bald, with wide, well-toothed jaws and no nose to speak of. Then there were their long, hook-clawed fingers and red eyes.

As Master Dusom explained it, Marrowdell's were simply a robust northern variety. That hadn't helped Aunt Sybb either. Though it was rare to see a mouse in daylight, or more than one. Roche, she thought with reluctant admiration, must have set a goodly number of traps.

"You know—Heart's Blood!" Tir dropped the sack, bright blood dripping from his hand. Before he could reach for it again, the house toad leapt from wherever it had been hiding to grasp a corner of the sack in its lipless mouth. Eyes half-closed in rapture, it dragged the sack, and protesting mice, out the door, grunting with effort.

Tir sucked pensively on his wounded finger, then shook his head. "So they have a use," he said wryly.

"House toads? Oh, yes." Jenn smiled with relief. "They never let mice indoors. And then there's eggs," she confided.

He frowned. "Eggs come from hens, girl."

"Have you seen any here?" Which was altogether pert, but he shouldn't sound like he knew everything. "Our eggs come from toads."

"From—" The former guard looked about to retch—which, to be honest, would likely be Aunt Sybb's reaction were she to ever know about toads and eggs, not that she'd be so crude—then steadied himself. "Ancestors Mad and Lost, what's next in this place?" He took a deep breath. "How does—where—?"

"You'll find eggs in its burrow. But you need these." Jenn reached in her pocket and pulled out the handful of pebbles she'd grabbed from the Nalynn jar. She couldn't help but give them a wary look, but they behaved as pebbles should and weren't the slightest bit appetizing. Tir took them with an appalled expression. "Give him a few to start, to show your good intentions. Whenever you want an egg, put a pebble in the toad's burrow the night before. After you collect the egg," she added, "it's best to replace it with a pebble right away.

One for one at least. Extra, if you can. They like—white ones best." She hoped he hadn't noticed her instant's hesitation.

The pebble on the Spine had been white. Which, Jenn told herself firmly, had nothing to do with anything. One of Peggs' expressions.

To Tir's credit, though he gritted his teeth, he closed his fingers over the pebbles and gave a resigned shrug. "Where's the burrow?"

"It won't be far from the house. Look near the hedge. Once you find it, just reach in and feel around."

"Ancestors Blessed," he muttered distractedly. He put the pebbles on the stove, moving one with the tip of a finger. "So. Who gave us the vermin?"

Too much to hope he'd forgotten, and too much to hope he'd forgive, either. Roche hadn't appreciated the sort of trouble he'd stir, playing his spiteful games on such men. "I can't tell you," Jenn admitted. "You'd scare him to death."

"Would I, now." The former guard actually chuckled. "I see. Well, if there's no more nonsense . . ." he let his voice trail away.

She sighed with relief. "Thank you. You're most kind."

"Me?" For some reason, this gave Tir pause. He regarded her with his light blue eyes and she was surprised to see a hint of red appear on his scarred cheeks. "If I were," he said rather gruffly, "I'd tell you what your father should. About Bannan."

She swallowed. "And what would that be?"

"Not to go playing girlish games with his sort, Jenn Nalynn."

Jenn felt her cheeks warm. "I don't know what you mean." Though she did.

Tir's eyes bored into hers. "He won't fool with a lass like the boys in yon village. Many's the time I've wished he would, but he falls hard or not at all. Now he's half a mind to challenge your Wyll. You give him cause to hope and there'll be trouble." She made to speak, but he wasn't done. "Is that fair?"

"Wyll wouldn't hurt—"

"Is that fair?" Tir was relentless. "Wyll has your promise. Heart's Blood, you made him a man to wed him, didn't you?"

She stared at the floor. "Yes." After a moment, a tear landed near her toes.

"Ancestors Dead and Diced, girl." His rough voice softened to a gentle rasp. "Don't you go crying. I want the truth, now. Which of them is it? Who's got your heart?"

Jenn raised her head. His face was blurred, and she blinked to clear her eyes. "I don't know."

"Well." He coughed. "Well, then. Hmm." A long pause. "There's only one thing for it," he said finally. "You leave them be, both of them, hear me? Neither's had time to find their feet in this Marrowdell of yours, let alone their own minds. While they do—while Wyll builds his house and I teach sir his farming—you search your heart. What's meant to be, will."

It was something Aunt Sybb would say. It was sensible and right and her spirit soared with relief. She'd go home and stay there.

"Thank you," Jenn said, and smiled from her heart.

Tir Half-face started, blushed, then bowed.

She hadn't meant to hurt him. She hadn't known she would.

Scant comfort, perhaps, but it took away that powerful, unfamiliar pain. Jenn hadn't betrayed their friendship.

Loath to step in Night's Edge, Wyll lurched along the Tinkers Road to pass it by, glad to be alone. That was the worst of life as a man, being surrounded by them and their things. They had no sense of respectful distance. His kind—

His kind. What was that, anymore?

The road turned to squeeze through the Bone Hills, flanked by solid lines of neyet. They grew thickest against the trapped ones, where none other would dare, for reasons no one knew. The neyet held the edge, or were stuck in it. They were brave and selfless, or ignorant. Which was which, Wyll supposed, hardly mattered. By holding the Verge and Marrowdell together, they'd be first to die if both again tore apart.

But not the last.

Dark thoughts. Darker, since allowing himself to be distracted.

The novelty of cart and farm, of rafters and tea, of conversation and games. So much confounded him. The girl's grace among her kind. How her eyes took the sun and gave back sky.

How his heart had shattered when she'd entered the Wound and he'd thought her lost.

Snarling, Wyll found an opening between two neyet and lurched through, gripping the nearest trunk as he heaved his bad leg over its roots. Bark cracked under his fingers. At once, ylings dropped to flutter around him and sing in protest, being unable to speak like the little cousins.

To avoid a branch falling on his fragile head, Wyll pushed into the open as quickly as he could.

The girl didn't know of this place, nestled close to theirs. She thought the forest solid to the hill, but it wasn't.

The neyet and their long shadows girdled a second meadow, smaller than Night's Edge, remarkable only for a patch of kaliia at its center too small to bother harvesting. An unimportant place. As Wisp, he'd passed through it every day and night of the girl's life without an instant's pause, for this was the way home.

Respecting the kaliia and its guardians, he made his way around, though it was harder going through the thick and untrampled wildflowers. He reached where the neyet played their little trick, the arm of their forest folding to almost, but not, touch their line along the road. Thus they hid this place from the rest of Marrowdell and gave him a path from Night's Edge safe from curious eyes.

If he took that path, he'd see the devastation of their meadow.

He chose the other way.

His feet crushed grass and scarred the moist soil. In his world, by now he'd be descending the steep winding path to his sanctuary, surrounded by clean, windswept rock. Unlike the little ones, like the kruar, as dragon he could cross at whim. The temptation to leave Marrowdell for the Verge choked him, but he would not.

Perhaps could not, as man.

The sei had left him the small magics, their potency now stripped by the girl's expectation. He'd no wish to learn what else he'd lost, and more sense than to challenge those who'd sent him here. If he could cross, his kind would be delighted to drop him in the foul river again, or worse.

So, in the girl's world, Wyll lurched through purple asters and golden grass, startled a rabbit and found bees. He lurched until something told him, here, and bade him stop.

Birds regarded him silently, then ignored him to be about their business.

The sun warmed his coated shoulders and stretched his shadow along the ground.

Yes. Chancy, trying to find a place here, that was there, but he knew where he was—or would be.

Safe inside the blue shimmering walls.

Home.

How pathetic he'd become, to have the sei's unpleasant hovel mean that to him.

He wasn't home, but this place was more his than any other in Marrowdell. Wyll took off his borrowed clothes and left them in a heap, as he'd left the villagers' unwanted gifts at the farm.

For a moment, he closed his eyes and tried to feel the air and sun the way they should feel, smell the meadow's scents as they should smell, but it was hopeless. He wasn't what he should be.

Still, it was pleasant, being here. Better than the dark. Peaceful. Warm. He settled himself on his clothes, having no desire to be damp, and set about his daily tasks as if this were a normal morning, and he, his normal self.

As if he waited for Jenn Nalynn in their meadow.

Lying back, good arm behind his head, Wyll sent tendrils of air seeking and gathering. The ylings were foolishly fond of flower petals to sew into their cloaks, and would risk themselves coming down to collect them. He plucked a few petals here, a few there, until the air sparkled with tiny specks of gold and purple and white, then lifted them above a neyet and let go.

Leaves rustled. He heard giggles and the scramble of small toes over bark.

Not a single petal made it to the ground.

Efflet, for their part, would shred any flowers that dared sprout within their fields and had no vanity, beyond a sensible fastidiousness about their claws. Serious, dedicated folk.

Wyll sent a breeze racing through the kaliia, tossing it this way and that. Almost at once, several stalks began to sway with more than their own weight as efflet, unseen in this light, clung to their tips and rode the waves. They didn't giggle, as ylings, but whispered their glee among themselves, ever so quietly.

Doubtless nyphrit lurked in shadows, anxious for darkness, ever hungry. They weren't his concern, being cheerless and grim and grateful only for his inattention.

For himself, Wyll idly gathered ripe seeds, those with fluffy white tufts or crisp parchment wings, and made them spiral into the sky until he couldn't see them with these eyes and higher still, so the wind of this world would find them and take them—anywhere. He did it for the girl, who mustn't and couldn't leave, and for himself, who wouldn't.

And because it was fun. His lips curved in the hint of a smile.

A smile that froze.

She was near. Coming to Night's Edge!

She mustn't, not alone. She mustn't see the ruin and think it her fault.

Even if it was.

Wyll struggled to his feet, remembered to reach for his clothes. Before he could dress, her anger lashed over him, a sharp, cold wind that stank of rot. Her angry shout struck like a blow. "You're not my father—or my aunt!"

Good. Blame him. There was nothing she could do to him he didn't deserve, but Marrowdell mustn't be ravaged. Her guilt then he couldn't bear to imagine. Wyll hunched against the bitter cold and waited for worse.

But the echoes of her fury tangled in the neyet and faded. He felt the sun's warmth again and took a careful breath.

Such a good heart, she had.

Such a fragile protection.

She mustn't learn how dangerous she was.

Wainn, who knew him, knew her as well. Unlike the truthseer, who understood discretion, he'd come perilously close to telling her too much truth. Wyll snarled to himself. Had he been able, he'd have ripped out Wainn's throat in that instant; what was one life against the safety of all?

How could he, regardless? Their lives—her life—depended on the girl's innocence. Her heart was so honest and full. How could she be happy here if she learned Marrowdell expressed her turn-born passions and expectations, if she knew how easily her moods could destroy those she loved?

And if she tried to leave . . .

She must be happy. And stay.

A bee circled Wyll's head. Ordinarily they knew better, since he was prone to spin their chubby bodies. Not to their harm; the girl liked honey and flowers. They'd buzz with such extravagant frustration until set free. Ordinarily he couldn't resist.

He felt the girl leave Night's Edge. Where would she go? The kruar played a docile steed to steal her attention; the truthseer, a storybook prince to win her heart. Being neither, all he could do for her was act.

She'd asked him to build a house in Night's Edge.

He'd try here.

But how?

Wyll sank back on his clothes. Listless breezes combed the meadow and brought dried grass to pile around him. A nest like a bird's wouldn't serve Jenn Nalynn. Frustrated, he shoved it aside and his hand slipped on something cool. Something that cracked.

And wept.

A crystal?

The small ones couldn't cross from the Verge into Marrowdell. Yet here one was, weeping its tears into the meadow. Wyll brushed grass aside and one became more.

And more. Before his astonished eyes, crystals grew up through the soil, grew and spread and locked one to the other until they encompassed a space, with him at its center, as large as the Nalynns' parlor. He could see the meadow still, though it was like looking through an empty pickle jar. Inside, sunlight became rainbows and glints of iced fire. The last few crystals laced like fingers overhead, leaving an opening wide enough for a dragon to fly free.

Wyll snarled. Didn't they know what he'd become?

Didn't they know they'd imprisoned themselves within the Verge, like the neyet?

Why were they here?

~ Fools! ~ he railed against them. ~ You'll break in the first storm and leave me anyway! ~

The world seemed to pause.

SNAP! CRACK!

He flinched and cowered as the neyet around the meadow suddenly went mad, raining branches and twigs until the sun itself was blocked and silence filled the dark.

A dark, Wyll was startled to realize as he cautiously moved, not filled with the tears of shattered crystal, nor pieces of broken neyet. Or bone.

~ Elder brother! I will save you! ~

~ I'm unhurt. ~

This assurance did nothing to stop the frantic, ineffectual scratching outside his—whatever this was, it wasn't a prison.

~ Hold. ~

With the greatest care, Wyll stretched fingers of air to learn the shape of his new surroundings. ~ Move aside, ~ he warned the little cousin. A door, a door for a man, that first. He flexed.

Crystal cracked, leaving the inevitable tragic puddle. Wood—for the neyet was now that—creaked aside. Sunlight flooded in . . . followed promptly by the little cousin, who stopped in the damp opening to blink at him.

Wind that wasn't his doing, wind that came of invisible wings, whooshed in past the sunlight and toad, wind laden with—of all things—moss. Small handfuls, all a claw could manage, but soon there was a floor, deep and soft. Efflet.

They'd nabbed a visitor for him as well, untimely in both daylight and the proximity of a possibly hungry little cousin. What appeared in this world as a large white moth tidied its wings with a momentary fluster, then bowed. ~ What news, elder brother? ~

Like a yling but not; the way a sei could be a dragon, but not. Marrowdell's moths were drawn to the affairs of others as this world's were to flame, an equally risky predilection for something frail and easily eaten.

~ We have a home! ~ the little cousin proclaimed, puffed as large as it possibly could without splitting its sides.

The messenger dutifully made its record, using a filed nail on a miniscule piece of well-scraped parchment. Done, the parchment was rolled and put with others in its satchel, then the moth, carefully avoiding the prideful toad, fluttered up and away through a gap in what was, Wyll supposed, his new ceiling.

He had a home.

Complete, it appeared, with house toad. He eyed the little cousin warily. ~ I trust you'll have a burrow. ~

~ May I? ~ It rocked on its stomach. ~ I am honored. I will do my utmost to protect our home, elder brother! I— ~

~ Yes, yes. ~ Wyll waved at it. ~ Go. ~

~ I must first relay a message to you, elder brother. From Jenn Nalynn. ~

Wyll leaned forward on his elbow, though it pained him, to put his eyes level with the toad's. ~ Do you mock me? ~ With menace. ~ You cannot speak as she does. ~

It didn't flee, though it shrank into itself and went pale. ~ We cannot speak, but we understand. Our elder sister taught us. ~

There was no such thing, not in this Marrowdell. Either the little cousin had gone mad or it bestowed the title on something else. Or someone.

It had to be the annoying woman from the mill, who could make herself ~ heard ~ albeit in a crude and painful fashion. The one, Wyll frowned, who'd refused to fear or help him. Why did she meddle in matters beyond her kind? ~ Wen. ~

~ Yes! ~ The toad perked up. ~ Our elder sister. She is wise and good and— ~

~ I will hear the message, ~ Wyll declared magnanimously, sitting back to be more comfortable.

~ Yes, elder brother! I am renowned for my oratory, and shall convey Jenn Nalynn's every word, while striving to capture each intonation, with complete description— ~

The dragon bared a man's teeth.

~ Though in this instance, a summary will assuredly do. ~ The toad blinked. ~ 'Very sorry. Not upset. Will make it up to you.' Then she kissed me. ~

The girl's apology he'd felt for himself. Faced with the toad's wide lipless mouth and warty skin, Wyll couldn't bring himself to believe the rest, though little cousins were the most honest of creatures. ~ She kissed you. ~

~ I can describe— ~

~ That won't be necessary. ~ The perfect lips of Jenn Nalynn were for her glorious smiles, not to bestow favors on a toad. He stifled a snarl and made an effort to be courteous. ~ I thank you for your oratory, most admirable and inestimable little cousin. Make your burrow nearby. Where ~ he warned ~ I won't step in it. ~

The toad waddled about, then hesitated.

~ What? ~

It waddled back to face him. If something so squat could look anxious, it did. ~ I would be honored to prepare eggs for you, elder brother. If you might happen to have . . . ~ It stopped, seized by an agony of manners.

Wyll was amused. Though they would never admit it, what small magic little cousins possessed dealt with the wishing of one thing into another, which meant having the thing in the first place, and there was a numbing nicety of rules involved in that. To make an egg required a pebble given to that toad by someone who wanted an egg, which was all well and good for brown or grey or black pebbles but caused an anguish of morals for the toad presented with one of the white pebbles they so desired for their queen's throne.

They were very good at making gems too, but those required the heart of a nyphrit killed by the defender of a home, and it lacked honor to encourage invasion simply to garner more gauds. Luckily for the little cousins, the villagers slept with open doors all summer and nyphrit weren't at all bright. He supposed this little cousin would do well; his home had no door to close.

~ I will take my meals with the truthseer, ~ Wyll decided. Jenn Nalynn would concern herself with pebbles and eggs when she came to live here.

If she did not . . .

The air held rain; their home needed a roof. He set himself to that task next.

And refused to consider the future.

SIXTEEN

"YOU KISSED A toad?" Peggs wrinkled her nose. "Don't tell Aunt Sybb."

Jenn peeled another potato for the pot. "Have you heard anything I've said?"

"Of course." Her sister dutifully counted off on her fingers, "You didn't kiss Bannan, though the moment was there. Nor did you kiss Wyll, who is, or was, a dragon. His sad condition isn't your fault, which is good news, and Tir has dreams, which isn't. You rode that giant whatever it is, Scourge." Smile disappearing, Peggs leaned forward and shook an admonishing finger under Jenn's nose. "And went into the Bone Hills."

Her list hadn't included the pebble or disappearing path. Jenn hadn't dared speak of them. Not because her sister would be horrified, and rightly so, but because words would make it all real again. What if she felt that dreadful craving? What if—

"What were you thinking?"

Jenn blinked. "When I kissed the toad?" she asked brightly.

The finger tapped her nose. "No, Dearest Heart," Peggs persisted. "The Spine."

"I thought I'd found a way to see what lay outside Marrowdell, without leaving," she answered truthfully, and had no trouble adding a deep, unhappy sigh. "But there was nothing to see."

"Then no need to tell Poppa—or Aunt Sybb—about that either." Her sister gave her a quick one-armed hug. "What matters is you're home, safe and sound. You are, aren't you?" She tugged Jenn's braid to make sure.

"Home to stay," she affirmed with great feeling.

Her sister gave her a searching look, then nodded in satisfaction. "Glad to hear it."

They pared vegetables in companionable silence. A gentle, steady rain had settled over Marrowdell, closing a curtain of peace around the village. All that could be seen through the kitchen window was the corner of their garden and the first of the bean poles. She'd made it home before the rain and in time to help Peggs in the kitchen. Radd was at the mill; Aunt Sybb took a nap, for once not restless or snoring. There might never have been strangers. Or wishes.

Or a curse.

"I like it at home." Jenn chose a plump young turnip to threaten with her little knife. "I know what I'm doing here."

"Away from them, you mean." Peggs, having the large knife, wisely rescued the turnip and her sister's fingers.

No need for names.

"Them and . . ." Jenn vented her frustration on a carrot, sending crooked pieces flying. "Them."

"Maybe it's time you told the Ancestors." Looking up from the turnip she was cutting into even little cubes, Peggs chuckled at whatever she saw on Jenn's face. "Couldn't hurt, could it?"

The tradition was to unburden oneself of secrets at the Midwinter Beholding, to greet the return of longer days with the Ancestors firmly on your side, well-informed of any and all transgressions. And hopes. It was about hope too, and Jenn had poured all of hers into the frosty air above their mother's bones each and every year she could remember.

Ancestors were supposedly beyond grief. Jenn had always imagined their mother enjoying her role as Blessed, watching her family grow, tending them with her love.

Each and every year, had Melusine heard her futile hopes, and wept for her cursed daughter?

"I'll think about it," Jenn said faintly.

"Good—"

"Hello!" Hettie appeared in the kitchen window, holding a dripping shawl over her head and shoulders. "Time for a cuppa?"

Peggs wiped her hands, grinning from ear-to-ear. "Of course. Kettle's hot. Come in."

As she bustled over tea, Jenn helped Hettie hang her damp shawl near the oven to dry. She leaned close to whisper, "I haven't told her."

Hettie sent her a grateful look, and squeezed her hand. "Such a good heart," she whispered back. "Do stay. I'd like that."

Usually the elder two gently shooed her upstairs. Pleased, Jenn nodded.

With Aunt Sybb abed in the parlor, they closed the curtain between the rooms. Jenn hopped up to perch on the counter, Peggs took a seat on a lower rung of the ladder to the loft, and Hettie settled on the flour barrel. They took their cups. Hettie rolled hers back and forth between her palms, her round pleasant face unusually serious.

Peggs considered her best friend, then said quietly, "What is it, Hettie?"

"You look so happy."

Jenn had to agreed. Her sister's contented bliss filled the kitchen like a warm fire on a cold night; it was impossible not to smile at her.

Twin roses bloomed on Peggs' cheeks. "I am," she admitted. "You've heard then. About—about Kydd." The uncomplicated joy when she said his name made Jenn glad—and a little envious.

"A Golden Day wedding, no less." Hettie chuckled at Peggs' look of dismay. "Dear Heart, did you honestly think to keep that secret? Lorra Treff's beside herself. If she could find a husband for Wen in time, you can be sure she would. Ancestors Witness, the woman would make one and fire him up in her kiln, if it'd work."

Peggs very carefully didn't look at Jenn.

Jenn very carefully pretended not to notice. She sipped tea, thinking of Wainn, who she was sure would marry Wen, then smiled into her cup, thinking of Wen, who she couldn't imagine would bother with a wedding, even for her mother. For the peace of the village, she hoped Lorra remained unaware of the leanings of her daughter's heart until becoming Blessed herself, which was a naughty thought she must admit to her own Ancestors when the time came.

"I'd hoped to tell you myself," Peggs told Hettie, chagrined. "You'll stand with me, won't you?"

"As if I'd let anyone else. But what of our Jenn?" The milkmaid turned to Jenn with a smile. "Who's to stand with you?"

Jenn's mouth opened and closed like one of Wen's fish. She vaguely recalled a list of Aunt Sybb's with names that had something to do with various roles at the wedding and who'd be best suited—or who had suitable shoes, she wasn't sure—but she hadn't paid attention, preoccupied by the novel concepts of husband and home.

"We haven't discussed such details yet," her sister said diplomatically. "But that's not what's brought you out in the rain, is it, Dear Heart?"

"No." Hettie bent her face to pay close attention to her tea. Strands of golden brown hair undampened by rain curled in the steam until tiny ringlets kissed her cheeks. The Nalynn sisters waited with outward patience, though Jenn was close to twitching when Hettie finally raised her head. "I'm with child."

Peggs took a calm sip of tea. "Tadd's or Allin's?"

Jenn gaped at her sister.

"Doesn't matter," Hettie shrugged. "There's but one I'd want, if he'll have us."

"Tadd, then," as matter-of-factly as if they discussed turnips. "Didn't I tell you?"

"That you did, Peggs." Hettie's broad smile dimpled her cheeks. "You were right. He's ever so much sweeter."

They were older, they were friends, and at ease with each other in a way, and concerning matters, Jenn couldn't pretend to match. Face hot, she slipped down from the counter. "I'll just go upstairs—"

"Jenn's kissed her first toad," Peggs announced, straight-faced.

Hettie's eyes twinkled. "Did he kiss you back?"

Picturing the patient toad, Jenn had to giggle. "Alas," she

exclaimed, pressing the back of her hand to her forehead, "he had no lips."

The curtain pulled aside. A becapped and sleepy Aunt Sybb blinked at the three of them.

"What's this about a toad?"

"Which is why I put pebbles out for the toad, sir."

At the moment, Bannan couldn't have cared less about the toad, pebbles, and any eggs to follow, though normally he would have been delighted to solve another Marrowdell mystery. "You told Jenn to leave." The words felt like broken glass. "To leave and stay away."

"Yes, sir. I did. Sir." Tir stood at parade attention, ready and willing to be chastised, though by the glint in the eyes above his mask he considered himself firmly in the right and willing to stay at attention however long it took his former captain to admit it.

"Stop that," Bannan grumbled as he stripped off his shirt and tossed it over the line. "This isn't the guard." He dipped his hands, wrists, and forearms in the water, then brought handfuls to his face. Taking his time, he cleaned sweat and dust from his neck and chest, under his arms, then finished by pouring the rest of the bucketful over the back of his head. He tossed back his wet hair and ran a rag over his face, feeling stubble. Time for another shave.

Tir hadn't budged.

Heart's Blood. The man was incorrigible. The truthseer glared. "How long?"

"I couldn't say, sir."

"I've a name." He wasted his breath; the habit would take years to break, if ever. As for Tir . . . he hadn't told the truth, or not all of it. Chewing on that disquieting fact, Bannan reached for his shirt.

As he pushed his head through, he grinned with sudden delight. Of course! "Why, you old romantic!"

"Pardon?"

"I beg yours, old friend. Ancestors Witness, you couldn't have managed things better. Wyll can't go to the village, can he? But I've errands. Many errands. I'll need to go there at least once a day." Errands meant the opportunity to take supper at the Nalynn table. Jenn might wear that pretty dress, with the little birds on it. They could sit on the porch . . .

"Best if I do any errands." The "sir" hung almost said; Tir hadn't relaxed a muscle. "While you stay here and farm."

"You—I—" Losing his temper wouldn't help, not if experience was any judge. With an effort, Bannan unclenched his teeth. "Why," he grated, "should I agree to that?"

Tir locked his gaze beyond the truthseer's right ear. "I promised the young lady you would. Sir."

He'd rushed matters, in the stable. Jenn needed time, time to learn her own heart, to choose between him and Wyll, or accept neither. All of which made sense, of a sort, and Bannan was inclined to agree, except for one thing. This hadn't been her idea. This was Tir's incomprehensible meddling.

Clouds had tumbled into the valley; the air promised rain. Marrowdell listened to Jenn's heart; she was troubled, he decided. Clasping his hands behind his back, Bannan studied his too-helpful friend. The man intended to outlast him and usually could, there was the rub. They were bound to get damp. "I suppose begging's out."

"Demeaning, sir."

"I could knock you flat."

"Unlikely. Sir."

Without so much as a blink. This was serious. "What about Wyll?"

"I expect you'll tell him, when the time's right."

"Oh, I will?" The dragon was not going to be pleased.

Tir, equally aware, had the temerity to add, "I'd take it as a kindness, sir, if you didn't mention my involvement."

"I'm sure you would." What good was knowing truth from lie when Tir refused to say a word that mattered? "Heart's Blood," Bannan swore, losing patience. "Enough, do you hear? Where'd this come from? You know I care for her." More than he dared say. "I'm no villain—"

Light blue eyes shifted to his, ice in their depths. "You're a moon-blind calf—Sir—and that's being right charitable." Tir shook his head in disgust. "I may not see Marrowdell the way you do, but Ancestors Witness, you're not seeing her."

But he did. Words trembled on his lips. How her eyes were endless pools . . . how her smile transformed everything and he'd give anything to have her smile at him . . . how pure light filled her slender form.

Ancestors Tormented and Torn. Tir was right. He was bedazzled.

And glad of it. "Don't speak ill of Jenn Nalynn to me," Bannan warned. "Friend or not, don't you dare."

"I'll say what needs be said, Sir," countered Tir as harshly. "Always have. Always will."

The two glared at one another. Bannan pressed his lips in a thin line, then grudgingly circled one finger. Make your point, that said.

"Granted she's a pretty thing and kind, with a smile to warm a stone's heart—"

"Jenn smiled at you?" Bannan flushed, ashamed of his envy. He was hearing the truth; what he felt about it didn't matter. Couldn't matter. "Go on," he said grimly.

"That's not all she is, sir, is it? Like her Wyll isn't just a crippled soldier. There's more, and it's not simple and it's not safe." The first raindrops reached them, beading Tir's bald pate. Neither man moved toward shelter. "Like this place."

"You saw something," the truthseer guessed, growing uneasy. "When you went down the road to find her." Was what he'd seen—that dreadful ooze from the forest—able to harm others after all? Had he put Tir in danger too?

"I saw the girl and that lad coming from the path, normal as could be—other than his carrying a lamp midmorning." Tir touched a suggestive knuckle to his head. "Why?" His eyes narrowed as if sighting a target for his ax. "That's why the fuss this morning. Something's wrong up yon hill. The way the lot of you were carrying on—I should have known it was about more than a girl falling off a horse!"

It was Bannan's turn to evade. "I told you of the curse. Jenn's not to leave Marrowdell."

"Ah, so we come to it," Tir announced with dour satisfaction. "Not to leave. For whose sake, I ask you?"

The obvious answer, the answer of a mother's love and life for her child, died in Bannan's throat. He'd seen Jenn Nalynn's power. He couldn't ignore its implications. Tir was right. Was the curse to keep Jenn safe?

Or to keep that power here?

"That meadow—or what's left of it. Tell me that doesn't fright you."

"We don't know—"

"Who does?"

Whoever promised Melusine her daughter would survive. The Ancestors, in his experience, weren't active in the affairs of the living. So who? Or what?

They didn't know.

The rain chose that moment to come down in steady sheets, soaking their clothes, enclosing them in formless gray. They could be standing anywhere, Marrowdell a memory, his farm a long-lost dream. Bannan felt a pang, as though he'd failed some unspoken vow.

"There's the other thing," Tir went on, relentless as a blade diving for an exposed throat. "Why the dragon? Horst and her family's what's kept her safe, by all accounts, not him. Ask me, it's like having an army keep a mouse from the cellar. A trap'd work better. Unless, sir, it's not a mouse in question at all, and the rest of us who need protecting."

There was no harm in Jenn Nalynn; he'd swear it with his last breath. That didn't make her safe.

He didn't care. Tir was a worrier, inclined to see trouble before anything else. Well and good in the marches, but little wonder Marrowdell's marvels confounded the man. "You may be right, my friend, and see more clearly than I," Bannan conceded generously, then half smiled, tasting sweet rain on his lips. "But it's too late for me, I'm afraid. My heart's found its home, here in Marrowdell, and its hope, with Jenn Nalynn. So come, Tir." Heartily. "Let's go in and drink to our bright future and the answers to all riddles."

"The drink'll be most welcome, sir," low and unhappy, "but I'll be honest. There's no future for me here, bright or otherwise."

The rain was warm; nonetheless, a chill fingered Bannan's bones. "What haven't you told me?"

"Sir." Tir's shoulders curled as if under a weight and he wiped his forehead with an unsteady hand. "Bannan. I can't stay. Not another night. Not even for you."

"What? Why?"

"I've—I've dreamed."

"I thought the toad kept you awake," Bannan said, feeling thick-headed. First, warnings about Jenn, now this? What next, reading portents in tea leaves?

"The dream did that." Tir's eyes filled with fear.

The truth it was, but the sun rising in the middle of the night would make better sense than this man being afraid of anything, let alone a mere dream. "A nightmare . . . ?"

"Worse." Tir's voice was flat and toneless. "Jenn knew. She said these ill dreams are what Marrowdell does. Those who can live here, like you, Bannan, don't suffer them. Those who dream can't bear to stay. It's why the villagers doubted you at first. There've been others who came to this valley, who wanted to live here. None of them lasted a night."

Wainn had worried about his sleep. He'd known. Were these dreams a test of some kind? Bannan struggled to understand. "You believe Jenn's responsible—that's why you sent her away?"

"No, sir," Tir protested with reassuring quickness. "She was sorry for me. The dreams drive her aunt, the Lady Mahavar, back to the city each fall. Poor brave woman." He shuddered, raindrops sliding down his mask. "They say the dreams are hardest to ignore near yon strange hills," so low Bannan had to strain to hear, "and not even the villagers dare sleep here. It's true. I nodded off an instant and . . ." Another shudder. "It wasn't as bad that first night, in the village. Jenn's to ask her father if I might sleep in his mill. It's all I can do."

Enough of this. Bannan threw an arm around Tir's shoulders. "We'll do better, I swear. Now for that drink," he announced, pulling his friend toward the house. The ground where the porch had stood was a puddle, fed by runoff from the new roof, so they splashed through what quickly became mud.

Jenn's clean floor stopped them in the doorway. Bannan wiped his bare feet with a rag. He found and lit his brand-new oil lamp, the other two having been smashed in the wagon. By that warm light, his new stove gleamed, ready for use, though he didn't see any pots unpacked. The ornate black door of its oven being as yet unhinged, the house toad had made itself at home inside and was presently asleep.

While Tir pulled off his boots, Bannan went to the stack of bags. Only one was open, but he was pleased to find it held what he sought. He turned, a bottle in each hand. "On one condition."

Tir pulled off his mask and scratched his beard with fingers and thumb. The skin below his eyes was bruised from lack of sleep. He'd been too caught up in his new life to notice, Bannan thought bitterly. He'd failed his friend.

Perceptive in his own way, Tir managed a hoarse chuckle. "It can't be besting me at 'stones, sir," he said. "Can't be done."

The truthseer offered a bottle. "Tell me why you sent her away. The whole truth."

Tir pried free the cork with his knife. Doing the same, Bannan waited.

His friend lifted his bottle. With the ease of long practice, he poured a goodly amount into his ruined mouth, head tilted so none dribbled out, then swallowed, throat working, eyes closing in reverence. When done, he gazed at Bannan. "To give a letter time to reach Vorkoun. And get a reply."

Bannan almost choked. Vorkoun? "You're writing Lila? Whatever for?"

"To save you, Sir," with some impatience, as if the task might not be worth the effort or was, as Bannan had claimed earlier, too late. "The baroness has the sense in your family, pardon my saying—"

Bannan took another, longer pull on his bottle, waving Tir past what was, after all, entirely fair.

"You listen to her, even when you argue like mad cats. Better than you listen to me, Ancestors Witness." Tir paused for more wine, then gave a decisive nod. "The baroness'll see the right of things. She'll know if you've stones rattling loose in your head or not."

The man had thought it through. "Go ahead," Bannan said cheerfully, making himself comfortable on a folded blanket, his shoulders against the wall. "For that matter, I owe my dear sister a letter of my own. I trust you won't mind sharing the courier's pouch."

Giving the bed a dour look, Tir crouched on his heels near the fireplace. He poked up the fire, then grinned sideways at Bannan. "Not if you pay, sir."

Their shared laughter filled the room like light, leaving an easier feeling, and the men settled to talk as old soldiers were wont, without thought of time.

A mostly empty bottle loose between two fingers, Bannan leaned in his doorway to watch Tir Half-face shoulder his pack and leave the farm. He refused to think it farewell. Radd Nalynn would take his friend in, he had no doubt. Tir had promised, fervently after the second—or had it been third?—bottle, to return the next day.

If he managed to spend the night in Marrowdell.

The rain had stopped; fat drops lined the roof edge, threatening unwary heads. Though well before sun's set, the lingering heavy clouds hurried twilight and Tir seemed to vanish beneath the old trees between one step and the next. Pouring the dregs of wine on the muddy ground, Bannan said with feeling, "Keep Us Close," and hoped he was heard.

A shadow moved across the farmyard, large and dark.

Scourge. "It's the Bloody Beast!" Bannan cheered rather unsteadily. "Off to watch Tir's back, are you? Good horse!"

The breeze along his cheek was damp and chill. "I do not follow Tir. I go to guard the road as the dragon can't."

Bannan straightened with a jerk, the bottle dropping from his hand. "Guard against what?"

"Those who may come."

If there was a risk—he turned too quickly, cursing as he staggered and had to grab the doorframe. His free hand stabbed past the barn, to where the Tinkers Road curved out of Marrowdell. "Who guards that? The other road."

"There is only one."

Which wasn't right. Well, it was right in a sense, but not right when it came to tactics, though it was unfair to have to argue tactics after—two, yes, two bottles each, which wasn't much for a soldier, but they'd been rushed . . . and maudlin, Tir leaving and all . . . and supper—he hadn't had supper, come to think of it. Tir Half-face could drink like a fish and never show it, which wasn't the point.

The point being tactics. Bannan steadied himself. Why was he arguing tactics with Scourge, who should know better? "You can't," he stated slowly and with extra care, "guard one end of a road and ignore the other. What if they—" he stressed the word, though he'd no clue who "they" might be, other than a worry of his strange not-a-horse companion's that was now his, which wasn't what he'd hoped for in any sense, "—come from there?" Another extravagant stab up the road. There. Perfectly sensible.

"There is no road beyond the valley," Scourge informed him, as if he was supposed to know such things and was being ridiculous. "Not in your Marrowdell. That's the turn-borns' crossing."

There certainly was a road, a well-maintained road, and roads, the truthseer knew, went places, even roads that sometimes flowed like silver water. So did crossings, which was a new word and as distracting as a feather to a kitten, but Bannan held to his concern. Rather than argue and be further confused, he switched targets and waved toward the Spine, the white of its rock stark against the clouds. "What about—what about—that, then? There's something," with conviction, "wrong with that."

"Only to fools who venture there." With amusement.

"Oh. Well, then." Bannan pushed himself straight, keeping a cautionary hand on the wood. "We're fine. You go guard everybody else then. Fine job. Good horse." He really should find the bottle he'd dropped, but it was getting dark. Or was it getting purple?

He blinked owlishly. "Sun's setting," he announced, relieved by how clear the words sounded. When he'd had too much wine, he had trouble letting go of "s's" which was singularly hilarious under the right circumstances and in the right company, but having had too much wine would not be a good thing tonight. Because . . . "I'm here alone," he realized. "Tir'sss left." He licked his lips and tried again. "Tir left and he sent away Jenn. He sent away Jenn!" because it was very important Scourge know.

And the shadow that was Scourge paused.

Encouraged, Bannan heaved a deep, heartfelt sigh. Then another. "Wyll'ssss. . . . gone someplace too. I dunno where. Being a dragon, I sssupposse. Now you—you're leaving me. Isss juss me, now. Me alone. By myself. That's—" he proclaimed with great seriousness, "—alone."

Before Bannan knew what was happening, Scourge was in his face. Without a word, not that words were what the not-horse used, the great beast lowered his head and shoved him, hard, with his nose. "Hey!" As he staggered back into the house, Scourge ducked through the doorway and followed, giving well-timed pushes with his nose until Bannan toppled.

Onto the mattress that was his bed.

"The floor was clean!" he protested.

Scourge was already gone.

As Bannan tried to sit up, something heavy plopped on his chest and pinned him in place. He craned his neck to find himself nose to nostril with the house toad. "The road's not a road," he informed it.

Unimpressed, the toad yawned toothily and settled itself.

Dropping his head back down, Bannan closed his eyes. The bed slowly spun with him in it, a familiar sensation after so much wine, but he found himself strangely content.

The others might leave him.

Marrowdell had not.

When and where families sat to supper in Marrowdell followed a comfortable routine. On days of hard shared labor, such as the harvest, lunch became the heftier meal, taken together close to the work. When families were busy at their own tasks, suppers were their time to gather and share the day's Beholding. The smells emanating from those kitchens could be a torment to anyone tardy to his or her table. Especially, the joke went, if you sniffed what the Ropps had burning on their stove—that family being prone to distraction—before savoring the tantalizing aromas from the Nalynns'.

Jenn wrinkled her nose. There was an aroma coming from Tir Half-face, who sat between her and Peggs, but she wouldn't call it tantalizing.

Aunt Sybb, fingers circled as she prepared to give the Beholding, gave her a glance that meant however a guest might smell was not to be acknowledged in any way.

"Hearts of our Ancestors, we are Beholden for the food on the table, including these uniquely shaped carrots, for it will give us the strength to improve ourselves in your eyes. We are Beholden for the opportunity to share this meal with our guest," Aunt Sybb nodded graciously to Tir, who turned an interesting shade of pink and sat straighter. "We are Beholden for the fine futures our young women have found for themselves—"

Peggs' turn to blush. Jenn folded her hands and held her breath. There was more to come. There had to be. Aunt Sybb had that gleam in her eye.

"—though we most earnestly hope it does not involve toads."

Radd made a small choking noise as he stifled a laugh. Jenn's cheeks grew warm.

"Hearts of our Ancestors," Aunt Sybb finished with satisfaction, "above all, we are Beholden for this time we are together, as family. However far we are apart, Keep—"

Tir surged to his feet, circled fingers over his heart. "Hearts of our Ancestors—!"

He'd arrived a smidge the worse for wear, as their father would say, and it simply wasn't done to interrupt the conclusion of a Beholding, which is why both Jenn and Peggs gave their aunt stunned looks when that gracious lady merely sat back and nodded.

"Hearts of our Ancestors," Tir repeated fervently, "we are Beholden for the fine hospitality shown by this family to someone who'd be served well enough by a spot on the porch, thank you, and scraps, if he deserved that much after—" a prolonged wet sniff, "—after deserting his captain." His voice rose a notch. "Deserted m'friend!"

Jenn eased as far from the impassioned and still-damp Tir as she could without being obvious, seeing Peggs do the same on his other side.

"Keep Us Close," Aunt Sybb prompted.

"'Keep Us Close,'" the rest murmured at once, including Tir who, the Beholding finished for him, hesitated before sinking back down.

"Turnip?" Peggs offered brightly. She'd been quick to add a seat and setting for Tir when he'd appeared at their door with their father just as supper was being laid out, refusing to take no for an answer. A kindness a lesser person might now regret.

"In return for accommodation, Tir's offered to help at the mill," their father announced over the clatter of dishes and serving spoons. He bestowed a pleased look around the table. "His uncle was a miller."

"But—" Jenn closed her mouth. She helped, didn't she? As for the heavier work, Uncle Horst was able and willing.

Radd's eyes twinkled. "I've boasted of your fine touch with the stones, Dear Heart. But we're lucky to have someone of Tir's experience in time for the harvest."

"Spent some years at it." Apparently feeling this a formal affair, Tir had left his axes at the door and wore his mask. To eat, he tipped it from his chin with a finger and adroitly slipped a spoonful behind. Jenn supposed he wasn't planning to drink until alone. "Yon's a fine mill," he complimented when finished chewing. Their father beamed. "Better'n the one at Endshere, 'cepting your water course."

Radd looked a little less pleased.

"More bread for our guest, Peggs," Aunt Sybb suggested.

"Water's the key. Have you thought of building a 'race?" Tir continued doggedly, oblivious to such bids for his attention. "To bring water to the wheel year-round," this to Peggs, who countered with an emphatic thrust of the bread basket. "Mill grain for others. Be a sawmill, off times. There's need." He stabbed his fork at the Nalynn parlor. "You could use some proper planks, if you don't mind my saying. I'd be happy to help."

"My thanks, but there's water aplenty when it's needed," Radd stated. "The mill runs but once a year, to grind our harvest, and we've no need for more, or interest."

Tir's eyes glinted with interest of his own, but he bowed his head. "Fair enough."

The rest of supper passed without incident. Their guest responded courteously to questions but offered nothing of his own. Aunt Sybb, as her habit, filled the silences with little stories of life in Avyo. Her stories tended to be instructive, particularly about the proper deportment of young ladies and the pitfalls of life alone for widowers who waited too long, but Jenn was delighted when tonight was something new. Their aunt regaled them with tales of the steamships that fought their way up the mighty Kotor River to Avyo, bringing cargoes across the Sweet Sea from Eldad, and the great barges, twenty or more linked together, that came down the Mila from the trade city of Essa bearing goods from mysterious Mellynne. In Avyo alone did cargoes from those domains mingle, for Eldad and Mellynne were separated not only by the southern mountain range, steep and impassable, but by their natures. Mellynne was the larger domain, content in its age and accomplishment; Eldad the upstart, pushing ever at boundaries. Only sailors and diplomats routinely traveled between.

Sailors who came through Avyo stayed at inns owned by the

Mahavars, their captains entertained at the home of Hane Mahavar and his lady. Little wonder Aunt Sybb knew their stories so well.

Jenn was enchanted.

Pie came and went. Tea, then another round. Still they sat, round-eyed, listening to tales of piracy, adventure, and the unending, oft-amusing, contests between Avyo's port authority and would-be smugglers.

"Parrots stuffed in a peg leg?" Radd protested with a laugh. "You can't be serious, Sybbie."

His sister's eyes glowed. "Quite serious. The birds fared better than the smuggler. His empty leg was confiscated as evidence."

Tir, who'd begun to slouch in his seat, straightened with a jerk to nod with sudden enthusiasm. "Smugglers always think they've found a foolproof trick," he volunteered. "We'd come across them in the marches, pretending to be shepherds hunting lost sheep or ladies looking for a quick—"

Aunt Sybb raised a finger the slightest degree, halting Tir midsentence. "Brother," she said equably, "I do believe the rain's stopped. Might our guest join us for a convivial glass on the porch? I'd enjoy hearing your experiences," she told Tir, a gently regal command. "Dearest Hearts," this to Peggs and Jenn, "feel free to take your leave. Our thanks for a most satisfying repast."

The sisters nodded at once, but Jenn glanced at Peggs, catching a flash of the same disappointment she felt.

Once their elders had left, they began to clear the table. As Peggs stacked cups on her tray, Jenn sighed. The sun was setting on another day; she felt her emptiness gnaw at her, though she'd had her share of supper and more tea than usual. Tir's stories would be the most interesting ever heard in Marrowdell, she just knew it, and would take her mind off everything, including her middle.

"I don't see why we can't hear his stories," she complained, but quietly. "They treat us like children and we're not."

Her sister pursed her lips then leaned close. "Silly goose. They didn't go out for stories. You saw them. Tir's beyond exhausted and so's Aunt Sybb, despite her nap. They're taking a quiet drink together, hoping to prevent the dreams."

She was a child after all, concerned for herself instead of others. Jenn thought of her earlier wishful belief, that she could simply want the terrible dreams to stop, and flushed. "Is there nothing we can do?"

Peggs' dark eyes were troubled. "Hope with them."

Stone swept upward to either side, its pale surface smooth and featureless except where it rippled uneasily, glistening wet, within her shadow. Jenn reached out and something surged forward to snap at her fingers. With a cry, she staggered back.

She shouldn't be here.

How could she be here?

The sun wasn't shining, yet she could see. She could see, but by a light unfamiliar, that cast her shadow in rainbows and broke over the stone like a wave. Light she could almost taste.

But light wasn't what she wanted.

A cramp flamed across her middle and she pressed her arms over the pain, empty of all but need.

She had to hurry. She had to hurry, or the pebble would be gone!

Which way? Jenn stumbled through bands of mauve shadow and green-gold light, gasping for breath, stumbling. She had to leave Marrowdell to be whole. She must leave.

She broke out into the meadow, which wasn't a meadow and was. She'd gone the wrong way, yet the pebble was here, in Marrowdell. She could see it, white and glistening wet, round as a caught tear and impossible to resist.

As she reached, wind battered her, like giant wingbeats. Wind that drove her to her knees and shrieked in thin wild voices. "STOP!!" "GO BACK!!!" "THE TURN-BORN FORBID IT!!" Wind that shrieked and wailed, as if she frightened what flew beyond reason.

And how could that be, when she was the one who crouched and cried in terror? Whose clenched fist pushed into her middle against agony . . . whose other hand stretched trembling fingers to the pebble . . . the pebble already sinking out of sight because she wasn't fast enough or strong enough or . . .

The ground shook as something pounded it! The wind faltered and fled, wingbeats rising and falling away, shrieks drowned beneath a ROAR!

Then silence.

The pebble sank from sight. Sobbing, Jenn scrambled forward on hands and knees. She plunged both hands into the ground, reaching with all her will and might until her fingertips touched the pebble and, with a sharp cry of triumph, she thought she had it. But it was too smooth and too small to grasp, and slipped from her fingers.

Without the pebble, she was empty. Jenn dropped her forehead to the ground and wept, arms locked in cold, unyielding stone.

"Go back, little one." A new voice spoke, ancient, filled with a dreadful patience. "Cross at the Great Turn. Only then may you be filled."

"I don't understand—" she tried to say, lifting her head to find herself alone.

No, not alone. The Bone Hills were closer, as if they'd moved when she hadn't been looking, their pale stone bulging and wet. They loomed over her and Jenn began to struggle. She had to pull her arms free before they moved again, before they crushed her, before . . .

Something warm and soft nudged her cheek. Breath, not the nicest-smelling but hot and wonderfully alive, stirred her hair. "I'm stuck!" she said desperately, as if it wasn't completely obvious her arms were encased.

"Wake up," the breeze ordered impatiently.

This was a dream?

The relief made her cry a little. Of course it was a dream.

And, in the way of dreams, once noticed, one woke.

Seeing where she was, Jenn screamed.

Bannan's eyes shot open. The thunderclap had been close enough to rattle the pots and he sat up, heart pounding. Where had that come from? It had been a peaceful sort of rain, last night. A little melancholy, but with no anger to it. What was wrong?

As he waited, tense, for the next clap, he saw the house toad in the doorless front entrance. To his deeper sight, it had a disturbingly martial appearance, cloaked in chain mail and braced as if ready for battle. With what?

The truthseer rolled to his feet, biting his lip as his head protested the quick change in elevation. Without making a sound, he eased across the floor to wrap his hand around the broom handle. With an unknown foe, he preferred a weapon with reach.

The toad guarded the front door. Bannan took up his post at the back, staring out at the privy. Small things moved in the hedge beyond, rustling its branches. Moonlight lay at his feet, gilding leaves and stones.

The thunder hadn't come from a storm, he realized with a chill.

It had been Jenn Nalynn.

The thunder was louder than her scream. Jenn cowered, shaking, but gradually regained her wits. She wasn't hurt. She wasn't on the Spine or surrounded by horrible stone.

Or in bed, where she should be.

She was in the carrots.

Buried to her elbows, which wasn't easy to do without a shovel even in rain-softened soil, with carrots to either side. Their fragrant tops tickled her nose. A moth hovered nearby, then two. They seemed amazed by where she was.

Trying not to think of how she could be where she was, Jenn tugged, but her arms didn't budge. She was stuck fast.

In carrots.

"You need a shovel," the breeze in her ear announced unhelpfully.

She looked up to find a great dark shadow against the starred sky. Scourge. Moonlight pooled in two deep scars in the soil near her, scars the size of his front hooves, where he must have reared and pounded down with all his strength. "You chased them away," Jenn said with wonder. "Like you calmed the river." Had the waves been like the wind and driven by wings? "Dragons. They were dragons." Not like Wisp. Dragons who could fly. "They're real?!"

"So are you." An amused snort. "You should be more careful in your sleep."

How was she supposed to do that? And how was she supposed to get out of the carrots, without waking the Nalynn household? This wouldn't be something she could explain to Aunt Sybb. Jenn managed to get first one, then the other knee between her arms, pleased not to rip her nightgown in the process, though it would be filthy. To no avail. No matter how hard she pushed and strained, her forearms stayed buried.

"Shovel."

Jenn sagged. "Which means someone to use it," she said miserably. Someone to witness the spectacle of her buried to her elbows, in the middle of the garden and night, not to mention in her nightgown.

Wainn would help, but he slept in the loft with Kydd. Uncle Horst would tell her father. Tir—he'd tell Bannan, she knew he would.

"Wyll," she whispered with sudden hope. "Can you bring him? Or summon him?" He'd have her free and clean in a heartbeat.

The breeze in her ear turned cold. "Would you risk him for so little? Dragons still rage nearby."

Moonlight bathed the Nalynn yard, finding nothing more exotic than the garden, privy, and hedge, but Jenn didn't doubt him. Not Wyll, then.

A house toad hopped into a patch of moonlight, gave her a dismissive look, then tipped its body to gaze up at Scourge.

The beast shook his great head as if annoyed by flies. "This little cousin claims help is on the way. I suggest," with dark humor, "you wait for it."

"Don't go—!"

But he was already trotting soundlessly away.

Jenn looked at the toad. "What sort of help?"

In answer, it sat and stared at her.

The vigil of man and toad continued, though only the latter knew what the vigil was for and the former had begun to stare longingly at the privy, standing in plain sight. Finally, Bannan couldn't wait. "I'll be right back," he whispered.

The farmyard was empty of all but a few moths, none of which appeared to have satchels. Nonetheless, Bannan kept a wary eye around him. One step. Two.

A warning croak!

Without hesitation, he dove for the ground with the broom against his body, rolling over and over before coming up to one knee and raising his flimsy weapon in defense.

A gust of wind rocked him. Bannan shifted to face it, only to be buffeted from the opposite side. He crouched lower, offering a smaller target. Wyll's tricks, but where was the dragon? The moonlight was generous and bright; he should be able to see him.

Another gust almost toppled him. The truthseer whirled around, broom swishing through empty air.

Desperate, he looked beyond the moonlight. There. And there. Glimpses, blurred at that, for what he strained to perceive was in constant motion. Man-sized, but not man-shaped. More than one, but he couldn't tell if three or fifty flew about. For they flew.

Through more than air. He was knocked over as something more substantial than wind rose through the ground to bump him aside.

Dragons!

Bannan held the broom by one end and gauged his moment, then swung with all his strength. The broom struck and shattered!

The wind stopped.

The glimpses were gone.

The farmyard was empty again.

Shaken, the truthseer tossed aside the remnants of the broom, rubbing his palms to ease the impact's sting. "Ancestors Daft and Idiotic." Could he be more a fool? He should have pretended confusion. Better yet, he should have ignored the wind gusts, made his way to the privy, and shut the door. Now the dragons knew something about their new neighbor.

He could see them.

Come morning, Bannan resolved, he was going to have a long talk with the dragon he knew.

Moonlight silvered Wen's wild hair and shone white over her nightdress. It missed her face, but glittered in the eyes of the house toads at her feet. Four of them. Under their stern regard, though she didn't know why, Jenn felt such guilt her glad greeting choked in her throat.

Wen stepped past the toads and went on her knees between the rows of carrots and beans. Lit, her face showed only mild interest. "Are you held or holding?"

"I'm—just buried," Jenn whispered. "Please help me. Did you bring a shovel?"

A small smile. "I brought better." She rose and moved aside. "They may scratch," she warned. "Hold very still."

" 'Scratch?' " Before Jenn could protest—for what good it would do, since Scourge had deserted her and she couldn't raise her voice without disturbing everyone—the house toads hopped beside her arms and started to dig.

Their clawed feet made quick work of the soil. Jenn closed her eyes and averted her face as best she could, trying not to flinch as yes, the occasional claw found her skin. But overall, they were careful and soon she was free.

Jenn sat back and wiped dirt from her fingers on her already filthy hem, eyeing the house toads. They squatted in front of her and eyed her back, their huge dark pupils giving them clear advantage. The largest had a familiar pattern of raised bosses and warts on its head, and she nodded a respectful greeting to the Nalynns' particular guardian.

It blinked.

That Wen talked to toads no longer seemed an oddness. "Thank you," Jenn said to the four, then looked up at the silent woman. "Do they understand what I say?"

"Of course. They also understand what happened and aren't happy. They protect the village. You put it in danger." Wen tilted her head as if listening. "There's no crossing here. You tried to make one. You mustn't do that again."

"I—" It was Jenn's turn to blink. The house toads didn't. Two opened their immense mouths, baring needle teeth. "How? I had a dream—"

"Because you went where you shouldn't." Wen offered a hand to help Jenn to her feet. "There are always consequences, Jenn Nalynn."

Her hand was cool and strong; Jenn didn't let go. "Help me," she pleaded, heart in her throat. She'd endangered Marrowdell. How could that be? She shivered; the night wasn't warm after all. "I can't hurt anyone. I don't understand how I could, but I wouldn't. I mustn't! Please. What must I do?" Tears filled her eyes. "How can I stop a dream? If I can't—if I'm dreaming like Aunt Sybb or Tir—I have to leave Marrowdell. But if I leave, they say I'll die. I don't—I don't want to die."

Something touched her. Jenn looked down to find the Nalynn house toad had placed its clawed foot over hers. The others gazed upward, their faces impossible to read.

"They say," Wen told her gently, "you should hope. The Great Turn is coming."

To hear the words from her dream made hairs rise along Jenn's bare arms. "What is it?"

"When all appears as it truly is, and anything is possible." Wen, who was taller, stooped to gaze into Jenn's eyes. "You've such a good heart. Rest lightly, Jenn Nalynn. Your dreams are your doing, not Marrowdell's." She bestowed a light kiss on Jenn's forehead, then smiled. "Find something safer to wish for, little one, before you close your eyes. And hope. Your time is soon."

Comforted, if no less bewildered, Jenn promised, "I will," and found herself yawning.

Wen walked away without another word, moonlight flowing through her wild hair. The toads had left when she wasn't looking, though an alarmed squeak from the hedge suggested they, too, had gone back to their nature.

"I don't understand any of this," Jenn whispered. But if toads could talk and a dream plant her with the carrots?

Anything must be possible.

Including, she yawned again, sleep. Before going in, Jenn cleaned the soil from her hands and arms as best she could without water, and brushed her sadly stained nightdress. On tiptoe, she snuck through the kitchen, avoiding the creaky plank, and climbed the ladder to the loft. Though so tired her bones hurt, an impulse stopped her partway up.

Moving as quietly as she could, though it was unlikely anyone would hear footsteps over their father and aunt's dueling snores, Jenn climbed down. She took the pebble jar from beside the fireplace and tiptoed outside again.

As if she'd imagined it, as if a dream, all was normal. A lamp burned at the Emms; the baby still woke for a late feeding, and Gallie used the time to write. Moonlight and shadow sculpted nothing more alarming than the hedge, larder door, and privy. Small things rustled at a distance, doing whatever small things did by night.

Without a whisper of dragons.

Had she imagined it? With a thrill of hope, she looked toward the garden.

Carrots lay strewn across three rows, and dark soil scarred the ground. There were holes—

Jenn tore her eyes away. Her body wanted to tremble. Her hands did and she focused on her nails, which would need a thorough scrub in the morning, and her task. She tipped the jar's contents onto the plank beside the wash tub and, by moonlight, sorted out the white ones, putting the rest back. She divided the result into four piles of three.

Little enough thanks for what the toads had done, but all she knew to do.

Satisfied, Jenn went up to the loft. As quietly as she could, she stripped out of her filthy nightgown and pulled on a clean one, then slipped under the quilt. Peggs mumbled something and rolled over, taking most of the bedding with her. Jenn tugged her share back and settled, staring up at the rafters.

Wish for something safe, Wen had told her.

So with all her heart, Jenn Nalynn wished for a lovely morning, with sunshine and dew on the asters and birds singing.

Then closed her eyes, to sleep without dreams.

The next morning dawned so blue and bright, so full of birdsong and busy bees, Bannan had to laugh. "Thank you, Jenn Nalynn," he told the sky. After a quick wash and shave, he filled a bucket for breakfast, eager to start the day.

Inside, he started a fire in his new stove, holding his breath until the flame caught, then set his makeshift table for one. He pushed the second of his new stools aside, along with his worries about Tir. The man was resourceful. If anyone could find a way to stay in Marrowdell, he would.

While water boiled for tea, Bannan laid a thick slice of ham to sizzle in his new skillet, only to stop midmotion as breezes chuckled through the room, collecting a plate, finding a knife, fork, and cup, then arranging them neatly at the table across from his. Bannan reached for more ham, grinning to himself.

Company, after all.

"Fair morning, dragon."

"It appears so, truthseer." Wyll lurch-stepped through the door. He'd slept outdoors by the creases and bits of moss on his clothes, and badly, by the dark circles beneath his eyes. His hair needed a comb, though his short beard was neatly trimmed—or was it always the same?—and he'd either washed or had his breezes scrub his skin. "Be grateful."

"For such a morning," Bannan inquired, at once wary. "Or something more?" Involving his escape from dragons, perhaps?

Wyll's eyes glittered, but all he said was, "This is Marrowdell. Where's the warrior?"

"Tir spent the night in the village." Bannan found himself unwilling to say more, not until he knew for sure.

Wyll, for a wonder, accepted the statement. "I slept in my new home," he announced with a casual air the truthseer didn't believe for an instant.

His heart sank. "You've built it?" His house didn't have doors yet.

"Yes." A breeze shifted the discarded stool back into position. "There's more to be done before it's fit for Jenn Nalynn."

Which wasn't quite the truth. Bannan hid his relief. "I take it 'more' includes a kitchen, since you're in mine."

"Perhaps I prefer your cooking."

"You'd be the first to say so," with a chuckle as he sliced potatoes and an onion into the pan. "Tir's convinced I can burn anything."

"Do you?"

"Not if I'm paying attention."

Wyll nodded, and perched on his stool. "Then I will not distract you."

Moments later, Bannan felt an unexpected glow of pride as he slid fragrant ham and crisped vegetables onto Wyll's plate, then his own. "Sorry there's no eggs."

Wyll glanced at the house toad, dozing in a sunny spot near the bed. The creature woke with a startled croak and took a prodigious hop out the door. "A duty neglected," the dragon said dryly. "There'll be eggs for lunch."

So they'd be sharing all their meals. Well, Bannan decided cheerfully, the coin for that would be information.

Once seated, he raised his mug and took a welcome swallow, then regarded Wyll over its rim. "Speaking of duty, Scourge spent the night guarding the village. Against what?"

"That's your first question?" Wyll appeared amused.

Bannan lifted a brow. Today was to be blunt, was it? "What should I ask, then?"

The dragon sipped his tea. "Are you not curious concerning eggs and toads?"

"Tir's explained why I haven't seen a chicken." He set down his cup. "I have, however, seen dragons. Last night. Friends of yours?"

Wyll tackled his meal, one hand wielding the knife, the fork as deftly handled by air alone. "I have no friends," with such calm certainty pity was impossible. "I trust you did nothing foolish."

"Smacked one with a broomstick." The truthseer stabbed a morsel of ham and demonstrated.

"I wondered at the haste of their crossing." Wyll almost smiled. "You've courage, Bannan Larmensu. Not much sense, but courage."

He shrugged. "Trust me, I regretted the impulse. But they left."

"Not," the dragon now a man cautioned, "because of you. It's—unlucky—to attract the notice of those who live in Marrowdell. They feared the consequences."

"You don't." Suddenly they'd arrived at waters of unknown depth, but Bannan could no more quell his curiosity than stop breathing. "Why is that?"

"Are all of you the same, truthseer?" Wyll remained amused. "Possessed of the same strength and abilities? Equally wise or foolish? These were . . ." A pause for tea. "Call them feckless youths, of more heart than brain. They tried to stop the turn-born." A flicker of silver beneath his lashes. "Had they bothered to ask me, I'd have told them they could not."

That name again. Bannan leaned forward. "Who are the turn-born? Scourge said they'd would be here soon. Are they what he guards against?"

Wyll's face went still. "Toads and eggs. Better to ask me about the little cousins, truthseer, and their admirable ways."

Advice, not outright refusal. A test, Bannan judged it. If he backed down now, he'd have let the dragon decide what he should know, so he waited, eyes fixed on Wyll's.

After a long moment, measured by their mismatched breaths and the uncaring trill of a distant bird, Wyll shrugged his good shoulder. "The turn-born? Cursed." He eased his useless arm within his jerkin, as if soothing an ache. "Powerful. We guard the edge on their behalf, not that they're grateful. Or gentle. I'll make you a gift, Bannan Larmensu, in return for this meal. Keep what you see to yourself, in their presence. The turn-born won't be pleased to find one such as you here."

The dragon gave him too much truth at once and dared him to understand. Bannan took a steadying breath, determined to find his way through, then paused, his eyes widening. "'Cursed' and 'powerful.'" He half rose from his stool. "Jenn Nalynn." Almost a whisper.

"Now, at last, you understand." Wyll lifted his cup in mock salute. "The girl is the sole turn-born on this side of the edge, unlike any others of your kind. This is why she must live with me and not you."

"So the dragons—" Bannan sat again, ignoring this last. "When you said they came to stop a turn-born, you meant Jenn. Why? Stop her from what?"

"The girl yearns for what's been forbidden. Her wishes have force, as you've seen." An eloquent gesture at his body.

Bannan narrowed his eyes. "What does she want?"

"To leave Marrowdell." With all innocence.

"To find what she wants," he countered impatiently. "Tell me what I don't know. What's been forbidden? By whom? These other turn-born? Where are they?!"

The dragon shook his head and turned his attention to his plate.

"Do not interfere in matters beyond your grasp, truthseer. What Jenn Nalynn desires is nothing either of us can provide."

The truth.

Bannan fought disappointment. There had to be a way and he'd find it. Wyll wasn't a man, despite appearances. How could he know a woman's heart?

"Perhaps I will show her my house after all," the dragon said smoothly. "When she comes today."

"She won't," Bannan snapped. "Jenn's staying in the village."

Wyll looked stunned. "Whatever for?"

"We've confused her. Ancestors Witness! If you were more than the seeming of a man," he goaded recklessly, "you'd know how hard this is for her."

"I know more of Jenn Nalynn than you ever will!" The dragon's fingers clenched into a fist; the knife folded. "This is your doing!" His eyes flared silver. Wind gusts shook the little house, a threat to the new shingles.

Bannan glared back. "Hardly. I'm to stay here. Tir's to run any errands."

Silver became an unhappy brown; the wind, a fretful whisper in the grass. "For how long?"

For letters to ride forth and be answered, as if letters and a distant sister could defeat dragons and wishes and the power of a heart's longing. For . . . he pushed his hopes aside. "It's up to Jenn Nalynn." Which was the truth.

The two sat in silence, breakfast cooling on their plates.

Until Bannan remembered the question unanswered, and his eyes shot to Wyll's.

"What does Scourge guard against?"

"Up you get, slugabed," Peggs said cheerfully. "It's a lovely morning."

No, it wasn't. Jenn snuggled deeper.

With a whoosh! the bedclothes were pulled off. "Muummfph!" she objected, keeping her eyes closed.

"Up!" Her sister shook the mattress. "I've the best news!" Joy in her voice. "Aunt Sybb's still abed! Sleeping like a baby."

Why was that a surprise? Sleeping was a very good idea. Everyone should be sleeping.

"Ancestors Lazy and Layabout! Jenn, get up. It's time for breakfast."

Her stomach rumbled. "Fine," she murmured into the pillow. "M'm up."

"No, you're not." The next thing Jenn knew, her pillow was whisked from under her head and heartily thumped on her backside.

"Hey!" Thoroughly awake, she grabbed Peggs' pillow, gave a "Whoop!" and launched into battle.

The pillow fight ended with them both on the floor, rosy-cheeked and laughing. "Oh, my," Peggs gasped. "We haven't done that for a while."

Jenn clawed hair from her eyes and mouth. "That'll teach you to steal my pillow."

"It got you up," her sister pointed out. "You don't want to miss this morning."

"It's true, then? Aunt Sybb's sleeping?"

"I doubt it, after the racket we made." But Peggs sighed happily. "It's true. The cider must have done it. I took a peek at her with Poppa and she couldn't look more peaceful."

At the mere thought, Jenn yawned.

"You, on the other hand, don't seem to have slept at all. What happened last night?"

"Last night?" Remembering, Jenn rose and began gathering the sheets. "We went to bed. I slept."

"Dearest Heart, you smell like carrots and your nightdress—the one on the floor—needs a boil in soap." Peggs' eyebrow lifted. "Tell me how that happens in bed."

She hesitated, hands full of sheets.

Her sister's gaze sharpened. "Jenn?"

"I will," Jenn decided abruptly. Couldn't her sister make sense out of anything? And, other than her unfortunate reaction to Wyll's powers, which was only because she'd worried about Kydd, and the overdoing of pies, only because, again, of Kydd, wasn't her sister the calmest, most reliable person in Marrowdell? "It happened in the garden," she began earnestly. Roses peered in the open window.

Peggs waited for the rest, a quizzical look on her dear face. "The garden?" she prompted.

Jenn took a deep breath. "The garden. I must have walked in my sleep. When I awoke, I was outside. I was—I found myself back on the Spine, or thought I was." She pushed forward, the words spilling out. "I was there because I needed something, and that's where it was. Or so I thought. Something I've needed desperately all summer; something," she finished with triumph, "that isn't in Marrowdell."

Peggs sat on the unmade bed, eyes wide. "What?"

"I don't know." Jenn sat too. "Last night, it looked like a white pebble."

Her sister's forehead creased. "Like the toads'?"

"No. Yes. But, different. It wasn't a real pebble. When I tried to pick it up, it sank into the ground, like it did the time before. When I went up the Spine." She gave Peggs an apologetic look. "I'd have told you, but I thought it was over."

"But it wasn't."

"No. Last night, the pebble was here. In our garden. Somehow I reached after it when it sank, but dragons stopped me before I could touch it and . . ." She continued with the rest, Peggs not interrupting, though her face went so white, her eyes were like dark holes themselves.

". . . the house toads dug me out," Jenn finished, turning her forearms to show the scratches.

Her sister sat very still. Too still. "I know it sounds like a dream," Jenn pleaded, "or a nightmare, but I swear . . ."

Peggs lifted a finger, just like Aunt Sybb when she wanted to forestall an interruption to her train of thought.

Jenn closed her mouth and waited anxiously.

Finally, her sister blinked and gave a brisk little nod. "Well and well again, Dear Heart."

This being far from the reaction she'd expected, Jenn blinked too. "Really?"

"Of course. We know how to keep you safe and out of the carrots. That's the first and most important thing. And Wen said it. We've hope!" She leaned forward to grip Jenn's hands. "Don't you see? The Golden Day."

Jenn, who didn't see at all, frowned. "My birthday or the weddings?"

"Neither!" Peggs had that gleam in her eye, the one that meant she'd decided on a course and wasn't about to be swayed. Kydd would come to recognize it, without doubt. "It can't be coincidence. An eclipse on the equinox? It must be this 'Great Turn.'"

Saying a thing with certainty didn't, Jenn was sure, make it so. Still, "Even if you're right," she said doubtfully, "what does that mean?"

"It means . . . it means . . ." Peggs sagged. "I don't know what it means," she admitted. "But it has to be important. The voice promised you could get your answer at the Great Turn and Wen said anything was possible then. Anything!" She squeezed Jenn's hands. "What if you can be rid of the curse? Find whatever it is you need so badly?"

Jenn's heart lifted. "Oh, Peggs." Thirteen days left. Too few a brief moment ago; all too many now. "How can I wait that long?"

Her sister's cheeks grew spots of pink. "I feel the same, Dear Heart, believe me, but we must be patient." Belying her own advice, Peggs released Jenn and surged to her feet, gathering the sheets so Jenn had to jump to her feet too. "Patient and careful," she said, plumping a pillow. "I'm glad you've decided to stay home. You must keep from that dreadful path. And we need to learn everything we can about the eclipse and this Great Turn."

"The equinox matters to the tinkers," Jenn mused aloud as she helped make the bed. "Maybe they know about the eclipse and—and about the rest. I could ask Mistress Sand." Her tent was Jenn's second home during the harvest; they'd sit and weave baskets from dried reedgrass, the soft-voiced tinker woman curious about what had happened in the village since the last harvest. Everything fascinated Mistress Sand, from the escapades of the piglets to Roche's latest prank, and Jenn made sure to tell her everything, except for Wisp and her meadow. Not because she didn't trust Mistress Sand, but because the other cared about the ordinary, not the extraordinary.

Having remembered that, Jenn went on glumly, "Though I doubt she can help."

"They won't be here till harvest anyway." Pausing, Peggs brought a lock of hair near her lips, then brightened. "But there's someone else in Marrowdell. Someone who knows about wishings and magic."

"But Bannan won't be here for days." Realization dawned. "You mean Kydd." Jenn pulled the quilt straight to hide her unease.

"Who else?" Her sister's growing excitement didn't help. "He had that book, didn't he? He may have more. I'm certain he will. He'll want to help, Dearest Heart."

Books their father and Aunt Sybb hadn't wanted in the village, if only in Wainn's clever head, being worried about some "old trouble." There were, Jenn thought distractedly, enough new ones.

Besides. Why would the village beekeeper, who painted for a hobby and wooed her sister with such awkward gentleness, own books of magic in the first place?

What had Kydd Uhthoff studied in Avyo?

Reading her face too well, Peggs sank down on the bed. "You don't want me to tell him."

"I'm not ready," Jenn evaded. "I'm sure Kydd would want to help. Maybe he can. But please, Peggs, let's not say anything, to anyone. Not yet." She added in a lighter tone, "After all, a sister-by-marriage who craves rocks and dreams herself into the carrots? I wouldn't blame Kydd for thinking less of me."

"I would!" By the fire in her beautiful eyes, Peggs was prepared to confront dragons, let alone her betrothed. "You're first in my heart, and always will be. I won't marry anyone so shallow!"

Poor Kydd was awash in dire straits, quite undeservedly. "You don't mean that, Peggs," Jenn protested.

"I certainly do."

What had Aunt Sybb said once? " 'The more you hold in your heart . . .' " Jenn quoted, and waited.

" '. . . the more your heart can hold.' " As she'd hoped, the fire in her sister's eyes subsided. Peggs pressed her hands to her heart. "You're right. Ancestors Witness, Kydd would never think less of you, Dearest Heart. I should know that by now." She almost smiled. "And it's true, what Aunt Sybb told us. I wouldn't have thought it possible, but once Kydd and I—once we knew how we both felt, my love for you and Poppa and Aunt Sybb grew so much—I swear I could burst, right now."

"Please don't," Jenn advised practically, though her own heart felt the same ache. Families looked after one another; she just wasn't ready to test the mettle of Kydd Uhthoff as part of theirs. "If things get worse," she temporized, "or if I need help, I'll go to Kydd with you that very moment and tell him everything."

Peggs looked relieved. "Promise?"

"Hearts of our Ancestors." Jenn retrieved her pillow from the floor. "What say we get breakfast? I'm famished."

The sisters placed their pillows on the bed at the same time.

Their eyes met.

"We'll be—" Peggs started.

"—married soon," Jenn finished.

Married, and no longer sharing this room, with its cozy window seat and memories. Most likely, Kydd would move in here, while she'd go to Wyll's new house.

"Dearest Heart—"

Before Peggs could say another word and have them both in tears and not at breakfast, Jenn seized her pillow and grinned.

"Defend yourself!"

The two hurried downstairs, trying to stop giggling.

"Who won?" inquired their father, with a grin.

"I did—"

"Did not!"

Radd Nalynn chuckled. "I declare a draw, for breakfast's sake. Go sit with your aunt. She's—" His lower lip developed a suspicious tremor and he coughed to cover it. "Go on with you," he ordered. "Wait. Take your porridge. I'm serving today."

Jenn and Peggs kissed him on his fresh-scrubbed cheeks, then hurried into the parlor.

"Fair morning," their aunt said in greeting.

Aunt Sybb looked more than rested. She looked radiant, with a rare color to her cheeks and lips. The sisters impulsively put down their bowls and hugged her, Jenn for her part trying not to sniffle. "What's all this?" their aunt chided, but fondly. "Sit now, and let me have my tea."

They sat, smiling at one another and their aunt. Aunt Sybb didn't quite smile, but gave them a benevolent look over her cup. She'd chosen the cream shirtwaist today, with its minimal lace, and wore her no-nonsense dark blue skirt. "I trust you're both ready for a busy day."

The spoon Peggs was using to dollop honey into her porridge paused midair. "Kydd and I'd planned a picnic—" She closed her lips over what was, for her, tantamount to an outburst, and gave a dutiful nod.

"A good start makes the best finish," Aunt Sybb announced primly, though her eyes twinkled. "You and your young men will have your whole lives together. Ancestors Blessed and Bountiful, we've much to prepare before that begins."

"Yes, Aunt," Jenn murmured with Peggs.

Their father arrived, his bowl of steaming porridge in one hand, a plate of slippery poached eggs in the other. He'd tucked a loaf under one arm and gripped a biscuit between his teeth. Jenn deftly rescued the eggs and Peggs the loaf as he sat, preventing catastrophe.

"Peckish, Brother?" Aunt Sybb inquired, her brow as high as Jenn had ever seen.

"Stocking up." Radd chuckled and waved the biscuit. "Today's the day, Sybbie."

"We're setting the stones?" Jenn sat up eagerly, then glanced at their aunt and sank back.

Peggs toyed with her spoon, head down.

"What's the matter, Dear Hearts?" Their father looked to their aunt. "Sybbie?"

"Ancestors Patient and Put Upon." Aunt Sybb waved her napkin at them, pretending to be exasperated. "Go. But you'll be working late and by lamplight."

This time, there was considerably more enthusiasm in the sisters' "Yes, Aunt!"

"Fools," Wyll replied, spearing a piece of ham. "He guards against fools."

The dragon's answers were slippery bits of truth. "Where's the harm in fools?" Bannan asked easily.

Silver flickered deep in Wyll's eyes. "Who would you fear coming to Marrowdell?"

"Ansnans." The name erupted from his throat. Heart's Blood, where had that rage come from? Discomfited, Bannan stood and retrieved the kettle. They were at peace. He was at peace.

And civilized. "Tea?"

Wyll's smile was unpleasant. "So you have enemies."

"I fought a war." However undeclared and thankless. "It's over. I'm a farmer now, not a soldier. Tea?"

"Who attacks dragons with a broom."

"Old habits. Let me pour for you." As he did, Bannan vowed, "I'll be more polite to such visitors in future."

"You'd be wiser to hide." Wyll shifted uncomfortably, then stood with a frustrated snarl. "My thanks for breakfast. I've work to do." He began to lurch away.

"Wait."

Wyll paused, twisting his head to look around. A demonstration of strength, standing upright at that moment, wildly off balance and with only one trustworthy leg. Strength and determination beyond any man's.

"Why should we fear fools?"

"Because what they would seek here," the dragon answered, "must never be found."

Once he was gone, Bannan discovered the sturdy squared logs of his house no longer seemed sturdy at all.

While Peggs heated water for dishes, Jenn nipped out to the privy. On her way back, she paused to check the garden. The holes and hoofprints had been filled, the carrots replanted in their row, more-or-less straight. A valiant effort, she assumed by the house toads, to hide the evidence. Alas, being carrots, they'd taken offense at being ousted from the soil and their tops had wilted. Rather than have Peggs notice and worry what might have happened, Jenn pulled the wilted ones out, leaving them to dry.

The pebbles were gone, she saw, and began to smile.

Her smile faded. In their place lay a rose, its stem neatly snapped. Dew sparkled like gems on the red velvet petals, and one leaf arched behind like a cradling hand.

Their mother's rose. She couldn't see the toads picking it. Had Wyll? Obscurely comforted, Jenn looked around, but saw no sign of him.

Well, she couldn't leave the rose lying out here. She took it up with care and brought it inside. "Look."

Peggs' eyes widened in wonder. She quickly dried her hands, following Jenn and the rose into the parlor.

"Ancestors Blessed!" their aunt said fervently.

Jenn laid the rose on the table. Fragrance filled the room like the deep toll of a bell. "I'm sorry, Poppa. I think Wyll did it."

He didn't appear upset. In fact, he looked rather pleased. "Why don't you take it to your mother?"

She swallowed, but nodded.

Back in the kitchen, the glorious rose in a most ordinary mug of water, Jenn whispered to Peggs, "Did you say anything to him—about my sharing with the Ancestors?"

"Not a word." Her sister looked unusually serious. "But maybe this wasn't Wyll. Maybe it's some kind of sign. An offer of help."

Jenn pushed her shoulder into Peggs' and dried another dish. "The Ancestors don't do that sort of thing."

"It's not as if we know," the other retorted, passing her a dripping spoon. "Once I'm among the Blessed, I'll want to help you."

"Hush!" Jenn hurried to press her hands—plus cloth and wet spoon—to her heart. "Hearts of our Ancestors, we'd be Beholden if you'd ignore my sister." With asperity, "You shouldn't say such a thing."

"Well, I would."

"Would what?" Tir Half-face leaned in the kitchen door.

Even with his metal mask, she could tell. His eyes were bright and bold. "You slept!"

"That I did, Jenn Nalynn, like a babe. I'm here to thank your father and offer my help before I head to the farm."

"Breakfast first," Peggs informed him, and bustled about filling him a tray.

"I'm glad," Jenn told Tir, and was. Both he and Aunt Sybb looked more themselves this morning, though admittedly their aunt, buoyed by the prospect of weddings, might not need sleep at all.

It was as lovely a morning as she could wish.

If she left out the slightly anxious part where she was now to head to the ossuary and confess to the Ancestors, best done before going to the mill, because their father would ask about the rose, without doubt.

And if she thought very positively, as Aunt Sybb would say, about having promised to stay in the village and leave Wyll alone while he settled, though she missed him and Night's Edge more than she could say and she could only hope the toad had given him her message.

Though she wondered, with perfectly normal and natural

curiosity, how Bannan was today, without Tir, and if he was content or lonely.

Most of all, if she ignored the small but growing and nasty feeling that she really mustn't cross the river and take the road and be anywhere near the path that led . . .

"Kind of you to say." Jenn blinked as the former border guard ducked his head in a self-conscious sort of bow, then held out a wrapped packet, his broad thumb trapping a coin against the darkened leather. "I'd like to send these letters. Your father said someone would be off to Endshere today. I can pay."

Letters. Jenn perked up. She hadn't thought of letters. She could write to Wyll and explain why she wasn't there, because he'd worry and fuss; she just knew he would. And—

"Keep your coin," her sister advised him. "We've an arrangement with the postmistress in Endshere. She's fond of our honey."

He leaned on the doorframe. "You send much mail?"

"A fair amount. The next bag goes with Uncle Horst before the harvest," Peggs chatted easily as she scooped porridge into a bowl. "Frann writes articles on weaving. She's had some published by her guild. Master Dusom corresponds with the university in Avyo. Gallie Emms keeps in touch with her publisher. Oh, and every fall, Lorra Treff sends her letter to the prince."

Tir's eyes narrowed. "What about?"

He thought of Bannan, Jenn realized with a jolt. Of how important it was that no one in Vorkoun—or anywhere with people who traveled and talked—learn a Larmensu had been the truthseer among the border guard. Hadn't Bannan asked her to keep his talent from the tinkers, who certainly went outside Marrowdell? He'd understood that risk; she should have.

Well, she did now. "Lorra calls the prince names and tells him how to rule Rhoth," she explained quickly. "Don't worry. Davi burns the letters without her knowing. Please don't say anything."

She saw the curve of Peggs' smile. So it wasn't a secret. Few things seemed to stay that way long in Marrowdell. Well, no matter what it took, Jenn decided, Bannan's past would. Not that anyone here loved the Rhothan prince, but there was no sense being careless.

Jenn took the packet, but not the coin, from Tir. "I'll put this with Father's," she promised, then looked up. "Would you do me a favor?" she asked shyly. "Would you kindly take a letter from me, when you go to the farm?" As a gleam appeared, she added hastily. "For Wyll."

"Only Wyll?" Behind his mask, Tir was grinning at her. She knew it. "So you've made up your mind, then?"

Her cheeks flamed.

Peggs, ever her ally, pressed the filled tray into his hands. "Why don't you take this on the porch, Tir? We'll let Poppa know you're here."

"That'd be most kind." He slipped out the door, leaving Jenn with her mouth half-open, then stuck his masked face in through the kitchen window. "Write your love letter, girl. I'll take it this afternoon."

The outrageous man vanished from sight before Jenn could do more than close her mouth.

" 'Love letter.' "

"Nothing of the kind," she denied hotly, still flustered. "I left without—it's not fair to—I—"

Peggs chuckled. "I think it's a wonderful idea."

Jenn gave her a suspicious look. "You do?"

At her most innocent, her sister took the leather packet and handed her the drying towel. "Of course. What is it Aunt Sybb says?" she mused. "Ah, yes. 'The spoken word's a chancy thing, but in his letters, you'll find a man's heart.' They'll write back. You'll see."

Jenn wasn't sure Wyll could write, though she shouldn't underestimate him. "I didn't say I'd write Bannan as well."

"Oh, but you must." A contented sigh. "Letters are so romantic."

"You write them, then," Jenn glowered.

Peggs pulled a slip of well-folded paper from her bodice. "I do." She fanned the note under her sister's nose. "Kydd's wonderfully eloquent." Jenn tried to snatch it, but her bright-eyed sister was too quick. "Some things are not for sharing," she stated firmly, tucking away her prize. "Write and you shall receive."

"I'm not writing love letters," Jenn repeated firmly. "To either of them!"

Though she wouldn't mind receiving one of her own, to see what it was like.

The village gate stood open to the road. It preferred being open, having old hinges and a rickety middle. Closing it did nothing to hinder escaped piglets anyway, and anything larger, with a mind to, could push it flat.

Past the open gate, the road flowed from Jenn Nalynn's feet to the trout path, to the bend, to wherever else it was inclined to go. Later today, it would take Uncle Horst and Roche, as well as Tir's letters, to Endshere, for the two went to arrange for Aunt Sybb's escort after the harvest. Riding back, they'd meet the twins and help bring the livestock home for the winter. Marrowdell was starting to feel the season's change and stir.

For once, Jenn didn't care about the season or the road, having another, closer destination in mind.

The path to the ossuary led off to her left, tidy and raked smooth, but narrow. By this time of year, the hedge became a little uppity, as Aunt Sybb would call it, and soon Master Dusom or Zehr would take a day to trim back the intruding growth.

Jenn didn't mind. The shadowed path was cool and peaceful, crisscrossed by single-minded bees and the odd spiderweb, and it was easy to duck under the branches. She needed the peace. Writing took more time and invention than she'd realized, particularly with Aunt Sybb keeping an eye on her handwriting.

Tiny birds hopped between the leaves, too busy stuffing themselves with berries to startle, and a butterfly with yellow spots landed on the flower in her hand, unrolling its long black tongue for a taste.

Melusine's rose.

The path opened on the patch of ground the villagers had claimed for their dead, carpeted in low-growing flowers. Moss surrounded the flat stones beneath the bench at one end and a grove of old trees softened the rock wall behind, their leaves rustling in the gentle breeze.

Sunlight shone through the sigils, casting the names of the Blessed on petal and leaf. Jenn laid the rose gently within her mother's. At the Midwinter Beholding, all was beneath a blanket of snow, and, to be honest, the younger villagers, herself included, struggled to stand quietly during the ritual and not stamp their booted feet to warm chilled toes, the feast and dance to follow being of greater interest.

Not so today. Today was a lovely morning.

Today she needed more than ritual. She needed to be heard and answered.

Answers. Jenn lifted her hands to let the sun write "Melusine" across her palms. Questions overwhelmed her. Dreams and dragons. Crossings and carrots. The Great Turn and the Ancestors' Golden Day . . .

What had their mother been like, before her nineteenth birthday?

A fine young lady of Avyo, of course, but what did that mean? Aunt Sybb's stories painted a life of appropriate behavior and proper protocol, which was well and good in public, but surely Melusine had her private moments and joys. Had she a place like Night's Edge? Had she other suitors? When had she fallen in love with Radd Nalynn?

How had she known he was the one?

It was terribly inconvenient, not to have those answers.

Or a mother.

Jenn brought her hands to her heart, giving Melusine's name back to the rose. She was here, she reminded herself, to share with the Ancestors, not complain about what couldn't be.

"Ancestors Dear and Departed," she began in a small, carefully solemn voice, "I suppose I'd better start with the wishing. That's pagan magic." Which the Ancestors would know, as they'd know about the books in the hives, and Uncle Horst and Melusine, and the secrets and hopes of everyone stretching back through time itself. Though they'd likely have to wait till midwinter to learn about Hettie and her baby-to-come, and she doubted Wyll would be inclined to share at all, having been a dragon and thus having no Rhothan Ancestors to listen.

Her wits were thistledown and clouds.

She composed herself. "The wishing wasn't Peggs' fault or Wainn's or anyone else's. I was the one who wanted—"

"Oh."

Jenn looked up at the little gasp to find Riss Nahamm standing in the hedge. Well, not in the hedge so much as come through it. Since the yard behind Wagler Jupp's house was on the other side of the hedge, where Riss hung laundry and tended a small garden, she was the most reasonable person to come through but . . . the hedge was there for a reason. Not even Wainn's old pony could force himself past those thick branches.

"I'm sorry, Jenn. I heard someone and—I'll leave you be." As Riss retreated the way she'd come, Jenn could see the thick branches had been cut away, leaving only thin ones, like a curtain. It was very cleverly done, though why anyone would want a secret door to the ossuary when there was a perfectly good path, she couldn't imagine.

"I'm not sure why I'm here anyway," Jenn admitted.

Riss paused, her long fingers lingering on the leaves. "It's a good place," she said softly, with a little smile.

Perhaps the secret door was for quick visits to her cousin, the way their father visited their mother. The ossuary was secluded for more than the peace of the Ancestors and living with Old Jupp had to be wearing at times.

Though that didn't explain why Riss wore her hair loose at this hour of the morning, nor the spray of pretty white flowers tucked above one delicate ear, nor did a visit to the Ancestors require a rolled blanket under one arm, since the bench was right there.

As for that lively sparkle in her eyes? Just like the one in Peggs' when she'd shown her love letter?

She didn't, Jenn decided, want to know. "I'll leave," she offered hastily.

"No need, Dear Heart." Spotting the rose, Riss came forward as if drawn. "That's Melusine's," she said with surprise. "I didn't know you could pick them."

"It picked itself." And had, as far as Jenn knew.

Riss smiled and briefly bent to touch a petal, her unbound hair rippling across her back like a red satin cloak edged in white. "I should have guessed. That's how it came to Marrowdell in the first place." At Jenn's expression, she chuckled. "Have you not heard the story? Of Melusine and this rose?"

The two had been close friends before she was born. Had the Ancestors listened? Jenn wasn't sure they did anything more than that, but it did seem remarkable to immediately find someone who could answer her questions.

"Not that one," she said eagerly. "Aunt Sybb told us how mother had to flee Avyo, because her family didn't approve of our father." Jenn hesitated, but it had been secret only from her and Peggs. "And about Uncle Horst."

Riss gave her a keen look. "He couldn't love you more. You must know that."

Jenn nodded, warm inside. For some reason, the sun grew a little brighter and warmer, as if it had slipped from behind a faint, high cloud. In the glade, it felt more like midsummer and perfume from the rose filled the air.

"Ah, the rose." Riss paused for an appreciative sniff. "Say what you will about them, the Semanaryas had a gift for roses. They grew them everywhere on their estate. This one climbed the wall outside Melly's bedroom. Handily so." She chuckled. "Before they were married, she'd nip out her window and down its trellis to meet your father, with none the wiser."

"So that's why she brought the rose," Jenn concluded happily. Could it be more romantic than this? "As a sign of their love."

"Not exactly." Riss' eyes shone. "She didn't bring the rose. The rose chose to come."

"Pardon?"

"You've heard Melusine's family tricked her into coming home that night, locking her in her old room?" At Jenn's nod, she continued, "Melusine packed what she could carry—having little Peggs, as well—and nipped out the window neat as could be. Only it wasn't a simple thing, climbing with such burdens and in formal dress, and she slipped. The roses caught her." A dimple showed. "Melly said the worst of it was trying not to swear while she pulled herself free of the thorns. Someone might have heard, you see."

Jenn winced in sympathy, having pricked herself more than once.

"She met your father and they fled through the gates," Riss went on. "It wasn't until they were well away from the city that Radd had a chance to tell her she had twigs tangled in her hair. Melly claimed the rose had escaped with her, and deserved a new home too. A better home. They certainly grew well. We all loved them." Her face grew thoughtful. "They were something of home."

Riss had been young then. Young and beautiful, with suitors and prospects and a full life ahead. Until that same night. "Have you been happy here?" asked Jenn without thinking, then blushed. "I'm sorry. I shouldn't—"

"Dear Heart, you should." Emphatically. "Sometimes we talk about the past as if it matters more than the present, and it doesn't." Riss grinned. "No matter what my beloved uncle claims."

Remembering parrots, Jenn grinned back.

Riss lifted her face to the sun and half closed her eyes. "Marrowdell, you won my heart long ago—"

"Marrowdell, was it?" said the man stepping into the ossuary.

Jenn's eyes widened. Riss, a blanket, and . . . Uncle Horst?

She couldn't have uttered a word if she tried.

His smile altered ever so slightly when he saw Riss wasn't alone, though it was no less warm. "Fair morning, Jenn. And to you, Riss," A small bow.

She inclined her head. "Indeed it is, Sennic."

Uncle Horst had a first name?

He carried a pair of the snips used for hedge trimming, which might have made sense except that he was supposed to leave for Endshere today. Worst of all, he wore a clean, if faded, linen shirt instead of his usual leather, and looked to have recently bathed.

Jenn realized she was staring when his smile faded. He looked down at Melusine's name and the rose. Twin spots of color appeared on his cheeks. When he looked up again, his face might have been carved from stone. "My apologies for the intrusion." Another, quicker bow, then he turned and strode away.

"Sennic—" Riss let her outstretched hand drop to her side. For an instant, disappointment curved her shoulders.

"I'm sorry." Jenn could feel her own skin flame. "I—I didn't know." Not that she knew now, but really, it couldn't be much plainer. "I'd have gone home," she finished lamely.

"Don't worry, Dear Heart." Riss sighed and shook her head ruefully. "It's not your fault. Sennic usually watches to be sure no one's come to visit the Ancestors, so he can slip through to my yard with none the wiser, but few are here this early. You took us by surprise, that's all." She spoke as if they discussed tapestries and not what they were, to Jenn's embarrassed dismay, apparently discussing.

She swallowed, determined not to ask.

The other woman gave her a knowing look. "Why do we meet in secret?"

Jenn blushed.

"We always have. Come. Sit with me." Riss put the blanket aside and drew Jenn with her to the bench. "It's a longer story."

"You've been told what happened at your birth," she began soberly. "Ancestors Witness, it was hard for all of us, losing Melusine. How your father stayed strong . . . but the two of you needed him, so what else could he do? Your lady aunt stayed as long as she could. And Sennic. He stayed too." She took Jenn's hand. "Not that we made him welcome, at first. Only your father—and my uncle, who understood such men—were kind to him. It was Uncle who suggested I give my home to this grim stranger, because it was close to the mill and your family, and as far from the rest of the village as could be."

Riss had lived in Uncle Horst's house? Which was, Jenn corrected herself hurriedly, the wrong way around. Wait till she told Peggs. "That was kind—"

"Not of me. Understand, Jenn. I wasn't the same person." The older woman sighed. "You asked if I'm happy here, and I am. But I wasn't, not at first. I was terribly angry, at everyone and everything. I hadn't wanted to leave Avyo. Why would I? Melusine left for Radd, but everything I had—it was there. I tried to stay—" Riss let go of Jenn's hands, and clasped hers together until their knuckles went white. "When the rumors started, I sought my Rhothan friends. Friends." The word was bitter. "They shunned me, afraid to be tainted by my Mellynne blood."

"Oh, Riss."

"There's worse. I'd no pride left," the other admitted softly, "only desperation. I went to suitors I'd once spurned. Offered myself to any who'd have me. I quickly learned that without the Nahamm fortune, no one would. I was sent on my way, to leave Avyo with my family and come here."

A rueful shrug. "Where I was no good company, Jenn, nor good neighbor. If Melly hadn't befriended me, I don't know what would have become of me. When the stranger came . . . when she died . . ." Riss took a ragged breath. "I flew into a rage. I blamed him for Melly's death. I blamed him for everything that had happened to me. I said things, horrible things. Give him my home? Never! My cousin stood by me." She dug her toe into the moss and looked where sun and sigil spilled the name "Riedd Morrill" on the ground. There were soft creases by her eyes and mouth, the sort left by a lifetime of kind smiles. She wasn't smiling now. "Uncle wasn't proud of us, but even he couldn't change my mind. I refused to look at the stranger, let alone speak to him. I shunned him, as I'd been shunned."

Aunt Sybb regularly pointed out that temper was more easily lost than kept, but Jenn had trouble picturing calm, pleasant Riss ever angry with anyone, let alone Uncle Horst. "You like him now," she ventured shyly.

Riss smiled. "I most certainly do." Her smile faded. "Then? It took a great deal to open my eyes to see the man he was. It took that winter, our worst. Day after day of howling winds and bitter cold. Everyone struggled. To care for their own families. To keep the livestock alive. Uncle took poorly after the Midwinter Beholding, so I stayed with him. Most days, we couldn't see another house through the snow; every night seemed likely our last. I might have despaired, Jenn, but each morning I'd wake to find water waiting and charcoal for our fire. There'd be a fresh hare or squirrel ready for the pot."

"Uncle," Jenn guessed.

"Yes, the stranger I hated. He cared for your family as his debt to Melusine; I couldn't understand why he helped us too. I didn't know him as I do now. As we all do."

Jenn nodded. If anyone in the village needed help, Uncle Horst was the first to realize it and act. Hadn't he been the one who'd heard Mimm Ropp's desperate cries? "He saved Cheffy from drowning," she remembered out loud, then shivered. The son, but not the mother. Mimm's name was on the ground, not far from their feet. She felt the prickle of tears. "It was Melusine all over again, wasn't it?"

"It almost broke him," Riss said. The words were blunt; her voice, gentle. "It would have, but for you, Jenn. You've held his heart since the moment you were born. You've kept it whole."

And came close to breaking it herself. Jenn sighed. "I shouldn't have doubted him."

"He's never made it easy for us." Riss shook her head. "When the thaw came and Uncle improved, all I could think was how we wouldn't have survived on our own, how selfless Horst was. How wrong I'd been."

"You apologized."

"I certainly tried. He's a proud man. After what I'd said to him about Melusine? I might not have existed. He wouldn't so much as look at me. I moved my things into Uncle's house and left mine empty for him, hoping he'd understand the gesture and forgive me, but it took your father to convince Horst to move from the mill and take it before mice went rampant." Riss tilted her head, her smile wistful. "Maddening man. I'd listen to him laugh with you, and hear him chat with Radd or Davi or anyone in the village. Not with me. He'd spend his free time here, planting flowers and training the hedges, humming as if he didn't know full well I could hear him from my yard."

Jenn leaned forward. "What did you do?"

"One summer morning, I'd had quite enough of being ignored and hummed at, thank you. I cut a hole in the hedge and surprised him. Right here. With a kiss." Her smile deepened. "Let's say he surprised me back."

It was, Jenn decided, as romantic a tale as any heart could wish—except for the part where it concerned Uncle Horst, who she couldn't possibly imagine as romantic. Riss, yes. She was lovely and kind and, until this moment, Jenn, like Peggs, had been more than half convinced by Aunt Sybb that their father not only should, but would court "that Nahamm woman" once Old Jupp had moved on, which would have been wonderful. Riss and their father, not, she thought with some guilt, losing Old Jupp.

Uncle Horst and Riss must truly be a secret if Aunt Sybb, who was usually infallible about people, hadn't guessed. "I don't understand," Jenn admitted. "After so long, if you and—" she swallowed and continued, "—why aren't you together? Why still meet like this?"

"I asked him to live with me years ago. To marry, if he wished. I told him everyone would be glad to see him happy. He said, everyone but him." Lightly said, making it worse to hear. "He believes that, Jenn. We steal moments together, hide our love, because to do otherwise would mean he'd forgiven himself for Melusine."

"I have," Jenn declared fiercely. "We all have."

"Yes, Dearest Heart. We have." Riss patted her hand, her eyes on the empty path and sad. "But he can't."

How hard could it be?

Bannan hefted the scythe and lifted its wicked curved blade high overhead, a grin spreading across his face. He'd seen the familiar implement used in fields all his life. One gripped, so, and cut with a bold swing. "Prepare for your beheading!" he warned, curling his upper lip at the chest-high grass between him and his garden. A few quick strokes, and he'd have a path through. And hay in the making.

Being alone at his first effort was not only more fun, but likely prudent. There was, Bannan was sure, a trick to it. Those with real skill made their tasks look easy, he'd discovered. Given time, and trials, he was sure he'd get the knack.

Swing!

The scythe swept down and across with gratifying power and speed. "I have you now!" Bannan crowed.

The grass bent aside, then sprang back up, unharmed. A bird landed on a stem, and began to peck at seeds, one bright eye regarding him.

"I can see that, sir. Cowering it is."

Bannan threw down the scythe and whirled. "Tir!" He rushed forward to take his protesting friend by the shoulders, searching his face. "Did you sleep? You look rested. Better. How are you?"

"Better, sir, than your grass cutting." Tir shook his head. "That's just embarrassing."

The eyes above the mask danced with life. Bannan gave him an affectionate shake then let go. "About time you got here," he said, making no attempt to hide his relief. "I might have cut off my foot. Show me what I'm doing wrong. I need to be superb at this by the harvest. To help the villagers," he added, to deflect any comments about impressing Jenn Nalynn.

"Don't bother with the scythe, sir."

Bannan shook his head. "I can learn—"

"Anything's possible, but doesn't change matters. I'm told this isn't usual grain."

"How so?"

"Doesn't need cutting." Tir gestured at the field beyond. "Falls over once it's ripe."

" 'Falls over?' " The truthseer burst out laughing. "You expect me to believe that?"

"The miller swore to it himself."

Bannan's brows knitted together. "Radd's pulling your leg, Tir." Which would be a change. His friend's pranks were legendary in the border guard.

"I've not your knack with the truth, sir, but I believe him. Besides," a sly look, "I checked every barn and shed. Counting this'un, there's but three scythes in Marrowdell. Even if these tinkers bring theirs, that's too few for such fields."

Water, always fresh, from their wells. Davi's forge, heated by a single large stone that never cooled. Grain that grew without pest or weed, only to harvest itself. Marrowdell's wondrous gifts, Bannan thought uneasily, couldn't have been better chosen to keep people here. Why?

And peril. He mustn't forget that. Scourge, sent to guard the road. The path to the Spine. The turn-born. He should tell Tir.

Who'd only just begun to sleep without nightmares.

While Bannan argued with himself, Tir continued, "There's no magic going to help us cut this, sir." His friend scowled at the overgrown farmyard. "That'll take sweat. But, first things first. I bear gifts." His hand went inside his jerkin and whipped out a creamy envelope with a grand flourish.

Driving off any thought of peril or magic. "Is that . . . ?"

"A letter from a certain farm maid? Most certainly it is, sir." As the truthseer reached eagerly for it, Tir pulled the oh-so-enticing envelope away. "For the dragon."

The truthseer let his hand drop. Of course it was for Wyll. Why would it be for him? "He'll be back for supper," he said, doing his best not to look disappointed.

"Ancestors Foolish and Fooled. You should see your face." Chuckling, his friend pulled out a second letter. "Here."

"Heart's Blood, Tir!" The curse was absentminded, Bannan's

attention all for the somewhat crushed envelope now resting in his hand. "She wrote to me?"

"Aie. And best you read the thing now and get it over with, before I teach you to cut grass."

The truthseer, already walking away with the unopened letter in both hands, didn't bother to answer.

Bannan sat on the branch to study the envelope. The Lady Mahavar's exquisite stationery, no doubt. His name wasn't on the front, but he trusted Tir not to mix the letters.

A careful slip of his finger broke the teardrop of wax sealing the back. He pulled out a small piece of paper, also creamy linen. The script was embellished at every opportunity with curlicues, but neatly done and easy to read.

To Bannan Larmensu, Salutations.

I regret to inform you that I will not be able to help unpack your kitchen. Under the kind and knowledgeable direction of our lady aunt, my sister and I have much to accomplish in the coming days, in addition to our accustomed tasks attendant to the tinkers' arrival and the harvest.

May the Ancestors grant you good health and spirits,

Jenn Nalynn.

Easy to read, and as warm as ice. He read it again and was just as discouraged. Yes, she hadn't wrenched his heart by mentioning her upcoming wedding, but that was simply her kind nature.

With a sigh, Bannan went to put the letter in its envelope. He stopped. What was this? More writing on the back, hurried and slanted, as if added in a rush.

I hope your new stove works as well as it looks. Uncle Horst says new doesn't mean better, but he doesn't even own a stove.

You need more pebbles for your house toad. Ask Tir.

Thank you for sending Scourge. He chased away the dragons. How did you know?

"Well and well again."

The hopeful little bird by his feet looked up.

"It's a letter, not crumbs," he told it. An honest, wonderful letter. A letter like her hand in his. Bannan nodded to himself as he folded the precious paper and tucked it carefully in a pocket. He'd use the envelope again. Hadn't she asked a question?

His face fell. If he answered truthfully, he'd have to admit Wyll had sent Scourge to the village and he, Bannan, hadn't a clue she'd been in trouble, from dragons or otherwise, and worse, that as a man, he'd be of no help whatsoever against dragons, other than, as Wyll said, to embarrass them with a broomstick. So much for her gratitude and good opinion.

Not to answer would be as good as a lie, something he couldn't and wouldn't begin; every word he put in her dear hands must be trustworthy. Trustworthy and interesting. Trustworthy, interesting, and draw her heart closer to his.

How hard could it be?

Daunted, Bannan went in search of Tir. Hopefully using a scythe would prove easier than writing.

There had to be something she could do.

Jenn scuffed her bare feet on the road. But what?

Her Uncle Horst had changed again, which went to prove how little she must know of her elders. Not to forget Riss, who'd promised, before she left, to tell her more stories of her mother.

And asked her, poignantly, not to tell anyone about her and Sennic and their years of secret love.

Secrets weren't comfortable. This one felt like wearing shoes; it pinched and the world tilted intolerably. Riss and Uncle Horst deserved to be happy. If she had her way, they'd marry on the Ancestors'

Golden Day too. The more weddings shared the dance, the better the dancing would be.

Another of their aunt's sayings, less happy, came to mind. The older the knot, the harder to undo. It applied to secrets, Jenn realized glumly, as well as to rope. She couldn't see how to undo this secret, or where to even start.

Bees droned past. Wainn's old pony nickered hungrily from the commons; someone must be picking apples. Marrowdell remained the same, regardless of secrets, and gave her advice.

It wasn't up to her to change things. Jenn firmed her chin. She'd promised to keep silent and she would. Any undoing must be up to Riss and Uncle Horst. All she could do was hope for the best.

Feeling a little better, she headed for the mill.

"Hello, Poppa," Jenn called as she came through the large open doors, blinking as her eyes adjusted. On spotting Uncle Horst, she almost missed a step.

He'd changed into his riding leathers and stood near the open mill casing. Radd and Tir were turning the crane on its pivot to bring it above the first millstone, the huge metal arms ready to take hold and lift.

"Hello," her father greeted, eyes on his task. "How was your mother?"

Tir looked mildly curious. Uncle Horst's face was set and expressionless, until their eyes met and she saw a plea in their depths. She gave the tiniest of nods. Lips pressed tight, he nodded back.

"Peaceful," Jenn assured her father. For Uncle Horst's sake, she added, "I prefer the Midwinter Beholding, though. Sharing faults feels more virtuous when I'm up to my knees in snow and half-frozen."

Her father chuckled, recognizing one of his sister's sayings. "You're in time to help the stones go in," he said, patting the crane's wooden upright. "Jenn's done that since she was taller than the case," to Tir.

Jenn smiled her delight. The millstones were almost as wide as she was tall, and two handspans thick. She loved how the crane floated them into place; how a finger's touch could spin them upright or flat. Their own magic.

Except, setting the stones brought summer to an end; it meant the harvest was nigh and so was everything else.

Uncle Horst gave a brusque nod. "I'll be on my way, then. The mist will be off the valleys by now. Anything more you want from Endshere?"

"No, no. What's on the list will do. Mind you leave the bandits in peace," her father grinned.

"They'd best leave me that way," Uncle Horst replied. It was an old joke; bandits on the Northward knew better than to ambush armed men on horseback.

But this time, there was something different in the old soldier's voice, something hard and almost hopeful.

They all stared at his stiffly straight, leather-clad back as he left. "What's got into him?" her father murmured.

Tir lifted his mask to spit to one side. "Sure he's coming back?"

When her father didn't answer right away, Jenn said, "Of course he is!" more sharply than she'd intended. "Uncle Horst belongs here."

"He'll be back with the livestock," her father agreed, which wasn't the same nor reassuring, not when his eyes remained fixed on the empty doorway and troubled. "Let's set the stones," he ordered, turning back to the crane. "The gears need greasing next, and there's oil to go on the leathers. Ancestors Witness, harvest's not going to wait for us."

Uncle Horst would be back, Jenn told herself. He'd be back to stay, and be married to Riss, and be happy all of his days.

She couldn't imagine Marrowdell without him.

She wouldn't.

He'd come for supper, not this.

Wyll regarded the envelope on his empty plate with dismay. The last such had sent him rushing to the Nalynns, which had been wrong, according to Jenn Nalynn, yet resulted in right, according to her father and aunt.

This was likely as fraught with expectation and possible failure.

Supper waited. He could smell it. He'd missed lunch and midafternoon tea. And snacks. He approved of snacks, which came at pleasantly unpredictable intervals, like successful hunts.

But first . . .

"It's from Jenn," Bannan explained, adding lightly, "I received one too."

Refusing to snarl at this, Wyll pried open the seal, as the old villager had shown him, and pulled out the part to be read. As he'd feared, it was in script, rather than the clear print of books. He worked his way, slowly, through the words.

Dearest Wyll. I must call you that, for who I see is different from Wisp, my meadow friend, though you're the same, of course, and I can't say I saw much of you as Wisp at all. Does this confuse you too? I'm very sorry if it does. I didn't mean for you to be hurt or unhappy. I asked the toad to tell you so. I thought only of myself and shouldn't have. I promise to do better in every way.

For a start, let me explain why I left the farm and why I won't see you for the next few days. There's so much to do for the weddings, although I think some of it is a little silly, which I would never say to Aunt Sybb because she wants everything to be perfect and proper for us. Tomorrow Poppa will set the millstones, which you know means the harvest is almost here and there's much to do for that as well. Roche's being broody and not helping, so Uncle Horst's taking him along to Endshere to fetch the mail and meet the twins. I love it when the livestock comes back. They pretend to be wild and snort, but they want petting.

I will write to you every day. You must write to me.

Jenn

"There's more on the back," Tir pointed out, and Wyll anxiously turned the paper over to read.

I meant to start replanting Night's Edge as a surprise, but I can't do anything about it now and the sooner we start, the sooner it will be back as it was.

Would you please spread any wildflower seeds you can find over our meadow? Asters would be especially nice. I'll collect what I can here.

Thank you for the rose.

The rose had given itself.

The seeds?

She meant well; he doubted restoring Night's Edge would be so simple.

Nor was Jenn Nalynn's other request. "She asks that I write," Wyll said, trying not to sound desperate.

"If you pen your passion quick enough, I'll take it with Bannan's tonight," offered the warrior, his eyes lively with mischief.

The man was writing too? Disconcerted, Wyll frowned. In the stories the girl liked best, letters were vital, as often as not leading to unforeseen conclusions. Unforeseen to him, at least; she'd sigh happily. "You wrote of passion?"

"Pardon?"

"Fair question, sir." Tir appeared vastly entertained. "Coming from a dragon."

"It's nothing of the sort." A sequence of expressions flickered across Bannan's face, none easily identifiable. Finally, "I'll answer this once. No."

"Good." Wyll put the letter and envelope aside. "I'm ready for supper." Still, this matter of letters was troubling. "I need paper."

"Just paper?"

"And supper."

Tir leaned back, hands behind his head. "Ancestors Famished and Faint, we'd have that by now, but someone won't share his fancy stove."

Bannan laughed and rose. "You can try it tomorrow," he said cheerfully. "Today's a celebration. Care for wine, friend dragon? I can't offer a glass, but I found cups."

Tir looked at Wyll and jerked a thumb at the truthseer. "He's in a rare fine mood for a man who can't cut grass to save himself."

"Who wouldn't be? Good company—" Hands protected by rags, Bannan pulled a crockery pot from within the stove, aromatic steam rising as he removed the lid. "—good food, and nothing but good in our futures."

Had he ever been this young? Wyll wondered.

Sausage stew in their bowls, wine in their cups, the three sat to eat. "Hearts of our Ancestors," Bannan commenced.

Wyll resigned himself to the delay.

"We are Beholden for this food, for it will give us the strength to improve ourselves in your eyes. We are Beholden for the chance to make our homes, for it gives promise to our lives." The truthseer smiled before saying, "We are Beholden for the kindness of Jenn Nalynn and others, for their help and encouragement—"

What had been in his letter from the girl?

"However far we are apart," Bannan finished, "Keep Us Close."

Tir echoed the words; Wyll didn't bother. He didn't care what she'd written to anyone else. "She will live with me."

Bannan lifted his cup and tilted his head. "We'll see."

Letters and a challenge.

Unknowing the stakes, they played their games. Like the toads and ylings, they built and created and believed themselves safe.

That nothing terrible and swift could happen, to sweep it all away.

"What I see are fools!" Wyll shoved himself from the table, the force rattling the dishes, and lurched to his feet. "For the girl's sake, I've warned you. Hide what you are from the turn-born. Be on guard as the Great Turn approaches, for others come to Marrowdell." He snarled. "Why do I bother? You are weak, weak and helpless. How dare you love her?"

The truthseer rose as well, his face gone pale.

"So it's love now?" Tir asked with a grin.

Wyll turned away and left, uninterested in the answer.

Hungry and furious, he made his way to Night's Edge to discharge his first duty. With its tall grass cut and raked, the farmyard was easier walking and fragrant. He didn't care, sending breezes to topple the piles. Seeds gathered like an angry swarm of bees behind him, and followed him to the ruin of their meadow and his content.

Wyll stopped at the path's end. The seeds roared past and flung themselves on the ground.

To wink into ash.

What had he expected? He wasn't turn-born, to will the course of nature this way or that. Just as well, the dragon growled to himself, wishing instead for claws and something to rend.

The turn would come soon, bringing the damp and the dark. Dragging his useless leg through rot and ash, Wyll hurried as best he could across Night's Edge, intent on his second duty, to write back to Jenn Nalynn.

Not that he knew how to write.

A powerful gust rocked him to one side. ~ WE TRIED! ~ A wail from the sky.

They dared much, crossing back so soon.

~ We failed! ~ from the other. ~ Why didn't you help? ~ from below.

As if he could do what they could not.

Last night, the girl had twisted the edge itself, yet remained innocent of her power.

Not so his peers. Having tasted that terror, now they sought his council. Swift to condemn him, smug at his penance. How quickly need renewed respect.

Fools.

Struck by a broomstick. Had he claws, he'd score their hides for that carelessness. Ignoring them, Wyll kept on his way. They crowded close, heedless and desperate, wingbeats raising choking clouds of dead meadow as they wailed like those already lost. ~ What can we DO?! ~

~ Can you write a letter? ~ he asked. Their confused silence amused him, but only for a moment. ~ THEN YOU'RE OF NO USE! ~

Ash darkened the sky as they scattered, to fall like gray snow.

Peace at last.

But no solution. Wyll snarled. To keep Jenn Nalynn safe and

prevent disaster, he needed to be a man, not a dragon, and write a letter.

How?

He worried at the question within the shade of the neyet and as he made his slow way home through the hidden meadow. He pondered as flowers and grasses wiped ash from his shoes and pant cuffs, breezes doing the rest, but nothing came to mind.

Once home, removing the comb from his pocket, Wyll let a breeze tidy and fold his clothes. The comb he'd taken; let Bannan find another. The regard for hair and clothing he'd discovered, having observed Bannan with his own.

He'd taken something else, too.

A book.

Bannan kept the volume by his mattress; they'd been watching him leave, not what followed out a window.

The books Jenn Nalynn brought to their meadow were nicer and better treated than this old and tattered thing, but it was paper and held words.

Words were a start.

He sat within his home, this sun's final light breaking through crystal and the remains of neyet, and used teeth and his good hand to rip the book apart, pages scattering on the moss like moth wings.

That was satisfying.

With more care, he let breezes shred each page until words and phrases drifted around him, tipped this way and that like flower petals. "Ands" and "thes." "Hes" and "shes." "Swords" and "heroes." "Forevers" and "never agains."

A few escaped through the open doorway.

With rare patience, Wyll picked through the words, arranging those he wanted, just so, on a bare piece of crystal.

Now what?

~ Attend me, little cousin, ~ the dragon demanded, well aware the creature crouched nearby. When the house toad appeared in his doorway, "fair" and "adamant" stuck on its warts, he pointed to what he'd made. ~ I've need of your tongue. ~

~ Elder brother? ~ It clamped its lipless mouth shut.

~ I will send these words, in this order, to Jenn Nalynn. Open your mouth and let me stick them to your tongue. You will then go to the village and show her. ~

The little cousins could change their appearance to better match their surroundings. This one went a sickly yellow and stood out. ~ I will do whatever you ask, elder brother, but are you sure about this? ~

~ Did you not boast she kissed you? ~

~ I may be wrong, elder brother, but I presumed that was more impulse than attraction. ~ It paused then said delicately, ~ There is also the girl's lady aunt to consider. She makes a most unpleasant sound if she encounters us in the house. ~

Wyll shuddered. Offend Aunt Sybb?

As if sensing he wavered, the little cousin concluded briskly, ~ Might I suggest another means of sending these words? One more pleasing? ~ It stopped and blinked at him, an immovable lump of virtuous opinion, waiting to be asked.

There was a lower level to stoop than sei and fate had hitherto shown him.

The dragon spared a moment to be grateful his kind had left, and the old kruar remained in the village.

Ask indeed.

~ What . . . ~ he made himself say it ~ . . . other means, esteemed little cousin? ~

~ Wait here, elder brother! ~ With that joyous cry, the toad hopped from sight, "adamant" and "fair" flying free to lodge in a crack.

Helpless to do otherwise, Wyll bided his time letting breezes collect the unused words from the moss; the stories the girl enjoyed implied this exchange of letters was only the first, so he should be prepared. The resultant pile was larger than the book had been; perhaps the words, having escaped, relished their freedom from one another. He could understand that.

~ Elder brother. ~

The dragon sighed, very quietly, and turned.

The toad was not alone.

Two ylings hovered above it, slender limbs dangling. Outside the turn, their shapes flickered and fooled; sometimes leaf and sometimes other. These took pity on his man's poorer sight, and gave him their true selves: creatures of delicate beauty, with bright curious eyes and tufted ears. Their fine hair gathered and splintered sunlight, so sparks of red and yellow and green danced around them, and they wore short tunics the color of sun-touched bark. Their wings were gossamer and they had four arms and two legs, with strong little hands at the end of each. One yling bore a quiver filled with fearsome spears, each the length of a man's finger; their barbed points poison-dipped. The other held a rolled bundle and a tiny basket.

Their cloaks, which took the seeming of leaves most of the time, were cunningly sewn of flower petals, spider silk, and seed fluff. The warrior's was mostly brown and yellow, to blend with shadow and light. With a trill to his companion, he took hold of the top of Wyll's doorway with one foot-hand and faced outward, spears at the ready.

In the Verge, ylings lived in cities suspended over calm lakes of mimrol, their snug buildings hung from threads that stretched from bank to bank, threads cleverly embedded with poisonous thorns to daunt even a careless dragon. At the turn, ylings would take flight to dance, dipping their thumbs in the silver liquid to weave ripples and rings. They were as lighthearted as their songs and feared no one.

Marrowdell's ylings had learned distrust and terror. Trapped in a strange land, they'd survived by hiding within neyet, posting guards against what would climb and attack. Worse, they were again betrayed. When the turn-born expected certain neyet to sacrifice themselves as wood for a village, the ylings in their branches had been forced to flee, only to face hordes of waiting nyphrit.

Warriors like this had cast themselves into those hungry jaws, so the rest could escape.

Bravery had no one size or shape. Nor, Wyll thought with the old pain, had worth.

The warrior's companion, cloaked in purple aster petals, floated downward to hover beside his rows of words. Her head tipped to one side, then the other as she examined them. All the while, her tall ears flicked nervously, as though she listened to something he couldn't hear or was unsettled this close to a dragon.

With a care that punished his twisted body, Wyll eased back. Ylings were quick to startle; he'd not thought to see any so far from their fellows or the safety of their neyet. Though he burned to ask how the little cousin convinced these two to approach him, he would not.

The yling unrolled her bundle on the crystal, revealing another cloak. Unlike that draped softly around her slim form, this was stiff and almost plain, save for a pleasing pattern of overlapped green. Cedar spice filled the air as she flattened the material with crisp pats of her little hands. Satisfied, she opened her case and took out a pair of needles that twinkled in the sunlight, as well as a spool of spider silk.

Then looked up at him and waited.

Did he imagine a smile?

Wyll let a breeze lift the first word of his letter to Jenn Nalynn and carry it to the cloak, setting it in position.

The yling pounced, her needles and thread moving too quickly to see, then moved aside, one hand beckoning with professional pride.

He leaned closer. Tiny paired stitches knit the ragged scrap of paper to the leaves below. Before his eyes, the stitches blurred away, the scrap's edges smoothed, and the paper with its word became part of the cloak. Yling magic. He moved his lips to read soundlessly, "Greetings!"

He would have a letter for Jenn Nalynn.

Wyll stared at the yling, confounded. ~ Why? ~

She startled up and away; the warrior sang anxiously as she settled back down.

~ You know what I am. ~ He had to understand. ~ You know what I've done. ~

Her ears twitched, but she didn't fly this time. With a flick of her hand, the tiny seamstress indicated the rest of the words.

~ Why do you help me? ~

Could that be another smile? He wasn't sure. She trilled and gestured again. I haven't time for fools, that said.

Feeling lightheaded, Wyll let the rest of the words float from crystal to cloak, the yling stitching each in turn, as if he were one of their own and deserving.

When finished, she awaited his inspection. Upon his nod, she rolled the cloak that was now his letter into a bundle and lifted with it into the air. The warrior dropped free to join her.

~ Wait. How are you— ~

More leaves than ylings, they giggled and were gone.

The house toad tried to sneak out the door with them. Wyll sent a breeze to scoop it up and hold it, legs dangling, in midair.

~ WHY? ~ he snarled.

Its immense eyes bulged larger, if that were possible. ~ 'Why?' elder brother? ~ with unconvincing innocence. ~ Why, what? ~

Why did crystals cross to shelter him? Why did neyet sacrifice their limbs? The efflet bring moss? And now . . . the ylings?

Did the small ones pity him?

Did they dare?

Enraged, the dragon snatched the toad from the air, its throat in his good hand. ~ How dare you forget?! You know this is my penance. All this is my fault! ~ He tightened his fingers and shook it. ~ You're trapped because of me! ~

~ Did you tear open the edge? ~ the toad argued placidly, legs swinging. ~ Did you abandon us and steal our queen? Did you go to war alone? ~

Flabbergasted by its impudence, Wyll let go.

The toad dropped to the floor, cracking crystal. Tears welled and the little cousin methodically stepped from the puddle before squatting to stare up at him. ~ You're no turn-born or sei, elder brother, you're dragon, flesh and bone. You're one of us, not them, and trapped too. ~

~ I RULED! ~ Wyll roared.

The toad squeezed its eyes shut while the angry echoes died away, then opened them again to stare in meaningful silence.

Insufferable creature.

Growling, he finally looked away. The little cousin was right. He ruled nothing, was nothing more than what cowered here, within the charity of the small ones. Why they cared for him, he couldn't understand, but that they did was dangerous folly. The girl lived far from the closest neyet. The river needed to be crossed. How would the ylings manage, without undo risk?

~ I am, ~ he conceded at last, ~ grateful. ~

No answer.

He turned his head the slightest bit. The last light of this sun filled his doorway, finding crystal tears, but no impudent, imprudent toad.

Say rather, honest, brave little cousin.

He hadn't looked for wisdom, in so small a size. Another lesson, late-learned.

But he was at fault, even if he hadn't been alone in it. At the last Great Turn, when meddlers here disturbed what they mustn't and weakened the edge, the mighty of the Verge had rushed to repair that breach. They'd been so wonderfully preoccupied, he'd known his moment had come. Not once had he hesitated to start his war. Not once had he paused to consider his responsibility to the very existence of the Verge.

Just as turn-born and sei hadn't considered the sacrifice of the small ones when they'd sealed the edge and saved the day, before expressing their displeasure with dragon and kruar.

Now, within his life, another Great Turn.

Let there be no fools this time.

Weary, yet for some reason at peace, Wyll stretched out on the moss to watch the turn through his door.

Night's edge swept down the flanks of the trapped and efflet emerged from their field to sit before him in their rows, claws knuckled at their breasts.

Company, all these years.

~ Greetings, ~ Wyll said to them, and nodded.

They looked at one another, then at him. As one, they gravely nodded in return.

With the passing of the turn, the efflet were gone. He heard their whispers amid the grain-heavy stalks. Not long now, the whispers seemed to say. Not long at all. They'd flee the harvest, taking refuge in the hedges around the fields, and woe betide any nyphrit who'd dared make nests in those branches over summer. The efflet would await winter's end, sculpting snow and ice into fantastical shapes that only efflet understood. Once those melted and the soil became soft again, they'd work their small magic and summon their beloved kaliia from the Verge, to sprout and grow here as well.

To the villagers' benefit, though Wyll doubted efflet saw it that way.

The efflet settled for the night as he did, peaceful still. They'd grow restless, as the harvest approached, and provide warning. There was time, yet. Time he would use. He would write letters to Jenn Nalynn. He would learn about being a man from the truthseer, surely a fair trade. Had he not warned the man to conceal his sight? In truth, more to avoid unpleasantness near his new home than because he cared how foolish or not the man might be, but Jenn Nalynn would care.

A certainty that didn't sit well in his empty stomach.

Hunger wasn't new nor worry.

Resting his head on the moss, Wyll closed his eyes and almost smiled.

A dragon writing a letter?

That was.

SEVENTEEN

To Jenn Nalynn, Salutations.

Thank you for your kind letter.

Ancestors Witness, you have been of inestimable help already, and I've Tir to assist me, so I urge you not to regret having to turn your attention to such important and pressing matters as preparations for the harvest.

I must tell you a remarkable thing. Large white moths enter my home by night. I sent an order for new windowpanes with your esteemed uncle. I shall leave an opening, however, for these moths are extraordinary creatures and I wish their continued visits. Each wears small boots, I swear by my Ancestors, and carries a tiny satchel locked with a jewel. I plan to watch for them again tonight, and hope to learn what's so important to a moth. You can be sure I will write and share with you what I discover.

May the Ancestors Keep You Happy and Well

Bannan L.

There was more on the back.

The stove lived up to its appearance. I look forward to the day when I may prove it to you.

The toad who lives with me has been well supplied with pebbles, and I look forward to eggs in the morning. Though Tir insists I collect them and not discuss their source, I consider myself privileged to have such a guest.

I claim no false honors. Wyll sent Scourge to the village, having knowledge of such dangers, and I am grateful beyond words that he helped you. My experience thus far with dragons involved a flailing broomstick and little result. Our dragon was amused.

I smile, sweet Jenn, to think of your hand in mine.

At this last, Jenn Nalynn felt altogether warm and she hurriedly put down the fine sheet of paper, glancing at her sleeping sister as if the act of reading such a line might somehow awaken her. It had not. Still, clearly this wasn't a letter to share.

In fact, she oughtn't keep it.

Though it was her very first letter. She picked it up again, with care, to look more closely at the writing. His writing.

Which involved his hand. The hand that remembered hers.

She put the letter down again.

Goodness, this business of letters was far more stimulating than she'd anticipated. She'd read it only once more, to be sure she had all the details, then put it somewhere out of sight.

Somewhere turned out to be inside a mitten, tucked to the back corner of her drawer. Though it was peculiar how often her eyes were drawn back to the chest.

The letter had been a distraction ever since Tir Half-face delivered it, folded inside a familiar envelope. He'd ducked his head to her in a manner Aunt Sybb would call decidedly cheeky and she'd done her utmost not to appear concerned when he'd told her Wyll hadn't sent a reply, because that would only encourage the man. To make matters worse, Tir had then, so casually, mentioned picking up her reply to Bannan's letter when he came to the Nalynns' for breakfast tomorrow, which left her no way at all to avoid such a reply.

Bringing the candle closer, Jenn picked up her quill and began to write.

To Bannan Larmensu, Greetings.

Thanks to your letter, I'm taking a greater interest in moths. They like Mother's roses and come to our window each night in summer. I've seen neither boots nor satchels, but have something remarkable of my own to report. This very night, one brought me Wyll's letter clutched in its legs!

As for our correspondence, Tir has been kind to carry it and I've told him so, but please tell me if this envelope does not arrive in good condition. He hints at a fondness for chewing paper and I fear for the corners, though he also claims your house is falling apart, which I do not believe at all. Peggs says he teases me, but I can't always tell. His mask gives him a most unfair advantage. Teasing or not, I'm glad he's been able to sleep, as has Aunt Sybb. They vow to take a cup of cider before bed every night.

Cynd told Peggs that Davi's finished your new hinges. You should have them tomorrow, with this letter.

Please feel no obligation to reply. Though I'd like to hear more about your Marrowdell. Mine is much of a sameness.

She'd filled the page already? But she had more to say and answer. She must write smaller, which Aunt Sybb wouldn't like. A person's script was evidence of their quality, she'd say. Bannan's would please her. His letters were crisp and sure, with extra ink on the down strokes and a nice flourish, though lacking in curlicues. Having believed curlicues assured a reader of one's adult and dignified and respectable nature, Jenn had strewn as many as possible through her first letter to Bannan.

A relief to stop.

An additional sheet or two would serve nicely, but the supply was limited, the more so since their aunt reserved most for wedding invitations.

As if everyone didn't already know and plan to come and wonder at her choice of a dragon turned man.

With a little sigh, Jenn turned her single page over to write.

Have you tried baking yet? We've starter for bread, if you need it.

Tir should respect your house toad. They are wise and clever. Ours helped me the other night, when I had some difficulty in the carrots.

You met dragons? What did they look like? Did they look like Wisp or different? Were they all the same? Wyll shouldn't make fun. I think you were very brave to flail at them.

As I recall, Bannan Larmensu, your hand in mine was either wet, muddy, or covered in Scourge's hair.

Jenn

That should put him in his place. Before her courage failed, Jenn put the letter in the envelope, tipped her candle to seal the flap with a fresh drop of wax, and put her reply aside to give to Tir.

Wyll's letter had no envelope, or paper for that matter, instead being a still-green leaf. She couldn't tell what kind, and it had the oddest texture, soft as cloth, but what was important were the words stuck to it.

Greetings!
I didn't send The beauteous flower
do not try." To cross again I warn of direst peril! danger
foreboding Bad
I cannot undo The meadow
undying gratitude be yours for Your words
Our domicile remains dry Now
You can dwell herein

As letters went, Wyll's first was, perhaps not surprisingly, brief and blunt. She chewed her lip. She should have known he'd be aware of what had happened. Had the house toad delivered her apology? She reread his letter, and couldn't be sure.

As for the words themselves? They'd been taken from a book, not written, which truly was clever of Wyll since she couldn't recall ever showing him how to write or print, just reading itself. She tried to pry "Greetings!" loose with a fingernail, but like the rest, it was fastened tight.

To obtain those words, however, Wyll must have destroyed a book, and the books closest to him weren't his to destroy.

They belonged to Bannan.

Whatever book it had been, she'd have to replace it. If Master

Dusom didn't have a copy he was willing to part with, she'd have to ask him to place an order by post.

Ancestors Baffled and Beloved.

The last time anyone from Marrowdell ordered a book, it had taken two years to arrive, and no one would admit to wanting it in the first place. The book itself went to good use, each villager taking it in turn to read. Something entertaining and fantastical, as Jenn recalled, about a winged pottery horse, a bitter old lady who gets her comeuppance, and a candy house. She and Peggs had decided Frann must have ordered it for Lorra during one of their battles, then thought better of it.

Replacing Bannan's book would be, Jenn was sure, a difficulty.

As for Wyll . . .

Dearest Wyll

How clever of you to make me such a letter and have a moth deliver it. I'm afraid I must rely on plain paper and quill, with Tir to deliver the result. He's happy to do so and I've thanked him. How do I thank the moth?

I'm glad the roof doesn't leak. That's very important in a house. Measure the windows for me, please, so I can make curtains.

I take your caution to heart, and promise to be more careful. Wen's told me to wish for what I should, not what I shouldn't, which I take as excellent advice. I'll do my best.

Aunt Sybb and Tir have slept without dreams. Isn't that a marvel?

Jenn

Jenn stopped, unsure what else to say. In Night's Edge, she'd talk to Wisp by the hour, and often be late home as a result; those conversations, as she thought of them now, had been thoroughly one-sided, filled with childish babble about this person or that, or daydreams about . . . what couldn't be.

Wyll, being visible and a man and sometimes grim and ofttimes sad, wasn't someone she could babble to any longer. A beloved friend, yes and always, but more like Uncle Horst than Peggs. She just knew he'd want to hear her sound adult and practical.

She sighed.

Peggs rolled over with a mutter.

As for the book? Jenn gave a decisive little nod. Dragon or no dragon, he mustn't destroy any more books. She turned the page and hesitated. How to broach the subject, without making things worse?

Mightn't Bannan have given Wyll a book he no longer wanted, to use for this purpose? Jenn shook her head. No, if he'd brought it with him into exile, the book was a favorite. Had been.

Ancestors Dire and Confounding.

She mustn't accuse Wyll of stealing the book, though she thought it entirely likely and wouldn't blame him. She'd discover the title for herself. Choosing her words with care, she added,

If you will need more words than you have at hand, please let me know. There is a book of rhymes I'm sure no one will miss with a splendidly broad vocabulary.

A book she'd have to borrow from Master Dusom's library and hope he wouldn't miss. His students wouldn't. The rhymes were older than Wagler Jupp and dreadfully dull, prized by the teacher solely for their excessive alliteration. She supposed she could ask him for it, but asking Master Dusom for a book led inevitably to him asking how she'd enjoyed it, and would she like another? He'd shelves of poetry; the whole business might never end.

Jenn put her reply for Wyll with the one for Bannan.

Wyll's clever leaf letter she left on top of the chest, to show Peggs in the morning.

Blowing out her candle, she sat a moment, gazing into the night.

Today's emptiness had been worse, as the sun set, than yesterday's. She'd need to wish even harder for a lovely morning, to keep her mind from . . . where it mustn't go.

But for all her good intentions, when Jenn closed her eyes, she thought of how nice Bannan's hand had felt in hers, despite mud or water or hair, and she smiled into her pillow.

"Mail's here!" Tir Half-face announced cheerily as he strode up to the porch. "And hinges."

With a nonchalant nod, Bannan finished pounding the next plank into place. He'd decided to use the well-seasoned lumber of his wagon to repair the loft floor, with any extra to be furniture, so he was piecing the porch back together from its original wood. "A pot of that foul brew of yours is on the stove," he said as he stood, wiping sweat from his forehead with the back of his arm. Another lovely morning, if unseasonably warm. With such cooperation, he'd have his house winter-ready well before snow. "We can get to the doors after that."

"Surely, sir," Tir pulled out a familiar envelope and waved it, "you'll want this first?"

If it was what he hoped, of course he did, but he'd have no peace if he succumbed too easily. Bannan smiled. "What I want are doors that close. Letters can wait."

Tir hadn't come alone. Scourge stalked behind, his great head bobbing behind the shorter man's. A breeze slid along the truthseer's jaw to his ear. "Letters? I remember letters. Shall I tell the girl about all those to women in Vorkoun?"

Hardly fair. "Do you want to be groomed again in this lifetime?" the truthseer threatened.

"Not looking for your help there, sir." With a chuckle, Tir ran his free hand over his bald pate as he slipped the plump saddlebags from his shoulder. "Though I'd take it kindly if you'd ask his bloody highness why I had to carry these, given he followed me the entire way."

Scourge snorted. "You didn't ask."

Tir swatted violently at his ear, almost dislodging his mask, then his eyes went wide as saucers. "I heard that!"

"I'm glad," the truthseer said dryly.

"No! You don't understand." His friend backed, arms out as if to protect himself, then turned wildly in a circle. "I heard a voice! A voice that wasn't a—" he froze in place, staring at Scourge. A hand pointed, finger outstretched. "Yours!" he shouted.

"Such insight." The kruar shook himself from nose to hindquarters.

"But—how?"

"Scourge?" Bannan couldn't stop smiling.

"I can be heard by whomever I choose." The breeze was amused too. "As for how? In Marrowdell, within the edge, I'm more of what I was."

And revealed it. The truthseer's mood darkened as he thought of what he'd seen, what he now could see anytime he looked deeper: the scars over Scourge's body, scars concealed by this light as a gleaming hide of black hair and dark brown mane and tail. He wanted to ask; he knew better. Scourge would tell him what he chose, when he chose. If at all.

Bannan made himself cheerful again by thinking of a new letter from Jenn Nalynn. If she'd written to him, and not just to Wyll. Who might not have written at all, he brightened, in which case, any letter must be his.

Wyll stirred from the doorway, where he'd leaned to watch Bannan work. He'd been quiet during breakfast and unexpectedly helpful afterward, using his magic with air to lift the planks into place. The truthseer had accepted that help with the sinking feeling whatever Jenn had written yesterday had given the dragon new confidence and silently cursed whatever impulse made him toss Wyll's discarded letter, unread, into the fire. Tir had been disappointed; he'd argued he wouldn't want someone reading his mail. Now, he wished he'd been less the gallant and more the scoundrel.

"I," the dragon said aloud, "am not restricted to whispers in ears."

The breeze turned chill. "So you're happy as a man?"

A flicker of silver. "Are you, as a horse?"

"Heart's Blood. It's like listening to an old couple bicker," Tir muttered, picking up the bags.

Wyll and Scourge glared at him.

"Well, it is." The former guard glared right back, undaunted. "What's between you, anyway?"

The right question. Bannan almost held his breath as the dragon and kruar swiveled heads to glare at one another.

"We're of the same world," Wyll said.

The breeze was like a blast from a forge; the men winced together. "Say the same war, and be honest."

"The same war." The dragon smiled unpleasantly. "Not the same side."

Tir grunted. "No surprise there." He swung the bags back over his shoulder. "So long as it's over."

Scourge stamped a great hoof. Wyll's eyes flashed silver.

Bannan and Tir exchanged wary looks. "Well?" demanded the truthseer. "Is it?"

"Yes. Over," the dragon replied, lips twisted as if the words left a sour taste.

"Well? Who won? You can tell us," Tir prodded, as if they discussed some disreputable but interesting wager.

Sometimes the man had no sense of caution whatsoever.

"No one," the breeze snapped.

"The end wasn't in doubt," Wyll smiled unpleasantly. "Until a truce was imposed."

Like Vorkoun, Bannan thought. Suddenly the sun didn't feel as warm as it should. What could force creatures like these to stop fighting? "By whom?"

"Those who pitied the kruar," the dragon answered, a wicked gleam in his eye.

With an enraged squeal, Scourge half reared and spun about, pitching forward in a flat run. He was out of the yard and pounding down the road to the village before anyone could do more than blink.

"Touchy," Tir observed.

"He doesn't care for the reminder." Wyll rubbed his withered arm, as if it pained him. "Nor do I. We've no interest in your world or in battle, truthseer. We wish only to be done with our penance."

"Yon bloody beast? What's he done to be punished for, other than being ugly?"

"I led dragonkind." Wyll looked almost amused. "Who do you think led the kruar?"

His former horse. Bannan shook his head. "Who ended your war and punished you?" he asked a second time. "Who could?"

"The sei." Wyll's eyes flashed silver, then faded. "Fear them not. Your world is of no consequence to them; theirs matters not to you. Between lies the Verge, where those worlds touch. Our home, once. Our battleground."

The dragon leaned against the strong logs of the house, his flawless hand resting on the windowsill. "It began as most conflicts do. One prize, two takers, neither willing to share. The Verge—the Verge is perilous and raw, potent with power. Beautiful. Beautiful in all ways." His voice was serene; wood cracked and splintered beneath his fingers.

"There was room for all, at first," Wyll went on. "Both kruar and dragonkind could live in it. Naturally, both claimed it. We don't," this with a certain dark satisfaction, "live together. The point came when it must be one or the other. I—I chose it be us. Things were going well, for dragonkind at least, but—let's say we'd picked a poor time to finish our dispute." No satisfaction now. Wyll noticed the windowsill and pulled his fingers free, then brushed their undamaged tips across the holes he'd made. "Disturbing the sei is unwise. They ended our war. Sent us to our own for justice, as is their way, then gave what was left to the turn-born, to serve penance for our kinds.

"Our war's long over, truthseer." Wyll straightened from the wall and slapped his withered arm with his good hand. "This is victory."

Once more, Bannan saw that ancient, terrible grief in the dragon's eyes. He could hardly breathe. With an effort, he broke that contact and made himself see just the man. Above the trim red-brown beard, Wyll's cheeks were pale as ash. Guilt and grief, Wainn had called him.

His body bore the lesser wounds.

"Heart's Blood," Tir swore. "These folk of yours. Sei. Turn-born. Sound like Avyo's meddling prince and his mewling barons. Always think they know better than them's what's done their bloody work. Interfering where they weren't asked and aren't wanted." His voice rose. "Who needs them, I say! You stick with us, Wyll. You stick close."

The dragon appeared dumbfounded.

Bannan took pity. "Who's for tea? There are fresh biscuits."

His friend snorted, the fiery glint in his eyes fading. "Your biscuits, sir? I've a pie, fresh from Peggs' oven, thank you, and letters for you both from the sister."

Bannan smiled. "Come, Wyll." He dared put a hand on the other's shoulder. "We'd best get our share of that pie."

Feeling the rock-hard tension of that shoulder, he thought he'd made a mistake, then the dragon relaxed. "I want my letter," Wyll proclaimed. "And a very large share of pie."

"Oh, would you, now?" Tir led the way, arguing as if they were any three friends. "I did the carrying, I get the biggest piece."

Bannan laughed. "We'll toss 'stones."

Later, Tir busy with the scythe on the overgrown farmyard, Wyll having gone home with his letter, Bannan sat on the porch and pulled out his. A butterfly perched on his shoulder, as if curious to read it too.

No too-short, too-formal note this, he realized at once. The page was covered with writing, without a curlicue in sight. He began to read, then had to stop.

She'd written to him from her bedroom.

His thoughts flew. Had moonlight touched her cheek or the warm glow of a candle? Had her hair been unbound?

He'd yet to see it tidy, let alone clean and loose. It would be beautiful, though. A river of silken gold.

Bannan waited for his blood to cool. Ancestors Blessed and Beloved, it was only a letter. He skimmed eagerly through the rest, surprised into a pleased laugh. So he'd failed to impress her with his cleanliness either. The life of a farmer, he was coming to realize.

A charming letter, lively with her voice and personality, warm and gracious. He reread how she'd thought him brave, and smiled.

She wanted more of what he saw. His smile faded and the butterfly flew up and away.

Not this time.

He owed her what he'd learned.

Bannan drew a heavy breath, then began to write.

Dear Jenn

Thank you for your kind letter.

I would appreciate some starter, especially if you would write instructions in its use. I'm reasonably adept at biscuits, but bread-making terrifies me. For your sake, I'm willing to try, but be prepared for abject failure and loaves like rock.

Tir is a scoundrel and outrageous flirt. Be wary of anything he says, especially if he's in a fine mood. I suspect he's made off with my comb and favorite book, just to watch me hunt for them.

My house isn't falling down, you'll be glad to know, and Wyll's been helping me with repairs. He shares my table without complaint and enjoys my biscuits, to Tir's disbelief. For myself, I'm convinced. You should see the number Wyll consumes at a sitting.

As for Wyll. He's told me something of his past that's helped me understand him, and that idiot Scourge. I feel I do both a service sharing it with you.

Dragon and kruar hold no love for one another, as we witnessed at their first encounter. I've learned since that Wyll and Scourge were warriors who once met in battle. That was long ago, and I believe they've each come to Marrowdell in search of peace, whether they realize it or not. I've known other old soldiers to do the same.

Being one myself, I assure you old habits—old hates—take time to fade. I find hope in how these two have made common purpose. Doubtless, they'll growl and bicker for life, but if they can co-exist, surely the day will come when I no longer think of Ansnans and Vorkoun with such anger in my heart. When I find peace, too.

My apologies for sharing such grim thoughts with you, instead of marvels. I vow to do better in my next letter.

Thank you, Dear Heart, for listening to mine.

Bannan

Before he could change his mind, he tucked his letter into their shared envelope, sealing it with the press of a heated knife to her latest dot of wax. What he'd said was real and true.

What he'd said, he'd not told even Tir.

That, for all the letters to the fine ladies of Vorkoun, who'd read his shameless banter, and not heard him at all.

Summer tried to linger, in warm afternoons and nodding flowers, but days grew shorter and shadows lengthened. Birds gathered in number, no longer interested in nests or song, whirling in busy clouds above fields they dared not touch. Bees hurried to fill their hives as the great sows gorged on fallen acorns, Himself watching sorrowfully from behind the gate because he would roam and forget where he belonged. Alyssa and Cheffy, sympathetic, brought him baskets of acorns, but it wasn't the same as freedom and the boar moped with immense drama while he ate. In the gardens, vines withered to bright yellow wreaths around ripe pumpkins and squash. On the crags, the first hints of red and gold appeared. Before long, too soon, the colors would spread like flame and summer be done.

Like the bees, the villagers used every moment of daylight to store what they could against the coming winter, tasks that meant not only comfort, but survival. Even the youngest felt the rising urgency and no longer grumbled as they threw themselves into their chores. In years past, Jenn recalled wistfully, she'd counted herself fortunate to slip away to her meadow and see Wisp once every few days.

This summer's end was different.

For one thing, there were letters. Letters and letters and letters.

Each evening, Tir would drop by on his way to the mill to give her Bannan's latest, and Wyll's would be waiting on the window seat or flutter in with a moth. Jenn grew anxious about leaving the window closed in case she missed one, though moths grew emboldened and Peggs worried about their clothes. Each morning, Tir would stop for breakfast and pick up her replies.

For another, this summer's end held impending weddings, one her own. Weddings, Jenn soon learned, meant sewing every moment she wasn't working in the garden or kitchen or helping Hettie make cheese or Gallie stuff sausage. Endless sewing. Not new clothes, or better-fitting old ones, which would have been fun, but household goods. Everyone with a length to spare brought it to the Nalynns. Jenn and Peggs hemmed sheets and cases, towels and curtains, and oh, the handkerchiefs . . .

Those would have been easier if she'd known what to embroider. Rhothan tradition, something Aunt Sybb inflicted with steely determination at every opportunity, held that good fortune could be sewn into a household. Her sister gladly stitched fantastical P's and K's on her work, twining the letters around one another until their father fondly observed both were nigh to illegible. Jenn settled for flowers and leaves.

She bit a thread and rolled the excess on a finger.

It wasn't quite fair to say she hadn't made up her mind whose initial belonged with hers.

It wasn't quite fair, she thought, that she couldn't.

The letters weren't helping. If Peggs fell silent, as happened whenever she thought of Kydd, which she did more and more often, Jenn would find words swimming up in front of her stitching. Bannan wrote of his Marrowdell, as she'd asked, regaling her with marvels. Toads in chain mail and roads of silver. Dancers in the old trees; hunters in the grain. He'd drawn the ruins he could see from his window, which was very interesting; he'd put a small lover's heart beside her name, which was unsettling and charming and altogether inappropriate. And the things he said?

She blushed and sewed faster. She could recite every word.

No cider for me. I keep your letters beneath my pillow. It's no wonder I sleep so well . . .

I wake each morning to sunlight and bird song, and my first thought is of you . . .

Dance with me, at the harvest? My sister, who taught me my steps, would tell you I'm a decent partner, who keeps to the measure and doesn't embarrass himself. Though if I had you in my arms, I fear I'd steal a kiss. Would you forgive me?

He was shameless.

And wonderful. For most of all, Bannan wrote of himself. Private, special things. The freckled girl in the bakery who'd won his five-year-old's heart with her cookies. Being lost in the woods with his sister, after they'd pretended to be hunters riding after wild boar, and how Lila had kept him safe and warm in her arms till they were found the next morning. The terrifying discovery he could see the truth or its lack in someone's face, and how his father had taught him the responsibility of a truthseer and its cost. Losing both parents. Gaining Scourge, who'd tossed him from the saddle twenty-three times before accepting him as rider.

Jenn could barely wait to read each new letter, an eagerness she managed to keep to herself only because she made herself read Wyll's first.

you Are being good careful . . .
I continue to build our magnificent castle it Has no windows . . .
why do We need a kitchen we can eat with him . . .
I do not know How to thank the small ones
they perplex me . . .
the harvest will Be soon and we will be Together always

Wyll was Wisp and loved her. She loved him. But with each new letter, the more Jenn understood Wen Treff's warning. A change in shape did not mean a change in nature. Wyll wasn't a man, not inside.

But he was her dearest, oldest friend. She'd made him what he was and he needed her. Eight bright and sunny mornings in a row, Jenn Nalynn awoke knowing exactly what to do. She would marry Wyll. She wouldn't write to Bannan again. She wouldn't read his letters. It had to stop.

Eight evenings in a row, she'd grown empty save for doubt. How could she not read and reply, when Bannan wrote from his heart to hers, and hers so needed his?

A voice interrupted her thoughts. "I know that face," Peggs said gently.

Jenn looked up from her stitching to where her sister sat beside her on the bench. Supper done, they'd sought the porch to take advantage of the last of the daylight. "This face?" She wrinkled her nose and squinted.

"No, Dear Heart. The one you get when you're thinking about Bannan Larmensu."

She had a face for that? Jenn felt warm. "I do not," she objected. "And you're wrong. I was thinking about—about how nice it will be to see Mistress Sand again."

The tinkers would arrive the day after tomorrow. A roasting pit was being prepared for a side of Bannan's ox; the meat, wrapped in moist sacking, would be left to cook till the welcome feast. In other preparation, Aunt Sybb's elegant bays, bored and sensing their journey home, were now stabled in the Emms' barn; come the harvest, they'd settle as willingly in harness to pull hoists as her coach. Brawl and Battle, who'd pull Davi's cart, dozed in the Treffs'. Tomorrow, the cows and calves and Good'n'Nuf the bull would be moved from the commons to graze the orchard. Wainn's pony always trotted eagerly in the lead, ever hopeful the villagers might have forgotten to pick the apples first. The sows and Himself would stay where they were, being gracious about sharing their space with the tinkers' wagons and beasts, and much less so about being ousted from their wallow.

Once the tinkers were here, clearing the fields and milling would take a hectic four days, all to be completed on the Golden Day, all including her birthday, their weddings, and, presumably, the Great Turn.

As if this wasn't enough to make her head spin, the very next unimaginable day, Aunt Sybb would leave for the winter, with Uncle Horst as escort. Kydd and Peggs would move into the Nalynn loft, it had been decided, and Jenn would live in . . . what? Whatever Wyll was building for them, not that anyone had seen it. Her father tried to hide his doubt, but he'd never been good at concealing his feelings, not the important ones. Aunt Sybb wasn't much better. She threw herself into wedding preparations with alarming fervor, and conversed, when she did pause for tea, about the preparations she would have done, had they been in Avyo and had another year.

"So you see," Jenn finished firmly, "that was my thinking face, not a face for anyone in particular."

"Hmm." Peggs said in a carefully noncommittal tone. Suddenly, she tugged the embroidery hoop from Jenn's unresisting hands and held it to the light. "Oh no. Dearest Heart—is it that time already?"

Jenn took the hoop back. She'd been preoccupied while she stitched, which wasn't unusual, and couldn't recall if she'd been doing a rose or a leaf.

She'd sewn a pebble. A white pebble.

Her sister was right. It was time. The sun was setting.

The hoop fell from Jenn's hands, to roll away on the weathered planks. A sudden cramp flamed across her middle and she doubled over with a groan she couldn't help.

Peggs' arms came around her, held tight. "Heart's Blood. Not again."

Again and harder to bear. "It'll pass," Jenn gasped, though she wasn't sure at all. The once-vague emptiness had grown to fierce hunger pangs and now? Now her stomach might be filled with burning coals.

"It's getting worse. I know it is. We must tell Poppa. Aunt Sybb."

"No. Please. There's nothing they can do but worry." More than they already did.

"Ancestors Distressed and Despairing. I'm worried enough for all of us." Peggs got that look, the one that said she'd made up her mind. Sure enough, "You promised me, Dearest Heart, if things got worse you'd talk to Kydd. Well, they're worse. We'll go tonight, after supper."

Unable to argue, Jenn clung to her sister and nodded. The pain faded, if not the emptiness. "At least it's not long now," she said, forcing cheer into her voice. "Till the Great Turn."

"Six days," Peggs agreed, with no more certainty than she. They trusted a voice from a dream. "Will you—can you—"

Easier to breathe, with the pain ended. "The question is," Jenn replied, retrieving her hoop and pulling out the offending thread, "will we finish our stitching by then?"

She knew what Peggs had meant. Could she last?

She must. That was all there was to it.

Jenn gazed up the road. Tir would be coming soon. With her next letter.

Maybe she shouldn't think of Bannan each night, or read his letter—and reread the rest—before bed.

But it kept that hunger at bay when nothing else could.

"Another letter, sir?" Tir gave a doleful shake of his head. "Seems to me you wrote one yesterday."

"Indeed I did." Clapping his friend on one shoulder, Bannan flourished the well-traveled envelope. "But Jenn wrote to me and I owe her an equally prompt reply." He offered, as he had each of the previous afternoons, "I could deliver it."

"I'll manage, sir." Tir took the letter. "No reason for you to leave this grand place."

A breeze nipped Bannan's ear. "This becomes tiresome."

"Who asked you?" Tir scowled. "Bloody beast."

Scourge rolled a dark eye to show red.

"Peace, the pair of you." As far as the truthseer was concerned, the situation had passed tiresome a week ago and was well on its way to driving him mad. But it was a delicious madness, hope-filled and inspiring, and wasn't it almost over? "Tir's right." At their looks, he added innocently, "Isn't harvest to start tomorrow?"

"The day after, sir. If these tinkers show up. I've seen no sign."

What he'd meant was no reply from Vorkoun, which was, Bannan thought cheerfully, Tir's problem and not his. He'd done as promised, and done it, thank you, long enough. "They'll be here. Then I must go to the village, mustn't I?" he asked, trying hard not to grin. "To earn my share of flour."

First letters, now this. Tir wasn't one to admit defeat, but Bannan could tell from his exasperated, "Yes, sir," that he'd won. "I'll let you know." Then his eyes gleamed. "Best I be going. I wouldn't want to be late to supper at the Nalynns."

The truthseer bowed. "Give them my regards." Tir might share Jenn's table, but it was his letter she'd read tonight.

Scourge snorted his impatience and headed off, though at a pace matched to the man's shorter steps. Bannan stepped out on the road to watch until they passed safely beyond the path to the Spine, smiling at the sight of Tir's hands gesturing, the kruar's head bobbing. A pair and conversation as unlikely as Marrowdell itself.

The day after tomorrow he'd take the same road at last, and see her dear face, instead of imagining it.

Have her smile at him.

She would, he thought. Smile. He felt sometimes she did, as she wrote him. Especially when she wrote what gave him hope.

I might forgive a kiss. Or I might not. I assuredly can't say ahead of time, since any kissing or forgiving would depend entirely on the circumstances, and such circumstances are highly unlikely to begin with . . .

Though I do love to dance. I would dance with you, Bannan. To see how well your sister taught you, of course . . .

I read your letters before I sleep. Within your words, I feel safe and happy, as though time isn't rushing by and taking me with it, as though anything might truly be possible. For that, I thank you.

He'd had his share of infatuations; Vorkoun abounded with soft skin and luscious lips, and he'd fallen in and out of love like clockwork. How could mere words on a page make his heart pound?

Because Jenn Nalynn wasn't to be found anywhere else. He'd looked for her all his life, without knowing what he sought.

Not long now.

After supper, Jenn and Peggs found Kydd Uhthoff up to his elbows in honeycomb and unsettled bees.

Which was, Jenn thought, slowing in case the bees blamed her for their imminent losses, to be expected. It was harvest time after all; honey and wax had their season, too. Wainn stood nearby, the hive's woven lid in his hands. Bees climbed across his eyebrows and ears and he smiled with closed lips, as though otherwise they'd be tempted to walk across his teeth.

Not a moment to interrupt.

Peggs, however, was undaunted. Hair bouncing on her shoulders, she marched straight to the open hive, with a brief nod to Wainn, and demanded of her future husband, "What do you know of magic?"

Kydd, who'd been gently sweeping bees from a comb with a wide brush, looked at his future wife with a strange little smile. "I wondered when you'd ask, Dearest Heart."

"You did?" Though taken aback, Peggs lost none of her momentum. "Well. I'm asking now. We need your help."

"I know a great deal about what purports to be magic, but isn't," the beekeeper answered enigmatically, and bent to coax more bees to leave. Then his eyes, keen and bright, lifted to Jenn. "Much less about what is."

Blood rushed to Jenn's cheeks. Bees droned by, more busy than annoyed. A few bumped into her; most stayed on their doorstep or hovered around the beekeeper as he removed the next comb. These were cleverly suspended from bars laid across the top of the hive and, if she hadn't been thoroughly flustered, she'd have peeked inside to look for Kydd's books.

A page of which she'd used. "I did some," she confessed. "I used a wishing from one of your books."

Wainn glanced up and smiled. "I wrote it down and Aunt Sybb knew the words. They rhymed."

"I was there," Peggs jumped in bravely. "I helped."

Jenn shook her head. "I did it. I threw the ash over Wisp and—and said the words." Her lower lip trembled; she closed her teeth over it.

"So now we have Wyll." To Jenn's relief, Kydd didn't appear upset. Or surprised. "You think it was the wishing."

"What else could it be?" Peggs asked before Jenn could.

"Indeed." The beekeeper slipped the honeycomb back in the hive and pulled off his sticky gloves. "There are wishings for any hope or desperation, our Ancestors being nothing if not inventive. I recall one for abundance in a marriage," he told them, solemn but for the twinkle in his eye, "that requires, among other things, a shellfish from the deep ocean beyond Eldad and a vial of powdered thighbone from one's most fertile ancestor. Even today, when civilized folk proclaim they no longer believe in magic, you can buy both in the markets of Vorkoun."

"If you buy powdered bone," Jenn objected, carefully not looking at her alarmed sister, "how can you be sure it's really the thigh? Or your ancestor's?"

"How—you—I—" Peggs sputtered.

"And not a cow's?" Wainn added cheerfully.

"Just so," the beekeeper approved. "Such are the arguments when a wishing fails. It wasn't the right bone. The words weren't said properly."

Her sister looked about to explode. "There'll be no magic or wishing about our wedding!"

Kydd chuckled. "Of course not, Dearest Heart. I wouldn't," he assured her, with a bow, "even if I could."

Mollified, Peggs gave a brisk nod. "Good."

"What do you mean, 'if you could?'" Jenn asked.

"Wishings aren't magic," Kydd said calmly. "At best, they're childish folly; at worst, elaborate hoaxes to take advantage of the gullible." He gave Jenn another too bright, too interested look. "Magic's what I found here."

"But—" A bee landed on Jenn's nose and she froze midprotest.

Other bees found Peggs more interesting, landing on her hair and arms. She held quite still, barely moving her lips to ask, "Might we continue this elsewhere?"

"At once. My apologies," the beekeeper said, easing a bee from Peggs' cheek with a finger and plucking another from her hair. "See how sweet you are?" he added softly, then louder, "Give us a moment to tidy up. We are almost out of light anyway, aren't we, Wainn?"

Wainn replaced the lid, making the bees happier and less interested in people, sweet or otherwise. The sisters helped gather the brushes and other beekeeping supplies while the Uhthoffs locked the buckets of comb in their larder, that sweetness being too tempting to leave in the open.

Kydd went into the home he shared with his brother and nephew, returning with a blanket, pitcher, and mugs. The blanket he and Wainn spread on a grassy spot beneath the nearest apple tree. The pitcher turned out to be filled with cooled tea, sweetened with honey, and Kydd poured as the sisters made themselves comfortable. Wainn stretched out on the grass, chin on his crossed arms, eyes closed. A moth lit on his shoulder. Jenn squinted, but saw neither satchel nor boots.

Kydd gave a cup to Peggs, fingers lingering, then passed one to Jenn. He settled, eyes lively with curiosity. "So you did magic."

She tried not to wince.

"Jenn Nalynn doesn't do magic," Wainn disagreed, which made her feel better. Then he added, "She is." Which didn't, especially when Kydd pursed his lips thoughtfully and raised his eyebrows.

"I am not," Jenn protested. She didn't want to be magic. Well, it might be fine and wonderful if she could see marvels like Bannan, or do the sort of miraculous things that filled stories, but not this. Not curses and horrid dreams and feeling ill for no reason every day. "I'm ordinary," she said desperately. "The most ordinary person in Marrowdell." She rubbed her arms, finding the air grown chill though the day had been summer-warm. Tonight they'd need an extra blanket. Which was ordinary. She would, she decided, pay greater attention to what was.

"Wainn meant no harm. Please don't be upset, Jenn," urged Kydd, sounding a bit upset himself.

"Too late for that," Peggs disagreed. She took Jenn's hand and squeezed it gently. "My dear brave sister. She's already suffering, Kydd. We must help her."

Jenn felt warmer at once. Who wouldn't, with such a champion?

"It's more than the wishing," Peggs explained, eyes flashing with determination. "Something's happening. Go on, Jenn. Tell them."

Where to even start? Wainn kept his eyes closed, appearing almost asleep. The moth tidied its wings while bees, not the least sleepy, droned by their heads.

The beekeeper gave an encouraging nod.

Once you dip your toe, take the plunge, Aunt Sybb would say, no matter how chill the water. Jenn gulped tea and began, "It started when I went up on the Spine . . ."

No one interrupted, not even a bee, though Kydd started a little when she spoke of dragons, and Wainn smiled when she spoke of Wen and the toads.

". . . the Great Turn, if it is the eclipse, is almost here. When anything is possible, whatever that may mean," she finished.

"The end of the curse," her sister stated firmly. "And whatever's making you sick. That, too." As if she'd settle for nothing less.

Kydd, perhaps well aware of his future bride's indomitable nature, went a little pale. "I see." His forehead furrowed. "Perhaps we should go to my brother. He knows more about eclipses and the stars than—"

"Master Dusom?" Peggs said faintly.

"Just Dusom, Dearest Heart. He's to be your brother soon," the beekeeper reminded her.

He wasn't yet, that look on Peggs' face meant, but all she said was, "We came to you."

"And I want to help." Kydd frowned in thought. "Jenn. This voice you heard. What can you tell me about who spoke?"

Terrifying might be true, but not, she understood, what he was after. "Old," she ventured. "Very old. And not—" she stopped.

"Not what?"

"Not like us," Jenn said faintly. "Not—a person."

Wainn opened his eyes and offered a finger to the moth. It stepped confidently atop a knuckle, wings fluttering. "I hear too," said the younger Uhthoff, eye-to-eye with the tiny creature. "Wen hears the best."

"Hears what?" asked Peggs. "Who?"

He gazed at them in mild surprise. "Marrowdell." The moth opened its wings and flew up and away. They all watched it disappear among the leaves.

Jenn sighed to herself. No doubt Wainn had a unique view of the world, as did Wen. If only it was easier to understand.

"I don't understand," Peggs echoed unwittingly. "How can a place speak?"

"Nothing would surprise me here," Kydd assured her, giving his nephew a fond look. Then he took a deep breath and leaned forward, an unfamiliar grimness to his face. "It's my turn to share a secret, dear ladies. One I meant to tell you long before now," this to Peggs.

"You left a wife in Avyo?" she teased, though Jenn noticed her sister's fingers had tightened around her cup. "Two?"

"No." He actually blushed. "Nothing like that. I—"

Peggs lifted one shapely eyebrow. "You don't like pie."

"I love pie," the hapless beekeeper protested. "I—"

"You—"

Jenn poked her sister's leg with a toe. Peggs feared what Kydd might say, for good reason. Marrowdell's secrets hadn't proved comfortable to learn, or safe. "Whatever it is," she promised gently, "we'll understand. Won't we, Peggs?"

Her sister gave the tiniest nod, her eyes troubled.

Kydd, to his credit, looked relieved. "I've not lied to you, ever," he said firmly. "You've already guessed I was a student, in part, of magic and wishings. Oh, I knew they weren't real. I knew so much on the road north." A rueful shrug. "And so very little, as it turned out.

"Imagine my feelings when we arrived in Marrowdell. I knew there was no such thing as magic and here was an endless fountain, waiting to be needed. Homes ready to live in. Grain that planted and tended itself. Magic, real magic, springing up everywhere I looked. Magic that had nothing to do with my books or understanding. Ancestors Witness, there were even magical toads!"

Wainn smiled.

"Because the Ancestors provided for us," Peggs countered, an unfamiliar edge to her voice. "That's what your brother teaches. That's why we gather to give the Midwinter Beholding. No one's ever called it magic."

"Not even Aunt Sybb," Jenn added, their aunt's distrust of Marrowdell's eccentricities being well known.

"No," Kydd agreed heavily. "And that's what you need to know about me, Dearest Heart." He shook his head. "I came here, my family shattered, Wainn injured and unconscious, and didn't see the lovely haven everyone else did. How could I? I knew better," this with a pained twist to his lips. "If magic was real, then so were the old stories about it. Stories that told me Marrowdell was a baited trap, that such gifts must have a terrible price.

"I insisted we leave, at once, but no one took me seriously. Everyone was exhausted and heartsore. They told me to be grateful. That the Ancestors were kind and generous and I should be properly Beholden.

"How could I be? I was terrified. When nightmares drove the other families away, I claimed they were warnings. When Wainn remained unconscious, I blamed Marrowdell, not his injuries. By the first harvest," a grimace, "I'd made myself such a nuisance, the village voted to tell Dusom to shut me up or send me away."

There was fire in Peggs' eyes. "No Nalynn would do that!"

"No Nalynn did." Kydd smiled slightly. "But most of the rest. I didn't blame them. I'd no evidence, no proof. Life was hard enough; they couldn't accept what made it easier might be tainted. Of course I couldn't abandon my family, so I pretended to recant, to be content, all the while ranting in private to my poor, patient brother."

He'd been like Riss, Jenn thought. Unhappy, but bound to stay. Worse, since he'd been afraid too.

Kydd continued, "Then, one night, I translated an Ansnan history text that described a terrible cataclysm in the north. It claimed priests wishing a path to the stars had brought down their wrath. Only a few escaped to flee south. They were named the star-touched, for though they were clearly mad, they were said to possess real magic.

"Magic. The north. And a cataclysm. I concluded it must have taken place here, in Marrowdell," he told them, eyes bright with remembered triumph. "The hills bear scars of the right age. I found what I believed were ruins."

Ruins Bannan had seen. Amazed, Jenn barely kept still.

"I had proof at last, that this place was too dangerous for us. I presented it to Duson and argued there could be another disaster at any time. He agreed with me, for once. Then," the beekeeper's eyes softened, "my brother asked me two questions. If we dared move Wainn, where could we go? And, if we died here, by magic or winter, what better place for our bones than with Larell's and Ponicce's?

"The answer to both was nowhere else. We were stuck here, trap or not, and from then on I stifled my fears. I waited and watched, expecting disaster."

"How dreadful!" Peggs took Kydd's hand in both of hers. "But—you don't feel that way now. How did you—what changed your mind?"

"The tinkers arrived. They . . ." he paused, his gaze seeming to turn inward, his mouth working without sound.

As if the words twisted away from him. "What did they do?" Jenn asked uneasily. "Kydd?"

His face cleared. "They were happy to see us," the beekeeper replied, which might have been the answer he'd first tried to give, or not. "They explained Marrowdell had been made by those who cared about the welfare of the lost or exiled, to be a new home for those with peace in their hearts. Best of all, Master Riverstone was able to heal Wainn."

The youngest Uhthoff rolled over to gaze up into the apple tree. "So I could tell you, Uncle. That Marrowdell was a good place and safe and we should stay."

Kydd reached out his free hand to tussle his nephew's hair. "The first words from your mouth." He ducked his head for a moment, as if overcome, then lifted it, his eyes suspiciously bright. "Marrowdell gave you back to us. I'd been wrong to fear its magic. Since then," a shy smile, "I've been entranced."

Wainn, speaking out. Wen, refusing to. "Because Marrowdell is magic," Jenn said, eyeing the apple trees, sky, and ground suspiciously. But they remained ordinary.

Like Kydd, Bannan had seen Marrowdell's magic right away. Well, she'd lived here her whole life and hadn't, which surely proved she wasn't magic at all. Greatly relieved, she picked up her tea.

"Well, then," Peggs said, so firmly Jenn paused, cup at her lips, to give her sister a worried look. "How do we make it stop bothering Jenn?" As if "it" was lumpy flour or mud on the floor.

Wainn frowned. "She should stop bothering Marrowdell."

Kydd frowned. "That's hardly—"

"It's Jenn Nalynn's fault," the younger Uhthoff insisted, uncharacteristically stern.

"It isn't!" her sister protested.

"He's right." Jenn put the cup down, her hand unsteady. Wen had said she'd put the village in danger. That she'd tried to go where she shouldn't. "The wishing worked because I did it. Because of—" she couldn't say the word, "—something about me."

"Yes, Jenn," Kydd agreed, his voice gentle. "I believe so."

"And that horrid pebble," Jenn said miserably. "It's my fault too."

"I see no other answer," he agreed, his voice gentle. "After all Marrowdell's done for us, I can't believe it suddenly means you harm. The pebble—or what it represents—must have something to do with your—" Peggs nudged him, "—special nature."

"You mean magic." She sighed. They were wearing her down with their belief, preposterous as it seemed. "I try to find something safer to wish for,'" she admitted. "Every night I try. But it's getting harder."

Her sister stroked her hair. "Sunset's the worst."

"Sunset." The beekeeper's gaze sharpened. "When the toads hide."

"Toads?" Peggs repeated blankly, so like Aunt Sybb Jenn would have laughed, but couldn't. The toads had come to her rescue, but they hadn't been happy with her. Not at all.

"Marrowdell's sunset is important," Kydd said. "The toads aren't the only ones who avoid it."

Wainn yawned. "Because sunset shows what's real."

"If you're lucky," his uncle qualified. "And they let you see them. At first, I couldn't, unless Wainn was with me. Even now, I rarely catch more than a glimpse. They're careful."

"Who are?" Peggs' eyes widened.

"We aren't alone," Jenn explained. "Bannan told me. In his letters." Which was no reason to blush, but she felt her cheeks grow warm anyway. "He says sunset's when he can see all manner of wonderful creatures." She'd tried to look for them herself, only to be disappointed. Lately she'd felt too ill to bother. Maybe she should hide at sunset too. At least then no one would see her discomfort.

"He sees the truth," Kydd nodded, unaware of the troubled turn of her thoughts. "Marrowdell is home to a host of other settlers, Dear Hearts, small and secretive. Some stay near us, as if we give them purpose. I believe—I hope—we have one as well, whatever it may be, that lets us earn Marrowdell's gifts."

Toads who traded pebbles for eggs. Guardians for the grain.

And dragons. Not so small, but very secret. What was their purpose?

"Wisp," she said uncomfortably, feeling a chill in the lengthening shadows. "He's looked after me."

"Yes," Kydd agreed, trading glances with Peggs. "At first, we all wondered that Radd let you go off on your own. Horst wanted to follow you, but Radd wouldn't permit him. He swore Marrowdell protected you."

Wisp's purpose.

His duty.

She was that to him?

Jenn had thought the agonizing emptiness at sunset was the worst she could feel. That learning the world wasn't what she thought, nor was she, the most frightening. Not so.

Now she must question a friendship as much part of her life as the sky or ground below it. The words were like slivers of ice in her mouth, or was it turning cold again? "He didn't have to be my friend to do that. Why did he?"

Kydd lifted his hands helplessly. Peggs shook her head.

Wainn bent his neck and regarded her upside down. "You became his."

About to object this was no answer, Jenn hesitated. Wainn blinked peacefully. She'd learned to pay attention to everything he said; it always made sense, if not right away.

She had become Wisp's friend, hadn't she? However it had started, whatever Wisp's reason for being with her, their friendship was real. In her heart, she knew it was. Jenn found herself able to smile, a little. "Quite the friend I turned out to be," she said weakly. "Look what he is now."

"Still yours," Peggs assured her.

Despite her so-called magic. It'd be easier to believe if she could see it. An extra finger or toe. Better yet, a rainbow of feathers in her hair, or hair that stayed clean.

In stories, people with magic were powerful and wise. She was neither, though admittedly she could be willful. Jenn sighed to herself. Aunt Sybb wouldn't approve of sulking over the state of things just because it displeased her. But she hadn't wanted magic. All she'd ever wanted was to leave Marrowdell and see the world.

Why wouldn't Marrowdell let her go?

Peggs, Kydd, and Wainn waited, patient and kind. A bee droned by, impatient and busy. Twilight was upon them. Shadows crossed their legs and cooled their toes.

Finally, Jenn held out her hands, palm up. "What should I do?"

Kydd ran his fingers through his hair, a rueful look on his face. "I wish I knew. My learning proved worse than useless here. That's why I tore up my books and used them in the hives."

"After I read them," Wainn pointed out. "I have all the words, Uncle, if you ever want them again."

Now that was magic worth having, Jenn thought enviously.

The beekeeper smiled. "For which I thank you." His smile faded as he met Peggs' eyes, then Jenn's. "You trusted me and came to me for help, Dear Hearts. I'm sorrier than I can say to disappoint you. Perhaps the tinkers—?"

"Don't be sorry." The youngest Uhthoff rolled over to regard him. "No one can help Jenn Nalynn now. It's her fault."

Peggs uttered a soft cry of distress; Kydd's face darkened. "Nephew!"

"It's all right," Jenn said quickly, though her heart plummeted in her chest and it wasn't. It wasn't right at all. "Wainn's just—just being—" Wainn, which should mean gentle and perceptive and often confusing, not this, not terrifying. "—honest."

"Honest or not, that's no way to speak to a friend come for our aid," the beekeeper snapped. "I expect better of you, young man."

She couldn't remember Kydd raising his voice in anger, least of all to his beloved nephew, but Wainn paid no attention. He looked directly at her, his eyes unfocused as though he listened to what only he could hear.

"Help yourself, Jenn Nalynn," he told her. "Your chance comes at the Great Turn. Seize it. Only you can."

Having made this startling pronouncement, the youngest Uhthoff jumped to his feet with a boyish grin. "I'm going swimming," he said cheerfully.

"Wait—" He couldn't leave yet. Not when he seemed to know more than anyone.

Wainn took her outstretched hand in both of his and went to one knee beside her. He brought his face to hers until their cheeks touched and all she could see of him was a brown eye framed by thick dark lashes. He smelled of roses.

"You found the way no others dared," he whispered, his breath warm on her neck. "Take it again when the time comes, Jenn Nalynn. Marrowdell will show you. Take it again and be your magic. Be brave and of good heart."

He lightly kissed her ear, then pulled away. "We believe in you." With that, the remarkable Wainn Uhthoff rose, gave a short unselfconscious bow, and walked into the growing shadows. To swim, presumably.

Jenn held very still, for once understanding all too well. Marrowdell expected her to go back up the Spine. She certainly didn't want to do that again.

Other than the treacherous part of her that did.

"We believe in you too," Peggs said, having heard only Wainn's final words. "You aren't on your own, Dearest Heart, and never will be. You have me. And Poppa and Aunt Sybb. Wyll—"

"And me," Kydd jumped in.

Peggs sent him a warm glance, then looked to Jenn. "You've us on your side, dear sister, and hope. Wen told you, didn't she? Wish for what's safe and wait. Be patient. You have what you need inside you—this magic. You can do whatever you must. I believe it." And, as if she had magic of her own, warm yellow porch lights began to wink through the trees, lit one by one. Marrowdell, settling itself for the night. Jenn heard soft voices and the lowing of the cows as they came to be milked. Someone sang. A lovely voice, a quiet, wistful song.

Riss Nahamm, Jenn thought, waiting for Horst, wishing her life and loves were different. For the first time, she felt envious. Life and love seemed so simple. She had to worry about magic and pebbles and . . . Help herself. Which meant, like Riss, keeping a secret. Only hers was dangerous. She couldn't let her sister or anyone, especially Wyll who would be angry, know she had to go back. They'd try to stop her.

Or worse, try to come with her.

They mustn't, she vowed, feeling much older than almost nineteen. The Spine wasn't safe.

Wainn was right. She was on her own.

"Jenn?"

She'd been silent too long. "You are the best sister, Peggs," Jenn said, finding a smile. "You're right, of course. Everything will work itself out."

"You can't be sure of that," Peggs countered. "We don't know what's happening to you or why."

"This is Marrowdell," Jenn insisted. "Kydd's right. We shouldn't doubt our own home."

The beekeeper looked as unconvinced as her sister. His eyes searched her face. "This sunset business will likely worsen as we approach the eclipse," he commented. "Covie has a stomach remedy. It might lessen your discomfort."

"I'll keep it in mind," Jenn assured him. Their concern warmed her heart, it was true, but at what cost? They couldn't help; they shouldn't try. And shouldn't they be happy? The moon was rising, the orchard peaceful and secluded.

The perfect place for lovers to meet. If only they'd notice each other more than her problem . . .

She wished they would, with all her heart.

The air softened and warmed, rich with the scent of roses. Her sister and Kydd moved perceptibly closer within the dappled shadow of the apple tree, their fingers intertwined, eyes on one another.

Which didn't mean she'd done something magic, Jenn thought with only the tiniest twinge. They were, after all, in love. She got to her feet, brushing off her skirt "I promised Poppa I'd stop in at the mill on my way home—" she began truthfully, since she also needed to pick up Bannan's latest letter, Tir having taken his supper there.

Both waited for her to finish with distracted, if fond, impatience.

"—I'll tell Aunt Sybb you'll be home later," she finished.

Jenn's smile faded once she left the pair. She walked by the still-busy hives without noticing the bees that bumped into her. She stepped out on the road without feeling the cool earth underfoot.

Distracted herself, but oddly, not by magic or pebbles.

She should, she decided rather desperately, have kissed Bannan Larmensu when she had the chance.

With each flash of the knife, the shavings thinned, curling as they drifted to the floor. Bannan rubbed his weary eyes with the back of his hand, but didn't straighten from his crouch over the wood. Almost finished.

Carving had passed many a tedious hour at camp. Some whittled, eyes on nothing at all, tinder accumulating between their boots. Others shaped arrows or walking sticks or forks. A few, like Tir, took dark pleasure in crafting faces to use as targets.

No words. No names. Nothing the enemy might find and pass to informants in Vorkoun. Regardless, everything went into the last fire before breaking camp, with the same care devoted to burying refuse and scuffing footprints. Anything to conceal numbers and intent, to hide.

Their enemy, naturally, did the same. In the marches, such was life.

A life, Bannan reminded himself, he no longer lived. A man without enemies was free to leave his mark in the world. Encouraged to do so, in fact.

He rubbed his thumb over the edge of the rose. By lamplight, it looked well enough. Returning to the initials beside it, he pressed the little knife carefully into the wood, deepening the J's lower curve. Next and last, the N.

There.

A moth fluttered to perch on one leg of the overturned bench, its head bent to examine his work.

"What do you think?" Curlicues had proved beyond his skill, but he'd done, he thought, a fair job, especially on the heart that held both rose and initials. Tradition held that to be the most important part anyway.

The moth reached into its satchel and solemnly removed a parchment no larger than a shaving. With an infinitesimal claw, it scratched away at that tiny surface, giving him an affronted look when he tried to peek at what it wrote. "Your pardon," he apologized, retreating to a more polite distance.

If it recorded him as possessed by hope and dread in distractingly equal measures, he couldn't deny it. Carving a sigil of love was one thing. To do so under a bench? A coward's choice, surely. What was he thinking? Ask Jenn Nalynn to sit on it and rejoice in private? "Lila needn't know," he advised the moth, though he'd no idea who or what read its little reports.

To be fair, his sister always understood what truly mattered; as often as not before he did.

Tease him over it? Oh, that'd she'd relish.

The moth finished and flew away. Bannan set the bench safely on its legs, hiding his love, and blew out his lamp. Night was settling around the edges of the farm, its shadows tucking in the trees and flowers. Something dipped and dove over the garden.

Something that giggled.

Smiling, Bannan waved a greeting, then yawned.

He went inside, leaving the door ajar; the village habit and a courtesy to his house toad, who was later than usual coming in tonight. Shrugging off his leather vest, the evening having turned chilly, he hung it on its peg, then climbed the ladder to the loft. A gentle breeze came through the open window, fragrant and cool.

Bannan readied himself for a good night's rest in what was, at last, a proper bed. The mattress might be straw, but it boasted imported silk sheets and two thistledown pillows. The sheets and pillowcases were slightly worn and bore the initials of Lila's sons; he valued them more for that.

The truthseer ran his fingers across the headboard. The wood from the wagon was rough, but could be, Tir had claimed, sanded and oiled to a fine finish.

Perhaps carved . . .

He shook his head. Not yet.

Jenn Nalynn's latest letter lay on the pillow, waiting to be reread. He took it to the window, tilting the paper to catch the faint remaining light, though he knew every word.

Dear Bannan

To my shame, I used to look forward to the harvest and my birthday with such selfish joy I didn't mind that it also meant Aunt Sybb would leave us for the winter. I confessed as much to Poppa today, while we swept the raceway. I thought he'd be disappointed in me, but he wasn't. He said it had made it easier for Aunt Sybb to go, seeing me happy.

How can I be happy now? I'm not that girl anymore. Everything's complicated, right down to the welcome feast. Davi's roasting your ox and wants me to thank you. I can't bring myself to do that, since your animal's dead because of Marrowdell. Because this place isn't like the rest of the world.

The world I'd hoped to see. Imagine it, Bannan. I could have met your sister, and seen Vorkoun for myself. Stood on every one of Avyo's great bridges and heard seabirds on the Sweet Sea. Taken the old caravan road to Mellynne and beyond.

I shouldn't write all this. Aunt Sybb would say "don't let regrets tarnish the future" and she's right. But it eases my heart to share mine, as I hope sharing with me about Lila and your life has eased yours.

Whatever my future holds, I shall face it. I take your courage as my measure, Bannan Truthseer, and vow to do what's best for those I love, as you have.

For that, for your example and the warmth of your friendship, I have no trouble thanking you at all.

Jenn

There was nothing on the other side.

"Dearest Heart, you're most welcome." Bannan pressed the letter to his lips, then folded it carefully. Little wonder the air was chill tonight; Jenn was troubled, despite her brave words, and he wished with all his heart he was with her, right now, kissing any regrets from her lips.

Which, however delightful a task, wouldn't help. He was part of what troubled her. The image of the dead meadow swam behind his eyes, a reminder Jenn Nalynn was no ordinary young woman. He risked more than losing her, if the dragon was right. He risked them all.

He kept her letters beneath his pillow, wrapped together in a square of faded yellow linen. Lila'd given him the token the day of their Blessed parents' internment in the Larmensu ossuary, saying not a word about it, then or since. He'd recognized the fabric as from the dress their mother had worn out to the gardens and the stables, and to play with her children. To the precious scrap, Lila had clipped the plain and sturdy brooch their father had worn when working around the estate, the elder Larmensu more at ease dressed like any stablehand than the lord of an estate. Don't forget who they were, those gifts said. And he hadn't.

Do what's best for those we love, she'd said.

And he would.

Tossing the pillow aside, Bannan took out the bundle, unfastened the brooch, and added Jenn's latest. Making sure it was securely pinned once more, he went to the chest at the foot of his bed, opened it, and laid the bundle gently inside.

He'd sent his reply with Tir. Done what was best for Jenn Nalynn.

Knowing that made it no easier to fall asleep.

Jenn climbed into bed that night, and did her best to think, not about magic or pebbles or dire warnings, but about safe and, above all, ordinary things. Maple candy came to mind. The unpleasant but needful taste of Covie's remedy, though that was too close to thinking of stomach aches and sunsets, so she thought instead, urgently, about the prickle of straw between her toes—

"You're in bed? I thought you'd be up writing. Did you light the candle for me?" Without waiting for an answer, Peggs went to the window and reached for a rose. Cupping a blossom in one careful hand, she took a long appreciative sniff. "What a night, Jenn. I told

Kydd how very brave I thought he'd been to stay for his family when he was so afraid of Marrowdell. Isn't it all amazing? Magic and old stories . . . I'm sure you'll be fine. He thinks so too. And did you see the moon? It was astonishing. The most beautiful I've ever seen." She began twirling around the room on her toes. "Only a day till everyone comes," she sang dreamily. "Only a day until the harvest." Her voice rose, "Then only four more," a twirl, just avoiding the end of the bed, "till our weddings! And the end of your curse, of course!"

"Hush," Jenn chided grumpily. "You'll wake Aunt Sybb."

Peggs stopped, fingers over her well-kissed and smiling mouth, eyes aglow.

Her own eyes felt like gravel. Jenn flopped over on her stomach. "As for letters, I'm finished with them," she informed her sister. "And tired."

"Your pardon. Good night, then, Dearest Heart." Her sister hummed, but quietly, as she changed into her nightdress, then brushed her hair.

Jenn rolled on her side. "I've nothing to say in a letter," she insisted, "that won't wait."

Peggs plumped her pillow. "Most reasonable."

Jenn flung herself on her back, arms outspread, and stared at the roof beams. "You think I should write."

Her sister blew out the candle and slipped between the sheets. "Move over. What I think isn't the question. What will they think, if you don't reply?"

Jenn rolled once more to give Peggs her share of the mattress, and muttered, "I don't care what they think. Men are a bother. Except Kydd and Wainn," she added hastily. "And Poppa." She drew a breath to continue the list.

"Go to sleep." A quiet chuckle. "Dream of dumplings."

"Warm, with butter and bits of bacon."

"There you go. I'll make some tomorrow."

Jenn listened to Peggs' peaceful breathing, barely louder than the crickets outside. She tried to think of butterflies and sunshine.

Letters.

Letters only made things worse.

Wyll's had been waiting on the window seat.

be careful be careful be careful
Do not speak to Strange persons when They arrive
I will protect you and Always yours Be

What did that mean? On the surface, someone new might be arriving. Being Wyll, she thought it more likely he admonished her against talking to Bannan and Tir at the harvest, which wasn't at all necessary or nice.

As for Bannan's . . . When she'd collected it from Tir, for once the former guard hadn't teased her.

He'd somehow known.

Her hand crept under her pillow, fingertips finding the cool smoothness of paper.

Dearest Heart

Forgive me if it slips out when next we meet. In the certain privacy of my thoughts, I call you by such tender names and imagine you smile. Yet a courtship by letter is no substitute for the trust and joyful knowledge gained from time spent together. I cherish every word you've written me over these past days. I do not count them as promises.

As hope, yes. I dare hold that in my heart. I burn with it.

Sweet Jenn, I beg you this once, do not reply. Let me hope with reckless abandon a while longer. Know that if you choose Wyll, I'll be the first to step forward to wish you both every happiness.

Know that I am here, if you choose otherwise.

Bannan

Both loved her.

Neither could help.

Neither should try.

The next morning, when Tir came to breakfast, Jenn Nalynn had no letters for him to take.

Wyll laid out his clothes, then awkwardly lowered himself to his mossy bed. Another night.

He detested night.

Night was dampness and chill. And danger. Nyphrit dared his door once he lowered his guard and slept. They were met and dispatched neatly by the little cousin to be sure, but that they dared approach at all . . .

The vermin had learned his new weakness. He could no more harm the vile nuisances than he could break Bannan's letter-writing fingers, satisfying as that might have been. The girl's expectation held him from worse than spilling ink.

Small and weak, nyphrit. In numbers, they were a threat not to ignore.

A moth fluttered in through his door, evading the toad's hopeful lunge with a flick of its wings. The dragon eyed it suspiciously. ~ There's nothing newsworthy here. Be gone. ~

Instead, it settled itself on the seat of his discarded trousers. ~ I bring tidings, elder brother. ~

The toad shifted to keep one bulbous eye on the moth, but wisely stayed silent.

Wyll, being more sore than curious, didn't bother to move or answer. He'd stood too much today, helping Tir and Bannan repair the larder. Why they wanted to store food in the ground was beyond him, but having such a store nearby was itself a pleasant prospect. Tir had given him a knowing look and suggested Bannan order a lock. He was welcome to do so. The dragon had no doubt he could open it.

The moth took a scroll from its satchel and waved it delicately. ~ Are you not interested, elder brother? ~

What interested Wyll, of a sudden, was the moth itself. He realized he couldn't tell if he'd seen this one before, or seen only this one;

unlike little cousins, moths looked and sounded the same. At the turn—he had no idea what they became, truth be told. The Verge didn't hold their like, so he hadn't cared.

Nor had he cared why they collected their tidbits of gossip. Now . . . now he wondered.

Wondering, the dragon pushed with his good hand and arm until he sat up. ~ Tell me your news. ~

The moth unrolled its scroll. ~ It is not mine, elder brother, ~ the small thing demurred. Reading his scowl correctly, it hurried on, toes fussing along the scroll's margin, large eyes dipping to read. ~ 'Your penance remains.' ~

That voice.

The toad cowered, eyes sunk into its head.

Those words. Wyll's blood froze. ~ What are you? ~

~ 'Keep her from harm,' ~ the moth read in a sei's unforgettable voice. ~ 'Your penance remains. Only you may know the truth.' ~

~ That's why I'm here, like this. That's what I'm doing! ~ He dared rail against it, when he couldn't against the sei. "I know my duty! I've set a guard. I've warned her— ~

The moth might not have heard. ~ 'Your penance remains. Ensure our peace, so long as she is as she is. Then, your penance will be complete.' ~

~ 'Is as she is?' What does that mean? ~ he demanded, desperate. ~ Alive? Dead? I don't understand! ~ He scrambled to his knee, arm outstretched. ~ Tell me! ~

~ 'Remember. At the Great Turn, all is possible.' ~ With that, the moth rolled the parchment and tucked it back in its satchel. Its wings twitched.

~ Wait! ~ The dragon threw himself forward, scattering moss and clothing and stacks of words. Crystal cracked as he fell, hard, the moth squeezing through his fingers and away. "Please!" He heard himself beg in his man's voice and closed his lips in shame.

The valiant little cousin leapt, too late. The moth disappeared into the night.

The moth that spoke for the sei. As a sei.

The moth that wasn't a moth at all.

Wyll curled into a morose ball, heedless of the damp from the broken crystal, of the mess.

The Great Turn. When all was possible. When what was possible? What was the girl to be?

They played games, the sei.

He hadn't thought they played them with Jenn Nalynn.

The dragon snarled in impotent fury.

Nyphrit slunk away in the dark.

EIGHTEEN

"ONE RARELY SEES such devotion to hemming."

Jenn glanced up at Aunt Sybb. "I want to do a good job," she said. She eased her grip on the needle, surprised to find her hand cramped and sore.

"There's good, Dear Heart," her aunt replied serenely, settling herself in her brother's rocking chair after a cautious glance beneath in case of toads, her hands on a paper-wrapped bundle she'd brought from the parlor, "and good enough."

Her finest needlework might be more than the hem on a dish towel required, Jenn admitted to herself. "I'm trying to keep busy," she explained. Today, the last and final before the harvest, was proving to be the longest she could remember. She'd done her chores—and some of Peggs'—with extra attention, then swept the mill floors until their father, normally pleased to have her underfoot, suggested she help her sister instead. Which she'd tried to do, but Peggs, for some reason, had picked today to clean out the stove and scrub that floor, humming happily all the while.

Which wasn't magic, but might be magic's fault.

Magic itself was proving decidedly uncooperative. Kydd hadn't believed the words and tokens from his book had mattered, that she'd somehow wished Wisp into Wyll by herself. So this morning Jenn tried wishing a dish dry, to no avail. Next, she'd looked their house toad in its limpid brown eyes and made a supreme effort to wish it wings.

The toad had fallen asleep.

It was all most discouraging. How was she supposed to accomplish something magical five days from now, if she couldn't put wings on a toad or dry a dish?

As for wishing at people, which she apparently could do? After last night, she'd not do that again, thank you, especially not at people she knew and loved. It wasn't fair, for one thing. It wasn't, she was quite sure, at all proper. She didn't need to consult Aunt Sybb to know what she'd say, if their dear aunt could bear to discuss magic in the first place. "Do nothing you'll recall with shame." She'd also say, "Now, Jenn Nalynn, how would you like that done to you?"

Though the latter had usually been about wearing Peggs' last clean shirtwaist or making faces at Roche.

So no wishing at people, a resolution Jenn feared she'd made too late. If she didn't know how she did whatever she did—if she did anything at all—how could she know what she'd already done? Could she really be sure what anyone said or felt or did around her had been their idea and not her wish?

Her life hadn't been the same since Wisp became Wyll. His hadn't either, of course, and she was truly sorry about that, but the more she'd thought about magic itself, the more it'd seemed the wishing and that morning had been the start of it all. Hadn't she'd wanted to have Wisp with her always, more clearly and powerfully than she'd ever wanted anything before?

There'd been another moment like that, she thought, glancing at her aunt with guilty pride. The haggard, worn look of days past was gone completely and not even powder muted the healthy glow of the older woman's cheeks. Her eyes shone like gems.

And hadn't she wanted, more than anything, for her aunt and Tir to be free of their nightmares?

Another saying came to mind. "A person of good character rises above her weakness and uses her strength wisely." Thinking it steadied Jenn. Whatever she'd done, however she did it, there'd been a moment when, yes, she'd made a choice. Not so wisely, in Wyll's case, but if she was responsible, hadn't saving Aunt Sybb and Tir from nightmares been very wise indeed? Bannan kept his friend; they kept the sure, loving counsel of their aunt.

But what else had she done?

Might do?

Hemming was safer. A stack of safely hemmed towels sat on the bench beside her and Jenn gave the empty basket a glum look. "I've finished everything," she complained without thought.

Aunt Sybb's well-drawn eyebrow rose skyward. "'Everything'?" But before Jenn could say a word and get herself in more trouble, the older woman patted her bundle and chuckled. "Then I've chosen the right time to give you this, Dearest Heart. For your birthday."

Jenn took the bundle eagerly, only to hesitate, fingering the knotted string as she searched her aunt's kind eyes. Had she been wrong? "You're not leaving early after all, are you?"

"Of course not!" Aunt Sybb ruffled like a distraught bird. "Ancestors Witness, wherever did you get that notion? You and your sister manage without me?"

"We couldn't," Jenn replied vehemently, content again.

"This is simply of more use today. It's a dress I'd intended you to wear on your first day as a grown woman." She smiled gently. "Since you'll be wearing a wedding dress that day instead, and have outgrown all others—yes, I noticed your legs, Sweetling, they're hard to miss—I thought you'd like it for tomorrow night. For the Welcome Feast and dance." At her blank look, her aunt's smile spread, making soft creases beside her eyes. "Your young man will be there, will he not? Now open it."

Jenn needed no further urging. She untied and rolled the string, tucking it into a pocket. The heavy waxed paper crunched and crackled as she unfolded it with care. "Oh." She lifted the dress, careful of the calluses on her palms.

At once she could tell it was different from any she'd seen. From the high waist down, the feather-soft fabric was elegantly patterned in black and white, that pattern, when she looked more closely, being of tiny millwheels and sheaves of ripe grain, arranged in rows. She'd seen such delicate artwork in books. How was it managed on cloth?

But there was more to wonder at. The dress was sleeveless. As if that wasn't bold enough to make Jenn blush, the bodice consisted of narrow strips of bright red, white, and black silk that would flow over the shoulders to plunge between the breasts, meeting in a complex knot sure to draw the eyes before being freed as long twirls of ribbon.

"The Nalynn colors, from when we had them. Now, it's not modern," Aunt Sybb told her, eyes bright, voice soft. "This was mine as a young woman. I wore it the first night I danced with my Hane." She gave a little cough and went on more briskly. "I'd have given it to Peggs for her coming of age birthday, but it suits your coloring and she wanted a—" Her smile faded. "You are happy with it, aren't you, Jenn? I assure you it looks much better worn."

Overcome, Jenn brushed her fingertips over the fabric. A treasure, this dress, full of memory and family and remembered joy. She couldn't ask for a more wonderful gift.

Though the notion of wearing it, in public, sent her heart racing. This was a woman's dress, proud and confident; the dress of a woman ready and willing to be noticed. And more.

"Oh, yes," she managed. "I'm happy—I'm beyond happy, Dear Aunt." She put the precious dress back in its wrap with great care, then rose to give her aunt a tender hug. "It's the most beautiful dress in the world. I'll treasure it always."

"There, then," her aunt said, clearly pleased. "When your sister's finished in the kitchen, you can try it on for us. I do believe it will fit as it is. You're taller than I was, but I admit in Marrowdell a hem sweeping the ground isn't practical. Though you must, truly must, wear shoes."

There was no arguing with that tone. "I promise," Jenn nodded and went back to her seat on the bench between the towels and her lovely new dress.

Their aunt folded her hands neatly. "Now, Dearest Heart, tell me what's wrong."

" 'Wrong?' " Jenn echoed. "Nothing's wrong, Aunt Sybb."

"I beg to differ," with sincere concern. "Look at you. You're skin over bone, pale skin at that. And I haven't seen your smile in days."

Jenn tried not to squirm, such a reaction being neither proud nor confident. She could use Peggs about now.

A breeze wafted the gauze curtains on the front windows and found its way through the open door, bringing the smell of soap in abundance. And baking bread. So much for help from there.

Before she could frame any reply, Aunt Sybb gave a decisive nod. "You've been confounded. No wonder you look worn, Dearest Heart. It's those letters."

" 'Letters?' " Jenn repeated weakly. "I thought you approved."

"I approved the first, which was seemly and courteous. It's not as though you and your sister have the opportunity to practice civilized discourse. I've often thought it was time you both took up writing memoirs—" Aunt Sybb caught herself before straying further. "Suffice to say, there's been far too many letters coming and going for simple courtesy, Jenn Nalynn, and not just with your future husband."

It was true. She lowered her head. "I meant—" What had she meant? Tir had warned her against playing games with Bannan, but it hadn't been a game, it had been wonderful and important. "—I meant no harm," she finished.

"I know, Good Heart." The older woman tsked gently. "Some men sing their way into your heart, others have a way with words. I'd have put a stop to your correspondence with Bannan Larmensu once I suspected, but I knew that clever rascal Tir would have outfoxed me." Said with some admiration.

"You needn't, Aunt. I've stopped writing to Bannan and to Wyll. They'll be here tomorrow anyway." A day and reacquaintance taking far too long to arrive. Jenn gave a listless sigh. "I wish it was over with."

"Because you've finished everything," her aunt reminded her. "The harder the work, the speedier the day." Her eyes twinkled. "I've a suggestion."

The mill was almost awake. Clean bags lay waiting in their stacks. Fresh grease darkened every moving part and the leather belts stretched between pulleys were clean and whole. Within their case, the stones rested, awaiting only power. All that moved were curious breezes and Radd Nalynn, his eyes sparkling with anticipation. The miller traced and retraced the path the milled grain would follow, knocking here, listening there, tugging and checking. Upstairs and down again. His daughters would chase him to be sure he ate.

Jenn Nalynn, having brought his lunch, eventually found her father in the basement, flat on his back in the stone raceway, his feet propped against a slat of the great wheel above. As he pushed, sun and shadow flowed across his body as the wheel smoothly turned on its axle. He gave a satisfied grunt.

"Your lunch pail and tea are upstairs, Poppa." She crouched down beside him and squinted. "The wheel looks good."

"It does, indeed," he said cheerfully. "I'd say we're as ready as can be." She moved out of the way as he slid from under the wheel. "You aren't planning to sweep again, are you?"

There not being a speck of dirt left in the mill, Jenn chuckled. "No, Poppa."

"Good. Help me check the gate, if you would?"

The gate had likely been "checked" several times already, but Jenn had no objection. While her father went upstairs, she walked past the wheel to the downstream end of the raceway and leaned out.

Here, the race opened on a tumble of large boulders, coated with a season's growth of moss and lichens. Shaded by the mill, the boulders would have made a fine place to stand and fish, except that the river itself was too far for a cast to reach. Between the mill and the first flow of water swayed a wide expanse of reedgrass, perfect for weaving baskets and mats once dried.

Hearing her father's knock from above, Jenn ducked back inside and went to the upstream side, that opening closed by a gate. Made like a door, of heavy wooden slats supported by cross members, the gate wasn't hinged, but rather suspended from a chain. By means of a geared wheel, the gate could be raised or lowered within its slot. Or dropped to instantly shut off the water's flow and stop the millstones, should the need arise. The 'stones spun fast enough to do serious damage to mill and miller if they went off kilter and came loose, not to mention the chance of sparks or a friction-caused fire should the grain and its flow not be right.

Milling was about respect, not risk, Radd Nalynn would say.

The gate rose smoothly and stopped where it should. Jenn called out, "It's good!" then bent to look outside. Instead of boulders, there was a path of smooth laid stone, like that around the village fountain, leading to the river. It was dry now, and sweetberry bushes met and twined overtop, making a cool green tunnel.

A red-eyed mouse, startled by the gate, glared at her before scampering to deeper cover. He'd best not linger, she thought.

Though he worked well and hard, Tir chafed at the oddness of a mill without water. Radd Nalynn, thoroughly enjoying his puzzlement, would only give a mysterious smile and promise he'd see soon enough.

Her father's head appeared in the wheel opening above her. "I'm going to shut it now," he warned.

Jenn waved an acknowledgment and climbed out of the raceway. A moment later, the gate plunged down, hitting bottom with a reassuringly solid thud.

She turned to leave, then stopped, looking back at the closed gate. It didn't glitter or show any sign of being other than ordinary. Yet once the hopper upstairs filled with grain to be milled, her father would turn the wheel, the chain would pull up the gate . . . and the river would enter.

Just Marrowdell's way; another convenience for those favored by the Ancestors.

No, Jenn realized for the first time.

It was magic.

She climbed the stairs in a thoughtful mood.

Her father sat on a bench, making happy little noises as he freed first a dumpling then a hunk of cheese from their cloth wraps. "Thank your sister, please," he said with a smile. "And my thanks for your help, Sweetling." Taking a bite of cheese, he nodded a question at the assortment of cleaning supplies she'd left near the open door.

"I told Aunt Sybb I'd finished everything I had to do for tomorrow," Jenn admitted. "She suggested I clean her wagon. 'Idle hands make an idle mind.'"

"That would do it," he replied cheerfully. "I'll help you pull it outside after my lunch. Come. Keep me company."

Jenn found a spot on the lowermost step of the stairs up to the attic. Sunlight slanted through the walls of the mill, painting bright bars across the floor. She stretched her toes into one, feeling the warmth, and asked as casually as possible, "When did you find out the mill was magic, Poppa?"

"'Magic?'" His eyebrows rose, then lowered. "Kydd Uhthoff's broken his silence at last, I take it."

"He said no one believed him."

"It's a hard thing, Dearest Heart, to raise a warning no one seems to hear. But we did," her father said, calmly taking a mouthful of dumpling. "And believed every word."

"If you did," Jenn frowned, "why did you stay? Why did you—" she couldn't accuse her father of lying, even if she was certain now that's what he'd done, what they'd all done "—not tell Kydd?" They'd let a young man suffer for months. Was this where the secrets had started? Once started, had a habit of secrets made it easier to keep Melusine's?

What was she to trust, then?

The light flickered on the floor, as if interrupted by cloud.

"We tried, Dearest Heart," her father said gently. "Kydd was the one who told us real magic had rules. That gave us hope, you see. We knew we couldn't keep travelling aimlessly, hoping for a place. Not without losing more of us. If there were rules here, we were willing to learn and obey them. Anything for a home.

"Kydd couldn't understand that. Had he been older, had he not just lost most of his family as well as being exiled . . ." he sighed. "Not even your mother could get through his grief and fear. When we asked for his help, all he'd say was we had to leave, that disaster could strike at any moment. Dusom could barely calm him."

To hear her father tell it, Kydd had been a boy who hadn't listened to his elders. To hear Kydd, the villagers, his elders, hadn't listened to him. There was more than one side to any tale, Aunt Sybb would say, and more than one truth.

Which went to prove, Jenn Nalynn told herself, her toes warm again, that listening and hearing weren't the same thing at all. She resolved to do better herself.

"Fortunately, Kydd made his own peace with Marrowdell," her father continued with a faraway look. "As did we. The magic here worked when most needed; it wasn't ours to control. We decided to give thanks to our Ancestors and to call anything magic their gift, perhaps truly for all we knew, and offer a Beholding.

"We also agreed not to question or trouble what was here, heeding Kydd's warning about those who'd built in Marrowdell once before, only to be destroyed. That's why Dusom didn't teach you and the other children about magic and wishings. We wanted to leave such things till you were old enough to understand and be properly cautious."

Jenn took great interest in twisting a bit of skirt between her fingers.

Radd Nalynn finished his tea. "Over the years, we came to love Marrowdell for what it was. I think by now most of us forget what's magic here and what isn't."

She had to smile. "Except Aunt Sybb."

"Except my dear sister. As for the mill?" Her father chuckled. "I thought some fool had built it in the wrong place and we'd have to tear it all down in spring and move it upstream. I was mortified when the tinkers, having been such help with the harvest, pulled the loaded wagons here, expecting me to mill the grain. I told them to go to Endshere. They told me," remembered wonder flooded his face, "to open the gate."

The tinkers again.

They'd known about Marrowdell from the start, how it worked, what it could do.

She would talk with Mistress Sand, Jenn decided with a tingle of new hope. Tomorrow, as soon as she could get her alone.

"That was a grand moment." He chuckled. "So be grateful to Marrowdell for its magic, Dearest Heart. It's made our lives what they are."

She couldn't argue with that.

Her father gathered up crumbs, shaking them back into the pail. "Let's get your aunt's monstrosity outside, shall we?"

Jenn jumped to her feet. Anything to keep busy.

Would tomorrow never come?

Tomorrow. Bannan twitched with impatience. How often had he wished time to slow; now it crawled, when he'd give anything to hurry it along. There was, he decided with a chuckle, nothing fair about it.

He'd hoped to settle his mind with work, as he had every day before this, but today, alas, when he needed distraction most? Nothing needed him.

After a dozen days of effort, his home was spotless. The doors hung open to the air on their new hinges. Two benches sat on the porch. The windows needed panes, but the frames were ready and he'd shutters to close in case of a storm. He had his bed upstairs, and shelves and pegs for his clothing. In the main room, more shelves and a table, plus benches before the fireplace. A lamp hung over the table; he'd claimed one end for a desk, marking that space with his books, less one, his quills and inkpot, and, a treasure, a ream of writing paper, carefully held in place by a jar of washed pebbles.

The paper had been a gift from his sister, the day he'd left. On feeling its weight, he'd joked he could write a book. She'd said not to bother, his letter-writing would do sufficient damage to the language and turned away, but not before he'd caught a telltale glisten in her eyes. He'd known better than mention it. Lithe and lethal Lila, the beautiful Lady Lila Marerrym Larmensu, the elegant and powerful Baroness Lila Larmensu Westietas didn't cry.

Though woe betide the guardsman she'd chosen for that afternoon's sparring session.

He'd write her another, longer letter and send it with Lady Mahavar, Bannan told himself. Perhaps he'd tell her where so many of the precious sheets had gone.

Thinking of letters only made him more restless.

The barn caught his eye, but it was well-swept, with bundles of sweet hay cut from his farmyard ready in its loft, in case the Ropps could spare him a milk-calf. Tir had helped him cobble together a small sty as well, since there might be piglets. Could and might, but nothing yet.

He glanced hopefully at the garden, but it too had been tamed, sufficient for this year. Neatly furrowed soil divided clumps of ripening beans from the tangle of vines around his fifteen plump squash. There were turnips, though thoroughly mixed with beets, and a stand of fine feathery green Davi Treff had assured him meant tender asparagus, come spring. He'd picked what apples the wild creatures had left him, sending those to the village. The Uhthoffs would press cider soon; he'd receive a share. Next year, he'd pick the fruit sooner, and learn how to dry it, As for the summerberries?

He'd eaten them as they ripened, as greedily as the birds.

Nothing to do. Nothing he wanted to do. Bannan turned again, gazing thoughtfully at the road. He dug at it with a booted toe.

Left took him to the river, the village, and Jenn Nalynn. But not today.

It also took him by the path. Not by night, he thought grimly. He'd learned that lesson.

Right was the way Wyll had gone. He'd left earlier, wanting to avoid the dark himself.

Nights were coming faster, of a sudden. The shadows of the old trees pooled along the road, though it wasn't sunset, not quite. Bannan hadn't thought he'd feel the shortening days so keenly, but life as a farmer was different. He'd learned to treasure daylight, rising with the sun and loath to go indoors.

In the marches, day had been for sloth. They'd cared for weapons and mounts, dozed or played 'stones. Night was the time to don armor and move out, or to stay quiet, sentries posted. He'd spent those hours with the fire to his back, staring into the dark. When a suspected spy was dragged into their camp, well, Captain Ash had stood behind a tall torch, watching for the truth, rarely seeing it.

Staring into darkness of another kind.

Not so here. Here, sunset meant pausing to see what fleeting wonders Marrowdell might reveal. Gradually, though elusive and shy, smaller things had shown themselves. Little cloaked dancers lived in the old trees, their hair as bright as sparks. They'd laugh and spin, then be leaves again. The dwellers in the grain appeared as pale, watchful eyes. They were winged and possessed of wicked claws; Bannan felt sorry for his ox. There were others, more wary. Not of him, he realized. The house toad in its glittering mail was relentless in its patrol of his farmyard.

Here night meant sitting by his fire, in his well-lit home, to reread her letters and write his own.

Not yet sunset. Not yet night. Nothing useful to do.

Bannan took a thoughtful step.

Then another.

Having taken two, why, what matter then to take another pair? Another four?

And, by then, well, he'd settled into an easy stride, a man out to stretch his legs and build an appetite for the stew on his stove. The old trees leaned closer and closer, not quite touching, leaves moving a little more than leaves alone should, but Bannan didn't try to see what might be watching.

Out for a walk, that was all.

Better still, he'd be a good neighbor, and visit Wyll. See his new house. Surely the dragon could use a little help in return for his.

Having given himself a worthy purpose, Bannan walked more briskly, eager to see what his rival had accomplished. As he went, he searched for any opening between the trees, but the massive trunks grew close, roots as thick as his body writhing from the ground to tangle with one another.

He frowned. Wyll had gone this way, hadn't he? Hard to tell. The road was dry; maybe Tir could spot a track in it, but that was beyond his skill.

The Tinkers Road. Scourge claimed it didn't leave Marrowdell, yet here it was well-packed, as if used.

Without ruts, as if not.

To his deeper sight, it flowed silver and hurried ahead of him, as if eager to be somewhere.

Where?

To answer such a pressing and interesting question, he need only go a little farther, and why not? Bannan decided cheerfully. The sun was still up.

He could hardly get lost.

Though stored in the mill all summer, the elegant coach still bore the dust and caked mud of its passage here. Plus cobwebs. Uncle Horst usually cleaned it. Wouldn't he be surprised?

Jenn wiped the back of her definitely not-idle hand across her sweaty brow, feeling grit slide along her skin, and grinned.

She was filthy. Again.

Aunt Sybb's coach, however, was now spotless. Its black leather gleamed, inside and out. The gilt trim around the windows shone, as did the brass rings of the curtains, and the curtains themselves were washed and pressed. The pillows their frail aunt used to protect her elbows on the journey remained in the house for now, but she'd cleaned the upholstery of both wide seats until it looked new. There wasn't a speck on the floor or cobweb in a corner. The lamps were polished and ready; she'd obtained some of Old Jupp's fine oil from Riss to refill them.

No time for supper, or need. On each of her trips home for hot water, she'd grabbed something from the kitchen, making Peggs laugh.

The boot, where the majority of luggage would travel, needed only a wipe but the coach box, where Uncle Horst would sit to drive Aunt Sybb's team, proved to have dried mud in every crevice.

Not for long. Jenn sat on top of the box, straddling the driver's padded seat with her skirt up to her knees, and whistled between her teeth as she dug her brush into the final join between wood and leather. She tossed her head, trying to keep soap-streaked hair out of her eyes as she worked.

"Now there's a portrait waiting to be painted."

Jenn straightened so abruptly she tumbled over backward, legs well over her head. She settled her skirt where it belonged before she peered over the roof edge.

Tir was so obviously looking elsewhere at the moment, Jenn's face flamed crimson. "If you're looking for my father—" the sun was almost at the Bone Hills, she realized in surprise, "—he's at supper." Peggs insisted he come home for at least one proper meal before the harvest.

"And sent me to bid you join us," with a bow that showed his bald pate.

"My thanks, but I've eaten," Jenn told him, which was true. It was also true that her middle was beginning to ache with a hunger having nothing to do with real and proper food. She resumed scrubbing, hoping he'd leave.

"Suit yourself," the former guard commented, in a tone suggesting she was only mildly demented to turn down a seat at the Nalynn table. He paused, running his fingertips over the side of the coach. "What's this? The crest's been removed. The Lady Mahavar is of a noble house," he added sternly, as if she wouldn't know her own aunt. "There should be a crest."

"I think Aunt Sybb hoped without the crest, the guards at the city gate might let her pass. But they still stop and search her belongings every time." It was her aunt's business and Jenn tried not to sound angry, but it wasn't easy.

Tir didn't bother. A fearsome scowl creased his forehead and he paused to spit meaningfully. "Heart's Blood! What ball-less dungholes did the Mahavars hire for the lady's escort? I'd like to see those city curs try any o'that nonsense with me there!"

"I'd like to see that too," Jenn assured him, and smiled.

His scowl eased away. Tir gave the coach a light rap with his knuckles, and looked up at her. "You need help keeping those rascals in line tomorrow," he offered gruffly, "you let me know, Jenn Nalynn."

Her smile softened. "I will. You'd best get to supper, before Poppa eats all the bread."

Tir widened his eyes in mock horror. "Then I'll be off." With a perfunctory bow, he headed off to the Nalynn house.

Jenn finished cleaning, then climbed down. A moth fluttered to a landing on the coach window, its open wings like scraps of white satin. She saw neither satchel nor letter in its claws and sighed, just a little. "My thanks for your service, friend moth," she told it, in case it understood.

Almost sunset. She didn't need to turn and look to know; she felt it inside, stronger than ever. Pressing her lips together, she endured the first cramp, then took a step, determined to put the brush in the bucket.

Instead, she staggered as the ground wasn't where it should be. She reached for the coach to catch herself.

And couldn't touch it.

The brush dropped because her fingers weren't there, where were her fingers? And she wanted to scream, but couldn't draw a breath, she couldn't, because she didn't have fingers, she didn't have toes, did she even have a mouth—

The sudden fire in her gut was so real, Jenn Nalynn gasped with relief. Somehow, she crawled on elbow and knee into the darkness beneath the coach, enduring in silence, thinking, as much as she could think at all, only of time. How long did it take the sun to go behind the Bone Hills? How many tortured breaths? How many more cramps?

At last, the sun set and she came to herself again. Jenn rubbed her hands in the cool rough dirt, overjoyed to feel fingers again; stubbed her toes on the coach wheel and almost cried with joy.

A dream, she told herself. A waking dream. That was all. Until she looked out to see the brush, lying where it had fallen. "What's happening to me?" she whimpered.

A cold little foot touched hers.

Jenn twisted, looking down. A house toad looked back. No, not one, but several, crowded together under the coach, legs overlapping stomachs, eyes on her. They'd taken shelter from the sunset.

So had she.

"It's all right," she said, as much to herself as the toads, and dropped her forehead to the cool earth. "It's over."

For today. What if tomorrow was worse?

Sunbeams slanted across Bannan's path, finding their way to the road past branch and through leaf. The Spine sank below the row of old trees to his left; ahead, where the road must bend, another of the Bone Hills rose into the sky, like a cloud caught against the earth.

He hadn't gone far before the air grew still and hushed. As it normally did, he reminded himself. The few birds left who sang by day were finished, and it was too early for the night's singers. His footfalls seemed loud and intrusive; without thinking, he fell into the old familiar stalk. Plant the foot so and put weight thus, avoid a regular pace and keep hand to sword hilt.

Finding no hilt, Bannan gave himself a little shake. This wasn't the marches, he reminded himself. Still, no harm in a quiet walk.

The Tinkers Road twisted left. He followed, to halt with a gasp.

Scourge hadn't lied.

The Tinkers Road didn't leave Marrowdell. It met the shadow of the Bone Hill and simply stopped.

Old trees erupted from the road's end, masking the lowest reach of pale stone beyond. Bannan walked to them, despite the shadow's bitter chill, and touched their trunks to be sure they were real. Nothing but a bird or toad could fit between. To his deeper sight, the road passed beneath the roots and was gone.

Which couldn't be right. This was the way the tinkers came, the way they left. The villagers had been confident.

The villagers didn't venture near the Bone Hills. How would they know?

The shadow deepened around him. The sun must be setting. This uncanny road was no place to be at night. He should go, now, and come back in the morning.

Then, as the last light of the sun passed them, the leaves in the old trees became something else, some things else, small figures, quick moving and cautious, that looked down at him, tilting their sparkling heads.

Grinning with delight, Bannan couldn't help himself. "Hello."

They took flight, some into the air, the rest running from branch tip to twig to hide in the shadows near the trunk.

"I'm sorry," he began to say, but he hadn't startled them.

Before his eyes, a dark hoof appeared in the air before the line of trees, then a leg, then a nose. Another hoof. Another leg and nose.

"RUN!"

He didn't need to be told twice. Bannan whirled and ran.

Once past where the road twisted, he stopped. He didn't doubt the warning, but he couldn't leave, not without seeing more. He crept back, putting himself behind a tree trunk. Holding his breath, he eased his head sideways until one eye could see past the bark.

Horses. Ancestors Witness, he'd run from horses. This was the dragon's idea of a joke.

Horses pulling wagons. Three wagons, filled with wooden barrels, a team of matched browns harnessed to each.

Bannan breathed again. He'd run from the tinkers. They must have some way through the trees he hadn't found. Abashed, the truthseer began to move into the open, lifting his hand in greeting. He hoped they hadn't seen him bolt like a startled deer.

There was no one to greet. The wagon seats were empty.

Why would horses pull empty wagons?

He flung himself behind the tree again, his blood cold. This was Marrowdell, he told himself. What he saw wasn't always the truth.

He peered out again, to take another, deeper look.

The road became silver and flowed. It no longer vanished beneath tree roots but soared up and into the sky, like a waterfall going the wrong way. The horses and wagons came from within that flow.

Horses? Their dark hides were overlapped plates of armor, supple enough to move with their bodies. Instead of manes, glinting crests like sword blades rose along their necks, catching fire in the sun's final rays. This had been Scourge, before his ruin.

Kruar.

The barrels became urns of brilliant blue crystal. The wagons remained wagons, though of unfamiliar design.

Beside each walked figures of light and stone.

Figures without faces, only masks.

Bannan pressed his back against the tree trunk and closed his eyes, fighting for breath. What had Wyll said? Cursed. Powerful.

Turn-born.

Ancestors Kind and Merciful, he had to calm himself. He had to get out of here without being seen or heard.

The hoofbeats came closer. Closer. What was he thinking? Scourge could smell a mouse under rotten potato peels. These kruar would catch his scent any minute. If he didn't want to be their mouse, he had to go now, calm or not.

He sidestepped roots to the next tree, then the next. Things scurried away. Something hissed. Only when he was sure he wouldn't be seen did Bannan jump out to run in earnest.

On the Tinkers Road.

Don't reveal what you are, the dragon had warned.

He should have warned him—warned them all—what the tinkers were.

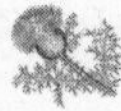

The turn had come. The efflet trembled and huddled together. The ylings cowered on their branches.

Wyll had no doubt why.

He snarled to himself, unhappy to be trapped as a man on the same side of the edge as the turn-born. When first one, then a second little cousin appeared in his doorway, he snarled at them, too. ~ What? ~

~ Elder brother, ~ they cried together, ~ the truthseer's at the crossing! ~

Wyll launched himself forward. He slipped on crystal and felt it break, heard the toads scramble out of his way, but couldn't slow. Not now. The fool. Curious, bright, interested in what he shouldn't be, always. Fool!

He lurched straight across the meadow, right through the kaliia, snarling and growling as he went. The efflet made no protest. Why would they? The grain could no longer be protected and they readied themselves to flee.

Wise efflet. He couldn't protect them.

Hurried, his body creaked and strained and tried to fail. The turn slid over and passed him as he pushed his way between neyet. Ylings trilled warnings. Nyphrit slipped into their holes. His useless foot snagged in a root and he pulled it free with a jerk that snapped bone.

The road at last. Wyll flung a breeze outward, "RUN!"

He hoped it found only Bannan's ears.

One breath. Two. He bided his time, furious at the truthseer, furious at himself, at this body. Bark cracked beneath his fingers . . .

A man came running. Wyll leapt, his good arm snagging Bannan's to jerk him to a halt. The man staggered or he did; they kept each other standing. "I saw them!" the truthseer gasped.

"Did they see you?" Wyll shook him. "Did they?"

"No. No, they didn't." Bannan swallowed, steadied, though his eyes were huge in his face and sweat beaded his forehead. "I saw them, Wyll," he said again. "Skin over stone. Skin over light. They wear masks for faces!"

"Go." Wyll shoved him toward the farm. "When you see them again, do not look so closely. See the tinkers."

"See tinkers." The truthseer gasped for breath then nodded. "Not turn-born."

No laggard in wit. "Just so." The dragon bared teeth. "Hurry now. They go first to your barn, to clothe themselves and wait for sunrise. They know better than pass the Wound by night. Go."

"But—"

"Get in your house, stay there, and ignore them. They'll find you when they're ready. Go!"

Bannan took an obedient step, only to pause and glance back. Though his face was pale, that inquisitive eyebrow rose. "Think they'll want supper?"

His broken foot howled, the turn-born—that potent nuisance—were heartbeats away, and Wyll found himself amused. "I suppose they might. They'll act as men and women, so long as they believe you see them as such."

"I will." Another perilous hesitation. "Thank—"

"Go!" Wyll turned his back on the truthseer. "Don't give them all my biscuits."

If he was smiling as the man hurried away, only the ylings could see.

He lost his smile as he waited. He'd been sent to guard the girl; she was safe for now, if through no act of his. His old enemy had returned to Marrowdell; they'd made common purpose, sure to confound those who knew both.

Unlikely the turn-born would notice, for tonight they crossed for their own peculiar concerns.

Five days from now, the light of the girl's sun would meet the light of the Verge in exquisite, fleeting harmony. The Balance. The next day's turn would come earlier here, then the next, as this world began its slide to longer, darker nights and winter. Something in that harmony and its change was felt, keenly, by turn-born. They offered no explanation, not that he'd dared ask, but long ago Wyll had come to believe the turn-born didn't choose to cross into Marrowdell for the Balance; they were drawn. Drawn, and compelled to remain until its turn, when they'd cross back to the Verge.

Why?

He hadn't wondered before his penance. Like any terst, the turn-born stayed to the boring flat terrain loathed by dragons. The terst themselves were boring, being similar to the girl's kind and content to toil each day. They coaxed crystal to build their dwellings, and preferred those stiflingly close to one another. They bribed efflet to grow their kaliia and traded with ylings for cloth. When permitted by their queen, little cousins would take hire, being dexterous and reliable workers, though they knew to count their earnings. The terst, like their turn-born, weren't completely to be trusted.

Why terst had left the untouched part of their world to settle the newly created Verge was beyond a dragon to guess. Their magic was trivial: the healing of broken limbs and wounds, which any dragon could do for itself and faster; the fermenting of grain, there being a drink they liked which no dragon could stomach, given its smell; and the wishing away of dreams, for the terst, like the girl's kind, sometimes found being between two worlds haunted their sleep. Like the small ones, they couldn't cross between.

But, sometimes, they gave birth to those who could.

Never on purpose, not once they'd learned the consequences of a child born within a turn. The terst moved their settlements farther from known crossings, to no avail, and did their earnest best to keep mothers from labor at that dread moment, or hid them in the dark.

Distance or darkness made no difference. Any newborn whose first breath came when the light of two worlds touched was bound to both.

Like the girl, terst turn-born were harmless while young; it was only when full grown that their power revealed itself, affecting the Verge and putting those nearby at risk. To the turn-born already grown and trained, busy negotiating their next collective expectation with exquisite care and interminable argument, such individuals meant potential chaos. A single turn-born, with differing expectation at the crucial moment, would stop theirs.

A solitary turn-born, unchecked by any other expectation, could devastate the Verge.

So turn-born lived together. Terst parents who suspected the worst would bring their infants to the nearest enclave, in hopes they were wrong. The turn-born could recognize some quality in each other; perhaps, like dragons and kruar, they sensed what didn't fully belong to either world. Regardless of how they knew, they took any new turn-born into their care, leaving the parents to mourn.

Wyll knew these particular turn-born, as well as any could. They came from the enclave nearest the crossings to Marrowdell, where he'd done his first penance. Few in number; they were always few. Determined. That, too.

And drawn to the other world, now.

Why?

He didn't know. Wyll stifled a frustrated snarl. How could he? They didn't discuss it among themselves. Like any sane dragon, he'd avoided them entirely until the sei dictated his penance and put him in the turn-borns' charge.

He'd managed to avoid them on this side of the edge, until today. The girl and her father grew preoccupied with the harvest, allowing him to sneak away to the Verge rather than share the too-close quarters of Marrowdell with turn-born. It would have to be this harvest when that sensible arrangement changed, with a Great Turn on the day of Balance.

Troubled, Wyll leaned against the neyet, caught in memory. At the last Great Turn, there'd been no village, no mill, nor villagers in Marrowdell. There'd been nothing to harvest, nor a river, nor crags riven and torn. The valley had been wild forest and stone. A place where kruar might cross to hunt rabbits and feisty young dragons might follow, to hunt kruar.

And be hunted. Wyll almost smiled, remembering. Were the odds not deliciously even?

The stealthy visits of a few turn-born had mattered no more than the growing towers of men, until the wise among the latter deciphered the time and the place, and the utter fools among them dared act. At the Great Turn, they'd cast their wishing and the trapped ones erupted in answer. Their vast arms had ripped free from the Verge and through the ground of this world, tearing at the barrier that kept both whole and apart until both were one.

In that moment of blending, confusion reigned.

Dragon and kruar, knowing full well where they belonged, took advantage. The small ones grew lost, straying into Marrowdell, while men spilled into the Verge and went mad. Towers crumbled, land heaved and split, and what might have happened next? Would the worlds separate once more or continue to blur together, until neither remained the same?

Busy killing kruar, such weighty matters had been far from his mind.

Except the sei were . . . bothered.

Having paid attention, they swiftly settled matters to their liking. To restore what was, the sei somehow sent the trapped ones back to sleep, sealing the halves of the edge so tightly this time that the only crossings left were where the barrier remained stretched between those now-still arms. The sei dealt with dragon and kruar next, then, having seemingly lost interest, though regrettably not in his penance, resumed their interrupted musings.

Leaving Marrowdell forever changed.

Stung by the sei's displeasure, dragon and kruar avoided their former playground. The turn-born, for whatever reason, could not. What had they thought when they'd first crossed into that new Marrowdell? One of scarred cliffs and crushed towers, with its river now split around smooth white hills that weren't hills at all, but the trapped ones left exposed. One now inhabited by neyet and ylings, by nyphrit and little cousins. Where efflet, confused but determined, called forth their precious kaliia to grow under a new sun.

That first crossing, they could have brought the small ones home, Wyll knew, feeling cold inside. Turn-born could cross with more than themselves. Instead, they'd found the new Marrowdell even more to their liking. They sacrificed neyet to make the village and the mill then, as if forgetful of what men had done once, waited for settlers to find them and stay. Once the valley again heard the voices of men, women, and children, the turn-born crossed before the day of Balance, pretending to be tinkers and friends. All, apparently, to harvest the kaliia of this world, instead of their own.

Why was beyond a dragon's imagining. He could ask them, Wyll thought. Did he dare?

No. The turn-born were unapproachable at best and this year's day of Balance held peril. They could be exposed, like any small one, by the coming Great Turn. They could be caught by an unraveling edge, should those come again with that dire knowledge and intent. Aware of such risks, the turn-born wouldn't be happy; did the air already have a storm's weight to it?

Hoofbeats sounded, deep and heavy, accompanied by the creaking protest of wooden wheels left idle for a year. Wyll braced himself and straightened.

A veritable cloud of ylings flung themselves in front of him, facing the road, each armed with tiny spears. Aghast, Wyll sent a breeze to tumble the little warriors up and out of sight. A little cousin, squat and sturdy, took position at his feet. He nudged it to safety beneath a thick root.

While Bannan ran home to make supper.

They were all mad.

Safety lay in avoiding undue attention. He'd calculated to a nicety how long it would take the truthseer to run to the opening off the road, to run inside his home, and, most of all, to calm himself and settle, so it would appear he hadn't run at all.

The kruar and their wagons, and the turn-born, came into view sooner than was safe.

Without hesitation, Wyll lifted his good arm in greeting, as he'd seen men do, and hailed them in his man's voice. "Welcome to Marrowdell."

Then let a breeze sweep road dust in their faces.

The kruar, being young and easily dismayed, plunged to a snorting stop. Unable to free themselves from the wagons or teammates, they shivered the blades along their necks in impotent threat, lips pulling back from their fangs. ~ What are you?! ~ they howled. ~ Who is this?! ~ ~ Death to it!!? ~

The dust dropped to the road. ~ Peace, little ones. ~

Wyll smiled, enjoying how a man's lips and teeth could express such complete disdain. Think what he might of Scourge, his old enemy would die before accepting "little one" from a turn-born.

One stepped from the rest, not so much closer, but to indicate she would be the one to converse. Sand-filled limbs, a mask formed into nothing so personal as interest. If appearance could be trusted, this was the turn-born who'd sent him to Marrowdell in the clutches of dragons. ~ Here, not there. Unclothed and alone. The villagers rejected you. ~

"I'm here to greet you," he replied aloud, inclined to daring. He might be safe; Bannan wasn't, not yet. Thanks to the girl, he spoke as well as anyone in Marrowdell. Could the turn-born do the same? "Like you, I save my clothes for them. As for alone?" He gave a modest bow. "Far from it. I'm to marry Jenn Nalynn at the end of the harvest. A shame you can't stay to watch."

The kruar stamped, shaking the edge. They'd like his dragon's flesh and bone beneath their hooves; having sworn their service to the turn-born for the harvest, they were bound to better behavior. A single tremor answered, deeper; Scourge, responding to challenge from his kind. The kruar rolled their eyes and grew very still indeed.

Wind howled through the tops of the neyet; turn-born temper, unimpressed, unrelenting.

Almost at once, the gale sputtered into a soft whisper, fragrant with the smell of warm leaves and late summer.

"She's come into her own," Wyll announced, as if they couldn't feel it for themselves. Jenn Nalynn's innocent and well-settled wish for fair weather held their spite in check. For now. Their number didn't matter. What did, as Wyll understood it, was clarity of intention. These turn-born knew what they wanted and how to accomplish it.

In that sense Marrowdell was safer with more of their kind than less, much as he disliked the thought.

~ And you, lord of dragons? ~ The turn-born took another step distant from the rest. Disagreement, perhaps. Or emphasis. ~ How goes your life as a man? ~

She mocked him, of course, as they all did and should. He was powerless, old, and broken.

But not futile.

Hadn't he saved the foolish truthseer, who should soon be within his walls and baking biscuits? Hadn't he had a letter from Jenn Nalynn, inviting him back to the village as soon as the harvest started? The little cousins called him one of their own.

He had, if not a home, then a purpose here. He mattered to Marrowdell.

The turn-born did not.

Knowing he shouldn't, knowing he mustn't, Wyll bowed once more, with what grace his twisted body gave him, and said with satisfaction. "I find it promising."

Cold burned his naked skin. He shivered so violently he lost balance and fell among the hard roots of the neyet. His eyelashes froze together and his lips cracked.

~ There is no promise for you here. ~ Words like ice. ~ There is duty and we will, most certainly, expect you to do yours. ~

His teeth clacked together, meeting in his tongue. Blood filled his mouth, choking his man's voice. ~ I know my duty! ~ he raged. ~ Do yours. Teach her! Make her one of you. ~

Astonishment.

He prepared to die for it.

Instead, a question. ~ Then leave her here, alone? Unchecked? ~

As turn-born must never be. Half-frozen, Wyll refused to falter. ~ She has a good heart. You could trust her. ~

~ Can we still trust you? ~

~ I KNOW MY DUTY! ~ he raged.

Silence. The kruar rolled their eyes.

~ Excuse our doubt. ~ The courtesy had an edge. ~ You have kept her happy, for the most part. The crop has grown well. ~ Warmth returned, a life-giving torment through arms and legs. He managed not to scream. ~ What heritage Jenn Nalynn may possess is the fault and curse of her world, not ours. We have forbidden her to cross to the Verge. Should she try again, we trust you know what to do. ~

They didn't wait for an answer. Kruar stepped forward; the wagons followed, no burden to their strength. The turn-born walked on

Marrowdell's road, beginning their magic. The villagers thought the harvest began tomorrow. In truth, it began now, with the building of the turn-borns' expectation.

The valley would bend to it.

Wyll pushed himself to a knee. Gripped bark to pull himself upright. Frost had burned his skin and found his heart.

His duty. Keep the girl on this side of the edge. Never let her cross, for her expectations would interfere with the turn-borns' and bring chaos to the Verge. Kill her, if that's what it took.

While the sei, who cared nothing for the worries of the turn-born or those who dwelt in the Verge, laid their own demand on him. Never let her leave Marrowdell, for if she stepped beyond, the edge would unravel along with her.

Kill her, if that's what it took.

The sei and turn-born agreed in one respect. Jenn Nalynn must stay where she was.

Or die.

Wyll spat blood and bared his teeth. His duty was to protect the edge, both the Verge and Marrowdell. He would decide how. Who knew better?

He'd do what Jenn Nalynn wanted. They would marry and live in his house and, as he had done in Nights' Edge all these years, he would make her laugh and be happy, keeping Marrowdell safe, keeping the Verge whole.

And she would live.

The coming night chilled flesh still covered in goose bumps. It was time to go home, to curl in moss, and rest.

Wyll lurched through the meadow, going around the kaliia. The path he'd trampled through looked like a wound. Dew stuck to his legs, clammy and wet. He couldn't stop shivering.

He couldn't help doubt.

He would do what Jenn Nalynn wanted.

But did she know what that was?

NINETEEN

MIST SWIRLED AROUND her feet, coiling up her body like warm silk. She tried to touch it, but the pale stuff slipped between her curious fingers; tried to taste it, but it hovered beyond reach of her tongue.

No matter. She danced, this way, that way, the mist her willing partner. Dancing was ever so much easier than untangling the bright threads of would she, should she, and why couldn't she? that filled her heart. She lifted her knee and twirled, the mist sliding by without a sound, and could have danced forever.

If dancing could be enough.

She stopped, the mist dancing alone until it missed her and settled, soft on her skin, like a question.

What more did she want?

She wasn't to, mustn't, and wouldn't. The bright threads turned blood-red and thick, the beat of her heart a struggle. There'd been a promise. Had she promised? But who? And why?

And for how long?

What she wanted was so small. It would be by her feet. It was there, right now, beneath the mist. Of that she had no doubt.

She'd only to stoop and . . .

Bands of mist tightened, holding her in place, refusing her. She cried out in silence. Fought, without moving. Did what she could, against mist and a promise.

Surrendered, heart empty.

Others stood before her, behind her, cradled in mist and faceless. They disagreed, that was all, and all there was.

All there could be . . .

Hot tears leaked from the corners of her eyes. They dribbled over her nose to join forces, then slid down her cheek to soak her pillow. If she moved, they'd only make a damp spot somewhere else and she'd wake Peggs, who'd worry.

As would sobs, so she wasn't, Jenn Nalynn told herself, to sob or sigh or do anything but lie here and leak. Something better would happen eventually. She'd run out of tears or fall back to sleep or it'd be morning.

She hadn't left their bed this time, or didn't remember coming back to bed. She supposed the bottoms of her feet could tell her, but looking at her feet would mean moving and a candle. By then, she might as well wake Peggs up to help.

At any rate, she'd rather not know.

Before bed, she'd done her best not to dream. Reread letters, thought of lovely mornings and butterflies and maybe pancakes with honey, which she did sincerely want, and avoided so much as an instant's thought of pebbles and being so empty she wasn't there at all.

She'd tried, but it had been so hard. Tomorrow, today now, everyone would be together again. How could she not think of that?

Another tear trickled across her nose. It left an itch.

Last night, most of all, she'd tried not to imagine how it would feel, to look into his eyes, his words in her heart, then have to turn away.

Jenn lay still, to wait for morning, and tried to imagine she could.

Bannan paused by the well to gaze at the sky. The Mistress winked at him, bright and familiar. The lovely Rose sat lower, above the village and Jenn Nalynn. Tomorrow, he promised himself. He'd see her tomorrow.

If he survived supper.

"Do you study the stars na?"

He hadn't heard the tinker approach. Had it come after him? Schooling his face, Bannan looked around. "Pardon?"

"Dusom studies them. Do you na?"

Their voices were soft and a little breathless, their questions marked by an unfamiliar sound as well as a rise. If he'd heard such in Vorkoun, he'd have assumed Rhothan was a language new to them or rarely practiced, though travelers from distant domains were uncommon so far inland.

Knowing he spoke to no man, the odd intonation made little hairs rise on the back of his neck. "No. I was admiring them. It's a lovely clear night."

"There will be clear skies for the harvest."

More than truth. Certainty. Dread settled in his stomach. Jenn Nalynn's effect on Marrowdell was unintentional. Were the turn-born from Wyll's world so sure in their power and knowledge they could make the weather they chose? What else could they do?

He'd rather not find out.

So far, other than their speech, the tinkers had proved unremarkable. A pair, looking like ordinary men, had come to his door to ask permission to spend the night in his barn. It had been their custom, they'd explained, but that was when the farm had been empty and they'd no wish to intrude.

Having made it home ahead of them by a dragon's grace, having listened as hoofbeats and the creak of wagons invaded his farmyard, having forced himself to put on extra biscuits and cut more potatoes into his stewpot without taking a look outside, because what was outside shouldn't be seen?

Ancestors Blessed and Beloved, Bannan thought he'd done marvelously to stand at the door, smile, and make them welcome to the barn, of course, and would they share his supper when they were ready?

Where was that fine courage now? In the dark by the well, for what light spilled from the house and porch hardly reached this far, Bannan couldn't have moved if he tried. His breath caught and his hands clenched, white-knuckled, on the handles of his buckets.

The tinker reached for one. "May I help na?"

It—he'd come to help. Of course he had. Heart's Blood, he had to stop suspecting everything they did, or he'd never last the night. With an effort he fervently hoped went unnoticed, the truthseer relinquished the bucket. "Thank you." They walked to the house together, Bannan matching his stride to the tinker's slower one lest the other fall behind and he'd have those eyes on his back.

The house was bright inside and should be; he'd lit every lamp, for courage and to make his home welcoming. The aroma of stew and fresh-baked biscuits filled the room as he entered, a room already full of strangers. There were seven tinkers altogether, plus a small white dog. The dog curled in front of his fireplace, chin on its rump. It looked like a hunter, with large pointed ears and a wiry coat, and kept its dark brown eyes on him as he piled steaming biscuits in a bowl and lifted the lid from the stewpot. Bannan had no trouble avoiding a too-close look at the tinkers, knowing what he'd see. He was sorely tempted to stare back at the dog, but knew better.

He tossed the 'stones in a high stakes game—did he not?—playing host to such guests. A strange euphoria roared through his blood, pushing aside fear if not caution. "You've picked the right day to try my cooking," he announced, with the bravado he reserved for those times the odds were stacked higher than a house against him. Tir would recognize it; for some reason, his typical response was to spy out the nearest exit. "Yesterday's tasted like soap, but I've high hopes for this stew." Bannan raised his spoon. "Come. Let me serve you."

"Our thanks." The woman called Sand stepped forward. He ladled a generous portion of stew into her trencher, for they'd brought their own, along with mugs and spoons, and added a biscuit. They'd carried the benches in from the porch so there'd be places for all, though he'd held his breath till sure none had noticed his foolish carving on the underside of one. As Sand took a seat, the rest came for their share, expressing gratitude in soft voices. They sat to eat without a Beholding.

Different ways. Bannan, who had no appetite, leaned over his bowl and prayed to himself, Hearts of our Ancestors, I'd be Beholden to see tomorrow.

They ate in silence, the tinkers as intent on their food as any weary travelers at journey's end. He studied them surreptitiously. The other six were men, or seemed so. Beardless, with straight black hair to their shoulders, he could see why Horst had thought him their kind at first, though the tinkers' eyes were the deep blue of a winter sky and his brown. Their faces were weathered, with ruddy cheeks and noses, and bright red lips. They were sturdily built, shorter by half a head than he, but he was tall for a Lower Rhothan. They'd given him names to use he didn't for an instant believe. Sand. Clay. Riverstone. Fieldstone. Chalk. Flint. Tooth.

Though the mere thought made his skin crawl, little wonder Jenn claimed "Mistress Sand" as friend and ally. Had Bannan met the tinker under any other circumstance, he'd have judged her someone's kindly mother, perhaps a shopkeeper; a strong and capable woman who put others at ease. She wore a sleeveless high-collared dress that fell to her ankles, the skirt narrower than those in the village, split at the sides to allow movement. The dress was dark brown and unpatterned, of a fabric he couldn't place. The men wore loose pants and jerkins of the same, unfamiliar in their cut, but comfortable-looking.

Like the men, Sand wore tall laced boots that might have been leather, and gloves without fingertips covered her arms from palm to shoulder. Over her dress was belted a loosely woven garment, like a shawl with wide sleeves to the elbow, gold in color and as finely made as any such work he'd seen in Vorkoun.

Clothes stored in his barn, till now. They'd planned ahead. For what?

Tucking spoon into trencher, Sand lifted a handful of the shawl. "Like it na?"

Caught staring, Bannan could only nod. "I've a friend who'd love such," he improvised.

Sand chuckled. "Made it myself and more to trade." She waggled the end in her hand. "Do you want this one na? A gift for your friend. All the same to me."

The truth, spoken like any tinker he'd met, stirred the tiniest doubt, for there was nothing here of the strange figures he'd seen on the road, nothing beyond the ordinary. He dared not look deeper and see, not when outnumbered and blocked from either door. Trust Wyll, he told himself. Trust the dragon.

Riverstone waved his empty spoon at Bannan's walls. "The man's setting up a home. He's hardly in need of fripperies."

"In Marrowdell, that means someone to set up a home for." She leaned her head toward Bannan and winked. "You heard. He has a friend."

Despite everything, he blushed. "There's a young lady in the village," Bannan confessed, finding it easy to sound the anxious lover. "I see her tomorrow for the first time in too long."

"Then a gift you must have. I'll pick the best from my stock in the morning." She gave a satisfied nod. "We'll settle the price later."

So he'd bought a shawl. As for the price? Tir knew his weakness at haggling and usually stepped in. "My thanks," Bannan said faintly, and hoped he could afford it.

"Ride with us to the village," Riverstone offered. "Fair return for our supper."

What mouthfuls Bannan had forced down his throat threatened to rise. He swallowed, hard, then bowed his head in thanks. Sit beside one of them, on a wagon drawn by kruar? That would be an entrance. "I trust you'll join us for breakfast first?"

"'Us' na?" Sand repeated, her smile fading. The others stopped eating to stare at him; the little white dog lifted its head. "Do you not live alone na?"

Too late to regret the slip; no time to worry over consequence. "My neighbor Wyll comes by for breakfast. He helps around the farm." Ancestors Brash and Bold, he was in for this much, why stop? "Could you take us both?" Bannan asked easily, while his heart hammered as it had when he'd urged Scourge down that impossible slope. "He's off to the village tomorrow as well. For the harvest."

The tinkers exchanged unreadable looks. The white dog's nostrils worked at the air. "We'll see in the morning." Sand rose to her feet. The rest followed.

They were leaving.

And he hadn't been turned to coal, or whatever they could do. Bannan schooled the relief from his face and stood as well. "Tomorrow, then."

Tomorrow. The village.

Tir. Jenn Nalynn. Aunt Sybb and all the rest.

Heart's Blood. He couldn't leave it at this. All he knew was that the tinkers weren't what they seemed. Should he risk the road by night, and their kruar, to raise the alarm? Or pretend to be blind and accept them as the others did? This was Marrowdell, after all, where toads wore chain mail and protected homes. Mistress Sand and the tinkers came to help with the harvest every year. They were spoken of as friends.

Did he not have his own secret?

It wasn't the same. The villagers knew what he was. The turnborn lied. Why?

Marrowdell was his home. As much as Horst or Scourge or toad, he guarded this road. "It's early," Bannan protested, accepting that duty though his heart, being more sensible, thudded in his chest. "I'd be a poor host if I didn't offer a sweet course."

Sand shook her head. "We've had our fill."

Out the door went Flint, then Chalk. Ancestors Awkward and Uncooperative. "I've wine," he offered hurriedly. What tinker could resist an evening cup? He could use one himself, when it came to it. A big one.

"Time aplenty to celebrate once the harvest is underway. Tonight, we must rest." Riverstone gave a small smile. "Our thanks for your hospitality, Bannan."

They left, four of them carrying out his benches. Bannan hastened after, careful not to step on the little dog. It was a glorious night, crisp and clear. Warm light spilled from his door and windows. He took a deep breath. "Surely you could stay a while longer, dear guests," he suggested, with all the charm he possessed. "I've lacked company."

"Where's the harm in a cup na?" Sand decided abruptly.

Their faces remained placid, but Bannan sensed the men weren't happy. Still, they nodded graciously to him before heading to the barn. The barn full of kruar and empty wagons and opened chests. Chests of clothing and what else?

Why were they here? In his world. Hers. What could they want?

The dog lingered too, standing on the porch.

Be the host, he warned himself, turning to Sand with a smile. He'd interrogated worse, surely. "What may I serve you, good lady? Tea? Wine? I've a stronger brew, all the way from Essa, though I warn it's an acquired taste."

She held out her cup. "Marrowdell's water, if you please. It's been too long since I've tasted it."

"Of course." As Bannan went to his well, the tinker seated herself on a bench. She faded into the dark wall beside the window, the dog a blur of white at her feet. With every step, he felt her eyes on him. Like him, she was curious and inclined to indulge that curiosity.

Ancestors Tried and Tested. He hoped he hadn't made a mistake.

The well brimmed with stars. He dipped her cup, ripples disturbing the night sky, and lifted it, full. Something moved near his feet and he almost jumped before realizing it was the house toad, squeezed flat against the stone. Until that moment, he hadn't noticed its absence, though it rarely left his home at night, not while he was awake.

Only a toad, but he felt better with it near.

Returning to the porch, Bannan bowed and gave the tinker her cup. Sand drank deeply as he made himself comfortable on the other bench, then sighed with content. "There's nothing like the water here." Before he could ask about water elsewhere, she continued, "Or the stars."

In Vorkoun, lights and chimney smoke made appreciating the night sky a matter of finding a rooftop, ideally with a willing lady, but leave the city in any direction and stars were as easily seen as here. And the same. "Marrowdell is lovely," Bannan agreed, skirting the perilous topic of a different sky and other stars. "I'm happy to have found my way here."

"In time to see the moon pass before the sun. Did you find your way here for that, Bannan na?"

Why would he . . . he gathered his wits. "An eclipse? No." Before he'd left Vorkoun, he'd heard some clamor about one, come to think of it, not that he'd paid attention. "I'm no student of the sky," he said for the second time. Ansnans cared where stars sat and how brightly the moon shone; in the border guard, they'd kept track only to guess when their enemy might move. "I'll look forward to it," he added lightly.

Then froze.

At sunset, he could glimpse the other world and see Marrowdell's secrets as they truly were. What might he see in an eclipse? What might anyone?

The turn-born, as they truly were?

Jenn Nalynn?

With great care, Bannan schooled his voice to polite interest, nothing more. "When will it take place?"

"The final day of harvest." Then, sharp and harsh, "The people of Marrowdell are kind and trusting. I am not. If not for the eclipse, why have you come na? Why now na? You'd best not mean harm."

The truth, if he'd ever heard it, and spoken like the person she appeared to be, rightly suspicious of a stranger and protective of those she knew. A person who cared. The little white dog growled and he knew he was in danger.

Bannan came close to sagging with relief.

If he was in danger, Marrowdell wasn't, not from Sand. About to answer honestly, the truthseer hesitated, trying to make out her expression in the shadows.

All at once, he saw too much.

A stern mask covered her face, or was her face. The thick hair above the mask was white, not black, and some nameless brilliance filled holes where eyes and mouth belonged. Where not gloved, a glimmer etched the shape of fingers and hands around her cup, and picked out grains of sand.

Hurriedly, Bannan looked away, where it was safe, to where lamplight streamed across the ground and small moths danced in its fringe. How to reassure this creature? "I swear by my Ancestors," he said fervently, fingers curved over his heart, "that I came to Marrowdell to make a new and peaceful life. The people here are kind, as you say. They've made me welcome and given me this farm. I'd do nothing to harm them." He looked up, making sure he saw only her shadowy form, and found himself saying as harshly as she'd spoken, "I'll let nothing harm them."

Silence stretched like a noose.

Just when Bannan was sure he'd made the mistake Wyll had feared, he heard, of all things, a warm throaty chuckle from the shadows.

Sand leaned forward to pat his knee with a hand that felt as real as his own mother's. She chuckled again. "Spoken like a young man in love," she said. "You should take her two shawls tomorrow."

Whatever Sand was, she believed him. "I'd best wait to learn the price," he returned, a little breathless. "I hope to buy a calf."

"In love and wise with his coin too. Lucky girl." He heard a swallow and a smack of lips, then the shadow that was Sand rose to her feet. "My thanks for the water. I'm glad we had this talk."

"As am I," the truthseer assured her, rising as well. He gave a short bow. "Until the morning, dear lady."

"I'm no lady," she said, a smile in her voice. "Rest well, Bannan."

"And you."

The little white dog strutted behind the tinker as she walked to the barn. Unable to resist, Bannan looked deeper, then chuckled to himself.

It was, of all things possible and improbable, a little white dog.

As if it had waited for the pair to leave, the house toad hopped to the porch, then through the open door.

Bannan wasn't ready to follow it. Instead, he stepped out into the farmyard. The sliver of moon had risen, but his eyes found the Rose again. "Tomorrow," he promised, his heart in his throat.

When he and Wyll, who was a dragon, would arrive in Marrowdell with the tinkers, who were turn-born.

Not to mention the kruar.

Doubtless the villagers would greet them as if nothing was strange.

Scourge, who was everything strange, had a knack for making himself scarce when a crowd appeared. Would he this time?

Tomorrow would bring what it would, Bannan told himself.

So long as it brought Jenn Nalynn.

Her skin crawled.

Her bones itched.

Something had to be done. And now. The feeling built and built, like a thunderstorm unable to burst, till Jenn could hardly lie still. If she knew what demanded doing, she'd do it, or stop it, if she knew how. Her thoughts scattered this way and that in exhausting fashion. If it kept up, she'd have to try Covie's stomach remedy. Or cider.

She managed to roll over without waking Peggs and stared at the sky through their window. Stars, still, or were they dimming at last? She'd guess dawn wasn't too far off, if there were birds singing, but what she heard was Peggs' soft breathing, and the peaceful snores of their aunt and father. Dawn wasn't, Jenn decided, close at all.

She wiggled her toes, one at a time, reassured to find them where they should be.

Right foot done. She started on the left. Little toe first.

All at once, there was a loud, steady rustle from outside, as though a strong gust swept through the fields, but no wind stirred the roses to either side of the window or cooled her face. At the same instant, the confused longings inside her faded away, so she might have fallen asleep then and there.

Instead, Jenn stared wide-eyed at the window, trembling so hard she couldn't believe Peggs didn't grumble or wake.

It hadn't been the wind. She'd heard the grain falling on its own, row after row. It had fallen because it was supposed to . . . because it must . . . because . . . because . . .

She wouldn't think it.

The harvest happened every year, dependable as the snow to follow. Marrowdell's gift, they called it, like the water in the fountain and the river through the mill. Marrowdell's magic, Kydd would say. In Aunt Sybb's opinion, the grain was defective in some way, with stalks that snapped under the ripe weight. Old Jupp warned each Midwinter Beholding they'd best prepare for the year it didn't. But it always did.

Always. Because . . .

Eyes shut tight, Jenn Nalynn clenched her fingers on the quilt. She wouldn't think it. Wouldn't.

But the thought found her, where she trembled, sliding cold and certain into place.

The harvest came, not because of Marrowdell, but because someone else wished it.

A wish she'd somehow felt.

Wainn's old pony was first to hear the new arrivals. As he had every year, he pricked up his small gray ears and wispy tail, to trot about the orchard whinnying like a much younger steed, bullying the calves and timid Good'n'Nuf. He didn't do it for long, and wheezed when he stopped, but the villagers knew what it meant and looked at one another with smiles.

Jenn heard the commotion from the loft and thrust her head out the window. The grain in the wide field across the river lay in neatly winnowed rows, as it should. She pursed her lips, then shook her head. Last night, she'd had the strangest thought about it, which only went to prove what Aunt Sybb said, an overtired mind played tricks best forgotten. Especially a mind full of notions of magic.

Impossible to forget what had happened yesterday. She lifted her hand into the sunlight and studied her fingers, newly grateful for each tiny crease of skin, thankful for the blunt sturdy nails at their tips. How she'd taken them for granted; how terrifying their loss, however temporary. The only good part of sunset, she shuddered, was that it passed quickly.

She had to hope tonight would be better.

After all, tonight, there'd be a Beholding feast to welcome the tinkers, sure to arrive today, and to give thanks for the harvest. Marrowdell's good fortune wasn't secret, though outsiders, unless they saw for themselves, felt they were being lied to, which didn't go well if one argued. Hadn't Tadd returned last fall with a black eye and loose teeth?

However it happened, and Jenn found it harder to believe harvests weren't like this outside Marrowdell, the village was about to be transformed. She pulled back inside the window. With a yawn that turned into a sigh, she sat on the window seat, kicking her bare feet. Ordinarily, hearing Wainn's old pony, she'd rush to the commons gate, to be first to greet Mistress Sand.

Nothing was ordinary now.

True, they'd all been up before dawn preparing, with every kitchen called into service. Bread stood cooling on windowsills, great pots bubbled with potatoes and turnips, and enough onions had been chopped to bring tears to everyone's eyes. Jenn had washed pots and pans while Peggs went upstairs to change; now it was her turn to get ready.

Preparing the harvest feast was a familiar, welcome busyness. Preparing to welcome all of those who'd eat it?

A quandary.

She'd brushed her hair till it crackled and shone, then, reluctantly, left it loose over her shoulders as her sister had instructed, pulling the sides back from her face in a single knot to keep it tidy. Hair like that expected to be admired. It invited touch.

Jenn curled up her toes. Would he notice?

Which he being a question she refused to ask herself, let alone answer.

Then there was her beautiful dress, hanging from a peg, waiting to dance.

She pressed the back of her hand to one cheek to find it warm. Surely the kitchen's heat, not, as Peggs claimed with a cheerful laugh, because she couldn't wait to greet a certain someone—the name carefully and significantly unspecified.

She wanted to be back in Night's Edge. She'd dig her toes in the fragrant grass and confess all her worries and hopes. Wisp might tickle her neck with flower petals to make her laugh and play with her hair. But Wisp and the grass and flowers were gone.

And it hadn't been play, when Bannan put his hands in her hair.

Her breath caught.

Wainn's pony whinnied again, louder.

It was morning, not night.

Night was for scandalous letters and moon dreams. Morning, Jenn told herself, was for what was real. Real meant accepting responsibility, as Uncle Horst had said, not knowing how right he'd been, for herself, her actions, and their consequences. She must learn what to do at the Great Turn. She must—she would—endure three more sunsets, without putting anyone else at risk.

Most of all, Wyll. Her truest, first friend depended on her. She would not fail him again.

Jenn pulled out the bundle of letters from Bannan Larmensu, secured by a well-washed yellow ribbon. His latest was there; their shared envelope sat on top. She ran her fingertip over the dots of cool wax along its flap, counting, remembering. Ten dots. One for each day she'd written him and he'd written her.

Squaring her shoulders, she went down to the kitchen.

Her feet barely touched the second rung when Peggs said, in no happy tone, "Must you?"

As shameless as his letter-writing rider, Scourge stood with his big ugly head shoved through the Nalynn kitchen door, as he'd done every morning to nicker plaintively for a bit of toast or, better still, sausage. Having forbidden him rabbits, Jenn had been unable to refuse, though her sister and aunt pointed in mute accusation to drifts of brown hair on the floor.

Jenn felt guilty about those too, though it was Bannan's job to groom the creature, not hers, and the once she'd done it . . .

She went briskly to the stove, opened the fire door, and tossed in her bundle, trying not to notice how quickly the yellow ribbon turned black, or how Peggs' understanding eyes held regret too.

"Shouldn't you be on the road, Scourge?" Jenn asked, forestalling any questions. She put hard-boiled eggs on a plate. "The tinkers are coming."

If the tinkers were coming, why, so would Bannan Larmensu, whose letters crackled and burned.

And Wyll would come too, she added to herself firmly. The harvest drew everyone to the village.

"Are you sure?" whispered a sly breeze, as Scourge daintily lipped her offering. The eggs were in their shells; he preferred them crunchy. "Are you like Wen, and understand the little horse?"

"If it isn't them," Peggs countered, "it'll be Uncle, with the twins and the livestock. In which case you," as she took the empty plate from Jenn and patted Scourge's neck, "need to be somewhere else."

The villagers had grown accustomed to Scourge, though few heard him speak. The old kruar was particular. He spoke to Peggs, but not Aunt Sybb, which was just as well; Wainn but not Kydd, much as the beekeeper longed to ask questions; Tir, of course; and Gallie Emms. For the first few days, Gallie had endured more than her share of Scourge's attention, the great beast having discovered she was the source of his beloved sausages. Loee being the size of a rabbit, her mother'd kept a wary eye on her baby when Scourge came begging, but it hadn't taken long before everyone realized it was more a case of protecting Scourge. Whenever Loee's tiny fingers clamped on one of his fetlocks, he'd stand paralyzed and trembling until someone took pity on him and coaxed the baby, who thought this a fine game, to let go.

It was such a sight, Jenn had written Bannan about it. He'd replied he couldn't wait to see for himself, but it did explain how he and his sister had survived crawling through the paddock. Tir, who might have teased Scourge unmercifully on the matter, could not, having been trapped himself for the better part of lunch by Loee's unrelenting grip on his little finger. With the current batch of sausages now safely locked in the smokehouse, Scourge had returned to pestering soft-hearted Peggs.

"I am somewhere else. I am here. Tir warned me there will be cows on the road. I avoid cows," the breeze assured them with a chill nip. "Revolting, smelly things. I don't see why you allow cows."

"You like cheese, don't you?" Peggs observed.

The answering purr was so deep it rattled cups. "Do you have more?" hopefully.

"None to spare." Her sister swept off her apron and hung it from its hook. She paused, her eyes searching Jenn's face. "I missed you at supper yesterday, Dearest Heart," she said, meaning, because Peggs was the most perceptive of sisters, sunset.

"I wanted to finish before dark," Jenn replied truthfully. "I was fine," she added, glad when Peggs looked more at ease.

And not as glad when Scourge turned his great head, to regard her in silence.

"Fine," she insisted.

"Well, then," Peggs nodded. "Are you ready to go, Jenn? We'd best hurry, if we don't want to be last to the gate."

Last would suit her, this once. Jenn decided she'd be even happier if everyone arrived and settled and totally ignored her, until, until . . .

Imagination failed. She'd just find a way to speak to Mistress Sand alone, avoid Bannan, and be with Wyll, that was all. As for tonight . . . there'd be dancing. There was always dancing. Risky, that. She'd best break a toe—really break one, if necessary—

"Coming?"

Jenn followed her sister into the parlor, gloomily eyeing the legs of chairs for their toe-breaking potential.

Aunt Sybb looked up from her writing desk, quill poised in mid-air. Her smile faded as her wise eyes searched Jenn's face. "Not so happy as we'd hoped, I see," she said quietly. "You look exhausted, Dear Heart. We missed you at supper last night. Is something wrong?"

If ever their beloved aunt must be saved from knowing too much about Marrowdell and magic, this, Jenn decided, was the time. But what to say?

"Jenn's dress," Peggs volunteered, doubtless realizing it too. "This one, not the lovely one you gave her, Aunt."

Jenn attempted to look concerned and not puzzled. Her dress was fine. Welcoming the tinkers was an event and those who wouldn't head into the fields today prepared for the occasion. Peggs wore her third best, while Jenn, after an exhausting turmoil over her choices, since her new dress must be saved for the dance and her third best was too short, had given in and put on her second best, with the little blue birds and new white ribbons.

"Not all the stains came out," her sister said meaningfully, gesturing at the skirt, which was perfectly clean and even pressed.

Clever Peggs. "It's terrible," Jenn said. She gathered a handful of fabric and held it up. "I shouldn't be seen in it."

"Indeed." By what effort their aunt hid her astonishment, Jenn couldn't guess, though Aunt Sybb was surely more accustomed to her youngest niece being oblivious to stains on her knees, elbows, and nose, let alone a hem. "You're welcome to stay with me, of course." She lifted her quill, then added calmly, "I expect there's no reason for your young man to be anxious upon his first return to the village."

She hadn't thought of Wyll's feelings. Or Bannan's, for that matter. Jenn smoothed her skirt, fairly caught. "Thank you, Aunt, but I should be there," she replied. "To be sure they—he—so everyone's happy."

"That's the spirit." Aunt Sybb gave them a fond smile. "Now off with you. You don't want to be last."

They weren't. When Jenn and Peggs stepped from their porch, Alyssa and Cheffy were still squirming by the fountain while Hettie straightened their collars, and, as the sisters passed by the Uhthoffs', Wainn stepped out with his father and uncle.

Once, Jenn would have waved then hurried on, determined to beat everyone to the gate. When younger, if she'd managed to sneak out, she'd be sitting in the oak by the river already.

This time, she stopped. Peggs gave her a grateful look.

The three walked up to them. "Fair morning, dear ladies," the eldest Uhthoff greeted. They aged well, Jenn decided as they returned greetings. Master Dusom's dark hair had grayed over his temples but remained thick, and he moved with the same courtly grace as his younger brother and son. If not for a slight bookish stoop, he would have stood a little taller than Kydd. His eyes fooled many a student, Jenn thought as she smiled at him. The lids were half closed most of the time, as if Master Dusom were sleepy or unaware, but the eyes glinting through those slits were fiercely intelligent and missed not a thing.

Meeting those eyes, Jenn remembered she hadn't actually asked Kydd not to tell his brother. Had he? She couldn't tell.

Meanwhile, Kydd had taken Peggs' hand and the two stood gazing at one another in mute wonder, as if they met for the first time. Jenn coughed impatiently and Master Dusom chuckled. "To the gate?"

She nodded and started toward the commons.

"Not that one," Wainn informed them.

"So this year it's the twins first," his father said cheerfully. "I believe you owe me a week's dishes," with a smile at his brother.

Having gathered her courage for Wyll's sake, Jenn felt cheated. "Do you think so?"

Wainn frowned, so slightly she almost missed it. "They'll be here soon," he said, which wasn't terribly clear, and started walking the way Jenn and Peggs had come.

Hettie called, "Wait for me!"

Peggs hesitated. "Go on," she said to Jenn, "I'll keep her company."

Because the twins were coming home, and Hettie had something to say to one of them. To Tadd. "I'll wait too," offered Jenn with a sigh, though she loved being there when the livestock first lifted their heads, smelling home, and began to low and neigh and call to the family they'd left for the summer.

Kydd smiled, still holding Peggs' hand. "And not be first?"

He teased her. Jenn eyed her future brother-by-marriage, who now knew all about her, or more than anyone but Peggs, and decided being teased was a good sign. "Never," she retorted, and ran to catch up with Wainn, who hadn't delayed.

In fact, he was in a hurry. She skipped and half jogged to keep with him as they passed Old Jupp's house. "You don't have to go so fast," she told him. "We're ahead of everyone else." They weren't the only ones impatient for the new arrivals, she noticed. Riss stood on the porch, shading her eyes with one hand. The morning sun poured down the road, making it all but impossible to see what moved on it.

She waited for Horst.

Who should rush to take her in his arms, Jenn thought with a pang. Instead, she just knew, he and Riss would nod civil greetings to one another, then Uncle would deliver the mail from Endshere and help settle the livestock. He'd inform Aunt Sybb about her escort and take part in the harvest. He'd stay busy and in sight and forbid himself the longings of his heart and hers until certain of privacy.

Which wasn't fair.

Tir Half-face emerged from the mill to stand beside Radd Nalynn, eyes as wary as if he was part of the village and the twins, newcomers.

They'd get along, Jenn knew. Allin and Tadd were friendly, curious sorts. They'd be coaxing stories from Tir the first chance they got, and always had some of their own.

Wainn stopped at the open gate. "Here we are," he announced.

"And first." Satisfied, Jenn clambered to the top rail and sat, swinging her bare feet. No doubt Horst and Roche had told the twins the news; when had there last been such an eventful summer in Marrowdell? The farm, now in Bannan's capable hands. Tir at the mill. Wyll—though they may not have said all there was about Wyll. Last and not least, the upcoming weddings. Considering what the twins had been up to with Hettie, they'd no reason to be disappointed that the Nalynn sisters were officially spoken for, though one twin was completely out of luck. "Do you see them yet?" she asked impatiently, shielding her eyes to squint down the road.

Wainn looked up at her. "Who do you think is coming, Jenn Nalynn?"

"Who—" she broke off. Why wasn't he smiling? She gripped the railing, suddenly unsure of her seat. "Who is?"

He shook his head. "Scourge should have guarded the road."

Another fair morning. Having spent a restless night listening for he knew not what, Bannan was up at the first hint of dawn. He was determined to be ready before the tinkers, or Wyll, could claim his attention. Nine days as a farmer had left him scruffy and unkempt; he'd shaved, what, twice? Jenn Nalynn deserved better. If she noticed. Of course, she'd notice.

What if she didn't?

The day being here at last, he'd find out, wouldn't he?

Stoking the fire in his stove, Bannan filled his larger pot with porridge and put it on to cook, then dumped in the last of the dried spiced fruit from his and Tir's travel rations. What was he saving them for, if not guests? The black wizened bits might not look appealing, but they'd plump nicely and add flavor.

The kettle was already hot, and the truthseer made himself a mug of tea, then poured hot water into his shaving cup. Towel over his bare shoulders, cup and mug in his hands, and shaving kit under one arm, he headed outside.

The kit was pure luxury, an oblong box of dark wood with a hinged lid, its outer surface inlaid with rare light woods. The fanciful design echoed the Larmensu crest, with fox faces peering out between stylized sunflowers. Bannan propped it on an upper limb of the fallen branch, a convenient height, and opened the lid. The mirror reflected blue sky and a jaw in dire need of attention.

The kit held a razor, its blade folded into a shell handle, strop, brush, and shaving stick. A farewell gift from his nephews and he'd thanked them gravely. Since they were too young to shave or shop, or to understand he was truly leaving and why, he'd known it came from Emon, the boys' father. They'd looked one another in the eye, he and the baron, and needed no words. Bannan opened the kit the first day on the road, once beyond Vorkoun's walls and eyes, and had managed to cut himself no more than three times whilst removing his beard.

Practice helped, plus respect for the splendid edge. He passed it along the strop before using the brush and hot water to draw a fragrant lather from the shaving stick he'd saved till now. Once that precious commodity was used up, he'd have to obtain whatever soap the men of Marrowdell used. Unless Jenn liked him smelling like a Vorkoun baron, Bannan thought cheerfully as he applied the warm lather to his cheeks, neck, and chin. In that case, he'd send for more, whatever the cost.

He drew the blade to his chin, wiped it clean on the towel, then prepared for the next pass.

"What's that smell?"

The blade halted above where his pulse beat near the skin. "Do you want me to slice my throat?" Bannan asked mildly, that pulse hammering a little more as he resumed shaving.

Wyll's face appeared beside his in the mirror. "Not before breakfast." The dragon squinted. "I'm glad I don't need to do that." His small reddish-brown beard remained as neatly trimmed as the first day they'd met. "Does it hurt?"

Bannan pretended to scowl. "If you want breakfast, let me finish."

If he'd hoped Wyll would leave him in peace, he'd misjudged the other's curiosity. Helping himself to Bannan's mug of tea, Wyll leaned on the branch nearby and watched intently. After a moment, a breeze found Bannan's ear, chilling the lather. "You survived the night. I'm impressed."

So, not about the shaving. Bannan finished his right cheek and glanced at Wyll. "The tinkers were fine company. We got along famously." He wiped the razor. "They're joining us for breakfast."

A flash of silver. " 'Us?' What did you tell them?"

"Only that you're my neighbor and occasionally helpful around the farm." He looked back into the mirror to shave his left cheek, stretching his lips to the side. "I assume they know the rest." There. Done and he hadn't nicked himself, despite distraction.

His distraction watched him rinse the razor, then bring up the ends of the towel to wipe the remaining lather from his face. "I brought back your comb," Wyll said without warning, and produced the missing item from inside his jerkin.

The dragon had looked tidier lately. "Keep it," Bannan told him. "I've another." He dropped the brush into its cup, closed his kit, then went to the well to splash cold water on his face and neck. Half-done, he stopped. Heart's Blood.

He straightened to stare accusingly at Wyll. "It wasn't just the comb. *Talnern's Last Quest*. You took my book!"

"I can't bring that back," the other said calmly. "I used the words in my letters."

"Ancestors Twice Put Upon and Tormented, Wyll, it was my favorite!"

"Then you should have put it somewhere safe."

The disgruntled truthseer washed up without another word, then smiled into his towel. *'Quest* was a daring adventure; its prose was, to be charitable, lurid. The poor dragon must have had quite the struggle to express himself from it.

Bannan tugged on the leather thong to free his hair. "If you need anything else, ask me first."

Wyll had a charming smile when he chose. "I'll try to remember. I do need breakfast."

"Speaking of breakfast, where are the tinkers?" The barn's big door remained closed. He hadn't cleaned and greased its wooden rail yet, so how they'd managed that without a racket, he couldn't guess.

"Meddling in the lives of others." Wyll lost his smile. "Have you not seen?"

A fair morning, with almost no dew, and a sky that promised heat. Somehow, Bannan knew the dragon meant more than weather. He glanced around the farmyard, finding nothing out of place. "What 'meddling?' "

"The efflet fled for good reason. Their kaliia lies dead."

This, he had to see. Bannan left Wyll to follow him indoors. He rushed up the ladder to the loft and looked out his window.

"Ancestors Blessed."

The grain, shoulder-high yesterday afternoon, now lay in tidy rows. All of it. Radd Nalynn hadn't been joking.

It should have taken days and sweat. A potent magic. More, a magic used to a particular purpose. Why? The obvious answer was to help the villagers.

He wouldn't have lasted a week in the marches if he'd accepted the obvious.

Feeling cold inside, Bannan shrugged on a shirt, then went back downstairs to consult the only expertise he had.

"They did it from inside the barn?" he began.

Wyll poured himself tea. "Now that they are within Marrowdell, they can do as they choose. Though why this?" A lopsided shrug. "Your guess is as good as mine would be."

The truth. Bannan's heart sank. "I thought you knew all about them."

"I was their servant, not their fellow." A glint of feral silver. "Despite the birth of Jenn Nalynn, I've avoided being here with the turn-born, nor was I interested in their doings." The silver faded. "Until now."

The truthseer clawed hair from his face and scowled. "That's not very helpful."

"What is not na?"

Bannan flinched. The house toad, hitherto asleep by the back door, leapt out and away. Prudent creature.

Wyll merely glanced at Mistress Sand. "My efforts in the kitchen," he said smoothly.

Recovering, the truthseer gave a short bow. "Fair morning, Mistress Sand. Allow me to introduce my neighbor, Wyll. I spoke of him last night."

"So you did." Her eyes glittered like frost. "Wyll, is it? I can see why you'd like to be carried to the village."

They weren't friends. Until this instant, Bannan hadn't realized they might be enemies. And here he was, stuck between them.

Wyll smiled. "Mistress Sand. I can see you're a kindly woman, gracious to grant a favor to those less able."

Shadows loomed in the doorway behind the tinker, who hadn't yet stepped through. Her companions, silent and watchful. The dog peered between booted feet, equally wary. The air fell still.

Except for a restless breeze that rattled the cutlery.

"Come in, come in," Bannan said hastily, before things went further out of hand. "Fair morning, all. I hope you—" Did turn-born sleep? Did they dream? "—were comfortable," he finished lamely. "There's porridge in the pot."

For an ominous moment, no one moved, then, suddenly as a blink, Mistress Sand smiled beatifically and came inside, offering him a bundle tied with string. "I picked out a shawl for you," she explained. "The gift for your ladylove na?"

Cutlery landed on the floor.

"Thank you." Bannan tucked the bundle under one arm, having no choice but to take it no matter Wyll's temper, and quickly stooped to recover the spoons. The little white dog got there first, sniffing hopefully. Meanwhile, the remaining tinkers filed in, avoiding Wyll as best they could within the small space, and helped themselves to porridge.

Oh, the morning was off to a fine start.

"Wainn, you can't leave it at that," Jenn pleaded. "Watch the road for what?"

But having made his ominous pronouncement, Wainn would say no more. She fell silent too.

The sun played its own tricks, darkening shadows, shifting them along the road. Twice she straightened, sure she'd seen something, only to sag back, having not. All the while, little chills played over her neck and shoulders, raising gooseflesh on her bare arms.

Then, something moved that wasn't a shadow. Somethings! "They're home!" Jenn shouted in relief and waved.

Her wave was returned by two of the three riders now in view. Two packhorses followed. Behind, the sun found brown hide, bright eyes, and tossing heads. The livestock, sensing their place, stepped lively and the riders did the same.

What had Wainn been thinking?

The gate shook as Hettie and Peggs climbed up beside her. They'd run ahead of Kydd and Dusom, doubtless Hettie's idea. "Oh, we're in time," the milkmaid exclaimed breathlessly, her face pale. "Look, there's the twins and . . . is that Roche or Horst with them?"

It was, Jenn realized a heartbeat later, neither.

Between the twins rode a stranger. A stranger in a green dress with yellow ribbons. A stranger whose lush black curls were topped with a wedding circlet of white summer flowers and trailing lace.

Hettie groaned.

"You don't know—" Peggs started.

"I do!" their friend despaired. "He's gone and married. Do you see? He's brought home a wife!"

Jenn couldn't tell which "he" from here. The three rode abreast, all of them faced toward the village.

Jenn and Peggs exchanged looks, then both put an arm around Hettie.

This was not a good start to the day at all.

Whatever Bannan had expected from coming into Marrowdell with the tinkers and Wyll, it wasn't to find the village deserted and the commons empty save for the two sows and their boar, who glanced up as a tinker from the first wagon opened the gate, then lowered their snouts again in supreme disinterest.

Four of the tinkers crowded together in the first wagon. Bannan and Wyll rode the second, with Sand and Riverstone in the third and last with their little dog. They'd let him put his pitchfork in the back with the barrels. They'd put other things in the wagons as well. Tents, poles, bags. From his barn, no doubt.

Bannan did his unobtrusive best to give their driver, Flint, as much room as possible. For his part, the tinker sat hunched forward, elbows on his knees, and stared straight ahead, thoroughly offended by Wyll's presence. Bannan was reminded of a certain lordling of Vorkoun too full of himself to take advice from someone as common-bred as Tir.

First ambush, he'd bled out in a ditch.

"Where's everyone?" Bannan whispered to Wyll, squeezed between him and the outside of the seat. Their wagon creaked up the slope beneath the oak tree, the kruars' hooves crunching on acorns.

Wyll didn't bother keeping his voice down. "Doubtless they've better things to do."

Doubtless the bundle on Bannan's lap continued to sour Wyll's mood. The truthseer hid a grin. He'd no intention of exposing his heart to the turn-born and, much as he enjoyed baiting his rival, the tide had turned. The dragon was now an ally. When the time came, he'd give the shawl to the Lady Mahavar.

But there was no reason to tell Wyll that.

"Seems odd, that's all," the truthseer commented mildly as they passed through the open gate.

Inside the pasture, the first wagon left the road and went up the slight rise toward the riverbank, then stopped. Their wagon pulled up next to it, Flint jumping down before it came to rest. "We camp here," the tinker announced, with a dour look at Wyll. "There's no place for you."

Not waiting for a reply, the tinker went to join his companions, busy unloading the first wagon with the economy of long practice.

Bundle under one arm, Bannan rose to take advantage of the extra height of the wagon. He shaded his eyes as he peered over the hedges into the village. "I still don't see anyone. Where's Jenn?" He glanced down at Wyll and lowered his voice. "You know, don't you?"

The dragon's lips twisted, but he didn't deny it. "At the other gate. Waiting for other arrivals."

She'd written of the summer stock. Ancestors Aloof and Abandoned, she'd gone to greet cattle instead of him? Bannan shook his head. Lila would love it. So much for the welcome he'd fondly imagined.

Or did Jenn Nalynn avoid a certain dragon?

Liking that notion, the truthseer grinned as he hopped down and offered his hand.

Wyll ignored it, taking hold of the seat's outside edge. As he rose, the kruar stepped briskly forward in unison, throwing him to the floor. The two turned their heads and snorted amusement.

Seeing silver flare in the dragon's eyes, Bannan stepped in. "Poor training. I'd have expected better."

If these kruar thought their flared nostrils and glares were impressive, they needed lessoning in that too. He knew an expert.

Wyll wrestled himself from the wagon to the ground, his fingertips leaving dents in the wood. "They are but horses," he dismissed with scorn. "As well expect courtesy from these pigs."

The third wagon stopped beside them, Riverstone and Sand looking none too pleased. Bannan gave a short bow. "Our thanks for the ride, Mistress." Courtesy was safer than whatever Wyll might come out with next. "We'll let the villagers know you've arrived."

Riverstone nodded. "Please tell the miller—" He stopped, his head lifting to stare toward the village.

As did Sand. Bannan glanced around, heart in his throat. All of the tinkers stood motionless, staring in the same direction.

He didn't dare speak, then realized he couldn't. The world had gone silent, as if pausing to stare as well. Why?

Sand gave a low chuckle, breaking the spell.

"—we'll head into the fields shortly," Riverstone continued as if nothing had happened. "Those who wish can join us there."

Wyll, meanwhile, let out a long breath, as if he'd held his.

Nothing for it but to go. The truthseer bowed again, thankful Wyll simply turned and lurched away with him. What had just happened? He gave the sky a suspicious look, but its benign and cloudless blue held no surprises.

The tinkers paused to watch them pass, a couple leaning their heads together to share some amusement. Kruar, still harnessed, snorted and stamped their challenge. "Ancestors Blessed and Beloved, Wyll, don't annoy them," the truthseer advised under his breath.

"My existence annoys them," the dragon replied calmly. "I need do nothing more."

Still, Bannan was relieved to glance back and see yellow tents rise on their poles, untroubled by a contrary breeze.

This close to home the most mannerly cattle and horses grew impatient, so those ahead of the small herd didn't pause, but rode through into the village, greeting those sitting on the gate with hasty nods. The look on the twins' faces reminded Jenn of the time they'd conspired to eat Roche's birthday cake before his party, an uneasy blend of triumph and the growing realization they may have been too clever for their own good.

A foreign bride? They should be worried. Or one of them should.

To be fair, the foreign bride seemed as pleasant and friendly a person as anyone could wish to meet, with bright eyes and a quick smile. Her dress was simple, but pretty; no city frills and nonsense, as

Covie would say when Aunt Sybb wasn't in earshot. Her bare feet hung comfortably as she rode a sway-backed chestnut mare who must be older than she was.

The three on the gate smiled and waved back as if it made no difference which twin was now married.

The yearlings and horses filed past, fit, fat, and shaggy. They'd had good grazing for the summer and soon would be loose in the fields. A couple called out and were answered by their kin in the orchard. Jenn was about to drop from the gate, to offer a pat and kiss a soft nose or two, when she noticed their ears were slanted back.

Which they shouldn't be. Uncle Horst and Roche would be following behind, to make sure none strayed, but the animals should be more interested in what lay ahead, not behind.

At the thought, she looked for Wainn. He'd stayed, eyes locked on the road, instead of leaving to help ensure the young and thoughtless cattle didn't stray and trample pumpkins.

He'd said Scourge should have guarded the road.

"We should go," Peggs said, but her voice was uncertain. She felt it too. Something wasn't right.

Another rider appeared. Uncle Horst. For some reason, he sent his gelding into a trot, shoving a path through the startled livestock. He glanced toward the three on the gate and Wainn, his face grim, then dug in his heels. The gelding broke into a canter, aimed for the knot of villagers waiting by the mill. Horst didn't look toward Riss at all.

"What's that about?" Hettie asked, but neither Nalynn could answer.

Roche rode up with the last of the livestock, the Uhthoffs' dappled mare serving as packhorse. Letting her go to follow the others, he reined to a stop, face flushed with excitement. "Go wait with the rest," he ordered, bold as you please. "We've guests coming."

Jenn was used to him being full of his own importance, but this? Peggs and Hettie scowled with her. "What 'guests?'" she said, not moving at all. "Who?"

"You'll see."

"Her family?" demanded Hettie. "Is that who?"

He made her wait for the answer, a nasty smile growing on his face. "Tadd's, you mean?"

Hettie stiffened in dismay.

Full of himself and spiteful, Jenn decided, not believing a word of it. "Roche Morrell," she cried, ready to burst with outrage. "You tell the truth. Right now!"

For an instant, she had the oddest impression everything stopped moving, everywhere. Which was silly, of course, because in the next, a bee flew past, a squirrel scolded, and someone shouted at a cow.

Roche's green eyes widened, pupils huge despite the bright sun. He stared at her as if he couldn't look away. "Allin married her," he admitted. "Her name's Palma. She's the daughter of the innkeeper in Endshere." Words kept coming, faster and faster, as if he couldn't stop. "Allin's been sweet on her since last summer, though I don't know what she sees in him. They married in Endshere because her parents can't leave the inn, and he's brought her here for the harvest, but they don't mean to stay, no matter what he says. Palma's father's retiring and leaving her the inn. Allin's to tend bar. I'm afraid he'll be a thorough grump and not let me keep running a tab—" He had to stop for breath.

"Why did you say it was Tadd, then?" Peggs demanded angrily.

His horse sidestepped as Roche flinched. Flinched, but answered. "Hettie fancies him. She'd never spread for me, just 'cause my mother married her father. I get mean when I can't have what I want. I wanted to hurt her."

The truth it likely was, though Jenn could have done with far less of it. He only did as she'd asked. Told. More shouted, really. Not that she'd imagined he ever would. Roche was all about evasion and half-truths; he loved to keep others guessing. But this . . .

This, she thought queasily, felt like magic. Her magic. She hadn't meant to wish at him or anyone. She must be more careful.

Jenn retreated behind courtesy. "Good of you to admit your—your faults, Roche," she said as charitably as she could.

"Bannan was right," he told her. "I wouldn't have married you. I said I would. I wanted to believe I would. But the truth is once I'd had you, I'd have left to look for something new. I don't want a wife. I just wanted to beat the twins to—" He pressed a hand over his mouth to smother the rest, face pale with shock.

So much for courtesy. "I'll tell Tir you gave them mice!"

"No need," Hettie said grimly. "Roche Morrell, I want you packed and gone, or I'll tell our mother about more than your sneaking off to hunt when you should be at work. Hear me?"

A scowl creased his forehead. He'd kept his hand over his mouth and now his fingers and thumb sank deep, whitening his cheeks, holding in whatever he'd otherwise say. It made him look, Jenn thought distractedly, like a soured old apple.

"Answer me!"

His hand flung itself away. Spittle-coated words burst from him like vomit. "You can't send me away! I'm going already. After the harvest, I'm leaving with Horst."

Uncle had given Wyll his ax.

Jenn's breath caught. Sounds from the village filled the air, the livestock settling, the flurry of excitement around Allin and his new wife.

Uncle had ridden by without looking at Riss.

"When he takes Aunt Sybb to Endshere," stated Peggs, the same fear in her voice. "That's what you mean."

"That's not what he means. Is it, Roche?" She had to know, whether it took magic or dropping him in mud. "You're telling us Uncle Horst's leaving Marrowdell forever."

"Yes," Roche answered, sending pain through her heart. "So am I. I hate it here. I've always hated it." With that, he ducked his head and drummed his heels into his mount's sides, sending it at a jolting trot into the village and away from them.

"Well." Hettie hopped down and dusted her hands. "Who didn't see that coming? I, for one, say we're better off without him."

"But . . . Uncle?"

Hettie looked up at Jenn. "Ancestors Daft and Ridiculous, don't tell me you believed his nonsense? Mean to the last, that's Roche."

"You're right." Peggs visibly relaxed. "He wanted to upset us,

Jenn. It was another of his lies. Why would Uncle Horst want to leave?"

Jenn fell silent. She believed. Uncle Horst wouldn't want to go. He loved them. But love wasn't enough, not if he'd some reason to leave. It hadn't been enough for him to be open with Riss, had it?

She pushed aside her own despair and longing, thinking very deliberately of how important it was that Uncle Horst make up his own mind. He wasn't like Roche, who should tell the truth more often. Uncle Horst was a remarkable man, exactly as he was, and mustn't be touched by magic. Ever.

Hettie had other priorities. "Palma, is it?" Her face lit with her wide, joyful smile. "Let's go welcome her. Coming, Peggs? Jenn?"

More likely it was Tadd Hettie couldn't wait to welcome, but, everything considered, matters were working out in that area better than they might. "I'll join you in a moment," Jenn assured them, having noticed Wainn still by the gate. He'd ignored all the arrivals, even Roche's antics, as if he mustn't look away from the road.

Hardly comforting, given Roche's claim of more guests. She turned to her sister. "If it's not Palma's family coming, who do you—"

Peggs had stopped, half on, half off the gate. "What's that?"

Jenn twisted around as "that" came into view with a toss of gilded horns and the ringing of bells.

The horns belonged to the tallest oxen she'd ever seen. They were more like horses than cattle, lean and long-legged, with delicate pale pink muzzles and large, wide-set eyes. Immense humps rose from their shoulders and gilded horns spiraled up and back to almost touch them, glittering against polished black hides. Gold glittered from their hooves and harness as well, harness adorned with little red bells.

There were seven of the noble creatures, harnessed in three pairs with one to the fore. A man in a stiff red robe walked beside that leader. His face was hidden beneath a broad yellow hat and, at the sight of them, he swung a larger, golden bell at each step to ring a deep counterpoint to the lighter music of the harness bells.

As if this entrance weren't remarkable enough, the oxen pulled not one, but three covered wagons, linked like beads on a string. The first had one set of wheels, the second two, and the third, when it came into view, had four. Otherwise, they were similar, each made of honey-colored wood, with inlaid black tile that formed a decorative pattern along the roof edge, then dipped to outline a curved and curtained window. A half window on the first wagon, which was the smallest; a large one centered on the side of the second, and two on the sides of the final, and largest.

The first wagon had a curtained front as well, and Jenn thought someone might be sitting behind it, but the material, though gauze-thin, was dark blue and hid the wagons' interiors quite effectively.

The elegant roofs were curved and so high Jenn was sure even Bannan could stand easily inside. As a final oddness, the wheels were made of some soft, black substance that made no sound at all as they rolled over the packed earth of the road.

It was, she decided breathlessly, simply the most marvelous way to travel.

Someone equally marvelous must be riding inside.

She couldn't wait to meet them.

"I'd say we've found them," Bannan noted. A colorful crowd gathered before the mill, including a trio who'd just dismounted. A solitary figure remained ahorse: Horst, leaning over in discussion with another man. Other villagers lined the road, guiding a small herd of cattle and horses through a temporary gate into the orchard. Whinnies and nickers and rumbles of greeting came from those already in that pasture. Bannan grinned as the two children went in hot pursuit of a yearling who slipped past them, intent on forbidden vegetables.

A bucolic scene, and a welcoming one. The air was rich with the scent of sun-warmed grain and roasting meat. His ox, the truthseer concluded, spotting the pit near the smith's house, and licked his lips.

All at once, a horse and rider pounded through the herd, sending heads tossing and two more escapees into the gardens. The man—

Roche—pulled his horse to a furious halt by the fountain, then jumped down, tossing the reins over his mount's head.

More Bannan didn't see, for an irresistible grip pulled him, not gently, around the side of the Morrills' house. "Get weapons!" Wyll commanded, eyes flaring silver. He released his hold with a hard shove and the truthseer staggered. "Go!"

"Heart's Blood!" Bannan made sure his bundle was safe, then rubbed his arm, another bruise for his collection. "It's just Roche—"

"Find weapons!" A breeze shoved him back another step. " 'Rouse the village!"

"Why?" Bannan's heart started to pound. "What's wrong?!"

"Go!" Infuriated breezes tore leaves and slammed clots of soil against the log wall. "Defend Marrowdell!"

He flinched and shielded his eyes. "All right! I'll get Tir." And his axes. "We'll scout—" For what? Ancestors Reliable and Trusted, he'd better have more than a dragon's tantrum before alarming the villagers. "What—"

"The bold suitors return!" An amused breath of air found his ear. Scourge wasn't in sight, which only meant he chose not to be seen. "Is your plan to hide and write more letters?"

"Useless old fool!" Wyll snarled and a vicious little wind whistled across the road, startling birds from the apple trees on the far side. Crack! A branch came loose and fell.

Scourge shied into view from behind a trunk surely too narrow to have hidden so much as his nose.

And charged.

"Heart's Blood!" The oath came at the same instant as a frantic thud of hooves—doubtless, Bannan thought numbly, Roche's horse running for its life—and an equally frantic scramble of footsteps as his former rider tore around the building, almost crashing into them.

While Scourge thundered across the road.

"Stay here. He's not mad at us," Bannan assured Roche.

It wasn't as though running would help.

"Useless," Wyll reiterated, standing his ground as the men put their backs to the wall.

Scourge plunged to a snorting halt, close enough to spray them all with dirt but not, thankfully, any closer. Bannan realized he'd been right to think his old friend something quite different from the kruar pulling the tinkers' wagons. It wasn't size, though Scourge was a third again larger.

It was the pure, unadulterated threat rippling from those curled-back lips to that upraised tail.

Roche whimpered. "Ancestors save me! He's going to kill us."

"That—" Wyll snapped the fingers of his good hand under Scourge's drooling fangs, "—for your help. You let them in, you great cow!!"

Bannan put his bundle against the log wall and took a step. "Let who in?" He might not have existed. The dragon and kruar continued to glower at one another. "Who?!" he demanded.

A low voice answered, "Ansnans."

Bannan spun on his heel to stare at Roche, hearing the truth, unwilling to believe it. "This is no time for jokes." Or nightmares.

The man was sickly pale but didn't back down. "I'm telling the truth. I can't help it," he added desperately. "Jenn told me to and now I can't stop!"

The truth. The moment in the commons. Sand and her fellow turn-born had been amused. Because Jenn Nalynn, however innocent, had enacted a just revenge?

"I hate it here," Roche went on. "The horrid dreams. The way everyone's so happy with their stupid little lives. I'll stay for the harvest to impress my family and be sure you don't look better than me, even if you are—" He gulped for air.

It was like watching someone topple from a cliff, Bannan decided. Dreadful, but you couldn't look away. Roche had best change his habits, or he'd condemn himself every time he opened his mouth.

"—and to see for myself if Jenn Nalynn marries this cripple when she could have had a real man, like me!"

Like that.

Bannan raised a hand to stop the flood, with a wary glance at the dragon, who still matched glares with Scourge. "I believe you." Ancestors Crazed and Confounded. The truth it was.

And Ansnans. Here. "Why would Ansnans come to Marrowdell?" he demanded, though sure of the answer. They'd come in search of Captain Ash. His entire body felt hard and heavy, the way it had before battle. Why had he abandoned his weapons?

A bee droned past. A moth perched lightly on the roof edge as birds sang. Voices rang out in the distance, cheerful and busy voices.

"Why does not matter!" The breeze stank of old meat and scalded Bannan's neck. "We find Tir!" A hoof slammed into the ground. "We kill them all! Squash them flat. Rip their flesh! Lick their blood as it pours out!!!"

Scourge was sharing; Roche turned green.

The eager violence was familiar, though having it put into words made Bannan grateful his mount had been mute all those years on the marches.

Violence that didn't belong here. That he'd chosen not to bring with him. Ancestors Desperate and Dire, he'd come here for peace. Where could it begin, if not with him?

So the truthseer said, almost calmly, "There's a truce."

The breeze sank to a fetid mutter. Wyll turned his head to stare at Bannan, silver glinting in his eyes. "Your truce matters not to me. These strangers are a threat!"

A threat, when the dragon didn't care about him or his past. "Wait. Roche," Bannan said, then sharper, "Roche!" when the younger man wouldn't stop staring at Scourge. With a start, he shifted his eyes to the truthseer. "Answer me," Bannan ordered. "Why have the Ansnans come to Marrowdell?"

"F— for the eclipse."

"The—" The truthseer closed his mouth, chilled to the bone. Sand had accused him. She'd known the danger. What had Wyll said about the men who'd come before, who'd built the now-ruined towers? That they'd been the spark to set two worlds ablaze.

Making the Ansnans a threat to this wondrous place.

To Jenn Nalynn.

Shaken, he turned to the dragon. "They're only men—"

"This is the Great Turn," Wyll said, cold and harsh. His silvered eyes were too hot to meet. "They think to meddle once more. They shall not!"

Scourge's head lifted, lips back over his fangs. "They must die," he agreed.

There was another way. There had to be. "Wait," Bannan heard himself said once more.

The dragon and the kruar looked at him.

"I can learn the truth," he offered grimly. "Let me talk to them first."

Captain Ash he would be again. For her sake.

Jenn and Peggs sat very quietly on the gate, so quietly that with any luck at all, no one of the group approaching from the village would notice and send them from what boded to be the most entertaining event in Marrowdell's history.

The strange train of wagons had halted some distance from the gate. It was that, or run over the house toad.

The toad, having leapt into the oxen's path, now squatted there like a large warty rock, refusing to budge even when the red-robed man shook his bell at it. In response, the toad merely puffed up and glared its indignation.

The man, nonplussed, tried to steer the oxen around the toad, but they, as if aware this was no ordinary toad, also refused to budge.

Curtains fluttered as the wagons' occupants noticed the delay.

"Who do you think's inside?" Jenn whispered eagerly.

Peggs leaned her head close. "No one from Endshere."

The sisters nodded wisely.

The front curtain on the lead wagon pulled aside and a head popped out. It was that of an older woman, though her scalp was bare. She shouted at the man in a language Jenn hadn't heard before, her meaning plain. He pointed his bell at the toad and shrugged.

"Welcome—" Jenn began.

The woman flung a gray scarf over her head and disappeared behind the curtain.

"You frightened her."

"Did not. What's Wainn doing?"

He'd stepped up to the side of the last, largest wagon. Now he rapped smartly on its wood.

That curtain drew aside, slowly. The youngest Uhthoff bowed a greeting and said something.

Which they couldn't possibly hear from this distance. Jenn hopped down at once, pausing to straighten her ribbons.

"What do you—Jenn, wait!" her sister urged, with a worried look toward the village. Master Dusom and Uncle Horst were in the lead, their father and Tir close behind. As, it appeared, was everyone else.

Wait. Everything was about waiting, these days. About behaving and waiting while others did things. Jenn shook her head in mute rebellion.

Abandoning Peggs, she walked as quickly as seemed proper. She dipped a half curtsy at the toad, nodded graciously to the robed man, and admired the giant oxen without getting too close. But her attention was all for Wainn and whomever he addressed.

So she jumped with a highly improper squeak when the curtains on the middle wagon were flung open and a smiling face peered out at her. "Fair, fair day, young lady!" boomed the owner of the face. "Have we reached the refuge at last? Is this the home of the mighty Celestial? We're in time, I trust?"

Jenn gave herself a little shake, then said as properly as Aunt Sybb could ask, though she struggled a bit to understand what he said, since he spoke with great enthusiasm and his vowels were either too long or too short, making even the normal words odd, "You've reached Marrowdell, good sir. My name is Jenn Nalynn."

"Gaienn Nalynn."

"Jenn," she corrected, though it wasn't polite to argue.

"Jeainn! Jenn! I have it. A splendid name. Jenn. Wait there, Jenn. Please. Right there. Don't go away." The curtain slid back in place, then the entire wagon shook as the stranger bustled around inside, clearly planning to come out.

Ancestors Witness. She hadn't planned to greet the newcomers herself, nor, she was sure, would their father be happy about it. At least what she'd seen of the man was pleasant and friendly: older, bald-headed, with big bushy eyebrows and brown eyes that crinkled cheerfully at the corners.

Wainn shook his head at her.

She pretended not to notice.

A door burst open at the back of the wagon, beside the tongue linking it to the next. Stairs neatly unfolded to the road, supported by chains, then the stranger stepped out, one hand holding the door-frame, the other keeping his hem from tangling his feet.

He wore a hat and red robe, like the man with the oxen, but his robe was much richer, with a panel of bright yellow from throat to hem and matching bars on the sleeves from shoulder to wrist. The material was finely pleated, with even the sleeves a mass of delicate, measured folds. Ironing the thing would take hours, she thought.

A resplendent, lordly figure who hopped past the lowest step and rushed to meet her with hands outstretched. "Hello and greetings, Jenn of Marrowdell!"

She took his hands—how could she not?—and managed a shy smile. "Hello."

"Dema Qimirpik. Were we not to greet the locals together?" A second man came from behind the last wagon. He nodded graciously to Wainn, but didn't pause, coming toward Jenn instead.

Who, about to be outnumbered by strangers, wished herself a little less bold. Nothing for it but to keep smiling, especially since her hands remained trapped in the soft, slightly moist grip of Dema Qimirpik. A name she'd need to practice.

"I saw her first, Urcet," claimed her captor, squeezing her hands gently.

Jenn blushed. To make matters worse, while Dema Qimirpik, though dressed like a woman, seemed a fatherly, friendly figure, the approaching Urcet was, well, he wasn't.

He wore tan trousers, topped by a short brown coat, belted and with pockets at chest and waist, over a creamy shirt with a collar open at the throat. A narrow black sash crossed from his left shoulder to his right hip, ending in a tassel tied with small, muted red bells, and a series of leather pouches hung from his belt. His shoes were polished to gleaming reflections and his hair, for his head wasn't shaved, curled tight to his scalp, black save for a round white patch above each ear. All of which being details Jenn noticed later.

He was the most beautiful man in the world. He had to be.

The skin sliding over smooth muscle and noble bone was as black as the oxen's hide. A gold bead gleamed from the one side of his broad nostrils and his bold dark eyes, large and slanted, had lids painted with gold. Generous perfect lips parted over shockingly white teeth as he began to smile at her, and his smile?

Jenn felt warm to her toes.

Fortunately, Peggs appeared at her shoulder as she stood staring. "Hello. I'm Peggs Nalynn."

The youngest Uhthoff followed behind, his face unusually troubled. "I'm Wainn Uhthoff. Why are you here?"

Releasing Jenn's hands, Dema Qimirpik smiled at Peggs and took her hands, in what Jenn now realized was his peculiar greeting ritual. "Urcet," he proclaimed, "we've come to a land of rapturous beauty. My heart may not survive it."

"Before you expire, my good dema," Urcet suggested dryly, his warm voice deeper than Davi Treff's, "you could introduce me. As head of our little expedition."

"Of course. Ladies—and you, young sir," this as Dema Qimirpik nodded to Wainn, "—it is my honor to present Urcet a Hac Sa Od y Dom, my esteemed colleague and fellow adventurer. We're here on a quest."

"You are not Rhothan," Wainn said bluntly.

Not Rhothan? Jenn's eyes widened.

"Indeed, we are not," Urcet agreed. He touched the fingertips of his right hand to the base of his throat and inclined his head. "I am

Eld. My companion and our servants are Ansnan. We accept that here we are—" he paused delicately, "—something of a novelty."

Novelty? From what Master Dusom and Aunt Sybb said, no one from Eldad ventured outside of Avyo, though perhaps that would change once they built their train.

As for Ansnor? Jenn's mouth went dry. The war was over, yes, but to judge by Bannan—

"I don't believe it!" A smiling Master Dusom pushed past Jenn and her sister. "Is that you, Qimirpik?"

"As you must be Dusom. We meet in the flesh at last."

The two clasped hands with every appearance of joy. "How did you—where did you—It doesn't matter." She hadn't known Master Dusom could babble. "You made it, Qimirpik! You're in time for the eclipse!"

"And in good company," the dema said, indicating Urcet. "My esteemed colleague from Eldad, Urcet a Hac Sa Od y Dom."

"Scholar Dusom." Urcet nodded graciously and Master Dusom bowed. From the looks on everyone else's face, their scholar had some explaining to do.

Wainn said no one in Marrowdell could help her, but he couldn't have known of the timely arrival of the dema. Heart alight with hope, Jenn eased back through the half-circle of villagers. These were scholars and friends of Master Dusom; being from other domains, they might know magic. It was certainly possible, she told herself, determined to make a good impression. So, while the rest exchanged greetings, Jenn went to where the Ansnan servant stood beside his team, staring in helpless frustration at the house toad.

"Fair morning,—" Did one say "good sir" to a servant? She'd never met one. Aunt Sybb hadn't said much on the matter, come to think of it, save the always useful advice to offer courtesy regardless of station. Jenn bobbed half a curtsy, "—good sir."

Up close, the servant's red robe lacked pleats or bands of yellow and was stained from hem to knee. His broad-brimmed hat was the same as the dema's, but he wore a scarf around his neck. His tanned face had wrinkles folding its wrinkles, as if he'd been plump once, so it was difficult to know if he frowned. Jenn kept smiling hopefully.

He said some words she didn't understand, then gestured with his bell, two fingers holding the clapper silent.

Was he pointing to the toad, the village, or shooing her away?

"I can help," she offered.

More words, none of which seemed polite. A definite, "go away," with the bell. He lifted his hand to the neck of the lead ox and gave it a morose little pat, as if to say, here we are, stuck in a wilderness with mad toads and stupid girls.

Well, this was frustrating. She wasn't stupid. He'd had all his life to learn Ansnan. The least he could have done before making this journey was learn Rhothan, like his master. She tried not to scowl. How hard could it be?

The woman in the first wagon called out something. The man turned his head and replied, not as loudly.

Really, how hard . . . Words were meant to be understood, weren't they? It wasn't magic.

But, Jenn thought suddenly, could it be?

How was the bigger question. Wishing. Wanting. Shouting. None of those felt quite right, not that she knew what right was.

She should be able to understand anyone, shouldn't she? If she put her mind to it, and really listened, of course she would. Why ever not? And be understood by anyone, if she spoke clearly, which she always tried to do, though sometimes she did speak too quickly for anyone but Peggs.

Trees tipped to listen. A butterfly paused as it sipped nectar, then fluttered away.

"—when the dema gives the word, Panilaq, and not an instant before."

Jenn blinked. So did the toad.

The servant did speak Rhothan. So much for magic. As for why he hadn't from the start? She shrugged. Other ways. They were from another domain, which of itself was a wonder and forgave all manner of strangeness. "I can move the house toad for you, good sir," she told him.

"I am Kanajug, not 'good sir.'" He shoved back his hat and leaned forward to peer at her. "You speak Ansnan."

"I regret to say I don't," she replied, a little embarrassed. Perhaps her appearance was as strange to him, so he couldn't tell she'd been here her entire life. Though in her defense, Jenn thought in her second-best dress she might pass for a well-educated and traveled lady. If she'd put on her shoes.

He stepped back into the ox. "You—you don't?"

"No." She wasn't about to mention her failed attempt at magic. "I'd very much like to learn—"

He thrust out the golden bell and rang it furiously at her, then turned and bolted—there was no other word for it—for the wagon.

"Did you understand that?" Jenn asked the ox. The ox and, leaning their heads inward, the six behind it, regarded her placidly. They were no help at all.

Well, she might as well do what she came to do.

Jenn went to the house toad and crouched in front of it, mindful of her dress. From its markings, it wasn't the Nalynn guardian; she had a feeling it might be Uncle Horst's. "Please let them in," she pleaded in a low voice. "They're friends of Master Dusom and ever so interesting." Especially the one named Urcet, a detail she didn't think worth the mention.

~ I guard. ~

Well, yes, that's what house toads did . . . Jenn paused mid-thought. She'd heard the toad. Only Wen heard toads. Until now.

This was astonishing. But how? Its thin lips remained sealed in a disapproving line. The words hadn't been whispered in her ear by a breeze. "How do you talk?"

The toad blinked back at her. ~ How do you hear? ~

Ancestors Patient and Put Upon. A listless jingle of harness bells interrupted what would likely have been a distracting conversation. Jenn leaned close. "Please let them pass. These are scholars from far away."

~ They may not pass. ~ The toad puffed itself up further, eyes fixed in an intimidating glare at the hoof of the lead ox. ~ I guard the road for our elder brother. I am an accomplished— ~

"I'm sure you are," she interrupted rather desperately. "You know what I've been enduring. Please, guardian. These men may be able to help me. Let them pass, for my sake."

It sighed and shrank.

Smiling, Jenn gently put her hands under its arms and picked it up. "Thank you."

Though it rumbled unhappily, the toad hung in her hands without a fuss.

Now the little caravan could come to Marrowdell. Just in time for the tinkers and the harvest and all manner of celebrations.

And the eclipse.

Surely a harmless event, since it took place high in the sky. The sky didn't trouble the ground, other than inflicting weather and tides. It couldn't.

Could it?

The house toad met her troubled gaze with reproach in its huge brown eyes.

It'd be her fault, those eyes seemed to say, if it did.

For all their power, the turn-born took frivolous risks. They could have stopped the girl's expectations at whim, but chose otherwise. Now a man who lied even to himself was doomed to the truth, and Jenn Nalynn? How long until comprehension dawned and she be confronted by her own? And what would happen then? Could a good heart save them?

Why would they not teach the girl? Restraint, if nothing else. She'd done something more, he could feel the unease of it in his twisted bones.

Wyll snarled to himself. Convincing them wouldn't be easy.

They cared nothing for him or his opinion.

Though they would care, deeply, who he'd let into the village if what the little cousins suspected was true. That these latest arrivals were of the same people who'd built their towers and cast their wishing, rousing the trapped ones.

"Talk, for what good it will do," Wyll told the truthseer.

"Listening's what will condemn them," Bannan replied, his eyes gone hard.

The dragon recognized the look, though he'd not seen it before on a man's face. His own lips stretched in answer. It wasn't a smile.

Bannan Larmensu readied for battle.

They all must.

TWENTY

MARROWDELL, SO DULL and ordinary at the beginning of summer, was at that season's end close to bursting with excitement and new people. Jenn was close to bursting herself, but with impatience. The tinkers' tents were up; she could see their yellow peaks from here. That's where she and Peggs were bound, to arrange everything with Mistress Sand and Master Riverstone, everything to include a place near those tents for the dema and his caravan.

They'd have been there by now, but Kydd had run to catch up with them, and they stood in the middle of the road arguing, when they should be hurrying to the commons.

"We can't let them in," he was insisting. "They're Ansnans. What if they've come to try again? If they disturb what they did before, they could destroy Marrowdell!"

If they'd asked whatever they'd wished at before wishing at it in the first place, Jenn thought with regret, nothing might have happened, but she was hardly the one to, as Aunt Sybb would say, "declare innocence and shout out blame."

Still, she refused to agree with Kydd. Not when the newcomers might help. "Your brother invited them," she retorted as calmly as she could. "He said they're astronomers, here for the eclipse."

"Dusom corresponds with dozens of scholars. He invited them all!" The beekeeper's face had that dangerous set to it; Jenn began to realize what her father meant when he'd said the villagers hadn't been able to reason with him, all those years ago. "Why did these come and no others? They have some other purpose, I swear it!"

"Well, we can hardly stop them now," Peggs pointed out, ever practical. "They've been promised supper." The upcoming feast having been mentioned by more than a few.

"You don't understand—" He was interrupted as Cheffy and Alyssa almost ran into them. The two slowed to apologize, then bolted after Roche's still-saddled horse, trotting around loose for some reason.

"Yes, I do," her sister said once the laughing children had passed. "But, Dearest Heart, didn't you tell us that when Marrowdell suffered its catastrophe, there'd been towers filled with those who knew magic? There's just the two of them this time, only one from Ansnan, with servants—old servants at that—in wagons. Surely it's not the same." She ended with a determined smile.

"As when I last played doomseer?" Kydd shook his head when they both made to protest. "Fear not, dear ladies. I learned that lesson." His face eased ever so slightly. "I have my concerns, but also my doubts," he conceded heavily, "including those you so rightly mention. Trust I won't run through the village shouting of disaster without proof."

Peggs went on tiptoe to kiss his cheek. "We'd listen if you did, wouldn't we, Jenn?"

She didn't hesitate. "Always." And smiled at Kydd until the trouble in his face diminished behind a smile of his own. "We'll watch them," Jenn assured him then. "Bannan and Wyll will help. And Scourge," there being little doubt the vigilant and nosy creature would get himself involved. If she had her choice, she'd rather watch the beautiful Urcet than the fatherly dema, not that she'd admit that to anyone. Especially Scourge.

The beekeeper appeared moved. "I couldn't ask for a better family."

"Speaking of family," Peggs announced briskly, though her fingers lingered on his shirt and her eyes shone, "someone best tell our dear aunt about the new arrivals." Sure enough, when Jenn glanced toward the Nalynn house, she spotted Aunt Sybb on the porch, book in hand to disguise any unseemly curiosity. "I'll see you in the commons."

"I'll let Mistress Sand know you'll be there as soon as you can," Jenn assured her sister.

Peggs left, Kydd's eyes following.

There was no telling what he might say to the dema, left on his own. "Accompany me?" Jenn asked.

The beekeeper gave her a look that said he knew exactly why she asked, but he smiled graciously. "Of course."

They headed for the commons at a far quicker pace, to her relief. When they passed Old Jupp's house, Riss waved from the open door. "Let's hope she keeps her honored uncle from confronting the Ansnans with his canes," Kydd murmured as he waved back.

First Kydd, then Old Jupp. Marrowdell was usually more welcoming, not that there was anything she could do about it. Or should.

They were almost to the fountain when an urgent breeze found Jenn's ear. "Come quickly, Dearest Heart."

"Wyll?" She looked around, but didn't see him. "Where are you? Is Bannan there?"

"What is it, Jenn?" Kydd asked, looking all around.

"This way," the breeze insisted, gathering force to tug at her sleeves and hem. It shoved Kydd into hasty steps forward and tumbled a bee. Even as they obeyed, the breeze kicked dust behind them, which was rude and unnecessary and threatened her dress, but she didn't try to argue. Not when it shouted, "Hurry! There's danger!" in her ear.

The tugs guided them to the Morrell house, then around its side to where an infuriated Scourge had Roche, Bannan, and Wyll pinned against the wall.

"Scourge!" she exclaimed. The beast snorted and Roche looked about to vomit.

Kydd jerked to a stop. "What's all this?"

To make it worse, Tir Half-face stepped around the back corner, hands on his axes.

Of course Wyll's eyes were silver, Jenn saw with a sinking feeling. His doing, this secret gathering. She had to calm him, quickly. "Wyll—"

"There's Ansnans come, sir," Tir interrupted sharply, speaking to Bannan. "Two men, a woman, with another man black as coal. Eld's my guess. I counted three of their cursed dolls, so that'll be the sum of them."

Why, he'd spied on them. How had he managed that? As for "dolls," she hadn't seen any; then again, she hadn't seen the far side of the wagons. Scourge bobbed his great head, eyes red and fierce.

"I know," Bannan replied in a strange, flat tone. He didn't look at her at all, despite her hair being clean and new ribbons on her second-best dress. "Why are they here?" To Kydd and Tir and Wyll.

As if she wasn't.

She understood why the truthseer would worry, and Tir, but there was no need. The dema hadn't come for him. She opened her mouth to say so.

"Dusom's invitation," Kydd spoke before she could. "I grant he's as surprised as anyone they came."

"For the Great Turn." Wyll's eyes almost glowed.

"If you mean the eclipse?" The beekeeper nodded. "It's the first in decades. Marrowdell will be, my brother swears, one of the best spots from which to observe it. I'm suspicious too, but with the truce—"

Jenn didn't listen to the rest. She was here, whole and entire, and neither Wyll nor Bannan cared enough to even look at her, as if she wasn't. So much for the meeting she'd longed for and worried over for days.

"Pigeons fuss; people converse," Aunt Sybb would say, not that Marrowdell had pigeons, but her point had been most instructive when it came to getting their father's attention. Growing flustered and loud, Jenn had learned early, did not work at all.

"Fair morning, Wyll," she said, cool and courteous. "And to you, Bannan."

Only then did Bannan look at her. Their eyes locked. His were ablaze; Jenn somehow stood her ground, hiding her now-trembling fingers in her skirt.

She hadn't thought being noticed would be worse.

She'd changed.

More than changed.

Bannan took a breath, or thought he did. If he'd worried his memory had been colored by fantasy, that no one could affect him as she had, here was proof. Ancestors Dazed and Dazzled, how could Jenn Nalynn have gone from lovely young woman to this haunting beauty in ten days?

A haunting beauty who did not look at all pleased to see him. He swallowed, hard, and thought better of chancing "Dearest Heart." "Jenn. It's—good to see you."

Scourge made a rude noise with his lips.

Hers, for a wonder, curved ever so slightly from their stern line. "And you, Bannan." Her cheeks gained a dusting of rose and she looked toward the dragon. "Wyll, you shouldn't be hiding back here. It won't make a good impression on Poppa or anyone else."

Wyll paled. "Dearest Heart—"

Scourge interrupted with another rude noise, clearly enjoying himself, then his head jerked up and aimed toward the commons, nostrils flared and red. Steaming drool dripped from his gaping mouth and a shudder ran along his flanks.

Caught the other kruars' scent, had he? Bannan didn't expect that to go well. Meanwhile, Jenn took Wyll's arm and leaned to say something in private.

Was it petty to hope that didn't go well? "Dearest Heart" indeed.

Using the distraction, Tir came close. "What's to do, sir?" he asked in a low voice, standing sideways, his hands on the well-worn grips of his axes. "About the Ansnans."

Bannan's blood boiled at the word, at the thought of them here, at their tricks. The dolls were a favorite. Ansnans counted by sevens, not tens, and the superstitious among them traveled in sets of that number. Whenever they couldn't, they'd bring dolls to make up the difference. Dolls. Dirty sack bodies with gourds for heads, their rotten skins carved with mocking smiles. The border guard loathed the things and burned any they found.

He forced a shrug. "It's not for us to make or break the peace, Tir."

"If they've come for you?"

His eyes found Jenn where she stood, nose-to-nose with poor Wyll. He lowered his own voice. "Our dragon fears they've come for something else. For the magic in this place. Be on your guard as never before. Tell me anything strange."

"Stranger than yon tinkers, sir?" Tir asked too innocently.

Bannan glanced at Scourge, who could hear a beating heart at twenty paces and doubtless heard every word. "Scourge told you."

Without taking his red eyes from the commons, the kruar curled lip over fang and sent a chill breeze to whisper, "Nothing's safe once turn-born cross the edge. We feel it. Dragons do. If you thought with your head, you'd leave Marrowdell, now."

"A song he's sung since last night," Tir commented. The eyes above the mask were grimly amused. "I said it'd take more than magical tinkers to pry you loose."

He'd die first; they knew it. "Treat them as you would any villager," Bannan cautioned, ignoring his "horse." "Watch over Jenn Nalynn. That most of all."

Tir gave the slightest of nods.

"Heart's Blood, I almost forgot." The truthseer stooped to retrieve his inconvenient bundle and handed it to his friend. At the raised eyebrow, he felt himself redden. "It's for the Lady Mahavar." He stressed the name. "I'd appreciate it if—"

The ringing of bells announced they were no longer alone.

Roche cowered and Tir was tense. Kydd looked worried again and Bannan—

Smelled wonderful.

Which didn't help anything and shouldn't matter, but he truly did.

He looked wonderful too. Working his farm had taken the shadows from his eyes and finished tanning where he'd shaved his beard. He fairly glowed with health, as Aunt Sybb would say, and, if not as beautiful as Urcet, was a fine figure of a man indeed.

And what was in that intriguing bundle he passed to Tir?

Bells rang and Jenn found herself unexpectedly grateful for that distraction.

And for Wyll, though she wasn't at all pleased to find him adding to the tension. "You needn't hide back here," she said kindly. "These aren't enemies."

"Dearest Heart." The silver faded; it didn't leave. "Trust me to know better." A breeze chilled her ear. "Stay away from them. Let us deal with this."

She'd been about to tell him how glad she was to see him, for she was, and to ask him about the talking toad. Instead, Jenn bristled. "If you can't be pleasant, Wyll, you'd best stay away."

Kydd tipped his head toward the road. "The tinkers will hear this lot coming. We should be there, Jenn."

"Coming," she said firmly.

With a final warning look at Wyll, Jenn Nalynn stepped back on the road with Kydd and hurried to the fountain, doing her best to smile. Bannan, who she was sure could and would be gracious no matter what, followed.

Wyll and Tir stayed behind, out of sight, with Roche and Scourge. That, she decided, was just as well.

Sending interested looks this way and that, Dema Qimirpik and Urcet walked in front of the oxen and their driver. Dusom, Uncle Horst, and her father walked with them, pointing out various sights. Most of the village, clearly in a festive mood, followed the wagons, including Old Jupp with his canes safely on the ground. She didn't see the Emms' twins, but someone had to get the livestock settled and they were likely in no great hurry to explain matters to their parents. Palma came with Hettie, their heads together and chatting like old friends.

Bees paused and hovered. Birds stopped singing and stared.

So they should, Jenn thought with growing delight. Between the magnificent oxen, their gilded horns gleaming in the sun, the exotic wagons, and the cheerful babble of voices and harness bells echoing from building to building, Marrowdell had its first parade.

The grand procession wound its way past the mill, then the Nalynn home, where Aunt Sybb and Peggs sat watching from the porch. Jenn's father waved at her, spotting the little group by the fountain.

"Stop!" Wyll launched into view, flinging up his good hand. Wind whipped dust and leaves into a frenzied cloud as he thrust himself between Jenn and the oncoming walkers. "Go back!"

The men stopped, coughing, arms over their faces. The oxen jerked up their heads, horns rattling together. There were cries of consternation from the villagers, most of whom couldn't see what was happening, and Old Jupp shouted something, cane in the air.

He couldn't have waited, Jenn thought with disgust. She stepped toward him. "Wyll! Stop!"

"These are my guests—" Dusom began to sputter, as Radd Nalynn gave his youngest daughter a despairing look. Her heart sank. She'd promised to control Wyll.

Before she could try, Kanajuq leapt forward, bell in hand, and struck Wyll on his bad shoulder.

As Wyll staggered and fell, Scourge charged from nowhere, knocking the old servant flat. The golden bell sailed up in a slow sparkling arc to land with a thump on the back of an ox. The offended beast bawled loudly, Scourge roared back, and the entire team began to stamp and bawl.

It was no longer a parade; it was a disaster.

At least the wind died as quickly as it started, dust and leaves dropping to the ground. Jenn crouched beside Wyll, who turned his head to look at her, face twisted with an emotion she'd not seen there before.

He was terrified. Her dearest, oldest friend. Forgetting everyone and everything else, Jenn ran her hand down his arm, feeling him tremble. "Did he hurt you?" She found his hand and laced her fingers with his. "Wyll? What's—"

"Uhhhh!" Qimirpik pressed his hands over his chest. As he did, his breath came out in a fog, as if the air was suddenly cold.

Urcet staggered back with a frightened cry, his breath visible too. He began a desperate chant, something about stars and blameless lives and resisting evil, and Qimirpik quickly joined in, adding a chorus of meaningless sounds that almost, but not quite made a nice harmony. All while frost rimed the edges of the wagons and coated the oxen's harness, and there was a dark shadow where the newcomers stood, but not over anyone else.

He could make a storm. She should have known he could bring winter. The servant shouldn't have hit him, but it had only been a bell and Wyll was a dragon, or had been. "Wyll," she pleaded, low so her father wouldn't hear. "Don't do this. Please stop!"

Wyll shook his head.

He tried to send the newcomers away, to make them unwelcome here. Which wasn't right at all and she wouldn't have it. She wouldn't! Jenn tore her hand from his. "I want them to stay!" she cried, having no idea what she did or what good she could do, but disagreeing with this, oh, yes, with all her heart.

Coincidence, surely, that the sun came out, as it should, to wipe away the shadow. That warm summer air settled over them all.

Until the frost was memory.

The dema and Urcet stopped chanting to stare at one another. Urcet looked entirely satisfied, and the dema said in an unsteady, but pleased voice, "The home of the Celestial, at last!"

"Did you feel it? We passed the first trial," the Eld exclaimed, slapping his thighs in triumph. "We did it, Qimirpik!"

They thought they'd saved themselves. Jenn's eyes widened. Had they? Did they have magic too?

"Manners, sirs," Uncle Horst scolded the gleeful pair. "You're in Rhoth. Speak so all understand you."

But they must have, Jenn thought, momentarily distracted. She'd understood every word. If they hadn't, she swallowed hard, how was that possible?

Dusom glanced at her father. "They claim to have worked magic."

Had she, back on the road, when she'd wanted to understand? It was all most confusing, though, she thought pragmatically, that would explain her newfound ability to converse with toads.

"Indeed we have," the dema said proudly. "It was foretold there would be trials to overcome. We're gratified to be tested so soon and succeed. Most gratified."

Judging by the beads of sweat glistening on his shaved head, the Ansnan was more than a little relieved, too.

Breathing easier, Jenn helped Wyll to his feet. "Aren't you sorry you did that?" she whispered. "These might be friends."

"These are fools." The disapproving breeze nipped her. "Dangerous fools. Stay away from them, Dearest Heart. For all our sakes."

"Why—"

"Let's keep everyone moving, shall we?" Kydd beckoned toward the commons. "We've harvest underway and only so much sun." His tone was light, but his eyes were troubled when they met hers. "Jenn?"

"To the commons," she said brightly. Like Wyll, Kydd was afraid. She wasn't sure what had frightened Wyll, but Kydd worried about something that had happened so long ago, trees covered the scars; if it had happened at all and not been a story.

Right now, she'd be much happier if it had been a story. Her magic grew more potent and less under control with every use, which made it worrisome to think that Ansnor might have mad and magic people, including, perhaps, the dema and his companion, who so worried her dragon.

Jenn made sure to take Wyll's hand before turning around.

To face the truthseer, who looked at her and saw everything.

This was the change.

Heart's Blood. How had he not seen it?

Jenn Nalynn stood before him, wearing light like skin, her eyes still huge and purpled with magic. The world itself had bent to her defiance, the turn-borns' will broken, for he'd no doubts who'd tried to remove the intruders with that touch of winter. Tried, until Jenn brought summer back again. She was glorious and powerful and . . .

Knew. Bannan saw the awareness cross her dear face like a cloud. No longer innocent. What the dragon feared had come to pass. Jenn Nalynn knew, if not everything, then enough.

And that he saw.

The truthseer bowed, sweeping his fingertips through dust and leaves, his heart aching for her.

There was altogether too much bowing going on, Jenn Nalynn thought, deciding she felt cross. Cross was better than anxious and much better than afraid. Cross let her walk past Bannan without a second glance, a glance she didn't dare take.

She'd seen herself change in his eyes, seen awe and something akin to pity in his face. Bannan knew. How could she doubt she'd done magic, when he saw it in her? When he knew, better than anyone, how that made her feel?

Cross made her take quick steps, but not so quick that she abandoned Wyll. He'd left his hand in hers as they walked to the commons, though it turned his every movement further off balance and was surely painful. His good foot left scars in the dirt. His other dragged and bounced.

His hand was warm and smooth, the strength in it oddly placed, so she wasn't sure at times if she held a hand at all. He was different. Special. She wouldn't blame him, Jenn decided. The caravan had surprised them all.

He must hear what she'd learned about herself, a conversation both urgent and daunting. "I've missed you and Night's Edge," she began as they passed the Ropps' barn. The cows would be brought from the orchard for milking, though it was likely the excitement would throw a few off. "I hope you've been—" happy trembled on her lips, to die unspoken. He couldn't be; she hadn't been. "—busy."

"Yes. I did as you asked," Wyll replied. "I built our house. I wrote letters. But our meadow remains as it was. I cannot restore it."

Jenn squeezed his hand, as much for her comfort as his. "We'll try together," she promised. They neared the open commons' gate and she had to smile as she spotted the familiar bright yellow tents, smile and add without thinking, "Mistress Sand might help."

Through his hand, she felt his intention to stop, there and then, but he couldn't and didn't; they had the village and caravan at their heels. A breeze toyed with her hair instead. "We are acquainted, Dearest Heart. Be prepared. They will not speak well of me and I ask you not try to change their opinion. Some things are impossible."

This time Jenn tried to stop, only to have Wyll's strong hold keep her moving forward into the commons. "What do you mean?"

He answered aloud, a hint of amusement in his voice. "Tinkers don't bother with those like me unless they must. It's their way. Don't take it to heart. I don't." This with a low chuckle.

"Like you." Did he mean crippled in body or not-always-a-man? Looking at Wyll didn't help. He'd set his young handsome face to such innocence Jenn couldn't bring herself to ask.

Then she heard a glad cry, "Sweetling!! Jenn!!!" and dropped Wyll's hand to run ahead and meet Mistress Sand.

Unlike Aunt Sybb, whose frail bones meant any embrace must be cautious, Mistress Sand was as strong and solid as could be. Jenn wrapped her arms around her and squeezed, almost losing her breath as the other generously returned the favor. "Look at you," Sand exclaimed, squeezing her again as if vision alone wouldn't do. "A fine lady, tall as your sister."

Before Jenn could do more than smile and say, "I'm so glad to see you—" she was passed to another for more squeezing. Master Riverstone. They were all here, Flint, Tooth, Chalk, and Fieldstone, every one glad to see her, including Kaj, the little dog who lived in Mistress Sand's shadow. By the final embrace, she felt hurried, bruised, and well-loved. And licked.

It was always like this, when the tinkers arrived in Marrowdell. Jenn was relieved to see the presence of strange faces did nothing to change the whirl of enthusiastic greetings or the bewildering speed with which Master Riverstone and Davi organized those bound for the fields. Daylight was precious; she felt that truth in her flesh.

Mistress Sand hadn't needed a warning after all. She and the others had been waiting at the gate. After greeting Jenn, and pointedly ignoring Wyll, who'd lurched away with a sneer before she could do a thing, the tinkers waved the dema and his caravan through with smiles and invitations to their tents. Did the newcomers need knives sharpened? Leather work? To trade?

Overwhelmed by the din of business and reacquaintance, to be truthful, unsure of her place in it, Jenn found herself easing away from the rest. It was then she saw Bannan Larmensu.

Was he coming to her? Oh, how she wanted him to—no. No, she didn't, she told herself hastily. She should run if he did. It was all most upsetting.

And unnecessary. For, without a look in her direction, Bannan walked over to Urcet and the dema, his hands out in the latter's greeting, smiling as if they were long-lost friends. Within moments, they might have been. Master Dusom joined them and their conversation grew animated.

Others might think it odd, knowing Bannan had fought the Ansnans most of his life, but Jenn understood, too well. He was doing what he'd told her he'd hated, using his magic to look for lies.

For himself? For Marrowdell?

Or for her?

She could ask, but that would be far too intimate a conversation to have with someone whose letters she'd burned this morning.

The truthseer wasn't alone on guard. Uncle Horst stood on the outskirts of the crowd, watching. Horst's oddness, they'd called it, to stay at the fringe of events. It wasn't oddness, Jenn thought. He cared for them and deserved better than to live out his life with strangers. She'd talk him into staying tonight, at the feast. There were too few nights left. She daren't wait; she wouldn't.

Master Dusom lifted his arm to point to the Spine.

Jenn's eyes widened. What was he saying?

"Jenn!" Allin came up to her, smiling widely, and there was no chance to find out. He'd matured over the summer, his sun-weathered face more like his father's than she remembered. He had little Loee cradled in one strong arm, her fingers tight around his thumb, and his mother and Palma followed behind. "Jenn, I'd like you to meet Palma Anan, from Endshere. We're wed."

As Gallie Emms looked elated, if a touch windblown, Jenn smiled at once. "Congratulations. Welcome to Marrowdell, Palma."

Up close, the young woman's face was cheerful and open, her eyes sparkling with wit. "Thank you. It's beautiful here. Allin didn't exaggerate." She waved an expressive hand. "And in time for your harvest. Put me to work. I'm no stranger to feeding a horde." With a wink.

"I see Devins! You have to tell him about your cousins." Allin grabbed Palma's hand and dashed away, Loee giggling.

His mother didn't go with them. "Ancestors Blessed and Bountiful, I'd have been happy to have our boys safely home," she avowed in her soft voice. "Who'd have thought I'd gain two daughters the same day?" Jenn did her best to look puzzled. Gallie, who read her face as well as anyone, chuckled warmly. "I see you know about Hettie, too. Good Heart, Covie and I've waited years for our children to leave games behind and stand together. I suspect Hettie and Tadd surprised only themselves." Her eyes twinkled. "Though I'd appreciate it if you didn't tell them I said so."

"I won't," Jenn promised, hoping their father hadn't been part of such discussions.

"It's all arranged. They'll join you and Peggs, on the Golden Day."

So soon? Jenn thought of Aunt Sybb's lists and the endless hours of sewing. "We'll share what we've done," she offered. Good thing Peggs had done such unreadable "P's" and "K's;" they'd easily pass for

"T's" and "H's" or any other letter. Her face fell. "I'm afraid all we have to spare are goods, not dresses."

Gallie's dimples deepened and she brushed gray-speckled curls from her damp forehead. "For the Ancestors' Blessing, I'm sure they'd marry in flour sacks, but that won't be necessary. I brought my dress from Avyo, why I don't know having two boys at the time, but now I'm glad. Wen and Frann can alter it." She gave a brisk nod. "Anything else must wait till after the harvest. Hettie and Tadd will live with us, of course."

There was no "of course" about it. Spring through summer, while the twins were away, Gallie used the loft to write. She'd written all manner of helpful books, with illustrations and lists, concerning what settlers and farmers should know, things those arriving in Marrowdell had not. Before Loee's arrival, she'd begun a new tome on the wildflowers of the north, with Peggs doing some of the many paintings she'd planned and the twins bringing pressed samples from their time in the neighboring hills. Gallie's work, under the name "Elag M. Brock" was widely published in Lower Rhoth; Master Dusom had copies, signed "Gallie Emms," on a special shelf.

All of which because the Emms' loft, especially in summer when the light was best, was perfect for Gallie's work, work important both to her and an untold number of readers.

"A busy morning," Uncle Horst commented, joining them. Before following the parade to the commons, he'd stopped to change his riding leathers for homespun pants and shirt. Had he stopped for Riss? Jenn couldn't tell. The other woman, face shadowed by a scarf, stood at a distance with her great-uncle, unobtrusively making sure he wasn't trampled by a careless ox or excited child. Or attacked the dema.

"And for you," Gallie replied. "Where did you meet our latest guests?"

His pale gaze flicked to the caravan then back. "Coming from Endshere. They'd stopped at the inn for a guide to Marrowdell, and happened on your son's wedding." He bowed, "Congratulations, Gallie. I know the Anans to be good, hardworking people. Palma's as wise as she is kind. Sorry to see Allin go," with a nod, "but he'll fit well there."

Allin wasn't the worry. There were new lines etched on Uncle Horst's face, faint and unhappy, and Jenn realized she couldn't wait till the feast. "You fit here, Uncle," she said. "Please don't leave us."

"Sennic?" Gallie asked sharply. "What's all this?"

His eyes closed. "Dearest Heart—"

Just then Battle and Brawl approached, fresh and eager to work, necks curved with pride under braided manes, feathers flying around their hooves. The three moved apart to let the team pass. Wainn, riding on the driver's box, lost his wide grin as he turned his head to look at her.

Once the cart rolled by, Jenn discovered Uncle Horst had led Gallie away, his head bent over hers as he spoke earnestly, a conversation she wasn't to share.

All around her, all of a sudden, people were talking and shouting, moving here and there. Oxen bawled, horses whinnied, metal 'forks clattered into the backs of empty wagons.

While she was quiet and still.

Alone.

As though she wasn't here at all.

The wrongness of it tightened her throat. This wasn't how she was supposed to be. She was part of Marrowdell.

She needed Wyll. Where was Wyll? Jenn looked around frantically but couldn't find him.

A butterfly came close, tempted by her nose, then left. Grateful to be noticed, Jenn let her eyes follow it through the bustle of the commons, a scrap of living color managing to miss or be missed by everything larger. It passed the caravan, then dipped where Bannan stood talking to those he'd called enemy.

He glanced at the butterfly, then looked at her as if he'd known she was there.

As if, by his looking, she was.

Her feet moved with her urgent heart.

"A hand with these, if you would, Jenn?" Frann dumped most of her stack of folded quilts into Jenn's arms with a relieved sigh, keeping the rest. Sweat beaded her face and she was short of breath, if not words. "Set them inside Mistress Sand's tent, now, that's a good heart. Lorra's had us running with her silly pots and now I'll be last there and late. Ancestors Laggard and Slow, if we'll ever be ready . . ." Muttering to herself, the older woman rushed away before Jenn could more than nod.

Saved by quilts. Jenn balanced the load, careful not to look where she mustn't.

She'd take her burden to the tent, then find Wyll.

Ancestors Foiled and Frustrated. First, Jenn Nalynn became magic incarnate and avoided him; now she ran errands to do the same. Oh, Lila would laugh.

She wouldn't laugh to see her brother play Captain Ash again, not that Bannan used the name. She'd understand how sickening it felt to slip back into that role, to lie as served his purpose, and to read their truth or its lack.

How his heart went dead as stone.

Thus far, what he'd heard had been the truth, but he'd yet to hear enough. A dema was the Ansnan equal of a Rhothan priest, and many, like Qimirpik, were scholars. A study of stars and sun was seemly worship; whatever this man sought in Marrowdell was not. Making Dema Qimirpik something other than the jolly fellow out for adventure he portrayed with such goodwill.

His companion? On the surface, the Eld was a dilettante, pursuing his curiosity in a land no other of his kind had seen. The source of funds, no doubt, since the wagons were Eld creations, with wheels that could be changed to roll along their metal tracks like an ox-drawn train. Cost of no concern, everything of the highest quality, down to the cursed dolls peering from the windows. Like the dema, Urcet was more than he seemed. There was passion in his eyes and gestures, an impatience that spoke of burning desire.

For what, being the question.

A question so far gently evaded. Bannan knew to be patient. If they came for Marrowdell's magic, he'd find out before the eclipse. Captain Ash would.

The truthseer kept his expression pleasant. He'd missed something, taking his eyes away to dwell on Jenn Nalynn. "Pardon?"

"I asked your opinion of our truce," the dema repeated.

" 'Freedom from conflict, however it happens, is the great step forward,' " Bannan said, shamelessly quoting the beekeeper. "I'm sure those in the marches were glad of peace."

"The 'marches?' Oh, that local trouble," Qimirpik blithely dismissed years of conflict and death. Ancestors save him from cloistered academics, Bannan thought, his smile freezing in place. "The area near Mondir's been unsettled far too long," the dema went on, this to the Eld.

The truthseer couldn't stop his frown. " 'Mondir?' "

"Vorkoun, you Rhothans called it." The dema wiggled his thick fingers. "Her proper name's been restored."

Dusom interrupted with something about locating the wagons.

They'd taken away his city's name. His home's. Somehow, more than the stink of Ansnan cattle, more than Qimirpik's smug face, more than memory, that shook him to his core. Hearts of Every Ancestor, he was Beholden Tir wasn't here, listening to this. He'd stayed back with Scourge to watch for any more surprises this day, reluctantly letting Bannan play scout.

"Now, dema. Vorkoun remains the name north of the Lilem," Urcet corrected. "Mondir will refer to the portion on the river's southerly bank, the part of the city built by Ansnans."

The south had better plumbing, Bannan thought numbly. Everyone knew it. Better plumbing but crooked roads.

The north . . . the Larmensu estate, now Lila's. The Westietas holdings. Vorkoun still.

Did the Ansnans expect him to be grateful?

"Are you coming?"

Heart's Blood, he'd been careless again. "Ready if you are," he said quickly. The wagons were about to head to the fields; a fair guess Dusom meant to join the others.

But the eldest Uhthoff had something else in mind. "Excellent. Urcet, Qimirpik, I'm sure the Spine will offer the best overall view of the valley."

When Dusom had pointed out the treacherous hill earlier, the truthseer'd thought it was merely to name it. "You mean to go up there? Now?" He stared at Dusom in disbelief.

"We've time for a quick trip," the villager argued, misunderstanding.

He couldn't allow this, he wouldn't, but how . . . "Surely you'd prefer to rest, good dema?" Bannan said. "The Northward's a hard road." He smiled his best smile. "It's not as if the hill's going anywhere."

"Truly said," Qimirpik agreed with a sigh. "I confess I'm exhausted, friend Dusom, and doubtless there'll be some fuss or other setting up the wagons before any of us can rest." He waggled his fingers at the servant who waited patiently by the oxen, bell tucked safely in his belt.

Had the man bravely smote a dragon in his master's defense, or struck a helpless cripple? Both, Bannan thought, deciding to be wary of him. As for Wyll, well, the dragon neither wanted nor needed his pity.

Urcet, who'd raised his gold-lidded eyes eagerly to the Spine, hid any disappointment well. "Indeed, dema. I should check the instruments after the journey. Tomorrow will be soon enough, thank you."

Too soon, in Bannan's opinion, but he'd done his best for now.

Dusom bowed his head. "As you wish. I do insist, good Qimirpik, that you be rested before tonight's feast. It should be splendid. Bannan here," with a look that warned the truthseer the other hadn't missed a thing and would have questions to ask in private, "provided the fine meat."

As if he'd come all this way to feed Ansnans. Bannan gave one of the short village bows in acknowledgment. "Until the evening, then."

"Until then."

He pulled away, not sorry to see Dusom bound for the mill; much as he respected the Marrowdell scholar, he was in no mood to discuss the Spine. Not with another man.

It was a topic for a dragon.

The first thing Jenn noticed, upon entering the tinker's tent and putting down the quilts, was that Riss Nahamm had cut her lovely hair.

Riss knelt on the red trading mat between Frann and Lorra, facing Mistress Sand. Samples and fabrics lay in colorful heaps, with more bursting from open sacks along the walls of the tent, and the three older women pored over their choices. They'd brought their own creations to trade, left by the open flap that was the tent door. Later, in another tent, Clay and Tooth would spread their tools, the former sharpening blades and mending pots, the latter working leather.

Jenn used to wonder what it'd be like to sleep in a room whose walls and ceiling billowed with every breeze, that spread light as evenly as snow. She and Peggs had done their best once with sheets; Aunt Sybb had caught them and made them do laundry a day early.

She didn't wonder why Riss had cut her hair.

The shorn ends protruded beneath the scarf she'd put over her head and tied beneath her chin. They curled and twisted, as though they'd fought the shears. Riss had worn her lovely hair like a cloak for him; whether Uncle Horst had told her he was leaving or Marrowdell spilled another secret, it was clear she'd do so no longer.

Numbly, Jenn exchanged nods with Wen and Cynd, who were setting out pottery for the tinkers' consideration; Riss' needlework lay as if dropped.

"Sweetling. I wondered when you'd have time for me. Here," Mistress Sand patted the mat to her left, Kaj having curled in a disinterested lump to her right. "Save me from these wicked women. They'll take all I have and leave me poor."

Frann laughed. "You'll do the same to us, Sand." She'd come in behind Jenn and sat at once, her flute by her side, as if the evening's music couldn't come soon enough, though the men were to leave for the fields and wouldn't be back till—

Sunset. Jenn dropped down beside the tinker, her mouth suddenly dry.

"Now, what did I put aside for my Sweetling . . ." Mistress Sand tossed tea cozies and brilliant shawls and lengths of lace up in the air as she searched, the woven gloves covering her own arms and hands catching Jenn's attention.

If she wore such protection, would her fingers stay with her during sunset?

"Do you have any gloves?" she asked, then blushed. "I don't mean to be rude—"

The tinker looked curious, not offended, and rocked back on her heels, arms folded across her chest. "Last I looked, young Jenn, it was summer. But," with her bold laugh, "never too early, is it na? Once I'm done with these fine ladies, I'll see what I have."

Lorra and Frann chuckled, their faces glowing. One love they shared was trade and, though hardly young anymore, gladly climbed aboard Davi's cart each fall to attend what they called Endshere's quaint little fair.

Which must be bigger than Marrowdell's, since this tent and mat was its sum.

Jenn realized she was still cross, and did her best not to be, but she needed to find Wyll, not be here. Being here alone would have been fine, but not with the others from the village, all keenly interested in gossip. Wen wasn't, but Wen was like the tent. Here and interesting in her own way, but apart.

Although being here, even with the others, was the perfect way to avoid Bannan Larmensu, who'd be leaving with the rest for the fields and safely gone for the day. Of course, for all she knew, he was avoiding her too. Why not?

He'd seen what she'd become.

She wasted time, being here, and there was little left before she'd be needed to take lunch to the fields, then help in the mill, and by then it'd be the feast when everyone would gather in a great noisy mass.

And now Riss had cut her hair. She sat still and too quiet, her eyes downcast. She looked so alone, Jenn ached for her.

"Sweetling na? I asked what news."

Pinned by the tinker's bright gaze, Jenn froze. "'News?'" she echoed faintly.

Sand laughed. "How quiet na? When I've heard such already! My my my." Each "my" was punctuated by the click of tongue to teeth. "I was surprised to meet the handsome new farmer." Her wink made Jenn blush. "I come here, and, la!, there are travelers from such amazing places. Then these fine ladies tell me of not one, but—how many weddings na?"

"Four," Lorra proclaimed, giving her silent, unwed daughter an exasperated look.

Three, Jenn knew about. "'Four?'" She glanced uncertainly at Riss, who sat still and staring down at the fabrics.

"Yours and Peggs'," Frann said cheerfully.

Which was two.

"The Ancestors smile on a Golden Day wedding." The words had trouble passing Lorra's gritted teeth. Wen smiled vaguely at her mother, then went back to arranging cups in a neat row. Cynd carefully didn't turn, but Jenn could see her dimpled cheek.

"Tsk, Lorra Treff. You make it sound ominous." Frann chuckled. "Jenn, the twins are marrying too. Gallie's convinced Palma to marry her Allin again and—" she paused for effect.

Lorra leapt in. "Our Hettie's settled on Tadd Emms," this with decided satisfaction. "There's naught but the Morrill boys left."

Wen's gray eyes touched hers with an unspoken message, so Jenn didn't mention Wainn Uhthoff, though it wasn't kind of Lorra to omit him. Mistress Sand hadn't mentioned Wyll, but that was just as well. He'd warned her she wouldn't like what she heard. Jenn smoothed her skirt and voice. "Four weddings. How marvelous!" she said, and meant it. "Aunt Sybb says the more weddings share the dance, the better the dancing."

Riss thrust herself to her feet. "Take what you want of what I brought, Sand. I've no love of it." As she turned to leave, Jenn was stunned by the look on her face. She'd expected sadness, not fury.

"Tell me about your wedding dress, Sweetling," Mistress Sand said, ever able to move past an awkward moment. "I'm sure I've something to go with it."

"Frann knows best," Jenn suggested, and that lady, who'd taken apart three dresses to make Jenn's and Peggs', needed no more encouragement to launch happily into a detailed description of flounces and darts.

Jenn herself only half-listened, her thoughts still on those who weren't happy at all, which was a mistake. A hearty laugh warned her the topic was no longer dresses, but what was under them. And worse. She snapped to attention as Mistress Sand said, "You've the truth of it, Lorra. Anyone can dance at a wedding. It's what comes after that makes it worthwhile."

All three were looking at her, not lace, Lorra and Frann nodding solemnly. Heat roared into Jenn's cheeks and she hastily got to her feet. "Couldn't agree more. Your pardon, Mistress Sand. I should help Peggs with lunch."

"Don't bond for life till you're sure of the plumbing," Frann pronounced. "That's what I say." The others nodded again.

She meant Wyll. She meant Wyll, who was as good and whole a person as anyone could be who'd started as a dragon and a broken one at that. He'd shown her his body, hadn't he, scars and healthy manhood both, which wasn't, Jenn thought, now thoroughly flustered, what she wanted to think about Wyll right now, in front of this too-interested audience. He was her friend. He loved her.

The rest blurred into some unimaginable future, beyond the Great Turn and Golden Day and her birthday. They'd deal with it, she told herself. "I'm marrying Wyll," Jenn declared. "I love him."

"That one na? You'd have to care for him all your life," Mistress Sand said, her face abruptly stern. "Pity's no reason to marry."

"I don't pity Wyll!"

More nods and shared looks. "She has far better prospects," Lorra stated, as if Jenn wasn't there listening. "This Bannan, for one. He's shown interest, Mistress Sand, and I'd say it's mutual. There have," in tone suggestive of more, "been letters."

" 'Letters,' " Frann echoed, wagging her eyebrows.

Was nothing private in Marrowdell? "I wrote Wyll," Jenn said defensively. "He lives with Bannan, who's also new to Marrowdell, so it was only polite to write him too."

"A fine thing, the manners you've learned from your lady aunt," Mistress Sand soothed, then she chuckled. "But you underestimate yourself, Sweetling. I've heard from this Bannan's own charming mouth of his love in the village, a love he hasn't seen for days. Who else but you na? Tell us. It's not only his mouth that's charming, is it na?"

A mouth she'd almost kissed. Jenn shook her head desperately, hoping to rattle sense into it. "I hadn't noticed," she retorted. Though he'd smelled wonderful and . . . "I really must go."

"Ancestors Delicious and Delightful, that's a man well put together," Lorra praised. "Almost as fine as my Davi."

"And a truthseer," Frann added with unfortunate enthusiasm.

Silence filled the tent.

There it was. Bannan had wanted to judge for himself if the tinkers should know; she should have warned him nothing stayed secret in Marrowdell. Filled with misgiving, Jenn looked at Mistress Sand.

Who, for a heartbeat, seemed someone else altogether. Someone cold and strange and angry. Jenn held her breath, hoping not to be seen.

Herself again, Mistress Sand smiled and tilted her head like a curious bird. "And what truths does Bannan Larmensu see na?"

She had to protect him. She didn't know how, or why she believed it, but Jenn knew Bannan had been right to fear discovery. The tinkers were her friends and Marrowdell's; they weren't Wyll's. And not Bannan's.

But before she could think of what to say, Wen came to stand behind her mother, her hair wild, her face tranquil, and spoke. "He sees me."

Jenn blinked; Frann gasped. Lorra Treff twisted on the mat to stare at Wen, soundlessly mouthing her daughter's name as if she was now speechless, and Cynd dropped a blue-glazed cup that bounced on the mat floor of the tent.

Mistress Sand pursed her red lips, the hint of a frown wrinkling her forehead. "Does he na?"

"Wainn likes Bannan," Wen continued in her dreamy voice. "As do I." Her light gaze fell on Jenn. "As do you."

She couldn't deny it if she'd wanted to, not once Wen Treff set them between the truthseer and harm. "Bannan's a good person and kind," Jenn said carefully. "Marrowdell's better for having him in it. And his friend Tir," she added, for no reason but to have everything and everyone in the open.

"Well." Mistress Sand slapped her thighs and laughed. "With all this liking and new faces, tonight's feast will be interesting indeed."

Just as Jenn began to relax, the tinker's eyes met hers and they weren't eyes, but glowing pits, like her mouth, lit from within . . .

Which wasn't right. Mistress Sand was her friend, her dear friend. Jenn stared back, determined to see the red lips and sparkling blue eyes she remembered, insisting . . .

And did. Sparkling blue, thoroughly cold. "My, my my," Mistress Sand said, clicking her tongue. "Interesting indeed."

While in the background, Lorra stood before her daughter, arms outstretched, and tried to say her name.

The blow had cracked something in the shoulder, that pain nothing to the hurt of the girl's radiant smile, aimed at the turn-born in their disguise.

Avoided by the others, equally glad to avoid them, Wyll found quiet and shade to one side of the gate, where a hitching post offered support. He leaned there and made himself watch, absently healing the bone. He endured as Jenn Nalynn ran into the open arms of first Sand, then Riverstone, while all around villagers poured past the caravan to clasp hands and pat shoulders. Even Roche seemed at ease with the tinkers and pressed forward, though he didn't speak.

The turn-born dared touch her, fondle her hair, claim her as friend, and all the while wish her dead.

Not all, of course, or not all at the same time, since Jenn Nalynn lived. True to their nature, the turn-born bickered and interfered with one another's expectations.

The dragon stirred at a thought. If not all . . .

Then who? Who among these turn-born favored her continued existence? Was there one among them who might prove an ally?

A desperate thought, but was he not desperate? The visitors the turn-born had warned against, his duty to keep out, stood in the midst of Marrowdell as welcomed guests. Like wind over a wing, they'd slipped his guard.

What guard? the dragon raged to himself. He'd let himself be distracted by home-making and letters. Appeased the villagers by abandoning his post, passed his duty to his old enemy. He should have known the kruar would fail too.

At the last possible moment, yes, he'd done what little he could. Sent dust up their noses.

Pathetic.

Leaving the turn-born to take matters into their own hands. Life had hung on a silk in that moment, twisting this way, then back. The villagers hadn't felt it start; the old kruar, who had some sense, had wrinkled his muzzle and given the sky a worried look as the air grew rank with menace.

No knowing what the turn-born willed, only that it was against those who'd breached Marrowdell's gate. Then, like a candle flame touched by breath, the threat had sputtered and was gone. Thwarted by Jenn Nalynn.

Proof she'd changed. Her expectations were no longer unaware longings. She'd learned of herself while he wrote letters from a ruined book and collected seeds that became ash. She'd come into power on her own.

He shouldn't be proud of her. The turn-born could well come to agreement now, to end her life. They might not be wrong.

Nonetheless, the dragon smiled.

"There you are." Having no respect for space, Bannan leaned against the same post. "I doubt anything will happen before tonight." He nodded toward the crowd in the commons. "It'll take time to sort that out, then we're off to the fields."

Wyll shrugged his good shoulder. "Any harm they intend waits for the Great Turn."

"The eclipse." The man nodded. "What happens then?"

"Light from the Verge spills into Marrowdell. To avoid being seen, the small ones will conceal themselves, as they do at a turn." If they could, Wyll thought restlessly. What rightly belonged in the Verge had its way of hiding from all but its light. The little cousins, like kruar, could seem less or other than they were; ylings sewed such magic into their cloaks. Nyphrit? The wicked things lurked in shadows by preference.

Like efflet, dragons wrapped themselves in the light of this world to vanish. When he'd wanted to amuse or distract the girl, he'd permitted her glimpses of his real self. A self now gone. "They should be safe," he finished.

"You aren't sure," the truthseer guessed.

"After the last Great Turn," Wyll said slowly, "the small ones were abandoned here. I don't know if any now live who remember. I don't know how much they understand if so." He must speak to the little cousins. Warn them to hide.

Above all, warn them to stay as far as they could from any trapped ones. Should the worst happen, some might survive.

What was he thinking? Wyll snarled to himself. He couldn't save them. He couldn't save anyone.

"And you?"

He didn't matter. "I'm a man, fool."

Bannan turned his head, staring with unwelcome intensity.

"A man," Wyll insisted, snarling aloud when the other half-smiled.

Whatever he saw or imagined, the truthseer wisely left well enough alone. "The dema and Urcet plan to view the eclipse from there." He pointed toward his farm and the Spine looming beyond, his face now grim. "What would they gain? It's not safe, that path," he continued. "I've seen it. Felt it. What's there, Wyll, worth the risk?"

The dragon showed his teeth. "The Wound. A trap for turn-born." He considered the man, then said the rest. "A crossing, for those able."

"Into the Verge." Bannan shook his head with wonder. "Ancestors Witness, these men have no magic. I swear to you."

"They have knowledge and belief." Wyll shifted, uncomfortable with the thought, never comfortable in this skin. Or in his own, truth be it. "Magic can be found here. Jenn Nalynn mustn't," with fierce emphasis, "be allowed near them. Or the Spine. Especially during the Great Turn."

"Heart's Blood." Though pale, Bannan gave a resolute nod. "Agreed. You'll have to tell her why, Wyll. The truth; all of it. About herself, about this place. It should come from you."

"I am closest to her heart," the dragon agreed, smug. "I'm glad you've come to your senses, truthseer. Not that you were ever my rival." It was important the man know his place.

The man chuckled, which was disconcerting. "We can discuss that another time, my friend. What matters is Jenn stays safe."

"It won't be easy," Wyll admitted reluctantly. "She doesn't care to be told what to do. In that, Jenn Nalynn is very much a turn-born."

The truthseer's lips quirked. "You could try explaining yourself."

Better still, he could lock Jenn Nalynn in the truthseer's new larder and leave her there until the Great Turn was done for this lifetime.

"She has to know," Bannan insisted. "All of it."

Wyll growled.

"Good," as if he'd agreed. "I'll leave it to you."

Man and dragon stopped to watch the commotion as the well-bred Ansnan oxen, realizing they were about to be pastured near the tinkers' horses, bellowed in protest. As they did their powerful utmost to turn and leave, the kruar, harnessed to now-empty wagons, snarled and stamped their opinion. Villagers and tinkers scrambled out of the way. Finally, discretion won and the oxen were unhitched and led, in haste, from the commons.

Bannan shook his head. "Heart's Blood, what is it about kruar and cattle?"

For all Wyll knew or cared, kruar mares threatened to turn their foals into the mindless things if they didn't behave. "There are none in our world."

"Your world. The Verge." The truthseer seemed to taste the words. "I'd like to see it."

Curious to a fault. "A pointless desire," Wyll said, amused despite himself. "The Verge isn't soft and peaceful like Marrowdell. You'd be killed and eaten. Or eaten alive. Though most likely you'd go mad. Then," he finished kindly, "be eaten."

"Is that so?" Bannan grinned, but didn't seem to expect an answer. He straightened. "Time to go. While I'm in the fields, Tir and Scourge will watch the village. I assume you'll stay and wait for Jenn?" A humorless smile. "While watching our new friends."

"I will." He would watch and wait, though while all others had been distracted by the cattle, the girl had slipped from the commons and gone home. She would be back. She always came back.

Wyll foresaw a problem. "The villagers may try to send me away again." Anger rumbled in his chest. "This time, I won't allow it."

"Oh, all's forgiven," Bannan assured him. "Horst and Radd let it be known you were protecting the village from strangers."

Wyll was nonplussed. "Why would they do that?"

"Because they love Jenn Nalynn." The bewildering man took a step away, then turned abruptly. A stride brought him back, to stand too close.

Worse, Bannan Larmensu placed his highly unwelcome hand on Wyll's good shoulder and bent to put their eyes on a level.

"And because I love her, dragon, I'll tell you something about hearts. Stop your worrying. I don't want your place in hers. I couldn't take it if I did. All I want, more than life, is my own." Fingers pressed and let go before he could snarl and break free. "There. I've said it."

Only then did Bannan walk away to join the others of his kind, as if satisfied he'd made perfect sense.

Wyll gave a violent shrug; only the girl's touch would he tolerate.

Only she had the right.

He settled back against the post, eyes half closed, to worry all he pleased.

TWENTY-ONE

SHE'D WANTED TO see what Bannan saw, the wonders Marrowdell hid from ordinary folk.

What a fool she'd been. Now Marrowdell changed before her eyes and nothing could be trusted, not even old friends. She was afraid to look anywhere, at anyone.

Jenn reached blindly for the kettlepot, only to have Peggs shout, "Stop!" and push aside her hand before it touched the hot metal lid. "Here." Her sister gave her a rag and sharp look. "What happened with Mistress Sand?" she whispered. "What's wrong?"

She whispered because they weren't alone. At the counter, Palma deftly filled cloth-lined buckets with bread bowls, hollowed from loaves and still warm. Riss, who no longer seemed angry but whose slaughtered hair drew worried second looks from everyone, added spoons, gathered from every household, to baskets of apples and sweet rolls. There'd be tea, hot and dark, for those who wanted it, but no honey or cream. Lunch in the field would be practical fare, quick to eat and hearty, and everyone helped.

Including Old Jupp, enlisted to sit in the Nalynn parlor with little Loee on his lap. Having relinquished his ear trumpet for a toy, he couldn't hear a word they said.

The rest could. "Nothing," Jenn whispered back. "I'm fine." She wasn't, not at all, but what could even the best sister in the world do when the world itself refused to stay safe? Louder, "The smell alone will bring them running."

A thick stew bubbled in the massive kettlepot. Jenn gave it a final stir, then replaced the lid and ran a stave through each of the thick handles. She took hold of her ends and gave a nod.

Peggs took hold of the others. "Coming through," she called, and everyone moved out of their way as the sisters lifted the heavy pot and carried it out the kitchen door.

The barrow waited outside, its open middle sized for the kettlepot. Zehr had made two of the labor-saving devices, one for the Nalynns and one for the Ropps. Hettie and Covie would be loading theirs too. The Treffs were busy with tonight's preparations.

Jenn wondered distractedly if poor Lorra had regained her voice, or if Wen had once more abandoned hers. She supposed she could ask a house toad, but she'd not seen one since the newcomers entered the village.

Though they would be scarce with the harvest, wise to avoid being underfoot when so many feet were in motion. Even Aunt Sybb who, well-rested for the first harvest anyone could recall, had stirred to pack lunches for those at the mill, causing a minor commotion when she'd insisted she could deliver the heavy pails herself. Tir, sufficiently scandalized to have the Lady Mahavar make his meal, had taken the pails from her, brooking no argument. Tooth and Dusom would bring their lunch with them, the grain wagon being expected shortly.

And shortly, those in the field would have theirs.

Jenn and Peggs pushed their barrow, with Palma and Riss close behind, down to the road and along it. A stalks wagon stood outside the Emms' barn, a rakeful on its way up, Cynd leading Aunt Sybb's bays, Gallie pulling the rope to steer the load. Allin leaned out of the loft door to guide it through, bared to the waist and already drenched with sweat.

"So you can work hard!" Palma shouted with a laugh. He waved, smiling broadly.

Jenn smiled too, happy for them. She'd miss Allin; they all would. The couple vowed to visit as often as the inn and weather permitted.

Just as well, she thought, smile faltering. Endshere could be the moon, for all the hope she'd go there.

Dema Qimirpik and Urcet claimed themselves most content to stay out of the way and rest from their journey, though as Jenn helped push the barrow through the commons gate, it looked as though their rest had consisted thus far of separating their wagons, hanging striped awnings over the windows of the larger two, and removing the arched roof from the smallest. A brass telescope now sat exposed and sparkling on a broad geared base, with other apparatus taking up most of what she'd wrongly assumed was the servants' living quarters.

And the person she wrongly assumed to be one of those servants still at work proved to be Wyll, busy poking his fingers into what clearly was instrumentation of the latest design. Instrumentation that would be costly, easily damaged, and not, Jenn thought in panic, for a dragon to poke.

"Go," Peggs suggested, taking the other handle.

Riss came to help, shifting her basket to a hip. "We'll manage."

"What's wrong?" Palma asked.

As Jenn hurried to save the telescope, she heard her sister explaining to Allin's new bride how Wyll was special.

Oh, there was no doubt of that.

The sun shone, the sky was an impossible blue, and Marrowdell's red-gold fields stretched out, ready to harvest.

As planned.

Bannan Larmensu paused to wipe sweat from his forehead and lean on his pitchfork, admiring the work of the turn-born.

Four wagons and teams, a driver and arranger in each. Five men in the rows, pitching. They worked the field nearest the village first, so the livestock could be let out of the orchard as soon as possible. No one had hesitated to set foot between the tall stalks, meaning the grains' lethal guardians had either fled or agreed to permit such trespass; Bannan had followed, doing his best to look nonchalant.

Three wagons for the stalks: Wainn drove Davi's team, grinning through the dust that masked all their faces in short order, with Kydd in the back arranging the dried stalks with his 'fork; the tinkers, Fieldstone and Clay drove their wagons, with Zehr and Anten in back. Davi had explained to Bannan, as he was new to their life, that despite a resemblance to straw, these stalks were nutritious and palatable. Yet another gift from Marrowdell.

The fourth wagon was for grain, being lined with canvas. Flint drove its team, Chalk in back to rake the grain level as it fell.

Harvest in Marrowdell. Ordinary stuff, Bannan thought, until you were part of it. Oh, then the strangeness showed. He lifted his next forkful of grain-heavy stalks and, as he'd been shown, tossed it in the air above the grain wagon.

The hard seeds rained onto the canvas, any chaff lifting away in a breeze. The same unfailing and courteous wind tumbled the now-barren stalks over the wagon to fall in a row; sweet and dry, and as ready to store as the grain was ready to mill. On the far side, big Davi and Horst pitched the fallen stalks from the ground into the waiting wagon.

The most remarkable part, Bannan decided, was that the harvest needed them at all.

The stalk wagons filled quickest, so as the first left, the third rolled behind the second, ready to take its place. In the village, the stalks, Marrowdell's "hay," would be raised into lofts.

There'd be no stopping until just before sunset. The tinkers, according to Kydd, spent that time secluded in their tents, for what they called their "Observance." The kruar, no doubt, would find their own way to be out of sight during the turn. Clever.

"Water?"

Taking the filled dipper, Bannan smiled gratefully at Alyssa. "My thanks." The girl and her brother ran water to the men and teams, a trip that would lengthen as they worked farther from the river and closer to the forest at the base of the Fingers, the aptly named Bone Hills to the north.

Across the valley from the Spine.

From here, it looked harmless, beautiful, in fact. The massive lumps of ivory stone gave it greater height than the other hills; the surrounding expanse of open meadow lent an almost majestic glow. He could trace the path up by gaps in the trees, see how it rose, folding on itself once, twice, thrice, nowhere too steep to climb.

Nowhere safe. Bannan frowned, thinking of the foul miasma staining the road that night, the pull of it once he'd paid attention. Jenn Nalynn had climbed to the top and returned. Had she been protected by innocence? By magic? Or was it simply that even malice slept, and luck was sometimes luck?

Whatever it had been, he couldn't believe she'd be safe a second time. As for the Ansnans—

"Ancestors Pricked and Poked." Roche tossed his forkful over the wagon with a grunt. "Must have been a good lay, to put you ahead of your brother."

Tadd Emms, to Bannan's right, turned crimson. "Heart's Blood, Roche—"

True to form, Roche had wasted no time spreading the news among the men that not only was Hettie with child, but she'd asked Tadd to wed her and be its father. Bannan put muscle into his next toss, trying to ignore the pair . . .

"And a baby on the way. Not mine. I'd have obliged, but she'd have none of me," Roche sneered. "Can't be sure whose it is, can you?"

The truthseer intercepted Tadd's furious charge with a hand to the younger man's chest, then looked over his shoulder at Roche. "It won't be pleasant, working with a gag in your mouth," he warned. "Control your gift, or that's what you'll have."

"'Gift?'" Roche spat. "What are you, old man? This is no gift."

Feeling Tadd ease back, Bannan nodded to the wagon and the not-so-patient Chalk. "Keep working."

Roche tossed his forkful with such fury that half landed on the tinkers' team, earning him a baleful look from the kruar. Tadd shook his head, but the truthseer, out of patience, stepped close. "Shut up and listen," he ordered in a low voice. Though sullen-faced, Roche obeyed. "You've been given a chance to change for the better. To become a man whose word's trusted, who can't be influenced to lie by others. Can you grasp what I'm telling you?" Bannan let his exasperation show. "Ancestors Witness, are you worth the trouble?"

The younger man kept his mouth closed with an effort that made his entire body shake and managed a single pleading nod.

The power of Jenn Nalynn, to wish this on him; Bannan almost shuddered. "It won't be easy," he said in a gentler tone, knowing better than make promises where magic was concerned. "I know you, Roche, better than you think. You've lied your whole life, to yourself as much as anyone else. Now you're choking on truths that want to spew forth like bile."

Something began to shine in Roche's eyes.

"Learn to govern your tongue. If you can't, start a new life where you know no one's secret and no one knows you. Live well, and the truth will become your strength, not your weakness."

Tadd had moved up to them. He'd listened and now regarded Roche grimly. "If he can't stay here, Bannan, he's nowhere to go. Endshere. Weken. Everyone knows Roche." He shook his head. "You idiot."

They should listen to Jenn Nalynn, who knew the world was a wider place, but Bannan held his peace. Roche shrugged, then gave a determined nod. He'd try, that said.

Meanwhile, there was a field to harvest, and none of them free till it was done.

The truthseer glanced over his shoulder. The village was out of sight behind the tall hedge. Above, the sky was cloudless, the air like a warm caress on the skin.

He'd done what he thought best, for Jenn Nalynn.

Now, it was up to the dragon.

The telescope was not only a marvel, it proved beyond doubt what Master Dusom had said, that Qimirpik and Urcet were astronomers. They'd introduced themselves to the tinkers as such, going on to include the two demini, the servants, who turned out to be the dema's students as well. Jenn wasn't sure what the distinction might be, since Kanajuq and Panilaq were surely too old to still be at their studies. Or to be servants, for that matter, though the silent pair went quickly about their tasks.

The dema had introduced the odemini next, these being, as far as Jenn could tell without actually touching one, dolls the size of Cheffy. With the curtains open, they stared from the largest wagon; it felt like staring though their faces were hidden by pleated veils. They wore robes like the dema's and weren't toys, since the dema named them as solemnly as he'd named the servants. Seven, Six, and Five.

Mistress Sand had laughed behind her hand.

Though only odemini were watching at the moment, Jenn walked rather than ran to the small wagon. This was her fault. Preoccupied with her own concerns, she'd neglected Wyll, that's what had happened. She shouldn't be surprised by the result.

"Stop that!" she whispered as soon and as loudly as she dared. Wagons weren't like houses. Their guests could hear what transpired outside, just as the tinkers could hear outside their tents. "Get away from there!"

Wyll lifted his head. "I've been waiting for you. You took a long time."

Meaning he'd been bored. Hands on a soft black wheel, she quickly leaned into the wagon. Nothing appeared broken. She gave a sigh of relief as she turned to the dragon. "You mustn't touch other people's belongings, Wyll. Not without their permission."

"They didn't ask permission to come here," he countered, unrepentant and not in a whisper.

"Wyll! Hush. Come with me."

He followed quietly into the small copse of trees near the pond. The caravan sat across the pond from the tinkers' tents. Jenn stopped where she couldn't see either.

Birds scolded from a lower branch and Satin, dozing in the shade like a mud-gray boulder, wrinkled her snout. Catching a familiar scent, she didn't wake.

Wyll surprised her by speaking first. "We need to talk, Dearest Heart."

"Yes, we do." Ignorance makes mistakes, Aunt Sybb would say. Knowledge prevents them. Comforted, Jenn put her hands on her hips, determined to educate her dragon. "People don't need permission, yours or mine, to travel the road or visit Marrowdell. Furthermore, it's our custom to be welcoming. You shouldn't have—" she strained for a neutral word and settled on, "—disrupted the dema and his caravan." She lowered her hands and finished miserably. "Everyone's upset with you again."

Upset? If the newcomers hadn't been thoroughly delighted by what happened, and convinced they'd defended themselves, the villagers would have sent Wyll away for good. Not that he needed to know.

Not that she'd have allowed it.

Wyll regarded her soberly. "Are you upset with me, Dearest Heart?"

Jenn sighed, then shook her head. "Of course not." She half smiled. "I've missed you."

"And I, you." He tucked a loose strand of hair behind her ear. "You've changed, Jenn Nalynn."

He didn't mean the hair. Closing her eyes, Jenn caught his hand and pressed it against her cheek. "Yes."

"Tell me."

Easier, with the world shut away and the warmth of his skin against hers. "I can do things, Wyll. To other people. Magic, Kydd calls it.

"It started, I think, when I—I wished you a man. Then I made Peggs and Kydd—" she skipped to, "—well, they might have done that anyway, and I'm almost sure I stopped Aunt Sybb and Tir's dreams, which was a good thing, but then I did something this morning to Roche to make him always tell the truth, which is going to get him in trouble, so that's not good, is it?" She opened her eyes to search his. "And I'm not sure at all those men stopped you, the way they say they did, when you tried to scare them away. I—" she swallowed, but made herself say it, "I think I did. I wished them to stay."

Silver flared. "Why?"

Hadn't he listened? "Wyll, I can do magic—"

"Why do you want them here?" he demanded, anger roughening his voice. "They shouldn't be, not now, not near you. They're dangerous!"

Like stones tossed in still water, the words disappeared, leaving change to spread behind.

Wyll knew. He'd known about her magic all along and it didn't matter to him, so long as she was safe. Jenn turned her face and pressed her lips to her protector's palm, unsurprised to taste ash. "You're my dearest friend."

"I am." Gently he reclaimed his hand, fingers curled around the kiss. "As you are mine."

"I am," she echoed. "Wyll. Friends help one another. I need to know—" Everything. Why did she grow up having Night's Edge and a dragon friend? Why did she have magic now and not before? Why did Marrowdell want her to stay? Why did she crave a pebble instead of kisses and why—oh, why—was she disappearing, for that's how it had felt, she admitted it, at the sun's last light of the day? The desperate questions spread like ripples, wider and wider, consuming all they touched.

Until they reached Melusine's promise and folded into one.

"What am I?" Jenn's breath caught. "I became this when I was born. What am I, Wyll?"

Wariness flickered across his face. "My friend."

"Since birth," she said, again sure. "What am I? Am I my mother's daughter?" Thunder rumbled in the distance, despite the clear blue sky. "My father's? Please, Wyll!"

Wyll looked her in the eye; she looked back, careful not to force an answer. No matter how desperately she needed to know, she would not.

After a long moment, an approving smile changed his face. "Yes, Dearest Heart. You are theirs."

The relief was so great, she trembled. "Thank you." She brushed her fingers over his sleeve, fretted at a button, then looked up. "But . . . if that's so, why am I magic?"

"Because you were born at a turn of light," the dragon said. "As such, you belong to the Verge as well as Marrowdell. The Verge is where I am from. It is—" As he paused to search for words, she waited, her heart hammering in her chest, for what he told her was strange and true and more important than anything. "—it is a place of magic, you might say. Those who are turn-born are able to impose their will."

Turn-born.

Those? She wasn't the only one.

In her dreams, hadn't others opposed her? Willed the grain to fall? While on the road, this very morning . . .

"It wasn't you," Jenn concluded, feeling blood drain from her face. "You didn't make it winter over the caravan, turn-born did. They're here, in Marrowdell, now. They're—" Her hand shot to her mouth, holding in the rest, and she stared at Wyll.

Mistress Sand, whose eyes and mouth hadn't been eyes or a mouth but holes filled with light.

And if Mistress Sand was one of them, then so was Master Riverstone. Flint and Chalk. Tooth, Fieldstone, and Clay. All of them. Turn-born and magic.

"Think of them as the friends you've always known," Wyll warned, which was the same as agreeing. "They have a purpose here and will brook no interference."

Jenn threw a wild glance in the direction of the tents. "But if I'm like them, if I'm turn-born too, shouldn't I go, couldn't I ask—"

His fingers closed like claws on her arm. "You're not like them," Wyll said sternly. "They're terst, from the Verge. They lie. They appear as men and women here so you and the villagers accept them. You're not like them," this with abrupt gentleness, his grip eased. "You have such a good heart, Jenn Nalynn. No," almost to himself, "all we need do is wait. The turn-born will cross at harvest's end. After that, we will live together and be happy."

Wyll feared them, she realized with an inner chill. What power they must have, to make a dragon afraid. Or was it what they were willing to do with it?

He told himself she was different.

Was she?

Of course she was. She was Jenn Nalynn, almost nineteen. An educated Rhothan lady, to hear her aunt, when she remembered her shoes. A fine young woman, to hear her father and sister, even in bare feet. "We'll be happy," she agreed. "So long as you," with mock severity, "leave other people's property alone."

"So long as you stay in Marrowdell, Dearest Heart." She hadn't lightened his mood. If anything, Wyll looked grimmer, with troubled flickers of silver in his eyes. "Though they know it not, these foolish men seek the Verge. If they attempt to reach it at the Great Turn, they could disturb what mustn't wake. You could show them the way. You must not."

She'd found the way no others dared, Wainn had said.

Only during the Great Turn could she cross, the dream voice had told her, and only then be answered.

Her heart sinking, Jenn finally understood. To save herself, she must return to the Spine during the eclipse, but that wasn't all. She must—somehow—use magic and cross into this Verge.

Where . . . what? If she went by stories, she'd face some trial or test. Succeed and be rewarded; fail and . . . succeeding was clearly better.

She'd rather find someone waiting there, someone sensible with a trustworthy face who'd explain what she felt at sunset and how to stop it. Her hopes soared. Maybe end the curse keeping her in Marrowdell!

After she crossed to the Verge.

As her path became more certain, if no less terrifying, it was as if Wyll moved farther away. He couldn't know. He mustn't try to stop her.

Jenn Nalynn wasn't sure he could.

"Dearest Heart?"

He awaited her promise. "I won't show the dema or Urcet anything of magic," she said solemnly. "And I'll treat the tinkers as I always have, as friends." It was as her father said, and Kydd. Don't look too closely; accept what was here. "Marrowdell has rules."

"Rules? Yes." A moth fluttered past and Wyll's gaze distractedly followed, then snapped back to her. "Rules to keep you safe," he insisted.

The thought, all warmth and comfort, abruptly twisted on itself. The wailing of the dragons rang in her ears; she would, if she closed her eyes, see the toads' reproachful stares. Wyll, watching, interfering, guarding. Forgiving her anything. Her mother's dying promise. Uncle Horst's vow.

She was turn-born and magic. Mightn't Marrowdell need to be safe from her?

It made such terrible sense, Jenn shivered and rubbed her arms, finding the air strangely cold.

"What's wrong, Dearest Heart?"

She couldn't look at him. "I'd never hurt anyone. You know that, Wyll."

"Yes, I do," he said at once, though she'd hurt him, hadn't she? Each of them lied to comfort the other, when she needed the truth.

Jenn lifted her face, desperately searching his. "You mustn't fear me. I couldn't bear it."

Silver flared in his eyes. "I fear nothing."

Brave dragon, to lie for her. He feared the other turn-born, why not her? "Please, Wyll. Don't be afraid of me," she begged. Teeth chattering, she could almost see her breath, which wasn't right at all.

"How could I be?" Wyll replied gently, his eyes brown again. "You've a good heart," the breeze in her ear, like the old days in the meadow. "The very best of hearts."

He was the very best of friends, she thought, comforted.

Just like that, it was summer warm again.

Dismayed, Jenn moved her hand through the air, fingers wide. "Wyll—?" Cold, biting cold. Her fingers stung and she cried out, drawing her hands to her chest. "Is it them?" she gasped.

"No." Wyll's arm came around her. "Be calm, Dearest Heart, and it will stop."

If she was calm?

Shaking like a leaf, Jenn burrowed her face against his healthy shoulder, his beard tickling her ear. With all her might, she thought of sunny mornings and dumplings with honey, as if this was night and she fought against dreams. She managed a breath, then another, smoother.

The chill left the air.

Because . . . She couldn't barely think it, let alone say it. ". . . Wyll?"

She felt his sigh. "Must you know? You could do what I say. I'm not used to explaining." This last as though he complained to someone else.

"Please. Tell me the truth." Jenn pulled back to see his face. "The way it turned cold, then warm again—was it them or—or was it me?"

"Yes," the dragon answered.

She tried to shake him; easier to push a tree. "Wyll!"

"Both." A little breeze chuckled in her ear, but he spoke aloud. "Dearest Heart. My friend. I swear I will tell you whatever you wish to know, no matter the consequences."

He made it her choice. He believed in her. Jenn summoned all her courage. "You say I'm turn-born. What does that mean? What happens around me? Why?"

His eyes gleamed. "To be turn-born, Jenn Nalynn, means not only your will but your feelings manifest around you. The terst turn-born have great self-control and work as one. They expect fair weather for the harvest and Marrowdell answers."

Such power. Jenn blanched, but nodded for him to continue.

"You can't undo that expectation now," he told her. "Only if you'd disagreed at the instant it began, as you did with the caravan, would it fall apart. So these—moments—of yours are stopped as soon as they start. To impose their will, turn-born must agree. Do you understand?"

They hadn't agreed with her in her dream and she'd lost her pebble. Jenn trembled, fighting back anger. Her feelings could manifest? She'd been anxious and the air chilled. Ancestors Desperate and Doomed, what if she'd been terrified? Or lost her temper; Peggs knew she had one. She could . . .

Jenn's eyes went wide. "Night's Edge. Oh, Wyll—"

"Easy."

"—Wyll, it wasn't the wishing," she gasped, sure now. Her despair and grief had destroyed their meadow. Heart's Blood, what worse could she do? "Help me," she begged, as emotions came crashing over her in waves. She was drowning. In fear, in worry, in dread. Thunder rumbled and she jerked in his hold. "I can't stop! Tell me what to do!"

"Do nothing," he whispered soothingly. "Wait."

Sure enough, the air calmed, though Jenn's heart pounded and she couldn't stop trembling.

"See?" The little breeze flipped up her bangs and tickled her neck. "Don't be afraid." Wyll kissed her forehead. "All's fine again. The turn-borns' expectation can't be changed now; the weather must be fair for the harvest. Anything else I'm sure they'll disagree with before harm's done." He set her from him with a wide smile. "Once they leave, Dearest Heart, I'll teach you their tricks so you can control yourself."

Wyll sounded suspiciously like someone trying to convince himself. "You know how?" she asked, wanting not to doubt.

"I will," the dragon promised. "You must live in Marrowdell and be happy."

Jenn made herself smile. "Another rule?"

"Your duty, as mine is to help you." Then, breath more than breeze, low in her ear, "Dearest Heart, Good Heart, if you answer to nothing else, answer to friendship. Trust I know what's best."

Words like those he'd said at Night's Edge. Words to keep her safe.

If only it was that easy. "I do, Wyll—" she began unsteadily. Maybe she should tell him the rest after all. Maybe she was wrong and he would help—

"Good." He half-straightened with a wince. "I'll watch these men. You'll stay far from them and away from the Spine."

As if she'd promised, which she hadn't and couldn't. She hadn't been wrong; Wyll mustn't know. Jenn said quietly, "I'd best get back. I left Peggs with lunch and Poppa needs me. I'll see you at the feast."

"Yes." Wyll frowned. "Davi said everyone sleeps in the village during the harvest. He offered me a hammock." The frown became anxious. "I don't like hammocks."

"I'll make sure you have a bed," she assured him. He deserved that and more. Her friend. Heart swelling with emotion, Jenn smiled. "Thank you, Wyll. For the truth."

"I was wrong to wait." His head lifted, eyes silver. A warm breeze whispered, "And wrong to fear. Marrowdell is in your hands now, Jenn Nalynn, as the Verge was once in mine. You will be wiser than I ever was."

Aloud, "Go." The dragon lurched over to lean on Satin, who didn't appear to mind. "If you need me, I'll be here."

Jenn nodded and left.

Despite her claim to be needed, she walked slowly. From no answers to so many, her thoughts whirled and slipped between them like a leaf loosed from a tree. She was turn-born. It was a name, a thing one was or wasn't by birth, with power that could be learned and controlled. That must be.

There were others like her and they weren't strangers. The tinkers, part of Marrowdell for as long as she could remember, beloved friends and helpers, were turn-born as well. They might be different and surely were powerful, but she'd been in their arms today. She refused to believe the warmth of their embrace had been a lie.

They cared about her.

And, she tensed, knew what she was. They must, to have entered her dream. Ancestors Blessed. She'd countered their—what had Wyll called it?—their expectation.

Her chin firmed. Rightly so. Freezing people in the middle of summer might be fine and good in the Verge, but it wasn't to be condoned in Marrowdell.

She had so many new questions. About Melusine's promise. About controlling what she could do. About—

~ He watches you. ~

Startled, Jenn looked up to find herself beside the largest wagon of the caravan. A house toad squatted underneath it.

In the window, one of the three odemini was gone, replaced by another, darker face.

Urcet.

He might have smiled and waved. Instead, he ducked out of sight. Jenn looked over her shoulder to where she'd left Wyll. He was hidden behind the trees, so she must have been too, but neither had lowered their voices.

She gave the dolls a sober look. "Don't go up the Spine, Urcet," she told him, sure he listened. "What's there is not for you."

It was hers.

There was a bucket of river water and a ladle to sluice it over head and hands. No towels, but the cool water felt too good to dry off anyway. Bannan shook drops from his fingers as he joined the others lined up for lunch, and watched for Jenn Nalynn.

Davi's draft horses stood resting in the shade by a hedge, bags of grain on their noses. He could hear their contented munching. The tinkers' horses rested as well and pretended to mouth grass. Every so often one would snap peevishly at a butterfly.

A new letter sat folded in his pocket, waiting for privacy and peace. He touched it, now and then, and smiled.

Not from Jenn, but Lila. Horst had brought it from Endshere, along with mail for the others. Tir had scampered off with a letter of his own, doubtless hoping the baroness would agree with him. Bannan's smile deepened as he stepped up to the makeshift kitchen. Lila had also sent a well-wrapped package, well in time for Jenn Nalynn's birthday. He hadn't opened it. That would be for her to do.

And if he imagined that glorious smile would follow? Well, he was a hopeful sort, wasn't he?

"Fair morning, good sir." The young bride from Endshere smiled back as she handed him a bowl of bread. They'd met before, in her family's inn. Not her doing, or her family's, that bandits had trailed them up the Northward; their good wishes had been truthful. No, his bet was on a shifty pair at a corner table, remembering their too interested eyes.

From the sparkle in hers, she remembered him well enough. "Thank you," the truthseer said. "Palma, isn't it? Bannan's my name. Congratulations." He gave a courtly little bow and she blushed. News of his settling in Marrowdell would return with her and her new husband, no doubt, to spread with every visitor to their inn. "I've a farm over the river now," he continued blandly. "I'll grow turnips. Turnips and beets. Ancestors Dutiful and Diligent, you can't have too many turnips." He circled his fingers piously over his heart. "Mainstay of life, turnips. Though beets have their place in the diet. Can't do without—"

"So true," Palma interrupted, her smile grown fixed. She hastily pressed a spoon in his hand, then waved him along as though shooing away a fly. "Stew's in the pots." Her attention turned hopefully to the next in line.

Hiding a grin, Bannan moved aside.

There were two barrows with stewpots, with tea and more food on the end of a wagon. Most of the village stood around in little groups, bread bowls in hand. On the way to fill his, the truthseer overheard Davi say to Clay they'd made good progress, despite the morning's slow start, then Zehr explaining to Anten how he'd rather be here than home while Gallie coped with both sons getting wed on the same day.

Bannan knew himself in no hurry for that day to arrive, especially now, with, Ancestors Battered and Bent, Ansnans and an Eld in Marrowdell planning something that could scare a dragon. Tonight's Beholding would express his sincere hope the Ancestors had no further surprises in store.

The quality of this meal would be no surprise, he was sure. "Fair morning, Peggs," he greeted, eagerly holding out his bowl.

The elder of Radd's daughters looked up with a pleased smile. "Bannan. How are you finding the harvest?"

"Ask me tomorrow," he grimaced and put a hand to his back. "Here I thought farming was the easy life."

Peggs laughed as she ladled stew into his bowl and handed it back. "You won't be the only one sore," she comforted. "Enjoy your lunch." When he couldn't help but look around, her smile faded. "Jenn's with Wyll."

"Then I'll see her another time." He'd no right to be disappointed, having pushed the dragon to talk to Jenn Nalynn. Bannan lifted his bowl appreciatively. "My thanks, Peggs." He turned to go.

"Bannan, wait." Peggs waved Riss to her, giving her the ladle. "I'll be back," she assured the other woman, then nodded for him to come with her, away from the rest.

Mere paces from the tall hedge, Peggs whirled and stopped him in his tracks, her eyes flashing. "Do you love my sister?"

As daunting as her lady aunt. Bannan didn't blink. "With all my heart."

"Hmm." She studied his face as intently as if she were the truth-seer, nodding as she came to some decision. "Bannan, Jenn's in trouble. Wainn says no one can help her, but—" her lip trembled then firmed, "—but I refuse to believe that." Said fiercely, for all she kept her voice low. "You must try. Please."

He tensed. "What's wrong?"

"It's—no, best you see for yourself," she told him. "Be with her at sunset. What's happening—it happens then, and getting worse, I know it. Yesterday, Jenn hid from me. From everyone." She reached out, an unconscious gesture, not quite touching his arm. "I haven't gone to Wyll. He's a bit—excitable—when it comes to Jenn, and I'm not sure he could help. Not this. I think—I hope you can, truthseer."

"I'll go at once," Bannan declared hoarsely, ready to run to the village. "Where is she?"

"Wait." Her fingertips, cool on his wrist, held him in place. "For sunset. When the light changes everything. Jenn's told me you see it, Bannan. What the rest of us don't. Another Marrowdell."

"I do."

Eyes dark with worry, Peggs said what sent a shiver down Bannan's spine. "Hearts of our Ancestors. When you look at my sister then, I hope you'll see her still."

It wasn't cowardly, Jenn Nalynn told herself, not to want to be seen at less than her best. Or shirking, since wasn't the hardest part of taking lunch to the fields when the pots and baskets were full and heavy? Peggs and the others wouldn't need her on the way home.

And their father did. He'd smiled with pleased surprise to have her back so soon and, being cheerfully oblivious to her second-best dress, straightaway sent her upstairs to help make ready.

Alone in the light-filled and airy attic, it didn't matter if her cheeks were flushed or her feelings were a horrid jumble sure to show on her face. Nor would she encounter Bannan Larmensu.

Which she mustn't, not yet. She wasn't ready.

Hard enough being calm as it was.

In a short while, right here, the milling would commence. The pulley assembly would slide along the greased roof beam, ferrying grain to the bin. From the bin, like a golden waterfall, the grain would plummet through an opening in the attic floor into the hopper. From the hopper, carefully controlled by Radd Nalynn, it would splash down to the millstones and be ground into flour. The flour, in turn, would flow smoothly down the chute to the cool basement and be bagged.

Filled, the bags would be hooked to a moving strap to be pulled back up to the attic. So long as all ran smoothly, the process wouldn't stop while there was light.

To make sure the pulley was ready, Jenn gave its ropes a little tug.

To make sure the weather didn't change in some untoward fashion, she sat in the opening, looking out over the village, and tried, very hard, to be serene and at peace.

"Easier said than done," she said morosely, letting her bare feet swing in air. As for her duty, to be happy?

She could be, and was, happy for those who were happy themselves. That wasn't what Wyll meant, but she couldn't decide to be happy herself. It didn't work that way.

A moth walked around the beam to rest on the sill's edge, keeping within her shadow. She offered it a finger; it shifted out of reach, but didn't leave.

"It can't be every feeling," she assured the moth. If it was, there'd have been no end of thunder or unseasonable air or rain when there shouldn't be. Ancestors Blessed, Aunt Sybb would have noticed by now.

Perhaps only unusual feelings could manifest. New or very strong ones. In her everyday life, other than frustration or being angry at Roche, she couldn't remember ever having very strong feelings.

Until her grief in Night's Edge.

Her despair on the road.

Such feelings were dangerous. Jenn shuddered. She might not be happy, but she wouldn't, absolutely wouldn't, be dangerous. She wrapped her arms tightly around her middle, and did her best not to feel anything at all.

The moth took tiny careful steps across the wood, within her shadow, to climb a fold of her skirt. Once there, it stopped and fussily tidied its wings, its big dark eyes aimed outward as if she was nothing more than a safe and handy perch.

Oddly comforted, Jenn leaned her head against the beam and closed her eyes. She needed to control her magic, like the other turnborn. Wyll promised to teach her once they left. But he didn't know everything. He didn't know she couldn't wait that long.

The river babbled close by and roared in the distance. Nearer, birds called one to another and people did too. Wainn's old pony sent up a plaintive whinny every so often, missing Battle and Brawl despite an orchard crowded with new and old friends.

A heart wasn't always sensible. Hers ached for what it couldn't have, too.

"Jenn!" Radd's voice rang up the stairwell. "Get ready! The grain's here."

Jenn sprang to her feet, hurrying to swing out the hoist, glad to leave thoughts of love and her perilous magic behind.

And let the mill's begin.

A trickle, like a finger, found the raceway first. More followed as the opened gate beckoned, darkening the stones, pushing leaves aside. Damselflies clung to waving reeds, then leapt into the air as the now-impatient water flattened all in its path.

While in the mill, the stones waited.

Water lipped the great wheel, slipping beneath and past and out. It kept coming, rose higher, and began to press. Inexorably, steadily, the wheel answered.

It turned full circle for the first time in a year and kept turning.

In the mill, gears passed the motion with a brisk clap of wood to wood. It became a dance as the runner stone began to spin above its partner, grain joining in at the behest of the tapping shoe.

Something banged in unwanted rhythm and Jenn's father gave the opposite side of the wooden case a sharp two-footed kick to settle it. Peace restored, he went back to working the stick and shoe that controlled the flow of grain from the hopper. His eyes were almost closed. Eyes mattered less, he'd say, than ears and nose and touch. After a few minutes, he was satisfied with the flow and left it to run. He crouched to open the little door on the side of the case, catching warm flour in his palm. Jenn watched as first he closed his fist, then opened his hand flat and sniffed. Not done, he rubbed the flour with a finger, then moved a pinch consideringly between thumb and finger, all while every part of the mill shuddered like something alive.

He held out his hand. Taking the flour, Jenn dutifully repeated his actions. The flour was silky smooth. She sniffed. No hint of scorched grain. "Perfect," she decided.

Radd grinned. "A fine start. Tadd?"

The twin stood over the opening to the basement, where the leather strap drew its waiting hooks up and past. "All's moving well, Master Radd."

"Then I'd best go," Jenn said, kissing her father on his already floured cheek.

She ran down the stairs. Tir nodded a greeting, his attention on the gears and wheel. She'd heard his surprised "Whoop!" when the water first arrived in the dry raceway, but didn't think it polite to remind him of his earlier disbelief. Some things in Marrowdell had to be seen.

She'd expected Tir. She stopped in her tracks, disturbed to find a turn-born standing by the flour chute. Chalk smiled, but didn't try to speak. It was noisy down here, between the slap of the wheel, the clapping gears, and the stones' rumble overhead.

A hand fell on her shoulder. Jenn started and turned, to find herself staring up at Master Riverstone. His blue eyes glittered.

Or did they glow?

Somehow, she made herself see the familiar friendly face of the tinker. She forced herself to return his smile, then pointed to the bag filling at the end of the flour chute as she ducked neatly from under his hand. Her task was to attach the next empty one and reopen the chute; Chalk's to remove the filled bag, tie its top, then hook it for transport upstairs.

But Master Riverstone got there first, gesturing he'd take her place. He half-shouted, "Sand wants to see you, Sweetling."

What could she do but get out of the tinker's way and nod? She wasn't afraid, Jenn Nalynn thought desperately. She loved Mistress Sand. She wasn't . . .

She was . . .

A chill wind whistled through gaps in the mill wall, startling Tir. It died as, together, the turn-born looked at her and shook their heads.

Jenn fled up the stairs.

Something was happening to Jenn at sunset, Peggs had told him. Something he must see for himself.

Did he dare?

The turn, Wyll called sunset, when light from the Verge slipped past that of this world, exposing what couldn't hide. Bannan had seen for himself, been charmed by Marrowdell's fierce toads and little wonders and flowing silver road.

He'd seen Scourge, as familiar as home and family, become something strange and old and distant. He'd watched tinkers become turnborn and seen the grief in a dragon's eyes.

What would he see tonight, if he dared look at Jenn Nalynn?

Nothing to alter his heart, the truthseer vowed to himself, digging his fork in the waiting grain. He'd glimpsed how light could fill her slender form, how her eyes shimmered with magic. As for her smile . . . oh, he'd witnessed its joy, if not yet earned his own. By any light, this world's or another's, how could she be anything but glorious?

Bedazzled he might be; for all their sakes, he mustn't be blind. If Peggs worried, she had reason. If Wainn believed no one could help Jenn Nalynn, that reason was dire.

Tonight, at sunset, he'd see for himself.

The sun being high overhead, all Bannan could do for now was to stop worrying and pitch. He'd liked to have worked close to Wainn or Kydd, either of whom knew more than he of magic and Marrowdell, but any chance of that would have to wait. The younger Uhthoff continued as the driver of Davi's horses, and his uncle stayed on the wagon.

The harvest progressed swiftly. Just as well. This closest field to the village was also Marrowdell's largest. Its southern edge followed the river, bending toward his farm; to the north and west its border was marked by a narrow forest of the old trees. Behind those rose the long, low sweep of the Fingers. The closer they worked, the louder the muted roar of the mighty cataracts beyond those Bone Hills. The sun made rainbows above where the crags split to let the water leave the valley.

Between those ruined towers. Ansnan towers, Bannan reminded himself grimly.

Allin and Devins arrived on an emptied wagon, gleefully ordering their brothers back to take a turn spreading stalks in the lofts. Kydd, Zehr, and Anten hopped down to pitch grain, Kydd offering his place to Bannan with a grin. The truthseer, shortly doing his utmost simply to avoid being buried in stalks, willingly traded back.

Which was how, by late afternoon, Bannan found himself paired with Horst. Having prided himself on keeping up with Tadd and Roche, he found himself speedily outmatched by a man twice his age. Horst dug in his 'fork as grimly as if he plunged it in an enemy's beating heart and whipped stalks through the air with a vengeance.

A man running from a secret. Wiping his brow, Bannan considered what else Horst was. An outsider, here. A man of war. They had that in common and more.

When Horst paused at last, forced to wait for the next wagon, Bannan approached. He received a curt nod.

It wasn't a welcome. Given Horst's mood, the truthseer hadn't expected one. "How soon are you leaving?" he asked bluntly.

Horst's head jerked around. "I don't recall my business being any of yours."

"It's not," Bannan agreed. "But we share an interest in Jenn's safety."

That grim pale stare locked on him. "What's this about?"

Making sure no tinker was close by, Bannan leaned on his pitchfork and lowered his voice. "There's something you need to know . . ."

The inside of Mistress Sand's tent smelled of sun-hot canvas and beer. Jenn let the door flap drop behind her. It had been down when she'd arrived, with Mistress Sand's white dog sitting guard outside with no friendly look, but she'd heard her name called and couldn't very well stand outside after that, not without showing as an indecisive shadow on the wall.

The inside of the tent was stiflingly hot, which it shouldn't be. There was a clever vent at the peak to let out heat and window flaps tied open on all sides. Jenn froze on the entry carpet, abruptly convinced what she felt was temper.

"Sweetling." The turn-born didn't rise from her seat. A chest had been set as a table in front of her, laid with a black-and-white-checked cloth. On it were two of Lorra's new cups and a round tray bearing seven small wooden boxes, each carved with a different letter. "Sit."

Another of the tinkers' folding chairs had been set across the table from Sand. Jenn unlocked her knees and made her way to it. She put her knees and feet together and sat very straight, her hands folded on her lap.

They were alone.

"I know," Jenn said quietly. "About you."

"Very little," Sand snapped, "if it comes from that dragon."

"Enough," she dared say back.

"Ah." The turn-born leaned forward to take the nearer cup, nodding at the other. "Drink with me, Jenn Nalynn. Tell me this 'enough' you know." Sunlight, filtering through the tent walls, was no match for the hot glow that replaced her eyes and mouth.

Jenn took her cup in both hands, taking a swallow of what was, as the smell promised, the tinkers' fine beer. But instead of being cool and refreshing, it coursed down her throat like fire. She sputtered and coughed.

"Tastes different now na?" Sand finished her mouthful with a smack of her lips, her face returned to normal. "My poor Sweetling."

And suddenly the air in the tent wasn't hot, but pleasant. Jenn caught her breath, eyes watering. "Why?"

"Again."

Rather than argue, she reluctantly raised the cup and took the smallest possible amount on her tongue, then swallowed.

It burned as before, but, now that she was ready for it, the sensation was strangely pleasing. Jenn took a braver mouthful and felt the fire all the way to her stomach. There it settled, a warm glow; a comfort, where she'd been so empty. "What is this?" she demanded, staring into her cup.

"The same we brew each year." Sand put hers on the table. "It's you who've changed, Jenn. Riverstone thought this would be your time. I disagreed; you're so young." She gestured at the boxes. "Still, we prepared. Now, Sweetling. Tell me what you think you know."

Jenn licked her lips. "You and Master Riverstone, all of you. You're not tinkers. You're turn-born."

Sand's answering chuckle was as rich as ever. "Silly dragon. We're turn-born and tinkers. Do you not have your trades na? Go on. Tell me the rest of his nonsense."

Wyll wasn't silly or nonsensical. "He told me you lie," Jenn countered.

"To protect ourselves, yes, we do." The turn-born seemed unperturbed. "To dragons and their like, if it amuses. Often does." She rubbed a thumb across thinned lips, her habit when considering a doubtful trade, then added, "Not to our own."

"Then you won't lie to me," Jenn declared. From wherever this courage sprang, she'd use it while it lasted. "I'm like you, Mistress Sand. Because of when I was born. Because of how—" At this, her voice failed.

"When and how were accidents," Sand dismissed. "They happen, despite all care to avoid them, and have consequences."

" 'Consequences?' " Jenn found herself on her feet. Wind swirled through the tent, tossing over stacks of blankets, smacking aside the door flap. "My mother died!"

Sand gave a single shake of her head; the wind fell away and everything settled back in place. "Very little," she repeated. "What more should you know na? Had Melusine come to us, we'd have kept her safe. Instead, she hid in our wagon. Unaware, we went where she couldn't bear to be. We brought her back, but it was too late."

They'd tried to save her mother. Save her from . . . Jenn sank back down. "You crossed," she almost whispered. "You took her with you to the Verge."

Dark brows hovered over glowing pits; she could hardly bear to meet that gaze. She dared not look away. "Perilous words," the turn-born said coldly. "Foolish dragon, to give them to you. He should know better."

It felt like a threat; it could be. Jenn stiffened. "I won't let you harm Wyll. Don't you dare try!"

Sand laughed. "Do worse than you na? I think not."

She flinched. "I meant—" But what could she say?

"You stole his shape, Sweetling, then pulled his teeth." The turn-born held out her hand, tipping her palm. "Poor dragon. You've left him nothing and useless. Up to us na? We'd end his misery." Eyes again blue, mouth again red, Sand reached for her beer as casually as if they discussed the fate of piglets. "What matters na? You. Your future. Forget those words, Jenn Nalynn. The Verge is not for you. You cannot cross."

But she must . . .

Somehow Jenn held in that desperate protest, covering the moment by taking another fiery swallow of her own. "Am I so different?" she ventured, careful to sound merely curious.

"The Verge is." Sand leaned forward, gloved elbows on her knees. "Sweetling, yes, you're turn-born. Melusine gave birth during our crossing; you drew your first breath in our wagon. But if we hadn't brought you back across, you'd have died. You don't belong there. None of your kind do. Trust me."

"Wyll doesn't."

"Dragons don't." The turn-born chuckled. "We're your friends, Jenn Nalynn, and always have been. Look." Sand spread the fingers of both hands over the small boxes between them on the table. "This is why I asked you here, as soon as we could be alone. You hunger. At each turn, it grows worse. Am I right na?"

"Yes." Tears filled Jenn's eyes, spilling cold down her cheeks. "Yes!" Relief made her tremble. Unable to say another word, she reached out.

Sand took her hands in a reassuringly tight grip, then let go. "Worse indeed," she said gruffly. "Poor Sweetling. We'll end that." A finger tapped each box in turn. "Take these with you, somewhere safe and quiet. Open them all and look inside—but don't touch. Not until you're sure which is right for you. Touch with bare skin, then taste."

Jenn's eyes had followed the tapping finger. At the word "taste," she stared up at Sand. She'd so wanted to taste the white pebble from the Spine, from her dreams. Was it here? Could it be? Hunger for it made her dizzy.

Horror at that hunger made her shake. "Why do I feel like this?"

"We all do, when our time comes." The turn-born reached to her shoulder and rolled the soft material of her long glove down to her elbow. The exposed skin was creamy white, the strong arm—

The strong arm—Jenn gasped—suddenly, the skin was glass and the arm of sand. Gorge came up her throat until her mouth filled with bile and beer.

And yet . . .

. . . wasn't it beautiful?

She swallowed hard; made herself look instead of run. To see that the clear skin held not only sand but light; the two blended, aglitter like a beach in sunshine.

Mistress Sand, the name now fraught with meaning, rolled up her glove. "The sand is of your world," she explained. "Born by two worlds' light, we must contain both. As a turn-born comes into power, the body empties to make room. Do you understand na? We, of the Verge, filled ourselves from your world. You must fill yourself from ours, Jenn Nalynn."

Another gesture, this time proud, over the boxes. "Since you cannot cross, each of us brought you something of the Verge. The first you touch to your skin shall be what completes you. You need do this but once, Sweetling. Now, tell us what you've chosen. We'll bring all you need."

"'Completes'—" She choked on, "—me." Having magic hadn't changed her from Jenn Nalynn. This? "If I refuse?" she heard herself ask, but Ancestors Doomed and Despairing, didn't she already know? Soon the turn would come when she'd vanish entirely, like the setting sun. Unlike the sun, she wouldn't come back. A single tear trickled down her cheek and the air in the tent grew chill and damp.

Sand frowned and the air warmed to summer again. She found a brown sack and began tucking the boxes neatly inside. "I see you need time to think, Sweetling. Our young grow up knowing and ready, but we could never agree when to tell you. Some doubted. Others hoped."

An impatient "tsk" with her tongue. "What matters the past na? We agree now." She thrust the filled sack at Jenn. "Help yourself."

The same command, as if Marrowdell's mysterious voice was here, in the tent. "Thank you." Though loath to touch the thing, Jenn accepted the sack. "Isn't this about the past, Mistress? The promise?"

For the first time, the tinker looked surprised. "What promise na?"

"Melusine's." Jenn gripped the sack. "Uncle Horst told me. Before she died, Mother said she'd been promised. 'My daughter will live, but only here. If she steps beyond the scarred hills, she will die.' Those were the words," she insisted when Sand shook her head. "Why Uncle and Poppa and Wisp wouldn't let me leave Marrowdell. I'm turn-born and cursed. You promised my mother you'd help me. And you have." She lifted the sack.

The tinker's expression mirrored Aunt Sybb's whenever a young Jenn had tried to argue the benefits of going barefoot. "Sweetling, your mother was giving birth and dying. She didn't speak to us. We said nothing to her. But that's good advice, however you came by it. Turn-born are part of the edge. We can't exist beyond it. Take a step too far na? My. My. My. Fray apart. Split and be emptied." She broke out in her deep laugh. "What does it matter na? If you could leave, why na? There's nothing outside we need."

Outside was a world, a wonderful one, Jenn wanted to argue, loudly. A world with domains and cities and oceans, populated with people who didn't have to swallow dirt to be whole and whose bad feelings couldn't hurt anyone but themselves.

A world she couldn't have.

"Be content here, Sweetling," Sand continued. "Marrowdell's no bad place." She pursed her vivid red lips, then nodded to herself. "Now, as for this farmer—"

Jenn stiffened.

"—this seer of truth. If you're careful, your friends and family won't ever know, but he'll see what you are. We would agree to be rid of him—"

"No!" Outrage made her voice harsh and strange. "Leave Bannan alone!"

Lightning flickered and died. Thunder sputtered.

Sand lowered her finger. "Such inconvenient passion, Sweetling."

"Please. You mustn't harm anyone," Jenn pleaded, doing her utmost not to be furious or afraid. "What Bannan thinks of me—what anyone thinks—it doesn't matter. It won't. I'm marrying Wyll and he knows exactly what I am." Hadn't he urged her to be happy so many times this summer? Hadn't Wen?

Not for her peace of mind. To protect Marrowdell. She saw that now. Along with something else. Something important. Jenn narrowed her eyes. "You can't hurt anyone. You can't do any magic if I disagree at its start."

"Bold Sweetling." Sand's laugh chilled her blood. "And how would you know na? Should we ask before we act na? Turn-born you are, but not one of us."

Jenn thought of the grain. Of the caravan and her dream. Her chin lifted. "I'll know," she said, certain. "Marrowdell is my home, not yours."

"My. My. My." A slow smile. A slower nod. "That it is," Sand acknowledged at last, then raised a brow. "And goes both ways. While we are here, you can do only what we allow. What of Marrowdell when we leave na? Flint and Chalk say you'll destroy what we've built here." She held up her hands, bending a finger of her right hand with each name. "Tooth worries." Another right. "Fieldstone doubts." Another on the right, the fingers of her left remaining open. Slowly, Sand folded in her right thumb, making a fist. "Clay fears."

They debated her fate, that's what Sand meant, and the numbers weren't in her favor. Jenn's eyes stung. The tinkers had been nothing but kind to her, all her life.

Until she had magic. This wasn't betrayal, however much it felt that way. The turn-born knew what she could do; they had every right to fear it. Didn't Wyll?

Didn't she?

"Mistress, may I ask what you and Master Riverstone think?" she asked, fearing the answer.

"The truth na?" Sand challenged, raising her fist beside her still-open hand.

The little boxes, sharp-cornered and hard beneath Jenn's fingers. Weren't they the truth too? Despite their concern, the turn-born understood her as no one else could.

Sitting still, she nodded. "The truth."

"Brave Sweetling." Sand lowered her hands. "The truth it is. Always, I've told the others you weren't like us. That you'd be different. Harmless as a rose, I said, and Riverstone agreed. Then we crossed and la. There was your mark, plain as plain."

"My—Wyll?"

"That? No." The tinker leaned forward. "Ashes and death. You know what I mean na?"

Night's Edge. Jenn gave a stricken nod.

"No different, then. Far from harmless. Riverstone had to ask it." Her eyes and mouth became blazing pits. "No matter our affection, dare we leave you alive na?"

For an instant, it was as if she'd fallen through ice, unable to comprehend, unable to scream once she did. As quickly, everything snapped back in place and Jenn drew a determined breath. "I know what happened. I won't do it again," she promised. They wouldn't need magic to be rid of her; they were seven to her one, each of them older and stronger. Or was it something simpler? The wonderful beer—she stared at her cup. Had she been poisoned? "I'll learn—"

A click of Sand's tongue. Did she have a tongue inside that hole of light? Would she, once "complete"? "Sweetling, we spend a lifetime learning and still must hold one another in check. Who have you na? And don't say that dragon." Her face resumed its disguise and she pretended to spit. "Couldn't save himself, could he na?"

This wasn't about Wyll; this was about her, her life. Jenn clutched the sack. "You brought these," she insisted, a chill wind whipping through the tent. "Why would you do that, if you mean to—if you plan to—" she couldn't bring herself to say it.

"Peace, child." Frowning, Sand offered Jenn her cup. "Drink. Go on. It'll do you good."

Having no choice, Jenn took a swallow. Poison or not, the liquid soothed as much as it burned. The wind died away as she found within herself a peculiar calm. "Mistress, will you kill me?"

"Much better," Sand nodded approvingly. "The question's been raised. You wanted the truth and that's what it is. Now I've told the others, every one, that I'll wait for the Balance, until your birthday, before I give my answer." Then, of all things, she winked.

Jenn's heart soared. "You don't agree!"

"How could I na?" Sand winked again. "They don't know you as I do. You're not one of us, Sweetling. You've been raised by your family, loving and loved. That smile of yours—it can't come from a heart like ours." Her own was almost wistful, then she scowled fiercely, "I've said you'd be different. I'll not be proved wrong, Jenn Nalynn."

"You won't be, Mistress. I promise."

"Good. Now, go and quickly," the turn-born ordered. "Decide what you need and show any of us the box so we can get more. The sooner you're complete, the steadier you'll be."

The boxes. How had she'd forgotten? Because she wanted nothing to do with them or that future. Jenn made herself keep hold of the sack. "Thank you, Mistress," she said numbly, bowing her head. "For the truth and for your belief in me." She gave the almost-full cup a regretful look. "And the beer."

"Take it with you," Sand suggested. "The taste you like na?" Her eyes and mouth glowed for a heartbeat. "That's from the Verge."

There was a way around the village without being noticed, if you were nimble and didn't mind a wet foot or hem. Once through the commons gate, Jenn curtsied to the oak. "May I pass?" With a slow creak of aged wood, its lowermost branch tipped, then pulled away from the hedge leaving a small, shadowed gap. "My thanks," she made sure to say as she passed through. The great tree could be grumpier than Old Jupp.

Jenn slid down the steep riverbank beyond, cup in one hand, sack in the other, digging in her heels to stop well short of the reeds. Bound for the mill, the river was full and frisky and not to be easily waded. She went along the bank, her feet squishing through warm soft mud, until she found a private, dry, and sunny spot. There she made a seat in the grass, putting the sack to one side.

She brought up her knees and balanced the cup on top in both hands, staring out, seeing nothing.

Turn-born. When Wyll had told her, it had—well, it had been an answer and she'd needed any and all. But the reality of it? Heart's Blood. Jenn sighed, aching inside from more than emptiness. Most of her kind, if she could call them that, thought her such a danger to Marrowdell, to all those she loved, that they were willing to kill her.

Mistress Sand believed she wasn't, which was a very thin thread to rely upon, now that she thought about it. Wouldn't Sand come to agree with the others, if there was another Night's Edge?

Wouldn't they be right?

Peggs always said she could find the good in anything. Where was it in this? Matters had been bad enough when she'd thought her curse was to be stuck in Marrowdell. Worse to be magic and hear voices and want pebbles.

Having everyone afraid of her? Her heart felt broken.

Now, the final insult. She couldn't stay herself. She had to become . . . what? A living jar of dirt. It couldn't be pickles or cookie crumbs or buttons of sentimental value . . .

She could let herself die.

After all, even with Mistress Sand's protection, even if she could control her magic and everyone stayed safe, what sort of life would she have? *We're flesh, not stone,* Covie had told Hettie. But she'd be stone and not flesh. Would she still like pie?

Would she still feel a kiss?

Or want one?

Jenn choked back a bitter sob. So much for Melusine's promise. She must have known about the turn-born and her daughter's fate; made up her "promise" to be sure Horst would stay and care for her.

"Stay and live like this." What mother could want that? "Step beyond the scarred hills and die."

Unless Melusine hadn't known and meant the Verge itself, not the road from Marrowdell. Had she been so shaken by her glimpse of that other world she'd have said anything to keep her daughter from it?

Jenn shrugged morosely. What did it matter? She wasn't a girl or a woman anymore. She was turn-born and cursed. The outside world wouldn't want her anyway. Who would?

A preoccupied bee droned by. Ants discovered her toes. A butterfly landed on the rim of her cup and she blew it away.

The Spine rose directly across from her, taunting and dangerous. Understanding her longing for it hadn't helped at all.

"Turn-born." Jenn Nalynn flung the cup and its contents in the river. "Monster!"

Wyll knew what she was, if not this. Bannan? Sand was right, he'd see for himself. Neither would repudiate her. They were better than that.

Even if they should.

She dared not despair. Dared not cry or be angry or anything normal. Overwhelmed, Jenn dropped her forehead to her knees.

~ What is wrong, elder sister? ~

She rolled her head. A house toad squatted in the grass, its eyes half-closed against the bright sun. "Do I become something else and live," she asked dully, "or stay as I am and die?"

It shut its eyes completely, becoming, to a casual glance, a lumpy stone. ~ Which is more honorable? ~

She closed her own. "Where's honor in this?"

~ There is always honor! ~ It sounded dismayed by her doubt. ~ I will explain. ~

"That's not—" She didn't get to say, "—necessary."

~ It is honorable to die, ~ the toad declared proudly, ~ if, by so doing, you protect others. It is honorable to live, if you have a duty to fulfill no other can. It is also honorable to die if your queen asks it, but you do not have a queen, do you? ~

Toads. Jenn sighed again. "Just a prince."

~ Yet you have those who love and need you, elder sister. ~

She opened her eyes. The toad gazed back, she'd swear with a smug tilt to its chubby body. "You're about to tell me," she said after a long thought-filled moment, "that it's more honorable to live for their sakes than accept death for mine. That if I have any chance to stay with Peggs and Poppa and Aunt Sybb—with Wyll and—and with everyone I care about and who cares about me—I owe them to take it."

It shifted cautiously. ~ I would never presume— ~

"You're right." Surely how very much she loved her family and friends was a kind of magic too. Jenn sat up straight and gave a firm nod. "I must help myself."

She reached into the sack and pulled out the boxes, arranging them in a row. The letters carved in their lids weren't the tinkers' initials as she'd thought, nor proper letters at all. She tried to make them out, but what magic let her understand what she heard didn't work for writing.

The house toad and a small brown bird watching, she brushed an ant from the top and carefully removed the first lid.

It contained a lump of something purple and shiny. To her astonishment, the lump slid quickly to one side as if to avoid the sunlight.

"Definitely not you," Jenn told it, replacing the lid.

The second box contained yellow feathers, or something like enough; the third, a disappointingly ordinary white sand—ordinary until it opened a bloodshot eye to leer at her. That box went back in the sack.

The fourth held pebbles, but they were brown and dull. The toad wasn't impressed either. The fifth, something dark green that stank like rotting turnip leaves.

The sixth box hissed and rattled when she touched the lid. Unopened, it joined box three in the sack.

"Last one," Jenn told the toad.

The white pebble could be inside. Her mouth watered as she slowly lifted the lid.

Fantastic gems sparkled and gleamed within, each facet holding her disappointed reflection. She closed that box and regretfully put it away with the rest. The turn-born expected her to choose from these?

Well, she couldn't.

They weren't right.

Nothing tempted her except the white pebble, which, as she considered how it sank through the ground, must be magical enough to be from the Verge, though why it had been in the meadow she couldn't guess. Or had it been left for her to find?

Disturbing as the thought was, it was worse to imagine the pebble, like the sand in the box, might have waited of its own accord.

She'd touched it with her bare hands. If it came from the Verge, according to Mistress Sand, that was that. Touch then taste then . . .

"Oh, no." She stared at the toad.

The toad stared back.

"It's my fault. That's what Wainn meant." Like Wisp and Bannan. Had she waited a day, she wouldn't feel drawn to both. Had she not climbed the Spine, any of these little boxes might have satisfied her. Well, not the eye or the moving purple goo or what hissed, but one of the others surely. The gems, preferably. She mightn't mind so much if she could sparkle inside. At least then she could show Peggs.

Jenn refused to think it defeat. Though it wasn't at all gracious to ask for a new and different gift, Mistress Sand had said she'd help. What better help than for the turn-born to cross back to the Verge and find her pebble? She'd ask, most politely, and hope.

She lifted her eyes to the Spine, its mounds brilliant white against the clear blue sky, like clouds.

If the turn-born couldn't find it by the Great Turn, she'd cross herself to look.

There was honor for you, she thought, with a nod to the stalwart toad.

To die trying.

Any other evening, especially after a day's hard work, Bannan would have been among the first to wrap his fist around a tankard of beer and fill his plate with steaming fragrant meat.

Not this night.

He'd stayed with the rest to see the animals cared for; not that the kruar required more than being free of their harness, but the livestock in the orchard needed to be coaxed into the now-cleared field. The Ropps' little bull, unwilling to concede space to the Ansnans' giant oxen, found himself to the fore and refused to budge; big Davi and two more men had laughingly pushed him through the hedge gate. The riding horses eagerly followed, kicking up their heels as they galloped across the wide open space. The rest of the cattle, the oxen, cows, and calves, came next, spreading out with heads down and mouths busy in full approval of their new forage.

Last, but not least, the fat old pony wandered after, with a nicker and fuss when he realized the draft horses and Aunt Sybb's team were to spend the night in their barn, a worry swiftly forgotten once the children tossed apple cores into the field for him.

Clean and dressed for the evening, Lila's letter safely put with his belongings, Bannan began his search for Jenn Nalynn.

The villagers were assembling for the welcome feast, so he headed there first. Platters and bowls of food covered the trestle tables laid along the path leading from the main road to the Treffs' and Emms'. The stretch between the former's home and the latter's barn offered a pleasing unobstructed view of the river and valley, so an abundance of benches and blankets and chairs had been set out wherever there wasn't garden. The tinkers had brought several of their barrels, tapping those to cheers and hearty applause. The barrels might not be the wood they appeared to others, but the beer looked and smelled as it should.

Lamps hung from poles and porches and even the branches of nearby apple trees. Candles ringed the fountain in the center of the village. None were lit. Not yet.

For the sun still hung over the Bone Hills, its low rays gilding the valley where it wasn't striped by long shadows. The crude log buildings took on a russet glow and the river sparkled like diamonds.

For the first time, Bannan found himself immune to Marrowdell's remarkable beauty. The turn was coming. He slipped through the gathering, avoiding pleasantries, fending off platters and jugs, looking everywhere for Jenn Nalynn. So intent was he, he staggered when Davi clapped him soundly on the back. "Fine work today, Bannan. We'll make a farmer of you yet."

"Good to hear," he said when he had his breath. Nodding toward the beer barrels, the truthseer made his escape.

Twice, he thought he'd spotted Jenn, only to be wrong. Once, he almost collided with the Ansnan dema and took a quick step out of the way. The dema and Eld, hosted by a smiling Dusom, mingled cheerfully with the villagers and tinkers. Their servants stayed close by the beer, eyes wary and tankards clutched to their chests as if chances to indulge were few and far between.

Horst stood apart, as usual, tucking into a plate of misguided ox. He was too adept a watcher to make his attention obvious, but Bannan was sure nothing the astronomers said or did went unnoticed. Especially now that Horst knew they might be here for more than the eclipse.

The truthseer hadn't told him of the turn-born or that Jenn Nalynn was one of their kind. There'd been no time or need. Simply passing along Wyll's warning, that the newcomers might try to use Jenn Nalynn as part of Ansnan magic, had been enough to put fire in the old soldier's eyes.

Tir should hear it all, but that had to wait. His friend would be busy in the mill with Radd until after sunset; Bannan had to find Jenn first.

Was that . . . ? The tantalizing glimpse of fair hair and round cheek was lost behind a forest of tall black feathers. As he attempted to peer around the hat without offending Lorra Treff, who mistook his attention and immediately smiled, someone took hold of his hand and tugged.

He glanced down to find the Ropps' youngest daughter, Alyssa, who wasn't smiling at all. "Bannan, you must come," she urged, tugging harder. "Your horse is starting a fight!"

Scourge. He'd wondered how long it would take, but now? Ancestors Witness, the beast had impeccable timing. The sun was touching the Bone Hills; in moments it would set.

Jenn . . .

As Bannan hesitated, an enraged squeal from the commons shocked the festive crowd to silence. A second brought worried murmuring, especially from the astronomers. "Your pardon," Master Riverstone said loudly. "Our horses play. We'll see to them."

Nods and relieved looks. The villagers went back to their party, Dusom busy explaining to the dema. That should be a conversation worth overhearing.

Knowing exactly how kruar could be, at play or otherwise, the truthseer nodded to Alyssa and headed for the commons.

Riverstone and Chalk were ahead, bound for their tent. As Bannan caught up to them, the latter turned and stopped in his way. "It's best to leave them alone. Our horses aren't the tame sort."

"My horse's there," Bannan snapped.

An eyebrow lifted in polite disbelief. "Why would—" A deep, bloodcurdling roar echoed through the valley and the other eyebrow rose in shock. "It can't be . . ."

So Scourge was adept at hiding from turn-born as well. Until, Bannan winced inwardly, now. "I have to go," he said as calmly as he could, stepping around Chalk. "Can't have a fight, can we?"

"What is it you see, man of truth?"

This was it, then. How they'd found out didn't matter; what did was what happened next.

Who did he fool? Whatever they decided, that's what would happen.

Though his heart thudded in his chest, Bannan kept his face pleasant. "Do we do this now, turn-born?" he asked grimly, with a meaningful nod to the gathering behind them. "Here? I'm not the one with secrets."

"Peace. We've no quarrel, Bannan Larmensu, unless you make one." Chalk smiled then laughed outright. "Sly old kruar. He brought you! His disguise na?"

The truth. All of it. For whatever reason—and he thought at once of Jenn Nalynn—the turn-born accepted his presence. He let out the breath he hadn't realized he'd held. "Scourge just wants to go home—" A pained squeal from the commons drew Bannan's head around. "Heart's Blood!"

He heard the turn-born shout, "Leave them!" as he broke into a run. He didn't look back.

The "sly old kruar" may have planned how to get here, the truth-seer thought furiously, but had he expected to meet six of his kind in Marrowdell? Well-armored, and for all Bannan knew, younger and stronger?

He'd bet on Scourge, no question.

Still. Just in case, he grabbed a pitchfork on his way.

Through the open window, Jenn watched the golden tinge on the crags consumed by darkness that moved steadily, stealthily upward. There was no stopping it.

All she could do was hide.

She'd returned to the tent with the boxes and her request, only to find Mistress Sand had left. She should have remembered. The tinker helped the Treffs each year with the welcome feast. Urgent as the pebble was, Jenn couldn't bring herself to risk Lorra and Frann's curiosity.

So she'd made her way home, to help Peggs. Her sister'd accepted her return without question or fuss, quietly keeping her busy.

Keeping her in sight, too, as the afternoon drew to an end. There was no fooling Peggs Nalynn.

Jenn hadn't tried. She'd stayed close to her sister, helping to set out platters and baskets, letting others do the fetch and carry. She'd waited for the tinkers and looked hopefully for Wyll, but there was no sign of either. Her dragon had promised to come tonight; she supposed he was busy too.

Then the wagons returned, those who'd worked the fields sitting atop the day's last loads, waving their pitchforks in tired triumph. The grain wagon went on to the mill while those not heaving stalks busied themselves with moving the livestock to their new pasture. Though every face wore a mask of dust and sweat, there was no mistaking Bannan Larmensu for anyone else.

Her eyes had followed him, her heart beating like a drum. Whenever he looked in her direction, Jenn would pretend to drop something under a table and crouch down. It was all quite exhausting.

It didn't help that Peggs tried not to smile.

Between trying to avoid Bannan and find a private moment with Mistress Sand, Jenn had felt sunset crawling closer and closer. Now, she understood the tinkers' daily observance; like the house toads hiding under Aunt Sybb's coach, they avoided exposure inside their tents. She couldn't face the turn in the open either, especially not in front of almost everyone she knew. But how to evade her determined sister?

Scourge. Just when it seemed Bannan had spotted her at last, the great beast had let out a roar, answered by the tinkers' horses. Everyone else had looked to the commons, including Bannan, and she'd nipped around the Emms' barn and home, quick as could be.

She owed Scourge a very large plate of hard-boiled eggs. In their shells.

So now, waiting for sunset, Jenn sat on the window seat and let the breeze from the river cool her flushed cheeks. Their father would stay at the mill as long as there was light, while Aunt Sybb happily held court on a chair Tir had placed for her in the center of the festivities.

She was safe, here, and alone.

Voices and laughter rose from the feast. After sunset, the lamps would be lit and the music begin. Quietly at first, to allow full stomachs to settle and dishes to be cleared. A foot might tap the beat. Heads nod slowly. There'd be satisfied smiles and peace.

The Beholding for the harvest would be said, pulling everyone together, then the tempo would rise along with the laughter. The eager would jump up; others tarry for another beer or take their turn on the drum. The hardest part was that the dancing need end, but all must be at work by dawn. Master Riverstone would hold firm; though he could be coaxed into an extra song or two.

Her extraordinary new dress hung on its hook. Jenn wore her former best, having lost her courage at the last moment. The pale green with white stripes was still pretty, though the bodice no longer allowed a deep breath and she'd caught Peggs giving her an amused look.

The last touch of gold left the crags.

Jenn braced herself, but the first cramp struck like a blow, driving the air from her lungs. Gasping, she stumbled toward the bed.

At her second step, she sank to her knees through the braided rug and wood of the floor, feet and ankles gone.

She tried to scream and couldn't, bent to push herself free but had no hands! No hands or wrists . . . She flailed her elbows uselessly, knowing she must be free before the turn ended or be stuck in the floor, which wasn't like dirt or carrots.

She'd die and be found like this. Peggs would have nightmares forever.

No. It wasn't going to happen. Rolling on her back, Jenn fought past her skirt to pull her knees close with what remained of her arms, trusting her feet and ankles followed.

All the while, the hunger. She shouldn't be here—she should be there, where she could find what she needed.

Another cramp shuddered through her and she whimpered. So much of her gone, the rest so empty. She couldn't bear it. She couldn't—

Something landed, where she'd once had a hand. A rose petal. As Jenn stared, another settled in the air below her knee, where she'd had a leg. Then more petals drifted through the window and more, until they coated her in red velvet skin, until it looked as though she had wrists and hands, ankles and feet again. Whole, again.

It wasn't true, but it was. Somehow, the illusion of shape helped her endure until, with a final agonizing pain, it was over. The sun had set. The turn passed.

As one, the petals slipped from her skin to the wooden floor, surrounding her with scent and softness as she curled into a ball and wept with relief.

Melusine's roses. She'd been right to come home.

And sensible, Jenn assured herself as her sobs became hiccups, not to have followed her first inclination, to lock herself in the privy.

That did not bear thinking about at all.

She'd survived, which did. Now to get back before the Beholding, or she'd surely be missed. Jenn wiped her face and went to stand.

She couldn't.

Her limbs. She could see them, touch them. They trembled and shuddered, but wouldn't obey.

The sky through the window was dark blue, lighter only on its lower edge. In a short while, the first star would show. The turn was over. Why wasn't she right again?

Jenn pinched the skin of her forearm as hard as she could, relieved by the pain. Her arm was there, but it wasn't, not all of it. She would empty, Sand had said, to make room.

Not yet. Not now. It wasn't fair! Jenn struggled but it was like trying to force her way through heavy snow. In the midst of all that was magic and strange, her once-best dress fought her too, its bodice a cage.

Then, of all things, a moth fluttered in through the window, landing lightly on the floor near her face.

"Help me," Jenn gasped. "Please."

~ Help yourself. ~

It was a much larger voice than was reasonable from so tiny a creature. Larger and older and, yes, familiar. Perplexed, Jenn blinked away tears. Had the moth been in her dream? "I mean to. I will," she said urgently. "But I have to move and I can't."

The moth regarded her with its round dark eyes as it absently used a leg to pull down and stroke one of the feathery plumes on its head, so like Peggs fooling with her hair while pondering what to do, Jenn felt a rush of hope. Would it help her? Could it?

The leg, dainty and white, released the plume and reached out to tap a rose petal.

"I don't understand."

Another tap, this impatient. ~ Taste. ~ A single wing flip took it a distance away.

There were petals against her face. Left with no other choice, Jenn touched her tongue to the nearest.

Fire!

She swallowed greedily, feeling the burn down her throat. Like the tinkers' beer but stronger, as if the rose held even more of the Verge. Best of all, her fingers twitched.

Jenn didn't question. With each touch of tongue to petal, more of her body answered until she could lift her head and use her fingers and wrists. With every swallow, she felt more herself, and more of herself.

Enough, she felt. Jenn Nalynn climbed to her feet, her limbs once again her own. The empty feeling was gone, replaced by that warm inner comfort. She crouched before the moth, bare feet crunching on now-dead and shriveled petals. "Thank you."

~ We promised. ~ In that too-large voice.

It looked like a moth, but wasn't. Of course it wasn't. It could talk, for one thing, which moths couldn't do, and had brought Wyll's letters. " 'Promised,' " she echoed, then her eyes widened. "You promised my mother—Melusine—that I'd live if I stayed here. Why? Who are you?"

It mightn't have heard. ~ You must cross at the Great Turn. Only then can you help yourself. ~

"Thank you. Yes, I understand that part." Jenn curbed the impulse to wish answers from it, sure such a magical creature would be offended and possibly angry. "But Mistress Sand's told me I can't cross. That I'd die in the Verge. She said they'll bring me what I need."

It curled its wings and body, abruptly resembling a white pebble.

"Yes! The pebble."

The moth tidied itself to its proper shape. ~ Turn-born cannot. They are too full of fear. You must cross at the Great Turn. We wait. ~ Suddenly, it wasn't a moth, or small, but huge and white and glistening wet.

Jenn stumbled back, knowing it was impossible that one of the Bone Hills could be in the Nalynn loft without the floor cracking or roof bursting or . . . but here one was and moving closer. She scrambled atop the bed and clutched Peggs' pillow.

The mass of stone vanished, as if it had never existed. The moth fluttered and tipped to land near her toe.

Jenn lowered the pillow. She opened her mouth and closed it, shaking her head. When nothing else untoward happened, she loosened the ties of her once-best dress and took a wonderfully deep breath. Only then did she speak, rather impressed her voice came out without a squeak. "Who are you? Why are you waiting? What do you want from me?"

To her amazement, the moth produced a tiny satchel from under its wings, then pulled out an even tinier parchment, just as Bannan had told her. Using the tip of one leg, it began to write at a furious pace.

Her answer?

No. For when it was done, the moth neatly replaced the parchment, then tucked away its satchel. Its wings opened.

She barely stopped herself from grabbing for it. "Please wait. Tell me."

It paused, tilting its head. ~ I cannot, elder sister, ~ it said in a small and fussy voice, quite different from what she'd heard from it before. ~ I bring tidings, when given me. I write what is new, when encountered. I wrote your questions, for they are new. Perhaps they will become tidings to those who can answer. ~ A leg wiped shakily over both plumes. ~ Perhaps not. I do not decide such matters. ~

Why, the creature was as confused as she felt, but less willing to admit it. "You came when I needed you. Thank you," she said, to be on the safe side, and climbed off the bed.

The moth flew up and out the window without another word, leaving her standing in the midst of fresh and shriveled rose petals.

On impulse, Jenn stooped to sweep up a handful, pressing them to her face to breathe in their fragrance. For an instant, it was as though her mother's arms were around her.

She lowered her hand. Melusine's roses were of Marrowdell

yet, somehow, of this mysterious Verge as well. "I'd much rather have you inside me than pebbles," she told the flowers at the window.

They turned as one to regard her, and she held her breath. Then, as one, they turned away again. Dark green leaves rustled, like a disturbed bird settling its feathers.

If it was an answer, she feared it was no. Still, she'd ask Mistress Sand about the roses tomorrow.

Hoping she hadn't been missed, above all hoping things would be better at tomorrow's turn, because today's had been hard enough, Jenn gently tossed the petals that had helped her out the window and made ready to rejoin the welcome feast.

Tir caught up with Bannan by the commons and, without a word, they vaulted the gate together. His friend, well aware of Scourge's tactics, had grabbed a pitchfork of his own. There was no close combat with a kruar.

Luckily, combat had yet to be joined. Scourge stood as if guarding the road from Marrowdell, neck arched until veins stood out, prancing in place. The other kruar, smaller but equally aroused, prowled like giant wolves in front of him. Heads down, lips back from their fangs, they made a moving wall of death incarnate.

"Bloody beast," Tir muttered as he and the truthseer ran forward. "What's he thinking?"

"He's not," Bannan replied. The turn was close, he thought suddenly. The kruar must want to be out of sight. Why would Scourge get in their way? "Hey!" he shouted, brandishing his makeshift weapon. "Over here!"

They were ignored.

Tir shrieked his war cry and Scourge's head jerked up.

The other kruar attacked.

Hooves slipped on grass and dug into ground. Heavy grunts and infuriated squeals mixed with the smack of body into body and the rip of teeth into flesh. Bannan charged with Tir, having no idea what they could do but determined to even the odds.

A blast of wind sent them toppling on their backsides, pitchforks flying. "Wyll! Heart's Blood," Bannan swore as Tir gasped for breath. Scrambling to his feet, the truthseer looked around furiously, spotting the dragon against a tree. "Let us help him!"

Not that any normal voice could be heard above the kruar. A cool breeze slid over his face to one ear. "They aren't fighting."

From Tir's sudden rigidity, he'd heard too.

It looked like battle. As Scourge knocked one of his opponents flying, two more snapped at his heels. Another lunged for his vulnerable throat and he whirled to present his shoulder instead, paying the price as fangs closed on that flesh and tore free a bleeding mass. The remaining two pounced, the first giving way with a squeal as Scourge locked his own teeth on its muzzle, but the other drove headlong between Scourge's front legs and heaved. The others joined in, pushing him up and back until he released his hold and began to fall over.

"They'll kill him!" Tir protested.

"Quite possibly," the breeze agreed. "He won't thank you for interfering."

The dragon was amused. While he couldn't tell if a breeze told the truth, Bannan trusted his instincts. He gestured, "Wait," to Tir. The man gave him a disbelieving look but obeyed.

Scourge landed with a thud that shook the ground, only to roll to his feet in a blur of powerful motion. He charged, catching his attackers off balance. As they scattered, then spun with open jaws, Bannan and Tir retreated to where Wyll stood watching. When close enough to be heard over the din, the truthseer shouted, "What do you mean, they aren't fighting?"

"What I said." Wyll pointedly looked anywhere but at the kruar. "They think the old fool's a hero. Their warlord returned from exile, to seek redemption at the Great Turn."

Another series of roars and a very loud, drawn-out squeal.

Tir, whose eyes hadn't left the kruar, abruptly tilted his head far to one side. "Ancestors Blessed and Bountiful!" He let out an admiring grunt. "Those are . . ."

"Mares," Wyll supplied dryly. "Yes."

Bannan turned in time to see Scourge most decidedly not fight with one kruar as the other five eagerly crowded close, snapping at one another. He quickly and politely looked away again. "I see."

"Bloody beast!" Tir exclaimed with enthusiasm. "He's doing another one!"

Eyes half-closed, the truthseer pinched the top of his nose and deliberately shook his head. "Must you watch?"

"As if he didn't," Tir retorted, but turned away, though he glanced over his shoulder every so often, once with a whistle.

"Scourge can go home?" Bannan asked the dragon, trying to ignore both squeals and whistle.

Wyll shrugged his good shoulder. "The sei exiled the old fool. Only they can permit it. Do hurry up." This as an uproar burst out among the mares. "We should leave," he added. "They'll want blood afterward. They always do."

Tir stopped looking over his shoulder. "What kind of blood?"

All at once, the commons fell quiet, so quiet Bannan heard music from the village. He turned.

Seven kruar, drool steaming from their gaping mouths, stood gazing raptly at them.

"Dragon's, if they can," Wyll replied, his smile as predatory as his man's lips allowed. "Yours may do."

Scourge stood with the others, sides heaving. The truthseer hadn't appreciated the sheer terror of being regarded with hunger by those wild red eyes.

It wasn't to happen now. "Scourge!" he shouted, stepping forward with a brisk clap of his hands. Anything to break that predatory glare. "Rabbits!"

With a loud "Whuff!" his oldest friend pricked up his ears and gave what might have been a nod, then slammed his head into his nearest new love, knocking her sideways. Scourge chivvied and chased the rest around, then, with a roar, broke into a gallop.

Full at the hedge. The mares followed, all running headlong at a barrier impossibly high for a horse.

Just as the sun went behind the Bone Hills, and the turn flowed over Marrowdell.

Manes became swords, hides became armor, and the kruar took flight.

Leading the fearsome creatures, jumping higher and further, plunging through the river beyond and up onto the road, their magnificent warrior king, naked of all but scars, needing nothing more.

Bannan found himself unable to speak.

Tir swore cheerfully under his breath.

"He'd better have them back by morning," Wyll grumbled. "Old fool."

But when the truthseer glanced at the dragon, he caught the hint of a smile.

Marrowdell's fountain stood ringed by cobblestones, then hard-packed earth. With the night sky above, candles around its rim, lamps hung from every likely branch and from ropes strung between, it became the sparkling center of an airy, beautiful hall. As lovely as any in Avyo, Aunt Sybb proclaimed kindly, though its dance floor could use some improvement.

The feast done, seats circled the lit space; chairs, benches, and blankets shifted to offer respite and a good view. Instruments waited near the commons gate, as did a table laden with barrels and tankards and pots of tea. But first, following the feast and sunset so all could attend, the Beholding.

"Hearts of our Ancestors . . ." Old Jupp began.

Marrowdell added their voices, from Alyssa to Aunt Sybb. "We are Beholden for the abundance of this valley, for it will give us the strength to improve ourselves in your eyes . . ."

Jenn nipped in between Peggs, who gave her a worried frown, and their father, who smiled. ". . . We are Beholden for the company of friends," she joined in with the rest, "for the harvest is a task beyond us alone. We are Beholden for the opportunity to gather in this Welcome Feast, to share your gifts. Hearts of our Ancestors, above all we are Beholden for Marrowdell, our home . . ."

As she spoke, she looked around as best she could beneath properly lowered lids. Everyone stood around the fountain, hands circled over their hearts, faces touched by the soft glow of lamps. The Uhthoffs next to the Nalynns, Kydd, of course, beside Peggs. The Emms and Ropps, with Palma and Hettie. Riss, with Old Jupp. The far curve was filled with Treffs, with hats and without, then Roche with Devins, as if no one but his brother would stand by him. The tinkers were next and Jenn acknowledged Mistress Sand with a nod when their eyes met.

A little apart, but still in the circle, Horst, with Tir and Wyll, though Wyll, like the tinkers, didn't even pretend to say the words. The dema and Urcet sat outside with their servants, as if watching a play.

There he was.

Bannan Larmensu.

He stood between Wyll and Wainn, taller than either, fingers circled over his heart. Being here at all, she thought with relief, meant that Scourge, who wasn't, must be fine.

Bannan said the Marrowdell Beholding as confidently as those born here and kept his eyes fixed on the fountain, allowing Jenn's to linger. Like the rest, he'd changed from his work clothes; unlike the other men, his white shirt was tied with black laces at the open throat instead of buttons and pants of leather, not homespun, clung to his strong legs. She'd held those pants, before Tir had taken them. The leather was glove-soft.

Which was not a proper thought during a Beholding. Hurriedly, Jenn looked away.

Then back, not done. Aunt Sybb would admire Bannan's knee-high black boots, polished to reflect the lamplight. Most of Marrowdell had bare feet. He'd tied back his hair, but an errant curl hung like a question mark over one eyebrow.

Her hair fell loose over her bared shoulders and back; strange, to feel it against her skin, but ever-so-reassuring. She no longer took skin or shoulders for granted.

Aunt Sybb said the last words alone, her voice full of such warm strength, Jenn's eyes prickled with proud tears. ". . . However far we are apart, Keep Us Close."

"'Keep Us Close,'" came the echo. The Beholding done, people began moving around, smiles on their faces.

Bannan raised his eyes, catching and holding hers. He didn't smile, perhaps because she wore Aunt Sybb's daring and adult dress, with shoes, and her hair was clean for once. She must look very different from the Jenn he knew.

For some reason, she couldn't smile either. For an instant, forever, they stood looking at one another across the open space.

Then she was surrounded. "You look beautiful, Dearest Heart," Aunt Sybb declared happily, coming close to adjust the long twisted ribbons down the front of the dress. She herself looked radiant, her elegant black shirtwaist and skirt topped by a lovely new shawl, golden and with sleeves. Bannan's gift; Mistress Sand's work. "Doesn't she, Radd?"

"Ancestors Witness," their father agreed, his voice thick with emotion. He'd missed some flour in his haste to wash up and attend the Beholding, and Peggs hovered with a handkerchief at the ready. "I shall visit your mother this very night and tell her how much like her you've become." He offered his hands to Jenn.

More than anything, Jenn wanted to run into his arms and stay there, safe from the world. Either world. Instead, she laid her hands on his callused palms and smiled. "I hope so, Poppa. Thank you. And you, Aunt Sybb. It's a wonderful dress."

As Master Riverstone and Frann retuned their instruments, Davi having produced his battered bass, there were murmured compliments everywhere, for Marrowdell wore its proud best. What better night for it? The evening was summer-warm, kind to bare arms and tired bones, and they'd reason to celebrate. Friends returned after a year's absence, larders filled, and, most welcome of all, the harvest well underway. There'd be a simpler gathering tomorrow night, as work took its toll, then all would meet again for the farewell dance, the night before the tinkers left.

Much as Jenn anticipated her birthday, this first night was always special though, to be honest, she'd paid heed to the dancing and precious little else. Tonight, Jenn found herself aware of much more. The little knots of conversation. Mistress Sand, with the Treffs. Her father and Tadd, waving tankards at Chalk. About the mill, she'd no doubt. Old Jupp, his ear trumpet aimed at Tooth, the pair laughing. Flint in earnest discussion with Dusom and Kydd. Clay listening to Tadd and Allin. Fieldstone with Alyssa, who was clutching a new doll and regarding him with wide-eyed worship.

How had she missed how Wainn looked at Wen, or how their fingers met in the shadows?

She'd lost sight of Bannan.

"Finally." Peggs took her hand and drew her aside. "Jenn, are you all right? Where did you go?"

"I changed my mind about the dress."

Peggs had brought them near a lamp; by its light, her face was drawn tight with worry. "Not the dress. Sunset."

Impossible, really, to fool her sister. "I thought I might be sick," Jenn admitted, trying not to squirm, "so I went to our room for the—for that time. I'm fine now. I'm here, aren't I?"

Her sister fluffed her bangs and drew a gentle finger down her cheek. "You look lovely and worn to the bone. An early night couldn't hurt, Dear Heart. With a second cup of Covie's remedy?"

The first had tasted like tar. Jenn grimaced. "I'd rather stay here," she confessed. Here, where there were people and lights, where she wouldn't, couldn't vanish. Music began to play again, louder and with a happy, irresistible beat. "There's dancing," she added, which was hardly necessary since couples were taking their places by the fountain, with Anten, who couldn't dance but tried his best every year, laughingly fumbling through the steps with his youngest daughter.

"Jenn! Peggs!" Despite her excitement, Hettie approached with the wary dignity of someone unused to shoes. Palma came with her,

her feet happily bare. "You have to hear this. Go on, Palma. Tell them about your book."

The soft light couldn't hide Palma's blush. "Ancestors Witness, Hettie. Allin's mother's the real author. She's famous. I just—just dabble."

"I'm sure everyone starts that way," Peggs said kindly. "Gallie must be thrilled to have another writer in the family."

"What are you writing?" Jenn asked, relieved to have a topic that wasn't about sunset or her stomach. "When can we read it?"

From blush to pallor, but if Palma thought she might evade such questions, she hadn't taken the measure of her soon-to-be sister-by-marriage. "It's a book about us," Hettie said proudly. *"Avyo's Forgotten Exiles."*

"That's—I haven't decided on the title," Palma protested in a low voice.

A book about them? Jenn exchanged astonished looks with her sister, then both stared at Palma. Peggs spoke with care. "It's illegal. The prince—"

"Won't live forever," the young innkeeper proclaimed fiercely. "Nor will the barons who profited. History deserves the truth!"

Jenn blinked.

Peggs' eyes sparked with fire of their own. "And the truth has found its champion! Good for you, Palma. Ancestors Tried and Triumphant. Good for all of us, I say. It's about time."

"Time we have to spare," Jenn insisted. When had she become the sensible sister? "The prince is old and fat. Aunt Sybb says it's a wonder he's lasted this long. Please be patient, Palma. And careful."

"So long as you finish," Peggs added, not to be denied.

Palma smiled. "Thank you." Hettie nudged her shoulder and she laughed. "You were right."

"What made you write about us?" Jenn asked, curious. She hadn't thought, until recently, there was anything in Marrowdell worth putting in a book.

"You want me to tell you now? But the dancing—" At their vigorous nods, Palma's face turned serious. She spoke with a storyteller's cadence. "All of you came through Endshere, on the way north. I was very young, but I remember the wagons, filled with everything you had. Your faces. Sad. Angry. Resigned. Afraid. I asked my parents why.

"They told me to be quiet and polite, for you weren't like us. You'd been rich. You'd lived in the capital in big estates, until being sent away by the prince. But you didn't look like rich people or bad. You looked like us, only lost.

"We gave rooms and food to those willing to stay the night." Palma's expressive eyes grew wistful. "I played, a little, with the children. They didn't know about farms, so I'd show them our sheep and chickens. Most wouldn't linger. Winter was coming. Came. The last wagon . . . if I close my eyes, I see it still . . . disappeared into snow."

Hettie frowned, then exclaimed, "Feathers! There was a black hen with the softest feathers. And a small girl in a red dress, who showed me how to hold it. That was you?"

"Yes!" Palma circled her fingers over her heart. "Ancestors Blessed and Bountiful. I wasn't sure anyone would remember me. Allin didn't, but he and Tadd were babes."

Peggs had been a baby too, Jenn thought, but Roche and Devins might recall a young Palma. Wainn too.

"The book?" Peggs nudged.

Palma collected herself with a little cough. "After that, I couldn't help but wonder what happened to you. All of you. I'd make up stories. When I got older, I had to find out." A smile. "I'd ask our visitors. Pieced together names and places. The more I learned, the more I knew I had to write. About the exiles. Their last night in Avyo. What happened." Determination firmed her voice. "I want to tell your story, the real one. It's important. People should know—" She stopped, as if embarrassed by her own passion.

No one spoke for a moment, then Peggs said huskily, "When you're finished, I'd like to read it. Please."

Jenn and Hettie nodded gravely. Palma looked grateful. "I—I wasn't sure how you'd feel, but I wanted to be honest. Coming here—" She didn't look at the sky or lights or fountain, she looked at the people. "—it's a dream come true." She sighed happily. "I want to talk to everyone."

"Not Roche," Hettie advised. "You can't believe a word he says."

Which, being no longer true, wasn't quite fair. Jenn made herself say, "I've heard he's taken a—a vow of truthfulness."

Peggs, ever her ally, jumped in. "I heard that too."

"A truthful Roche?" Hettie looked skeptical, but shrugged. "Well, if he thinks to find someone like you, Palma, Ancestors Witness he'll have to improve himself."

"Exactly," Jenn said, a little too heartily. She went on, "Palma, you should start with Old—" she corrected herself, "—Master Wagler Jupp."

"'Jupp?'" Palma's eyes widened. "The Secretary of the House of Keys? He's here?!" Her voice actually squeaked on the word.

"He is." She beamed. "With chests full of documents. He's writing his memoirs—"

"Why didn't Allin tell me? I have to meet him. Hettie, you must introduce us!" She twirled to go then back again, her mass of hair confused enough to slide over her face. "Wait. I need my notebooks—"

"What about the dance?" Hettie protested.

Palma gave her an incredulous look. "Do you know what an opportunity this is?"

"I know Old Jupp's been in the beer and will be dancing himself once the music starts." Peggs chuckled. "You may want to leave your questions till tomorrow. After his nap."

"I can take you to Riss Nahamm, his great-niece," Jenn offered, holding out her hand.

Though the innkeeper looked crushed, she rallied with a smile. "Sorry. It's just—to be so close—"

"I understand." To want to know, to see for herself? That desire had been everything to her once, before pebbles and magic and curses. How remarkable, that Palma would find hers here, in Marrowdell.

If Marrowdell let her stay.

Full of trust, Palma gave her hand. "Lead on, Jenn Nalynn."

As she did, Jenn wished with all her heart that Palma sleep as well as she would at home, with only sweet dreams. She wished and . . .

"Here you are."

Mistress Sand stood in her way.

Jenn stopped, Palma stopping with her. She met the turn-born's blue-eyed gaze and refused to let hers waver. This, she would have.

The pipe sent up a cheerful and familiar melody, the flute followed. As more villagers rose to dance, Sand gave Jenn a tiny nod before smiling at Palma. "Greetings again. I've heard there's to be a second wedding na? Congratulations."

The innkeeper's daughter blushed. "Thank you, Mistress."

"Stop by my tent in the morning. I've something pretty for you." Sand glanced at Jenn. "Before you rush away to dance, a word na?"

"I'll come right back," Jenn promised. "I want to introduce Palma to someone."

Nodding, Sand took a seat.

Mulling over what had happened, or not, Jenn led Palma to Riss Nahamm.

Riss had dressed for the dance in green satin. It had been her best dress when Jenn was little, then gifted to Cynd years ago. Covie'd worn it since, though Gallie couldn't, as well as Frann and Wen. Peggs had had it last year, adding yellow ribbons. The ribbons were gone and Riss had wrapped a heavy black shawl over her shoulders despite the warm night. Her wounded hair curled against her pale cheeks and neck, and her eyes were haunted until she saw Jenn. "Fair evening, Jenn. Palma."

What had she been thinking, to bring a stranger to Riss when she was so unhappy? As Jenn regretted her decision, Palma crouched before the seated woman. "I'm writing a book," she said eagerly. "It's about you—about all the exiles. Their struggle. Leaving Avyo. May I—I'd like to—I mean I—" Words failing, she looked beseechingly at Jenn.

"Palma would like to speak with Master Jupp," Jenn supplied. "Tomorrow, if possible. I mentioned his memoirs."

"Of course." Riss' face lit with real pleasure. "The injustice of the past is my honored uncle's favorite topic. I fear you'll find him hard to stop, once started."

"I wouldn't want to," Palma declared stoutly.

Riss smiled. "Come, sit with me." She made room on her bench. "Tell me about your book."

"If you'll pardon—" Jenn began, then stopped, pleased to find neither paying attention. She walked away, rather satisfied with the night so far.

She saw Kydd lead her sister to join the dancers around the fountain and felt a little wistful, but she wasn't here to dance. Not tonight. She had to talk to—

A figure moved from the shadows. "Would you teach me this, Jenn Nalynn?"

Jenn started, a little, but smiled politely at Urcet. He'd changed his brown coat for a sleeker one, embroidered in red and gold. The same black sash crossed from shoulder to waist, with its muted red bells, but he'd left the pouches and belt behind. He was, if possible, more beautiful than before; Jenn found herself chilled, not warmed.

He'd spied on her from his wagon. And she wasn't, Jenn knew, to talk to him any further. Which had to include dancing.

"I'm sorry," she said, looking around for a reason and having no trouble finding it. Wyll was coming toward them as quickly as his leg allowed, silvered eyes catching the lamplight. "I must honor my betrothed with the first dance."

Urcet leaned close. He smelled of spice and beer. "And me with an explanation, girl," in no friendly tone. "How come you to speak Eldani?"

She did? Really, it was no stranger than speaking moth or toad, Jenn decided and drew back, giving Urcet her aunt's quelling stare. "Enjoy the festivities," she suggested haughtily, and went to meet her dragon.

To forestall anything unfortunate, which, from Wyll's expression, could be anything indeed, Jenn slipped her arm through the crook of his good one and urged him, firmly, toward the dancers. "I'm so glad you found me. It's time for our first dance."

He came without argument, though there was menace in the lingering look he shot at Urcet and she was sure they shouldn't be left together.

Master Riverstone's pipes, Frann's flute, and Davi's bass were being accompanied, more or less in tempo, by an assortment of pans and kettlepots enthusiastically struck by whomever felt so inclined and had remembered to bring a spoon. Jenn's spirits lifted until, despite her shoes, she was half dancing as she pulled Wyll along.

He stopped short and she almost fell. "Try, Wyll," she coaxed. "You might like it." Old Jupp was out there, his canes a minor hazard, but as sure-footed as if the music moved his legs for him.

"What I like is watching you dance, Dearest Heart," he reminded her, for hadn't she danced in their meadow times without number? He'd whirl daisy petals and dizzy bees as her partners, catching her in his little breezes when she'd twirled herself once too often.

Before she'd destroyed Night's Edge.

Sobered, Jenn nodded and looked for a suitable place for Wyll. There were others who sat and watched, or paused to catch their breath, but not all would appreciate the dragon's company. "Let's find you a—ah!" Spotting Wainn, she brought Wyll over to him. "I'll be back. There's someone I've to talk to—"

"Oh, we'll take care of him." Tir Half-face appeared at her shoulder, a pair of brimming tankards in each fist. His eyes were mischievous over his mask. "I promised friend dragon I'd introduce him to a proper drink."

"It stinks," Wyll protested as he took one.

Wainn took another and grinned. "It's good," the youngest Uhthoff assured him. "To the harvest!" He clicked his tankard against Wyll's.

Who looked so dubious Jenn had to bite her lip to keep from smiling. "Keep out of trouble," she advised. "I won't be long."

She had to speak to the turn-born. That first.

"Keep an eye out for Bannan," Tir called shamelessly after her. "Can't miss him. He's in those tight leather pants you like."

Jenn hurried into the shadows between lamps.

Where her blush wouldn't show.

He hadn't lost sight of her for an instant.

Or dared approach.

Bannan shifted around an apple tree to keep the dancers between him and Jenn Nalynn, pondering the nature of courage.

Where was his?

Fled. Vanished. Nonexistent. Was it the dress? Old-fashioned it might be, but wearing it, she was magnificent.

Or the look she'd given him, at the end of the Beholding? When it seemed her eyes went straight to his lonely heart and laid it bare . . .

He was in well over his head tonight, without a single drink to blame.

"Truthseer."

At the quiet word, Bannan tensed and looked around, expecting a turn-born. Seeing Horst, he relaxed. "Any news?"

"Their servants'll have sore heads tomorrow," the old soldier informed him. "The dema seems harmless. The other?" He lowered his voice. "Ancestors Witness, you were right, Bannan. This Urcet plays some role and, whatever his purpose, he won't be easily discouraged. A ruthless man and dangerous." An unspoken question hung in the air.

"The sole Eld in all of Upper Rhoth can't disappear, my friend," Bannan grinned. "No matter how clever we are."

"Inconvenient," Horst said mildly. "Let's hope Marrowdell acts for us."

The dreams. Of course. Remembering Tir's anguish, the truthseer grimaced. "Heart's Blood. I never thought to wish nightmares on a man."

A grim laugh. "You won't have to. Newcomers arrive full of themselves, only to slink away before breakfast the very next day, tails between their legs. It's kept life simple. Till you."

"Sorry to disappoint," Bannan grinned.

"A man endures what he must." A real smile. "Speaking of which . . . our Jenn looks lovely tonight, don't you think?" Horst's smile faded. "The very image of Melusine."

The "image" sat with Sand, the two in earnest conversation. Lamplight gilded her hair and sent shimmers along the ribbons that flowed between her breasts.

Bannan coughed.

"Are you going to hide from her all evening?"

"I wasn't—" At Horst's knowing look, he stopped any pretense. "It's for the best."

"Is it?" Horst put a hand on his shoulder. "I've known Jenn all her life, Bannan. Her family's like my own and, Ancestors Blessed, there's strength in the Nalynns you'll not find elsewhere. Let her know how you feel. Trust her to do what's right."

"It's myself I don't trust," Bannan admitted wryly.

"A man of honor." The hand fell and the old soldier's voice softened. "Don't let honor steal your happiness—or hers."

"Horst—"

But the man was gone.

Bannan's eyes found Jenn. She'd risen to her feet, smiling down at Sand. Horst was right. He avoided her tonight for the same reason he'd carved her initials where they couldn't be seen, to appease his prickly honor. How could he look the dragon in the eye if he courted his betrothed in earnest?

According to Horst, by refusing to follow his heart, he gave no credit to Jenn Nalynn. Lila would be more blunt. Thought so much of himself, did he, that he could sway such a wondrous heart from its course with a mere dance or a kiss?

Jenn swayed with the music, wanting to dance.

Trust her.

Bannan straightened his shirt cuffs and screwed up his courage. Man against dragon, then. A dance there would be.

Any kiss would be up to Jenn Nalynn.

Mistress Sand gestured to the apple tree overhead, her bracelet sliding up her gloved arm. "It's true what's rooted in the edge draws across something of the Verge. Melusine's roses are special, Sweetling, without doubt. But . . ."

"But?" Jenn urged, though her heart sank.

"What's of this world can't complete such as you. Just as well, I say. Fill yourself with something that has its own opinions na?" She feigned a shudder. "I wouldn't."

She hadn't thought of it that way. Jenn shuddered too.

"Don't you worry. Flint and Chalk will cross in the morning." Sand gave her a look, more curious than concerned. "If you're sure none will do na?"

"I'm sure. I had a dream about white pebbles," Jenn said truthfully. "I can't stop thinking about them." The words dried her mouth and she took a quick swallow of beer.

"Sure you haven't been talking to toads na?" The tinker chuckled. "Foolish things and their stones."

In fact, she had, but that was something she didn't feel she should share with the turn-born. Jenn's eyes fell on Sand's bracelet. Unlike the villagers, the tinkers didn't change to fancier clothes for an occasion, but the ever-businesslike Sand would wear a sample of the jewelry she'd brought to trade. Not that those in Marrowdell could afford it. The band of silver was set with polished amber, a tiny sprig of green leaf trapped in each piece. Trapped as she was. "You're right," Jenn said soberly. "There's no other way, Mistress. Today's sunset—"

"Sunsets happen to worlds," Sand corrected when Jenn paused. She tilted her palm. "You say you want to learn. Learn this. Along the edge, where worlds touch na? Not sunset. Turn."

"Today's turn," Jenn said with care, "was—difficult." She held in a shudder. "I sank through the floor."

The turn-born's eyebrows rose. "So much gone, so soon na? My my my." The click of her tongue seemed pensive. "Different in more than I'd thought," she said at last, then gave a nod. "Tomorrow's turn, be in my tent, Sweetling." Sand tapped the side of her tankard. "What's from another world na? Keeps you whole."

Overwhelmed, Jenn closed her eyes for a moment. When she felt calm, she opened them to meet Sand's understanding gaze. "Thank you—"

"Tsk. It's the same for us," the other said gruffly. "The flour we take home, kaliia grown by your light na? We bake bread. Brew it with mimrol and spice from the Verge." She took a swallow then smacked her lips. "Marrowdell's taste. A comfort till we cross again." A wink. "A treat, that too."

"Beer." Jenn gave her own a startled look. "That's why you come to Marrowdell?" She'd expected something more—magical.

"Beer," Sand said smugly, "is why we built Marrowdell. This—" her gesture took in the village, the dancers, and all those watching, "—is why we come. Nothing like it in the Verge, Sweetling. Not for such as us."

Impulsively, Jenn laid her hand on Sand's gloved one. "You could stay longer. You'd be welcome."

"Ah, that's my good heart. Easing dreams, thinking of us," the turn-born's expression softened. "We don't belong on this side, Sweetling, any more than you belong on ours. The time for the harvest is all we can bear. The turn of the Balance na? Easiest to cross, with all we must. No, we can't stay, but I take it well you've asked. Very well."

It was a moment so like others they'd shared as simple friends, Jenn found herself saying, "May I ask another kindness, Mistress?"

Sand narrowed her eyes. "Not for that dragon," she guessed with dismaying accuracy and no good temper. "We're none of us glad he's here and none of us glad of his duty."

"I know his duty," Jenn defended. "To make me happy. But Wyll does more than that—he's my dearest friend. I just—I just wish you'd think better of him."

The turn-born scowled and took a long drink. A small growl came from beneath her chair as Kaj vouchsafed his opinion.

It wasn't no. "Please?" Jenn dared. "You don't know him as I do."

"Nor wish to." Sand lifted her tankard toward the dance floor. "They're playing your favorite," a dismissal. "Dance, before the night's done. Tomorrow we'll take care of you." Without looking at Jenn, she added, "As for the dragon—" with a face as if eating something sour. "You've made him a man. We might—might, I say, I don't promise—deal with him as one."

Having won more than she'd hoped, Jenn stood and smiled. "Thank you, Mistress."

Sand glanced up. "Go on with you." She didn't smile.

But there was a wink.

Jenn needed no encouragement. The dance was one she loved, with a happy tempo and complex steps. She wandered along the edge of it, looking for Peggs, who was the best partner, but Kydd had her sister twirling in his arms. Wyll was busy with Tir and didn't care to dance.

Where was . . .

"May I dance with the most beautiful woman in Marrowdell?"

Jenn schooled her face before turning to Roche; after all she'd done, he didn't deserve her disappointment too. "I—"

"Promised the first to me," Bannan Larmensu interrupted with a graceful bow, and swept her into the lamplight.

Heart's Blood, if only he'd waited for any other song, but seeing Roche step forward, hearing him say what was true, for tonight Jenn Nalynn outshone the very stars?

Bannan stepped up to Covie, bowed, and looked longingly past her shoulder at Jenn, presently curtsying to Old Jupp. He'd taken his chance and must bear the consequence.

The old country dance was one he knew, thanks to Lila. The steps took partners coyly away from one another, then back again. They might as well be writing letters, the truthseer thought glumly, as Jenn's small hand found his only to lift away a beat later. There was a moment in each other's arms, but, as that was a rollicking high step and spin along a row of clapping spectators, Bannan found himself less aware of holding her and more anxious to avoid her toes.

Jenn stepped firmly on his and they both went off balance. She laughed like a peal of bells and he couldn't help but do the same, his heart taking flight. "Shoes," she mouthed before turning to curtsy neatly at Roche, who'd joined with his mother for a partner.

Most of Marrowdell had, Bannan realized as he held hands with a beaming Hettie and swung her about. The rest sat around. Tir considered dancing a waste of drinking time and, between spins, he could see Wyll with his friend. The tinkers sat and watched as well, but the dema had hooked his robe through his belt and was leaping around in time with the music, if not his fellow dancers. Urcet was deep in conversation with Dusom and Radd, doubtless about his plans for the coming day.

The Lady Mahavar smiled and nodded at him when their eyes met. Gallie sat beside her, foot tapping as she nursed tiny Loee.

Bannan found Jenn once more in his arms. Their eyes met and, wonder of wonders, she began to smile . . .

The music stopped.

As the dancers, including Bannan, exclaimed their dismay, Davi strummed his strings. "Great news!" he bellowed, then moderated his voice to loud. "Hettie. Tadd. Come here, please. Right here, where everyone can see you."

Dismay turned to anticipation. Since no one else was moving from their spot, Bannan didn't. It kept his arm around Jenn's slender waist. She didn't appear to mind.

Perhaps she didn't notice.

Regardless, it was permission of a sort and he was unashamed to take advantage.

Hettie and Tadd, holding hands, made their way to the open space before the musicians. Both were breathless, their eyes bright. "What can't wait till after the dance?" Hettie demanded and everyone chuckled.

"Horst, you old sneak," Davi ordered cheerfully. "You get out here too."

Bannan felt Jenn stiffen. At her whispered, "Uncle. No—" he looked down to meet eyes smudged with worry and understood.

Horst stepped from the shadows into the lighted space. "Ancestors Witness," he said, his smile plainly forced. "Is there such a thing as a tactful Treff?"

Unrepentant, the big smith grinned. "Not at a time like this, my friend." Another strum. "Go on. Tell them."

"Tell us what?" Hettie asked.

"Tadd. Hettie." Horst's smile warmed as he turned to the pair. He circled his fingers over his heart. "Hearts of our Ancestors, we're Beholden you've come to your senses at last."

Friendly laughter at this, though not from Jenn or Bannan. He looked around and saw other somber faces. Zehr and Gallie Emms. Riss. They'd come to stand by the edge of the crowd, along with all those who'd been seated.

They knew.

"I've a gift for you," Horst began. "I'd intended to wait as long as I—I'd planned to present it at your wedding." Bannan saw his throat work before he continued, "But Davi's right. A time like this . . . well, there's no keeping it secret now, is there?"

The laughter following this was light and scattered, as the villagers began to realize something more than gifting was happening.

Radd, smiling until now, suddenly frowned. "What's this about, Horst?"

"I'm giving Hettie and Tadd my house," the old soldier announced, strong and clear. There were soft gasps, then a hush.

Davi strummed again. "Ancestors Blessed," he said smugly. "I told you it was good news. Now, Horst, before anyone fusses, where'll you be hanging those bear claws now? We've room—"

"I won't need it, thank you." Horst looked at Radd. "I'm going home. It's time."

"What?" the miller demanded, his face drained of blood.

Strings snapped. The baby cried. Bannan felt Jenn tremble.

"No. No. Don't leave for our sake." Hettie touched Horst's arm. "You're just being kind. Too kind. So many times—so many ways. You saved—" her voice shook "—you saved Cheffy from the river." She tried to smile, tears now streaming down her cheeks. "You can't leave. You needn't. We don't need a house, do we, Tadd?" He shook his head fiercely, equally overcome. "We're to live with Zehr and Gallie and Loee. Marrowdell's your home too."

Horst kissed her forehead. "Ancestors Blessed and Bountiful, child, it's done. I'm glad the house won't be empty. It came to me as a gift. Honor me by being happy in it."

"Hettie's right. Your home's here," Radd said solidly. "Give the house, Horst. We'll find—"

"Heart's Blood. Leave be." A violent lift of his hand; a warning. "I can't stay."

Accept it, Bannan wished the miller, for everyone's sake. But he hadn't the power of Jenn Nalynn and her father wasn't a man to settle for evasion. Not in this.

Radd Nalynn stared at his old friend, his mouth working. "Ancestors Witness," he said in a strained voice, "you're the brother of my heart. Whatever this is about, we'll deal with it together. Tell me."

"Don't!" Riss broke from the crowd and came forward, startling everyone. "Let him go, Radd," she pleaded, eyes fixed on the troubled miller. "As you love him, let him go as he is."

"This is nonsense. Horst," Radd tried to lighten his tone, "let's take a bottle on the porch, and give the dancers their floor—"

"You don't know what I've done." So harshly said that Tadd pulled Hettie back and Bannan felt Jenn's arm tighten around his waist. "You'd send me away yourself if you did!"

"I forgave you Melusine!" Radd shouted. "Trust me." His arm swept out to include the village. "Trust us. Ancestors Great and Generous, Horst, we're your family! Now—now and forever." His voice gentled. "One day, our bones will rest together in her dear company."

Riss covered her face with her hands and rushed away through the crowd.

Horst drew himself straight and tall, his face terrible to behold. "Melusine doesn't lie here."

"W-what are you saying . . . of course she does."

"I stole her body and gave it to the Semanaryas." When the miller gaped at him, speechless, Horst took a menacing step forward. "Fool! Did you truly think returning a ring would call off their hounds? That they'd take my word? Your peace—Jenn's—had a price. The ring's what lies here. Not your wife's bones."

In the horrified silence, the sound of Radd's fist striking Horst was like thunder.

Horst knuckled blood from the corner of his mouth with a strangely satisfied look.

Then lightning snapped and crackled, just missing the trees. Villagers ran for shelter as the storm's wind howled around them. Bannan tried to move with Jenn only to find his arm empty. He glimpsed her by flashes, her face distraught.

Suddenly, the storm was gone, as if it had never been. People halted, looking around in amazement.

The storm was gone, and with it, Horst.

Sand stood with Jenn in her arms. She looked to Bannan with a frown. "Take her from here."

So he did.

Bannan spread a blanket on the ground and helped her sit; he thought of her fine new dress and Jenn knew she should thank him.

But she couldn't find words. Uncle Horst was gone. Her father, who couldn't swat a fly and was never angry, had struck his truest friend, drawing blood.

Her mother—she'd said Beholdings over nothing, all her life. Her father had taken comfort, from nothing. Jenn thought she should be angry too, but she wasn't. Uncle Horst was gone and there was a hole in her heart.

Bannan sat beside her, shadow against night, helping by his silent presence as Sand had helped by stopping what could have been a greater disaster.

Together, they sat and looked out over the dark river. Music had started again behind them, muted and quiet and without the deep thrum of Davi's bass. No more dancing, not after that. Doubtless, some would be talking, trying to make sense of it. Those not working the fields tomorrow would start to tidy up, though the beer would likely flow a while longer, to soothe nerves.

She should go to her father, but she couldn't. Not yet.

The slide of water through reeds was its own music; the darkness, comforting walls. In stories, Jenn thought numbly, it wouldn't be proper of her to sit with Bannan, alone and apart, not when she was to marry someone else in three days. In stories, this would be romantic and fraught with—with whatever it could be.

Stars gazed down, cold and uncaring. Aunt Sybb, she knew, would understand and approve. They were all heartsick, tonight, and taking what refuge they could.

Pulling off her shoes, Jenn rested her chin on her knees and let tears flow down her cheeks. At least she needn't fear her grief, not tonight; the turn-born would protect Marrowdell.

"Horst believed you'd hate him, once you knew the truth," Bannan offered gently. "He couldn't bear to stay and find out."

"I don't. How could I?" She hesitated, wiping her tears. In the dark, his face was indistinct, impossible to read. Was hers? "You do believe me."

He understood what she meant. "They call it being a truthseer, but I hear a lie just as well. Not that I'd ever doubt you, Jenn Nalynn. Horst shouldn't either. You or Radd."

"Poppa just needs time," she agreed, hoping she was right, then sighed. "Poor Riss."

"'Riss?'"

"She and Uncle—" Jenn blushed and was glad Bannan couldn't see it. "They've been lovers for a long time. In secret."

"Ah. That explains—" his turn to hesitate.

She wiped her face. "What?"

"He told me to forget honor and ask you to dance."

Honor. Uncle Horst had thought of her, had thought of them, even as he prepared to leave his own love behind. "I'm glad you did," Jenn replied in a small voice. "It's hard to believe he's gone. Marrowdell won't be the same." She shivered. Did she cause it, or was the night turning cool, as harvest nights were wont to do?

Without a word, Bannan shifted to shelter her bare back and shoulders against his warm chest, wrapping his arms around her like a blanket. It was the most unromantic of embraces and Jenn sank into it with a grateful sigh, laying her head on his shoulder.

Strange, how lying in Bannan's arms made her feel better. Safe. She wasn't safe at all. Hadn't she almost died in her bedroom? As for better, having learned just today what she was and what it meant, it was hardly reasonable to feel any improvement in her lot whatsoever.

She just, most truly, did.

A squeal echoed along the valley and she felt Bannan's chuckle. "Scourge's having quite the night." He sounded pleased. "I suppose if the herd's late for the harvest, I'll have to explain to the tinkers."

"They know what you are," she warned.

"And are taking the news well, all things considered."

That was good news. Jenn let herself enjoy the rise and fall of his chest for a moment, then, though she was sure of the answer, asked quietly, "Do you know what they are?"

Bannan laid his cheek against her hair. She felt his nod.

"What—I am?" she went on, her voice barely a whisper. "Why there was a storm and then—then not? What I can do?"

Another nod.

Bannan held her, like this. As if nothing she was or could be frightened him.

As if he knew how afraid she was.

"I've something to tell you," Jenn said huskily. If she didn't, if she vanished tomorrow . . . "In case—if anything happens—if I'm—I'm not here anymore. I want you to know why. To explain—to my family. To Wyll. Would you do that, for me?"

He went rigid, his arms strong around her, but his voice was reassuringly calm. "I promise."

"You've seen Mistress Sand and the others. Seen how they are, inside? What they are?"

"I have. It's remarkable."

That was one word for it.

Stone, not flesh. For an instant the enormity of it overwhelmed her. She'd live, if she could. But what was she to become? How would she feel? What would there be to love? To exist, without love . . .

Jenn gathered her courage. Don't squander the Ancestors' gift,

Aunt Sybb had said. Live each moment. Yes, she'd meant not to daydream when one could be productively employed, but the words . . . fit. She was herself, tonight.

Not something to waste.

"I'm like them," Jenn began, carefully. "I mean—I—I will be. I need white pebbles. I found one on the Spine, that day. I didn't know it was magic and from the Verge. I didn't know it would matter if I touched it, but now I have and it's—I have to have it, Bannan. I'm empty and unless Mistress Sand finds my pebble, unless they can bring me more—what I need to be filled—filled like them—before the Great Turn, I'll have to go up the Spine, I'll have to cross into the Verge to find it, even though she says I can't—that I'd die—" words began to pour out but she couldn't stop, "—but I must, the voice told me, I must help myself. If I don't get the pebble, I won't—I'll be gone." She twisted to see his face. "It's happening already, during the turn. Every day. Today, the sun set and I lost—I lost—my legs and feet and my hands and my wrists and—" She choked back a sob.

"Dearest Heart. Hush." Stroking her hair, Bannan drew her into his lap, cradled like a child. "We'll find it. I swear it with my life's blood. I—" Before he said another word, Jenn kissed him.

It was a desperate, teary, stolen kiss and shouldn't have been romantic at all. But when she pulled away to see what he thought of it, Bannan Larmensu slipped both hands into her hair and brought her mouth back to his with an urgency that made her heart pound.

For a dizzy time, nothing mattered and she most heartily approved when his hands strayed over the shoulders bared by her daring dress and didn't he gasp wonderfully when her hands strayed too and found leather?

~ Elder sister? ~

She was not going to listen to a toad, not when—Ancestors Blessed and Blissful, now his hand found her breast and oh why hadn't anyone told her how delirious it would make her feel and whatever he was doing, he mustn't stop—

"Heart's Blood!"

Not only did he stop, but Bannan heaved violently onto his side, in so doing sending the house toad tumbling from his back to plop like cold soggy pudding on her breasts.

Pudding with little sharp claws.

Jenn shoved it off indignantly and sat up, fumbling her bodice together though both toad and man had most certainly seen what there was to see.

~ Elder sister, someone's coming. ~

It could be Wen and Wainn, who, come to think of it, probably relied on the toads for such warning. Or one of the men looking for a discreet shrub. Or—it didn't matter who. "Someone's coming," she warned.

Instead of helping her to her feet, the dress being awkward, Bannan leaned in to kiss her once more, so thoroughly Jenn might have forgotten the toad and whomever approached entirely except that the truthseer ended the kiss, put another, tender one on the tip of her nose, then stood, offering his hand.

All of which left her quite breathless and grateful it was dark.

Ancestors Hot and Bothered, it took all Bannan had to help Jenn to her feet and release her hand, instead of flinging them both down on that wonderful blanket under the blissful stars and—

And what? he scolded himself, fighting the rush of desire as he watched her slender silhouette tidy ribbons and hair. A hasty toss, when she was heartsick and needing comfort? She deserved far better. Was that a tear in her beautiful dress? Bumbling oaf. He'd acted like she was his first. Though, in his defense, her passion had matched his and—he collected the blanket, grateful for the dark.

Ancestors Witness, he could do better. Hearts of our Ancestors—as he folded the blanket and tucked it under an arm—I'll be Beholden the rest of my life for the chance to do better with this woman as often as possible, for as long as we live.

Without toads, he added, glaring at the creature in question.

"Did you say something?" Jenn whispered.

"No." Heart's Blood, had he prayed aloud? A crash and muffled oath from the shadows saved him. "Someone's coming."

"This way." She collected her skirt and shoes in one hand, offering him the other.

Holding hands, stifling giggles, because, despite everything, suddenly it was fun to dash in the dark like naughty children, they ran between garden rows and around privies and behind the Emms' barn. There, Jenn pinned him against the log wall for a long and distracting kiss, before pulling him after her again.

He could, Bannan decided cheerfully, do this all night.

They wound up at the Nalynns' back door. A lamp shone on the front porch, but not here. Jenn stepped on the shadowy step and turned. "Bannan."

A fleeting chill to the air. Their evening was done. To show he understood, and, in honesty, to remind himself, Bannan put his palms against the log that ran atop the doorframe. "My thanks for the dance," he said lightly. Then, not lightly at all, "I won't let you vanish, Dearest Heart, I swear by every Ancestor I can claim. You'll have what you need, though we leave this world to find it."

"My mother died after crossing, Bannan." Despair thickened her voice. "Mistress Sand forbids it. She said people don't belong there. I don't—I don't even know how."

"Our dragon worries too. But we're not any people, are we? You've their power; I've my own." As he tried to see Jenn's face, the rich scent of roses filled the air and a moth landed near his fingers, tugging free its parchment. Marrowdell paid attention, he thought with a burst of joy. "If we must, we'll find our way without Sand's help. You've done the impossible once," he reminded her gently. "You wished a dragon into a man." The thought of Wyll brought a twinge of conscience.

"I did," she sighed. "But a wishing to move between worlds? Even if we found the words in Kydd's books, even if what he believes is true and I—I'm able to make them work, what if we need tokens too? Marrowdell isn't Vorkoun."

No, Bannan realized with a start. It held a caravan fresh from

Ansnor. What might the dema have brought besides a telescope? A possibility not to share until he was sure; he wouldn't build false hope. "We've time, Dearest Heart," he said instead. "You aren't alone in this." The night was full of roses and magic. His heart sang with hope of his own. "In anything." He sank to one knee, one hand outstretched, the other circled over his heart. "Hearts of our Ancestors, all that I am, is yours. I love you, Jenn Nalynn. Will you—"

Her finger covered his lips. "Don't say it," she pleaded, her voice unsteady. "Whatever's to come, all that I am is yours, Bannan Larmensu. I do love you. I have," she said simply, "since we first met."

The truth and wondrous. He kissed her fingers and caught her hand. Rising, he pressed it over his heart, covered with his own. "Then I've no shame. Marry me, Dearest Heart, and not Wyll."

"There'll be no wedding." She pulled her hand from his and stepped out of reach.

Something was wrong, when nothing should be.

Bannan carefully lightened his tone. "A kiss, then. Before we part for the night." He opened his arms.

To his dismay, Jenn retreated another step. "It would only make things worse."

"How so?" he asked softly. "I know the truth, Jenn Nalynn. You love me as I love you. How could a kiss be wrong?"

"Because of what's to come," she said with quiet resolve. "I'm to be stone, Bannan. To give up my flesh and become a—a thing of magic. Right now, this moment, I love you. I love Wyll. My family. Will I then?"

"Jenn—" Faced with such courage, what could he say but the truth? "I don't know."

"Nor I," so gently, his heart hurt. "That's why I won't kiss you again. Right now, this moment . . . I'd believe it our last." Another step back and away. "Leave me with hope."

Then Jenn Nalynn was gone, leaving him in the kitchen doorway, too stunned to move.

Trust her, Horst had said, and been right.

Save her, Bannan told himself. *That, above all.*

He roused to turn and look over the river, past field and forest, raising his gaze to the bleak mounds of the Spine.

And knew what he had to do.

Night and damp. He hated night and damp. The dragon restrained a snarl as he straightened from his hiding place.

~ They were not pleased, elder brother, ~ the toad said anxiously. ~ I but did as you commanded— ~

~ You acted well, brave cousin, ~ Wyll assured it, stumbling as his good leg cramped. His body hated being bent and motionless even more than standing, but he hadn't dared move until the girl and the truthseer went out of sight. Hadn't dared be seen.

So that was it. He glared at the Spine, thrust against the stars. Only turn-born could bring an object into Marrowdell; they would never risk the Wound. This pebble Jenn Nalynn had found there, that she had to have? Something else had brought it from the Verge.

The sei. It had to be.

Bait in a trap, but it made no sense. The sei had their own world and, unless disturbed, rarely left it for the Verge. To come here? Why?

What didn't he know?

~ Your pardon, elder brother, ~ the toad ventured. ~ But shouldn't I follow them? They may—ah—continue. ~

Despite the grimness of his thoughts, Wyll found himself smiling. ~ They very well may, little cousin. They very well may. ~ For so long, for her sake and Marrowdell's, he'd sought happiness for Jenn Nalynn. He'd been prepared to do whatever she wanted.

At last, he knew what that was. For a moment, her joy and delight had warmed the night, thanks to Bannan Larmensu and her own heart. Like being bathed in her smile.

The turn-born hadn't disagreed; perhaps, in this, they couldn't.

The rest likely thought it was the beer.

The drink smelled as foul as his dragon-self remembered; admittedly, the taste had been bearable. Had he the stomach to drink sufficient of the stuff, doubtless he'd be listening still to Tir's tales of the many well-endowed women he'd married and left behind. Wainn had been fascinated; Wyll unconvinced.

But the brew left a trace of the Verge on his man's tongue, to remind him of all he'd lost, and he'd wanted no more of it. He'd followed Jenn Nalynn, when Bannan had taken her from the disruption caused by the old soldier's confession, knowing she was upset. He'd listened, appalled by the girl's secret and her pain.

Let them be, to find happiness, until Roche and others came stumbling.

Now Horst had fled, Tir was drunk and maudlin, and both truthseer and his former enemy were distracted by urges they surely could have postponed.

Better to be a dragon. Mate all at once, just the once; the business over and done before an enemy could take advantage.

Not that his kind were of use in this.

He was left to rely on what—little cousins? Frustrated, Wyll sent an irate breeze to whistle and snap over the ground, relenting as the faithful toad shrank into a contrite ball, eyes shut.

Jenn Nalynn needed his help, not this. ~ Forgive my temper, inestimable little cousin. ~

The eyes popped open, disks reflecting the rising moon. ~ There is nothing to forgive, elder brother. Will you send another letter? ~ it asked hopefully.

The time for letters had passed. ~ Guard them both, ~ he ordered.

Leaving the toad, Wyll went in search of a more potent ally.

Nyphrit rustled in the deeper shadows as he passed. They hunted scraps from the feast, he supposed, uncaring. The little cousins would attend to any who grew too bold. When he reached the edge of the lamplight, Wyll looked for the turn-born of sand.

He found her where she'd been throughout, seated apart where she could watch the villagers yet reach the beer table unimpeded. She was with the one full of red earth, Clay, and the dragon stopped at a safe distance. Music played, though no one danced. He waited with deliberate patience to be acknowledged.

At last, Sand waved her fellow away and gave him a grudging nod.

The small white dog, perhaps remembering dragons and their appetites, showed a tooth as he approached, then slipped to shelter behind his mistress. Wyll twisted himself into a chair, accepting the pain.

"Tell me, lord of dragons," Sand said, leaning back to laugh at him. "Was it you warmed our Jenn or a man born and whole na? I've coin on the answer."

It deserved none. Before he spoke, Wyll looked for moths then gave his attention to the turn-born. "The sei are meddling."

"Sei na?" The mockery left her face. "Their business is none of ours."

"When it is here? When it is her?"

She gave him a bemused look. "You've gone mad, I see. Flint said you would."

Wyll showed his own tooth. "The sei want the girl to cross at the Great Turn," he told her, sure of that much. They'd thrust their secret on him, that the girl mustn't step beyond the edge or all would unravel with her, without giving him the rest. Why they'd let her live. Why she had to live. "They've given her a reason—a hunger. I don't know their purpose."

"What a dragon doesn't know na?" Sand took a drink. "Everything. Sei don't cross. They can't, is the way of it, any more than little ones. So sei aren't here and don't want and can't meddle." She pointed a finger at him and wiggled it. "That hunger our Sweetling feels na? No more than proper. Time comes, a turn-born empties and must be filled. We'll bring her what she needs from the Verge."

Sei were here. He'd heard them. Arrogant, insufferable turn-born, their bodies hollowed out and stuffed. How and why—he hadn't cared. The thought didn't trouble him, any more than the difference between a kruar's entrails, preferably steaming on the ground, and his own, preferably whole.

Wyll snarled to himself. He should have guessed what was happening to the girl. His ability to feel her distress or know if she was happy had lessened of late. Because he was now a man, he'd thought. Because she tried her earnest best to contain her feelings.

No. It was because with each day, there was less of Jenn Nalynn. To survive, she must become turn-born inside too.

He sincerely hoped Aunt Sybb wouldn't think it his fault.

"What she needs is the white pebble," Wyll said sharply. "Did she tell you? Where she found it?"

"In a dream. A strong one, I grant." Sand made a dismissive gesture. "What matters na? Our Sweetling's not terst." Explaining anything they didn't understand. "We'll find some thing like." Fingers stroked her gloved arm. "Let her touch. Let her taste. She'll be complete, dragon, and content."

"It wasn't a dream. The pebble's real and she's touched it."

"Impossible." The turn-born narrowed her eyes at him. "None of us brought such a thing here."

As he'd feared. "She found it on the Spine." Wyll saw horror on her face; he shared it. "The sei left it for her. As bait—" The air in his mouth turned ice cold, locking his tongue.

"To reach the Spine means entering the Wound and it would never let one of us escape. You lie, dragon," with utter menace. "To what purpose na?"

His body, already cramped in the chair, prickled with frost. He forced words through numb lips, "No lie—truth. We must save—save her!"

His breath thawed. He sat, shivering, in the cruel chair, waiting for the cold to leave his heart.

"If this is the truth," Sand said very quietly, "then saving our Sweetling becomes—a difficulty. The Wound—it's not beyond belief it could use such a lure. Oh, there's something in that void, dragon, despite what your kind believes. Something that hungers for us. We hear it whisper. Say our names. Wail in fury when we resist it. Having Jenn Nalynn," she concluded, pale and set, "it should have swallowed her whole. Release her. She's not terst. A bad taste, maybe. Then why summon her back na?"

"The sei—"

"Are beyond our knowing." With a dark scowl. "They play their games on the Verge side of the edge, Dragon Lord, and care nothing for Marrowdell or the Wound or what happens to any of us. No, this is about what waits there. If you're right—and truthful—the Wound wants Jenn Nalynn. She can't go back to it. She must be stopped."

His duty? "I won't kill her," he stated, bracing himself for her rage.

Sand appeared amused. "Of course you won't."

Turn-born trickery. Wyll gripped the chair's arm, feeling it crush and splinter within his hand. "Try to force me and I'll kill you!"

"Of course you can't." She leaned back again, studying him. He refused to lower his eyes. Sharp little gusts of wind kicked dust at their feet, the worst he could do to her, but it said something, that he dared. "Bold dragon," she acknowledged. "Peace. I was first to hold the babe. Think you love her more na?"

Wyll glared. "I didn't think you loved at all."

"Most don't." Her continued amusement confused him and he lowered his head in threat. "Peace, I say. You don't remember me, do you na? I was the size of Alyssa when you stole me from my family."

"You all smell the same." There'd been such a child, hidden long and well. Unusual, for terst to cling to their turn-born, but not unheard; once her existence had been discovered, he'd been sent to retrieve her. As he recalled, he'd left the village in shards.

For the fun of it.

"I remember you," Sand replied. "And that other life. Well enough to treasure our Sweetling as if she were my own. I'd not want her harmed."

"So long as she stays here," Wyll snapped, as he wouldn't have dared in the Verge.

She wasn't used to being contradicted; he saw that in her face. But instead of lashing out, or sending him from her, the turn-born nodded. "If Jenn could cross—cross and survive na? There's needful magic we do, dragon, tending the Verge for the good of all. She could disagree or worse. Being different, being from here, she could attempt what we'd not imagine. We can't harm our own, so yes, dragon, you were sent, your duty to kill our Sweetling if it came to it. I've hated you ever since."

Honesty from a turn-born. It was almost pleasant. "Now?"

"Now I know you couldn't touch a hair on her pretty head." A startling laugh, loud and long. "You love her too. You've proved it."

"I have." Suspicious, Wyll hesitated, then glowered. "How have I?"

He tensed as Sand leaned too close and winked. "We can't act against the nature of a thing. We only help it along. Do you understand na? Jenn Nalynn couldn't have left you weak and helpless, great lord of dragons, unless that's what you wanted to be."

It wasn't true. Wyll uncoiled and surged to stand, the chair falling over behind him. "I wanted to stay strong!" The villagers gave him startled looks; the turn-born looked to Sand, who shook her head. "I'm her protector!" he railed. "Why would I want to be useless?"

"Who's always been the greatest threat to our Sweetling na? You." Sand half-smiled. "How better to keep her safe than pull your own teeth."

He hated being out at night. Hated chairs. Hated standing. Hated being near any of the terst turn-born.

Especially this one.

"Dragon." Sand had lost her smile. "Wyll."

Jenn's name for him, from a turn-born. The strangeness of it gave him pause.

Stranger still, she rose to her feet. "Walk with me."

He'd prefer to tear out her throat. Surely that fierce bloodlust meant he'd not wanted to be weak, but had had everything taken. Fangs, claws, wings.

Power.

"We do her no good standing here," the turn-born reasoned. "The villagers will start to worry about you more than Horst. We'll get questions we don't care to answer. Come."

"Where?" he growled, but his shoulder bent, his body twisted, and he'd taken a step with her before realizing he would, so what did it matter?

Sand went by the table to put down her tankard, waving with a smile to those still by the beer, then took the road that led to the commons, to the river, to Night's Edge. Beyond. The white dog trotted behind them, at a distance.

"What you've told me is disturbing," she said quietly. "If true—don't bristle at me—" as he stopped, "—if the Wound tricked Jenn into touching something of the Verge, we must find it."

Mollified, he resumed walking. "The Spine. It'll be there."

"There's where we'll die and to what good na? No. We must look elsewhere." She shook her head. "Aiee. We aren't dragons, to fly. Abandon the harvest na? We'd suffer. The villagers would leave. What can we do na?"

Honest hate, now honest desperation. "You ask me?" Wyll stared at her shadowed face.

"I'd ask the stars if they cared. Well na?"

"Would you ask the sei?"

"If I knew how," she said, surprising him most of all. "Though their answers aren't safe to want, are they na?"

If they had answers and not more opportunities for his penance. The turn-born keeping to his pace, Wyll lurched through the open gate and thought. Lamplight glowed within two of the newcomers' wagons, curtains drawn to hide those inside, and torches burned on poles outside the tinkers' tents, casting light like pools of warm gold. Beyond, moonlight and shadow and the Spine.

"Look on the Verge side of the Wound," he suggested abruptly. There, it was a thrust of stone, jagged and windswept, with its own crooked path from the lands below; a place worthy of dragons, if it didn't bleed poison and death. "You needn't climb or go close. Search the loose stones along its base. Some from the summit should have dropped there."

"A day's travel from our crossing," she protested. "Treacherous."

"There or here." Turn-born couldn't be trusted, he snarled to himself. They didn't listen.

But Sand gave a slow nod. "I'll send Flint and Chalk."

"Those two?" He scowled. "Why?"

"None safer." Was that a smile in her voice? "They can't agree."

And thus couldn't make expectations without the others. The dragon smiled.

The dog barked a warning.

"Hallo!" Tir, running to catch them, came to a quick and awkward stop when Sand and Wyll simply stopped to wait. "Wyll," he exclaimed, as if surprised. "Glad to find you. We've been waiting. C'mon back. There's beer," with solemn certainty.

The man's breath stank of the tinkers' brew, his surprise was feigned—nothing else in Marrowdell moved as the dragon did—and as for waiting? It was, Wyll realized with real surprise, a rescue.

"Beer na?" Sand chuckled. "Sorry, friend Tir. Riverstone's about to put in the corks. The harvest's just begun."

"Too right." Tir draped his arm around Wyll's bent shoulders. "It's time I showed my friend here where he's sleeping. C'mon, Wyll. They're stringing hammocks between the trees. S'all cozy."

Wyll didn't budge. "I'm not sleeping in a hammock."

"He's with us," declared Sand.

Tir's unwelcome arm tensed. Not as drunk as he pretended, the warrior, nor about to relinquish him to the turn-born. Which was a waste of gallantry. Faced with a hammock? "I'm sleeping with them."

"Hard work deserves a good rest na? We've room and bedding to spare, Tir. You're welcome too."

"That's very kind, Mistress." Tir stepped away from Wyll, now clearly concerned for his own situation. "But—"

"Very kind and generous," Sand agreed in a voice to end any argument. "Riverstone will tell Bannan. All to rest well for tomorrow na? Come."

Moments later, Wyll found himself standing in the trade tent, a blanket under his good arm, watching Tir.

The tent was lit by small trays of burning oil, set atop short metal poles arranged around the center trading area. The oil was mimrol, the poles of no metal found on this side of the edge, and Wyll found himself feeling unexpectedly at home.

He yawned. "I want to sleep."

"Not yet." The former guard, sober the instant Sand had bid them good night, was on some kind of hunt. He pulled apart piles of blankets, opened any unlocked trunks to rummage through their contents, and finally went on hands and knees to peer under the low table. He rocked back on his heels. "Ancestors Bound and Baffled. Nothing."

"What are you looking for?" the dragon asked wearily.

"I'll know when I find it." With that unhelpful answer, Tir circled back to the trunks.

Wyll ignored him, sending breezes to collect the best of the blankets—yling work, like the tent and the turn-borns' clothing—into a cozy nest away from any opening. After dealing with turn-born, he was tired, sore, and in a thoroughly foul mood, tonight, more than usual. That Jenn had been happy . . . that Sand wanted to help? He couldn't deny those were to the good.

That a turn-born believed he'd want to be this futile?

The dragon snarled and made his way to his corner. The only thing worse would be if the old kruar found out . . .

"Hear that?" Tir padded noiselessly to the door opening. "Ancestors Witness, it'll be those Ansnans. Up to some mischief in the dark."

"They study stars," Wyll said to be annoying.

"Horst, then, bringing his horse from yon field." As Tir eased open the door flap, the dragon heard hoofbeats.

But a little cousin had watched the old soldier slip away from the rest, going for his horse and few belongings, abandoning his post. Wyll supposed Horst was out of Marrowdell by now. Regrettable. He began the arduous process of lowering himself onto the tempting softness.

"Heart's Blood. What's he—Wyll. Wyll!"

There'd be no rest till he answered Tir's summons. Wyll straightened with an effort, and lurched across the uneven, too-soft floor of the tent. "What's wrong?"

The other pointed.

Reluctantly, Wyll stuck his head into the damp night air. The white shirt shone in the moonlight. "It's only Bannan."

"On a stolen horse." Tir's voice was low and grim. "Where's he going on it, that's what I want to know."

At the moment, he was going sideways, the horse sensibly unwilling to venture from its fellows in the dark, especially with kruar ahunting. Wyll grinned. Scourge's rider, defeated by a farm horse? Even riding the way Jenn rode Wainn's old pony, namely bareback and with a contrived rope halter, the outcome was inevitable. Sure enough, with a slobbery shake of its head, the horse settled into a resigned walk toward the commons gate.

The one leading to the ford.

"Do something," Tir said in his ear, his breath rank. "Stop him."

"Maybe Bannan wants his own bed too," Wyll said nastily and pulled back inside.

He was grabbed by the shoulder and hauled forward again. "With an ax?"

Wyll shrugged himself free. He supposed the object strapped across Bannan's back could be an ax, albeit a very large one. If he'd armed himself? "He goes for Jenn Nalynn," he concluded aloud. Scourge claimed the truthseer had been lured by the Wound, like any turn-born. "If he takes that road by night, he won't come back. I—"

"We have to stop him!" As Tir made to leap from the tent, doubtless to shout and cause a deplorable commotion, Wyll took hold of his belt. The man struggled, using very unkind language, but what a dragon chose to hold, he held.

Wyll sent a chill breeze to snap at the horse's head. As the animal shied, Bannan and ax flew in the opposite direction. Satisfied, he released the belt and Tir staggered from the tent, with a glare over his shoulder, to help his friend to his feet.

The horse trotted away with a relieved snort.

The dragon headed back to his nest, slowly enough that the two men, arguing in furious whispers, entered the tent first.

Bannan threw off his friend's hand, then saw Wyll.

He'd relish the dreadful pallor on the other's face if they were enemies, though the cold determination in those eyes might give him pause.

If he were a man.

"You would die for nothing," the dragon said bluntly. "The turn-born will search for her pebble tomorrow. Come and sleep." Then he smiled, a very small smile. "I promise no more toads."

"Toads—" from pallor to flush. "Heart's Blood. You were there." Bannan's hand pushed through his hair, an interesting array of emotions vying for expression. Guilt won. "Wyll, I—" the words stuck in his throat.

"Sir?" Tir looked from one to the other. "What's this about?"

"A blanket," Wyll answered with wicked satisfaction. "He made Jenn Nalynn happy on it."

For no apparent reason, Tir began to choke.

The truthseer's face went bleak. "All that matters now is saving her."

Had the man not listened? "Her happiness is—"

"Enough!" Bannan thrust out his hand as though to fend him off. "Leave be." He lowered the hand and his voice, shaking his head. "Just . . . leave it be."

There'd been no denying her happiness. What could have gone wrong? Wyll looked to Tir for an explanation, but the man's eyes were on his friend, and strangely sad.

The girl was home, that much he knew. Safe in her bed, he guessed. Wyll shrugged. The truthseer must have displeased her or failed as a lover. He would have to make the effort himself, then.

"The turn-born search tomorrow," he said again, firmly. "Get some sleep."

He turned to his nest, only to stop in dismay. A white moth was perched atop his blankets, a strip of parchment at the ready.

"A visitor." Bannan came to stand beside him, then went to one knee. "Marrowdell," he greeted the moth, giving Wyll an expectant look.

As if they should talk to it. As if anything to do with the sei was a good idea or safe. Sand had the right of it. Had he the courage, the dragon snarled to himself, he'd squash the moth and take the consequences.

It took a different sort of courage to ask, ~ What do you want? ~

~ I bring questions, elder brother. ~ Spoken like the small thing it was. Wyll wasn't ashamed to be relieved.

"It has questions," he said aloud.

Tir had come close. Now his forehead creased. "Ancestors Blessed, does everything here talk?"

"Don't scare it," Bannan cautioned his friend.

~ Tell me, ~ the dragon ordered.

The creature fussed a little with its wings, giving Tir a decidedly worried look.

Wyll summoned his own patience. ~ Pray continue, little cousin. ~

Mollified, the moth consulted its tiny scroll. ~ 'Who are you?' ~ it said in the girl's voice, sharp with fear. ~ 'Why are you waiting? What do you want from me?' ~

He tensed. The girl had confronted something.

The moth went on in its own voice, ~ Do you have the answers, elder brother? ~

The dragon scowled. ~ How could I? ~ he said irritably. ~ I wasn't there. ~

The moth tucked away its parchment and fluttered into the air.

~ Wait! Who would know? ~ He sent a breeze to force it back. Blankets tossed, the tent walls strained against their pegs; unaffected, the moth flew through the open door and was gone.

The truthseer rose to his feet. "What happened? What were the questions?"

"I'm not sure," Wyll admitted. "It overheard Jenn Nalynn. She asked: 'Who are you? Why are you waiting? What do you want from me?' Do you know the answers?"

"No." Bannan looked to Tir. "Jenn knows about the turn-born. That can't be it."

"First Ansnans, now moths with mysteries." Tir rolled his eyes. "Ancestors Bored and Baffled. To think, sir, I'd almost hung up my axes, this Marrowdell being such a peaceful place."

"Tir—"

"Don't have to say it. Sir."

Bannan shook his head and put a hand on the other's shoulder. "If I don't, you'll hound me for days. You were right. There's peril here as well as marvels. Though I'm not sure your axes will help. Wyll?"

He was tired, sore, and wanted his bed. Nonetheless, the dragon stayed where he was, frowning at Bannan. "Jenn said nothing to you of this?"

The truthseer raised an eyebrow. "I thought you were there."

"You took the blanket and ran."

Tir coughed.

"No. We—no. Jenn said nothing about someone waiting."

But a thought had struck the truthseer; Wyll could see it in his face. "What is it?"

"What's up the Spine—how sure are you it stays there?"

Despite his ignorance, or because of it, the man asked a terrifying question. "The trapped ones are caught within the edge itself and can't move," Wyll replied. "Not in either world. Be grateful. The last time they but flinched and Marrowdell bears the scars."

"What's trapped?" Tir asked sharply. "Who?"

"He means the hills," Bannan exclaimed, as if a puzzle had been solved. "The Bone Hills."

"No, sir." Tir stumbled back a step. "Moths can talk and dragons be men and yon river flow through the mill only when there's grain to grind, but this is madness. They're stone!"

"What they are, or were, or will be, only the sei know." The dragon grinned wickedly. "Still want your axes?"

The warrior collected himself with a ferocious frown. "They'd make short work of you, that's for sure."

Not as he should be. Wyll bristled. "You—"

"Peace!" Bannan interrupted. "If the hills can't move, what could?" he persisted. "This Wound. What is it?"

Another question launched straight at what was to be feared. Wyll couldn't decide if the truthseer's willingness to confront the worst was admirable or appalling. "The edge never healed in that place. What remains . . . what that means . . . no one knows. Those able to sense the Wound feel a profound dread." He let them see his shudder. "Some are drawn. Those lured too close are not seen again. Dragons," he hastened to add, "are not such fools."

"Yon path up the hill?" Tir ran a hand over his bald head. "I've gone past it day and night. Seems ordinary to me."

"Be glad of that," Bannan told him. His eyes narrowed. "I've only felt it at night. Why?"

"This sun counters it. Darkness gives it strength. Both. Neither. What does it matter?" His leg pained him, but there was always pain.

"Day or night. If you risk that path, you put yourself into the Wound and you won't come back."

"Jenn did."

"Are you not hearing, sir?" Tir snapped. "You can't go up there."

"If the turn-born fail, we've no other choice!"

Grabbing the fool by the throat to draw him close, Wyll bared his teeth and wished for fangs. He ignored Tir's attempt to intervene, ignored Bannan's hands as they battered at him. He waited until both gave in and went still.

Then, staring into the truthseer's defiant eyes, feeling his breath, he spoke with the hint of a growl. "I'll find another. Jenn Nalynn is my life and my duty, Bannan Larmensu. For her sake, for yours, don't attempt the Wound until I say it's her last hope. Give me till the Great Turn. You know I speak the truth."

The other couldn't nod or answer, but some of the defiance faded from his eyes.

"Well enough." Wyll eased open his hand and turned away, lurching in slow steps to his pile of blankets. He lowered himself down, used a breeze to draw another blanket over his head and body, and closed his eyes.

If the men murmured or moved, he neither noticed nor cared.

Tomorrow, he would cross.

For Jenn Nalynn.

TWENTY-TWO

BREAKFAST DURING THE harvest was early, hearty, and, above all else, full of excited chatter about the night before and the coming day.

Jenn picked at her plate, Peggs stared at hers, and Aunt Sybb kept lifting her mug of tea then setting it down gently, untasted. Up, down.

Only Radd Nalynn ate with appetite, but he did so in a forbidding silence no one dared break.

It was, Jenn thought, the saddest meal she'd ever forced down her throat.

Their father finished and pushed his plate away, rattling it over the cutlery.

Aunt Sybb put down her cup with a thud and splash of tea. As the rest of her family stared at her in shock, she said, lips thin, "At least we know."

"Sybbie—" Her brother made a quelling gesture.

"Don't you 'Sybbie' me, Radd Nalynn," she snapped, eyes afire. "And don't you sit there looking like this is the end of the world two days before your daughters' weddings." A nod to Jenn who tried to be inconspicuous. "And birthday."

He scowled and stood. "I'm for the mill."

She rose as well, her frail body straight and stiff. "All this time, we've waited in dread for Melly's family to send someone else. We both knew her ring wasn't proof. I wish Sennic had told us. He would have, but he feared you'd react like this—"

"He stole her body! He took her!" Radd's anguished cry startled the house toad from its hiding place under the heat stove. "Don't you understand? Melusine's gone . . ." Jenn and Peggs sat, pale and still, as their father sank down and sat, hands over his face. "And so's he."

Ignoring the toad, Aunt Sybb came around the table and placed her hands on his shaking shoulders. "Not from our hearts. Never from our hearts." She laid her cheek tenderly against his head. Her eyes found her nieces, then looked meaningfully toward the kitchen.

Peggs rose quietly, drawing Jenn with her. Once in the kitchen, she freed the curtain separating the rooms from its hooks and let it close.

Jenn sat on the ladder, her hands in her lap. Peggs stood by the sink and picked up a dish towel, then put it aside and went to trim the lamp. Sunrise was still but a lesser darkness behind the mill; late and later, with winter's coming. Uncle Horst was no stranger to the dark or to sleeping outside.

It didn't make it feel right, that he was out there. "He'll go to Endshere," she whispered. Find a bed, a hot meal.

Peggs' eyes were suspiciously bright. "He won't stop so close. I heard him speak once of Thornloe. It sounded like a place—a place he liked."

The great port on the Sweet Sea. As far from Marrowdell as a Rhothan road could take him. "He could go anywhere," Jenn said numbly. The world was too big.

"Ancestors Witness, we're his family." Peggs' chin threatened to quiver, then she firmed it and gave a determined nod. "We'll write. We'll tell him to come back. We'll send letters everywhere and surely one will find him. What's wrong with that?"

Jenn had shaken her head. Now she grimaced. "We don't know his real name; he won't use the one we do. Uncle Horst lied to Mother's family to keep me secret. Don't you see? He won't let himself be found by anyone. He'll make himself—" she shivered as she said the word, "—vanish."

"So he's truly gone." Her sister sighed and reached for her apron, tying it on with a quick sure bow. "Best we cook."

Jenn blinked. "Pardon?"

Peggs gave a wan smile. "It's what I do, Dear Heart, when I can't fix the world. I make sure people are fed. Haven't you noticed?"

She'd thought Peggs just liked cooking, which made it convenient for her not to, but this made such sense to her sore heart, Jenn rose to find a basket. "I'll get turnips."

And as they cooked, while Aunt Sybb consoled her grieving brother and the rest of Marrowdell roused to the harvest, she'd tell her dear and wonderful sister why there'd be only one Nalynn wedding on the Golden Day.

And why she must be with the tinkers, when the sun set on this one.

Warm soft lips moved over his eyes, nose, and mouth. She'd changed her mind and come to him and Bannan lingered in that wondrous waking moment until he realized those warm soft lips were also hairy.

He jerked up, furiously scrubbing drool from his face with a sleeve. The massive shadow that was the kruar's head lifted away with an amused nicker. Tir rolled over with a snatch at blankets and a muttered, "Bloody Beast." The pile over the dragon didn't stir at all.

Scourge had pushed his front half through the door opening, in so doing lifting most of the tent wall free of the ground. Before he could do worse, Bannan tossed aside his covering and got to his feet. "Outside. And have a care."

The kruar eased back out. He followed, rubbing his neck. The dragon hadn't broken it; he could have, easily. Whatever Wyll's seeming, no man had such strength. He'd have to offer thanks they were on the same side at the evening's Beholding.

Dawn was near enough to dim the Mistress and hide the Rose. Lamplight glowed in the Ropps' barn. Milking, he guessed, hearing a cow, and stretched with an involuntary yawn. Ancestors Weary and Worn, farmers slept less than soldiers. What life had he gotten himself into?

Closer at hand, their purr so low and intense he felt as much as heard it, the kruar mares stood together, chins on one another's backs, tails slapping lazily.

"Mine."

At the smug note to the breeze, Bannan's lips twitched. "Did you leave any rabbits?"

"Rabbits, yes." Scourge gave a purr of his own. "No wolves."

At least they hadn't gone for the village livestock, something he suspected had more to do with the kruar aversion to cattle than compunction. Was that why Marrowdell had no sheep?

A curiosity for another day. Bannan looked across the pond at the unlit Ansnan wagons, tucked against the tall hedge, and frowned.

Scourge bent his neck to follow his gaze. "Attack as they sleep," he suggested cheerfully, eyes red.

Bannan laid his hand on the kruar's shoulder, avoiding the fresh gashes. "We don't want to attack them."

"We do!" Scourge shook his head, drool flying, and showed his fangs. The mares lifted their heads and showed theirs.

He gave the bloody-minded beast an absent pat. "They may have what I need, old friend. A magic to cross into the Verge, if the turnborn won't help."

Scourge sidled from under his hand, turning to lower his head and stare. "What's this?" The breeze was hot and fetid with menace. "That dragon tricks you to your death, so he may have her!"

"We're both trying to save her. Wyll's not the problem." And might not be the only answer, he realized all at once. "What do you know about the Wound?"

The mares whined. Scourge lifted his head to aim one startled eye at Bannan.

"It's dangerous to those who notice it and draws them to their death. Heart's Blood, I know that much. I need more, Scourge. How to pass it safely—"

The breeze was chill enough to nip his ear. "You cannot. It bleeds."

The miasma he'd seen with his deeper sight, staining the silver road, came from the Wound. That it was blood of some kind? Ancestors Aghast and Fearful, he wanted to deny it was possible, but if the Bone Hills were other than stone, anything was. Bannan steeled himself. He had to know. "Wyll told us the Wound was where the edge hadn't healed. Is it a void?"

A lip curled in disdain. "You asked a dragon? They are oblivious to the ground until we pull them to our traps. Then, they care." Scourge lifted a hoof, let it drop without sound. "Kruar miss nothing. At the last Great Turn, the sei caught something in a trap of their own. Something hungry for turn-born. Kruar were first to find it, stuck within the edge. We named it the Wound, for it bled into both worlds. We couldn't—" the breeze turned pensive, "—reach the flesh."

Bannan's own crawled. "How can it be—how can it still bleed?"

Now he was regarded by the other eye, as if what he asked was so troubling, Scourge had to be sure of him. "My mates tell of changes during my exile. There came those able to feed on what the sei left in their trap. Kruar do not contest them."

An undying creature, fed upon by what the fearsome kruar avoided. Jenn Nalynn, being lured to it. Grimly, Bannan raised his eyes to the shadowed Spine. "What bleeds can die."

"Not always," the breeze in his ear warned. "And sometimes, not at all."

"Eggs?"

The dema lifted his plate with a pleased smile and nod. Despite his blue-black skin, Jenn had the impression Urcet blanched at the thought. The odemi, Panilaq and Kanajuq, weren't at the Nalynn table or any other. Apparently they'd had too much beer last night and nothing would wake them, leaving their masters to wander from kitchen to kitchen in search of breakfast.

Unless, she thought worriedly, they'd come straight to hers.

"Is there more tea?" Urcet asked. He'd emptied a pot already, touching nothing solid. She hadn't noticed he'd been much into the beer, but perhaps the tinkers' unusual brew didn't sit well on so foreign a stomach.

Or he hadn't slept. She'd wished away Palma's dreams and not thought of these men. Jenn glanced guiltily at Qimirpik, relieved to see he appeared his jovial self. He'd left off his hat, seeming well at home.

"I'll get more," she told Urcet. If he'd dreamed, so be it.

Hers had been dark. She'd tried to stay awake, to hold on to the smell of Bannan's warm skin, the touch of his hands and mouth, the way she'd felt; she'd fallen asleep, to plunge into a nightmare where every time she reached for him, her fingers slipped over stone.

Aunt Sybb resumed the conversation paused by eggs and tea. "Last night had its pleasant moments," she said delicately. "I'm sure you'll enjoy the upcoming festivities even more, though certainly our little village can't match the Hac Y. You must be sorry to miss it."

Jenn returned with the tea to see Urcet press fingers to throat and bow his head in gracious acknowledgment. "You know our ways, Lady. I'm honored."

"The Mahavars regularly host merchants and diplomats from Eldad," Aunt Sybb explained, giving her a nod of thanks as she poured. "The Hac Y celebrates intellectual achievement, does it not? Most admirable."

"Thank you. Accomplishment should be rewarded." Something guarded left Urcet's face and he smiled for the first time. "Eld treasures scholars and inventors. During Hac Y, entire cities fly the banners of their most successful innovator. Structures rise in honor of the finest minds. I myself hope for the day—"

"And so you should," Aunt Sybb slipped in adroitly as he paused for breath. "While our celebrations aren't on such a scale, I daresay you've never attended a Rhothan wedding on the Golden Day Blessed by our Ancestors, let alone four at once."

"I, for one, can't wait.' The dema waved a forkful of egg. "What do you say, Urcet? Collect the Celestial's Tears, then dance the night away in the company of these sweet brides?"

Jenn fumbled the teapot. " 'Tears?' "

"Dema!" The Eld half-rose from his seat. "We agreed not to speak of this."

Twin outbursts at her table, coupled with peril to the tea, drew Aunt Sybb's eyebrows together in mute disapproval. Qimirpik merely chuckled. "Sit, Urcet. There's no keeping secrets in a friendly little place like this, is there, good lady?"

"Quite impossible," the lady agreed, bending a finger to indicate the teapot would be safer on the table, near her hand. " 'Celestial's Tears?' So your visit for the eclipse has a religious connotation." She steepled her fingers, eyes aglint with implacable interest. "Do enlighten me."

Jenn knew that look. It was the one she'd receive if late, or messy, or without shoes, and meant any explanation best be compelling. Hoping to stay for this one, she did her best to be unobtrusive, but Aunt Sybb glanced at her with another look she knew.

"I'll be in the kitchen," she said faintly.

Once there, Jenn put a finger to her lips as her sister looked up, to let her know there was something worth overhearing. Not that they should. Aunt Sybb expected the pretense of privacy; when she entertained a guest in her parlor, though it was simply the front half of the room, the sisters would make sufficient noise in the kitchen to prove they weren't listening or interested. More often than not, Jenn would slip out the kitchen door and run to her meadow, while Peggs busied herself with pie.

This time, without a word, the two stood close behind the curtain. Even now, Peggs had a distracted, thoughtful look. Her sole response thus far to hearing the sum of Jenn's dreadful secrets had been to agree Hettie would appreciate the dish towels. Jenn knew her sister. Faced with a problem she intended to solve, Peggs Nalynn would say nothing until she had a plan.

Though it seemed unlikely she'd find one this time, Jenn was obscurely comforted to see her so-wise sister chewing a lock of hair.

She wasn't by what she heard.

"My anxious colleague and I," the dema was saying, "share a curiosity about magic. I won't bore you with how the old ways became the roots of Ansnan philosophy and today's modern and more reasoned intercourse with the Celestials . . . unless you've an interest?"

"I studied," Aunt Sybb demurred, raising her nieces' eyebrows. "By magic, I assume you refer to the pagan Rites of Petition—what we'd call wishing."

"Oh-ho!" From the sound, the dema slapped his thighs. "See, Urcet? No need to obscure our intentions. Indeed, good lady, we are on a wondrous quest, with such a rite to cast. Will it work? Will it not? Only a valiant effort can answer. The place must be right. The time. You're familiar with what ancient Ansnans believed of an eclipse?"

"That the sun hides earthly sin from the Celestials, allowing it to flourish by day. Whenever the Celestials fear for the souls of the faithful, they push the moon in front of the sun so they may look down from the sky instead. Tea?" A pause. Jenn could picture their aunt's graceful, dignified hands lifting the pot and pouring. "Much like checking on errant children, wouldn't you say?"

Urcet laughed.

The dema sounded a little less happy. "More than look down, good lady. An eclipse was when the Celestials opened their gate for those pure of soul, so they would live forever in paradise."

"There, Urcet, our faiths part company," Aunt Sybb commented dryly. "All of us, pure or not, await the end of life in the sure comfort of becoming Blessed Ancestors to those who follow."

"To check on them, like errant children," the Eld echoed and laughed again. "We Eldani have no commerce with stars or our dead. Though my mother would warn me that if I skipped a lesson, the house grini would bite off my nose while I slept."

A nose intact and adorned with a gold bead. Fascinated, Jenn wondered if there was a connection. Not that it mattered. This rite of the dema's? The time and place for it could only be the eclipse, atop the Spine. But these tears they were to collect? It was all she could do not to wish the dema to the point.

"As an astronomer, I view such beliefs as allegorical. Stars cannot touch the ground or order the moon." The dema grew cheerful again. "Everyone knows the Celestials witness and judge our lives from their lofty place in the sky."

"You've come to be judged, then, Dema Qimirpik."

"Me?" His astonishment seemed sincere. "I attempt pure intention, good lady, with all goodwill, but a pure soul? A lifetime of discipline and penance is no surety of that. No, as my deeds are witnessed, let me be so measured." A hesitation, then, "Though I confess to you, the great Refuge of the demas was built for that purpose, long ago. Those who lived therein sought nothing else than paradise."

"And settled for nothing less," Urcet said lightly.

"What do you mean?"

Jenn looked at Peggs, who gave a tense nod. Was this it?

The dema coughed. "Stories, of course, grow in the telling. Stories of blame for disgraceful deeds can be trusted the least. Still, those from that time have common threads. All agree the demas of the Refuge came to believe themselves pure and grew impatient for paradise. Seventy-one years ago, yes, there was an eclipse like the one we anticipate. So much is fact, is it not, Urcet? According to story, these demas gathered in the highest of their towers and, waiting until the moon hid the sun, and in view of the Celestials, cast a Rite of Petition to force open the gate to paradise."

They'd tried to cross into the Verge, Jenn thought with sudden fierce joy. They'd had a way to do it. A way these men might possess. Bannan had hoped for a wishing and here it was. Words and tokens both. Hers for the taking.

So Peggs wouldn't read that determination in her face, Jenn turned back to the curtain.

"Predictably, the endings are the same. The Celestials, enraged by the arrogance of these demas, did stretch forth a Hand to wipe the Refuge from the earth." Qimirpik chuckled.

Peggs touched her hand, her face pale. She shook her head in mute warning and Jenn gave a nod to show she understood. Something terrible had happened that first time. Kydd had guessed. Wyll had known. It mustn't happen again.

But it wouldn't, if she took charge. She'd be careful.

"A cautionary tale indeed," Urcet said dryly. "We hadn't expected to find its inspiration the instant we saw Marrowdell."

"How so?" Aunt Sybb asked rather grimly.

"The Celestials' pale and mighty Hand grips the valley to this day." Qimirpik's chuckle became a boisterous laugh. "Good lady, your face. Oh, please don't think us mad. What you call the Bone Hills, and name the Fingers and Spine. Unusual rock, yes, doubtless exposed by a quaking of the earth. But to those consumed with guilt and remorse, who saw their world crumbling around them? I think you'll agree they could seem the stuff of stars, come alive."

She didn't know about stars, but the Bone Hills? Jenn's heart pounded. She'd looked within and seen something there. They'd crowded her in the carrots, which she'd hoped a dream until one forced itself into the Nalynn loft. That, she was unhappily sure, had been real, however strange. Did that make them alive?

She certainly hoped not. From Peggs' tight lips, she felt the same.

From the parlor came an unusual clatter, as though someone dropped a fork.

"Your pardon, good lady," the dema said with instant remorse. "I don't mean to upset you."

Aunt Sybb didn't drop things. Peggs and Jenn exchanged worried looks, but before either could move, there came a controlled and firm, "A fanciful interpretation indeed. Urcet, you've not eaten. Would biscuits and honey be more to your taste?"

While their aunt disapproved of eavesdropping, she did expect such hospitable suggestions to be overheard. So at Urcet's murmured thanks, Peggs hurriedly put biscuits on the stove to warm, paused to rattle dishes, then returned to the curtain.

The dema continued. "The surviving demas and odemi scattered to the far corners of Ansnor, to live out their lives in disgrace. Mondir, the holy city that supplied the Refuge, was abandoned to—forgive me, good lady—abandoned to the heretics of Rhoth. Given the times, you understand, their wild tale was given credence it wouldn't find today."

"Yet here you are," Aunt Sybb said, pouncing like a toad on a mouse, "with a rite of your own."

"The tales have their basis in truth," Urcet said impatiently. "Tell the lady of the Tear."

"I was getting to that," Qimirpik replied. "It was claimed the survivors died horrible deaths. Or they went mad. Most intriguing? All returned with magic in their blood. To heal. To see the truth. To create fire from air. Not unheard of in Ansnor, or Rhoth, for that matter, but to affect so many, at once? Hard to prove or disprove, since these people hid themselves away. But you can see why we'd be interested."

Something was burning. Jenn sniffed, then pointed in alarm at the stove. Shaking her head, Peggs ran to retrieve the biscuits, putting aside the couple with blackened bottoms.

"The Tear."

"Yes, yes. A dema brought with her a remarkable stone. She claimed it was a Tear shed by a Celestial, in grief over their—"

"White as a pearl," Urcet interjected. "It fit in a man's palm, yet no one could hold its weight more than an instant."

Her pebble?!

Jenn stifled a gasp and Peggs clutched the honey pot to her bosom.

"There were other claims," the dema said testily, as though his colleague was telling the juiciest parts. "That the Tear caused terrible dreams. That magic failed near it. It was deemed a punishment visited on the guilty. Not long afterward, the stone disappeared. Buried. Stolen. No one admits to knowing. We're here," he finished, "to summon another."

She might not need to cross at all, Jenn thought, heart pounding with hope. With this rite, she could call her pebble to her.

"Why would you want such a thing?" From Aunt Sybb's tone, she wondered more about the sanity of her guests.

"For proof," said Urcet boldly. "These rites and wishings . . . your pardon, good dema, good lady, but are they not the bread of charlatans and fools in both your domains? But the Tear?" Jenn could hear the hunger in his voice. "What they did in this valley at the last eclipse brought forth something of demonstrable power. Power like the magic of Mellynne.

"We of Eld must understand such magic," he went on, impassioned. "The Naalish are rumored to employ it as others use fire or steam, yet refuse to share or trade their knowledge. A matter of contention between our governments. But now we have new and wise friends in Ansnor, and magic? That's to be found, right here."

Aunt Sybb laughed gently. "What's here is a quaint little village, nestled among interesting, but hardly exceptional rock. You've traveled for nothing, good sirs, other than the eclipse. The Naalish spread tales to impress foreigners. You've been fooled. There's no such thing as magic, here or in Mellynne."

A bold assertion, even for their aunt. How could she ignore the wishing and Wyll, let alone the toads? Jenn frowned in puzzlement.

Peggs finished loading a tray with the basket of almost burnt biscuits, the honey pot, and a bowl of the dried fruit Aunt Sybb relished for her constitution. She canted an eyebrow at her sister, mouthing the words "Trust her" as she stepped around the curtain into the parlor.

Peggs had the right of it, Jenn realized. However much Aunt Sybb disapproved of Marrowdell's magic, she wouldn't give such a secret to these strangers.

"That may be what we'll prove, good lady," the dema responded tactfully. A pause, as if he shrugged. "Then, as you say, we'll have an excellent view of the eclipse and, not to forget, dance at your weddings."

"But if the rite works, there'll be a concrete result. A manifestation." Urcet, however reluctant at first, seemed bent now on convincing Aunt Sybb. "Not as it was when we were tested yesterday. Something to take with us. Proof to silence nonbelievers."

Take her pebble? A chill wind shifted the curtain and rattled the pots behind her. Jenn bit her lower lip, fighting her outrage. The air warmed and she briefly closed her eyes in relief.

"Thank you, Dear Heart. Good sirs, two biscuits surely. Some of the fruit. I insist. A most beneficial start to the day." Then, as Peggs came back around the curtain, "So I take it what you would do here has not been approved by either of your peoples. Why," Aunt Sybb asked with deceptive ease, "should we?"

"We mean no harm—" the dema began.

"I'm no fool," her tone sharpened. "I fear you may well be. If this magic of yours works, what's to say it won't bring a second catastrophe to Marrowdell?"

"If you believe—and we do not—" Qimirpik emphasized, "—that the rite cast by the demas of the Refuge was in any way responsible, be reassured, Lady Mahavar, please. That they made such an attempt is anathema to all Ansnans." He blew out a quick hard breath. "Never, never, would we do so. May the Celestials witness and judge. All I seek is the Tear and, in all honesty, I seek it to satisfy my own curiosity concerning its nature."

"While I share no gods with my esteemed colleague," Urcet added smoothly, "the rite we wish to perform is a simple finding spell, attuned to what we've learned of the Tear. Cast at the eclipse, far from the village, and at the highest point we can reach. It will be utterly harmless."

If they believed any magic harmless, it proved how little they knew. If hers could so easily get out of control, their rite could as well. Jenn doubted either of them had any idea what their magic would do, only that they hoped it would do something.

Worse, she suspected what Urcet wanted wasn't the same as the dema. Qimirpik, other than being a foreign person of different beliefs and a little bewildering at times, she judged overall a pleasant and decent sort. The Eld? Urcet, she feared, was after an accomplishment to impress his domain. For that, he wouldn't settle for a stone. He'd want whatever power could tear down the Refuge and fill people with magic.

The pebble was hers. It wasn't selfish, but true.

Her eyes met Peggs. They nodded as one.

The dema and Urcet mustn't do any magic in Marrowdell.

The only magic, Jenn resolved, would be hers.

Before dawn, the commons filled with the bustle of those making ready to harvest the first of the two fields on the far side of river. Wyll being still buried in blankets and the tinkers not in sight, Bannan and Tir took advantage of a communal porridge pot left on the table by the gate, helping themselves as well to tea and honey. They took this welcome bounty to a bench from last night.

When done, Tir gave a satisfied grunt. "Ancestors Kind and Generous, they feed us well, sir. I made sure to tell your sister. Speaking of sisters . . ." He produced a rumpled envelope. "Care to read what yours said to me?"

Bannan regarded his friend over the rim of his cup. "Not particularly."

"I can read it to you."

"Don't bother."

Replacing his mask only emphasized the mischief dancing in Tir's eyes. "But there's an entire page on your taste in women. Sir. And in such language!"

"Heart's Blood!" The truthseer half rose to his feet, then sat back down and made himself go on more calmly. "I'm in no mood for commentary. Hers or yours." He rubbed the back of his head and managed a rueful smile. "At least Lila didn't order you to drag me back." Though he wouldn't have been surprised.

The mischief became something darker. "I wish she had."

"Too late." Bannan put a hand on Tir's shoulder. "I'm glad you're with me, old friend."

Blue eyes narrowed. "Someone's to make sure you don't go doing anything stupid. Sir." Then gleamed. "Not on your own."

"I appreciate that."

The former guard stood. "I'm for the mill."

Bannan nodded. "Keep watch."

"Oh, I always do, sir." Tir gave a grim laugh. "Tho' here, I'm never sure what for, one day to the next."

"Trust the toads."

Tir stared at him, then left, muttering under his breath about proper watchdogs and what was wrong with cats?

Bannan pulled out his own envelope. Leaning his elbows on his knees, he held the precious thing in his hands as he gazed across the river. Dawn's blush had reached the mounds of the Spine, painting one side a pretty pink, leaving the other drenched in black. "Ah, Lila," he whispered. "I wish you were here, too."

He'd read her letter by the light of a turn-born's lamp, before falling asleep beside a dragon.

He pulled it out, and read it again.

From Baroness Westietas, Lila Marerrym Larmensu, of Vorkoun
To Bannan Marerrym Larmensu, of Marrowdell

Little Brother, if this reaches you unsealed, by all means cut something important from the person who gave it to you or I will. With a dull knife.

Salutations

So now you're a farmer.

You never did grasp the difference between a weed and a flower. Or a sword and scythe. Be careful with the tools. The north's no place to chop off a foot.

Can't say I saw that coming, you settling on the land. Thought you'd wind up a magistrate or librarian. The family could use a librarian. Suppose there's time for that yet. I'll send the books you've requested but one. Hard as it is to believe, there's not another copy of Talnern's Last Quest *in all of Rhoth. You have appalling taste, little Brother.*

But the best of companions. Don't tell Tir I said so. His letter? Ancestors Treacherous and True, it was a masterpiece of guile and blunt speech. Be careful of that man. I was almost afraid to respond lest he think I was proposing.

Dragons, is it?

Bannan snorted and shook his head.

It'll interest you then they've been in my dreams of late. Impolite creatures. Flying through walls. Coming up through carpets. Speaking—shouting—not that I understand, but I know somehow they speak. Deadly things. Beautiful. Wild. I'd be smitten if they didn't look liable to eat the boys.

Gifts of yours, little Brother? I'd be glad to know they're real. This world could use dragons.

As for this Jenn Nalynn. Don't try to fool me. We're both very good at protecting what matters most to us. I read your truly incredible descriptions of this woman. Heart's Blood. Did you think I wouldn't see the shape of what's missing? She's not safe to love. Not a rival. Something about her.

Tell me, little Brother. If I see her in a dream, will I be afraid or glad?

Do you even know?

There was more. About the family, about Vorkoun. A new invention of Emon's. She'd ended with "Give Scourge something bloody for me."

"Do I know?" Bannan asked himself, then gave a sure nod, putting away the letter and getting to his feet. Jenn Nalynn would never be something his sister should fear.

He put his dishes with Tir's in the bucket of soapy water by the table, bowed once in the direction of the Nalynn home, then went to the commons.

The tinkers were hard at work already; five tinkers, not seven. Bannan guessed Flint and Chalk had crossed the ford while they'd been at breakfast and looked for them down the road, but they were already out of sight. They searched for Jenn Nalynn's pebble where he couldn't. If they succeeded, she'd become one of them in truth.

Ancestors Witness, she couldn't know what that meant; none of them could. She'd lost hope, that was all. He'd hope for her.

And more. Bannan walked briskly up the small slope to the caravan. The curtains were open, the three odemini staring out. Ignoring the dolls, he went around to the back of the largest wagon. "Fair morning," he called, rapping on the door.

The only response was a choked sort of snore from underneath. The truthseer bent down to find the source. Panilaq lay on a heap of blankets, her mouth agape, with Kanajuq sprawled over her legs. The pair appeared more unconscious than asleep. "Sweet dreams," Bannan told them as he stood.

He lifted the brass door latch, toyed with it a moment, then let it fall. No use rifling through their things until he knew what he sought. That meant a conversation. Unfortunately, the harvest would keep him busy—and across the river—for the day. He'd have to wait for the evening meal, an awkward time to try and get the dema to himself, but it might be his last chance. If Horst was right about Marrowdell and the nightmares, the newcomers could be forced to leave.

If Scourge was right about the Wound and what fed . . .

Hope, he reminded himself.

The truthseer returned to those gathering, drawn to join Dusom and Davi by the smith's wave. "I've no one to spare for the mill," the latter was saying, busy with a buckle on Brawl's harness. "Horst's gone. Flint and Chalk haven't shown for work." He straightened. "Bannan here's to drive Flint's wagon—"

This was news. "I am?"

"So I'm told." Davi grinned. "Riverstone's taking the other," he continued. "Cynd's to fork grain. Your friends will have to wait or go on their own."

"They can wait." The elder Uhthoff looked more relieved than concerned. "The Spine's not somewhere I'd send them alone."

It was somewhere he'd tried to go, armed with fury, a stolen ax, and no good sense. Bannan winced. What had he been thinking? He owed Jenn better, not to mention Roche's poor horse.

As for the kruar. Truth on the surface, but Davi wasn't beyond a joke. "I'm to drive the tinker's wagon?"

"Riverstone told me you could handle them."

Dusom gave the kruar a doubtful look. They stood peacefully enough, one pretending to chew grass.

More likely a bone. Scourge had a disconcerting habit of tucking one of those deep in his jaw for later.

A breeze slid along his neck and found his ear. "They've promised to be horses for you." An afterthought. "They won't talk. Not to prey."

"Charming," Bannan muttered under his breath. Louder, to Davi. "Oh, we've an understanding." Horses, were they? He walked to the nearside kruar and gave it—her—a friendly pat on her darkly dappled rump. An ear twisted back, a lip curled over a fang, but she tolerated him.

"A braver man than I," Dusom commented. "I'll tell Qimirpik, then get to the mill. Radd's not doing well today."

Bannan nodded in sympathy. Horst's leaving and his reason hung like a pall over the otherwise lovely morning. The men readying the wagons were subdued and unsmiling. The tinkers were no happier. They didn't like being apart, whether from distrust or honest concern.

He'd lain awake most of the night, remembering the soft feel of her skin, the passionate throb of her heart against his, the full, rich taste of her lips. Remembering that Jenn loved him. Trusted him. That they were going to fight for her life together.

And, if they won, that might be the end.

He'd heard that terrible truth in Jenn Nalynn's voice, carried it like a weight now. If they succeeded, she'd change from flesh and blood to—to whatever a turn-born was, inside.

Skin of glass, heart of stone, lips of light.

Would she still love him? Could she?

Hope, he told himself.

"Bannan?"

"Sorry," he said numbly, then rubbed his head. "Wasn't the best night."

Dusom's face darkened. "No." He cheered with a determined effort. "Ancestors Witness, there's no cloud without sun behind it. We're Beholden you're here, Bannan, you and Tir." His gaze rested on his brother and son, standing with Anten. "And look to happier days ahead."

As he turned to leave, Bannan reached out to stop him. "Dusom," he said quietly. "Have a care with your guests."

The elder Uhthoff gave him a keen look. "Because they seek to do magic that might tear Marrowdell apart again?"

The truthseer let his hand drop. "Kydd."

"My wise brother." Dusom grimaced. "Once more, I hope he forgives my doubt. No, this warning came today, from his soon-to-be aunt by marriage."

"The Lady Mahavar?" The truth it was. Bannan raised a brow. "I thought she didn't believe in magic."

Dusom chuckled. "To live in Marrowdell is to believe." Bannan glimpsed a bit of Wainn's joy in his father's eyes. "Our Sybbie finds magic somewhat like her youngest niece. Perplexing, unpredictable, and impossible to keep in shoes. She prefers, shall we say, not to encourage it." His gaze narrowed. "Which in no way makes her foolish. That lady's courage is greater than any of ours, as is her wit. Don't underestimate her."

"Never. I've a formidable sister," Bannan admitted, "and I'm sure even Lila would defer to Lady Mahavar."

"Good. Keep count of your fingers—" with a nod to the placid-seeming kruar, "—while I keep my eye on certain foolish men."

Bannan bowed to the man who'd raised Wainn and taught Jenn, brushing his fingertips over the cool tips of grass. He began to see how Marrowdell had weathered so much, so well over the years.

"Please. Where is he?"

Unblinking, the house toad regarded her and said not a word.

Not that it spoke, but Jenn knew she would hear it if it had something to say. She sat beside it on the rim of the village fountain and regarded it back. The toad gradually paled to match the stone, save for its dark limpid eyes.

A bee droned by. Birds sang. The sun warmed her toes. Despite everything, or because the turn-born intended it, Marrowdell was its normal self.

And hid her dragon. She'd looked for him in the commons, but found only Satin among the trees. He wasn't in anyone's kitchen or the orchard. There'd been no time to look elsewhere, between making lunch and filling the cistern—which had made her cry, a little—and she'd so hoped when she'd found the toad.

The unhelpful toad. "I must talk to Wyll." Any more of this and she'd be tempted to push it in the water.

"He's busy." Wainn sat down on the other side of the toad, which closed its eyes in bliss and leaned against his leg. "How are you this day, Jenn Nalynn?"

Was Wyll busy or the toad? Guessing the former, Jenn sighed to herself. As for how she was? "More knowledgeable," she offered wryly. "Aren't you driving Davi's team?"

"Roche and Devins are unloading my wagon at the Treffs'." Wainn gave her a sidelong look. "Wen sent me. She said you've lost hope."

Jenn pressed the heels of her hands against her eyelids. "She's right," she admitted. She let her hands fall to her lap and opened her eyes. "I'm not giving up. I won't. I'll do what I must. It's just—after . . . I—I don't see any future. I can't."

"How can you?" His forehead wrinkled beneath his hat. "It hasn't happened yet. While you wait for it, Wen says to do happy things, like Kydd. Get ready for your birthday. Dance."

All summer, she'd waited to be nineteen, to be adult at last and free. Now? She'd stay eighteen forever if she could. About to say as much, Jenn hesitated. Wainn hadn't mentioned her wedding, yet she'd told only Peggs and Bannan.

The toad. She winced inwardly. "You know I'm not getting married with the rest."

"I do. Wen does." Wainn's frown deepened. "Does Wyll?"

"Not yet." Jenn tapped the house toad lightly between its closed eyes. "That's why I'm trying to find him."

Wainn's face cleared. "Wyll's busy."

She couldn't help but laugh. "So I hear."

"You should ask," he told her, serious again. "Before you change his future. Ask him."

Advice he'd given before; advice she should have followed. Jenn shook her head. "This is different, Wainn. I'm giving Wyll his freedom."

Someone shouted and he leapt to his feet. "The team's ready," he said with an eager grin.

Then Wainn Uhthoff gazed down at her, something ancient and stern in his eyes. "Ask him if freedom's what he wants."

She'd have asked Wyll but, either by accident or some dragonish design, Jenn hadn't found him by the time she was needed to set out the evening meal. Tonight would be peaceful, with no formal Beholding or dance. Master Riverstone would play his pipes and there'd be quiet conversation and perhaps the odd game, but most would seek an early bed.

The meal was the main event. Savory steam rose through slits in the great meat pies, the practical destiny of leftover ox. The Treffs had made their squash soup, swirled with cream and spice. The Ropps put out platters of cheese and baked apple. There were roasted vegetables and thick slices of bread.

Jenn couldn't eat. She'd let the others take lunch to the field, though it meant missing the chance to see Bannan. She'd cleaned house and helped Aunt Sybb pack, trying not to grow melancholy. The day had sped by, as if sunset pulled the world toward it.

She could feel it.

"What's that about?" Hettie whispered, pointing with her chin as the two put out plates.

Jenn looked down the trestle table to where Riss and Lorra stood arguing in front of the soup. Suddenly, Riss threw the ladle on the ground and walked away.

"Who knows?" she replied, though she could guess. The soup was—had been Uncle Horst's favorite.

An unexpected tap turned them both the other way. Old Jupp tapped the table leg with his cane a second time, to be sure of their attention. His wisps of white hair stood on end, though he was impeccably dressed, and he waved his ear trumpet impatiently. "Well? Where is he?"

Exchanging a worried look with Hettie, Jenn asked, "Is there anything we can do for you, Master Jupp?"

At the first word, he'd lifted the trumpet and aimed it at her. When she finished, he scowled thunderously. "You can answer my question. Where is he? Where's Horst? The harvest's no time for him to be off on one of his fool trips."

"Last night . . ." Hettie began unwisely.

"I was there," he snapped. "And heard. Drunk and maudlin. Little wonder, between weddings, babies, and foreigners. I'm sure Radd and Dusom took matters well in hand and talked sense into him. Tell me where Horst is, please." This last with such absolute authority Jenn felt her shoulders straighten.

She looked past her reflection in the trumpet. Despite the stern set to his wrinkled face, Jupp's eyes were desperate. He knew, Jenn realized, shaken. He knew about Riss and Uncle Horst and feared the worst for her.

Her courage failed. "If I see him before you do," she promised, "I'll let him know you're looking for him."

Hettie, ever kind, nodded. "Meanwhile, Master Jupp," she said, her eyes suspiciously bright, "would you have time for Palma?" She beckoned to the young woman, standing near the kettles. "Has Riss told you? She's writing a book about us—about the exiles. I know you were busy this morning—" Unsaid, afternoons he napped. "Here she is." Before the poor man could do more than open his mouth.

Palma curtsied, still drying her hands on her apron. "Master Jupp. This is an honor."

"I've no time," he said testily. "I'm looking for Horst."

The innkeeper read the situation at once. "Then I won't trouble you, good sir," she said smoothly. "I've borrowed a copy of Lehman's *Avyo As She Was*. Master Dusom assures me there's an entire chapter on—"

The trumpet shook in Old Jupp's hand. "Lies, all of it. Poorly written ones. I've the documents to prove it. You come with me at once—what's your name?" She murmured it. "Palma. I insist!"

Jenn gave her a grateful look as the pair left. "Hettie," she asked thoughtfully, her hands full of forks, "How was Palma this morning?"

Hettie's wide smile was as glad as she'd ever seen it. "Ancestors Blessed, Allin had to wake her for breakfast. I thought Zehr would burst with joy." Her smile flickered and faded. "The only time he looked happy. Oh, Jenn. We didn't need his house!" All at once, she looked ready to cry. "I tried to tell him."

"We all saw," Jenn assured her. She put an arm around her friend's shoulders. "Think how much comfort Uncle Horst will take, knowing you and Tadd and your beautiful baby—" winning a tremulous smile, "—are living happily ever after in his house."

Hettie hugged her back. "I will." She sighed, then her smile firmed. "Thanks to you, Good Heart, we'll have towels and sheets. Ancestors Witness, my needlework's fit for curd bags at best. You're sure you've kept enough for yourselves?"

"She's sure," Peggs said as she joined them. She shed her apron and tucked it under the table. "Jenn? Time to go."

"Go where?" Hettie raised her eyebrows. "Now? We're not ready."

"We won't be long." Her sister slid a determined arm through Jenn's. "Mistress Sand's asked us to help bring something from her tent."

Such "somethings" often being exotic sweets, Hettie's face lit with anticipation. "Hurry, then," she said, shooing them along.

Jenn let herself be led, arm-in-arm. "Peggs. What are you doing?" she whispered urgently, forcing herself to smile at those they passed.

"Getting you where you need to be, Dearest Heart," her sister said calmly. "There's another two pies in the oven," she told Gallie, who nodded. "Check the pickles, please?" to Covie.

Then, low and fierce. "Did you think I'd let you go alone?"

Jenn squeezed her arm, drawing Peggs close. "I think," she said unsteadily, "I've the best sister in the world."

Her sister squeezed back, then freed her arm in order to give Jenn's braid a tug. "I do," she countered. "And I won't let you be without a home."

Admittedly a consequence of not marrying Wyll Jenn hadn't thought through, but it wasn't, she decided at once, her sister's problem. "I'll find—"

"No need, Dearest Heart. It's settled," Peggs said in that she-knew-best voice. "Kydd and I can live with his brother."

"It's not settled," she protested. "I'll find somewhere. The Ropps could use my help." With Hettie gone, she could share a bed with Alyssa. "Or the Treffs."

Another step and both said, "Not the Treffs," at the same time.

The sisters exchanged shy looks. "I mean it, Peggs," Jenn insisted. "I'll find a place. Besides—" she found a smile, "—who'd cook for Poppa?"

"You could learn," Peggs rejoined, but they both knew who loved to cook and who didn't.

And both knew, but wouldn't say it, that where Jenn lived in two days' time wasn't as important as making sure she did.

The lane bent past the Treffs, to meet the main road. The sisters left the shade of the apple trees, their feet silent on the packed red earth, and fell silent themselves.

The tinkers' tents rose above the hedge surrounding the commons, golden in the late day sun. She didn't need to see the light; the by-now familiar emptiness within told her. The turn was coming.

"They're back!" Peggs said, startling her.

Davi's wagon rattled first through the commons gate, muddy drops flying from Battle and Brawl's feathered feet. More had dried in pink spots along their flanks and clung to the wagon's wheels and front.

Wainn stood on the stalk-laden wagon, reins in hand, grinning face well-freckled. He looked to have jumped in the river himself, perhaps to shed the worst of it, but it hadn't, Jenn thought as she grinned and waved back, done much. Cleanliness would wait till the wagons were unloaded and teams cared for; the waiting meal would doubtless prompt most to the quickest possible wash of face and hands.

Wainn turned into the Ropps' lane, their loft next to be filled. The first of the tinkers' wagons came right behind, its pile of stalks topped with dusty harvesters who jumped down to help or hurry to their respective homes. The grain wagon followed, passing the sisters on its way to the mill.

"Jenn," Peggs said carefully. "Could that be Bannan?"

The final wagon came through the gate. Its driver was the right height, but caked in mud from head to toe. His team was no better. Seeing them, the driver smiled, teeth white against the cracking layer of dark red.

A smile she'd know anywhere. "It's Bannan." Though she felt unexpectedly shy, Jenn waved with her sister. "I wonder what happened."

"Maybe they missed the ford," hazarded Peggs.

True, the river was deeper, its bottom silt, to either side of the broad, unmissable stone path.

She'd like to have lingered, to watch Bannan take the wagon to the Ropps', but there wasn't time to waste. "Let's go."

Stepping carefully to avoid the mud, the sisters made their way into the commons. There was no sign of Wyll, but Qimirpik and Urcet were doing something with their telescope, the servants hovering nearby with tools. Five luxurious chairs had been arranged under the awning of the caravan's largest wagon, the dolls reclining in three. Disappointingly, blankets covered the dolls up to their veiled heads, hiding any detail.

The Ansnans made the turn-born seem normal.

"Which tent?" Peggs asked quietly as they approached the tinkers' encampment.

"I don't know." It hadn't mattered before. During the tinkers' brief observance, everyone else in Marrowdell would be preoccupied with cleaning up from the day's work and, of course, getting supper.

Centermost was the trade tent, where Mistress Sand held court. Nearest was the one in which Clay and Tooth plied their trades; farthest where the tinkers slept. Before the sisters had to guess, the flap of the sleeping tent opened and Riverstone beckoned them inside.

Kruar as horses? The truthseer'd had no complaint, up to the moment when, on the last trip across the ford, his team had gleefully plunged wide to drench him with muddy water.

He spat grit. The near kruar turned her long head to regard him, he could swear, with amusement. Both beasts were coated in mud; knowing Scourge, he imagined they relished it. Having thought of his old friend and the pranks he'd played over the years, Bannan's sense of humor returned. "My thanks for the shower, ladies," he said with a bow, and began to strip their harness, wasting no time. The turn was coming and they wouldn't appreciate a delay on his part.

Teeth snapped near his ear; a hoof just missed his boot. He grinned as he pulled free the last strap and gave the kruar a hearty slap on the rump. "Be good."

She growled and kicked, not too close, then both broke into a trot. The other four joined them, jostling as they went through the commons gate. When a deep roar in the distance brought answering squeals of delight, Bannan laughed and shook his head.

His smile faded as he gathered up the mud-caked harness. Jenn had seen him in all his filthy splendor and smiled, if too briefly. She'd be with the tinkers by now; he'd no doubt Peggs would stay with her, no matter what the tinkers thought.

Earlier in the afternoon, from the field, he'd seen Flint and Chalk return. Had they succeeded?

The village youngsters, energy unquenched by a day spent delivering water, stood nearby with soapy buckets, waiting to clean the leathers. Bannan handed the kruars' harness to Cheffy, then, with a hasty apology, took one of the buckets. Stripping off shirt and boots, he closed his eyes and dumped hot soapy water over his head and shoulders.

As he used his palm to clear suds from his eyes, Alyssa, giggling, handed him a rag and a bucket of rinse water. "Ancestors Blessed," he said fervently. Another moment, then he was, if not clean, at least free of the worst of the river bottom.

The hopeless boots he left with the harness. The shirt received a quick dunk and rinse. He wrung it out as he walked, then pulled it on wet. His hair, he clawed back from his face and left to drip down his back.

Riverstone had made it clear he wouldn't be welcome at the turn.

They were welcome, Bannan Larmensu thought grimly, to try to keep him out.

Mistress Sand set four cloth bags on the small chest serving as a table, then spread her fingers over them. "Only you will know. Is it here na?"

Jenn exchanged a final look with Peggs. There'd been no comment from the assembled turn-born when both sisters entered the tent, other than a chill to the air she'd denied almost without thought.

Her sister gave her a brave smile and nodded.

She lifted her eyes to the others. Sand sat on a pillow on the other side of the chest, the rest on stacks of blankets arranged around this central open space. As sleeping arrangements went, the tinkers' were disappointingly ordinary.

As spectators, they were anything but. The turn-born revealed themselves, each body filled with its particular substance, each head topped with white hair, every face a mask over light. Peggs, Jenn realized almost at once, couldn't see the change, not yet. She would at the turn.

"Sweetling."

"Yes." Jenn's eyes found Flint and Chalk. "Before I look, I want to thank you."

The expressions on the masks couldn't change, but they inclined their heads.

Her feelings a tangle of anticipation and dread, Jenn tipped the contents of the first bag onto the chest. As smooth white stones rolled out, she gasped. They'd found her pebble and more! Her mouth watered.

The stones stopped rolling, to became ordinary rock.

Jenn swallowed and reached for the next. When she opened the bag, something small and white leapt out, skittering across the chest in a blur of too many legs. Peggs squeaked as it dropped from the chest to run over her skirt. Kaj, curled up and asleep, aroused in an instant to give chase, barking furiously. There was a scramble, a moment of digging, then a decidedly final crunch.

"Not that," Jenn said faintly.

Her sister gave her an appalled look.

Before matters worsened, she grabbed the third bag and dumped its contents.

A globe of purest white landed on the chest with a loud "crack." Before her horrified eyes, fissures grew over its surface, deeper and deeper, then, all at once, giving way.

An orange jelly slowly, steadily, inexorably oozed forth, followed by a "plop" as a round green yolk joined it.

Jenn turned her head to glare at Flint and Chalk. "A white pebble," she said, making the words as clear and distinct as possible.

"Don't blame them, Sweetling. What looks one way in the Verge na?" She clicked her tongue. "Might not here. Try again." Her fingertip poked the fourth and last bag closer.

Wary of another egg, Jenn opened it with more care. But what came out when she gently tipped it wasn't an egg or a stone or even something that scampered.

It was fine black ash.

Her heart gave a sickening lurch of recognition.

Ash that sparkled silver-white, looked at a certain way. Glittered emerald green, another.

"Jenn? Is that—is that what I think it is?"

Jenn shook her head at Peggs, not because her sister was wrong, but that wasn't the question to ask. That wasn't it at all. She looked up at Sand. "Where did they find this?"

"They searched near the Wound. On the Verge side."

Jenn didn't let her eyes fall, though the brilliance where Sand's should be burned and left images dancing at the edges of her sight. "And you believe them?" For once, she welcomed the frustrated anger building inside her. The turn-born understood emotion. They'd feel hers, even if they stopped what it could do. "I made this." Satin and hair, Melusine's toy block, her map. She rubbed her finger in the ash, touched it to her tongue. It tasted as she'd thought it would.

Like Wyll.

"I made this," Jenn repeated harshly. "I used it at Night's Edge to wish my friend into a man and it disappeared with him. It wouldn't be near the Spine or the Wound. It would be wherever Wisp fled."

"His hiding place." Sand slowly rose to her feet. "I was there at the sei's summons. I watched one complete your wish. For the sei, I sent the dragon back to Marrowdell. Why na?"

The others, disturbed, stood as well. Riverstone shook his head emphatically. "We don't question the sei, here or in the Verge. They punish the dragon lord as a lesson to his kind. Don't give them cause to punish us!"

"I'm no fool." Sand turned to stare at Flint and Chalk. "But you na? You were to take the dragon's advice, not go to his home."

"Trust that old fool?" Chalk protested. "Going near the Wound is madness."

"We couldn't take the risk," agreed Flint.

"Now you think as one na?" Sand made a disgusted sound. "Tomorrow, I'll go myself."

She couldn't, Jenn thought, seeing the same fear cross Peggs' face. Without Sand, the others could agree that she was too much trouble, too dangerous. To be rid of her. For all her brave talk, she had little doubt the turn-born could do what they pleased.

"Flint and I will do it," Riverstone announced. "He can be spared." With a glare of his own at that turn-born.

Just as Jenn went to thank them, a cramp struck and she doubled over, her arm sweeping the chest clear. Peggs took hold of her. "It's happening!" she cried.

"Close. Not yet," Sand said briskly. "Tooth. Clay. A place for our Sweetling, so the turn passes her quickly."

The turn-born gathered blankets and made them into a bed. Jenn sat down, arms pressed to her middle, Peggs at her side. When Sand brought her a tall cup, she asked hopefully, "Beer?"

"Stronger. Drink it. All of it."

Jenn raised the cup, grimacing at the smell. The dark liquid wasn't anything pleasant. "What is this?" she delayed.

Peggs put a reassuring hand on her back. "Ancestors Witness, it can't be worse than one of Covie's remedies."

It could, Jenn suspected, but nodded and took a cautious swallow. Sour as unripe sweetberry, with the consistency of syrup, it tasted purple, which wasn't a taste yet suddenly was, and burned like a hot coal to her stomach. "Whoa," she gasped.

"From home," Riverstone explained.

The Verge, unblended with Marrowdell. Remembering the rose petals, Jenn drank as quickly as she could. Her eyes watered from the heat of it and her hands began to shake. At once, Peggs' fingers covered hers, helping hold the cup.

"Don't look," Jenn urged, meeting her sister's compassionate gaze. "During the turn. Close your eyes."

"You brought her here," Sand disagreed. "Why else na?"

Not to have Peggs see her as she became. "I didn't—she came—"

"Hush, Dearest Heart." Peggs lifted her head to regard the turn-born, spots of red on her cheeks. "I came for my sister," she declared. "And to see the truth. You've lied to us from the beginning. When Kydd tried to convince the rest to leave, you lied to him too—or worse—" with a grimness Jenn had never heard in her sister's voice before. "You lie and you hide. If you're the friends you claim to be, you'll show yourselves to everyone!"

"My. My. My." Sand chuckled and lifted a hand to the other turn-born, bringing it around in a grand gesture, palm up, at Peggs. "See it na? Melusine's fire! You want to know why we hide na?" She leaned close; Peggs didn't move. "Because we're like Marrowdell itself. Too strange. Too different. Only a few can bear it. Your mother understood, Sweetlings."

"Our mother?" Shocked, Jenn hardly felt the next cramp. "What do you mean?"

"She knew," Peggs said, almost a whisper. "Our mother knew what they were."

"That's why she hid on your wagon." Jenn's eyes widened. "She knew you could take her where Horst couldn't follow." Like Wen and Wainn. Like Bannan. Poppa'd as much as told her outright. How could she not have understood? Melusine Nalynn had loved Marrowdell because she'd seen it for what it was.

"Melly was our friend." Riverstone stepped up. His crystal mask had the strong features of the face he showed the world, its cleft chin and hooked nose, but none of its warmth. His voice, though, was tender. "We helped her roses. You can't imagine our grief—"

"It's time," Sand broke in. "Sweetling. The milk na? Should help. It does us. We'll see na? You must lie still."

Jenn laid down, her body so rigid she couldn't tell if the stack of blankets made a soft or hard bed. Peggs sat beside her on the floor, taking her hand with a valiant smile. "I won't leave you, Dearest Heart."

And she wouldn't, no matter what she saw. Not her sister. Jenn rolled her head to look in the direction of the setting sun. "It comes."

The tent grew dim. The turn-born, perhaps for her, perhaps because they must, appeared as tinkers once more. All seven stripped their gloves and stood with arms outstretched, as if daring the light to expose them.

Flint, Fieldstone, and Clay were nearest the door.

The turn found them first.

Peggs' fingers clenched around hers as their faces became masks, their hair shocks of white above. She was silent as that otherworldly light poured from the holes once mouths and eyes.

Though she flinched, just a little, as their arms became glass filled with flint, brown stone, and red clay.

The turn passed and three rather self-conscious men lowered their arms.

Jenn braced herself as the turn came closer and closer, but it didn't help, nothing helped. She cried out as pain ripped through her . . . lost Peggs' hand, or did she lose hers . . . her hand was found again and warm . . .

Then the turn closed in and she emptied . . .

"Jenn!"

Tinkers. Turn-born. Peggs, her face distraught. The dog, teeth bared. Bannan didn't care who or what else was there as he rushed to the figure writhing in agony. "Jenn!"

He dropped to his knees. Ancestors Despairing and Doomed, she was fading before his eyes, her dear face barely discernible, her skin little more than a hint of purple. The blankets beneath showed through her arms.

Peggs, with incredible courage, clung to that shell of hand with both of hers. Her eyes flashed to him. "Help her!"

The only magic he possessed was the truth. How could that—

Jenn's ghostly face turned to him as if she spoke. As if she knew he was there. Wasting no more time in doubt, the truthseer desperately looked deeper.

And found her! Her eyes were like the edge of night itself, purpled with magic. Against the cream of her skin, her lips were rose red and parted in wonder. Trembling with relief, he bent to press his lips to hers.

And touched nothing.

Bannan flinched back. The horror in Jenn's face mirrored his own. "I see you," he told her, told himself. "You're not gone, Dearest Heart. I can see you."

She just wasn't here.

But she lay on top of the blankets, that much he could tell. And Peggs held something, if only the memory of a hand. "It's almost over," he promised, looking to the turn-born to be sure.

Mistress Sand, busy pulling on her gloves, gave a small nod. "The light from the Verge fades sooner than your sun's. There. See na?"

A small hand slipped into his, like a bird to its nest.

Bannan glanced down to find Jenn Nalynn gazing up at him. "I stayed this time," she said with such relief his heart ached. Then her eyes suddenly twinkled. "You're dripping on me."

"At least it's not mud," he said, a ragged edge to his voice. He helped Peggs ease her to sit. Their eyes met over Jenn's head, shared a fear.

For she felt . . . different. Fragile, as if she might shatter. His fingers were loath to leave her shoulder.

Jenn covered them with hers. "It's over," she said gently. "I'll be better in a moment."

Heart's Blood. "What about tomorrow?" He looked to Flint and Chalk. "You didn't find it," he accused, rising to his feet. "Why?"

"Why are you here, truthseer na?" Riverstone demanded, stepping in front of the others.

Sand clapped her hands. "What's done, is," she said sharply, looking from Bannan to her fellow turn-born. "What's waiting na? Supper and those hungry to eat it." More gently, to Jenn, "Tomorrow."

Jenn nodded, climbing to her feet before he or Peggs could move to help her. "My thanks."

Sand shrugged. "Thank us then."

As the three headed out of the tent, Bannan going last to be sure Jenn was steady, he wasn't surprised when Sand beckoned him to stay.

"I'll take care of her," Peggs assured him when he hesitated. As Jenn frowned, ready to protest, her sister hooked a firm arm through hers and pulled her along. "We can't leave Hettie to serve my pies, Dearest Heart. She cuts the pieces too big for the plates."

The flap dropped behind them.

Bannan turned to face the seven turn-born. None looked happy. Fair enough. Neither was he.

"For what you did to help her," he said with the villagers' short bow, "I'm grateful."

"You, last night na?" Sand pursed her lips and made a kissing noise. "We—" a gesture to the rest, "—enjoyed."

The truthseer flushed.

"We meant no trespass." Riverstone shrugged. "Jenn Nalynn controls her passions, but hasn't learned to keep them private. She will."

"She'll still have feelings?" It came out before he could stop it.

"For you na?" Sand asked astutely. Not waiting for an answer, she sat cross-legged on the floor, the panels of her dress draped neatly over her tall boots. The men followed suit. "Sit."

Bannan sat, schooling his expression to polite interest, unable to keep his heart from pounding like a drum.

"A trade, truthseer," Sand proposed. "Our Sweetling hides something from us. Say what and I'll tell you what to expect in a turnborn's bed."

"I think not." Though, Ancestors Tempted and Torn, his curiosity on the subject was close to pain. That Sand mentioned the topic at all? A good sign. "I like surprises," he finished.

Sand raised a brow. "Not all are pleasant."

He forced a chuckle. "That's the way of life."

"So it is." She considered him, then tried another approach. "Being what you are, you know when I speak the truth. Am I right na?"

Trap or opportunity. He nodded warily, prepared for either.

"What you saw happen to Jenn Nalynn at this turn was far worse than has happened to any of us." A finger went up; her first truth. "Isn't terst, might be why. Born between worlds, might be why. We don't know." Another finger rose; the second truth. "We can help her through tomorrow's turn. The Great Turn na?" Her other hand lifted, turned palm down. "We cannot. It will last beyond her enduring and past any help of ours. All we can do is provide comfort. Do you understand na? Unless Jenn is complete and whole, she will empty and be gone before your sun shines again. Is this the truth na?"

Unable to speak, he gave a terse nod.

Riverstone leaned forward. "On the Day of Balance, truthseer, we leave the village at midday. We need time in your barn to pack what remains there—with your permission na?"

The trunks? He waved them past the inconsequential. "You have it."

"The Great Turn will take place two hours past dawn," Tooth volunteered. "We will remain in our tents."

"If tomorrow we fail her," Sand told him, "bring her to us for the Great Turn. We will ease her end as best we can."

"Let her die. That's your advice?" Bannan's hands wanted to grab the turn-born and shake her. He flattened them on his thighs. "You can help Jenn—you must!"

"My my my." She had him and knew it. "What you know, tell us now. Keeping a secret's worth nothing if she dies. I love her well," she added, looking him in the eye. "What more can we do na?"

The turn-born offered him the truth, dared him to accept it. With an inner apology to Jenn Nalynn, he did.

"Jenn has heard a voice. It's told her she must help herself. That to find what she needs, she must cross at the Spine during the Great Turn."

A daunting silence filled the tent.

"She doesn't know how," Bannan pressed. "If you want to help, teach her!"

Sand rocked back and forth, her gloved arms across her middle. "Even were we willing . . ." she said at last, then looked to Riverstone. "Tell him."

"During a Great Turn, the edge becomes brittle, like thin ice." The tinker shook his head ominously. "We don't dare to cross then. Jenn cannot."

"Disturbing the edge could wake the trapped ones!" this from Flint, in a tone of near panic. "We could all die!"

The dragon's fear. What sort of place was Marrowdell, that the very hills could come to life? The truthseer pretended a calm he didn't feel. " 'The trapped ones,' " he echoed. "The Fingers and Spine. The Bone Hills and Marrowdell. Your names?"

Sand stopped rocking. "The first settlers'," she surprised him by saying. "The landscape troubled them and they left, but the names na? Stayed behind." She nodded at Flint. "He's right. What's exposed in this world has its roots in ours. Disturb it na? We don't dare and won't. She mustn't cross then."

Something else said she must. A game, Bannan decided with rising anger, tossing Jenn Nalynn like a nillystone across a table—but for what? "If it's so dangerous, why does Marrowdell want her to do it?"

" 'Marrowdell.' " Sand drew a finger across closed lips as she studied him, eyes a blaze of light. The finger dropped. "You know of the Wound." Not a question. "Yet you, like the dragon, believe our Sweetling hears another voice. A voice to obey."

"Sand—" Riverstone shut his mouth to keep in the rest of his protest. The other turn-born sat, grim and still.

"They let me speak," Sand observed. "They know I must. What we are, na? Cautious, careful, safe. Know our power and our place." She raised a finger, wagged it. "Know not to disturb those greater. Wise na? We think so. In the Verge, the sei are greatest of all, man of truth. If—and I still do not believe—if the sei are here and call our Sweetling na? We will not interfere." She tipped over a palm. "If the Wound calls our Sweetling, we won't aid her to that death."

He'd gambled and lost. There'd been but a faint chance; nonetheless, her refusal felt like a blow. Bannan swallowed what he might have said and bowed his head graciously.

"To act, we must agree," Sand said more gently. "Understand na?"

Meaning she couldn't help, but the rest couldn't harm. The turn-born stood aside, for better or worse. He nodded.

Riverstone rose to his feet, the rest doing the same. "We'll hunt the pebble at first light," he promised. A gesture sent Tooth to retrieve a tall bottle. "For our Sweetling. It may soothe."

"I'll make sure she gets it," Bannan said with a short bow.

He thought they were done, but when he went to the door, Sand slipped past to lift the flap for him. "Jenn must not make that journey alone," she whispered. "How brave are you na?"

He met the turn-born's blazing eyes. Whatever she read in his produced the smallest of smiles.

"Well, then," the erstwhile tinker said loudly. "To supper, before the food's gone!"

"We shouldn't have left him," Jenn argued, though it was futile trying to sway Peggs when she felt firmly in the right.

Sure enough. "We're the ones late for supper. Will you hurry?"

Already half-trotting to keep up, she dug in her heels and pulled. Hard.

Her sister twisted around, dark hair swirling like a cloud. "Heart's Blood!" Suddenly, her face crumbled. "Oh, Jenn—"

They hugged one another right there, in the middle of the commons, Peggs weeping on her shoulder.

"It's all right. He saw me," Jenn whispered. "Bannan saw me and I was—" Saying "real again" wouldn't comfort her sister, though it was true. Something in his eyes had kept her safe, kept her here. "I was better this time," she finished lamely. "Please, Peggs. I'm fine." Then a horrible thought struck her. "You aren't upset because—because of how I looked, are you?"

Peggs pushed back. "Of course not!" She sniffed. "I was shocked to see Mistress Sand and the others for what—as they are—but who wouldn't be?" Pulling a newly embroidered handkerchief from her bodice, she blew her nose with a vengeance. Over it, her eyes were red and troubled. "I couldn't feel your hand," she mumbled. "I thought I'd lost you, Dearest Heart." She lowered the 'kerchief. "I didn't let go. I wouldn't."

"I know." Jenn kissed her sister's damp cheek then tipped her head to the village with a small smile. "Hettie and the pies?"

The elder Nalynn drew herself up. "What are we doing still here?"

Waiting for Bannan, Jenn thought wistfully, with a look over her shoulder. But there was no sign of him outside the tinkers' tent and Peggs, reminded of responsibility, wasn't to be denied again.

When Devins wasn't looking, Jenn slipped the pie from her plate onto his and stepped back into the shadows. His was a healthy appetite. She'd none, but it had been easier to let her plate be filled than to argue, especially with Peggs.

A hand took her empty plate. "Try this."

"Bannan."

He didn't smile as he held out a cup. "A gift from our friends."

The gift was having him back and safe. Jenn took a quick swallow. More of the purple-tasting milk, it settled in her stomach, easing the ache there. As for Bannan? "You saw me, Dear Heart," she said softly, cradling the cup, knowing what drew those fine lines at the corners of his mouth and tensed the muscle along his jaw. "You made me real again."

At this, the brown of his eyes took on that apple butter glow, but there was nothing happy in the look he gave her. "You were almost gone."

"Well, I'm here now." Somehow, she'd become the one to offer reassurance and comfort; perhaps, as Aunt Sybb promised, facing her trials had given her strength. Jenn put her arm through his. "Come with me."

She was tempted to lead him deep into the welcoming night, to kiss away his unhappiness and forget her own. Resisting that urge was difficult indeed; it didn't help to be quite sure that if she asked, or merely hinted, this remarkable man she loved with all her being would sweep her up in his strong arms and carry her—well, somewhere close, because if they reached that state she wouldn't want him tired nor could she possibly wait.

Jenn found herself breathing a little faster than she should.

Being sensible, she led Bannan through the apple trees to where Riverstone and Frann sat playing a quiet song. After dipping a polite finger in the water, they took a seat on the fountain wall, where everyone could see them, but not overhear a quiet conversation.

They didn't touch, they couldn't, for so many reasons but above all because neither would risk hurt to Wyll. She laid her hand on the stone; casually, he put his nearby.

Which shouldn't have been intimate, but, oh it was, since there was a warmth along the side of her little finger which could only be from Bannan's hand, and surely he felt the warmth from hers which led to another distracting series of thoughts about warmth and feeling she let flow and tingle, it being a silly, happy thing to sit so properly and think otherwise.

Wen would approve.

Reluctantly, Jenn withdrew her hand and put it on her lap. They had matters to discuss. She could think of only one reason the tinkers had kept Bannan back, and it was important he not listen. "Mistress Sand tried to convince you I shouldn't try to cross, didn't she?"

"She pointed out the difficulties, yes," Bannan replied easily, his eyes on the musicians. "What she really wanted was to know what you've kept from them."

"Oh." Jenn studied his profile but he'd assumed his dauntingly polite public face. "You told her," she guessed. "I don't mind," she added quickly. "Mistress Sand is a friend, I'm sure of it."

"She is. I tried a trade," he admitted, which was, as she thought of it, a very apt approach with a tinker. "In return, I asked them to teach you to cross. They refused. They don't know what speaks to you or what it might want. That you hear this voice? That it wants you to cross? They're terrified, Dearest Heart. I heard the truth of it."

Hadn't the dragons howled that the turn-born forbade her to cross, back when she'd understood none of it, or herself? Jenn blew out the breath she'd unconsciously held and collected herself. "Thank you for trying. We'll find another way."

His mouth curved in a smile. "That's the spirit."

"I may have already," she said. "Dema Qimirpik has an Ansnan wishing—a rite—to bring my pebble here, from the Verge."

Now he did look at her. "Your pebble?"

"He calls it a Tear from the Celestial, but when they described it—Bannan, it's the same, the very same. Urcet wants it to prove there's magic, but it's—" Jenn stopped before "mine."

"Yours," he agreed, finishing for her. "Well well. I'd planned to talk to our fine guests tonight. This will help."

"They don't know," she cautioned. "What magic really is. What it can do. They're—" one of Aunt Sybb's sayings came to mind, "—playing with fire inside a full tinderbox, that's what they're doing. We can't allow it."

"Then, Dearest Heart, we'd best take away their matches, hadn't we?"

Her smile started deep inside, where the turn-born remedy had eased her emptiness, rising through the heart he'd filled with his, until it was all she could do to only smile at Bannan Larmensu and not throw herself in his arms.

"Jenn Nalynn," he whispered huskily, smiling himself. "'What magic really is.'"

If she kept gazing at him, and he at her, they'd cause, if not scandal, then certainly interested comment. She broke away first, deliberately looking for her dragon in the gathering. "I haven't seen Wyll today. Have you?" He might be avoiding her for a reason, now that she thought of it. "I hope he didn't sleep in a hammock."

"Sand made us welcome in her tent," Bannan explained, easing her concern only to add a new one. "Wyll sent the toad, by the way."

Jenn covered her mouth with her hand and stared wide-eyed at the truthseer.

Who grinned, unrepentant. "He wanted to warn us someone was coming."

Wyll approved, that meant. Of—of—but how could he? Her thoughts flew. Because he didn't want to marry her, that was why, which would be sad in a way but really for the best. Or was it because he was a dragon inside and thought differently about . . . about what shouldn't, she began to frown, have been discussed by the two men—maybe three if Tir'd been there—in a tent! "What exactly did you—"

She stopped as Aunt Sybb approached. Bannan stood and bowed.

"A fair night, Bannan. Jenn, dear—" The lady paused, looking from one to the other. "Your pardon. Am I interrupting?"

"We were just—what's wrong?" she asked in sudden alarm, for Aunt Sybb's hem was dusted with flour, her shoes red with mud, and her eyes were full of worry.

"Your father. I can't find him. He has to eat."

Bannan was quick to offer his arm as the elderly lady wavered on her feet, helping her to sit. She murmured her thanks and looked up at Jenn.

Who flushed with guilt. How had she not noticed her father's absence? Too concerned with herself, that's what. "I'll take him a plate—"

"He's not at the mill." Almost fretful. "He wasn't at home. You have to find him."

Jenn took her aunt's hands in hers, dismayed to find them ice-cold. "I know where he'll be," she assured her gently. "Please. Rest here."

"Go," Bannan told her, sitting beside Aunt Sybb. "I'll find Peggs and see both safely home."

She nodded gratefully and left.

First, to gather some help.

By lamplight, the roses were blood red and black, trailing over the lines of roof and wall, nodding overhead. She'd need a ladder to reach one; not that the flowers would let themselves be picked.

"I'm here for Poppa," Jenn whispered. The roses bent to regard her. "He thinks Melusine's gone and it's breaking his heart."

Leaves rustled.

She lifted her hands. "He needs you."

There was a snap somewhere in the darkness overhead, then a single bloom tumbled down. It landed, dew-damp flower and stem, across her palms, and had not a single thorn. Jenn closed her eyes and breathed in its heady scent. "Thank you."

Holding the rose, she walked through the circles of light cast by porch lamps, then left those behind. The soles of her feet knew the road, her urgent will shortened it; she arrived at the opening to the ossuary within heartbeats and wasn't surprised at all.

The path was dark, but a glow lit the end. As Jenn went toward it, she heard a sound she couldn't place at first, then did.

A shovel?

She stepped into the opening, uncertain what she'd find.

A man stood waist-deep in Melusine's resting place, her name writ in lamplight across his bent back, sod and clods of dirt splayed around him like battle wrack. As if sensing Jenn's presence, he slowly straightened and turned. Sweat and tears streaked the flour on his face into a savage mask, and she didn't know who he was.

The scent of roses floated in the air, more than one rose, more than a hundred. Jenn took a desperate, deep breath. Saw him do the same.

All at once, the stranger's face became her father's beloved one, though gaunt and worn. Leaning on the shovel for support, he looked up at her as if he couldn't believe his eyes. "Jenn?"

Rose in hand, she slid into the hole. "Oh, Poppa." She took him in her arms and held tight. "We've worried," she scolded through her tears. "You missed supper and Aunt Sybb went all through the mill looking for you. I told her I'd find you."

He held her then, patting her back gently. "You found me being a fool. There there. You shouldn't have climbed down, Dearest Heart. Look at your dress. Come now."

They helped each other out of the hole and collapsed, more than sat, on the dirt-splattered meadow grass. A moth landed above Mimm Ropp's bones, but offered no comment. A pair of eyes reflected the lamplight; a house toad sat nearby. Comforted, Jenn handed her father the rose.

Taking it, he closed his eyes and inhaled slowly.

"Poppa, didn't you believe Uncle Horst?" she asked carefully.

Her father let out his breath and gazed at her, spots of red appearing on his cheeks. "I wasn't looking for your mother's bones."

"Then why?"

"Her ring. She wore it, always. The thought of it in the ground . . ." His voice shook.

True, one properly buried bones, not belongings; Rhothans did, Jenn reminded herself, newly aware there could be other ways considered equally respectful by those who followed them. "Maybe Uncle Horst wanted to leave you something of her, here," she ventured.

"Who knows what went through his thick head?" but gently said. "I'd hoped to find it. You and Peggs have so little of your mother and now, now we've less than we thought. Your pardon," this in a more normal voice. "Excuse the rambling of a foolish old man. I've troubled you and my dear sister for nothing."

Radd's hands were filthy, the nails were broken and bleeding; he hadn't just used the shovel. The hole he'd dug was deep and dark, its sides crumbling, and what soil showed in the light was riddled with small brown stones aglint with gold. To find a ring in that?

Bannan believed. "'What magic really is,'" Jenn repeated softly.

Despite her father's protest, she jumped into the hole where her mother's bones had been and reached down, fingers touching the dirt.

And dared to believe too.

Her fingers closed over something small, cool, and smooth. She froze in place, afraid to look in case she was wrong.

"Jenn?"

Holding her breath, she straightened and held out her open palm. A ring lay there, its intricate weave of gold glittering in the light, its tiny roses with their ruby hearts sparkling as if new.

Eyes aglow, Radd Nalynn plucked a rose petal and used it to pick up the ring then enclose it, safe from the dirt on his fingers. He trembled as he tucked the tiny bundle inside his shirt.

He helped Jenn from the hole, keeping her hand in his. "Ancestors Dear and Departed. You're so like your mother, Dearest Heart. It gladdens my heart you've her gifts too." He smiled at her puzzled look. "Melusine could find whatever was lost; bring what was lost home again. She brought us to Marrowdell. It wasn't an accident," gently, as if she'd objected, but she hadn't. "We came where she belonged. Where we all did."

So she wasn't as she was by a turn of light, not entirely. Some of her magic, maybe the best of it, was part of her.

"Come, Poppa. We'd best get back," Jenn said, feeling lighter than she had for days. "Aunt Sybb's waiting."

He grimaced. "Wait till Sybbie sets eyes on the pair of us."

Nothing was different, but everything was. Jenn giggled and the moth lifted into the air. Her father laughed. When they finally stopped, gazing at one another, she saw signs of a new peace in his face.

"If we hurry," she suggested, "we might make it home before she does." Which they surely would, if she helped shorten the road.

"You go ahead. I can't leave this," he said ruefully, nodding at the hole and dirt.

About to help, Jenn glimpsed movement. Three toads came to squat by the first in the lamplight. A rustle in the hedge promised reinforcements. "It'll be looked after, Poppa," she declared.

With a curtsy to Marrowdell's toads, Jenn Nalynn took her father home.

Bannan Larmensu found Dema Qimirpik under a trestle table. His legs, at any rate. They were bare, as were the Ansnan's feet, and flailing about as the man attached to them attempted to crawl in farther. Given the dema's proportions were more generous than the table's, the mood of those watching ranged from perplexed to amused. The few items on the table had been hastily rescued.

The truthseer looked for Urcet. The Eld stood at a distance and, by his expression, would prefer to be anywhere else, with anyone else. Embarrassment at his colleague's antics or impatience?

A satisfied grunt, a perilous tip of the tabletop that had more than a few grinning, then Qimirpik wriggled out. Though it was educational to discover that a dema wore skin and nothing else under his formal robe, what mattered was revealed hanging stoically from his hands.

A house toad.

The spectators' mood changed in a flash. "Let it go," someone ordered gruffly. "Leave it be," from another.

Qimirpik's smile faded. "I mean no harm," he protested, holding the creature gently to his chest. The toad stretched a long and lazy foot, otherwise unperturbed. "It's remarkable—so large." He appealed to his unsympathetic audience. "The eyes—they're unusual—"

"Put it down!" This, sharply, from Gallie Emms.

"He won't hurt it," Bannan said to the villagers, taking pity. "Unusual and revered, good dema," he told the man. "I suggest you observe Marrowdell's toads from a distance."

"As you wish." With great care, the dema bent to lower his captive to the ground. The house toad struggled free just before it touched, hopping back under the table with an offended croak.

Crisis averted, the evening's last stragglers broke apart, heading for their homes and bed. Bannan stayed by the dema. He'd seen Aunt Sybb safely off earlier with Peggs, both concerned over the miller, and known he could do no more. The tinkers had gone to their tent at the same time.

Slick as butter, Tir Half-face appeared beside Urcet with two cups and a bottle. Bannan didn't care where his friend had obtained the brandy and hid his satisfaction as the pair left together, presumably after a comfortable spot to enjoy the fine drink.

"My thanks." Qimirpik brushed at his robe. "I intended no offense, but it's difficult to avoid mistakes when one travels. Local customs, mores, strictures. Stars above, I swear they multiply the farther I go from civilized climes. I'm sure you've noticed."

Bannan's smile faded.

The dema gave him the briefest of looks, then deliberately went back to fussing over the hang of his pleats. "Have I mentioned I'm good with dialects?" he continued. "A hobby. Your friend with the mask—from the hills of Upper Rhoth, without doubt. The tinkers are something of a puzzle, I'll admit, but I'll solve it. I always do."

Perhaps not this one. "What have they told you of themselves?" the truthseer asked curiously.

"Little enough," admitted the dema. "Those of that profession aren't the most forthcoming, of course, but these have traveled well beyond what you'd expect, that I'd swear to."

True, if not in the way he likely meant. Bannan lifted a brow. "How do you know?"

"Observation, my good Bannan." Qimirpik tapped a finger beside his eye. "The bracelet Mistress Sand tried to sell me? Such amber is found in Mellynne's foothills, nowhere else. Master Riverstone's pipe? Ah, I've seen one similar but once, and that owned by a fellow dema whose family came from a valley so far to the east, I vow, it's hard to credit you're still in Ansnor. The people are white as snow and bray like asses instead of laugh, stars be my witness. You don't believe me?"

Settling his hip against the table, Bannan grinned. "They're traders," he argued, beginning to enjoy the man despite himself. "Bangles and pipes change hands, move from place to place. It's not surprising."

"Not like the surprising Jenn Nalynn, hmm?"

At the abrupt switch, the truthseer tensed before he could stop himself. Grateful for the lamplight, he managed a casual, "In what way?"

"Why, the good lady speaks Ansnan as my mother taught me!" Qimirpik slapped his thigh and nodded. "Moreover, Urcet claims her grasp of Eldani, a difficult tongue to master, is beyond reproach. To find such talent and scholarship hiding in a crude—forgive me, but we're men of the wider world—farm village? A crime!"

"The villagers are well educated," he replied mildly. Jenn Nalynn, in his hearing, spoke only Rhothan, and that with a charming accent reminiscent not merely of Avyo, but of that city's elder citizens. She also spoke to toads. In Rhothan, not toad. Whatever toad might be.

Magic? Bannan smiled to himself. If so, it was clever magic indeed. At a guess, Jenn had wished to understand and be understood, rather than try to learn the languages themselves. The turn-born, with their oddly accented Rhothan, must have chosen the other path. Or could they? he thought suddenly. Could they agree to change something about themselves? If not, they'd be forced to learn the language of Marrowdell the ordinary way.

"An interesting group, in truth." The dema's gaze sharpened. "And you, my good Bannan, late of Vorkoun, late of her guard, and once of her nobility. You've arranged for my esteemed colleague to be preoccupied for a reason. Shall we retire to the comfort of my caravan to continue our conversation?"

Fairly caught, the truthseer stood away from the table to bow. "Lead on, my good dema."

The servants were awake and alert this time. Panilaq took herself to the middle wagon, by the rattle of dishes to prepare the requisite Ansnan hospitality. After a surly glance at Bannan, Kanajuq stirred to drop the metal stair and open the door to the largest wagon, going ahead to light a lamp, then climbing out again.

"Welcome, welcome," Dema Qimirpik said cheerfully, lifting his robe as he bounded up the stairs.

A step at a time, Bannan followed behind. He passed through the door, bare feet sinking in lush carpet, and found himself within what was more salon than wagon.

The roof arched well over his head, crowned in glass to admit the witness of stars. The rest of the ceiling was painted black, but that color was obscured beneath the gilt of handwritten prayers.

The rest of the wagon resembled the interior of a ship. Other than the curtained windows to either side and doors at each end, every bit of wall space was in use. Ornately carved cupboards and racks lined the tops; below were narrow worktables cluttered with star charts and papers and instruments. Cushioned benches waited before each, hinged to fold away.

A wider, luxuriously padded bench under the rightmost window housed the three odemini, belted in place. The dolls, Bannan was glad to see, faced the now-closed curtain.

Under the left window was a gleaming dining table, hinged as well, but presently extended into the middle of the floor. A pear-shaped lamp sat centered on the table, its wide lower half encased in gold filigree, its upper a network of crystal and faceted red gems. The light it cast was pleasant, though reflections danced over the walls with their steps. Two elegant chairs, upholstered in red and gold velvet, stood waiting, as did a pair of fluted glasses.

What was Ansnan and what was Eld?

"Sit, sit." The wagon rocked and reflections jiggled as the dema took his own suggestion and claimed a chair. "Panilaq!" he bellowed, pounding a fist on the table. The lamp rattled. "Pardon the delay," this as Bannan sat and pulled his chair to the table. "My odemi are worthy and diligent, not quick. Pani—!"

Before Qimirpik could finish his second summons, the old woman climbed into the wagon, a tray in her hands. The deep carpet kept her to an anxious shuffle, the tray tipping so its contents, a large glass carafe and platter, slowly slid to one end then the other with each step. Bannan held his breath, but miraculously, she made it to the table.

The carafe proved full of wine, the platter a less-than-artful arrangement of soft white curds surrounded by brown crisps. A dainty bowl of salt had been forced into their midst. Panilaq filled the waiting flutes before weaving her way out of the wagon.

"Ah." The dema surveyed the offering with patent delight. "My colleague—" he wrinkled his nose, "—prefers I not bring out Ansnan fare. But I trust you're familiar?" With that, he set the salt bowl between them.

Bannan moistened the little finger of his left hand in his mouth, then dipped it in the bowl. Deftly scooping curds on a crisp with his other hand, he took a generous bite and immediately sucked the salt from his finger. Timing in the mouth was crucial. Done well, the salt tamed the bitter spice of the curd while the crisp's heat flared, a pleasant, if eye-watering sensation. Done poorly? The only recourse was to spit the awful combination out; even so, the foul taste would linger for days.

The truthseer chewed, swallowed, and smiled at Qimirpik. As Captain Ash, he'd learned the trick of it to lull Ansnan captives. Now, he did the same to impress his Ansnan host. He should have bet Tir on the likelihood of that.

Having taken his own first taste, the dema touched the rim of his glass to Bannan's. "Before I ask what you want of me," he said, "allow me to apologize. I'm not a worldly man, Bannan. My attention's been here," a finger to his head," and there," a gesture to the night sky revealed through the ceiling window. "I was wrong to speak lightly of the marches and of your city. It was a long and bitter conflict, won by no one. My presence here, as your former enemy, must seem an insult. That, I deeply regret."

The truthseer regarded the Ansnan, then touched his glass to the dema's and took a sip. The wine was dry and strong, with a harsh bite to it. Much like history, he thought ruefully. "I thought I'd come far enough to leave the past behind," he confessed, giving truth for truth.

Qimirpik nodded. "The stars have seen what we wish forgotten. It's my belief they remind us at the least convenient time." He leaned back, arms crossed over his ample belly, and asked calmly. "Are we still enemies?"

Bannan half smiled. "I doubt, good dema, we ever were."

"Excellent. Because I must confess," with a contented sigh, "I like this Marrowdell of yours. I'd be sorry to leave a moment sooner than I must."

"You've slept well," the truthseer deduced, unsurprised. There was something about the other man, a lightness of spirit, that suited the place.

"Better than I can remember." Qimirpik's affable features took on a guilty cast. "Unlike poor Urcet, who was afflicted by terrible dreams. He plans to take a sleeping draught rather than risk another such night." The dema sipped his wine, then added keenly, "We're being tested, aren't we?"

The truth wouldn't daunt this man, Bannan judged. "In a sense. Not everyone can live here. Those who can, sleep free of nightmares." Or have Jenn Nalynn's magical help, he added to himself. "The dreams will worsen. Your companion may demand to leave."

"Urcet?" Qimirpik's face eased. "Nothing would please him more than to believe he faces a trial. His deepest desire is to prove himself." A chuckle. "I have no such ambition."

"To come this far," Bannan probed, "unarmed and trusting a truce with its ink barely dry? If not ambition," he looked the other in the eye, "then what?"

In answer, the dema rose and went to a cupboard, taking out a rolled parchment. After Bannan lifted their wineglasses clear, he spread it on the table, using the carafe and salt bowl to hold it flat.

It was a print of a painting, marked with neat scholarly notes along the margins. The buildings were stylized, the lettering within the art so old-fashioned as to be illegible to Bannan's eyes, but he recognized the subject without difficulty. The dragon had carved the likeness of those soaring towers from dirt and flower dust, before wiping them away with a breeze.

"Pick a height in Ansnor, you'll find a refuge perched there, full of those seeking to be closer to the stars. Some are older than recorded history, others last but a single avalanche, but in truth, Bannan, almost all are small, modest structures. Unlike this." Qimirpik's ink-stained fingers stroked the parchment. "The Great Refuge of the North. Generations labored to build it. The rich impoverished themselves to see it done. Understand, Bannan, this wasn't a retreat, where petitioners could seek peace and solitude for their worship. No, this was built in a place rich in magic, to use that magic. My forebears saw themselves the equals of the Blessed Celestials and demanded entry to paradise." His hand flattened over a tower. "Little wonder they came, in the end, to utter ruin."

As dragon and kruar had settled the Verge, drawn by its power, those ancient Ansnans had settled the valley that would become Marrowdell. Neither outcome, Bannan thought uneasily, had led to peace. "A mistake made once mustn't be repeated," he urged. "If that's why you've come—"

"I've no wish for magic or power." Qimirpik took his seat, his eyes lifting to Bannan's. "I've come for something harder to find." A wistful smile. "To believe again."

The truthseer narrowed his eyes. "Here, among Rhothans."

"Where else? The course of my life—" the dema stabbed his chest with a finger, "—was set when I replied to a heretical Rhothan astronomer. I realized this Dusom Uhthoff must live where we'd challenged the Celestials and was willing to scandalize my fellow demas to satisfy my curiosity. But—" with a charming shrug, "—as the years passed, my distant friend showed me a love for the stars could be—should be!—free of self-interest and presumption. Our arguments, and there were many, drove me to discoveries I couldn't have imagined. The status I now enjoy among Ansnan's scholars, I owe to him."

The truth, but not all of it. "And your loss of faith," said Bannan.

Qimirpik sighed. "I don't blame Dusom. Prayers failed me, those I sought for reassurance bickered and contradicted themselves. Smoke from steam engines dimmed the stars above my refuge and where were the miracles? The Celestials tested me and I despaired of them. Then came Dusom's invitation to come here, to view the eclipse. I had hope again. So here I am."

"To perform more magic. How will that restore your faith? This rock you plan to summon . . ." Bannan let the words trail off as he refilled their glasses, his every sense tingling.

"Urcet can have the Tear." With that unexpected assertion, the dema paused for another crisp and curds, pulling his salted finger from his mouth with a satisfied pop. "It's why he came and how I could. As for me, Bannan? I shall bare my soul to the Celestials during the eclipse, here, where my predecessors committed their heresy, and ask forgiveness for their crime and my doubt. I dare not hope. I will not falter." He carelessly rolled the parchment then tossed it aside. "But none of this is why you're here, is it?"

Ansnan and enemy. Meeting a gaze as wise and kind as his father's had been, the truthseer put aside the last of his anger and abandoned pretense.

Jenn Nalynn had said it. There was another way.

Bannan Larmensu leaned back, and lifted his glass to Dema Qimirpik. "I'd best start with the dragon . . ."

Efflet carried him over the river, an awkward and painful process Wyll was glad to have done before the others awoke. He'd crouched in damp grass by a hedge until the sun peered over the crags, unwilling to confront the Wound by dark.

And found himself with unwanted company.

The kruar mares passed him with nary a glance, though the last wrinkled her snout and sneezed. Behind them trotted the one Wyll most wished to avoid this day.

The old kruar, being his obstinate self, stopped in front of the dragon, dipping his head to regard him. ~ Why are you here? ~ He snorted dubiously. ~ Is there a threat? ~

~ Why I'm here is my business. Don't you have horse work to do? ~ Wyll added evilly. He wrinkled his man's nose, sure any smell came from the blood drying on the kruar's sweat-stained hide. ~ Bathe first. ~

Scourge didn't take the offense he'd hoped. Instead, his big head came unpleasantly close, nostrils flared with interest. ~ You're up to something. What? ~

~ If you're lucky, ~ the dragon sneered, ~ it'll kill me. ~

~ I'll end your miserable life when it suits me, ~ the kruar said pleasantly. A mare paused by the river to glare back at them, nickering a summons. Scourge rumbled a reply, then, ~ Explain. I won't leave until you do. ~

~ Stay, then. ~ The dragon pushed by his ally, lurch-stepping his way down the road. ~ I promise not to die in a less than satisfactory manner. ~ Which wouldn't be rid of him. ~ I need fresh clothes, ~ Wyll added sourly.

~ Bathe first! ~ Snorting at his own joke, the old kruar abandoned him, splashing across the river.

Finally.

Wyll gave his attention to the road, wary of ruts, careful to set his good foot where it was flat. A fall would cost precious moments.

The girl was running out of time.

The dragon snarled at the Wound and kept his distance as he passed. The opening was bright and welcoming at this time of day, slanted sunbeams giving the lie to the dark beneath the trees. Bright, welcoming, and untrustworthy. He twisted to face it, uneasy until it was well behind.

Abandoned only for a day, the farmyard felt emptier than that, as if Bannan had never come or as if he'd never be back. Wyll hunched his shoulder and avoided looking at the porch and the house and the new larder door, though his stomach reminded him he hadn't eaten.

Easier to hunt, hungry.

Turn-born walked the road behind him; he heard their voices and steps, took care not to be seen. They'd take their own path and he wished them success.

Rely on it? He'd depend on nyphrit first.

Beyond the barn was the hedge, beyond the hedge, the kaliia field to be harvested tomorrow. The girl's path linked each with the next, ending at Night's Edge. Wyll took it, trampling grass and wildflowers, sweeping aside webs, and startling a rabbit that stopped to stare, nose atwitch.

Did it wait for her?

In case, he sent a little breeze to drop clover flowers at its feet. The fool creature leapt into the deeper grass and was gone.

They knew better than trust him, though he'd not harmed any since she'd come into his life. He still frightened rabbits, Wyll thought morosely, if nothing else.

Night's Edge. He threw himself forward and ash swirled around him. Small sticks protruded from the ground, snapping underfoot like bones. Forced to throw his arm over his mouth or choke, the dragon kept moving, eyes half shut. Nothing had grown. He'd come to be sure.

Perhaps he'd hoped.

But their meadow was lifeless and Jenn Nalynn was doomed, unless those beneath notice could find a way.

Step, twist, push forward. Step, twist, push forward. His man's body was awkward at best and a trial to move over uneven ground, but worked. Here. Refusing to think further, Wyll made his way through the gap in the neyet to the hidden field, then turned toward home.

There. A glitter where one shouldn't be, marking a cave of crystal and dead wood, carpeted in moss. Stray words were stuck here and there inside, remnants of his letter-writing. He'd gaze at them, pondering the nature of "woolly" and "checkerwork" and "enchantment." There were words he doubted and words that made him curious. Some were amusing to say. "Rapscallion" was a recent favorite.

~ Welcome, elder brother. ~ The house toad, able sentry and busybody, another favorite word, peered from under an aster. ~ Is there something you require? ~

He required his proper form. That being beyond a little cousin's magic, Wyll ignored the question. He took another step and paused, feeling his way.

Yes. Here. The crossing.

~ Elder brother? ~ with deep apprehension. ~ What are you doing? ~

~ What I must. ~

He could do this, or fail. There was but one way to know.

He didn't need to see, to find where he'd once belonged, but to cross? As dragon, he'd stood here and simply left Marrowdell behind.

As man?

Only turn-born could carry more than themselves. Wyll removed his shoes and shed his clothing, dropping the encumbrances carelessly to one side. The little cousin hastened to take position near the pile, either confused or sensing a task it could undertake.

Wyll drew a breath scented with flowers and growing things, let it out again, and between the in and out of air . . .

He crossed.

No flowers where he stood. No flowers and the ground was tipped and the sky was falling and he collapsed with a scream onto naked rock, overwhelmed and struggling to understand what was wrong.

He'd crossed as a man. That was all. Calming himself, Wyll forced open his watering eyes, determined to see.

Colors were colors but others were tastes. Touch sang in his ears and shivered his bones, while the sound of his own breathing scalded his skin. He stood, or tried, and something moved, or did it fall? With a flinch, he fell again, hard.

This body lied. It couldn't be trusted. Wyll rose to his feet again, weaving because nothing assured him what was up or down.

So be it. He knew. He knew this place better than any other. The expanse of orange and green and nameless color were hills and flats and distant plains. What appeared ribboned stone above, threatening to fall and crush him, were the roots of Marrowdell's kaliia showing through the sky and harmless.

The effort to reconcile knowledge with what he saw and felt was like being remade and, for a fleeting instant, Wyll dared imagine his man's form wouldn't last here, away from the girl.

But as the Verge shook into its familiar shape around him, he remained the same.

Shape didn't matter. Form couldn't. Once he believed where his foot would land, he moved it, twisted, and wrenched himself along the stone rise. Not to where the river of mimrol curled and flowed, for that led to the turn-borns' crossing. Not to the steep, winding path to his sanctuary. There was no point hiding.

He was here to be found.

Wyll chose a place where stone met sky to wait, relishing the wind needling his bared skin almost as much as the plunge into cloud below.

Before long, air pulsed against him, driven by great wings.

Dragons.

They rose from the clouds, descended from the sky, circled him at a cautious distance. Silent, for a welcome change, though he supposed they were at a loss, seeing him thus.

One swooped, the wind from her wings knocking him perilously close to the edge. Daring. Stupid. They were, Wyll reminded himself, much the same. He sent a wind of his own, knocking her back and into two of her fellows. The three roared and clawed at one another as they tumbled, pulling apart short of the clouds to regain the sky.

At a more respectful distance.

Questions began. ~ Why are you here? ~ ~ Why are you that? ~ ~ What do you want? ~

Wyll waited for silence to return. Some settled below, clinging to the stone, fanged heads twisted to keep him in view. Others rode the air, scaled sides catching the light, so many the sky glistened like the surface of a great ocean.

Glorious, his kind.

When they weren't fools.

Once sure of their attention, Wyll bared his teeth. ~ You've carried me before. Carry me now! For all our sakes, I must reach the base of the Wound. ~

Those on the stone launched themselves with wild cries of dismay. Those in the sky spun and whirled, colliding with one another in a mass confusion of wings.

~ COWARDS! ~ he roared after them, but to no good. The dragons fled as if he actually could hurt them.

As if he would.

He should have known. Beardless younglings. They'd found him entertaining in his fall and stayed to watch, but hadn't they scattered from any threat? A dragon worth fearing wouldn't come near him, wary not of him—not anymore—but of the sei's interest.

There was no help here.

So be it. Wyll turned toward the Wound. It loomed above all other thrusts of stone, linked at its foot to this and other hills by a crooked, rock-strewn ridge. That was the way, for those with two strong legs. A day's walk, if not an easy one, for the terst turn-born.

For him . . . he started walking. It would take what it took.

~ Why are you here? ~

Knowing that voice, Wyll twisted around as one last dragon climbed onto the flat with him, claws cracking the stone. Emerald green, with awkward limbs and malformed head, the sei settled on its haunches, regarding him with flat golden eyes.

He stared back, too afraid to so much as blink.

Again, deep enough to shake bone. ~ Why are you here? ~

The little cousins were braver. The truthseer. Jenn Nalynn, the bravest of all. Thinking of her, Wyll found he could speak. ~ I've come to save the girl's life. ~

The sei's head turned improbably on its neck, its expression like the old kruar's when puzzled. ~ At the Great Turn, all is possible. ~

The moth had said the same. Wyll scowled. Riddles, when he needed answers. ~ Why wait? You showed her the pebble, knowing what she was. She suffers. Let her have it now! ~

The head snapped upright, misshapen jaws agape in threat.

He braced himself, but nothing prepared him for the speed of the sei's pounce. Claws dug in, ripping through skin at shoulder and thigh, taking hold deep in his flesh. Wings unfurled, the sei launched itself into the air, with Wyll hanging below.

To drop him for his impudence. He waited for death.

But the claws gripped, blood sliding over his skin, and the first heavy beat of wings brought a surge of hope. For whatever reason, it was taking him to the Wound.

There'd been a time he'd dreamt of flying. This painful jerking through the air was nothing like his memories of riding the wind. The sei, lacking grace, forced its way through the sky. They followed the ridge and Wyll watched for the turn-born, but they were nowhere to be seen.

The gathering of dragons wouldn't have frightened them; the arrival of the sei must have sent them scampering for cover.

He didn't need them. His plan was to find a fallen pebble and leave it at the crossing for Sand to bring to Marrowdell, that turn-born being the only one he halfway trusted. In his darkest dreams, he'd not thought to ask a sei to help.

In his darkest dreams, he'd not imagined entering the Wound itself, but instead of slowing to land where the ridge met the upthrust stone, the place where pebbles, white and otherwise, should lie waiting, the sei's wings beat harder and faster, taking them straight at that stained cliff.

Before they hit, its body tilted and began an impossibly steep climb. His useless arm and worthless leg scraped and banged against the uneven rock, but still the sei climbed. The wall glistened with something dark.

Or was it white?

Still it climbed, entering a cloying fog that burned his nostrils. The thick stuff swirled around the beating wings. Something dire gibbered and shrieked in the distance; the dragon snarled in answer, thoroughly outraged.

Better to be dropped, than a plaything of the sei.

Anything was better than to be brought here, to the Wound itself, where even turn-born weren't safe and no dragon dared fly. A clean fall, from this height, might do what it hadn't before. He might die this time. Wouldn't that annoy his old enemy?

Before he could struggle free, they broke through the fog and reached the top.

As the sei flew slowly over featureless bare rock, dread filled Wyll until he could hardly breathe, not that the air wasn't already foul. Because he saw nothing, meant nothing.

Dragons knew in their bones. The greatest danger didn't show itself. Didn't roar or give warning.

It struck.

Then the landscape changed. Ahead, neyet ringed eruptions of familiar pale stone, their wooden arms woven into a fence. Or was it a wall?

Where their broad bodies entered the ground, for the roots of these were in Marrowdell, things prowled, slipping between gnawed branches, flashing teeth before they ducked from sight.

Nyphrit, naked and gray. Larger than any he'd seen and in greater number.

Something oozed outward from each encircled stone, between the neyet, dark where it flowed into cracks and fissures, opalescent where caught by light.

The sei groaned and spasmed, driving its claws deeper in his flesh.

Needful agony he could endure; this was insult. Wyll growled in protest and, for a wonder, the creature's grip eased slightly. ~ What are you showing me? ~ he demanded.

~ At the Great Turn, all is possible. ~ With this unhelpful reply, the sei aimed for the largest of the stones.

Seen from above, their arrangement matched the mounds of Marrowdell's Spine, though not their shape. This one, in that world, would be the centermost. The path to its summit was here a crooked line of rock descending from empty sky. The edge was perverse.

The sei flew lower as it crossed the ring of neyet, forcing the dragon to contort or risk his good limb to their upward reach. ~ All is possible, ~ it intoned again. ~ Even this. ~

They passed the ring of neyet, to hover over the rise of pale stone. Buffeted by the sei's powerful wingbeats, clenched in its claws, Wyll stared down.

An eye, larger than them both, opened to stare up.

Better than a mouth, he calculated coldly. An eye was vulnerable, even one rimmed in night's edge blue, its center flecked with stars. An eye meant something alive that could, by a dragon's sure reckoning, be made dead.

Alive and, by the way the eye tracked them, aware. ~ You put the others to sleep, ~ he accused the sei. ~ Why not this? ~

~ There was an opportunity for penance. ~

Being trapped as stone between two worlds wasn't punishment enough? Of course not, Wyll thought grimly. They made examples, the sei. Of the dragon's lord. Of the kruar's general.

Of whatever this had been.

A tear leaked from the eye, falling round and white, to land with a bounce and rattle.

A pebble.

More lay gathered, a talus of suffering. What the sei had given Jenn Nalynn; what she had to have! Wyll grinned with triumph. ~ Take me down there, ~ he commanded, forgetting what carried him. ~ It's what I've come for—what the girl needs! ~

The sei swept down, but not to land. Somehow, it forced itself and Wyll into the narrow space, one wingtip brushing through the twigs of the neyet, the other stroking the side of the trapped one.

Nyphrit leapt for his dangling legs, claws reaching, jaws snapping. They dropped back atop one another, so thickly were they packed. Others, Wyll saw with rising horror, were oblivious to the temptation of new prey, busy eating the one who couldn't escape.

The sei, point made, took them higher.

~ Why? ~ he shouted. ~ Why make it suffer? Why ask her the impossible? ~

The emerald head bent and twisted, the eyes regarding him molten. ~ We ask nothing and do nothing. We are not in her world or of it. ~

Wyll looked down at the trapped one, meeting the gaze of that ancient eye, unable to tell if it felt pain or fear. But he had no doubt. None at all.

~ This is one of you. This is a sei. ~

The legends said the powerful had tried to reach from this world to the next, in their failure creating the edge and the Verge and becoming trapped. How had he not understood? Who could but the sei? This one was caught in both worlds. This was what had spoken to him, as the moth.

And this, he thought with growing fury, was what lured the turn-born, the truthseer, and Jenn Nalynn. Easy to see what killed any who came too close, but why call them to their death?

~ What does it want? ~ he asked desperately, since only a sei might know.

But the sei become dragon gave no more answers. ~ At the Great Turn ~ it said for the third time ~ all is possible. ~

It flew him back to where he'd crossed without another word, letting him drop from a height. The breath knocked from his body, he reeled at the edge of consciousness but fought to stand, unwilling to show it weakness. Blood pooled at his feet.

The sei hung, no longer bothering to flap its wings, like a poorly drawn dragon pinned to air. ~ You must return to her world. ~

Without the pebble. Knowing above all Jenn Nalynn mustn't cross alone to retrieve it. Wyll snarled his defiance.

~ You know the truth. No other. ~

It reminded him of his penance and showed him another's. Did it think to cow him? Wyll's lips pulled from his teeth. ~ How much truth? ~ he asked, all menace. ~ You sent me to keep her within the edge, warned if she left it would unravel and everything I care for die. Yet instead of sending me to end that threat, you put me with her, let me learn to love her, help her make me this! ~ He slapped his crippled side with his good hand.

Then he shook his head, like a man. ~ I don't care about my penance, ~ he told it wearily. ~ I don't care about my life. Can you not understand? If you want the girl to live, help me bring her what she needs. ~

~ We will not. Ensure our peace, so long as she is as she is. Your penance will be complete when she is as she must become. ~

This was new. Wyll stared at the sei. ~ You want her to cross, as much as the trapped one does. You want her filled with its tears. Why? ~

A flash of green, a whirl of glittering ash, and what had been comprehensible became large and vast and so much more than dragon or man that he staggered but refused to fall.

~ WHY?! ~ Wyll shouted with all his might, cracking rock. ~ ANSWER ME! ~

The sei paused.

Then, to his astonishment, the sei spoke.

~ It is not trapped. It chose to stay and hold the edge, doing penance for our curiosity. At the last Great Turn, others pulled it too far into their world. It is wounded, it weakens, and, soon, it will die. When its hold fails, little cousin, the edge will fail with it. ~

He was beyond caution. ~ Then save it! ~

~ We cannot. It must be healed in both worlds, by someone of both. Long has it called to the turn-born for help, but they refuse to hear or die. ~ The shape and voice grew fainter and more distant. ~ The girl is the promise and last hope. If she becomes as she must, if she does what she can, if she lives, she will save it and so the edge. At the Great Turn, ~ a whisper, like a cold caress, ~ all is possible. ~

The sky became a white moth, soft wings stretched to the horizon, eyes like twin suns.

Then was gone.

Wyll looked out over the Verge. Had he a dragon's eyes, from here he would see mimrol lakes, sparkling with the ylings' webbed cities; villages of terst, their crystal homes surrounded by fields of kaliia, their children at play; that way, so near the limit of the Verge the turn-born shunned the place, the white palace of the toad queen; beyond the palace, the endless rolling plain that marked the beginning of their world, as Marrowdell's crags marked the start of hers.

If the edge failed, both worlds would survive. There'd be dragons and girls and insufferably pompous sei and princes.

But if the edge failed, there'd be no places seething with magic. No breathtaking Verge, no beautiful Marrowdell, and no Jenn Nalynn.

No turn-born, which he could live with, but to lose so very much else . . .

His cursed man's eyes clouded with tears. He'd wanted her happy and safe. Now he must help her attempt the impossible.

So be it.

Move before his body failed him. Reach the crossing and get back. Knowing what he must do was easier than accomplishing it. Among their many faults, sei never grasped the frailty of others; having seen one being eaten alive, Wyll supposed they couldn't. Still, he would have preferred help that didn't leave him dripping blood and, yes, he gasped at the grate of bone, mostly broken. His body claimed what strength he had to heal itself; there was no arguing with that dragon imperative. He staggered on in a daze, weaker by the breath.

The crossing was near, the sei's one mercy. He fell more than stepped on the place, refusing to faint till he smelled flowers again.

And, when he did, he lifted his head to find himself being regarded not only by the alarmed toad, but by the old soldier, who sat cross-legged by his shoes. A horse stood grazing a short distance away.

Horst raised an eyebrow. "Are you going to die, dragon?"

"Not today," Wyll promised, then let the dark claim him.

TWENTY-THREE

IF SHE FELL asleep, the morning would come faster. If it did, Jenn reasoned, so would the next.

Which could be her last.

This being dire enough to keep anyone awake, she lay beside her sister, whose gentle snores went to prove some people believed events would unfold as they should so long as everyone was fed and well-rested.

She shouldn't think that. It wasn't fair or true. Peggs slept because she was truly exhausted, and no one cared more about what might happen to her than her sister.

Lying in the dark made it hard to be hopeful, that was all. It would have helped if she'd found Wyll. He'd been gone the entire day. When asked, no one could remember him sharing a meal or being nearby. Mistress Sand had given her a startled look, and asked the other tinkers, but none had seen a dragon. Jenn couldn't help but worry. What if, having seen her with Bannan, Wyll didn't care to be seen by her?

At least their father was, if not happy, happier. He'd shown Melusine's ring to Peggs, who remembered playing with it, and Aunt Sybb, who cried, just a little, to see it again and remember far more. He'd brought out the summerberry wine and poured them all a glass, and they'd made a Beholding, there and then, for Uncle Horst and asking the Ancestors to keep him safe wherever he was or went.

So it had been a good evening and tiring. Tomorrow would be busier, since as well as finishing the harvest and preparing for the farewell dance, Aunt Sybb must finish her packing, and as if that weren't sufficient, there was a wedding feast to plan. Smaller, but no less important according to their aunt, was the quandary of heads; more precisely, what went on them. Rhothan tradition held that a bride wore a wedding circlet of lace atop her hair, preferably a family heirloom. As each new bride added her own bit of lace, the oldest of these, so Aunt Sybb said, trailed over shoulders and back like so much frail and yellowing froth. In most families, new ones were made every few generations. Peggs would wear their mother's, Hettie her stepmother's—that of their mother, Mimm, being saved for Alyssa, and Palma was to wear Gallie's, though the latter was a compromise of some difficulty, since little Loee should properly inherit it.

Which left Jenn, who hadn't yet told Wyll there'd be no wedding, so couldn't very well tell anyone else. Only that morning Aunt Sybb had proclaimed the business of her circlet taken care of as she'd brought her own—it being wise, as she always said, to be prepared rather than caught without. Unfortunately, she'd concealed her treasure from everyone but the mice.

Her circlet was now in shreds.

Wine, tears, and honest fatigue conspired to send Aunt Sybb to bed when she'd otherwise have stayed up all night to somehow make a new one. It would be, she'd pronounced firmly, tomorrow's priority.

Finding Wyll was hers, Jenn vowed. She lay awake, staring into the dark for an interminable time. Finally, she mouthed the words. "Where are you?"

"Downstairs," a warm little breeze whispered in her ear.

Wyll!

Careful not to wake Peggs, Jenn slid from under their quilt and grabbed a shawl. She padded down the ladder quick as could be, then through the unlit kitchen, stubbing a toe on a basket left where one usually wasn't and biting her lip not to cry out. Finally, she was through the door.

Lamps on porches and barn doors had been extinguished for the night. Stars crusted the sky, but beneath all was dark upon dark. Jenn moved by feel. Here was wood, here was flagstone, here was dew-wet grass.

And there, movement, man-sized and bent.

"Wyll!" She hurried to him and would have embraced him, but something in how he stood made her stop and wrap the shawl about her shoulders. "I tried to find you," she said. "I need to tell you—" there was nothing for it but to spit it out, though he hadn't so much as acknowledged her presence, "—I'm in love with Bannan, not that I don't love you too, but it's different because you're like a brother and my dearest friend and he's—well, with him it's not like that at all. So I can't marry you, even if I married anyone, which I won't, not without knowing what I'll be as a turn-born though really, when it comes to it, I'm not ready to marry at all." Having delivered that in one breath, she quickly drew another. "Do you understand, Wyll?"

He came closer with an ominous growl, but it wasn't like his growl, more the sound of stone against stone, and the shape she'd thought was Wyll grew larger and paler and loomed so near she put out her hands to stop it.

Only to find herself alone in the dark, holding her pebble. A dream? No, it had to be real. She had her pebble at last. About to bring it to her lips, the small stone grew impossibly heavy and with a despairing cry, she had to let go.

"Dearest Heart. Jenn!" A breeze swirled around her, strong and warm like arms, then snapped against her ear.

Startled awake, Jenn stood for a moment. Outside, in her night-dress, again. At least this time she wasn't buried in the carrots. "Wyll. I was dreaming. I dreamed you were here."

"I am here." The same shape approached, this time moving like her dragon. "Are you awake now?"

She pinched herself to be sure. "Yes. Did I—was I talking?" She truly hoped she didn't have to break his heart all over again. "Did you hear what I said?"

"Yes." The breeze straightened her shawl and played along her cheeks, then abruptly stopped. "You're less than you were."

Which, however true and horrible, wasn't, she frowned, what she needed to hear. "The turn-born gave me a drink that helps." She tried to see him, and couldn't. "Wyll, please. What's happened—just happened. I was wrong to wish you into a man, and wrong to try and force you to marry me. I hope you can forgive me—"

"Yes," Wyll said, dismissing love, marriage, and all else. With his next words, she knew why. "I found your pebble."

"Did you bring it?" she asked, heart in her throat.

"I could not," with such bitterness she reached for him, but he evaded her touch. "A sei is caught between our worlds and dying. The pebbles are its tears and it calls you to save it."

Well, she'd expected a quest or task. Helping a dying—whatever a sei was—sounded like something she'd want to do anyway, Jenn reassured herself, fighting to stay calm, and tears were much nicer to contemplate than most of what the turn-born had brought her from the Verge. How fitting the dema used the same word for her pebble, though, her thoughts jumped, why would he?

Covie, however, was the one with any healing skill. How was she to save it?

Wyll waited, invisible in the dark and silent, so like Wisp when he wanted to avoid a topic that she realized with a shiver there must be more and worse. "Tell me the rest."

"The sei is besieged by nyphrit. Doubtless others lie in wait along the path up the Spine. They are deadly, Dearest Heart. They will kill anything, anyone who dares approach."

She should have been frightened; instead, Jenn struggled to contain her fury. Block her from what she must have? "I will dare," she said grimly, when she could speak again.

"Not alone." The words caught on some tightness in his throat. "We will—" a movement, as though he staggered. "Not alone."

Hands outstretched, she went to him. What her hands found was soaking wet and ice cold. "What have you—no matter." Jenn whipped off her shawl and laid it over his shoulders, then put her arm around his waist. "Come with me," she ordered, urging him to the house.

"I hate the river," he grumbled, but didn't protest as she led him into the kitchen. Finding the ladder by feel, she settled him against its support, then hurried to light a lamp and put more wood into the cookstove.

She shot worried glances at him. More had happened to the dragon than a dunking. His shirt bore dried bloodstains and his good arm was held as if it pained him or as if he cradled damaged ribs. "The nyphrit," she guessed, horrified he'd taken such a risk.

"A fall. I'm almost healed."

Almost healed at dragonish speed meant he'd been badly hurt since she'd last seen him. Her hands wanted to tremble as she poured hot water for tea, adding a generous dollop of honey to his mug. Gently putting it into his shaking hand, Jenn crouched before him, eyes searching. "You shouldn't have gone," she whispered.

"Did the turn-born bring anything useful?" he asked. When she shook her head, his eyes glinted silver. "Then I should have gone." The silver was replaced with brown. "Is there food, Dearest Heart? I'm hungry."

"I'll make something," Peggs offered, coming down the ladder. She eased past Wyll, and went to work. Within moments, a thick blanket replaced the light shawl around his shoulders. More wood went into the stove until it crackled and snapped and the kitchen grew toasty warm. Another lamp lit, then she pulled out knife and board, preparing thick sandwiches with a calm efficiency for which Jenn was unutterably grateful. She rose to her feet to help.

"The lost is found." Radd came in through the kitchen door, yawning as he poured himself a cup of tea. The curtain to the parlor remained closed, though it was unlikely Aunt Sybb would sleep through much more.

"I fell in the river," Wyll volunteered. He'd stopped shaking, his hair beginning to dry in the heat from the stove.

"Again?" Their father chuckled. "I'll find you something dry to wear."

"Wyll's hurt," Jenn said, but when she went to pull aside the blanket, Wyll gently resisted.

"There's something I must say."

The three paused, looking at the dragon.

Wyll rose to his feet, the effort draining the blood from his face, but managed a short bow. "Radd Nalynn, father, brother, and miller," he announced. "I regret to say I cannot marry your daughter. That one—" He had the gall to point.

"Don't change the subject," Jenn fumed. "You're hurt and need attention."

"Let the man speak," Aunt Sybb interceded. She stepped past the curtain, fully dressed and impeccably powdered. "May I inquire, Wyll, what's brought about your change of heart?"

"My heart hasn't changed," the dragon answered, his glance at Jenn alive with mischief. "However I have recently learned—" He was going to say Bannan and the blanket and the dance, she just knew it, and braced herself for their aunt's reaction, which might be tolerant but at this early hour might be anything but. "—I've other obligations."

Jenn relaxed.

"I see." Aunt Sybb fixed her with an unreadable stare. "Your feelings on this, Jenn Nalynn?"

"I'm fine," she said quickly. "In truth, I may have been—hasty."

An elegant brow lifted. "Well, then," the Lady Mahavar pronounced. "Dry clothes, Radd. The poor man is dripping on the floor. I believe we should sit to a proper breakfast, if you and Peggs would be so kind." Then, without any change in her expression, she added, "This is what comes of toads. Mark my words, Jenn Nalynn."

Jenn dropped a quick curtsy. Peggs turned toward the sink, her shoulders shaking, Radd chuckled, and the house toad, who'd tucked his head under the curtain to see what was about at such an hour, gave a toothy yawn.

While the dragon sipped tea and looked insufferably smug.

Until Jenn met his gaze and saw the dread he couldn't, or wouldn't hide.

All day long, clouds lurked beyond the crags in every direction, never quite tumbling into the valley. Bannan wondered if the turn-born tired, having kept the weather fair these past days, but even they looked at the horizon and frowned.

Tir lifted his mask and spat. "Isn't natural, sir. Just say'n."

He shrugged. What was, here? "So long as it holds off till we're done."

They harvested the field next to his farm; it lay farthest from the village, split into a deep wishbone by the first of the Fingers, and those working its ends found themselves shadowed by the forest. Hedges hid the ruined meadow, a mercy. Bannan gazed wistfully, every so often, at the rooftops of his home and barn.

An empty barn, for now. Davi promised a share of stalks from the village once the tinkers left; Anten a couple of piglets from Satin's next birthing.

Bannan dug in his 'fork and pitched. How could he plan for the future, when tomorrow loomed as ominously as the clouds?

"Ancestors Broody and Glum. There's that look again." Tir tossed stalks into Wainn's wagon. "Sir."

"Stop calling me 'sir.'"

His friend grunted and lifted another 'forkload. "Bannan. You could cheer up. There's another dance tonight."

Riverstone and Flint were absent, having crossed to the Verge in search of Jenn Nalynn's pebble; the other turn-born drove their wagons. Everyone shifted duty to put Kydd, Allin, and Tadd in the mill; it being tradition for a prospective groom to cook for his to-be-bride and her family the night before the wedding, each of the three needed to stay close to a kitchen. Ribald jokes at their expense lightened much of the day.

Wyll was in the village too. There were no jokes about him, the villagers unsure if they were relieved or insulted to learn the strange man had rejected their beloved Jenn Nalynn, the tinkers puzzled. The dragon wouldn't care what any of them thought, only Jenn, and acted, Bannan judged, to spare her what he could.

Roche, who would have spoken up and not pleasantly, had

volunteered to help the dema today. Just as well, the truthseer thought grimly, his temper tried enough by his so-helpful friend.

"Here, I'd have thought you'd be singing," Tir went on, persistent as a blood fly. "Yon lovely farm maid being free again."

Bannan stabbed his pitchfork in the sod. "Heart's Blood! Will you leave it be?"

Wainn looked down, his eyes somber within the shade of his broad hat. The truthseer waved an apology for slowing the work.

He tried to free the 'fork, but it was well and truly stuck. Without a word, Tir lent a hand; together they pulled it out. "It's not tonight on my mind," Bannan explained. "It's tomorrow. What might happen."

"Wouldn't let us do that in the guard," Tir came back smartly. "Fret over what might and what mightn't and who knew what else? Those that did, didn't last."

"Tir—"

"You've done what you can, haven't you? We're ready as can be. Now take my good advice," in a lighter tone, "and give it to someone who could use some herself. Along with a dance or five."

Bannan shook his head. "More 'good advice?' "

"Only kind I give," Tir asserted. His eyes twinkled. "Bannan-sir."

"I think—no, I'm sure—that's worse." The truthseer gave up. "Call me what you will."

"Sir!"

They fell back into the rhythm of dig and pitch, side by side.

Bannan couldn't help but see the Spine with each lift of his head, stark against the black, torn clouds. Tomorrow he'd be there with Jenn Nalynn, to cast Qimirpik's rite and summon her pebble to Marrowdell. The tokens and words were in a pouch secured around his waist, beneath his shirt. He wouldn't part with them.

But tonight, he would most certainly dance, if the lady was willing.

Leaves turned on the heights, geese flew overhead, and, almost overnight, Marrowdell took on the faintly shabby look of autumn. Thick-coated horses and cattle spread out over the empty field, finding favorite spots from last year or making new ones, together wearing a path to the river. Despite the lingering warmth and green, everyone looked to the sky and nodded wisely to one another. Tomorrow's equinox might mark the end of summer, but this far north, winter was what followed.

Refusing to think of winter or tomorrow for that matter, Jenn wrestled the barrow containing the sum of her worldly possessions across the sod, taking the shortest path to the Emms' kitchen door. Once Gallie had heard the news, she'd rushed to the Nalynn kitchen. Jenn was as near a daughter as could be, she'd declared fiercely, and would have a home with them as long as needful.

There being no arguing with that, with Peggs being off delivering a cold lunch to the field workers with Hettie and Palma and Aunt Sybb visiting the Treffs', Jenn straightaway emptied her share of the drawers and clothes chests into pillowcases, leaving only what she'd need for the night and morning in the loft.

"Just run your things upstairs, Good Heart," Gallie greeted her cheerfully, Loee on one hip. "Mind the mess. We'll sort it all later."

The "mess" Jenn discovered to be the densely scribbled pages of Gallie's current manuscript, hung like laundry between the rafters. She worked her way between lines, careful not to dislodge any, and found a bed made up and ready. There were two in the room, but the rightmost was still covered in books, as were the chests for clothes. Where the Nalynn loft had a window seat, Zehr had built in a desk, presently obscured by paper.

Which would stay there, Jenn hoped, seeing no reason Gallie couldn't use the loft for her writing so long, she ducked, as they came to an agreement on the hanging of literature.

"Thank you again," she said, climbing down the ladder.

Gallie wiped her forehead with the back of her arm. "Ancestors Blessed, it's no more than your mother would have done." Her kitchen was filled with steam and curls of sausage; the twins, Jenn guessed, having enlisted their mother's help to prepare their grooms' portion of tonight's feast.

"Here, let me," she offered, taking the bundle of baby and receiving a grateful smile. Sitting herself on the ladder, Jenn gave the sleepy-eyed infant a knuckle to gum, smiling at the sensation. "Gallie, what do you know of my mother's gift?" she asked gently, keeping her eyes on Loee.

"Your father's the one to ask such things."

She looked up. "He's told me Melusine could find things. And bring things home."

"That she could." Gallie's face lightened. "When the twins wandered—you know how they are, one eggs the other into worse than either alone—I'd tell Melly and she'd call them for me. Before Zehr could get his boots on to go look for them, there they'd be, coming home." She sighed. "A sad sad day, when we lost her."

Jenn chose her words with care. "So she had magic."

"'Magic.'" The other woman put down her knife and gathered onion bits in her cupped hands, giving Jenn a keen look. "Yes, you could say that." She dropped the onion in a pan, then pulled down a sausage coil. "But it wasn't the kind with words and bits of dead animals."

"You mean wishings," she supplied.

"Yes. What your mother did required none of that nonsense. What Melly wanted found, was found. What belonged in a place, arrived there. This place," Gallie moved her knife in a generous arc "was where we needed to be. And of course, we needed the tinkers."

Jenn managed not to jostle the baby. "'The tinkers?'"

Gallie smiled. "We'd fields of grain, but what could we do with it? I remember the meeting. Davi and the rest shouting ideas how to harvest it, not that they knew how or we'd tools; Radd worrying about the mill. Some thought we should send to Endshere and sell the grain to any willing to come and help. Young Kydd kept arguing we should give up and leave.

"Melusine said not a word that night, but the very next day, the two of us were sitting on the porch, she with Peggs, me with my babes, and she told me to expect company. We needed friends, she said, and friends she'd found."

The turn-born could have taken what they needed from Marrowdell; they could have turned the villagers into puppets to do their bidding.

Was it because of Melusine they'd come as friends?

"Look at that. Here. I'll put her to bed." Jenn relinquished the now-sleeping baby to Gallie, who tucked her gently in the cradle behind the ladder. "I hope I haven't upset you, Dear Heart, saying such things about your mother."

Jenn smiled. "Not at all."

"Because you're the same. You always have been." Gallie straightened, brushing a lock of damp hair from her high forehead. "Haven't you noticed how we all come to you when something's lost?"

"Yes, but—" She'd thought it part of her reputation for being good-hearted which meant, as far as she'd been concerned, an inability to say no to any request, from help finding a button to, what was much more fun, locating a missing piglet. "Oh."

Hadn't Bannan found his way home by coming here?

If so, it hadn't been her doing, Jenn decided firmly. Bad enough her feelings could change the weather; she'd no desire to change people's destinies and wouldn't. Finding buttons and piglets was sufficient. "Thank you again, Gallie, for letting me stay. I'd better get back and help Peggs with the dishes."

Gallie nodded. "I'll see you later, then. The sewing?"

Added to the many unusual chores of this day were emergency alterations to Hettie's scant wardrobe, necessitated by her newly expanding waistline. "We'll be here," Jenn promised.

The best part of being together to sew, Jenn thought, was that Peggs couldn't fuss over her having moved out in front of Gallie, Aunt Sybb, Hettie, Palma, Lorra, and Frann. It was also wonderful simply to be with their aunt, who'd be leaving soon.

The worst part was sitting still on a day when so much else had to be done. To sew, which, no matter how one tried, couldn't go any faster. Not that she was in a hurry for the day to end, but Aunt Sybb had made daunting lists.

And there was the circlet.

"I could wear my own," Palma offered, though her fingers didn't leave what lay in her lap. Her earnest gaze went to each of them. "Couldn't I?"

Jenn lowered her eyes to avoid it. The circlet was of spun silver, with ropes of tiny pearls to hang below, and would be perfect over Palma's lush black hair. If only it had come from another source.

Before leaving the sewing circle, Riss Nahamm had placed a faded velvet case on the Emms' table. Inside had been this.

"Yours was lovely, Dear Heart," Gallie said kindly. "But its flowers have faded beyond use. Fresh are a joy, but with the season's change, we've none suited in bloom. You're welcome to wear mine, if you'd rather."

"Thank you, but you should save it for Loee, should she wish it." The innkeeper chewed her lower lip, then ventured, "There are roses—"

Seven heads shook at once. "We don't cut Melusine's roses," Peggs explained hastily. "It's a tradition."

"My apologies." Palma gazed down in her lap. "This is the most beautiful thing I've ever touched. I—I'm overwhelmed."

Aunt Sybb's tiny cough gathered their attention as effectively as a magistrate's bell. "Treasures have value only when put to good use," she said firmly. "Wear it and be happy, Palma. Keep it for your daughters' joy or pass it to another. Remember the circlet is a symbol, honoring those who gave us love and life, and a promise, to live a life of love."

Peggs' eye shone; Jenn was sure hers did too. No one moved or spoke, but everyone smiled.

Did Aunt Sybb blush? If so, she regained her composure, lifting her pen. "Now, let's go over our lists."

Arms around a basket overflowing with clean wet laundry, one of the items not on any list but needful just the same, Jenn stepped on the porch and turned sideways to get through the door. She tried not to notice that Aunt Sybb's cases were full and strapped for the trip to Avyo; she couldn't help but notice who was sitting inside the parlor.

Urcet rose with Kydd, who said at once. "Let me help with that."

Not when the basket contained Peggs' simples and nightdresses as well as some of her own. "I'm fine," Jenn said breathlessly, maneuvering her awkward burden through a room made smaller by their presence. She'd be even better if her dragon hadn't filled the Nalynn laundry tub with bedding whisked by a breeze from her and Peggs' bed, including the pillows, then curled up in it for a nap, but after the night he'd had, she could hardly begrudge Wyll some comfort.

Though it meant doing the laundry at the Ropps', their tub not presently soaking workwear, and then walking back between wagons and everyone in a hurry.

Remembering her manners, she blew sweaty bangs from her forehead and paused, balancing the basket on a hip. "Tea?"

"No, thank you."

She shifted the basket, not to make too fine a point. "If you're looking for Peggs, she's at the Emms."

Urcet touched his hand to his throat. "We're here for an audience with you, good lady."

Jenn glanced at Kydd. Seeing the grim set to his mouth, she nodded. "Give me a moment, then."

Once in the kitchen, she pulled the curtain across and got to work, fingers flying as she pegged laundry to the lines strung over the stove. They were for Peggs' sake, though with the twins now settled, her undergarments should be safe outside. Their father'd be grateful if so, since he walked into the laundry as often as not. Kydd, being taller, surely would.

Kydd, being who and what he was, must have talked to the Eld about magic. Now, they were here, waiting for her. She chewed thoughtfully on a peg as she hung the last nightdress. Because of the harvest, she hadn't seen Bannan yet today; with no way to know if he'd spoken with the dema, or the result, she'd need to be careful with Urcet.

Finished, Jenn paused to tidy her braid and be sure her feet weren't filthy. Taking off her apron, she grabbed a bowl of apples, Aunt Sybb's training being impossible to ignore, and slipped past the curtain.

The men rose again to bow. Flustered, for bowing made this a formal occasion, Jenn gave a token curtsy and put the apples on the table so hurriedly two fell off and rolled.

Kydd caught one in each hand, and gave them a peculiar look, as if suddenly reminded the apple trees had been strangers here too, once. Jenn took advantage of his distraction to sit herself; she folded her hands and waited. "Let intentions reveal themselves," Aunt Sybb would say, usually followed by "first to speak's the last to listen."

The men sat as well, Kydd placing the apples in the bowl. "Our honored guest has come with a proposal, Jenn," he said, proving Aunt Sybb right, as always. "One I believe you should hear for yourself."

Jenn turned to Urcet and waited.

The bead twinkled at the side of his nose as the Eld smiled. "The wealth of knowledge contained in this small valley continues to impress. Kydd," a gracious nod to the beekeeper, "knows more about Ansnan magical rites than anyone I've met. A shame we didn't correspond, as your brother with the dema, before my coming. I'd have saved considerable time and funds."

Kydd smiled too, but it wasn't a smile that warmed his eyes. "Anything's possible."

Waiting in silence having proved useful, Jenn gave a small, experimental cough. It didn't sound like one of Aunt Sybb's; nonetheless, Urcet waved a hand. "Excuse my digression, good lady. I appreciate that you're busy." With a flourish, he produced a slender brass case, displaying it on the palm of his broad hand. "Here is the Rite of Petition, to open the door to paradise. If you help me cast it, Jenn Nalynn, I'll give you the Celestial's Tear."

Stunned, Jenn looked from the case to Kydd.

"Urcet's well aware you're someone special, Dear Heart," the beekeeper informed her, his lean face without expression. "He came to me for advice, as your soon-to-be brother, and I said you might be interested in such a trade. Let's hear him out, shall we?"

This was the Uhthoff who'd stood up to an entire village, who'd named her magic and loved her sister. Trusting him, she nodded.

"First, we want to see it for ourselves, Urcet. The complete rite."

"Proof. Of course." Putting the case on the table, the Eld pressed the ends, then pushed his thumb firmly against its polished upper surface. The case popped open, revealing a folded paper and three flat-sided glass vials, their tops sealed with wax. "I ask your discretion. My esteemed colleague doesn't know." Urcet emptied the case, standing up the little vials, unfolding the paper. "He refused to countenance bringing such to Marrowdell, in case we offended the stars."

He chuckled as though the dema was foolish, but he wasn't, Jenn thought. Urcet was, to do what he wanted and not listen to warnings.

Kydd held out his hand for the paper. "They're only words until said at the proper time and place. And—" blandly, as the other man hesitated, "—by someone of magic."

Urcet gave her a hungry look. Jenn felt herself blush, then pale.

The beekeeper sharpened his voice. "The rite."

"As you wish." The Eld and Jenn watched intently as Kydd read what was inscribed.

Done, he tossed the paper on the table and lifted an eyebrow. "You've the tokens?"

Urcet folded the paper with care, first, returning it to its case. "I've the tokens." He didn't offer them.

Kydd rested his elbows on the table and put his artist's hands together. Pressing lips to fingertips, he regarded the Eld, then leaned back. "What's the price, these days, for a dragon's heart?"

A . . . ? Horrified, Jenn was about to object, but something gleamed in Kydd's eyes and she held her tongue.

"No more than its worth," Urcet said smoothly.

"I've no doubt you paid far more than that," the beekeeper

assured him. "They saw you coming, good Urcet. Dragon's heart? A chicken's. A goat's. You've fallen for the oldest ploy out there. Impossible ingredients for impossible magic."

"You lie." The Eld closed the brass case. "You seek to discourage me. To stop me casting this rite and bringing magic to my people." He thrust himself violently from the table. Apples spilled. "I will not be denied!"

As quickly, Kydd was on his feet. "Cast it as often as you want," he suggested, ice to the other's heat. "I guarantee nothing will happen, other than possibly the relief of gout, for what you've brought is a word-for-word translation of the Rhothan wishing to that purpose. I suggest, good sir, Dema Qimirpik is not so much a fool after all."

The two men glared at one another.

There was not to be a brawl in the parlor, the night before her sister's marriage, especially not a brawl between her sister's betrothed and a man half again his size. Jenn stood, welcoming the sudden bite to the air, glad to see the Eld lose his certainty and stare at her in dismay. "You've come to a place you don't understand," she told him sharply, "to take what isn't yours. While I admire scholarship, I suggest, good sir, you've a great deal to learn."

Kydd ducked his head and smiled as the air warmed again.

Urcet looked, if anything, more alarmed, but met her eyes without wavering. "It is plain that I do, Jenn Nalynn," he conceded, touching his throat. "If you wish me gone from Marrowdell, I will depart before the sun sets on this day."

Before the turn. If only he'd brought real magic. A rite with words and tokens to let her cross into the Verge.

But he hadn't. And if all the dema could do was summon a pebble, he couldn't help either.

Send them away? That was hardly fair. Jenn sighed and gave herself an inward shake. The two men stood watching her, each with his own intensity, and whatever happened tomorrow, as Peggs would say, today had to be finished first. Which meant tonight's dance, a thought that lightened her spirit, a little.

"Ancestors Witness, the more dance at a wedding," she said to

Urcet, "the better. Please stay for the eclipse and enjoy what else Marrowdell has to offer. I'd not have such a distinguished visitor leave thinking us poor hosts."

His mouth worked, as if something about this struck him more deeply than she'd expected, and he touched his throat with the fingers of both hands before turning and walking out the door.

Kydd bent to kiss her forehead. "Well done, Dear Heart."

"Was it?" She sank into the nearest chair. "He'll be angry at the dema."

"Protest being found out?" The beekeeper grinned. "I suspect Urcet will do a fine job of observing the eclipse and otherwise avoid magic for the rest of his visit with us. After all, he's met the real thing." With a satisfied bow to her.

Seeing his relief, Jenn knew she mustn't spoil the feeling or this night, though as far as she could tell, matters weren't at all resolved. "Magic doesn't do dishes," she said practically. "I've promised Peggs I'd clean up—" she began to smile, "—and hide anything breakable before you take over the kitchen. And don't worry. Poppa's promised to finish at the mill in time to join the feast." For, with this being the harvest dance, everyone would eat together.

He pretended a look of horror, but couldn't hold it, breaking into a laugh. "Ancestors Witness, I've no intention of missing a chance to prove myself."

She rose and touched a finger to his heart. "You already have." Lightly said, not lightly meant.

Kydd caught her hand in his. "Not until you're safe," he declared. "Whatever tomorrow brings, my new sister, you won't face it alone."

He was wrong. As Jenn gazed into his earnest face, that certainty settled around her heart, sure and oddly comforting.

Alone was how she would be.

"I couldn't ask for a better brother," she told him. "Be ready after breakfast. Now, enough of this. Go." She smiled. "Tomorrow's your wedding."

"Three weddings. And your birthday. Peggs' arranged the gifting to be before the ceremony, so—" All at once he blushed, looking years younger. "Ancestors Forgetful and Slow. That's a secret. Was a secret. Pretend to be surprised?"

It was silly and sweet and so far from what occupied her thoughts that she was too startled to answer right away.

"Peggs hopes to make you happy. We all do."

"I'll be properly surprised," Jenn assured him.

If she was there.

"What's that about?" Tir sat straighter, though the mound of stalks shifted under his weight and the wagon was moving at a clip that said Battle and Brawl were equally aware their work was done once they reached the village.

Bannan saw what had caught his friend's sharp eyes. Roche and Kanajuq were using sledges to hammer in supports for the small wagon, it having been moved to the center of the most open part of the commons, the telescope wrapped in protective canvas. He sagged with relief. The dema must have done as he'd promised and found some way to keep Urcet from the Spine.

"I'd say they've decided to view the eclipse from here."

"Ancestors Gullible and Taken, glad I didn't bet on it." Taking off his hat, the other wiped his bare head. "Rarely seen a man as set on his way as yon Eld. Going up there was all he'd talk about. That and his best friend's sister—"

"Tir." Absently. It should be good news, but Bannan felt a shiver of doubt. "What—"

Not a shiver. A breeze had slipped down his neck. A breeze that whispered, "Come! Now."

The dragon, and in no good mood.

"A summons from Wyll," the truthseer advised his friend, sliding down from the pile. "Keep an eye on them," he added as Tir made to follow, pointing to the caravan. Scowling, the former guard settled back.

The wagon behind was pulled by kruar he'd driven yesterday. Seeing him on the ground, the mares did their best to run him down, snorting their amusement. Evading their rush, Bannan bowed, then turned and made his way across the commons, urged by breezes that nudged him along as if there was no time to lose. However alarming that was, he kept to a walk, not about to rush headlong with everyone watching.

Wyll stood outside the tent nearest the river; not the one assigned them for sleeping, but where Jenn Nalynn had gone to be helped through yesterday's turn and would do so again today. Bannan threw an involuntary glance over his shoulder, but the sun rode above the Bone Hills still.

As he approached, he saw Wyll was without his boots and wore an ill-fitting shirt and pants. Moreover, his face, hands, and feet bore the scabs and yellowing bruises that, in a man, would be days-old wounds. He held his good hand cupped to his chest, as though over a pain.

What had happened yesterday?

Worse and worse. Tossing aside the pitchfork, Bannan lengthened his stride.

"Inside," the dragon said aloud when he was close enough, leading the way into the tent.

They'd prepared for the turn. Despite the sunny afternoon, the pole lamps set around the centermost mat were lit. There was a low table at one end, with Sand in her accustomed place behind it, and the stack of blankets made ready, on which Jenn Nalynn would lie. For now, the little white dog claimed it, tail covering its black nose, eyes alert.

Riverstone stood to one side, outside the lamps. Flint sat in a far corner, knees drawn to his chest and head down.

Something was wrong. Something new. "What's happened?" Bannan demanded.

"The Wound almost claimed them," Sand answered. "By day."

"It strengthens—" Riverstone began.

"Weakens," Wyll interrupted. "I've seen for myself. I know the truth."

There was no pebble on the table, no sacks, only an ewer and cups. They'd failed, Bannan thought bitterly, no matter the excuse.

"What truth na?" she asked grimly.

Wyll lowered his hand. A bedraggled moth sat on the palm, pinned by his thumb over a wing. "Do you know what this is?"

Sand made a dismissive gesture. "A pest with too much curiosity. Don't waste our time, lord of dragons."

"Imagine it much larger." Wyll held out the moth. "Imagine it filling a sky."

There was something implacable in the dragon's voice, a note Bannan hadn't before heard. That, or something in his face drew Sand to her feet. She came around the table to stare at the moth.

Then gasped and stepped back, her face filled with horror. "Sei!"

"It can't be," Riverstone objected, coming forward.

"Yet is." Wyll released the moth. After tidying its wings, it flew to perch on the stack of blankets, the little dog jumping out of its way. The moth took out its parchment, clearly intent on recording what happened next. The turn-born stared at it.

"A sei in Marrowdell," the dragon continued. "Most of it lies between but this," a flick of fingers at the moth, which lifted its plumes as if startled, "this much is here. To spy. To interfere. Above all," he said heavily, "to summon help."

"Help?" Bannan looked from Sand to Wyll. "I thought they were gods."

Sand shook her head. "Sei are powerful beyond our knowing, yes, and act as they choose, but they are no more gods than is a dragon. What do you mean, help na?"

"What we've named the Wound—what almost claimed you today," with a disdainful curl of his lip, "is a sei, caught in the edge. It's dying and calls to the turn-born for help, but you don't listen. If you do, and go to it, you die, because what's killing it—" Wyll bared his teeth in what wasn't a man's smile, "—will kill anything else."

Scourge had told him this much. "What's up there?" Bannan demanded.

"Nyphrit."

The name meant nothing to him, but it did to the turn-born, who exchanged quizzical looks. "Such are a threat to little cousins," Riverstone argued.

"These are like no nyphrit you've seen before, in dreadful number. They could clean the meat from a kruar before it screamed." The dragon smiled. "Only a sei could have endured this long."

"Go on," Sand said grimly.

"Kruar, dragon, turn-born. We've each had our part of the truth, but never all of it. Until now." It wasn't triumph giving Wyll's voice such compelling strength, the truthseer thought, but despair. "I saw it for myself, carried there by a sei who told me, 'The girl is the promise and last hope.' They've known since her birth. The one trapped here helped her survive; the others, helpless here, made me her guardian."

It wasn't a game. These beings, whatever they were, had meddled in Jenn Nalynn's entire life. "To what end?" Bannan asked harshly. "Did they tell you?"

"They told me," a grimace. " 'At the Great Turn, all things are possible.' The dying sei needs Jenn Nalynn to cross and save it. If she does, she will live and the Wound be healed." The dragon pressed his lips together, as if there was more.

The truthseer would have asked, but Sand spoke first. "Save a sei na? We couldn't do it. How could our Sweetling na?"

"We must help her. All of us."

The truth.

Against hordes of whatever nyphrit were, in another world. The truthseer shook his head, not in denial but protest. "What can we do? What can Jenn do? This is unfair, Wyll. She's—" he stopped himself. Jenn Nalynn was many things; helpless wasn't one of them.

That didn't make her a slayer of monsters. Or the savior of one.

Flint rose to his feet, eyes and mouth ablaze. "We hold the edge as much as any. Do more! Why are we lured to our deaths na? The sei could have explained. Told us what to do. Why not na?! Are we not worthy na?!"

The turn-borns' attention, and Wyll's, snapped to the moth. Sand gave a dismayed cry.

The dragon laughed.

"What did it say?" Bannan looked from one to the other. "Tell me!"

Flint and Riverstone shrank back. Sand cowered.

"This sei blames them," Wyll answered with grim satisfaction. "When first called to hold the edge, to help it, the turn-born were afraid and refused to listen. All of them."

Meaning they'd agreed. The truthseer stared at Sand. "Is that what you wished? Not to understand it?"

She knew what he meant, but spread her hands in a helpless gesture. "I wasn't yet born, but even if I'd been there, truthseer, I wouldn't know. What we do, whatever we've done na? Becomes part, becomes real. For us as much as the Verge."

"To undo this na?" Riverstone shrugged. "We could do more harm. We dare not."

"Still afraid," the dragon accused. "What use are you?"

"Enough. I've this." Bannan pulled the pouch from his belt and held it up. "It's Ansnan magic, to call Jenn's pebble from the Verge to Marrowdell."

"Useless. The girl does as much in her sleep." Wyll looked at Sand. "We need your help—all of you. She can't do this alone."

"Hello. I thought—"

They turned.

"—I'd come early." Jenn Nalynn stood in the opening to the tent, framed in sunlight, or did sunlight pour through her? Her gaze went from him to the dragon, paused thoughtfully at the moth, then came to rest on the turn-born. "I'm glad to find you all here. We need to talk about tomorrow."

Wyll's eyes were silver and hard to meet, but his anger wasn't at her. Mistress Sand looked unhappy, which might be about her. Riverstone and Flint? Aunt Sybb would say the pair looked rattled; they hadn't found her pebble either, Jenn decided. Bannan, though he smiled to see her, was pale under the harvest dust.

She'd interrupted an argument; easy to guess the topic. Jenn came into the tent and sat on the stack of blankets beside the moth. It tucked away its parchment and stepped on her offered hand, walking up her arm to her shoulder. "The others are on their way. And Peggs. We don't have much time." The turn. Would she feel it the rest of her life? "We need a plan."

"Yes." A careless wind swept through the tent, stealing pillows from the tinkers' beds. Wyll settled on the resulting pile with a satisfied grunt. A breeze tickled the hairs of her neck, then found her ear. "They've been humbled. Hurry, Dearest Heart, before they remember their pride. Get their aid."

She didn't smile, but she gave him a warm look.

The turn-born sat more slowly. Bannan hesitated, then sat as well, his eyes intent.

"My my my." Sand clicked her tongue. "Tomorrow na? Your birthday. Three Golden Day weddings, though not four," with an unreadable glance at Wyll. "Our farewell. You'll come here, to be safe, during the Great Turn. What more needs be said, Sweetling na?" she asked. "Besides what you'd like for a treat."

Pretend, Sand suggested. Pretend to be carefree and happy, before slipping away from her family and friends to die.

"You think I'll fail," Jenn accused. She'd come knowing what she must say, and what she mustn't. She dared not lie, not that she would, but if she was to save herself—if she was to save them—it started now. "I won't fail. Not if you help me. Please tell me, Mistress, what is a sei and how does one save it? For tomorrow I will cross."

Wyll half smiled. Bannan looked to Sand as if to remind her he'd know the truth. Flint shook his head and went off to sit in a corner.

Sand pursed her lips and glanced at Riverstone.

"You're sure what you saw na?" He pointed to the moth on Jenn's shoulder. At Sand's nod, he sighed. "Then what we know is yours, Sweetling. Turn-born do not dispute what a sei desires.

"As for the rest . . ."

The turn came and went. Knowing what to expect hadn't helped. Nothing could. Seeing her beloved face disappear before his eyes, fading beyond even his deeper sight, had been like losing her there and then. Peggs had sobbed in silence; Wyll had fled the tent, his face terrible to see. When it was over, what remained of Jenn Nalynn was nothing more than light within a shell if he looked too closely. For all that, despite it, she rose and thanked the turn-born with courtesy and grace, the only one of them able to speak.

Bannan found Wyll by the gate, staring at the Spine. The dark blue sky hung behind the bleached stone like a curtain, hiding that other world. A world he'd see for himself tomorrow.

"Jenn's gone home with Peggs." Needing the support, he leaned his arms on the top rail. "I have to believe . . ." He coughed the huskiness from his throat. "With her courage, anything's possible."

A breeze tore through the mighty oak by the ford, rattling acorns and rustling leaves. Its branches creaked a protest; the little wind subsided.

"No, it's not fair," he agreed, resting his chin on his arms. Bannan turned his head to gaze at Wyll. "You held something back. What?"

"What I can say, I have. What I can't changes nothing." The dragon's eyes flared silver. "Jenn Nalynn must succeed."

They'd made what plans they could. He and Wyll would wait at the tinkers' tent; Jenn would be there as soon as she could slip from home. According to the turn-born, all she need do was seek her pebble. The edge was weakest between the tallest mounds of the Spine; step there during the Great Turn and she'd cross into the Verge. By holding Bannan's hand, she'd bring him with her.

How to save the sei? They'd exchanged helpless looks, then shrugged. Hopefully, it would tell her how. As for how to fight through hordes of slavering nyphrit . . .

"We could use some help." The kruar and the terst turn-born wouldn't risk the Wound; Jenn wouldn't risk her family and friends. Just as well, in his soldierly opinion. Fear of any kind worked for the enemy.

"I'm here to seek it."

Bannan raised his head. "From what?"

"Don't be hopeful," Wyll warned, a snarl behind the words.

Something small, like a leaf and not, danced in the air. A house toad squatted by the gatepost. How could he not hope, when Marrowdell was so much more than it appeared?

Suddenly, the air filled with wings. Bannan gasped and moved his feet as something unseen pushed up and through the ground.

Dragons!

He saw nothing, heard nothing beyond the murmur of the river and the clatter of dishes back in the village, but there came a pressure, a call as powerful as any horn. His blood quickened. This was a summons to battle. More, to glory!

The air emptied.

Wyll raised his hand, then let it fall. "I don't blame them," he said at last. "If turn-born dare not interfere in a sei's workings, how can dragons?" He turned away. "The fools trust me with their fate."

Grief, not disappointment. The truthseer frowned. There was a question no one had asked, perhaps knowing the answer. He asked it now. "What happens if the sei dies?"

"It must not," came the disquieting reply. "More I cannot say and you needn't know. Now go, Bannan Larmensu. Join those who celebrate and see if you can make Jenn Nalynn smile. I must rest."

The heart of the village was aglow with light and music. Appetizing smells wafted past the hedge into the commons and Bannan's stomach told him how long it had been since that quick lunch in the field. Leaving Wyll, he strode quickly past the now-empty tinkers' tents and the pond. One of the sows regarded him sleepily then closed her eyes.

Tir Half-face eased from the shadows, matching his steps. "What's to do, sir?"

"Tomorrow morning, we go up the Spine," the truthseer informed him. "I'll want your spares."

"Steel against magic?"

"Against flesh and blood. There'll be creatures trying to stop us. Nyphrit, they're called. Like the mice here. Bigger, I'm told."

"Ancestors Glorious and Grim." There was light enough to see Tir drop his hands to the axes in his belt. "Give the word, sir. I'm ready."

Bannan shook his head. "Your post's at the gate." Before the other could object, he went on, "Keep Jenn's family and friends here and safe. Make sure Urcet doesn't change his mind." Sensing, if not seeing, the other's thunderous scowl, he added, "Don't worry. Wyll and Jenn have their magic, I've my own."

"Yours, sir, pardon my saying, is hardly a weapon." Though unhappy, Tir didn't argue; he understood the stakes and no one would pass him. "My spares are in the mill with my kit. I'll sharpen the edges tonight. Mind you don't cut yourself."

"I'll do my best." The truthseer grinned without humor, then nodded to the caravan. "Anything new with our friends?"

"That lot?" Tir raised his mask to spit. "Aie. They're going to cook one of their cursed dolls."

Adjusting their number. Bannan raised an eyebrow. "Someone's joined them."

"Or will. Could be they expect reinforcements. Without Horst," Tir shrugged, "who's watching the road into the valley?"

"Scourge and his lady friends roam the woods." The truthseer chuckled. "Pity anyone who tries to pass them."

"Bloody beast," more cheerfully. "Could be they plan to take someone, then. I know you trust the dema, sir, but with all that's going on, is that wise?" A grimmer tone. "Ancestors Witness, they're Ansnans."

"Stars witness, we're heretics who worship our dead and probably boil kittens." Bannan clapped Tir's shoulder. "This is Marrowdell, not the marches. I'll go and ask about the doll while you, my distrustful friend, wash off the harvest and change. There's to be a dance, as you've said so often today."

"You dance. I'm for the feast and the beer." Lightly said, but his hand found Bannan's shoulder, fingers digging deep. "It's no bad way to spend the night before a battle."

It wasn't.

The two parted company, Tir for the village, Bannan heading to the caravan. Sure enough, there was a pyre of smooth shaved sticks in front of the middle wagon. He sniffed, nodding as he smelled an aromatic oil. They'd come prepared.

Ansnans did. For an instant, the truthseer saw another pyre, already lit. It had been in the center of another patrol's camp, one seemingly abandoned, and they'd worked frantically to douse the flames and pull out half-consumed dolls. Fifteen, in sum. The number of Rhothans taken prisoner that dreadful night.

Prisoners now freed, he told himself, forcing a smile as Qimirpik spotted him and came forward, his hand out in greeting.

"Welcome! I'd hoped for more witnesses, but everyone's busy. Come. Come."

Urcet was nowhere to be seen, perhaps, Bannan thought, unwilling to be part of an Ansnan ritual. The odemi, Kanajuq and Panilaq, were waiting, the former with a blazing torch, the latter with a bucket of water. The three dolls sat in chairs and the veil of the leftmost had been lifted, as if its painted eyes, large, black, and round, should survey the proceedings.

Roche Morrill stepped from the wagon, pausing on the lowermost stair when he saw the truthseer. He was fresh scrubbed and dressed in a fine linen shirt. A flush mottled his cheeks, but he came the rest of the way. "Bannan."

Smiling broadly, the dema waved to the younger man. "Good Roche wishes to see Ansnan for himself," he announced. "We're about to adjust our numbers—for luck, I've told him," this as he placed a hand on the other's back to urge him toward the dolls. "Can't have too much when traveling."

Bannan gave Roche a sharp look. "Does your family know?"

"Soon enough." His look was met with a defiant one. "The world's larger than this hole. Dema Qimirpik's offered to teach me astronomy. I've no interest in that, but I want a chance to be special. To do what no one here can. I'll earn my way. I'll work." The voice might be sullen, but the words rang with truth; not that Roche could help that.

Whatever else, the boy had courage, to leave not only his home but domain. He might have a bright future after all. "Then accept my congratulations," Bannan said. "I wish you the best."

Roche blinked uncertainly, but he was given no chance to say another word. The dema pointed to the unveiled doll. "There you go. Make room. Make room."

They'd told him what to do, for Roche didn't hesitate. He picked up the doll as he might a child, supporting its torso and legs, and carried it to the waiting pyre. Laying it down, he took the torch from the servant and looked up at the sky. The Mistress showed, if nothing fainter. "By the stars' grace." He touched the flame to the oil-soaked wood. "I, Roche Morrill, take your place in this company."

He looked queasy as the doll's clothes charred away and the wood of its head and body caught fire, but the dema gave a loud "Whoop!" and took the torch, tossing it carelessly on top to produce a shower of sparks. "I, Dema Qimirpik, bear witness."

The elderly servants echoed the words, together and with enthusiasm. Roche might be Rhothan, but he was strong and young and used to hard work. Having his help would ease their lot for the journey home.

The truthseer bowed and said, "I, Bannan Larmensu, bear witness."

"Excellent. Wine, Kanajuq. Wine for everyone. This is a great day!"

Roche looked more bewildered than happy. He wasn't used to being the center of attention for the right reasons, Bannan judged. The truthseer circled his fingers over his heart. "Hearts of our Ancestors," he said solemnly, "we are Beholden for the fresh start being offered this man. And," a nod to the dema, "for the quality of his new friends. However far we are apart, Keep Us Close."

"'Keep Us Close.'" Roche said unsteadily. He held out his hand. "My thanks for your advice, Bannan Larmensu. I hope you find in Marrowdell what I couldn't."

Bannan clasped it with both of his. "Thank me by writing to your mother. Often."

There was already a subtle change in the other's bearing. A new confidence. Roche nodded. "I will."

"Wine!" urged the dema, a full glass in his hand. "This is a moment to celebrate!"

"It is, and my thanks, but I can't stay." Bannan indicated his dusty clothes. "There's the feast—"

"And Jenn Nalynn." Roche actually smiled.

"And Jenn Nalynn," Bannan agreed, smiling back.

Nothing was held back from the farewell feast. Tables creaked under the weight of platters and bowls, although this year's differed in that three of the offerings were the grooms'. Radd Nalynn kept refilling his plate, Kydd having proved an excellent cook. The Ropps took dutiful mouthfuls of Tadd's sausage stew before urging it on others, a spice having been mysteriously added that didn't agree with his to-be mother-by-marriage's stomach. Allin had no better success, his bread pudding being discreetly whisked away as there was something unnerving about its consistency. Hettie and Palma were not impressed, but Devins collected on bets with both twins.

Though the purple-tasting milk was all her body craved, Jenn Nalynn sampled every dish but the pudding, going back twice for her sister's summerberry pie. Tonight, she belonged here. Tonight, she was no different from Hettie or Peggs or Cheffy or anyone else in Marrowdell and she intended to live every moment to the full.

An intention her sister must have read, for Peggs didn't hover or fuss or even give her those thoughtful, worried looks. Instead, the eldest Nalynn daughter was all smiles and laughter, a vision of such beauty Jenn began to worry Kydd would walk into a tree.

The second loveliest woman in Marrowdell, however, didn't smile or laugh. Riss sat by herself, holding a ring of tapestry on her lap like a shield, and Jenn's eyes wandered to her more and more often. Finally, she excused herself from a lively discussion about waterworks in Eld and how they differed from Ansnor's between her father, Urcet, Tadd, and Dusom, a topic she'd ordinarily find fascinating, and, filling two tankards with beer, went to sit beside Riss.

The older woman tucked her needlework in its sack and stood. "Your pardon, Jenn. It's time I went home."

No, Jenn thought, it was time Riss began to heal. "Do you wish you'd never met him?"

"Heart's Blood!" Green eyes sparkled with fury, or were there tears? Riss sank back down. "What sort of question is that, Jenn Nalynn?"

"An honest one." Offering one of the tankards, Jenn waited until Riss took it. "You're so unhappy."

Staring into the drink, the other brought her lower lip between her teeth, then said quietly, "Ancestors Witness, I wish I'd met him sooner. Before all this. I wish we'd met when we were free to love and stay together the rest of our lives." She drank, deeply. "The sad truth? I wouldn't have loved him then. I wouldn't have noticed him, wouldn't have understood him, wouldn't have guessed the person he was or cared. The Hearts may move us at their whim, but we must be ready when they do. I wasn't."

"The circlet—" Jenn hesitated, unsure how to ask.

Riss almost smiled. "Don't worry. I'm glad Palma's excited to wear it." The almost smile disappeared. "More than glad. Of the things I most regret . . . my friend Sisyl came to say good-bye. She brought the circlet to show me. Her mother'd had it made by our favorite silversmith, you see, just as I'd hoped mine would do. I was so bitter and angry, I stole it." She sighed. "Ancestors Petty and Foolish, I don't know what I thought to accomplish. I could never marry in it."

Jenn touched Riss' arm. "Aunt Sybb says, life's trials make us the women we are. Whatever you think of your past, Riss, it's made you someone we all love. Especially Uncle Horst and he's—" with emphasis, "—no fool."

"No. No, he's not." Riss sniffed and drank a little more beer. "Ancestors Blessed. I miss him. I'll always miss him." She looked at Jenn. "How strange. It helps to say it."

Jenn smiled. "Then you should try saying it to someone else," she suggested gently. "My father, for instance. He misses Uncle Horst too."

"Radd?" A sudden dimple. "And risk your lady aunt thinking I'm interested at long last?"

"You knew?"

Finally, a smile. "Since Melusine's passing, Sybbie makes a point of taking tea with me just before she leaves, for the company and to discuss, in exquisite good taste, of course, her brother's many virtues. In case I become interested."

Why . . . why that was . . . exactly what Aunt Sybb would do, now that Jenn thought about it. "Oh. Has that been awkward?"

"Not really." Riss lifted her cup toward where Radd Nalynn stood talking. "Your father shows up the next day to apologize and share a glass of wine."

Jenn almost choked. "He knows?"

"From the start. Radd asked me not to tell. He didn't want to spoil her hopes and, between us, I think he feared she'd try to pair him up with Lorra or Frann next, though Sybbie's wiser than that." Riss laughed, the first time in days. "Your aunt's a treasure."

"She is." Jenn couldn't wait to tell her sister.

As if Riss' laughter had been a sign, Covie and Cynd bustled up to claim their friend, their faces wreathed in relieved smiles. Jenn took her leave.

There was no rush, not tonight, for the feast to end and the Beholding to start. Just as well, since the dema was late, and his servants, along with Roche who'd been helping them all day. More importantly, because she did have favorites, Bannan and Tir had yet to arrive and Wyll was nowhere to be seen. He'd promised he wouldn't leave the village tonight. Truth be told, she wasn't sure he had his strength back, but she wouldn't underestimate him.

Master Riverstone, Mistress Sand, and the rest were here, being congratulated and thanked. There was a great deal of backslapping and tankards raised to one another, the harvest having been successful, and the tinkers' wagons would be loaded with their share in the morning.

Jenn refused to think about the morning. She wandered contentedly through the gathering, admiring Alyssa's new ribbons and Cheffy's new-to-him shirt, walking a little faster when she overheard Lorra ask about the coming eclipse and Dusom launch into an explanation of what to expect, and a little slower when she noticed Aunt Sybb was talking with Old Jupp.

Which was just as well, or she'd have run right into Wainn and Wen. "Fair evening," Jenn greeted the pair, her smile fading when they didn't smile back. Thinking she understood, she added quickly, keeping her voice down, "Wyll made up his own mind. You can ask him."

"And you've made up yours," Wen said. She'd added a ribbon to her wild hair, a concession, no doubt, to her mother, and wore a dress that had been Covie's and didn't fit her slender frame, but in that instant, she looked like a queen. Not a story queen, but the grim kind from history books, who'd order armies with a crook of a finger, and were liable to have heads removed rather than debate.

What Wen was, whatever she'd become, in Marrowdell, for the first time, Jenn felt a thrill of fear. She looked to Wainn for help, but his eyes swam with grief and he shook his head. "You want to go alone, but you mustn't."

How? How they knew didn't matter. Gathering her courage, she turned back to Wen. "I will go alone. The sei told me to help myself; that anything's possible at the Great Turn. That seems plain enough. I needn't risk anyone else. I won't."

Wen tilted her head, as though listening to an unheard voice, then her gray eyes glittered. "'Anything's possible,'" she echoed carelessly, lacing her fingers with Wainn's as if it no longer mattered who saw. "But what risk love will take is not yours to decide, Jenn Nalynn. You aren't being fair."

"I know." Jenn laid her hand over theirs. "But it's my love that won't let me do otherwise."

Though they remained unhappy, Wen bowed her head. "Ancestors Dear and Departed. You take all our hearts with you. Be careful of them."

"I will. I promise."

Wainn gave her a searching look. "Know who you are," he said abruptly.

She couldn't see why she wouldn't; then again, the youngest Uhthoff saw a great deal she didn't. Jenn nodded gravely.

"And dance," he added, his face making one of its lightning changes from solemn and wise to simple and kind. Suiting action to words, he took Wen in his arms and whirled away into the night.

"Wen?" Lorra may have missed the hand holding, Jenn thought with a mild wince, but she hadn't missed that. Wen's mother approached like an oncoming storm, hat aimed skyward, hands clenched in her skirt to lift it from her rapidly moving feet. "Wen Treff!"

"If you'll excuse me," Jenn said hastily, moving out of the way. "I'm looking for my aunt."

" 'Keep Us Close.' "

Heartfelt, those words. Bannan murmured them with the rest, faintly amazed he'd known these people so short a time. He'd miss the indomitable Lady Mahavar more than a little. Marrowdell wouldn't be the same without her.

"Yon's a special lady," Tir said solemnly. He'd circled his heart with one hand, balancing an overloaded plate in the other, and now reached for the tankard he'd put aside for the Beholding. "Those Avyo clodheads best not give her any grief." This last a dark mutter into his beer.

Music started up, light and lively, turning sobered faces glad again. "Worry about it later," Bannan advised distractedly as Jenn Nalynn's searching gaze found him across the circle. He bowed an invitation and she smiled and came.

As she crossed what was now the dance hall, dancers moved together behind her, arms outstretched, laughing. He let his eyes feast as she neared, seeing her do the same. The green-striped dress was a far cry from the antique gown, though delightfully snug under her breasts, but whatever she wore, she'd be glorious. There was a glow to her golden hair from more than lamplight, a vibrancy to her skin that owed its source deep within. If he dared look deeper—but he wouldn't.

Not tonight.

"Fair evening, Bannan Larmensu," Jenn said with a saucy curtsy. Her eyes were aglow too, full of life and, yes, that was mischief, he was sure of it.

"And to you," with a full bow. Her feet, he noticed, were charmingly bare. "May I have this dance?" as he rose.

Her hand slipped into his. "If you can keep up, good sir."

From then on, time was measured in laughter and the trill of pipes. At one point, Uncle Davi scattered the dancers, carrying both niece and nephew on his broad shoulders, everyone clapping as the children giggled; at another, Radd and his sister took the floor alone for a lovely waltz that brought tears to no few eyes. Later, the grooms, wedding bands around their waists, were urged into the center to show off their dancing prowess. Bannan wasn't surprised when the elated beekeeper leapt higher and longer than either of the younger men.

Every so often and not often enough, the pipes would slow and someone sing. Jenn would drift into his arms and lay her hands on his shoulders; his hands would find her warm waist and their eyes would meet. They may have moved to the music or stood like statues; he neither knew nor cared. More than once, not often enough, his head would lower or she'd rise on her toes and their lips meet in a sweet, stolen kiss.

But the night wasn't endless. A bell rang, right when he least wanted an interruption, and the music stopped. "Midnight supper," Jenn told him, taking his hand to pull him to the tables.

Which wasn't, Bannan thought, what he hungered for. He pulled her into the nearest welcoming shadow and planted a far more satisfactory kiss on those warm and willing lips. Then another. And another. And suddenly, somehow, the ground wasn't moving under his feet as ground should, but sliding away and taking them with it.

Leading to a breathless state of things involving a sturdy tree trunk or was it a bench? There were uncooperative laces that gave just before being broken, followed by the disappearance of his shirt and a feverishly tender mutual exploration and . . .

Heart's Blood, what fiend invented such undergarments?!

Laughing, Jenn Nalynn pulled him to the soft grass to show him the trick of it.

And some time after that, the air filled with the scent of roses as Bannan Larmensu discovered what it meant to give everything of himself in love . . .

To someone who joyously did the same.

Jenn woke and smiled. Whatever the day and fate brought, last night had been everything she could have asked. And more. She turned her head to see Bannan lying beside her. He hadn't commented on the blankets or pillows until they'd been well used indeed.

Her smile deepened. Peggs had told her of this private spot, hidden by the mill and hedges; as Aunt Sybb always said, it was best to be prepared. She lifted her arm, shedding rose petals. Those had been a gift.

She looked up to check the sky. Overnight, the old trees had leaned close to roof their little bower. Seeing her attention, the branches spread apart.

The stars were dim. Almost dawn. Her long-awaited birthday.

And time.

It was a wish she'd made before and often. A simple thing. To slip away unnoticed while her father and her sister and her aunt slept, so she could run to Night's Edge and Wisp before anyone insisted on breakfast or chores. Sometimes it had worked. Sometimes, she hadn't made it through the kitchen door.

That was before she was magic.

Now Jenn Nalynn made the same wish, without doubt or hesitation.

After such a perfect night, you deserve to rest.

Don't notice me.

She could feel her magic flooding Marrowdell with peace, pouring through windows and doors, finding its way into tents and wagons. Bannan sighed contentedly and rolled over, his arm leaving her stomach.

Jenn rose, shedding more petals, and pulled out the clothing she'd brought stuffed in a pillow. Her plainest shirtwaist, her too-short skirt. Her hair she braided with flying fingers, but as she tied the laces on her shirt, her fingers lingered on well-loved skin and she smiled to herself, then at Bannan.

There was no time to waste. She intended to be on the Spine before anyone woke. The baby would probably rouse first, though like everyone else, tiny Loee had stayed up for the dancing and late supper.

The turn-born? Marrowdell was hers. Catching them asleep might not be fair, but she'd not have them interfere.

As plans went, she'd hopefully thought of everything, but as Jenn started to leave, she discovered she hadn't. The house toad, clearly not the least asleep, took another waddling step forward, then stopped. It blinked and yawned to show its sharp teeth, then settled on its belly. ~ What's needful, elder sister? ~

Jenn put her finger to her lips, then pointed to Bannan, hoping it understood. She dug her hands into her skirt pockets, hoping to find . . . yes. She put the pebble, ordinary but white, near the toad.

It turned to watch her leave with a soulful expression, but didn't argue.

Don't notice me.

Jenn made her way through the village. The mill was dark, as was Old Jupp's place. Her father was in his hammock, snoring gently. Roses turned with a rustle and slip of leaves as Jenn hurried past, but made no other comment. The toad and roses might be awake, but the horses stabled at the Emms' weren't.

Don't notice me.

Jenn dipped her finger in the fountain, then paused to wash her face in its cool clear water, drying her hands on her skirt. Candles guttered in their bowls, the odd lamp glowed faintly, and their light helped her avoid the occasional tankard and overturned plate. The chairs were still out, though empty, the festivities clearly having continued long enough for those usually obsessed with tidiness to leave it all for morning.

Don't notice me.

All quiet at the Uhthoffs, but she started when Devins' whistling snore echoed through the door of his house. The Ropps and Treffs slept as soundly as the rest and Jenn climbed the gate to the commons, holding her wish firmly in mind, daring to think of nothing else.

She passed the caravan. Passed the sows, asleep with their heads on their boar. She didn't so much as glance at the tinkers' tents, instead looking where she had to go.

Which was just as well, because otherwise she'd have tripped over Tir Half-face.

He lay on his sleeping roll, axes clasped in his hands, in front of the gate to the ford. Bannan's precaution, Jenn decided as she stepped around him. Hers, she thought, was simpler.

Don't notice me.

Over the gate and down the slope. The great oak shivered as she passed, but not enough to rouse Wainn and Wen, asleep in its branches. They'd waited for her and she loved them for that.

And wanted them safe.

Jenn stepped into the river. With the milling done and the gate closed, the water was its normal placid self; the work of an instant to wade to the other side. Once across, she paused to look back.

Everyone she loved was there, asleep and safe. Dawn was a promise beyond the crags, its first glimmer like the lifting of a curtain. She nodded, took a deep breath, and turned to face the Spine.

The road was a pale sliver quickly lost in darkness, but Jenn didn't hesitate. Her feet knew it, though laden wagons had crunched its stones and changed its ruts. This was her road and with each step she went faster or the road shortened, for before she'd taken three deep breaths she was there.

At the path to the Spine.

Like something wicked leaving on a light to tempt a weary and not very cautious traveler, that being a story Jenn would have preferred not to remember at this moment, needles of early sunlight stabbed through the dense undergrowth, illuminating the way.

That was to the good, she told herself. It was a rutted, twisty, and sometimes untrustworthy path. Light could only help her climb faster.

She took a step, then another, feeling that she didn't so much enter the Wound as leave Marrowdell behind.

Well, if this was to work, Jenn thought determinedly, that's what she must do.

She held up one hand as she walked, in case of webs, but there were none.

Just rustling.

Not like the roses but nasty and furtive, more and more from either side and she remembered the red-eyed squirrels in the trees that hadn't quite seemed right. She put all her will into her wish.

Don't notice me.

But they did.

~ Elder brother! Elder brother! ~

Wyll snarled. He'd finally found a position that hurt less than the others and this was his reward? He refused to open his eyes. ~ Leave me be. ~

Blissful silence. Then a toad landed in the middle of his sore ribs. ~ WAKE! ~

His hand aimed for its throat, but the little cousin, being wise or more alert, leapt away. Something began to stir in the dragon's oddly dulled mind. ~ What's happening . . . ~

~ She went alone! She's in the Wound! ~

Fully awake, Wyll struggled to his feet. The turn-born lay in their beds, unconscious or asleep, though light came through the windows of the tent. He thrust himself through the door flap to find Tir lying on the ground by the gate and no one in sight.

When he thought of Jenn Nalynn, of that warm and special feeling that told him where she was and how, his head turned to face the Spine. She was there, and afraid.

The little cousin squatted nearby, understandably pale.

~ How long? ~

~ I came as quickly as I could, elder brother. I tried to wake the truthseer, but couldn't. ~

She'd put them all to sleep. All! Except . . . ~ Why was I affected and not you? ~ Wyll demanded, offended.

~ Perhaps ~ it temporized hastily ~ because you are a man in shape, elder brother. ~

This useless body had betrayed him.

No longer.

Wyll sent breezes surging through the valley. ~ AWAKE! ~ he commanded.

One rolled Tir from his bed into the gatepost. As the man awoke with a curse, another breeze startled the livestock awake, the old pony leading a short-lived stampede. A baby cried and roses snapped and voices began to shout.

Though sorely tempted, Wyll merely shook the tinkers' tent.

He'd done what he could here. Now to see what he could do there.

Ignoring Tir's shout, the dragon went through the gate, splintering the cedar rails. He drove himself into the river, falling forward, struggling up with a snarl and spit.

Then was lifted!

Efflet!

Claws gripped him everywhere and they flew with all the urgent speed their small bodies could manage. ~ Brave little cousins! ~ he praised as they carried him along. ~ Find her! ~

Before it was too late.

TWENTY-FOUR

MICE.

But like no mice Jenn had ever seen. Their gray naked shapes came out of the shadows, dropped from branches, mewling and whining and whimpering in their eagerness to attack. The size of yearling pigs, they rose on their haunches between slow steps toward her and flexed their claws, red eyes hot with hate.

Nyphrit. That's what Wyll called them.

Whatever they were, they hadn't attacked yet. There was nothing for it but keep on, so she did, twisting and swerving to avoid them. The path fought her too, the ground slimy and uneven. Whatever magic helped her get this far abandoned her now.

Jenn started to run.

The nyphrit crowded close, catching at her skirt, scratching her legs, but couldn't keep up. She turned the first bend in triumph.

And stopped, her heart in her throat.

The creatures filled the passage ahead. She threw a panicked look behind. They'd left a narrow path open.

A trap or an offer to let her leave?

One began to move toward her, drool dripping from its open jaws. Others followed. Closer and closer.

Magic. She had magic, but what good was it if she didn't know what to do? Create a storm? She could be that afraid, if she let herself, but then what? A storm great enough to kill them could bring the trees down on her too, let alone what might happen to Marrowdell.

A trick or lure. If she could think what they'd want more than her and wish it, but they drooled as if starving and looked to her for their meal—

Then the first leapt! Jenn threw herself to the side, but it wouldn't be enough. She was going to fail, right here, because she'd—

With a grunt the creature convulsed and dropped, an arrow bristling from its side. Squealing in fury, the others backed away, but didn't leave.

Uncle Horst stepped into the open and notched another arrow. "This way!" he ordered. "I'll hold them."

He'd stayed to guard her. She'd wonder how he could be awake later. Her relief to see him mixed with her fear until she put a stop to both. "I can't go back." Jenn got to her feet. "I have to reach the top." Before he could object, she gave him the truth. "It's what my mother promised."

"Where's Scourge?" Bannan demanded, dressing as he half ran.

Tir had made the choice to find him. Whether that was the right choice remained to be seen, he thought grimly. Using her magic, Jenn could already be at the top. Alone.

"Haven't seen his bloody majesty since he and the ladies took off again last night. But Wyll's gone after her."

For all the good a toothless, crippled, dragon-turned-man could do. Bannan took the axes Tir proffered and thrust them into his belt. Wyll would do what he could, he knew, feeling a chill that had nothing to do with magic. They all would.

Why, Jenn?

He should have guessed. Should have known. She'd such courage. She'd never risk anyone else.

The first person to fool him, the truthseer told himself bitterly, and she'd done it with the truth.

Their hasty passage through the village was noticed. Kydd came to them still doing up his shirt; as others emerged from their homes, their sleepy curiosity quickly become concern, then alarm. Before any more could follow, Bannan stopped and put out his hand. "Keep them here."

"Where's Jenn?" the beekeeper demanded. "The eclipse's started."

Bannan shot a look to where the sun hung just over the crags. He couldn't see any change, but took the man's word. "She's gone ahead. We've no time to waste. Explain what you must, but—" he grabbed a fistful of the other's shirt and stared into his eyes, "—everyone stays here. Swear it."

Kydd nodded grimly, understanding, the truthseer knew, far more than he'd said. "Go."

Releasing his hold, Bannan clung to one thought. Jenn Nalynn. He pounded down the village road, Tir at his side, vaulting the gate in one smooth motion. He heard what sounded like cheering from the direction of the caravan, but didn't bother to look.

Mistress Sand stood outside the turn-born's tent. "Save my Sweetling!" she shouted.

The far gate was next, lying in ruins. Bannan looked a question at Tir.

"Dragon." His friend tossed his mask aside and drew his axes with a wicked twist to his gaping mouth. "Let's not be outdone."

Splashing across the river, their feet hit the other side as one. Wishing for his sword and pistol, though Ancestor's Witness, as well wish for his entire troop, Bannan drew his axes and focused on nothing but speed.

It wasn't far to the cursed path, but before they reached it, there came a splintering crash and groan, as though half the forest fell at once. Bannan grabbed Tir and pulled him back as leaves and branches rained down on the road.

It took a heartbeat. When the air cleared, they looked at one another in dismay. The opening was now blocked by a twisted mass of wood.

"Find another way," a calm voice informed them.

Bannan and Tir turned around. "Wainn?"

He stood as if he'd been waiting for them, his pole with its dangling lamp in one hand. "Those old trees aren't like the rest," he confided. "Wen says they've gone mad, being part of the Wound. They want to stop you."

"Where do we go then?" Time was wasting. Bannan could feel it. "Is there another path? I can't let her cross alone!"

Wainn tipped his pole at the forest. "Go up."

Climb that jagged slope, through the wild growth of old trees. Mad trees.

Tir followed his appraising look and paled. "Sir. You can't, sir. We'll cut a way through." Going to the jumble of wood, he attacked the nearest branch with his treasured axes.

Had they every ax in the village at work, it would take days to clear.

Having one hope left, Bannan brought his fingers to his lips and gave a soundless whistle.

Scourge had always heard it, had always come. It had been the one surety in his life, that whistle and his oldest friend's answer.

And, just when Bannan was about to despair, there came the thunder of hooves.

"I've two arrows left," Uncle Horst said quietly. "And this." He patted the short sword at his side.

The arrows spent had brought them to the next bend. His aim was unerring and, with each new death in their midst, the cowardly creatures had given way. But not far and not for long.

The Great Turn was coming. Jenn felt it crawling through her flesh. "I have to do this, Uncle." She put her hand on his shoulder. "You don't. Please—"

He shook his head, as she feared he would. As she'd known he would. "When I let fly this time, start running. Don't look back, Dearest Heart."

Jenn swallowed and nodded back. Standing on her toes, she kissed his grizzled cheek, then gave him room.

The old soldier moved ahead, notched his bow, and let fly. "Run!"

Her feet obeyed before she could be afraid. A nyphrit fell, bowled back into the others by the arrow's force. As she ran into that gap, another arrow whistled through her hair, grazing her cheek, to plunge full in the throat of the next creature lunging for her.

"For Melusine!" There was a flash of light beside her. A sword dipped and came away bloody.

As the nyphrit converged, snarling and howling, on this new threat, Jenn ran through. Two strides, three.

Heart pounding, arms pumping, she dodged and ran and did her best, not thinking of what happened behind her.

Suddenly a pair dropped from an overhanging branch to block her way. Heads lowered, claws flexing, the dreadful things closed in. She had to back away.

A wind came from nowhere and everywhere, knocking the nyphrit to the ground.

"Wyll!" She spun around.

Only to see Uncle Horst go down beneath a writhing mass of claws and teeth.

Scourge pranced in place, his shoulders lashed with sweat, his nostrils wide and red. "Why are you here? Why are we here? What is this?" With dark surmise. "It's that dragon's doing, isn't it?"

"Take me up the hill," Bannan pleaded. "That's all I ask."

"Up there?" The breeze turned numbing cold. "No! Up there is death. Today I cross and petition to return home. Today I may lead my people once more. Why—" as if they tried some trick, "—would I want to die? Why do you?"

The sound of ax to wood stopped and Tir turned to give the kruar a disgusted look. "The dragon's the brave one, then."

Scourge half-reared. "He's an old fool!"

"You're right," Bannan said heavily.

"I am? I am! He's a fool."

Shaking his head, the truthseer went up to the great beast and laid his hand on the hot sweating neck, then reached up to scratch that one spot Scourge could never quite reach. "You've saved my life countless times, old friend. Time I thought of yours. Go. I shouldn't have asked this. I'll find my own way. My thanks for all you've done, for myself and my forebears. It's more than enough."

The huge head twisted to bring an eye to bear. "'Done?'" the breeze said dubiously. "'Enough?'"

"He means it's time you retired, you old bag of bones," Tir said acidly. "Go tell stories to your foals."

"Hush, Tir. You've been my comrade and companion, Scourge. I wish you well." With a final pat, Bannan turned away to search for the easiest entry into the forest.

For any. Roots writhed and overlapped, waiting to snag an ankle. Branches with cruel thorn-like twigs laced overhead. He tried his deeper sight, only to flinch as he saw the miasma flowing where there had been ground and what sucked at the life of the trees.

Nothing mattered. Blinking free, he made to step over the first root.

A familiar nudge in his back sent him staggering into a tree. "Bloody Beast!" he snapped, whirling around. "If you won't help, leave be! I have to save her!"

"Then don't waste time," the bloody beast replied smoothly, a fire in his eye.

He didn't wait to ask or doubt. Securing his axes, Bannan stepped on a root, took hold of Scourge's excuse for a mane, and leapt astride. The kruar spun on two legs to snort an unmistakable comment at Tir; continuing to spin, he reared with a roar and launched himself at the impenetrable forest.

Heart pounding with renewed hope, Bannan laid himself along that massive neck and held on with all his might.

As the efflet dropped him, Wyll saw the old soldier fall but had no time to mourn. Nyphrit in appalling numbers whined and scurried through the neyet, gathering to attack in greater numbers. Those he'd pushed from the girl had regained their feet.

Oh, for fangs and claws and above all his own power. He'd turn them inside out and have them eat their own children. He'd . . .

All he could do was push them aside. The girl might do more, but she stood, shocked and motionless. She'd cried out his name so joyously. Now she saw for herself what little use he was.

The nyphrit changed their tactics, sending forth some to taunt while others slunk to attack. Something bit, holding to his bad arm. Something else had his good leg. Wyll shook them off, but a dozen more followed.

A nyphrit about to leap at him snapped in confusion as red scored its haunch. An instant later it was in pieces. Another squalled and died.

Efflet!

The nyphrit stopped moving, staring up with their red eyes. There was ominous movement in the branches above and to the side.

~ Careful! ~ he shouted. These weren't the nyphrit of hedges and holes. These weren't just larger . . .

Before he could cry another warning, nyphrit dropped from the branches, claws outstretched. Caught, injured, efflet became visible.

The nyphrit ate them alive.

He couldn't care, he mustn't, the girl was what mattered. If she failed, they'd all die, from efflet to old pony. But as more and more efflet were torn apart, Wyll scooped up one that fell close and tucked it in his shirt, snarling his own warning at the nyphrit who tried to snatch it, mouth gaping.

"Wyll! This way!" The girl had found a branch and swung it to clear her path. The sly things dodged back and pretended fear. They toyed with her, he knew. They lured her from him, took her where greater numbers waited in ambush.

Perhaps they wanted to tear her apart before the sei.

Even now, if he could, he'd warn them, tell them how killing the sei would loosen the edge and they'd die too. But the words burned to ash before he could utter them.

She vanished around the path's final twist.

Wyll flung his breezes, lurched forward, tried to follow. They played with him too, attacking from one side, then another. Those he could reach with his good hand died, broken, but the rest cared not. His wounds bled, exciting them further.

~ Elder brother! Bring them to us! ~

What nonsense was this? He shook his head, blood spraying. With nyphrit clinging by claw and tooth to him, an awkward and unbalanced weight, Wyll struggled forward. He would reach Jenn Nalynn. If he could do nothing else, he would put himself between her and danger. Let them eat him first.

~ Yes, elder brother! This way! ~

TWENTY-FIVE

JENN DROPPED HER stick and tried not to step on a toad.

She hadn't known there were so many. Hadn't known, she blinked in astonishment, their mouths could open like that. The house toads pounced and swallowed with a methodical thoroughness, making short work of any nyphrit foolish enough to stay on the ground.

While above? Above was a curtain like spider's silk, that glistened and gleamed and sliced any nyphrit that attempt to leap through it into very small pieces. Those who sought the safety of branches?

She couldn't quite make out what happened to them. It looked as though leaves, which clearly weren't leaves but she had no other word for them, were throwing tiny spears, and anything struck fell to the ground.

To be eaten by a toad.

"Dearest Heart! Are you all right?"

Was she all right? Aghast, Jenn hurried to Wyll, trying to find a place that wasn't bloody to hold him. "We have to take you back—"

"Scratches. But this?" He surveyed the battle with clinical interest. "This is—unexpected." In much the same tone Aunt Sybb would use for some combination of clothing Jenn had thrown on in the morning without looking.

"They're winning." Jenn suddenly sobbed. "If they'd come sooner—they might have saved Uncle Horst!"

"He gave the ylings time to set their trap," Wyll said sternly. He pushed her onward, adding, to her horror, "There are more nyphrit. Now go. The little cousins have opened the door for you and defend it. You must cross. The Great Turn is nigh. Find your pebble."

Her pebble. Jenn's mouth watered and she looked to the massive trees that stood like gateposts at the end of the path. That was the way to the Spine, to her pebble, to whatever she must do.

Before she could take a step, several toads left their battle to line up in her way. ~ Wait, elder sister! ~ one told her, eyes bulging.

A chorus. ~ He comes! ~

"It seems," Wyll said dryly, "they know something we do not."

If he lived through this—Bannan stopped there, certain he wouldn't but determined, regardless, not to fall off.

For Scourge climbed through this strange dark forest as if born to it, finding footholds where common sense said there were none, sliding his bulk and hapless rider through gaps where any sense of any sort shouted none existed. Bannan would have closed his eyes long ago, but he'd forgotten how. Forced to look, he did his utmost not to comment.

It didn't help that the kruar was purring. If he'd thought he'd tested the capabilities of this creature before, he was sadly mistaken. Poor Scourge. Bored silly in the marches, where there were roads and tracks and slopes that weren't perpendicular. Here, at last, he was in his element.

Scourge's head and neck lunged violently, not for the first time, jaws snapping closed over some unfortunate thing. Bannan slipped forward and barely caught himself.

Purring and hunting. "Ancestors Dire and Distracted."

An ear flipped back, conveniently avoiding a sharp twig. "That was pleasant." The breeze chilled. "No longer. We near the Wound. Be ready."

Bannan braced himself, for what he didn't know. There'd been no pull, no sense of something ominous and waiting as he'd experienced that very first night. Then again, this wasn't night.

"Now!"

They broke into sunlight and chaos.

Loathsome gray creatures flowed like nightmares. Most were heaped over one another in a heaving mass, the outermost baring teeth and claws in threat as they noticed the new arrivals. These were nyphrit?

Heart's Blood, Jenn had come this way.

Scourge roared with delight as he charged.

A sword flashed from the pile, skewering two nyphrit. Without thinking, Bannan jumped from Scourge's back, landing hard but rolling to his feet, axes out and slashing in the same motion. Three down, another two. They died easily but their number?

The pile diminished as those quarreling over a share of one prey grasped there was another nearby. Bannan fought his way closer, but Scourge, head, hooves, and jaws equally lethal, made it there first.

The kruar drove his head down and pulled back up, a man dangling from his jaws. The man swore like a soldier and slashed out with his sword. Nyphrit fell back, whining as if conceding their morsel.

"Easy, friend." Bannan dodged the sword as Scourge dropped his find and spun about exchange insults with the pacing nyphrit. "You're—" safe? He couldn't lie. "—not alone."

The sword point dipped and the man crumpled. "Heart's Blood." Tearing a strip from his shirt, Bannan wiped the mask of blood from the face. Horst. Who else? "Horst!! Listen to me. Where's Jenn?"

The old soldier clung to consciousness, how, considering his wounds, only the Ancestors knew. "Kept going. The dragon too. Leave me. Hurry!" His gaze was serene.

And implacable.

Bannan nodded. He helped Horst to sit, back to a tree, and put his sword in his hand.

Nyphrit watched with avid interest.

Mounting Scourge, the truthseer didn't look back.

Shadows darkened, and the sunlight glistening along the threads winked away. The air chilled and Jenn gasped and doubled over, the cramp a warning. The Great Turn was underway. She couldn't wait, no matter what the toads wanted.

Just as she opened her mouth to say so, a horse and rider thundered up the path.

She didn't, she thought with frustration, need rescue. She needed to be left in peace to do what she must. Well, she'd had a certain amount of rescuing, to be fair, but really, now all she needed . . .

Was for Bannan to drop from Scourge's back and wave the toads out of their way. "Hurry!" he cried to her and, of all things, began to run up the path.

Her path.

Spurred by an unfair outrage, Jenn ran after him. "This is my quest!" she shouted, somehow unsurprised when he glanced over his shoulder and gave her a reckless grin.

All at once, they were in the meadow.

Jenn was relieved to find no nyphrit waiting. Perhaps they needed the shelter of the old trees. Marrowdell stretched below, but it didn't look right. This early in the morning there should be long velvet shadows and sunshine sparkling on the river.

Instead all was strangely dull. She shivered and looked for the sun.

Most of it was gone.

As, she noticed numbly, was most of her. She began to sink through the ground. "Bannan!"

He swept her up in his arms. "Which way—there!" This as a moth fluttered from the grass between the two tallest mounds. As they came close, something vast moved within the stone.

They entered the place between and stepped from dim light to none.

"You know what to do, Dearest Heart," whispered the breeze in her ear. "Search for your pebble and you will cross. Beware—"

But the rest of Wyll's warning was lost as Jenn, beyond desperate, wanted to find her pebble . . . wanted to find it NOW . . .

The world folded on itself.

She was gone.

Instead the warm, vibrant woman he'd held only last night, in his arms was something cold and hard that reflected clouds and sky or glinted. The familiar golden hair, caught in a braid, the farm maid's shirtwaist and faded skirt, mocked his grief. Smooth glass turned to him instead of a face. Arms and hands of glass. Feet.

They were too late.

"Bannan? What's wrong?"

Ancestors Blessed, her voice was the same. He closed his eyes, then opened them. Maybe it was this place . . . "Look at me, Jenn. What do you see?"

"I see you," with puzzlement, then alarm. "Why?" A hand of glass lifted. "Oh, no! Oh—"

He pressed his face into her hair, smelling roses. "You'll be all right," more plea than promise.

"Did we—have we crossed?"

Pulling himself together, he looked over her head. "We must have," Bannan said wonderingly.

He'd stood on the flat top of the Spine, between mounds of bone-like stone, his feet on sod. Impossibly, he now stood at the top of a narrow rocky path that sprang into being in midair.

And led down. To a plateau wreathed in fog, where . . .

Jenn suddenly squirmed in his arms. He tried to set her down gently, but she forced herself from him and almost fell. Whatever else, she was solid once more. To his concern, she set off on that path, although surely she saw what he did . . .

Or did she?

"Wait!" He threw himself after her and took her arm, held despite her protest. "Tell me what you see down there."

. . . For something of astounding size lay sprawled on the outcrop below, partly buried within the stone, the rest heaved up as though, at the moment the stone hardened, it had been about to pull free. Trees, of a kind, surrounded the exposed flesh, if it were flesh, while between tree and flesh? Bannan was unhappily sure the moving gray masses were nyphrit, in incalculable number.

"My pebble," she declared, fiercely trying to pull free. "Let go!"

His heart sank. But he released her and followed.

Despite what lay ahead, Bannan couldn't help but look beyond. This was the Verge and he was here, in the land of dragons and kruar.

It was the world he'd glimpsed from Marrowdell. Rivers and lakes of silver sparkled in the distance. Feathered forests of purple and gold rose along the rims of valleys, and not all the valleys were in the ground. The landscape intertwined with the sky, so that down and up became a question of where one looked. The sky itself was half rainbow and half . . . and Ancestors Blessed, what was that, in the distance?

His foot slipped.

Fingers like iron steadied him. ~ Pay attention, ~ the dragon snarled.

Stones rattled and bounced off the path as Scourge pressed close behind. ~ Home! Home! ~

He wasn't hearing them—yet was.

But what mattered ran too far ahead, braid bouncing on her back and feet flying with absolute confidence. "Heart's Blood. Jenn!" he shouted. He went as fast as he dared, then threw any caution aside and ran as well, hearing the dragon and kruar coming behind.

He only hoped Scourge wouldn't run them over.

She couldn't see, really. She didn't need to, for her pebble was so close. It was like her dream, where she only had to hold out her hands and it would come.

~ You have crossed to petition us. ~

That was from her dream too. She was to ask, which was only polite, but she was empty and glass and well past desperate. "I've come for my pebble!" she told it. And wouldn't settle for less, not this time.

~ Come to me. ~ A slightly different voice, if either were voices. This was almost familiar. ~ Please. ~

All at once, she felt a powerful tug, as if anything could make her run faster. Her feet might be glass but they managed the rock as well as her flesh ones, maybe better, to be honest, because by now she'd have scraped her heels or stubbed a toe.

Jenn shook her head, feeling abruptly more herself. Why wasn't she waiting for Bannan, who she could hear came behind? How brave he'd been, to cross with her, to stay with her. But when she tried to slow down, the tug wouldn't let her. It was desperate too, and running out of time.

The Great Turn. She'd forgotten her purpose here was more than the pebble. She was to heal the sei and that could only be done during the eclipse. But there was no sun here, or none she could see, and the light was very odd, or dim, or her eyes weren't right.

Time. It might be different here or the same, but regardless, she had to hurry.

Close now. Too close. Red eyes had spotted them and nyphrit, those not eating the poor giant creature, began to mass where the path met the plateaus. Bannan threw himself forward, but Jenn Nalynn would get there first. She ran as if oblivious to the waiting threat.

She was turn-born and glass, he tried to tell himself. Surely she was safe from them. A gamble nothing in him would accept. "Jenn! Wait!"

A shadow darkened the sky.

Bannan threw himself down. It was, Ancestors Mad and Driven, it was Scourge leaping over his head, a naked Wyll somehow hanging on to his neck.

The kruar landed, hooves slipping and scraping on the rock, then recovered. Rather than run, he jumped like a crazed goat, no longer constrained to the truthseer's pace, covering huge lengths of the crooked path with each bound.

Bannan hurried after, sure he could hear the dragon swearing.

Something was in her way. Jenn squinted and tried to make it out, but it was probably, she decided, grass. Hadn't there been a meadow at the other end of this strange path? She gasped for breath now, which was reassuring in one way but since she couldn't feel a mouth, she was afraid to know how.

The path evened at last. Relieved, she began looking for her pebble.

To find herself face-to-face with a nyphrit.

Not one.

Hundreds.

They waited, staring at her. For her to move, she thought. For her to give them an excuse.

It wasn't fair. She was so close!

They sat on their haunches, flexing their claws, daring her.

They shouldn't, Jenn thought, beginning to feel more angry than afraid. They really shouldn't.

Suddenly, their eyes left her and lifted. Before any could do more than snarl, a massive dark shape leapt over Jenn's head and landed in their midst.

"Scourge?" It was, with Wyll, who couldn't possibly ride, somehow clinging to his back. The great warhorse moved almost too quickly to see, tossing nyphrit this way and that, crushing more under his hooves. Wyll was using his breezes to clear a path—for her. They did it for her.

From hundreds to thousands. A wave of nyphrit appeared at the edge of her vision, running atop one another in their eagerness for battle. They'd overwhelm her protectors, tear Bannan apart as they had Uncle Horst . . .

No, Jenn Nalynn decided, they wouldn't.

She didn't like nyphrit. What she really liked, and what properly belonged in a meadow, were rabbits.

Just like that, red eyes became soft brown, drooling muzzles shrank to cute furred noses, and rabbits replaced every nyphrit.

That, Jenn Nalynn thought happily, was more like it.

The power of a turn-born.

Wyll dropped from the kruar's bloody back, staring as rabbits bounded away in all directions. Scourge huffed and snorted, still in a fine battle rage, but there was nothing left to fight.

And nothing to contest her.

Glittering like ice, the creature who'd been Jenn Nalynn walked toward the imprisoned sei, meadow sprouting behind as her whim changed bare rock.

And the dragon moved out of her way.

TWENTY-SIX

THINGS WERE WORKING out much better than she'd expected, Jenn thought. Why, this place was nice enough. Almost as pleasant as Night's Edge.

It wasn't, of course. This was where she'd find her pebble. She knew exactly where it was now, just over there, at the base of that white hill. Not a hill, she supposed, but as creatures went, a big lump didn't seem as dangerous as the nyphrit had been.

She'd taken care of them, hadn't she?

Which was fine, but there was still something wrong about this place. If she tried to look at the sky, it was all twisted and the wrong color. If she looked into the distance, nothing made sense.

Perhaps, she thought, that was why she'd been summoned here. To put things right. She closed her eyes to keep out the confusion, and wished, very clearly and strongly, for things to be nice and normal and real again, just like at home.

She opened her eyes hopefully.

To find herself standing in the dark.

"Jenn Nalynn!" The love of his life had turned a multitude of slavering, albeit small, monsters into rabbits. Bannan laughed as he ran. If only he'd had her in the marches . . .

His feet caught as the ground under him sprouted asters and daisies. He fell, face first, into what felt like thick sod, and stared, bemused, at what appeared a line of ants.

What was she doing? Climbing to his feet, Bannan moved more cautiously. Jenn was still too far away to hear his voice, but meadow spread from wherever she'd stepped, consuming the plateau.

Meadow, he thought grimly, that didn't belong here.

Scourge stood surrounded by flowers and rabbits, looking as discomfited as ever he'd seen him. Wyll leaned on the kruar's shoulder, staring after Jenn Nalynn. As the truthseer approached, he turned a face full of grief. "She's destroying the Verge."

"I'll stop it," Bannan heard himself promise.

Not that he knew how.

What had she done?

It wasn't an ordinary darkness. Jenn knew that, just as she knew she didn't dare take a step, for there was nothing to stand on. Something she'd wished had gone wrong, again. Why hadn't she been more careful, thought harder, been wiser?

"Jenn."

Her name, in his husky voice, wrapped around her like sunshine. Though she hadn't thought her eyes closed, it was as though they'd opened.

Bannan, right there, standing in the dark. She saw him, she realized with a shiver, by the light coming through her own skin. Lifting her hands, she held them near his face, to better see him. "Dearest Heart," she whispered, when she saw the fear in his eyes.

"You have to stop," he told her. "You're changing this world into ours and you mustn't."

"I saw no world. I want to," she explained earnestly. "I want to see what's real more than anything."

The fear left his face, replaced by understanding, then compassion. "Ah, Jenn. You wanted to see wonders, didn't you? The world beyond Marrowdell? It's here, Jenn Nalynn, waiting for you. Let yourself see. Remember my letters?"

Which was so odd a request she frowned. "Of course I do."

"The rivers of silver. The sky like a rainbow from one end to the other."

He'd written of them. Of more. They were here? "I didn't see them."

"I couldn't see Scourge for what he was, Dearest Heart, until I accepted he wasn't what I thought. Look at the Verge again, and see it as I do. See the wondrous place it is."

It wasn't wondrous if it contained nyphrit, Jenn thought, but something in her responded to his voice, to the certainty in his eyes. "The sky . . ." she began.

And there it was, like no sky she'd seen or imagined. Jenn gasped and staggered, feeling his arms warm around her. "I've got you. Don't worry about up or down." He laughed. "They aren't as important here. Can you spot a river?"

This time, as if she saw with his clear sight, there it was. A ribbon of the finest silver, winding its way into . . . into a forest of feathers and up, which was truly strange, into a valley of . . . and buildings . . . buildings of crystal.

All at once, the Verge stretched out before her like a glorious painting. In the distance, as if singing to her heart, dragons.

And closer, shaking his head, her dragon. "Leave the rabbits," Wyll advised, an odd smile on his face. "But stop the meadow. Please."

What did he mean? Jenn pulled free of Bannan to look around and winced. A meadow, a perfectly fine and normal Marrowdell meadow, was growing outward from where she stood as if she'd spilled it like milk.

Stop! she wished.

It did, daisies nodding in surprise.

This, Jenn knew, was exactly why Mistress Sand and the other turn-born hadn't wanted her here. She would have, she feared, a great deal to explain. But first. "I have to find my pebble. And save the sei."

Bannan bowed. Wyll nodded, his pride in her shining in his eyes. She chose to ignore Scourge's interest in the rabbits.

There were trees in her way, but cooperative ones that lifted their branches to let her pass. Jenn nodded her thanks.

There were a great many rabbits, most looking quite puzzled. Some had already discovered the clover of the meadow and were nibbling contentedly.

~ Help me. ~

Stepping between rabbits, Jenn went to the wall of stone. This was where her pebble waited. This was where she'd had to come. "What do I do?" she asked, laying her palms against the stone.

But it wasn't stone, it was an eye larger than the world, and from that eye dripped tears of pearl white.

Without need to think, Jenn leaned forward and opened her mouth, not that she had one, but there was something she did like that and . . .

A tear landed on her tongue and she swallowed.

It burned!

More than the tinkers' beer or milk, more than the time she'd scalded her wrist on the kettle. It was pain yet wasn't . . .

Because it filled that hollow within, and helped make her whole again.

She drank tear after tear, knowing the moment she'd had enough, pressing her lips to the stone eye in thanks.

"How can I help you?" she asked it. "What do you need?"

~ Bring me home. ~

It was home, Jenn thought. At once, something told her she was wrong, that it wasn't quite. Melusine's magic, to bring the lost home again.

A turn-born's, to find the way.

A little pull, she decided. Like . . . THAT.

The eye closed as the hill sank into the ground. All around the plateau, other smaller hills disappeared. It felt right, Jenn thought, beginning to smile.

Everything did.

"Jenn?"

She reached for Bannan's hand, then, seeing her own, brought it before her wondering eyes. "Look at me!"

Her skin was glass, but inside was pearl, warm and aglow. It was much, much better than being filled with rocks or buttons.

Then, for some reason, she remembered what Wainn had said. "Know who I am," she whispered. Was it possible? Could it be that simple?

Yet as she looked, the pearl faded and her skin took on its familiar hue. She touched her fingers, the nails, turned over the palm to see streaks of dirt. Brought both hands to her face, to feel a mouth and eyes and a nose. "What am I?" she asked.

Bannan caught her hands in his. "I look at you," he said gently, "and see Jenn Nalynn."

~ What about me? ~ Scourge stomped a hoof, then startled them all with a roar. ~ I demand my right to petition! ~

~ We hear you. ~ The voice seemed to come from everywhere at once.

The kruar snorted, seemingly unimpressed. But when he spoke next, it was with quiet dignity. ~ Is my penance fulfilled? ~

~ It is, Lord General. ~

Scourge lowered his head as if overcome, then to Jenn's surprise, made a whuffing sound toward Wyll. ~ And his? ~

~ I don't need you to ask for me, ~Wyll said acidly, eyes silver.

~ You needed me to get you here, ~ the kruar retorted.

~ Without me, you wouldn't have lasted this long! ~

"Wyll," Jenn interrupted. "Ask!"

The silver left his eyes. ~ It doesn't matter, ~ he said gently.

It mattered to her. "Is his penance fulfilled?"

The voice seemed amused. ~ We leave that to you, turn-born. ~

Her. It was up to her? "Yes!" Jenn said at once. "Of course."

Nothing changed. Wyll stood there, naked as when she'd first seen him as a man, except for streaks of blood and bruises starting to bloom. Too many bruises, she thought with regret, all on her behalf.

"It's up to you," Bannan whispered in her ear.

He was, she thought, giving him a thankful smile, almost right.

Going to stand before her first and best friend, Jenn asked, "Wyll, what do you want to be?"

He touched her cheek, a breeze ruffling her bangs. "I want to be Wisp," he told her, "and your friend."

"Always," she whispered. Then she kissed him on the mouth, tasting ash, and, stepping back, made her wish.

A blade like ancient bone, long as her longest finger, the tip like a needle, the underside of its elegant deadly curve serrated. A tuft of wiry hair, curled like the end of a beard. Breath like steam. Skin like woven chain, as fine as the best linen.

Glimpses. Wyll gazed back at her, still a man.

She faltered. "I hadn't seen enough."

~ I see the expectation of this turn-born. ~ A new voice, strange yet familiar. Jenn looked up to meet the emerald eyes of a dragon, though it didn't seem quite a dragon for as she looked at it, for an instant it was a moth.

All at once, a ball of flame came crashing down, consuming Wyll! As Jenn screamed and Bannan shouted, the fire died, leaving a huddled shape, coated in bright green ash. She held her breath as the shape struggled and moved, ash drifting away.

Away from silver scales and a long face, with glittering amethyst eyes and nostrils breathing smoke. A beard did indeed hang below fanged jaws. A shudder, and ash fell from a wing, stretching out and up as though amazed to be free. More ash and a tail ending in deadly spikes swung through the air. A foot, with claws just as she'd glimpsed. Another foot, larger.

His other side. Jenn's heart panged as the ruin of first one, then the other leg appeared, as the old, healed, but dreadful scars along one side came clear. The wing, still aglitter with ash, was held tight against the body. It was withered . . . useless . . .

It was not! "No!" she cried, adding her wish. Insisting on it!

And the wing, curled against his side, unfolded, a perfect match to the other. The dragon curled his neck to bring his eyes to stare at it.

With a shake, the last of the ash came free.

And winked away.

~ What am I? ~

"Wisp," she said fiercely. "And my friend." Jenn put her arm around Bannan, blinking away tears of joy. "Thank you," she said to the green dragon, which wasn't, she decided, remotely as handsome as Wisp.

Who was more than handsome. As he stretched his wings, his tail supporting his crippled side, the polished surface of his scales reflected the light. His eyes were every bit as expressive as they'd been as a man's, and Jenn smiled when they found hers.

And suddenly, there were dragons everywhere. Blue and gold and red and colors she couldn't name. They filled the air, almost touching, though they gave the sei wide berth. Others, to her amazement, flew up through the ground. "Me and my broom," Bannan said in her ear.

~ You have served your penance, Dragon Lord, Lord General, ~ the sei told them. ~ You may return to your kind. ~

~ At last! Farewell, truthseer, turn-born! Dragon, may we meet in— ~ perhaps thinking better of "battle," Scourge finished with ~ — the hunt! ~

With that, he ran off, tail flagged, kicking his heels at any dragon that came too close. As he made his way along the ridge connecting this plateau to the next, kruar appeared from their hiding places to run behind, their crests glittering.

Jenn felt Bannan sigh. "Be happy, old friend."

She looked to her friend, who hadn't left. Though it was the hardest thing she'd ever done, Jenn said to Wisp, "Go. Be happy."

With a fierce roar, he launched into the sky, scattering his kind. They whirled in a dance of color and motion, then, as suddenly as they'd come, the sky was empty.

The dragons, her dragon, were gone.

"Horst." Bannan shook his head grimly. "We had to leave him."

Jenn tucked her arm in his. "I know." Crossing back had been, as Mistress Sand promised, a matter of being there, and wanting to be here. Here was the Spine and the path down. A path she no longer feared. This was no longer the Wound, but a path like any other. Though, from the rustling, there were a few nyphrit.

Rabbits, she warned them.

There were two less mounds on the Spine, and those left were sunk deeper in the ground. Explaining that she'd leave to the astronomers.

Bannan stopped at the first bend, turning to her. "You could wait here."

"It's all right. I'll come."

Jenn had braced herself, but she gasped as she saw Uncle Horst's body, slumped against the tree. "Is he—?" There was so much blood. He couldn't possibly . . .

The truthseer dropped to one knee beside him. After an endless moment, he looked up. "He's alive, but not by much. We have to get him to the village." He lifted the other as gently as he could.

They could use Scourge. "I'll get Davi and his cart."

"The trees blocked the path," he warned.

"That much," Jenn promised, "I can do."

In the end, it was Urcet and Roche with the small wagon, the telescope left in the commons. The long-legged ox proved nimble and the old trees listened when Jenn demanded passage, though they'd shed some branches that had to be moved. And though Urcet and Roche paled at how quickly the road passed on the homeward trip, they made no comment.

"Sweetling na?" Mistress Sand came out of her tent, with Master Riverstone behind her. Seeing what they brought, she made a sound of distress. "Bring him inside, quickly. We have our ways," she added, giving Jenn a look full of meaning.

They'd helped Wainn, Jenn remembered, and nodded gratefully.

"Please. Anything you can do. Uncle—" Her fingers stroked the unconscious man's hand, then she looked up. "He saved me, as much as anyone did. I shouldn't have tried to go alone."

"If you hadn't," Sand said soberly, "who's to know what would have happened na?" As the others worked to move Uncle Horst, she came close, her eyes suddenly aglow. "Sei. Can it be na?"

"It wasn't a pebble." Jenn took a deep breath. "But I feel—I feel myself again. As if nothing had happened. Whole."

"What's in you, Sweetling, is nothing we'd dare touch," the turnborn told her, which was hardly a comfort, then she added what was, "All's well, I say. Now go reassure your aunt. She's refusing to hold the weddings until she knows you're safe, and no one argues with that fine lady."

"No," Jenn almost smiled. "No, they don't."

"I'll take your word for it, sir."

Bannan, razor poised at his throat, paused to regard his friend in the mirror. "We crossed to the other world. The Verge. And back."

Tir gave a contented grunt. "S'long as I don't have to."

"You might like it." The truthseer smiled to himself. "There are dragons."

"That's not as appealing as you might think, sir." But Tir's eyes gleamed above his mask. "You say the bloody beast stayed behind. I won't say I'll miss him—"

"We both will." Shave done, Bannan rinsed his blade. "But he deserves to live his own life."

"Speaking of that, sir. Bannan."

When his name came out, things were serious. This time, however, he suspected the best, not the worst. "I take it you're leaving Marrowdell."

Tir leapt to his feet. "Knowing if you hear the truth's one thing," he said suspiciously. "Spying out a man's secrets is another altogether."

"Peace, my friend." Bannan turned and raised an eyebrow. "Lady Mahavar's offered you service in Avyo, hasn't she?"

"The good lady needed an escort to Endshere, sir, and who else was to do it? And as I told her, Endshere's not good enough, what with her guardsmen being lax at best, so I'd go to Weken and on—" Tir stopped and rubbed a hand over his head. "That obvious, was it?"

"That obvious." Bannan put his hand on the other's shoulder. "And I couldn't be happier. Get her safely here again, come spring." He pushed gently. "Both of you."

Tir nodded, eyes agleam. "I confess I'd worried if you could manage without me, sir, being alone as you are and helpless. But I know you will. She loves you."

"It's that obvious?" the truthseer asked, bemused.

"To a blind man," Tir said with complete satisfaction.

"Jenn, do you have any?" Peggs sounded desperate.

"I'm looking." Jenn couldn't help her smile. Who'd have thought, after the morning's wild adventures, she'd be frantically hunting hairpins.

Who'd have thought she'd be without Wisp or Wyll.

Which was, she reminded herself, because he was finally being who he should be, where he should be, without some fool girl interfering. "Found some," she exclaimed, stuffing them in her mouth and turning to her sister.

Who, despite a few stray hairs, had never been more beautiful. "What?" Peggs asked, giving her dress a worried look. "Is something else wrong?"

"Nothing," Jenn assured her, mumbling through the pins. "Nothing at all." She climbed on the bed to fix Peggs' hair. "There. You're perfect."

"Hardly," her sister said, but happily. The dress, their mother's, was wedding blue, the bodice thick with silver thread. Melusine's circlet crowned Peggs' thick black hair and her eyes sparkled with joy.

"Now, you?" She captured Jenn's face in her hands and searched it, finally nodding. "I can't believe the difference. And you're sure there's no—ah—rocks?"

"No rocks. Or gloves." She raised her arms, sleeves falling back to reveal skin. "That's how terst look like us. Wainn knew. I'm who I am. If I want to look like them, I can. I'll show you," she offered shyly, "if you like."

Peggs nodded at once. "Please."

Undoing her laces, Jenn let her shift fall to her ankles, then did.

It wasn't so much a wish, as an inward, ticklish stretch, that left her glass, light, and a sei's tears.

She stood on the bed and waited for her sister's opinion. It mattered, Jenn suddenly realized, more than anything.

"Ancestors Blessed," Peggs whispered. Her fingers trembled as they touched Jenn's arm, then her face. Just as she began to worry, her sister's face lit with a smile and Peggs poked her in the ribs, making her giggle. "You feel like you," Peggs announced with satisfaction, as if that had been of greatest concern, then shook her head wonderingly. "But how you look, like this? I've no words for how strange and beautiful you are, little sister. Kydd will want to paint your portrait."

"I'm not," Jenn said firmly, pulling on her shift, "posing like this for your husband."

Peggs laughed, then sobered. "Everything's better now, isn't it? Even Wyll?"

She nodded. Bannan had thought to say that he'd given Wyll his horse, as his former rival saw no more reason to stay, but Peggs knew the truth. "Much better," she said. "He's free now and happy."

Otherwise, the Great Turn had passed with no greater incident, so far as Marrowdell was concerned, than a minor rumbling of the earth that sank those portions of the Bone Hills on the Spine. Of more interest and import was poor Horst being mauled by what everyone assumed to be a bear. But they had him back, and he'd heal, surely a sign this was the Ancestors' Golden Day.

And soon, the weddings.

"Hurry up," she ordered her sister. "Kydd's waiting!"

Marrowdell gathered under a cloudless sky, to inform the Ancestors on their Golden Day of the union of families, as Rhothans did. Other weddings might be more formal or less; others, Jenn was sure, weren't as much fun. For this was a time of joy and hope, and only smiles would do.

The brides were beautiful, every one. The grooms, well, there was no doubt Tadd and Allin hadn't been as clean in all their lives, and their mother had surely tied the bands around their waists, but Kydd Uhthoff? He wore his brother's best long coat, despite the weather, and looked like a lord.

Except, Jenn smiled to herself, when he saw Peggs. Dignity was part of the man and grace, but that boyish grin took years from his face.

For the Wedding Beholding, the three couples would stand on a carpet. There being none large enough, a quilt had been laid out by the fountain, but no rug could be finer, Aunt Sybb had declared, given the quality of the work. Frann had actually blushed. The Beholding itself was led by the eldest of the bride's family. There being three brides, two being connected to the same family, and none of Palma's relations in the village, all had agreed Master Jupp should be asked instead.

The twins and Devins, Hettie had informed Jenn and Peggs with a grin, had promptly placed bets on whether Old Jupp would remember to be there.

They'd lost, of course. An event like this was tonic to a gentleman of past responsibility and honor. Well ahead of time, he arrived with Riss on his arm, wearing his finest tall hat and prepared to do his duty.

"Did you like it?" Alyssa whispered as they waited for him to be ready. "I made the string."

Jenn smiled down at the child, touching the painted bead. "Very much," she whispered back. As Peggs had planned, her birthday gifts had arrived before the weddings. The colorful bead, on its freshly braided string, was from the Ropps and had been originally carved by Zehr Emms. The Treffs had given her a book of poetry remarkably similar to the one she'd thought to borrow from Master Dusom. Devins and Roche, not to her surprise, had given her a rather familiar jar of pickles. Riss and her great-uncle's gift was one of her beautiful tapestried pillows. The Emms shouldn't have brought her a gift, since they'd given her a roof and bed, but nothing would do but Gallie give her a candlestick that had been Lorra's last year. The dema and Urcet had gotten involved as well, though as guests it wasn't expected of them, giving her a small brass telescope. Hettie couldn't keep her eyes off it, so Jenn knew who would get it next. The tinkers brought her a keg of beer, Flint giving a wink, and Jenn had immediately promised to share it.

As for Bannan Larmensu? He'd looked mysterious and said his present would come later.

She could hardly wait.

Poppa had kissed her forehead, then looked her in the eyes to say she was now adult in the eyes of the law and free to make her own choices. Aunt Sybb had smiled, adding, "Something you've always done, Dearest Heart." With Peggs, they'd taken her in their arms, and that moment had been the best gift of all.

"Hearts of our Ancestors," Master Jupp began, and, as one, villagers, travelers, and tinkers all, Marrowdell raised fingers to circle their hearts.

"I wish to make you an offer, Jenn Nalynn."

Jenn finished running the knife through the cake before she looked up at Urcet. "Of what?" she asked, trying not to sound doubtful, but it wasn't uncommon, Aunt Sybb had warned, for weddings and especially the celebrations thereafter to provoke certain urgent longings in those not yet wed.

He'd dressed for the occasion, resplendent in black, red, and gold.

She thought he looked a little less exhausted, which might have had something to do with her wish earlier today. She hoped so.

Having her attention, the Eld touched fingers to throat. "Let me show you the world. Come. Travel with us. I'm aware you aren't held by—" the fingers fluttered dismissively, "—legal constraints. Surely, a woman of your education and talent wants more than what's here."

She did.

Or, she had.

"There's more to Marrowdell than you might think," Jenn said without irony. "But thank you. Very much. I trust—you've enjoyed your time here?"

Dema Qimirpik, as if he'd watched, chose that moment to join them. He lifted a hand as if to pat Urcet on the shoulder, but smiled broadly instead. "Enjoyed? My companion's been inspired!"

"How so?" she asked politely.

Before Urcet could answer for himself, the jovial dema continued with enthusiasm. "Why, he's decided to pen a fantastical novel, full of magic and all manner of adventure. No names, of course. Authors are highly regarded in Eld."

Why, the clever . . . Jenn ducked her head to hide a smile, quite sure who'd planted the seeds of that face-saving notion.

"The best are." Urcet gave a self-deprecating shrug. "I have my research. It remains to be seen how well I write. I could have used—" with a dour look at Qimirpik, "—experience in casting a rite."

"No doubt we'll manage something back in Ansnan. Now, good lady, what do you think of our offer, for it is mine as well? Or is your fate here, in this lovely valley?"

"It is, Dema Qimirpik." But that wasn't, for the first time, a hard thing to admit. Jenn smiled. "I hope you'll visit us again."

Urcet looked to have swallowed a pickle, but the dema smiled warmly. "As the stars witness," he said with a bow, "that's my hope as well. I've felt closer to them here than I have in—" He stopped there. "Travel does so broaden the horizon. Does it not, Mistress Sand?"

"That it does." The tinker wore her finest today as well, and Jenn thought there was a contentment to her face that hadn't been there before. "Then there are those of us who stay close to home."

His eyes twinkled. "Surely not you and your fellows, good lady. I'd say you've traveled most of us all."

Jenn tensed, but Mistress Sand merely smiled. "Traveled na? Ah," her eyebrows lifted. "You noticed Riverstone's pipe and this—" she pulled her sleeve back from her gloved arm to show the bracelet of silver and amber. "You have an eye, you do, but trade goods have wings of their own, do they not na? We stay close, as I said."

He looked disappointed, then cheered. "See, Urcet? This is why one must confirm the details. Mistress, my compliments on your fine beer, but have you tried our Ansnan wine? I insist."

"And I accept," Sand said smoothly, then smiled at Jenn. "First, we've another gift for our Sweetling's special day."

"I don't need—" Jenn began.

Happy murmurs began spreading through the crowd, a way opening up.

It was a makeshift stretcher, Tooth and Chalk at one end, big Davi at the other. On it, propped up with pillows, wan but smiling, was Uncle Horst!

Jenn threw her arms around the turn-born and hugged her tight. "Thank you!"

Sand hugged her back. "No thanks are needed, Sweetling," said so only Jenn could hear. "Healing's a terst skill. One we use too seldom. It was time we agreed and a worthy cause for it."

As the stretcher was set down, in a shady spot with a good view, the tinker said loudly, "It wasn't as serious as it first looked, but the man needs time to heal. And someone to sit on him till he does!"

This brought a laugh, and even Horst smiled ruefully.

"And beer!" someone shouted. "Welcome home!" It became a cheer, glad and loud, and Jenn could see how it affected him.

All at once, the villagers encircling Horst gave way, quickly. Old Jupp smacked a final shin with a cane, then came to stand by the stretcher. Everyone exchanged curious looks.

Jenn held her breath.

"You missed the weddings," Old Jupp accused. "I gave the Beholding. It was superb."

"Your pardon," Horst said quietly. "I regret I was—"

Thwap! went the cane. "I'm not done."

Alyssa giggled and was quickly hushed.

"You missed your wedding, in point of fact."

It was almost comical, how Horst's mouth hung open after this, with no sound coming out, but it wasn't, not really, and no one spoke or coughed. Jenn's heart began to pound.

Old Jupp smiled and lifted his hand. "We can remedy that."

Riss Nahamm stepped from behind Covie and Cynd, both of whom looked torn between tears and smiles. She wore the dress of wedding blue and silver Hettie had worn earlier, the brides having changed for the feast. On her head . . .

Jenn blinked, then smiled.

On her head was a circlet of red roses.

Melusine's.

"Welcome home, my friend," Radd Nalynn said, coming to take Riss' arm and lead her to Horst. "To stay, this time."

"Is this real?" Horst cried out in a desperate voice, rising on an shaking elbow. "It can't be. I've died and—"

Thwap! went the cane again. "The man's doubtless fevered," Old Jupp pronounced gleefully. "You can see he needs proper care. Your thoughts, Niece?"

"I think," Riss said, dropping to her knees beside the stretcher, "you're absolutely right. Sennic, Dearest Heart, I—"

Jenn wasn't the only one surprised by how much strength the wounded man had left.

And, to no one's surprise and everyone's joy, there was a fourth Golden Day wedding after all.

He'd been to another world and back, experienced marvels, magic, and bloodshed—not to mention four weddings and an eclipse—but get Jenn Nalynn to himself? Caught by yet another happy villager, Bannan smiled and nodded and agreed the Ancestors were exceptionally generous today, doing his utmost not to look obvious as he scanned the gathering. Where had she gone this time? He understood there was work to be done, work those newly wed were exempt from for the day, but surely—

"Bannan?"

Holding in a sigh, he turned to smile at his latest accoster, a smile that warmed when he found the Lady Mahavar at his side. "A splendid day," he assured her.

Her eyes twinkled. "A splendid day for hunting eggs," she corrected, tipping her head just so toward the Nalynn home. "If you take my meaning . . . ?"

"I do." Heart soaring, the truthseer bowed, fingertips brushing the ground, then rose to plant an impulsive kiss on her soft powdered cheek. "Thank you."

Ancestors Blessed and Bountiful, that won him a dimple.

Bannan didn't waste time. Tir lifted his tankard to him as he passed, knowing full well, the scoundrel, where he went and why. Past the fountain, up the slope. There was the house.

Roses turned to look at him, their petals aglow in the late day sun.

He paused to bow to them as well, for he valued their good opinion.

Then it was around the log wall and by the tidy garden and there she was.

Or there her skirt was, for Jenn Nalynn was on her knees and elbows under the hedge. When she sat up, cheeks flushed with triumph and hands full of eggs, he stepped forward and bowed. "Jenn Nalynn."

"Bannan Larmensu." She put the eggs in her basket, then accepted the hand he offered to rise to her feet.

Neither let go. They stood like that for an endless moment, content to gaze at one another, until the corner of her mouth deepened in the start of a smile. "Did you come to help me find eggs?"

Reluctantly freeing her small fingers, Bannan pulled the strap from his shoulder, bringing around the narrow tube. "I came to give you this."

Then, because she wasn't just Jenn Nalynn, not anymore, he sank to one knee as he held it out.

"Bannan—"

He smiled, understanding her sudden doubt. "I'm not proposing. Not today," he warned, his smile wider. "This is my gift. Happy birthday, Jenn Nalynn."

Jenn's first thought was relief. She'd planned to be ready—hoped to be ready—oh, wanted to be ready—to learn the consequences of what she'd become. Last night . . . last night in Bannan's arms had shown her how very much she would regret if, as turn-born she . . . she stopped there, for her second, better thought.

A gift, for her birthday. Something she hadn't seen in his home or wagon. Putting down her basket, she sat on the grass, for it wasn't right for him to kneel before her as if she were a queen, which she most certainly wasn't, though she quite liked the glow in his apple butter eyes and how it made her tingle.

That had to be a good sign.

Jenn took the tube. Its dark leather, now that she held it, proved to be carved in an ornate design, worn with use; the strap was new and stiff. Replaced, she decided with approval, for this clearly was a family heirloom and precious. The metal clasps were polished and glittered like gold. Perhaps they were. Altogether, it was the finest thing she'd ever been given and much too rich for Marrowdell.

Whatever was she to do with it?

When in doubt, Aunt Sybb would say, give an honest compliment, advice usually applied to her brother's turn in the kitchen and the result, but could, Jenn realized, apply to such a gift. "It's very well made," she ventured. "And very useful," she declared with rising enthusiasm, since Kydd would enjoy such a case for his paintbrushes, so here she had next year's birthday gift for her new brother and likely something he'd share with Peggs, making both happy. In the meantime, "I'm quite sure I will use it—often. Thank you."

Bannan, who'd sat, one arm on a knee, chuckled. "While I'm glad you like the case, Dearest Heart, the gift's what's inside."

The case, she almost protested, was more than enough. She'd have settled for the way the endearment left his mouth and found her heart. Another good sign, surely.

Distracted, Jenn undid the clasps, which freed the top third of the tube from the rest, and, because she didn't expect that to happen so smoothly, the contents didn't wait to be pulled free but spilled out.

And unrolled, covering her lap with color.

A map.

Lila had done more than well, Bannan decided happily. The cartography was superbly detailed, yet elegantly done. "Do you . . ." he looked up at Jenn and words failed him.

Tears filled her eyes and her lips trembled. She trembled, even her fingers shaking as they hovered over the parchment.

What had he done? He was an idiot. Worse than an idiot. How else could she react, shown all she couldn't have? "I'm sorry, Dearest Heart," he said desperately, reaching to take the offensive thing away. "I don't know what I was thinking—I—"

Her hands stopped his. "No. It's perfect," she said with such determination his heart ached. "I had a map once. Like this. Well, not really. Mine had holes in it and the roads ended at the border with Ansnor which I knew wasn't right and . . ." her voice grew steadier, then filled with wonder. ". . . this shows Avyo's bridges . . . and look . . . there's more to Mellynne?" Her finger traced the western expanse of that domain, with its many cities, then went back to Avyo. She lifted it to touch where the Sweet Sea met the coast.

And laughed. A moth he hadn't even noticed took flight. The air filled with the scent of roses and birds sang in the hedge as if surprised by spring. "I found the ocean!" Jenn exclaimed. "Look, it's right here and much much bigger than all of Rhoth. What's it like?"

"I don't know," he admitted. "Lila's sailed on it." Then, because

Jenn Nalynn was glad again and anything was possible, he dared go on. "We'll ask her when she comes to Marrowdell. I want her to meet you."

A flicker of worry in those glorious eyes. "Are you certain she'll want to meet me?"

Her concern was real and not to be trifled with, so Bannan carefully didn't smile. "I don't believe we could stop her, Dearest Heart."

"I could." All at once, she wasn't Jenn Nalynn but turn-born. Skin of glass, light and pearl . . .

And magic incarnate.

The map. A gift of love. A treasure. Jenn Nalynn let it fall to the grass as she stood. That dream was over. Beyond her family's home, by the fountain, those she loved gathered in joy and happiness, well into the beer and summerberry wine, full of laughter on this perfect day. She would not let regret or despair or anything else enter her and touch Marrowdell.

She dared not.

Bannan rose to his feet as well, but didn't back away. The compassion in his eyes made her tremble. "Turn-born," he acknowledged, refusing to avoid the truth, knowing perhaps better than she why this was the shape she'd taken.

"Is that all I am?" she asked desperately, reaching for him with a hand that wasn't a hand, but glass and tears and light.

For a wonder, he smiled. "Shall we find out?" Before she knew what he intended, he'd untied the bows at the top of her shoulders and eased the dress over the curve of her breasts.

Jenn gasped.

Breathing deeper himself, Bannan touched the side of her neck with one finger, then traced a loving line to the hollow at her throat and over, then down.

Down to what became flesh and warm and felt—

She gave a most unmagical squeak.

Was the Jenn Nalynn who'd drunk the tears of a sei, who had such unimaginable power, the same woman he'd loved last night? There was, Bannan decided cheerfully, only one way to be sure, for both of them. His hands eased their way inside her dress and . . .

"Ancestors Tried and—!" Jenn grabbed him by the ears and pulled his mouth to hers.

. . . no, Bannan thought, reeling. This wasn't at all the same woman.

This was . . . whatever this was, she was everything wonderful about Jenn Nalynn and more.

Whatever she was, could love and be loved.

Jenn Nalynn felt as though she danced on air as she took the eggs into the kitchen, for Aunt Sybb wouldn't want her to neglect her task even when that task had been, as she would put it, to "help things along." Things had been helped. Her marvelous new map of the world safely in its carrying case, Bannan had promised to help her write a thank you letter to Lila, because his sister had chosen it and Jenn wasn't too sure how you wrote a baroness. He'd laughed at that and refused to explain why, pulling her close for a kiss.

Jenn found her aunt on the porch, peacefully surveying the activity around the fountain. The tinkers had lingered longer than usual, and the music from Master Riverstone's pipe joined that of the birds. The older woman smiled a greeting and Jenn took a seat on the bench nearby.

"How went your egg hunt, Dear Heart?" At her blush, Aunt Sybb nodded with satisfaction. "I'm so happy for you. For you both." She gazed over the village. "For everyone."

"You could stay another day," Jenn said wistfully.

"My heart grows impatient for my own love." Aunt Sybb patted her hand. "I'm sure you understand."

At last, she did. Jenn leaned over and kissed her aunt's soft cheek. "Please bring Uncle Hane with you, one day."

"Maybe I will, Dearest Heart. Maybe I will." Another pat. "And your Wyll. He's proved a true friend and a remarkable man. I trust you'll be seeing him again?"

"Wyll's gone," Jenn said simply. "He's Wisp again and free."

"Ah." Aunt Sybb raised an eyebrow. "But not a—" she paused, delicately, and pointed under her chair.

"Not a toad, Aunt. I promise."

Her aunt looked relieved. "Well, I'm glad that's settled. Now, here comes my brother with some tea. My thanks for your company, Dearest Heart, but I'm sure you'll want to say your farewells to Mistress Sand and the tinkers. They'll be leaving shortly."

Jenn rose. "I will." Impulsively, she crouched before her aunt, taking her hands. "Aunt Sybb, I've listened to everything you've told me, truly, even when it didn't seem I did, and I want you to know how much your words have helped me, especially these past weeks. You're wise and kind and I want you, very much, to take care and come back to us. Please."

"Ancestors Blessed." Aunt Sybb blinked as though overwhelmed, then smiled. "Of course I will, Jenn Nalynn. However Far We Are Apart—"

"Keep Us Close," Jenn finished, and, though she didn't know if magic worked outside of Marrowdell, she did know one thing.

She'd just made a wish.

The pile of small white pebbles was, quite simply, extraordinary. Wainn had found her and brought her behind the great oak tree to see it. Wen was already there, along with three house toads.

Jenn picked up a pebble to be sure it was the plain sort, then put it down and looked at Wen. "It wasn't me." She looked at the toads and inclined her head. "Though these are well deserved."

The toads didn't blink, maybe loath to take their eyes from what was to them, treasure of the highest order. She'd meant to ask Wyll, or Wisp, why the toads preferred white pebbles. Jenn sighed.

"You didn't go alone," Wainn said smugly.

"About that," Jenn began, looking from one to the other. The timely arrival of the toads and Marrowdell's other small defenders hadn't been coincidence. Don't look so hard at a kindness, Aunt Sybb would say, that you forget to be grateful, which was, she thought, exactly right. So instead of asking, she smiled, from her heart. "Thank you."

Wen looked at Wainn, he at her, then both smiled back.

While the toads edged up to the pile of pebbles, touching them with their toes as if to be sure the stones were real.

"What do you think?" Jenn asked. She sat with Mistress Sand in the second wagon. The turn-born had stopped beside the path, to feel the difference for themselves, and Master Riverstone had gone so far as to walk a few steps before coming back, shaking his head in wonder.

"What I think na?" Sand put her gloved hands on her knees and shook her head. "I think Melusine should have ridden like this, with us, and not died. Then I think, if she had, we wouldn't have you, Sweetling, and this—" a gesture to the path, "—would still be killing us and a sei would still lie dying. What I think na? It's best not to think too much."

The wagons started up again, the others walking alongside.

"I understand, now, why you didn't want me to cross alone. Not," Jenn added hastily as Sand gave her a worried look, "that I did anything terrible. There are," she confessed, "rabbits. And a little meadow. But Bannan showed me how to see the Verge for what it is and—" remembering, her breath caught, "—it's magnificent. I won't cross again if you tell me not to, Mistress—" she owed them that, "—but may I? I can't leave Marrowdell and I want—I'd like—to see more."

"My. My. My." Sand clucked her tongue, abruptly in a much lighter mood. "Such care and good sense. I'm sure the others would be glad to have you come and visit, after what you've done. Besides," with a wink, "you're part sei now. Who are we to argue na?"

Jenn wasn't sure about that.

"As for more na?" Sand held out the arm with the bracelet, its polished amber like little eyes. "Happy birthday, Jenn Nalynn."

She wasn't giving her the bracelet, Jenn thought, puzzled, but a riddle. "I don't understand."

"Didn't the dragon tell you na?" Sand laughed outright. "Turn-born aren't always truthful." She shook her wrist, making the bracelet jiggle. "The dema has a sharp eye. This pretty thing comes from Mellynne. I traded for it in Channen myself."

Jenn stared at her. "You? But turn-born only exist within the edge—"

"The edge is where our worlds overlap, Sweetling. We call our side the Verge and we've yet to find its end. Why would Marrowdell be all there is on yours na?"

Because she'd believed it. Because she'd accepted that her life would be confined, yes, but in a place she loved, with those she loved. Heart pounding, Jenn asked with the greatest care, "What else is there?"

Sand smiled. "Anywhere touched by magic, Sweetling. When you're in the mood to explore, we'll show you the crossings we know. Maybe how to find your own na?"

She could leave Marrowdell. Not only for the Verge, which was astonishing, but to visit the places on the map?

"I thought I'd lost my dreams," Jenn admitted.

Sand winked again. "You can't lose dreams, Sweetling. Only misplace them for a while."

Which sounded so much like Aunt Sybb, and was so much more than she'd hoped, Jenn Nalynn's smile began in her heart and grew until the turn-born laughed aloud and clapped her hands, then pulled her close. "That's what I've waited to see," Sand whispered huskily. "That's what I wait for all year. You be happy, Sweetling."

It was affection and, Jenn realized, earnest advice. She hugged the tinker. "Thank you. More than I can say."

The wagons pulled into Bannan's farmyard, golden in the low

rays of the sun. When Jenn jumped down, willing to help with the bags, Riverstone stopped her. "You've your own work to do," he said, and pointed. "We've agreed."

Toward Night's Edge.

"I'm not sure—"

Sand lifted down her little white dog. "You don't need us. Do what your heart tells you." She winked. "We'll see you next year or sooner. And your handsome farmer."

Jenn hugged them, everyone and Sand twice, then rubbed the little dog behind the ears. Feeling generous, she looked to the tinkers' horses, but they curled their lips and she kept a prudent distance.

Then, tucking her hair behind her ears, she took the path to Night's Edge.

It was like coming home, or would have been, had there been anything left but ash and death. Jenn stopped where she'd stood that day.

Where she'd wished away her friend.

She stood long enough for the ash disturbed by her footsteps to drift back to the ground. Bees passed her, bound for living places, and she watched her shadow lengthen as the sun sank toward the Bone Hills. Not yet, something told her, though in the village they'd be refilling lamps for the wedding dance. Dema Qimirpik had promised to show them the steps to an Ansnan one favored by young couples.

Bannan was there, waiting.

But Sand was right and she belonged here, where her magic had done its worst. Only she could make this right. If she couldn't, so be it.

This had been her favorite time of day, before. The sun's rays poured gently on the valley, making everything appear better than it was or perhaps, she wondered, being officially a year older and hopefully a little wiser, they merely revealed beauty hidden by the brighter busier light of full day. When she'd planned to leave Marrowdell, this was the view of it she'd wanted to remember. When she'd believed herself trapped here, this was the only one that eased her heart.

A moth fluttered nearby.

Now, Jenn agreed, feeling the coming turn of light not as pain, but as a joy that made anything seem possible.

Night's Edge.

As she loved it . . .

As it should be . . .

She wished it, with all her heart and will. At first, she wasn't sure, then thought, was that a hint of green? With the thought, the hint became a wash sweeping from hedge to forest, covering the ash. Not any green, but the green of spring, new and vibrant and unstoppable.

Leaves popped and stems grew and flower buds nodded. She danced to keep from squashing any, not that it seemed they could be squashed.

The turn came, pouring blue down the Bone Hills, that weren't hills, she knew now, but the sei who was, like her, part of Marrowdell, part of the Verge.

The turn came, and flowers opened, which flowers usually didn't because this was the start of night, but Jenn was so very glad to see them. Daisies and asters. Summerberries and thistles. A late-flying bee streaked in and landed, surely surprised but willing.

The turn came and now she could see it as Bannan did. How there were quiet creatures in the hedges who bowed, claws to their breasts. How the turn flowed past and the old trees came alive, lit with dancers, their hair like stars. How the road was lined with guardians in chain mail, their eyes like coins. Everything in Marrowdell had a shape and a life and something to risk.

And had risked. For her.

"Thank you," she said numbly, sinking down into the flowers. "From my heart, thank you."

A daisy tumbled into her lap.

A voice softer than petals warmed her ear. "You're welcome."

"Wisp?" Jenn scrambled to her feet. "Wisp!" Oh, it couldn't be, but if it was . . .

"I am! I am!" Flowers flew in dizzying spirals, the bee hapless among them, and caught at her hair and skirt and whirled her in circles until she fell, laughing. "I am."

As smug as ever.

"And here."

Jenn turned to find herself facing her dragon. "I can see you." Just. In the twilight, he was blue shadow and silver shimmer, his eyes deep wells. Perilous, in the way of truly wild things.

Precious, beyond words. "Are you—" it was selfish to say it, because hadn't she so much joy in her life, but the words slipped out, "—back?"

The proud head tilted. Steam rose in curled tendrils. "Where else should I be?"

She narrowed her eyes. He was being difficult. "You know what I mean."

"Ah." Her bangs flipped. "What I mean, Dearest Heart, is that I'm your friend. That is what I want. That is what I am. Always."

Then, suddenly, wings opened and beat and he rose into the air. "When you dance with the truthseer, tell him the little cousins have sewn his book back together. There are some holes, but I'm sure he can fill in the words. Tell him any should do."

"It was you!" She'd been sure of it. "Wisp, you can't take books."

"Books. Books. Books." Leaves and flowers whirled upward. "Come tomorrow, Dearest Heart. Bring thistles!" With that so very familiar request, and a most unfamiliar roar, Wisp flew into the night sky and disappeared.

Jenn Nalynn stood in her meadow, staring up. If she cried, and maybe she did, the tears were glad and warm and fell on flowers.

Was he back? Really?

She circled her fingers over her heart and whispered, "However Far We Are Apart . . ."

"Keep Us Close," whispered her best and dearest friend.

The dragon settled to watch the girl walk home, though the Wound was no more and the evening barely dark. His pleasure, not his duty, but they were, were they not, the same?

The little cousins knew. Despite enough nyphrit hearts to cover themselves in gauds and glory, they patiently stood guard along the road and at every doorway. Including his own, much to his chagrin, but there was no arguing with them. Though they could be puzzled. He'd managed the pebbles without any the wiser, and, best of all, without having to touch water.

Efflet cuddled against him. He couldn't very well stop the silly things and they were, he had to admit, better than damp leaves.

Dragons were nearby. Curious, appalled. Whatever their reason, he ignored them.

Those closest suddenly scattered.

Ignoring them too, the old kruar stalked from the forest. ~ Are you going to lie here all night? ~

~ If I wish. ~

Scourge snorted. Then, slyly, ~ There's another bear. ~

Wisp blew steam. ~ So now you need help hunting? ~

~ From a toothless dragon?! ~

~ Old fool! ~

Together they watched the lamps being lit in the village. Music spread across the valley for those who cared to dance.

The dragon gave a pensive snarl. ~ A bear. ~ The efflet, ever sensible, crept away.

~ Maybe two. I'll go first! ~ Scourge whirled and plunged back into the shadows.

She'd saved them all, Wisp knew. Jenn Nalynn. His charge all these years, his worry and joy. He'd thought to protect her, and she'd turned everything around, to protect everything he cared about.

And some he didn't.

The edge was solid again. The sei, safe again in its mad penance, held their worlds together. And, most important to him, if not to the sei or other dragons, the girl was happy.

He stretched his wings, free of pain, if not of scars, and went in search of bears.

If the old kruar found them first, he'd be insufferable for days.

Concerning the Denizens of Marrowdell

Allin Emms, son of Gallie and Zehr, brother of Loee, twin brother of Tadd. Came to Marrowdell as a babe. Tends livestock.

Alyssa Ropp, daughter of Mimm and Anten, sister of Hettie and Cheffy, stepdaughter to Cynd, stepsister to Roche and Devins. Born in Marrowdell. Helps in dairy.

Anten Ropp, brother of Cynd, father (with Mimm) of Hettie, Cheffy, and Alyssa. Widowed then married Covie. Stepfather of Roche and Devins. Tends the dairy.

Aunt Sybb (the Lady Sybb Mahavar, nee Nalynn), sister of Radd, aunt to Peggs and Jenn. Spends summers in Marrowdell. Wife of Hane Mahavar. In Avyo, they own several of the better riverside inns.

Bannan Marerrym Larmensu, brother of Lila, rider of Scourge. Former Vorkoun border guard who went by the name of "Captain Ash." Truthseer and, in Marrowdell, farmer.

Battle and Brawl, Davi Treff's team of draft horses.

Cheffy Ropp, son of Mimm and Anten, brother of Hettie and Alyssa, stepson of Covie, stepbrother of Roche and Devins. Born in Marrowdell. Helps in dairy.

Covie Ropp, mother (with Riedd) of Roche and Devins, stepmother to Hettie, Cheffy, and Alyssa. Widowed then married Anten. A baroness in Avyo. Tends the dairy. Village healer.

Cynd Treff, nee Ropp, sister of Anten, wife of Davi. Aunt to Hettie, Cheffy, and Alyssa. Gardener and seamstress.

Davi Treff, son of Lorra, brother of Wen. Husband of Cynd, Anten's sister. Uncle to Hettie, Cheffy, and Alyssa. Village smith.

Devins Morrill, son of Covie and Riedd, brother of Roche. Stepbrother of Hettie, Cheffy, and Alyssa. Stepson of Anten. Came to Marrowdell as a boy. Tends the dairy.

Dusom Uhthoff (Master Dusom), father of Wainn and Ponicce, husband of Larell (widowed), brother of Kydd. Formerly professor at Avyo's University of Sols. Village teacher and helps tend the orchard.

Frann Nall, former business rival and now friend of Lorra Treff. In Avyo, holdings included riverfront warehouses. Village weaver and quilter.

Gallie Emms, mother of twins, Tadd and Allin, and baby Loee, wife of Zehr. Author and sausage maker.

Good'n'Nuf, Ropps' bull.

Hettie Ropps, daughter of Mimm and Anten, sister of Cheffy and Alyssa, stepdaughter of Covie, stepsister of Roche and Devins. Came to Marrowdell as a child. Village cheese maker.

Himself, boar.

Horst (first name, Sennic), former soldier. Took the name of Horst from baby Jenn, who continues to call him Uncle Horst. Hunter and village protector.

Jenn Nalynn, daughter of Melusine and Radd, sister of Peggs. Born in Marrowdell under magical circumstances.

Kydd Uhthoff, brother of Dusom, uncle of Wainn and Ponicce. Came to Marrowdell as a young man. Formerly a student at Avyo's University of Sols. Tends apple orchard. Village beekeeper and artist.

Larell Uhthoff, mother of Wainn and Ponicce, wife of Dusom. Died by misadventure on the Northward Road.

Loee Emms, daughter of Gallie and Zehr, sister of Tadd and Allin. Born in Marrowdell.

Lorra Treff, mother of Davi and Wen. Great-aunt to Hettie, Cheffy, and Alyssa. Formerly head of Avyo's influential Potter's Guild. Village potter.

Melusine (Melly) Nalynn (nee Semanaryas), mother of Peggs and Jenn, wife of Radd. Died by misadventure.

Mimm Ropp, mother of Hettie, Cheffy, and Alyssa, first wife of Anten, sister of Cynd. Died by misadventure.

Old Jupp (Wagler Jupp), great-uncle of Riedd and Riss. Former Secretary of the House of Keys in Avyo. Currently writing his memoirs.

Peggs Nalynn, daughter of Melusine and Radd, elder sister of Jenn. Came to Marrowdell as a babe. Village's best baker and cook.

Ponicce Uhthoff, daughter of Dusom and Larell, sister of Wainn, niece of Kydd. Died by misadventure on the Northward Road.

Radd Nalynn, father of Peggs and Jenn, husband of Melusine, brother of Sybb. In Avyo, owned mills and a tannery. Village miller.

Riedd Morrill, father of Roche and Devins, husband of Covie, cousin of Riss, great-nephew of Old Jupp. In Avyo, was a baron and served in the House of Keys. Died by misadventure.

Riss Nahamm, cousin of Riedd, great-niece of Old Jupp. Came to Marrowdell as a young woman. Creates tapestries and cares for her great-uncle.

Roche Morrill, son of Covie and Riedd, brother of Devins. Came to Marrowdell as a young boy. Hunter.

Satin and Filigree, sows

Scourge, the Larmensu warhorse. In Marrowdell, his true nature is revealed.

Tadd Emms, son of Zehr and Gallie, brother of Loee, twin of Allin. Came to Marrowdell as a babe. Tends livestock.

Tir Half-face (Tirsan Dimelecor), former Vorkoun border guard. Bannan's friend and companion.

Wainn Uhthoff, son of Dusom and Larell, brother of Ponicce, nephew of Kydd. Came to Marrowdell as a young boy. Injured by misadventure on the Northward Road.

Wainn's Old Pony

Wen Treff, daughter of Lorra, sister of Davi. Came to Marrowdell as a young woman. Talks to toads, not people.

Wisp, the dragon/Wyll, the man, Jenn Nalynn's dearest friend and greatest enemy.

Zehr Emms, father of the twins, Tadd and Allin, and baby Loee, husband of Gallie. A fine furniture maker in Avyo. Village carpenter.

The Making of Marrowdell

A TURN OF Light takes place in a world of my imagining, but that imagining took its inspiration from a particular period and place in history. I was fascinated by the situation faced by the first European settlers in north-central Ontario. They arrived, many having spent their lives in cities such as London or Paris, hoping for a new and better life. Families climbed from carts and wagons at roads' end to face a daunting landscape of lakes, rock, and trees. Vast and harsh. Unforgiving and unforgettable. We call it the "land between," and nothing they'd experienced could have prepared them for it. But they not only endured, they thrived.

Today, you can drive the roads these settlers used, from Ottawa to Renfrew, through the Haliburton Highlands, and, if you keep going, you'll get to our house. Along the way, you'll pass what they left behind. Little villages named after battles in another hemisphere, or favored pets. The remnants of cabins made from logs bigger than any tree in sight. Lilacs where the privies had been, for flowers smell better, don't they? Most of all, the massive barns, older than this country, some in use, others vanishing within new forests.

And in every village, down by the water, you'll find a mill—or its memory. For the early settlers didn't stay to their cabins or little farms. They built, having brought more than themselves and their belongings. They brought knowledge and skill. While blizzards howled, they wrote letters home and painted by lamplight. They raised children, to bury too many. On fine summer days, they put aside work to canoe the peerless lakes and learn the names of wildflowers, because this land had captured their hearts.

I'd had the notion for this story for a very long time, but hadn't a clue where to set it, only that I wanted something special, with capable people who were out of their element. Then, one fall afternoon, we were driving home along the old road with its modern numbers. Mist was pooling in the valleys and the light had that quality my husband the photographer so loves, that makes anything seem possible.

We passed one of the long-abandoned pioneer barns just as the sun found it, burnishing the wood, spreading gold down the slope below, to lose itself in a forest like the edge of night.

And Marrowdell was born.

We Can Help With That

I set off, quite literally, to learn as much as I could about the people who would have lived then and there; not to recreate an historically accurate village, but to come close enough to make my settlement a rich and workable one. What I knew about pioneers could fit in a thimble. There'd been that month in grade 5, a smattering from a Canadian history class in high school, and the odd bits one gleans about a place by being curious. I won't get into the joyous months of research that ensued or how many books I read. What matters here? The people who've helped me breathe life into Marrowdell, for I didn't do it alone.

I love water and human ingenuity; no surprise, then, that I fell in love with mills. I happily climbed in and through all the derelict gristmills I could locate, then found a true gem. Watson's Mill, Manotick, is an operational gristmill on the Rideau River. While it's far grander than the one in Marrowdell (though what I imagine Radd Nalynn would have owned in Avyo) the principles are the same. I was privileged to interview Master Miller Cam Trueman, not once, but twice. Cam answered my eager questions, volunteered fascinating details I couldn't have found any other way, and even ran the mill just for me. While Roger documented the visual, I scribbled madly in my notebook. To top it off, just before publication, Cam very kindly read over the mill scenes from *Turn*. While any errors in fact and leaps of fantasy

Roger Czerneda Photography

Watson's Mill, Manotick, Ontario

are mine, I was thrilled beyond words to have his support and approval. Thank you, Cam and Watson's Mill.

Roger Czerneda Photography

Author with miller, Watson's Mill.

Early on, I discovered I had only to mention I was researching early settlements and farm life to be offered help. My thanks to Judi and Andy Williams for lending me two books that were of immense help: *A History of Domestic Space: Privacy and the Canadian Home* (1999) by W. Peter Ward, UBC Press and *Sisters in the Wilderness—The Lives of Susanne Moodie and Catharine Parr Traill* (1999) by Charlotte Gray, Penguin Books Canada. The latter led me to the books of Susanne Moodie and her sister, as well as their letters.

Also, I must thank Roger's hockey buds. Several of these fine gentlemen are farmers. When I asked them what to call that little window thing in the top of a barn—a term I couldn't find in the otherwise excellent *Looking For Old Ontario: Two Centuries of Landscape Change* (1999) by Thomas F. McIlwraith UTP—I was faced with such an earnest combination of goodwill and growing perplexity I felt guilty. (It turns out there's actually no name for it that everyone uses and we won't get into the "diamond cut-out" issue at all.) Nothing would do but I be taken to the real thing. Thank you, Jim and Nancy Partridge, for letting me wander through your magnificent barn, and thank you, John and Nancy Nicoll, for the loan of your very helpful book.

I must also thank Ron Gostlin, Manager of Muskoka Heritage Place, Town of Huntsville. Ron unlocked the gates pre-season so I could step back through time. (The wonderful things people do for writers!) It wasn't until I walked around the log buildings and barns that I came to appreciate what I'd read of how people lived inside

Roger Czerneda Photography

Model of Marrowdell by Julie Czerneda

them. Small, yes, but strongly built. Bright, too, so long as the sun was up, with generous windows. Compact by necessity, but well-organized.

Roger Czerneda Photography

Author at Muskoka Heritage Place, Huntsville.

My measurements from the pioneer village, coupled with research into the farming and acreage needed to support a settlement like Marrowdell, determined the scale and contents of my model landscape. It took me a month to build and was worth every minute, allowing me to immerse myself not only in fantasy, but place.

Sometimes, it's getting the small details right that most please an author. Playing with my grandfather's tools. How to make lye—or beer! Learning the smell of whey. Scourge's itchy fall shed owes its veracity to the mighty Duncan and Doranna Durgin. The consequence of wandering cattle to a pumpkin patch? Thanks, Lydia Cook! And I owe the names of Rhoth's rivers to Janet, Willem, Leora, and Mila Chase.

I've been changed by what I've learned of the lives, loves, and homes of those first settlers. Those familiar with Ontario may notice some unexpectedly familiar names in this book. As my small tribute to the source of my inspiration, most of my character names came from the pioneer settlements and roads in this area, and the families who built them. Anten and Ansnor. Uhthoff and Emms. Devins, Horst, and Zehr. More. By all means look them up.

May their history come to life for you, as it did for me.

We'd Like to Invite You...

I love using my next book to formally thank those who've had me as a guest at their conventions the preceding year. This time? Years. And exceptional ones at that. I must mention as many people as I can (and production allows). If you skip this section, you'll miss fabulous folks. I fear, despite my notes and feverish rereading of emails (tricky, through the corpses of three hard drives), I'll miss more than a few myself. If you know you belong in this list, do me yet another kindness and write yourself in for me.

For hosts past have become the enduring, beloved friends of the present, and I can never thank you enough for that.

Conscription 2009, Auckland, New Zealand: Kevin Maclean, Jan Butterworth, Simon Litten, Stephen Litten, Maree "Salmon" Pavletich, Barbara and Peter Clendon, Sally McLennan, Malcolm Fletcher, Lorain Clark, Alan Parker, Teemu Leeisti, Norman Cates, Lynelle Howell, Nalini Singh, Helen Lowe, the fabulous writers who attended my workshop (SpecFicNZ), Peter and Anne Hamilton, Mike Hansen, Lisa Baird, Russell Kirkpatrick, Joffrey Horler, Andrew Robins, Glenn Younger, and Louise McCully.

Other New Zealand Hosts: Paul Brown of the Manukau (now Auckland) Library. Lyn McConchie (and friends) of Farside Farm. Lance Lones and Henri and Steve Reed of Wellington.

Conjecture 2009, Adelaide, Australia: Damien Warman, Juliette

Woods, Adam & Ruth Jenkins, Sean Williams, Judy Downs (Dymocks Books), Alison Barton (and son Joshua) who showed us the Warrawong Sanctuary and platypus, Helen Merrick, Cheryl Morgan, Justin Ackroyd, Ewart Shaw (Radio Adelaide), Catherine and Steve Scholz, Michal Dutkiewicz, and Bill Wright.

While we were Down Under, Karina Sumner-Smith looked after the homestead and my Poppa. Thanks are inadequate. We're forever grateful.

And then there was Worldcon . . .

Anticipation, 2009, Montreal, Canada: Terry Fong, René Walling, Eugene Heller, Robbie Bourget, Byron Connell, Andrew Gurudata, Sylvain St-Pierre, Lance Sibley, James E. Gunn, Christine Mak, Brian Maged, Dave Anderson, Bruce Farr, Ian Stockdale, Jim Mann, Ruth Leibig, Randy Smith, "Taz," Ruth Hansen, Linda Ross-Mansfield, John Maizels and Alexandre Simone and all the others who wore black with such exceptional skill (aka the Hugo and Masquerade Video/Tech Crews), masquerade green room staff, and my dapper and eloquent co-hosts: Jean-Pierre Normand, Yves Meynard, and Sébastien Mineau. And the hordes (I kid you not, there were hordes) of hard-working folks who made this a memorable and wonderful experience.

At this point, I confess none of the above would have happened (and I'd likely have left my head in a box at LAX), but for the astonishing competence and calm of one person, Ruth Stuart, Liaison Extraordinaire. Three cheers!!!

Since and before then: Thank you to the concom of Polaris, Ad Astra, and SFContario for your ongoing enthusiasm and support. You are treasures. Thank you, CanCon, for letting me be your Viral GOH. Rick Wilber? It was an honor to participate in your Women Who Write SF conference at USF. Last, and not at all least (nor really in any order by this point), thank you KeyCon, for a wonderful event and for bringing my beloved editor to Canada as GOH.

I'm done. Not because there aren't more of you to thank, or because I've run out of kindnesses to acknowledge, but because in remembering you, I'm truly overwhelmed. I love you guys. And I won't forget.

The More Usual Acknowledgments

First of all, I want to thank you, my readers and friends (and Roger's hockey buds), for your patience. When all this started, none of us—especially me—expected *A Turn of Light* would take almost four times as long to write as any of my previous books. I thought I'd need an extra few months, fantasy being something new, but years? Suffice to say I'm extremely grateful for the understanding of those of you who knew I was still alive (there was mail) and even more how those who really really REALLY wanted me to write Esen or Sira next instead (there was, as I mentioned, mail) supported my choice. You all deserve house toads.

Among those who had to be exceptionally patient? David "Digger" James, who won the bid at a charity auction to give names to an entire family in Marrowdell an embarrassingly long time ago. Thank you, David! When he gave me his name and that of four women, I knew the result would be interesting. And it was. Meet the Treff household: "Davi" (David Trefor James), "Lorra" (Lorraine Vivian James), "Wen" (Gwen Veronica James), "Cynd" (Cindy Hodge), and "Frann" (Fran Quesnel). I'm honored to include your names in my story and hope you love the characters who bear them as much as I do. (And don't mind the strange bits I made up.)

There are three other names in Marrowdell from the real world.

"Alyssa" was Alyssa Donovan's birthday present via another auction. How fun is that? Happy belated birthday! "Palma Anan" was in celebration of our dear friend Shannan Palma's doctorate. Finally, I owe "Hettie" and her smile to the incomparable Henri Reed of New Zealand. (Made you blush, didn't I?)

Spending so long, and so much of myself, on one project meant I relied more than usual on my friends, in person and online. Anne Bishop, thank you for all those postal cheer-ups. Kristen Britain and Janny Wurts, thanks for believing I could do that fantasy epic stuff. To the awesome John Howe and incredible Ed Greenwood, thank you for making me cry for the best of reasons. Jana, Ruth, Jihane, Janet, and Chris? Fun ride, wasn't it? I hope you enjoy the result. Kristine Smith, I owe you more than you'll ever know. Thanks for sharing the dark as well as the light. Onward, in truth!

As for the rest? To thank you here is impossible. Instead, let me say this, to each and every one, with hugs to follow. YOU ROCK!

When it came to waiting for *Turn,* the one person I worried most about was the one person who knew exactly how long it would take, my editor-dear, Sheila Gilbert. Sheila, being both wise and kind, never burst my endless "oh, I'll be finished soon" bubbles. Instead, she encouraged me along my wild and wacky genre-shift, surer than I something good would come of it. Such trust. Nothing could have meant more. Thank you, Sheila, for letting me indulge in whimsy. For making toad jokes. For believing in me when I couldn't. I wouldn't have dared this leap without you.

I would like to thank Matt Stawicki for his beautiful cover art, Kenneth May for saying such nice things about my first-ever map, and G-Force Design, Dora Mak, Paula Greenberg, and Jackson Typesetting for the incredible quality of this book. Josh, you're my hero. Marsha Jones? You might be free of questions about contracts and e-pirates, but not of me. Thank you for your help, friendship, and your kindness to my Poppa.

Speaking of family . . .

Thank you, Scott, for your help developing the Ansnan culture and names. And for making us so proud and happy, always. Thank you, Steph, for your encouragement all along. We're proud of you too. Poppa, thank you for listening to, well, everything.

Roger? Whenever I looked too far ahead and doubted, because every so often I did, you'd cue Wisp's theme on the big speakers, pour me a glass of my favorite wine, and say: "You're having fun writing this. Nothing else matters." For that, even more than your wonderful photographs that brought Marrowdell to life for me and for cheerfully missing holidays and doing extra so I could keep writing, thank you from the bottom of my heart. Always.

This book started with someone. It's fitting it end with that person too. A few years ago our daughter, Jennifer Lynn, told me she'd enjoy having her name used for a character in one of my books. I said I would, but only if she read "her" story before anyone else. What began as a private mother/daughter notion grew to a true collaboration. Jennifer read every scene, most of them multiple times. She gave me feedback on plot, character, and pacing. (For Xmas, she gave me the stupendous house toad you see in my photo.) We consulted on cover sketches and copy, on every detail imaginable. When Jennifer reached the final page of *A Turn of Light* while sitting in an outdoor café in Thailand, she stopped a rather mystified pair of tourists to take her picture as she read. Why? To send to me, then and there, so I could share the moment.

Jennifer? It's been a privilege sharing it all. There was always to be a happy ending. Because of you, every word of this story has been filled with joy.

However Far We Are Apart,
Keep Us Close.